Chapter and Hearse

By the same author

The Religious Body
A Most Contagious Game
Henrietta Who?
The Complete Steel
A Late Phoenix
His Burial Too
Slight Mourning
Parting Breath
Some Die Eloquent
Passing Strange
Last Respects
Harm's Way
A Dead Liberty
The Body Politic
A Going Concern
Injury Time (short stories)
After Effects
Stiff News
Little Knell
Amendment of Life

Catherine Aird

Chapter and Hearse

MACMILLAN

First published 2003 by Macmillan
an imprint of Pan Macmillan Ltd
Pan Macmillan, 20 New Wharf Road, London N1 9RR
Basingstoke and Oxford
Associated companies throughout the world
www.panmacmillan.com

ISBN 0 333 90764 7

1 3 5 7 9 8 6 4 2

A CIP catalogue record for this book is available from the British Library.

Typeset by Intype London Ltd
Printed and bound in Great Britain by
Mackays of Chatham plc, Chatham, Kent

Dedicated to

Peter Lucas

of happy memory

Contents

A Change of Heart 1

Due Diligence 15

Time, Gentlemen, Please 31

Cold Comfort 50

Chapter and Hearse 63

The Widow's Might 77

Handsel Monday 92

Preyed in Aid 110

A Different Cast of Mind 130

Examination Results 135

Child's Play 148

Like to Die 162

CONTENTS

Dead Letters	176
Gold, Frankincense and Murder	189
The Trouble and Strife	210
Losing the Plot	221
A Soldier of the Queen	234
Touch Not the Cat	242
Exit Strategy	251
The Wild Card	257
Coup de Grâce	265
Dummy Run	279

A Change of Heart

'There's a girl downstairs, sir,' reported Detective Constable Crosby, 'who is saying that the hospital's killed her granny.'

'They've been killing grannies over there for years,' responded Detective Inspector C. D. Sloan drily. 'Par for the course, if you ask me.'

'No, no, sir, it isn't like that at all.'

'You mean granny wasn't one of Dangerous Dan's patients?' said Sloan.

The worryingly high casualty figures for Mr Daniel McGrew's surgical operations at the Berebury and District General Hospital were a byword throughout the county of Calleshire, but not a police matter. So far, that is.

'No, sir. One of Dr Edwin Beaumont's.'

'Ah, that's different.' Sloan frowned. 'He's one of the physicians, isn't he?'

'One of their top ones . . .' began Crosby.

'I'd always heard,' mused Sloan, 'that he was one of their good ones too.'

'Nothing known against,' responded the constable promptly, police-fashion. He hastily amended this to,

'I mean, yes, sir. They say over there that he's very highly thought of in his own line.'

'Which is?'

'Hearts,' said Crosby succinctly. It seemed appropriate for the time of year. The constable was still debating the wisdom of sending a Valentine Day's card to a nubile young lady on the police station's switchboard. 'And this is all about hearts.'

'And her granny's heart in particular?'

Unlike most of the rest of the police station, Sloan had refused to be drawn on the matter of the Valentine. As a happily married man, 14 February no longer held any terrors for him and he meant to keep it that way.

'Too right, sir.' He glanced down at his notebook. 'A Mrs Hilda Galbraith. The granddaughter is called Susan Merton and she insists her grandmother had always wanted to live.'

'Don't we all, miss?' Detective Inspector Sloan asked Susan Merton gently. She was young and pretty and very upset.

'I didn't mean Granny wanted to live for ever,' said the girl carefully, 'or that we wanted her to, even though she brought me up after my parents died. Of course she knew she would die one day. Everybody does . . .'

Sloan nodded sympathetically.

'And there's that bit in Shakespeare saying golden lads and girls all must come to dust, isn't there?' Her eyes began to mist over. 'Granny loved Shakespeare.'

'Yes?' said Sloan encouragingly. The Immortal Bard

was particularly good on the subject of death, but he didn't think this was the moment to say so.

'She'd known for ages that she could die suddenly at any time. She'd even told us where her will was and what sort of funeral she wanted and everything. You see, she had had a bad heart for ages.'

'Ah . . .'

'Besides, Inspector, she'd slid back from Thomas Hardy's "all-delivering door" more than once.' She frowned. 'Granny used to say that that poem of his called "A Wasted Illness" described what was happening to her very well.'

'Really, miss?' As far as Detective Inspector Sloan was concerned, poetry – however distinguished – was not usually something that was given in evidence. And evidence was what counted in police cases, not allegations.

'Anyway, Inspector, she'd had it spelled out by Dr Beaumont when she asked him – and we all knew it, anyway. You'd only to look at her blue lips. And she kept on having these terrible attacks of breathlessness.'

'I see,' murmured Detective Inspector Sloan, although he wasn't at all sure that he did. Mrs Hilda Galbraith's number sounded to him to have been pretty nearly up anyway. Not, of course, that it should make any difference to a potential murder inquiry. On the other hand, it did add to the statistical likelihood of a natural death . . .

Susan Merton said, 'Her son – that's my uncle Colin – came back to see her whenever he could, of course, but he's been through a nasty divorce and only just got married again, so it isn't easy for him to get down here now . . .'

Sloan made a mental note.

'And he's had to start a new job up in the north. His own firm went bust, you see . . .'

Quite automatically, Detective Inspector Sloan made a written note of the name Colin Galbraith.

'Although – ' Susan Merton's face started to crumple into tears – 'I'm afraid he didn't get here in time today.'

'Ah . . .'

'He's on his way back now and I know he'll be very upset when he arrives.'

'I'm sorry,' said Sloan simply.

The girl took a deep breath and tried to steady herself. 'But Granny always wanted to go on living as long as she could. I know she did.'

'Don't we all?' said the policeman again.

'Oh, no, Inspector.' She stared at him. 'A lot of the patients in the hospital don't . . . especially the old ones who are very ill.'

As Sloan turned over a page in his notebook, he was reminded of an ancient character in one of Geoffrey Chaucer's *Canterbury Tales*. He was the old fellow in 'The Pardoner's Tale' who spent his days searching for Death without being able to find him. Now, their Mr Daniel McGrew, decided Sloan, could probably have done something for him . . .

'Sometimes they even ask you straight out when you're admitted there,' Susan Merton was saying.

Sloan came back to the present, keeping his pen at

the ready. 'They ask you if you want to die? Are you quite sure of that, miss?'

'They ask you if you want to be actively resuscitated,' said the girl spiritedly, 'which comes to the same thing, doesn't it?'

'Well . . .' It wasn't only lawyers who could split hairs, of course. Doctors could be sophists, too.

'And sometimes if you're really ill, they don't ask you at all,' declared the girl. 'They just let you die.'

Sloan made a noncommittal noise well down his throat while he thought about this. Crosby appeared to be concentrating his mind on a pair of shapely ankles. If it hadn't been for the tear stains, the girl's face would have been really striking too. It was oval-shaped, with eyes of a deep, deep brown and hair to match. He couldn't see any young man hesitating about posting any number of Valentines in her direction tomorrow.

'I don't mind that,' said Susan Merton more matter-of-factly. 'In fact, sometimes I think it's better if the doctors do do the deciding themselves . . .'

Detective Inspector Sloan mentally reserved judgement on that too. He wasn't either a medical man or a theologian and these were muddy waters for a mere policeman.

'Those who aren't ever going to get better, for instance,' went on Susan Merton. 'The hopeless cases.'

Sloan made a note. Hopeless cases or not, policemen – mere or not – had a duty to see that the law was kept. And killing was unlawful. Not keeping alive might be something different, but that was not for him to say. He was, after all, only a policeman.

'Sometimes those who are in what they call

intractable pain too,' continued Susan Merton, twisting her handkerchief into a damp knot.

'Like your grandmother?' Sloan suggested tentatively.

'No, not like my grandmother,' she said at once. 'She wasn't in great pain.'

'Are you then alleg— That is, miss, are you then suggesting,' he asked, 'that your grandmother's life-support machine was switched off without consultation?' His knowledge of the law on this point was a bit shaky. If someone was going to say that the patient had been thus intentionally killed, then 'F' Police Division at Berebury stood a good chance of making legal case history.

'No,' responded Susan Merton promptly. 'She wasn't on a life-support machine.'

'So, miss,' asked Sloan, his pen still hovering above his notebook, 'what exactly is the problem, then?'

She sniffed and said in a muffled voice, 'They – Dr Dilys Chomel, that is . . .'

'And who might she be, miss?'

For the first time something approaching a smile flitted across Susan Merton's face. 'Uncle Colin calls her God's representative on the ward, but she's actually Dr Beaumont's house physician.'

Detective Constable Crosby lifted his eyes from his study of Susan's ankles. 'Who's God?'

She looked at him, surprised. 'Dr Edwin Beaumont, of course. He's the consultant in cardiac medicine there.'

Detective Inspector Sloan, who was older and thus

more experienced in the obeisance exacted by the medical hierarchy, hadn't needed to ask.

'Dr Chomel's very nice,' went on Susan Merton, 'but she was actually off duty when Granny . . . when . . . when it happened.'

Sloan made another note.

'Dr Beaumont,' said the girl, 'had already asked Granny whether or not she wanted to be resuscitated if she had yet another heart attack . . .'

'And?' asked Sloan, leaving aside Dr Chomel's niceness as not really germane.

Susan burst into tears. 'And Granny had said she did want to be. Definitely. I know, because I was there when Dr Beaumont and Dr Chomel discussed it, and so was Uncle Colin. He'd come down specially to see Dr Beaumont about Granny.' She swallowed visibly. 'Neither of us wanted her to die either.'

'So why, may I ask,' said the police inspector sternly, 'are you now saying that the hospital killed Mrs Hilda Galbraith?'

'Because they didn't even try to save her,' she sobbed. 'That's why.'

Sloan stiffened. 'I must remind you, Miss Merton, that it is a very serious accusation to make.'

'They just let her die,' insisted the girl flatly, 'and I think that's the same as killing her, whatever anyone else says.'

At the Berebury and District General Hospital Dr Dilys Chomel did her best to cast a professional gloss over Mrs Galbraith's death.

'We have a policy here, Inspector,' she hastened to assure him, 'of taking the patient's wishes into account in our decision-making processes as well as our own medical view of their future quality of life.' She added the latest medical mantra: 'Illness is a partnership, you know.'

Sloan ignored this fashionable concept and got straight down to the tried and tested police agenda of first checking what he had been told. 'Could you then, doctor, tell me exactly what Mrs Hilda Galbraith's own wishes were in this respect?'

'Ah . . .' began Dr Chomel.

'I take it you did know them?' He must remember that the old lady hadn't been on oath when she told her family she wanted to live. She might, he thought sympathetically, actually have wanted to be allowed to turn her face to the wall in peace, untrammelled by oxygen masks, needles and tubes, leaving herself undisturbed by the distress of her nearest and dearest, yet letting them happily believe that all that was medically necessary was being done for her.

It was what he himself would have wanted.

'I think,' said Dr Chomel cautiously, 'she may have changed her mind about the whole thing. At first she told us that, if it was ever called for, she wanted us to attempt resuscitation.' The house physician always put in that little rider about *attempting* resuscitation rather than just doing it. The popular view was too optimistic a one.

'Ah . . .'

'It isn't always successful, you know, in spite of what you usually see on television,' she sighed, 'and after being on the ward for a little while, I'm afraid the patients do get to realize this.'

'I can see that might be the case,' agreed Sloan, bearing in mind that Mrs Galbraith also might have said one thing and later agreed to another. After all, it was a free world – even in hospital. 'But after that?'

'She must have told – er – someone else on the staff here that she didn't want it tried after all.'

'What makes you say that, doctor?'

'Her notes.' She hesitated. 'As you will see, Inspector, they're quite clearly marked and that's why the crash team wasn't sent for. Look, there . . .'

Both policemen peered at the patient's records.

'You will observe,' said Dr Chomel, 'that we had her down as a "122".'

'Meaning what exactly?'

The house physician explained that the figures had succeeded the letters 'DNR' on the admission records of patients at the Berebury and District General Hospital. 'In most hospitals, Inspector,' she said awkwardly, 'those letters stand for "Do Not Resuscitate".'

'I see.' Sloan thought he was beginning to see quite a lot now.

'And some people,' the young doctor said ingenuously, 'take exception to that decision being visible on the chart at the bottom of the bed.'

Detective Inspector Sloan said that he could see that they might.

Detective Constable Crosby said that he would have done.

'So now we write "122" instead,' she finished lamely.

'One, two, that'll do,' chanted Crosby insouciantly.

Dr Dilys Chomel, who came from a culture that did not encompass English nursery rhymes, looked bewildered. 'That way,' she said, 'now only the medical and nursing staff know.'

Detective Inspector Sloan, for one, did not for a single moment believe this; but then, he was in the disbelieving business. Any half-intelligent patient or visitor could have worked it out for themselves.

Dr Chomel wasn't in the disbelieving business. Not yet, anyway.

'And if a visitor should ask what the "122" means,' she went on hastily, 'they're told that it's the extension number of the doctor who has to be informed of any emergency.' Active medical resuscitation was not a problem in her own country. Few people there lived to their three score years and ten, let alone any longer. They also shared an unshakeable belief – completely at odds with contemporary Western medicine – that 'what will be, will be'.

'But I take it they weren't told that the patient would be dead by the time that doctor was contacted?' enquired Detective Inspector Sloan. Hippocrates, he decided, would be surprised at quite how far medical ethics had come since his time. 'If he or she was ever to be contacted, that is . . .'

'No,' she said, looking uncomfortable.

'The best of both worlds,' he murmured.

'This and the next,' remarked Crosby incorrigibly.

Sloan resolved that as soon as they got back to the police station he would give his assistant something more serious to think about than the sending of a

Valentine. Such as when to keep quiet during an investigation . . .

Unfortunately the detective constable had more to say. 'Do they have a secret sign too, doctor, when they want to reuse your liver and lights?'

Dr Chomel's command of English, though good, was not up to this. 'No, no,' she said when Crosby explained. 'For organ transplants we need the written consent of the relatives.'

'I can see that your resuscitation procedure looks good on paper, though,' said Sloan absently, his mind now elsewhere.

Dr Chomel still looked uncomfortable.

'Having to be good on paper,' Sloan said kindly, 'is half the trouble these days.'

Dr Chomel looked even more uncomfortable.

'So who,' piped up Detective Constable Crosby helpfully, 'wrote this number "122" on the patient's notes, then?'

'I'm not entirely sure,' Dr Chomel said with obvious reluctance, 'but it does explain why the crash team wasn't summoned.'

'Someone must have put the number there,' said Sloan ineluctably.

'Yes, Inspector.'

'Someone who knew what the numbers meant,' concluded Sloan aloud.

'Yes, Inspector.'

'Narrows the field a bit, doesn't it?' said Detective Constable Crosby chattily.

'Ye-es,' she agreed, her uncertainty now patent.

'Someone must have done it here, in the hospital, too,' continued Sloan.

'Yes.' She gulped and suddenly blurted out, 'I'm afraid that it's written in green ink.'

'Is that significant?'

Her voice fell to almost a whisper. 'Dr Beaumont always writes his patients' notes in green ink.'

Sloan nodded. Idiosyncrasies were important in establishing the pecking order. 'To be different?'

She shook her head. 'No, Inspector. He says it's so that there can't be any doubt who's written them.'

Dr Edwin Beaumont treated the police visit to his home as a tiresome interruption. 'Don't tell me that the relatives are complaining the patient wasn't well treated,' he began testily.

'Only in a manner of speaking,' said Sloan, explaining.

'If you think,' the consultant said crisply, 'that I am going about administering a *coup de grâce* to every very old patient blocking one of my beds, Inspector, you are mistaken. And I have statistical records to prove it.'

'It seems that someone did,' said Sloan mildly. 'In green ink.'

'Clever,' conceded the medical man. 'Very clever. But not done by me.' He took out his pen and wrote down the numbers on a sheet of paper. He handed pen and paper to the policeman. 'Or with my Waterman pen nib. Check with your tame specialists if you like.'

'I doubt if that will be necessary, sir,' said Detective

Inspector Sloan. 'But if I might just borrow your telephone to talk to Dr Chomel . . .'

The physician pushed it towards him.

'Dr Chomel? Inspector Sloan here. There's something I want you to do for us. Now, listen very carefully . . .'

The two policemen were back at Berebury police station with a surprised Colin Galbraith under arrest on suspicion of causing unlawful death before Sloan expanded further.

'What counts in police work, Crosby, is evidence – hard evidence – not just suspicion.'

'Yes, sir, but . . .'

'What we needed to do was to get the old lady's son to write down those letters in the presence of an impeccable witness . . .'

'Dr Chomel,' said Crosby, faint but pursuing.

'The courts trust medical doctors,' said Sloan elliptically, 'even if all their patients don't.'

'Yes, sir, I know that, but . . .'

'So we had to get Colin Galbraith, who after all must have needed his share of his mother's money after a contested divorce, a new marriage and a failed business if anybody did . . .'

'I'll say,' said Crosby, who had had the perils of matrimony spelled out to him in the canteen by the cohort against the sending of the famous Valentine.

' . . . to write the letters "122" down without suspecting that we knew anything was amiss.'

'But what I don't see, sir, is why you got Dr Chomel

to get Galbraith to sign a statement that he didn't want a post-mortem performed on his mother. That's got nothing to do with it.'

'Nothing,' agreed Sloan cheerfully. 'What was important was getting him to date it.'

Crosby frowned. 'What's the date got to do with it?'

'With today's date, of course,' said Sloan.

'Today's date?' said Crosby, adding after a moment's thought. 'The 12th of February?'

'The graphologists don't mind if you use letters or figures,' said Sloan. 'Or which pen.'

'So . . .'

'Whether you write down 12 February or 12.2 and the year, you've got to use the figures 1 and 2.'

'One, two, that'll do . . .' remarked the constable.

'Exactly. Anyone can use a green pen but your handwriting characteristics can't be disguised. Distance-killing, you could call it, writing in that death warrant. By the way, Crosby . . .'

'Sir?'

'If I were you, I think I'd send that Valentine card for 14 February after all . . .'

Due Diligence

'I must say I don't like the idea at all myself,' said Simon flatly. 'Otherwise, of course, I can see that it would be a very good place to live.'

'Quite,' said Kenneth Marsden, the estate agent, patently unperturbed. The word was one he was very fond of using with his clients. It implied agreement without actually spelling it out. 'Quite.'

'Nor me,' chimed in Simon's wife, Charlotte, quickly.

Too quickly.

'Quite,' said the estate agent again. Kenneth Marsden had found that this all-purpose word equally usefully concealed disagreement without actually spelling out the fact to prospective purchasers of attractive properties newly on the market in rural Calleshire. 'I do understand, naturally. It was all very, very unfortunate.'

'I mean,' said Simon Cullen, 'it's not every day that something like that happens in someone's house.'

'Quite so.' The man from Messrs Crombie and Marsden, Estate Agents and Valuers, paused and then said judiciously, 'On the other hand, it has at the same time to be remembered – ' Kenneth Marsden was also in the habit of making all unwelcome pronouncements in the impersonal tense – 'that there are very few domestic properties in this country – especially genuinely old ones such as the Manor at Cullingoak – in which, over the years, somebody has not died . . .'

'Naturally,' agreed Simon, 'but this death was really only the other day, wasn't it?'

'Which is why the present owner wishes to dispose of it so quickly,' said the estate agent smoothly. He changed the subject with the skill born of long practice. 'By the way, how did you happen to hear about the Manor being up for sale? We shan't be advertising it until the end of the week.'

It was Charlotte Cullen who answered him. 'Somebody at work mentioned it to me, and I rang my husband and got him to collect the key when he was in Berebury so we could see over the house while I could fit it in. I've got to go abroad for the bank tomorrow.'

Kenneth Marsden translated her coded message without difficulty. There would be no problems over money or mortgage with any purchase was what she was actually telling him.

'But the lady of the house didn't just die, did she?' persisted Simon.

'My husband meant houses in which there has been a fatal accident,' spelt out Charlotte for him. 'Didn't you, Simon?'

Simon Cullen did not respond to this.

'I do understand,' Kenneth Marsden hastened to say soothingly. Actually he understood a great deal more: he now knew which of this couple it was who metaphorically wore the trousers. This knowledge was something that was as important to him now as it would be to any experienced negotiator.

'The publicity,' pointed out Simon.

'Unfavourable,' conceded the estate agent immediately. He allowed a little pause to develop before he said obliquely, 'You yourselves would, of course, be benefiting from this to the extent that the property has been placed on the market at a substantially lower price than it would have been had the – er – unfortunate accident not occurred.'

'We do appreciate that,' murmured Charlotte Cullen. 'It is an important factor in our even considering purchasing a property such as this. I must say, though, that I agree with my husband that it is a very nice house.'

Within the privacy of the partners' room of Messrs Crombie and Marsden, Kenneth Marsden had described this particular instance of his lowering of his valuation of the house as 'blood money'. To his eternal credit, the vendor had not demurred at his suggested figure. Indeed, for a money man – he was a stockbroker – Mr Wetherby had shown very little interest in the prospective sale, only in disposing of the property at the earliest possible moment.

Needless to say, Kenneth Marsden did not say either of these things now. Instead, he nodded his agreement with Charlotte. 'Yes, indeed, Mrs Cullen,' he said easily. 'It's a very fine example of its period.'

Charlotte, who was rising rapidly through the upper-middle echelons of the Bank of Calleshire, where she worked, leaned forward and said, 'Actually it was the price which first attracted my husband.'

'I'm sure,' said Kenneth warmly.

Simon said nothing.

'I hesitate to use the word "bargain" in these particular circumstances,' went on Kenneth Marsden, matching spurious frankness with superficial – if seemingly transparent – honesty, 'but there's no denying that if it weren't for the – er – tragic incident there, the Manor at Cullingoak would be much more highly priced than it is today.'

'My husband,' began Charlotte again, 'was quite taken with the actual property too . . .' She turned towards Simon and said, 'Weren't you, dear?'

Simon had long ago decided that Charlotte must have read in a women's magazine that where the wife was the money earner, it was important that she deferred to her husband on each and every occasion when this was at all possible. And that her constant litany should be, "I'll have to ask my husband." That this should only be when his answer wasn't important went, Simon knew, without saying.

'The kitchen needs a bit of work doing on it . . .' said Simon spiritedly. 'And the larder window needs fixing.'

He made both statements without any fear of being described as a 'house husband'. Charlotte had never ever brought herself to tell the world that her husband had been made redundant from his job at the metal works in Berebury and therefore that he stayed at home while she made the money – and quite a lot of money it was these days too, to be sure. He wasn't complaining about that. It was her end-of-the-year bonus, she had told him, that was going to make buying the Manor at Cullingoak possible.

When asked what her husband did, Charlotte always replied with perfect truth that he was a bimetallist. Since she moved in the world of corporate banking, this was almost always taken by her office colleagues to mean that Simon was an economist who was concerned with the monetary system in which two metals are used in fixed relative values and not – as he actually was – someone trained in the coefficients of expansion of all metals.

Charlotte never disabused them of this misapprehension, and when the more knowledgeable responded with remarks such as, 'Gold and silver, I suppose,' she would say uncertainly, 'I think so, but I'm afraid it's not really my field . . .' That people did not talk much about their work went without saying in all banking circles, and the conversation would move on.

'I dare say that the owner might agree to that sort of repair being taken into account,' the estate agent was saying to Simon, without for one moment revealing how very useful it was in a negotiating situation to have a few small bones to chew over. The smaller the bone, the better, of course. In the world of the estate agent, work on a larder window was easily conceded, and the cost of an upgraded kitchen something to be wrested from the owner after a nominal struggle.

'Who is the owner anyway?' asked Charlotte casually. 'He wasn't around.'

'A Mr Wetherby,' replied Kenneth Marsden, adding, 'He's naturally still very shocked at losing his wife, you know, and not too keen on going back to the house.'

'I'm not surprised,' said Charlotte Cullen. 'Poor man.'

Simon gave Marsden a hard look. 'And I take it that the whole place has been rewired?'

The estate agent looked pained. 'I can assure you that the house's electrical system was the very first thing that was checked after the accident. It was found to be all in good order – ' he gave a slight cough – 'in spite of everything.'

'Everything?' queried Simon.

'Mrs Wetherby's electrocution seemed quite inexplicable. Mr Wetherby was at work when it happened and so wasn't able to help much with the coroner's enquiries.'

'Then there shouldn't be anything for us to worry about, should there?' said Charlotte in the same decisive tones as she had used to wind up many a meeting at the bank.

'No,' said Kenneth Marsden automatically.

She raised an enquiring eye in her husband's direction and went through her usual routine. 'What do you say, Simon? It's up to you, of course, but I must say I like it . . .'

'Me too,' he said meekly.

'Right.' She turned to Kenneth Marsden. 'You can tell Peter Wetherby that we'll take it.'

'I don't think you'll regret it,' said the estate agent heartily, shaking hands as they left.

Simon Cullen was inclined to agree with him when, six weeks later, he and Charlotte had duly moved into the Manor at Cullingoak. The larder window had been fixed and the men were due to come that Monday morning to improve the kitchen layout. Simon had no hang-ups about doing the cooking, belonging as he did to the very workman-like 'if you can read, then you can cook' school of *haute cuisine*, but equally he saw no point in ever working under less than optimum conditions. Actually he brought to the task of cooking the same attention and care that had served his previous employers very well until the advent of the world decline in the heavy metals industry.

'Now, then, Mr Cullen,' said the foreman, 'before we get started, can you just check that this plan here is how you want it all doing? Measure twice and cut once, as my old boss used to say.'

Simon switched the electric kettle on as a gesture of good intent before he joined the man peering over the drawings laid out on the kitchen table. 'That's right,' he said after duly studying the design. He pointed to the larder door and with his hand sketched an imaginary journey round the kitchen in the direction of the stove via the work surfaces and the kitchen sink. 'Store, wash, prepare, cook, serve . . . that's how it should be.'

The foreman scratched his head. 'I hadn't thought of it like that.'

'Only if you're right-handed,' said Simon. 'The lady who lived here before must have been a southpaw.'

'Both her hands had burns on them,' the man informed him ghoulishly.

'Though they never did find out how she got them,' chimed in his mate, Fred.

'Electrocuted in the utility room, she was,' said the foreman lugubriously. 'But don't you let that worry you. They went over that room with a fine-tooth comb after it had happened.'

'Couldn't find a thing amiss, though,' said Fred in his role as Greek chorus. 'They never did work out what went wrong.'

'Really?' said Simon, absently moving in the direction of the worktop. The kettle had come to the boil and switched itself off. 'Tea?'

'Milk but no sugar for me,' said the foreman, undiverted. 'Thought it must have been something to do with the ironing board, they did, because that was lying on the floor beside her when her husband found her. There was a pile of nearly dry washing in the laundry basket beside her too.'

'And,' supplemented his assistant eagerly, 'because she always did the ironing while she watched her favourite afternoon programme on television.'

'My wife too,' said the foreman. 'Thanks,' he added, cradling the mug between his large, dirt-ingrained hands. 'I don't know which channel, though,' he added in the interests of accuracy, 'because I'm not there then.'

Simon decided that this was not the moment for quoting that famous question, 'But what was the play like, Mrs Lincoln?'

'Two lumps for me,' said his mate, stretching his hand out for his tea. 'They thought she died just before the programme came on at four o'clock . . . and that's what the man who did the post-mortem said too.'

'Pathologist,' supplied Simon.

'But they never found out how she came to be electrocuted,' repeated the foreman, addressing himself to his drink. 'Never.'

'Funny, that,' murmured Simon Cullen.

'It said in the paper that her husband was at work at the time it happened,' expanded the foreman.

'At a meeting all afternoon,' chimed in Fred. 'It said that too. About a dozen people there with him all the time.'

'My wife spends a lot of her time at work in meetings,' said Simon. 'I know, because she tells me when not to ring the office.'

'If you ask me,' opined the foreman, pushing back his chair, 'most meetings are a waste of time. Let's get started here, Fred.'

Simon swept up the empty mugs and drifted off to take a look at the utility room with new eyes. It was situated off the kitchen and housed the central-heating boiler and the washing machine, as well as all the impediments associated with living in a sizeable house in the country – including Simon's new green wellies. The Wetherbys' ironing board had gone and Simon had stood the Cullens' one there in its place, but otherwise the room looked very much as it must have done in the days of the previous occupants.

Propped up beside the ironing board and the radiator was the clothes horse which Simon and Charlotte had brought with them from their old house. In fact, the only relic of the Wetherbys' regime was one of those old-fashioned wooden airers, which could be lowered by a thin rope, loaded with damp washing and then hoisted back up to the ceiling above the boiler to dry.

Simon examined everything in the room with his customary care but was no wiser at the end of his survey. In fact, had he but known it, he reached the same conclusion as the investigating authorities had done – that something had electrified the metal of the ironing board.

When he gave the men their tea in the afternoon he said, 'You might just put a lick of paint on that small scratch on the radiator in there next time one of you has a paintbrush in his hand.'

'No problem,' said the foreman. 'No sugar, thanks.'

'Two lumps for me,' Fred reminded him. 'Worked out how it was done, have you?'

'Done?' said Simon.

Fred gave him a knowing wink. 'They said the husband had got a lady love tucked away somewhere.'

The foreman set his mug down and said sapiently, 'What he had got was an unbreakable alibi, so you mind what you say here, Fred.'

Fred bridled. 'There's no smoke without fire. Besides, don't forget that most murderers are widowers.'

'Because they've killed their wives.' Simon nodded. 'I've heard that one before.'

'Remember,' pronounced the foreman magisterially, 'it didn't say anything about that in the newspapers – not even the Sunday ones.'

'What else did it say?' asked Simon, adding in spite of himself, 'I suppose it is theoretically possible that the ironing board was live – electrified, that is – a long time before Mrs Wetherby touched it.'

'Not before one o'clock it wasn't, insisted Fred vigorously. 'Ivy Middleton was here all that morning. She put the dirty washing in the machine and started it up before she went home, like she always did, dinnertime.'

'That's right,' said the foreman. 'I was forgetting about Ivy. She touched that ironing board and she didn't get an electric shock, did she, Fred?'

Simon and Charlotte hadn't kept Mrs Ivy Middleton on to do the rough housework. As Charlotte had put it so pithily when she – they – paid for the Manor, 'They could afford Cullingoak Manor – just – but not the extras as well.' Ivy had rated as an extra and so Simon saw entirely to the running of the house.

'There could have been some cable and a time switch,' he said in spite of himself. It was just as well Charlotte was at work. She wouldn't have approved of his wasting the workmen's time – let alone his gossiping with them – like this. 'You know, an electric wire from the nearest power socket to the ironing board timed to come live after Mrs Middleton had left.'

'Now, if I may say so, that's where you're wrong,' said the foreman placidly. 'The police thought of that too.' He took a swig from his mug. 'It so happens that there wasn't any such timer in the house or garden, and, believe you me, they searched for it.'

'I can quite see that they would,' murmured Simon.

'And,' the foreman added, tapping the table with his forefinger for greater emphasis, 'they had a witness that the husband – Peter Wetherby, that is – didn't leave the house before the police arrived, so he couldn't have hidden a timer anywhere outside the house.'

'Got it in for him, haven't you,' said Simon, 'this Peter Wetherby?' Suddenly something about the name jarred in his mind. He couldn't quite place the memory but it was there, somewhere.

'Ironing boards don't become live on their own.' The foreman shrugged, starting to get to his feet.

'I reckon,' said Fred, 'it was suicide.'

'Suicide?' echoed Simon.

Fred nodded. 'I think she connected a wire from the socket to the ironing board herself and her husband came home and found her and removed the evidence pretty quickly. Didn't want anyone to know she'd done it because of this other woman, see?'

The foreman said, 'You're a great one for your theories, Fred, but it don't get the work done . . . Come along now, let's get started here or we'll never be done.'

Over the next few weeks Simon had to agree that Fred's suicide theory was the most tenable. Something like a kettle flex could have been plugged into the nearest power point and bare wires at the other end made to touch the metal of the ironing board. Turn the switch on, clasp the ironing board and Bob's your uncle. A married man becomes a widower in no time at all.

And all that the husband would have had to do before he rang the police was put the proper plug back on the appliance – the work of a moment – and no one would be any the wiser. Oh, and perhaps change the face of the plug in the wall in case there were burn marks there too.

He gave this thought whenever Charlotte was away – she was away rather a lot these days for the bank. At least he thought it was for the bank until the bank telephoned urgently one weekend to talk to her and he referred them to their conference and they said they weren't having one.

That was when he remembered what it was about the use of Peter Wetherby's Christian name that had bothered him. Charlotte had known it even though the estate agent had only given them his surname.

Now he came to think of it, she had known too about Cullingoak Manor being for sale for a low price before it had been advertised . . .

It still didn't explain how Mrs Wetherby had died while her husband was well away from the action unless it had been by her own hand.

Simon Cullen was rapidly coming to the conclusion that it hadn't been.

That was when he laid his plan.

'Darling,' he said to Charlotte the next evening, 'I think I'm going to have to have a couple of nights away next week. Uncle George wants me to go up to Yorkshire to see him.'

'Fine,' she said. 'Remember me to the old boy. Not that I've seen him since the wedding.'

'No more you have,' he said, since his relations weren't much liked by Charlotte. 'I'll go on Tuesday and be back Thursday evening. That all right?'

'Fine,' she said. 'By the way, before I forget, I may be a bit late back on Friday – we've got a big meeting at the bank Friday afternoon.' She smiled. 'Salary review committee – mustn't miss that.'

'Not on any account,' he agreed gravely.

Simon studiously avoided the utility room when he got back to the Manor on the Thursday evening – he and Charlotte had a quiet evening together.

'You might switch the washing machine on first thing, Simon,' she said as they went upstairs. 'I went through my summer things while you were away ready for the autumn.'

'They'll be all beautifully ironed,' he said, 'by the time you get home.'

'It's getting too chilly to wear them now. I must say I was quite glad of the central heating when I got in yesterday.'

'The afternoons are getting cooler,' he agreed amiably.

As soon as Charlotte had left for work on the Friday morning – the day of her big meeting – Simon entered the utility room very carefully. He didn't switch on the washing machine, though. Instead he examined the room with extreme caution. There was indeed a plug in the power socket and a length of flex tucked away behind the radiator and then running, almost out of sight at ground level, to the nearest leg of the ironing board. Fred had been right about that anyway.

But he wasn't into metals and Simon was.

Also behind the radiator, firmly taped to it, was

what he had been looking for – that which would make the whole thing live.

But not just yet. Not until the central heating warmed the radiator.

'Clever,' he murmured to himself appreciatively. 'Very clever.'

It was a short metal bar which neither the police nor anyone else would have looked at twice had they noticed it lying around. It was half copper and half steel lengthways – the principle on which thermostats often work. And it was pressed firmly against the back of the radiator, the copper part set alongside – but not touching – one of the two wires in the flex.

This had been scraped bare. He checked that the central heating was set to come on at three o'clock as usual – Simon thought it would take about an hour to warm up enough to make the copper expand and complete the electrical circuit. Then he went back to the kitchen to wait for something to happen to establish that he was alive and well before lunch.

At twelve o'clock their next-door neighbour came to the door. 'Your wife has just rung me, Mr Cullen, to say she thinks she can't have put the telephone back on its hook properly because she keeps getting the engaged signal.'

'I'll check,' he said, knowing it would be so. 'Thanks for letting me know. Like a coffee?'

'Some other time, if I may.'

'I'll look forward to that,' he said, and meant it. His neighbours really were very agreeable people indeed. Getting to know them in future was going to be a pleasure.

When Charlotte got back at six o'clock he was out of sight, behind the utility-room door. She went straight there, calling out his name as she did so. He did not answer, but when she was right inside the room and standing, puzzled, in front of the ironing board, he stepped out quietly from behind the door and gave her a gentle push towards it. She put out her hands to save herself, and screamed as she touched the ironing board.

At the trial, before pronouncing a life sentence, the judge described Peter Wetherby as a clever, calculating and callous killer of the two women in his life.

Time, Gentlemen, Please

'I don't like it, Sloan,' declared the Superintendent heavily.

'No, sir.' Detective Inspector C. D. Sloan hadn't for one moment imagined that he would. Change was undeniably in the air and, just like the Victorian hymn writer, Superintendent Leeyes invariably associated change with decay.

'In my young days,' Leeyes was rumbling on, 'the police force was the police force and MI5 and MI6 were the secret services.'

And, exactly as it said in the old hymn, the Superintendent always saw change and decay all around him too.

' "And never the twain shall meet",' muttered Sloan under his breath. 'Like East and West.'

'What's that, Sloan? I didn't quite catch . . .'

'Nothing, sir.' The Inspector coughed. 'You were saying that in your day . . .'

'Then the police did their job and the secret services did theirs.'

'I'm sure, sir.'

The news that it had been ordained from on high that in future members of secret services MI5 and MI6 were to work hand in hand with the police in the tracking down of major criminals had been received at Berebury police station with what a professional diplomat would have called 'some considerable reserve'.

'Moreover,' said Leeyes flatly, 'when that lot got up to something in the course of their activities which wasn't legal, we weren't told.'

'Quite, sir.' Metaphorically, Sloan averted his eyes too.

'Not that we wanted to know, of course,' he added hastily. 'At least they spared us that.'

'Not our problem,' agreed Sloan.

'Now,' he said morosely, 'if they overstep the mark, we'll get the blame too. Bound to.'

'Clandestine operations usually make for difficulties,' said Sloan sagely. In his opinion they were almost as risky as stings.

'And why, Sloan, they should imagine for one moment that a bunch of out-of-work old cloak-and-dagger merchants should be able to nail our drug traffickers and big-time fraudsters any better or quicker than we can beats me.'

'Yes, sir. Me too,' said Sloan, noting with detached interest that the Superintendent's famous territorial imperative extended to Calleshire criminals as well as to its good citizens.

'Which is not to say,' pronounced Leeyes trenchantly, 'that I am suggesting for one moment that the Serious Fraud Squad couldn't do with some proper help.'

'No, sir . . . I mean, yes, sir, I'm sure it could.'

He opened his hands in gesture. 'I ask you, Sloan, what *is* the force coming to?'

Detective Inspector Sloan, who from bitter experience knew better than to attempt to answer his superior officer's rhetorical questions, made no reply to this.

'I suppose they haven't got anything else better to do these days,' carried on Leeyes ruminatively. 'Not now, seeing that the Cold War is over.' He sniffed. 'I understand that today it's not so much a case of "know thine enemy" as knowing who on earth your enemy is in the first place.'

For one wild moment Sloan considered mentioning that in an international context this fragile state was known as 'peace', but he soon thought better of it.

'The secret services just don't think they've got any real enemies left,' insisted Leeyes. 'That's their trouble.'

'Well, we have.' Detective Inspector Sloan was under no illusions about this. 'More than enough of them.'

'Oh, yes,' Leeyes unhesitatingly concurred with him. 'There are still plenty of bad boys around in Calleshire. No doubt about that.'

'And so these – er – secret services want to borrow our enemies so that they can keep going, do they, sir?' asked Sloan, aware that even in these politically correct times 'enemy' and 'criminal' were still always spoken of as male.

'Right first time.'

'And we,' ventured Sloan carefully, letting several

tricky revolutionary situations abroad pass unmentioned, 'at least have the benefit of usually knowing who our enemies are.'

'You name it, Sloan, and we've got them on the job. Fraudsters, drug dealers, confidence tricksters, car criminals – the lot.'

'Quite so,' said Sloan. Like change and decay, criminals were all around. And with them always too.

The Superintendent pushed a directive across his desk. 'According to this, Sloan,' he quoted mincingly, 'we've got to feel free to enlist the aid of MI5 and MI6 in our struggles with serious crime whenever we may want their assistance.'

'Right, sir,' he responded neutrally. Detective Inspector Sloan was head of the tiny Criminal Investigation Department at Berebury police station and such serious crime as there was in this corner of Calleshire usually landed on his desk first. He got up to go. 'I'll remember that.'

'Wait a minute.' Leeyes stayed him with a raised hand. 'I'm afraid the Assistant Chief Constable wants to put in his ha'p'orth too.'

'Yes, of course, sir. When are you going to see . . .'

'Oh, not me, Sloan.' The Superintendent looked out at a clear, golfing sky. 'I'm going off duty now. You.'

The Assistant Chief Constable, who was both a police officer and a classicist, welcomed Sloan with a genial, 'Ah, Inspector, come in and hear what our secret services are up to . . .' He waved Sloan into a chair the other side of his desk. 'Sit yourself down.'

'Thank you, sir.'

'I'm not sure all this isn't in direct contravention of the Civil List and Secret Service Money Act of 1782 – as revised in 1978, of course – but ours is not to reason why.'

'Probably repealed by now, sir.' As far as Sloan was concerned, the older the statute the better. Laws that had stood the test of time were usually good ones.

'I'm afraid that MI5 and MI6 are taking this business of closer cooperation with the force quite literally.'

'Really, sir?' responded Sloan. 'I must say, myself I don't quite see how they can help us. Not in the short term, anyway.'

'Help us, Sloan?' echoed the Assistant Chief Constable stoutly. 'I should think not, indeed! The very idea . . .'

'Sir?'

'I can assure you that the boot is quite on the other foot.'

'Sir?'

'You've got hold of the wrong end of the stick, man. They want us to help them.' The Assistant Chief Constable fingered the message sheet before him and frowned. 'At least, I think that's what they mean. Their prose is what you might call a trifle opaque.'

'They've got a problem?'

He smiled thinly. 'Yes, I think we may say that. Of course, I'm only reading between the lines, which I understand is what you do with their messages before you swallow them.'

'On our patch?'

'Four times over so far.'

'I see, sir.' Sloan leaned forward. 'They need our help, do they? Might I ask in what way?'

'In the matter of establishing the assignation procedure of certain enemies of the state.' The Assistant Chief Constable suddenly looked remarkably cunning. 'Unless, of course, Sloan, they are just testing us out. Seeing if we are any good at playing their sort of wide games – that sort of thing . . .'

'A dummy run?'

'Quite possibly.' He tapped his desk with an elegant gold pen. 'Except that I wouldn't like this force to be thought of as dummies in any sense – if you take my meaning.'

'No, sir. Naturally not.'

'What they have said to me – ' the Assistant Chief Constable contrived to project doubt into every word – 'is that they have two suspects – that is to say, two people with – er – different loyalties from ours . . .'

'Spies . . .' supplied Sloan, wondering if this term too had now become as politically incorrect as almost every other expression in hitherto common usage.

'Shall we say "agents of another power", then?' suggested the Assistant Chief Constable helpfully.

'Very well, sir.'

'And that they, whoever they are, are meeting,' said the Assistant Chief Constable, 'somewhere in your manor here for the exchange of – er – of whatever it is secret agents hand over these days . . .'

Sloan nodded. With Kipling it had been letters for a spy; with Sherlock Holmes it had been plans – the Bruce-Partington Plans; with John Buchan it had been something to do with the Thirty-nine Steps . . .

'Money?' he hazarded, coming fully into the twenty-first century.

'That's quite possible, Inspector. As even infant criminals seem to know these days, money leaves too much of an audit trail if you transfer it by any other method than hard cash in the good old brown envelope.'

'So what exactly is their problem, sir?' Detective Inspector Sloan knew a good deal more about the importance of audit trails now than he had done before money-laundering had joined the older, simpler crimes in the Newgate Calendar.

The Assistant Chief Constable tapped the message sheet. 'How the two parties – whoever they are – get in touch with each other to arrange the handover.'

'So that they can be stopped?' enquired Sloan diffidently.

'So that their communications can be intercepted,' the senior officer amended, suddenly looking very cunning again. 'And, for all we know, tampered with and sent on.'

'And when they do meet,' hazarded Sloan, 'it will presumably then be established who they are? I take it identities are wanted . . .'

'Got it in one, Sloan.' He frowned. 'No, that's not quite right.' He fingered the message sheet again. 'They know who one of them is.'

'Ah . . .'

'What they don't know is who she's meeting.'

'She?' said Sloan.

'Codenamed Mata Hari,' the Assistant Chief Constable said apologetically. 'These people haven't got any imagination, you know.'

'And what they want to know, you say, sir, is who she's meeting . . .' It sounded all very *Boy's Own Paper* stuff to Sloan.

'That and how they make their – er – '

'Assignations, sir?'

'Exactly.'

'Not by telephone?'

'Tapped.'

'Letters?'

'Intercepted.'

'E-mail?'

'Don't ask me how, Sloan, but these clever johnnies tell me that they've got that sussed out too.' No one, except perhaps Superintendent Leeyes, remained more Luddite in his attitude to computer technology than the Assistant Chief Constable.

'Coded advertisement?'

'Apparently their code breakers can't work out anything in the daily newspapers that could possibly mean "Meet me outside St Ninian's Church in Berebury at eight o'clock on Friday morning", or words to that effect.' He twitched his lips into a grin. 'And I'm told it wasn't for want of trying either. For their sins, they even went through all those Baucis and Philemon advertisements.'

'Beg pardon, sir?'

'Baucis and Philemon were Ovid's couple to whom the gods gave the gift of growing old together like entwined trees.'

'Ah.' Sloan's brow cleared. He should have remembered that the Assistant Chief Constable was a classicist first and a policeman a long way second. 'I'm with you, sir. The "Lonely Hearts" columns . . .'

'I understand there was no shortage of volunteers for the research,' said the Assistant Chief Constable drily, 'but much good it did 'em . . .' He paused and then, scholar that he was, added punctiliously, 'In that respect anyway.'

'Radio transmitter?' suggested Sloan.

'First thing they looked for.' The Assistant Chief Constable wrinkled his nose. 'Old hat anyway, these days.'

'Internet?' Sloan made another effort to come into the twenty-first century.

The Assistant Chief Constable said 'They're quite sure that Mata Hari – sorry, but that's how they will refer to their female suspect – doesn't have access to it.'

'Don't they have Internet Cafes now, sir?'

The Assistant Chief Constable said gloomily, 'They've been tailing her for weeks . . . Mata Hari, indeed. You'd have thought they'd have been a bit more original, wouldn't you?'

'And her opposite number?'

'Always male so far.'

'How do they refer to him?'

'You're not going to like this either, Sloan.'

'Sir?'

'They're calling him George.'

'They do have a precedent,' Sloan conceded stiffly. The boundaries between spy, traitor, defector and double agent were something that in the ordinary way he didn't have to explore. But, like those between crime and sin, they were as intertwined as that couple with the odd names whom the Assistant Chief Constable had just mentioned.

'And they've seen him once – but so briefly that it didn't help much.' The Assistant Chief Constable waved a memo in the air. 'They got a camera shot of his back, here in Berebury, that's all.'

'But they exchanged something?' Detective Inspector Sloan, like most policemen, remained ambivalent in his attitude to criminologists, but Loccard's famous exchange principle that all contacts left traces on both objects, inanimate and otherwise, had been ground into him when a young constable as firmly as the twelve times table.

'He came up behind her and took something out of her hand without speaking or looking at her, and then walked on without a pause or looking back either.'

'So he knew where she would be and when,' concluded Sloan without difficulty.

'And conversely, presumably she knew when and where he would come,' said the Assistant Chief Constable, 'because I gather she didn't even look up as he lifted whatever she had for him . . . She just went on strolling along.'

'But what nobody knows is exactly how they made the arrangements . . . Is that it, sir?'

'The problem in a nutshell, Sloan.'

'And,' pointed out the Detective Inspector, 'they think that George was probably aware that she – er – Mata Hari, that is – was being kept under close observation.'

The other man nodded. 'That's right. Because by approaching her from behind, he didn't let our people see his face.' He straightened up. 'Except we must remember that they're not really our people, Sloan.'

'No, sir.' That was the trouble with the secret services. No one was ever really sure whose people they were . . .

'How they think we can help, I don't know.' The Assistant Chief Constable scratched his chin. 'I can't see the point of waiting by the spot where the exchange happened to see if it happens again, can you?'

'No,' said Sloan, adding vigorously, 'and in any case, sir, if that's what these types want, I can see no reason why they shouldn't do the surveillance themselves. It's the force who are short of man power.'

'Quite, quite,' said the Assistant Chief Constable pacifically. 'On the other hand, it would be good to get them off our backs so that we could all return to proper policing.'

'So it therefore follows,' said Sloan, in the manner of a schoolboy proving a theorem, 'if the secret services are so sure that Mata Hari and this character whom they call George haven't been in touch by any other means, that there must have been a sign or a plan, separately visible to them both, bringing them together in some other way.'

'We're all agreed on that, Sloan, but their people have looked everywhere and can't find one.' The Assistant Chief Constable squinted modestly down his aquiline nose. 'That's why they've come to us, and we don't want to let them down, do we?'

'So when and where did all this happen, sir?' enquired Sloan stolidly. The larger question of whether or not the police wanted to help the secret services, he left unanswered.

The Assistant Chief Constable waved the message sheet in his hand. 'Outside St Aidan's Church at ten o'clock on Tuesday morning last week . . . and I may say they mounted a watch there too on Tuesday this week.'

'No joy?'

'Not there. All the action was over at St Barnabas's at twelve noon instead.'

'The other side of town.'

'That's what's irking them, Sloan. As you know, Berebury's by no means short of churches. Comes of being an old medieval settlement, I suppose.'

'And their next encounter?'

'Just in front of St Ninian's at nine yesterday morning.'

'That's my mother's church,' remarked Sloan absently, his mind elsewhere. 'I suppose they could be going through all the churches in Berebury alphabetically. That would be easy enough for anyone to arrange.'

'They'd thought of that. You're forgetting St Catherine's.'

'So I am, sir.'

Detective Inspector Sloan had been doing his best to forget the ultra-modern St Catherine's Church ever since it had reared its ugly metal spire in the middle of the old market town. Even worse than the tower was the series of shiny spikes where a traditional church would have had flying buttresses.

'But it was the rendezvous at St Peter's at nine this

morning that got the secret service boys really wound up, Sloan. You know, that old church down by the riverside that isn't used any more . . .'

'Redundant,' said Sloan pithily, 'although if you ask me there's more sin down in that part of the town than anywhere else.'

'Quite so. Well . . .'

'If ever a patch needed a church,' averred Sloan feelingly, 'it's the Water Lane district.'

'Perhaps.' The Assistant Chief Constable frowned. 'They tell me Mata Hari and someone else . . .'

'Who wasn't George?'

'A new face – or, rather, a new back. They did their exchange dead on the first stroke of the church clock.' He scratched his chin. 'From all accounts it went like clockwork too, which is more than it did one day last week . . .'

Detective Inspector Sloan looked up. If there was one thing every police officer found worth investigating it was a deviation from the norm. 'What happened last week?'

'Apparently, Mata Hari was outside St Olave's all that morning, but no George. It was raining and she got soaked, but he never showed and neither did anyone else.'

'And next time?'

'Your guess is as good as mine, Sloan.'

'Actually, sir, the time and place might be a guess,' said the Detective Inspector, 'but, if past performance is anything to go by, the meeting will be outside a church.'

'Ye-es, I suppose that's so.'

'And on the hour.'

'That too, Sloan, now you come to put it like that.'

'On past performance alphabetically, saving St Catherine's – ' Sloan knew what it was those high spikes there reminded him of, so many mantraps – 'it should be St Thomas's . . .'

'Mata Hari and her friends do seem to need a church, all right,' agreed the Assistant Chief Constable pensively, 'which is funny, when you think about it.'

'They seem to need the outside of one, sir, anyway,' amended Sloan.

'And something by way of a clock.'

'St Ninian's doesn't have one,' said Sloan, almost without thinking. His mother's arrival there went by the sound of the church bells. All he ever had to do was to get her to the church door on time. She was always telling him it was an interesting church doorway, but he couldn't for the moment remember why.

'Right.'

'And it can't be the church bells,' said Sloan knowledgeably, 'because St Olave's doesn't have a ring any more.'

'Nowhere near enough young bell-ringers coming forward these days, Sloan. Too much like hard work – pulling a rope and counting.'

Sloan paused. 'There's one more thing, sir . . .'

'What's that?'

'All these meetings you've told me about have been in the morning.'

'So they have, Sloan.' He tapped his pen on his desk. 'Now, why should that have been, I wonder?'

'Perhaps this precious pair need daylight to come together, sir.'

'Good point, Sloan.' The Assistant Chief Constable leaned back in his chair. 'But not for recognition . . .'

'The recognition would seem to be a bit one-sided, sir. That's if Mata Hari only has something lifted out of her hand from behind.'

'True, but – er – George must know whose hand from which to do his taking.'

Sloan wrinkled his brow. 'On the other hand, she may not need to know who's coming up behind her to collect the – er – dibs. It might even be safer that way.' Dibs wasn't a word he relished using. Like the name Mata Hari, it smacked of an earlier, more melodramatic era.

'Perhaps, Sloan, there's something else they need . . .'

'Fine weather?'

The Assistant Chief Constable nodded. 'Could be, Sloan. Now what sign, I wonder, could there be which doesn't work in the rain.'

'There must be something,' said Detective Inspector Sloan. There was a pair of tribes in Borneo he'd read about which only went to war in daylight – that was because they were frightened of the dark – and in fine weather because the rain spoiled their martial feather head-dresses. 'They'll have a reason for using the front of all those churches . . . bound to.'

'Something which needs the sun perhaps?' The Assistant Chief Constable frowned. 'There can't be that number of handy sundials in the middle of Berebury, though.'

'And the sundial only tells the time, sir. It wouldn't

tell them when to meet.' The rim of the sundial in the municipal park said something sententious about its only recording the sunny hours, but he did not say this. 'These meetings, sir, that the secret service said were all outside churches . . .'

'Yes?'

'Did they mean outside the church doors?'

'I'm not sure if they were as precise as that, Sloan.' The Assistant Chief Constable peered at the notes on his desk. 'Why?'

'Churches usually face east . . .'

'Agreed. So?'

'So their entrance doors are usually on the south and north sides.'

'Granted.'

'Although sometimes, of course,' went on Sloan, 'they have a west door too . . .'

The lean, intelligent face of the Assistant Chief Constable took on a look of close interest. 'Are you telling me, Sloan, that none of the action will have been on the north side of any of these churches?'

'If that is the case, then it might perhaps indicate that we are thinking along the right lines, that's all, sir.'

A little smile played along the other man's lips. 'Am I then right in thinking that an extension of this proposition would be that our two suspects wouldn't have met on the west side of any of the churches either?'

'Yes, sir. Not if the meetings all took place in the morning, sir, which you said they did. The west side only gets the afternoon and evening sun and the north side none at all.'

'I did say they were in the mornings,' said the Assistant Chief Constable. 'All of 'em.'

'And if their signal needs the sun, that would explain why the meeting outside St Olave's was fouled up by the rain.' Like the warriors of Borneo, Mata Hari's contacts too would have had their reasons for not liking bad weather.

The Assistant Chief Constable stroked his chin. 'Go on.'

'But if they're working their way round the Berebury churches alphabetically, it wouldn't explain why they left St Catherine's out,' said Sloan. He'd learned long ago not to bend facts to suit a theory. Defence counsel always found a chink in faulty armour.

'They didn't leave St Peter's out though,' remarked the Assistant Chief Constable, 'just because it's not being used now.'

'So, sir, it wasn't something hidden in the church notices in the porches . . .' His own mother, now, was always able to draw accurate conclusions from innocent-looking flower rotas.

'That follows, Sloan. St Peter's in, St Catherine's out . . .' He sat back and regarded his notes with a pensive air. 'Doesn't make sense, does it? We're like those chaps looking for a sign from the East.'

'The Three Wise Men . . .' There was something beginning to niggle at the back of Sloan's mind now.

'Well, it looks as if we two wise men can't help our – shall we say our "confrères"? – with the answer to their little problem after all.'

The niggle at the back of Sloan's mind was turning into a positive irritant.

'Pity, that, Sloan,' murmured the Assistant Chief Constable wistfully. 'I should have liked the force to have come up with . . .'

'St Catherine's Church is post-war,' Sloan said suddenly.

'The 1960s architects have a lot to answer for,' observed the classicist urbanely.

'But the other churches are all old and Anglican,' said Sloan.

'I don't know that that gets us very far, Sloan . . .'

'Before clocks, sir, churches had to have ways of telling folk when to come to services . . . those who couldn't read anyway.'

'Agreed, but what about it?'

'They had something called mass clocks on the church masonry.' The niggle in his mind had clarified into a memory. 'Usually on the porch door.'

'Well?'

'The priest put a little wooden peg into a hole in the stone and then scratched a line outwards from the hole.'

'But I don't see . . .'

'The congregation would know it was time for church when the shadow from the peg fell on the line.'

'Are you telling me that there's one of these mass clocks on all these churches?'

'There's one at St Ninian's,' said Sloan. 'Scratch dials, they're sometimes called.' He paused and then said, 'It would be easy enough to make a little hole and draw a line on the stonework of the others if they hadn't got one already.'

'Except St Catherine's, which hasn't got any stonework.'

'All metal and glass,' agreed Sloan, 'more's the pity.'

'And no one would ever notice something like that on an old church, would they?' The Assistant Chief Constable reached for the telephone. 'Right, Sloan, we'll tell these intelligence types where the next meeting will be . . .'

'And when, sir . . .'

'Amazing where a bit of ratiocination can get you, isn't it?'

'Sir?'

'A Latin word,' said his superior officer airily, 'for a conclusion reached by reasoning.'

Cold Comfort

Sixteenth-century Scotland

Sheriff Macmillan hadn't at first heard the sound of the approaching bagpipes but the hall-boy at Drummondreach had. Upon the instant, the lad uncurled himself from the rush-strewn floor and reached for his own set of pipes, listening intently the while. He began to pump up the bag under his arm even as he scrambled to his feet, making ready to carry out his duty of first identifying and then heralding any new arrivals at the policies of Rhuaraidh Macmillan, Sheriff of Fearnshire.

Cocking his ear in the direction of the distant pipes, the boy echoed his response with the preliminary notes of a lament. That sound, though, brought the Sheriff to the entrance hall of his dwelling place quickly enough, even though the other bagpipe players were still a mile or more away.

'They're playing "The Fearnshire Lament", my lord,' said the boy, his own acute hearing demonstrating one of the many advantages of youth to the older man. 'I ken it well . . .'

'Aye,' said the Sheriff crisply. 'I hear it quite clearly myself now . . .'

Rhuaraidh Macmillan stepped back more than a little thoughtfully while the hall-boy took up the bagpipes' chanter again and made to answer those heard from afar but as yet still unseen. The playing of that melancholy tune carried its own sad significance to the Sheriff. It meant not only that those coming near approached in sorrow rather than in anger but that a man was untimely dead somewhere nearby and within his jurisdiction.

It meant more than just dead, of course.

That particular lament told both Sheriff Macmillan and the hall-boy at Drummondreach that the death being announced by the playing of the dirge was of a known clansman. It was not some enemy or stranger of no consequence who was being thus sung. It foretold rather that a man had died from within the tight little circle which comprised the close-knit aristocracy of the Fearnshire clans.

'Who'll it be this time?' he pondered aloud. The Sheriff's writ ran among clansmen all tied by generations of auld alliances and ancient fealties. Rumour had it that the new Queen in Edinburgh – she who had lately come over from France – had referred to them as unruly tribes, but that was not to understand their allegiances to the land and its people, both of which had been established in these northern parts for time out of mind.

'I think I can see them now, my lord,' said the boy.

And it must be said, the Sheriff admitted fairly to himself, there were men around too who were locked together by equally ancient enmities. Memories in the

Highlands were long and unforgiving. Perhaps this was what Her Majesty at Holyroodhouse had been told . . .

Perhaps too it was different over in France.

'There's three of them, my lord,' announced the hall-boy, peering out.

Sometimes, of course, the Sheriff reminded himself as he scanned the horizon, the enmities were still red and raw, just like the scars on Murdo Ross's face. These were still livid from an altercation at hogmanay with Black Ian – Ian Tulloch – of Eileanach. The man had drawn his dirk at Murdo Ross – kinsman and friend – over the delicate matter of which of the pair should at the turn of the year first-foot a certain young lady at Achnagarron, and Ian Tulloch hadn't been seen at Eileanach or anywhere else in Fearnshire from that day to this.

The pipes were calling to each other now like urgent vixens . . .

Moreover – and this was where the Sheriff's responsibilities came in – that lament also meant that the death was of a Fearnshire man who should not have died: that is to say that he – whoever he was – had not died in his bed of a sore sickness or old age.

Thus, according to the old custom of the country, it followed ineluctably that the Sheriff of Fearnshire had duly to be told, and that he had a duty to enquire, had to inspect, had to pronounce and – if it were then proved that the death had been unlawfully at the hand of another – had to punish. What happened in France might well be different, but this was Scotland and, as far as Rhuaraidh Macmillan himself was concerned, this was how things were going to stay, new Queen or not.

The drone of the other pipes could be heard quite clearly now and soon a little gaggle of men hove into view, hurrying down over the brae.

The hall-boy, the keener-eyed of the two, took his lips off the chanter long enough to say, 'Angus Mackintosh of Balblair, my lord, and a Mackenzie . . .'

'Colin of that ilk,' observed the Sheriff without enthusiasm. The man was a troublemaker.

'And Merkland of Culbokie, Younger,' said the hall-boy, resuming his pipes.

Rhuaraidh Macmillan advanced towards the threshold and waited for the men to reach him, sniffing the air as he did so. It was a little warmer today and not before time. Spring, he decided, must really have come to the Highlands at long, long last – and that after one of the darkest, coldest winters in living memory. It was the same each year, though, he conceded to himself. He always began to doubt the return of warmer weather and then, suddenly, like the midges, it was upon them.

The drone of the pipes died away as the three visitors drew near. Colin Mackenzie stood forward as self-appointed spokesman, while Angus Mackintosh and young Hugh Merkland kept a pace or two behind him.

'We've found Black Ian,' announced the man Mackenzie breathlessly. 'Ian Tulloch . . .'

'Dead,' added Hugh Merkland.

'Long dead,' supplemented Angus Mackintosh.

'And Murdo Ross is away over to the west,' said Mackenzie, adding meaningfully, 'today.'

'Just as soon as he heard Black Ian had been found,' chimed in Angus.

Colin Mackenzie said, 'You'll no' have forgotten, Sheriff, that it was Ian Tulloch that struck Murdo Ross.'

'I remember,' said the Sheriff shortly.

Striking any man was bad, striking a relative or friend much worse. Doing it with a weapon in the hand was never likely to be forgotten, still less forgiven. Even worse was the crime of following a man to his own dwelling place and assaulting him there – otherwise known as hamesucken. And that was what Ian Tulloch had done.

'Murdo Ross was off like the De'il himself was chasing him,' contributed Hugh Merkland, 'as soon as he was told the news.'

'Perhaps the Devil was chasing him,' said Mackintosh insouciantly. 'How can any man tell what Satan looks like?'

Merkland ignored this and went on eagerly, 'Will we be going after him for you, Sheriff?'

'You will not,' said Rhuaraidh Macmillan firmly. 'You will be first telling me where you found Black Ian dead.'

'In a barn at Eileanach.'

'More bothy than barn,' put in Angus Mackintosh.

Merkland said, 'The men were taking the sheep up to the hills for the summer . . .'

Sheriff Macmillan nodded. The annual movement of the sheep to the higher ground was a late spring ritual in Fearnshire. The French had a special word for it – *transhumance* – not that the new Queen would be likely to know about it, for all her regal French connections. Summer pasture for sheep would not be one of the concerns of her world . . . She had others, though, from all accounts. Mostly to do with the heart, he had heard.

' . . . and when they got up there the drovers tried to open up the place as usual but they couldn'a get in,' Merkland was saying.

'How did you know he was dead?' asked the Sheriff.

There was a pause while Mackenzie shifted from foot to foot. 'He was hanging from a beam.'

'We saw him through the cracks in the wood,' vouchsafed Colin Mackenzie. 'We couldn'a get in either, you see.'

'Dead long since, with a bang-rape round his neck,' supplied Angus Mackintosh.

'Someone must have been after the hay,' said the Sheriff.

A bang-rape was a rope with a noose used by thieves for carrying off corn or hay. It would do fine for hanging a man too.

'Maybe so, Sheriff, but they didn't steal what hay was there,' said Angus Mackintosh. 'It's still strewn about in the bothy.'

'Ian's axe is there too,' said Mackenzie. 'It's standing against the wall.'

'Nobody could get in to take it, you see,' contributed Hugh Merkland. 'The door was barred on the inside.' He waved a hand. 'It still is.'

'So why then did Murdo Ross go away to the west when he heard?' asked the Sheriff, not unreasonably. For a man to take his own life in these parts was rare enough, but a man who had harmed friend and family might well feel that he should. 'If the door had been barred on the inside by Ian Tulloch . . .

'Anyone,' sighed the Sheriff, 'who had reached man's estate could have told Black Ian that remorse was the most difficult – in fact, the only intolerable – emotion with which to live.'

There was an uncomfortable pause and an uneasy shuffling of feet as it became apparent that not one of the three wished to answer his question about Murdo Ross.

'Well?' demanded Rhuaraidh Macmillan.

Eventually Colin Mackenzie said uneasily, 'We couldn'a see anything there, Sheriff, that Black Ian could have been standing on . . . before . . .'

'Nothing at all,' said Merkland.

'Not a thing.' Mackintosh of Balblair endorsed this. 'We looked.'

'Whoever had put him there must have taken it away with them,' said Hugh Merkland, adding, 'Whatever it was.'

'I see,' said the Sheriff.

'Now shall we go after Murdo Ross for you, Sheriff?' said Merkland impatiently. 'He'll be well away by now.'

'No,' said Rhuaraidh Macmillan at once. 'You'll come with me back to Eileanach. First I must see the body.'

Now, *super visum corporis* was a phrase Her new Majesty at Edinburgh, a daughter of Mary of Guise or not, would surely understand. They said she was good at the Latin as well as at the French. It was her lack of comprehension of the Gaelic, indeed of nearly all matters Scottish, that was the worry . . .

*

Mounted on his palfrey, his clerk riding a little behind him, the Sheriff led the party out towards the broad strath above which lay Ian Tulloch's lands. The journey took time. The bothy was far away up in the hills, alongside the route of one of the old coffin roads over to a clan burial ground and already halfway to the west as it was.

His mount stumbled and slipped from time to time as it tried to pick its way over the bare stony track towards the rough building. What was possible for men on foot and hardy sheep was not so easy for a horse. Spring might have come to the lower-lying ground, but higher up winter had only just left. Rhuaraidh Macmillan could see that even higher there was still snow and ice lying on the side of the ben. On a north-facing hillside, both could linger all summer.

'There, Sheriff – ' Colin Mackenzie pointed. 'You see yon bothy over there?'

'Aye,' agreed Macmillan, automatically noting that any footprints in the snow leading to the building were long gone. And so were any footprints in the snow leading away . . . Equally, any marks made by footprints on the ground since the thaw would have been overlaid by those made more recently by men and sheep.

'Look, Sheriff, through this gap here . . .' Colin Mackenzie already had his eye to a crack in the door.

Rhuaraidh Macmillan reluctantly brought his horse to a standstill on the track. There would be those – and plenty – who held that Murdo Ross had been well within his rights in exacting his revenge on Ian Tulloch for raising his weapon – if he had, that is – against

Murdo in anger, let alone in jealousy; who would insist for all time that Black Ian had received only his just desserts for an attack on a life-long friend – to say nothing of one with blood ties.

That, however, was not the law and the law must be served above anger and jealousy. This applied in Fearnshire if not any longer in Holyroodhouse in Edinburgh. Aye, there was the rub. Rhuaraidh Macmillan straightened himself up in the saddle. The difference was that he himself was responsible for the upholding of law and order in Fearnshire. Who exactly it was who was responsible for law and order and not anger and jealousy triumphing at the Scottish court today was not for him to say . . .

The Sheriff dismounted and bent his eye – albeit unwillingly – to the crack in the wooden door of the bothy.

What the three men had told him was true. Swinging from a high beam without handholds to reach it was a body. That it was of Ian Tulloch he was in no doubt. 'Black' might have been how the man had been known in his lifetime; it was assuredly an accurate description of how he now looked many weeks after his death.

The Sheriff's gaze travelled down from the suspended body to the floor. What the men had told him about that was true too. There was nothing at all there which Black Ian could have climbed on or kicked aside to jump to his death. All that was visible was a large damp puddle on the floor, surely greater by far than could have come from the body above. He put his shoulder to the door of the bothy and found, as the others had done, that the entrance was still firmly barred against them.

'Shall we batter the door down, Sheriff?' asked Hugh Merkland, always a man of action rather than thought.

'No,' said Rhuaraidh Macmillan sternly. 'Wait you all over there while I take a look around.'

He walked slowly and carefully round the outside of the bothy. Ramshackle it might be, but it was still proof against the elements and animals. Deer would not have been able to get in there any more than the four men could. The primitive building had never boasted windows or a chimney.

'Murdo Ross'll be away over the hills by nightfall,' murmured Merkland restively. 'We'll no' catch him now.'

'And Black Ian didn't have any other enemies,' said Colin Mackenzie with emphasis. 'None at all.'

'Och, one enemy's enough for any man,' put in Angus Mackintosh of Balblair, stroking his chin sagely. 'Isn't it, now?'

'Black Ian was his own worst enemy,' said the Sheriff, stepping back to examine the roof. 'He didn't need others. You all know that.'

'Aye, that's true,' conceded Colin Mackenzie, nodding. 'The man should never have taken cold steel to a kinsman right enough . . . What is it that you're seeing on the roof, Sheriff?'

'Nothing,' replied that official with perfect truth. 'It's quite sound.'

'It would need to be up here,' observed Angus Mackintosh, looking round the bleak countryside. 'If the wind had once got under it, yon roof would be away up over Beinn nan Eun in no time at all.'

'Or down in the loch,' said Merkland.

Colin Mackenzie pointed down the hill. 'It's a wonder Black Ian didn't just jump into Loch Bealach Culaidh there – if he had a mind to make away with himself, that is.'

'It's hard to drown if you're a swimmer,' remarked the Sheriff. 'Or if the water's frozen.'

'It's hard to hang yourself from a high beam without having anything to hold on to or stand on to get you there,' said Hugh Merkland. 'I still think we should be away after Murdo Ross . . .'

'No,' said the Sheriff quietly. 'Tell me, is that Ian Tulloch's own axe I saw in there?'

'It is,' said Mackenzie.

'Ah . . .'

'Man,' exploded Merkland, 'you dinna need an axe to hang yoursel'.'

'Ian Tulloch did,' murmured the Sheriff.

'But . . .' Merkland's eyebrows came together in a ferocious frown.

'He couldn't have done what he did without an axe,' said the Sheriff. 'Or something like it.'

'But it's rope you need to hang yoursel',' protested Colin Mackenzie. 'We all know that.'

'Mind you,' said Rhuaraidh Macmillan, 'I'm not saying that Black Ian didn't need the rope as well as his axe.'

'But . . .' Hugh Merkland began his objection in turn.

The Sheriff said, 'He needed the rope afterwards.'

'Afterwards?' echoed Merkland.

'After he had used the axe.'

'But . . .' began Colin Mackenzie.

'And the rope together,' said the Sheriff.

'I still don't understand,' said Colin Mackenzie.

'Neither did Murdo Ross,' said the Sheriff, 'and that's why he's away to the west in such a hurry.' Rhuaraidh Macmillan gave the door of the bothy another great shake. 'It's barred right enough and by my reckoning it was Ian Tulloch himself that put the bar on the inside there.'

'And so,' demanded Colin Mackenzie truculently, 'how did he get himself high enough to hang himself from that beam without anything to stand on?'

'Ah,' said the Sheriff neatly, 'he did have something to stand on.'

'But there's nothing there,' said Colin

Mackenzie. 'Nothing at all.'

'There's nothing there now,' said the Sheriff patiently. 'There was something there that he could stand on at the time.'

'That's taken itself away?' growled Colin Mackenzie derisively.

'In a manner of speaking, yes,' replied the Sheriff. 'But it was brought there by Ian Tulloch himself using the bang-rape and his axe.'

Colin Mackenzie drew himself up and said with dignity. 'I'm thinking that you are for making fools of us, Sheriff.'

'Is it the Little People we're going to have to thank for killing Black Ian, then?' chimed in Hugh Merkland scornfully.

Angus Mackintosh asked instead, 'What is there, then, Sheriff, that Black Ian could have brought here with an axe and a noose that's gone away on its own after he used it?'

'A block of ice,' said Rhuaraidh Macmillan, pointing to where some still lay unmelted further up the hill-side. 'Now will you be away, all of you and find Murdo Ross and tell him to come back?'

Chapter and Hearse

'Sloan,' barked Police Superintendent Leeyes down the telephone, 'you're wanted, and quickly!'

'I'll be right over, sir.' Detective Inspector C. D. Sloan didn't exactly click his heels together, but he did get to his feet pretty smartly.

'No, not by me. Don't come to my office.'

'Sir?'

'It's the Assistant Chief Constable who's asking for you.' The Superintendent didn't even try to keep his amazement at this unlikely event out of his voice. 'Don't ask me why.'

'Me, Sir?'

Detective Inspector Sloan did a rapid mental revision of his past week and work. As far as he knew, he hadn't blotted his copybook in any way, but you never knew. With the Police and Criminal Evidence Act in operation, even not offering a suspect a cup of tea was capable of being misconstrued by a defence solicitor.

'You, Sloan. He says,' said Superintendent Leeyes, 'that it's a sudden emergency.'

'I'm on my way.'

*

The Assistant Chief Constable – a gentleman copper if ever there was one – received him with his customary courtesy.

'Ah, Sloan, there you are . . .' If there was anything urgent pending, it certainly didn't show in his manner. 'Take a seat.'

'Thank you, sir.' It wasn't going to be a disciplinary matter, then: rebukes were delivered to a man standing. On the carpet, if there was one.

'A little problem has cropped up this morning in connection with the Minster.'

Sloan sat down. That explained one thing anyway. Calleford Minster was not in Superintendent Leeyes's 'F' Division and the Superintendent took as narrow a view as did the Coroner as to what was and what was not within his jurisdiction.

'And,' continued the Assistant Chief Constable unhurriedly, 'it's got to be resolved before tonight.'

'I see, sir.'

'By half past seven, actually,' said the Assistant Chief Constable.

'Time is of the essence, then, is it?' ventured Sloan.

'It was and it is,' said his superior enigmatically.

'And the problem?'

'There are two problems,' said the ACC, 'and one of them is murder.'

'Ah!' And the victim, sir . . .' Every case had to begin somewhere and every case – every murder case anyway – had a victim. 'Do we know . . .'

'Oh, yes, Sloan. There's no doubt about that. The man's name was Lechlade. Walter Lechlade. Exact age unknown. Probably about forty.'

'And his occupation?' If unemployment carried on on its present-day scale, a man's occupation – or lack of it – would soon cease to be worth recording.

'Precentor and prebendary,' said the ACC.

'So this Walter Lechlade was a clerical gentleman, then, was he, sir?' Sloan wasn't quite sure of his ground here, but the words sounded ecclesiastical enough and they were talking about cathedrals.

'That's the whole trouble,' said the ACC gently.

'The Church looking after its own?' suggested Sloan. It had, after all, been known to happen.

'Well,' conceded the ACC, stroking his chin, 'I must say it was all hushed up at the time. Nothing written down and so forth.'

'People will always try . . .'

'Until Peter Quivel – he's the Bishop in the case – started making a fuss.'

'Ah,' said Sloan. 'Truth will out.'

'I'd very much like to think so, Sloan, but I'm afraid the bishop had his own axe to grind.'

'It happens,' said Sloan, without thinking. He pulled himself together and got down to business – he wasn't here to philosophize. 'And the time of this murder, sir?' After all, the ACC had said himself that time was of the essence, hadn't he? 'Is it known?'

The ACC looked down at a pile of notes on his desk. 'Between one and two o'clock in the morning.'

'And where exactly?' Detective Inspector Sloan opened his notebook from sheer force of habit.

'Between the cathedral and Lechlade's own house nearby. That is, in the lane between the Bishop's Close and Canon de Derteford's house at the corner of Bear Lane.'

'Not a very usual hour for a clergyman to be out and about, sir, if I may say so.' Sloan tried not to sound at all censorious. Time was when it would have been relatively safe to be abroad at that time of night, but not these days. Small wonder, though, that someone had wanted the whole matter hushed up.

'Oh, yes, it was,' said the ACC unexpectedly.

'Not a sensible hour even so, though,' insisted Sloan.

'He was in the Cathedral Close,' the ACC reminded him.

'But was it secure?' said Sloan, unimpressed.

'Well, no, it wasn't actually. That's the whole point. But it ought to have been, Sloan, and I must say you've got to the heart of the matter very quickly.'

'Thank you, sir.'

'You see, the gates to the Close should have been shut at curfew . . .'

'It's good that these old customs are kept up, sir, isn't it?' put in Sloan. 'It's still done at eight o'clock every evening at the Minster, I believe.'

'Yes,' responded the ACC briskly. 'But what happened the night Walter Lechlade was murdered, Sloan, was that not only was one of the gates – the south gate – left open for his murderers to come in, but it was also left open for them to get out.'

'Murderers?' Sloan sat up. 'Was it a gang-killing, sir, then?' They didn't have a lot of those in the mainly rural county of Calleshire, thank goodness, but the ways of the city were bound to reach them in the end.

'I suppose you could say that it was, Sloan,' agreed the ACC thoughtfully. 'I must say I hadn't thought of it in that light myself . . . More of a conspiracy, you might say.'

'And the gateman given something for his – er – forgetfulness?'

'He was indeed,' said the ACC warmly, 'and probably not what he expected either.' He prodded the pile of papers in front of him. 'He – the gateman, name of Stonyng, Richard Stonyng – said that the Mayor hadn't told him to shut the gate.'

'What had it got to do with the Mayor, might I ask?' Criminal investigation and local government usually met head on over fraud and planning law, not murder.

'Quite a lot. The cathedral had been in dispute with the civil authorities about their boundaries for years.'

'It's not unknown, sir.' It had always been a great relief to Sloan that property disputes were civil not criminal matters. He added a trifle sententiously, 'Good fences make good neighbours.'

'Good neighbours the city and cathedral weren't,' said the ACC emphatically, 'In the old days, men on the run from the Mayor and commonalty used to jump over St Peter's churchyard wall and take sanctuary in the cathedral – much to the city's annoyance.'

'Men have always tried to escape from justice,' observed Sloan, who carried several scars on his person to prove it.

'I suppose,' said the ACC, who had been at school at Eton, 'that you could call it a sort of Wall Game. Anyway, it seems that the man on the gate . . .'

Sloan glanced at his notebook. 'Richard Stonyng . . .'

' . . . took his orders from the Mayor that night.'

'And the Mayor's name, sir?' prompted Sloan, his pen poised. Office holders always had recorded names.

'Alfred Duport.'

'And where, sir, does he come in, or don't we know?'

'Good question, Sloan. First and foremost, he seems to have been in cahoots with the Dean against the Bishop.'

'That's bad.' It sounded an unholy alliance to Sloan.

'Very. But not unknown in English history,' said the ACC grimly. 'In this instance, the *casus belli* . . .'

'Beg pardon, sir?'

'What? Oh, sorry, Sloan. The cause of their dispute was the appointment of John Pycot as Dean of the cathedral . . .'

'Not popular?'

'Not with Bishop Peter Quivel anyway. He said the election had been rigged.'

'And as it was the Bishop who – er – blew the gaff, do I take it the Dean had something to do with the death of the pre . . . the other clerical gentleman, sir?' Rigged elections were not usually the province of a detective inspector, but murder was.

'You've got it in one, Sloan,' said the ACC, beaming.

'Not a lot of brotherly love lost?' observed Sloan. That, at least, could be safely said about most murders.

'None.'

'But why should it have been Walter Lechlade who got killed, then?' asked Sloan, anxious to get at least one thing clear.

'Pro-Bishop, anti-Dean,' said the ACC succinctly.

'So where does the Mayor – Alfred Duport – come in, then?' asked Sloan for the second time.

'Friend of the Dean,' said the ACC.

'But the Dean wasn't the murderer, surely, sir, was he?' ventured Sloan, although he was naturally prepared to concede that it wasn't what you knew that mattered but who.

'John Pycot didn't kill Walter Lechlade personally, if that's what you mean,' said the ACC, 'any more than Henry II actually killed Thomas à Becket on an earlier and much more celebrated occasion.'

'That, sir,' observed Sloan, greatly daring, 'is a fine point.'

'Oh, the King was morally guilty,' conceded the ACC, who didn't have to deal with split hairs on a daily basis in court. 'No doubt about that.'

'And did penance,' said Sloan. There had been a picture in his history book of a barefoot Henry, in sackcloth and ashes, making his way to Canterbury in the snow to be flogged that had stayed in Sloan's mind since he was a small boy.

'The Dean did penance too,' said the ACC.

'For helping get rid of another turbulent priest?' asked Sloan, his memory stirred now.

'For getting rid of a priest,' amended the ACC.

'Really, sir?' Sloan's mother, who was a great churchwoman, was forever insisting that she didn't know what the Church was coming to. It was beginning to sound as if she might be right.

'From all accounts,' said the ACC drily, 'it was the Dean who was turbulent.'

For reasons that Sloan had never enquired into, his

mother always blamed any present-day trouble in a cathedral on Thomas Cranmer and his statutes – perhaps he should have listened to her more. Detection was a more arcane business than it seemed at first sight.

The ACC was still talking. 'History, Sloan, says that Walter Lechlade was a peaceable enough fellow. Not that that saved him, of course.'

Detective Inspector Sloan nodded. Being peaceable was no insurance against being murdered. 'How was he killed?' he asked, the policeman in him taking over from the erstwhile schoolboy and the inattentive son. There had, he remembered, been another Archbishop of Canterbury as well as Thomas à Becket who had been done to death in office. His name had stayed in Sloan's memory from his history lessons purely because of the manner of his murder.

The ACC consulted his papers again. 'Two blows on the skull and the arm from knives, swords and Danish axes.'

'Not a lot of those about, sir.' With that other archbishop, St Alphege, it had been ox bones.

'There were then, Sloan.'

'Then?' Sloan's pen stayed suspended above his notebook, a suspicion confirmed. 'Do I take it, sir, that we're not talking about the here and now?'

'Yes and no,' said the ACC, quite unabashed. 'More of the there and then, perhaps, than the here and now, but some of both.'

'Might I ask where?'

'Exeter, Sloan.'

'And when?'

'November 1283.'

'When the Mayor and the Dean murdered this Walter Lechlade . . .'

'The Precentor . . .'

'With a Danish axe?' Their pastry must have come later.

'No, no, Sloan. The actual murder was done by others, orchestrated by three vicars and a canon . . .'

With Thomas à Becket, thought Sloan, it had been four knights, but the end result had still been the same spilling of brains.

'In fact,' murmured the ACC, 'one commentator called 'em satellites of Satan.'

Sloan said he wasn't at all surprised.

'Henry de Stanway, clerk in holy orders, John de Wolrington, Vicar of Ottery St Mary, John de Christenstowe, Vicar of Heavitree, and Canon Reginald de Ercevesk,' recited the ACC. 'Almost the Four Horsemen of the Apocalypse, you might say.'

'Caused a bit of a flutter in the dovecotes, that, I dare say, sir.' There had been other clergymen who had hit the headlines, but Sloan didn't think this was the moment to mention them.

'The Bishop appealed to the King for justice.'

'And which King would that have been, sir?'

'Edward I of blessed memory.'

'The Hammer of the Scots?' More of those history lessons had stuck than Sloan had appreciated.

'He was known as the English Justinian,' said the ACC, who had had a classical education.

'I didn't know that, sir.'

'And he came down to Exeter at Christmas 1285.'

'Two years later?' In Sloan's book, justice delayed was justice denied.

'This is where it gets interesting, Sloan.'

'Really, sir?' Interesting, he decided, it might be; urgent – today, this minute, urgent – he couldn't see how it could possibly be.

'The case was begun on Monday 24 December . . .'

'Christmas Eve?'

'Christmas Eve – the judges were Roger de Loveday and Richard de Boyland – and then it was adjourned for Christmas.'

' "The hungry judges soon the sentences sign",' said Sloan, quoting Alexander Pope, ' "And wretches hang that jurymen may dine".' They had that piece in their speeches each time at the Berebury Magistrates' Annual Dinner.

'It wasn't like that at all,' said the ACC a trifle plaintively. 'No, they all kept Christmas Day in high old style and then, on St Stephen's Day . . .'

'Boxing Day.'

'They found Richard Stonyng . . .'

'The gatekeeper . . .'

' . . . guilty of murder.'

'For not shutting the gate?' Sloan was sensitive about gates. There had been one terrible week in his schooldays when the boy who had been detailed to play brave Horatius, Captain of the Gate, had gone down with mumps. Sloan had been the unwilling understudy and anything to do with gates, fearful odds, ashes of his fathers and temples of his gods still struck an unhappy chord.

'For opening the gate to let the felons in before the

murder and for not shutting it after the deed was done to keep them in.'

'I see, sir.' Dereliction of duty or complicity he would have called that himself, but apparently the judges had reckoned it murder. 'An accessory before and after the fact,' he said neatly.

'And as for "Mr Mayor, sirrrr" . . .' baaa'd the ACC in the tones of Larry the Lamb.

'Alfred Duport,' supplied Sloan. The ACC's literary background had obviously been broad enough to have included *Toytown*.

'Found guilty of consenting to and planning the felony and receiving and harbouring the felons.'

'Aiding and abetting,' translated Sloan.

'And then on Holy Innocents' Day . . .'

That, thought Sloan, couldn't have been judicial irony, surely?

' . . . all those who had pleaded benefit of clergy . . .'

'That, sir,' said Sloan, 'was some sort of establishment cop-out, wasn't it?' He knew that, like sanctuary, they didn't have it any more, although it was true to say that the only criminal clergymen to come his way officially had certainly been attempting – one way and another – something for their own benefit.

'A way of exculpation of men of the cloth grounded in a text in the First Book of Chronicles,' said the ACC, admitting that he'd looked it up. 'Chapter sixteen, verse twenty-two.'

Sloan decided he really would have to pay more attention to his mother's interests in future.

The ACC shuffled the notes on his desk and read out, ' "Touch not mine anointed and do my prophets no harm." And all they had to do to prove they were clerks in holy orders was to be able to read the first verse of Psalm fifty-one. The Miserere.'

'So the clerical conspirators got off?' concluded Sloan doggedly.

'Handed over to their bishops, except the Dean, who was sent to a monastery.'

'And the actual murderers, sir?' Sloan knew who he meant – the ones with blood on their hands, which was as good a definition as any he knew.

'Escaped abroad.'

Detective Inspector Sloan, currently coming to terms with the vagaries of the Crown Prosecution Service, sighed and said, 'Not a very satisfactory outcome, sir.'

'There was one more puzzle.'

'Sir?'

'The records are a bit shaky, but afterwards they wrote down that the Mayor had been hanged on St Stephen's Day.'

'But,' said Sloan, frowning, 'surely that was before he was tried?'

'It has been known.'

'Lynch law.' That was the only law the police were pledged not to uphold.

'Actually, Sloan, it was known as Lydford law. Punish first and try afterwards.'

Sloan said he thought 'Try first and don't punish afterwards' was more the vogue these days.

The ACC said, 'What they meant was that the prisons were so awful that often those who were accused died from gaol fever before they could be brought to trial – which is rather different.'

'Yes, sir.' Sloan paused. 'I take it that this has all been written up somewhere?'

'Admirably.'* The ACC patted a thin, square grey book on his desk. 'I can't think why no one's made a play out of it.'

What Detective Inspector Sloan couldn't help but wonder was how something that had happened in the year 1283 could suddenly become enough of an emergency this morning for him to have been summoned post-haste from dealing with latter-day criminals who only ever pleaded broken homes and unhappy childhoods.

'You think it hangs together all right, Sloan, do you?' asked the ACC.

'Yes, sir.'

'I've made myself quite clear, I hope?'

'Perfectly, sir.'

'And you found it an interesting case?'

'Yes, sir.' He ventured a modest pun. 'What you might call a top-brass rubbing-out.'

'The difficulty is,' said the ACC, surreptitiously making a note of this, 'that they have a literary and historical society attached to Calleford Minster. I belong myself.'

'Really, sir?'

'And they've got a bit of a problem.'

'Sir?'

'Yes, indeed.' The ACC leaned back in his chair.

* Frances Rose-Troup, *Exeter Vignettes* (Manchester University Press, 1942).

'Their secretary's just rung me to say that tonight's speaker has been taken ill and would I step into the breach with something suitable.'

'I see, sir.' The quotation 'Once more unto the breach, dear friends, once more' could, Sloan felt, safely be left to the Chairman in his introduction.

'I thought I would tell them about this murder,' said the ACC.

'The cathedral interest.' Sloan nodded.

'I'm calling my talk "Another Exeter Riddle", Sloan, because there were some famous medieval Exeter riddles . . .'

It all seemed quite open and shut to Sloan. He said restrainedly, 'Should go down very well, sir.'

'It was helpful to rehearse it with you,' said the ACC unblushingly.

'Thank you, sir.'

'I thought I would begin with a quotation.'

'It's often done, I understand, sir.' It was always done at the Berebury Magistrates' Annual Dinner.

'From Shakespeare.'

'Naturally, sir.'

'This one.' The ACC squinted modestly down at his notes. ' "Some men are born great, some achieve greatness, and some have greatness thrust upon them . . ." '

The Widow's Might

Anthony Mainwaring Heber-Hibbs knew to a nicety the moment at which to step out from under the shelter of the canopy outside the airport lounge and into the hot sun of Lasserta. It was immediately after the aeroplane had trundled up the runway, come to a final standstill and been linked to the landing steps.

And not a moment before, the heat of the sun in Lasserta being what it always was.

He stood forward now but doffed his topi only as the cabin door opened and the first of the passengers began to stumble out into the open air after their long journey from England.

It wasn't by any means every visiting group that the Ambassador turned out for in this manner. There had been a party of archaeologists the month before that he hadn't so received and last week a posse of forensic accountants had similarly landed at Lasserta airport without being officially welcomed. They had arrived to look into the flourishing money-laundering industry for which the sheikhdom was renowned, Lasserta being one of the most efficient of the world's rapidly diminishing number of tax havens, while the archaeologists had been searching for signs of a really ancient civilization in this antique desert land.

Her Britannic Majesty's Ambassador had allowed both those other parties to touch down without affording them any diplomatic niceties. The East Calleshire Regimental Association – in this instance, a group of widows and orphans – came into a rather different category. The accountants had talked about 'widows and orphans' as well, but they had referred to them in a financial context as potential assets for someone – he wasn't quite sure whom. His secretary too sometimes spoke of 'widows and orphans' when she was producing reports, but why he never knew or asked.

These widows and orphans – the Calleshire ones – were quite different. And something had given him cause to think that they weren't going to be exactly assets either . . .

The people coming off the aeroplane now were real widows and real orphans from an ill-fated Anglo-Lassertan military campaign of some twenty years ago which had come to be known as the Engagement at Bakhalla. This disastrous action had strayed uncomfortably near the Sheikh's palace at Bakhalla, hence its name.

Anthony Heber-Hibbs had deemed it appropriate – the words 'appropriate' and 'inappropriate' were much used in diplomatic circles – that he give this particular tour a polite reception.

He therefore advanced, a model of civility, right hand outstretched, towards their leader as she reached the bottom of the steps. Mrs Norah Letherington, a woman clearly born to command and looking every inch the late Colonel's lady, responded with a firm – albeit slightly damp and sticky – grasp.

'Is it always as hot as this here?' she asked faintly as the heat rising from the airport tarmac hit her in an advancing wave for the first time.

'I'm afraid so, madam,' he said, replacing his formal headgear before the sun got at what was left of his hair.

Mrs Letherington blinked in the glare of the sun and beckoned her trusty lieutenant forward to be introduced. 'This is my deputy, Miss Ann Arkwright.'

The Ambassador bowed towards a sandy-haired woman whose freckled skin would doubtless soon begin to suffer from the sunlight.

'And – ' Mrs Letherington half turned as a young man in crumpled jeans and grubby T-shirt appeared at her elbow – 'this is Colin Stubbings, who is acting as our military adviser for the tour.'

Only years of training in the diplomatic service kept the Ambassador's eyebrows in place rather than raised to his hair-line as he surveyed an unattractive youth who had not quite outgrown acne. Anthony Heber-Hibbs charitably attributed the incipient beard to the difficulties of shaving on a long-haul flight, but not even charity could cause him to forgive the libidinous logo on the young man's T-shirt.

'Your adviser?' he asked politely.

'Colin has made a special study of the Anglo-Lassertan campaign,' she explained quickly, sensing his reaction, 'especially the Engagement at Bakhalla.'

'Has he?' responded the Ambassador without enthusiasm.

'He's a student of military history at the university,' she went on, 'and naturally, since he lost his father out here – George Stubbings was a Sergeant in the action – he's always taken a particular interest in what went on in the campaign.'

'Quite so,' said Heber-Hibbs, hastily pulling himself together. 'Well, I mustn't keep you standing here in the sun. Very bad for you all, especially if you're not used to it. Now, I understand that you're staying at the Coningsby Hotel in Gatt-el-Abbas, so . . .'

'That's where the general staff holed up during the Bakhalla campaign,' Colin Stubbings informed him. 'Miles behind the firing line. And well out of danger, of course.' He shrugged. 'Lucky for some, you might say, but not for my mother.' He hitched his shoulder in the direction of a large woman in a floral dress now descending the airline steps as if her feet hurt. 'Most of dad's platoon got wiped out.'

'Colin,' Mrs Letherington informed Heber-Hibbs, perhaps feeling some further explanation was warranted, 'was awarded the Tarsus College History Prize for an essay on what Anthony Eden should really have done when Nasser annexed the Suez Canal.'

'Did he indeed,' murmured the Ambassador.

'Instead of what he did do,' added Colin Stubbings gratuitously.

'Naturally,' said Anthony Heber-Hibbs at his smoothest. 'It wouldn't have been a matter of speculation otherwise, would it? Only fact – which always gives one so much less scope, don't you think?'

'I don't mind telling you that it's fact that we've

come out here for,' announced Stubbings bluntly. 'To find out what really happened at Bakhalla.'

'Ah,' said Anthony Heber-Hibbs.

' "Theirs not to reason why", of course, "Theirs but to do and die",' quoted Stubbings, 'and die they did.' He sniffed. 'Not much of a poet, Tennyson, but at least he got Balaclava right.'

'Yes, indeed,' agreed the Ambassador, hoping that there had been no other parallels in the Engagement at Bakhalla with the ill-fated Charge of the Light Brigade, or, come to that, with the Charge of the Heavy Brigade either.

'Someone had blundered,' declared Stubbings firmly.

'The Earl of Cardigan, I think,' murmured Heber-Hibbs. 'Or was it Lord Lucan? I'm afraid I'm not an authority on the Crimean War.'

'I meant someone had blundered here in Lasserta,' asserted Stubbings. 'And we don't know who.' He paused and then added ominously, 'Yet.'

'It's too soon for us to be able to examine the official records, you see,' murmured Mrs Letherington obliquely. 'The thirty-year rule and all that.'

'We have to wait another ten years before we can look at them,' put in Ann Arkwright from the sidelines. Her voice quavered slightly. 'I lost my brother out here and I'd really like to know how and why before then.'

'It's ten years to wait only if the records aren't embargoed for another fifty years after that,' said Colin Stubbings. He sniffed. 'I wouldn't put it past them to do that either, things being what they were at Bakhalla.'

'I quite understand,' said Heber-Hibbs readily. Like

almost everyone else he knew, the Ambassador considered thirty years much too soon for official records to be available to the general public. He did his best to sound sympathetic. 'Difficult for you.'

Personally Heber-Hibbs favoured a hundred-year rule, and, given the choice, he would have advised the authorities to leave records undisturbed for at least another hundred years after that for the dust from any battle to settle. Mercifully the Anglo-Lassertan campaign had been only twenty years earlier – well and truly inside the thirty-year rule. This, he was now beginning to realize, was something to be profoundly thankful for.

'It's what they usually do with official records when there's something they want to hide,' asserted Colin Stubbings trenchantly. 'Mark them down as not to be opened for another fifty years.'

Mr Anthony Heber-Hibbs, a man grown old in the Diplomatic Service, decided against enlightening the lad with the truth. What actually happened to records that might damage the reputations of either the living or the great and dead was much simpler than merely placing them under a dated embargo.

They were lost.

Without trace.

Accidentally on purpose, you might say.

'And we shall want to visit the cemetery, of course,' Mrs Letherington was saying, her face clouding. 'My husband's grave . . .'

'I quite understand,' responded Heber-Hibbs gently. 'And naturally if there's any way in which my staff and I can be of assistance to your party . . .'

The Ambassador summoned his Military Attaché as soon as he got back to the Embassy.

'Christopher,' he said, 'you'd better fill me in. I have a feeling that this party means business. What exactly went wrong at Bakhalla?'

'Nobody really seems to know, sir.' He frowned. 'That's the whole trouble.'

'Which is why the widows and orphans have come out here with their battle guru,' deduced Heber-Hibbs. 'To find out. Go on.'

'It would appear that one platoon of the East Calleshires suddenly wheeled away from the main action and disappeared out of view.'

'Never seen again?'

'Not alive,' said Christopher Dunlop ominously.

'It's happened before, of course,' remarked the Ambassador. 'It's not the first time.'

'Sir?'

'The lost Legion of the Ninth. Went missing north of Eboracum – that's York to you and me – around AD 117.'

'Never seen again?'

'Neither dead nor alive,' said Heber-Hibbs. 'Like the lost army of Cambyses. That disappeared in a desert too.'

'Cambyses, sir?'

'King of Persia. Herodotus tells us that the king lost thirty thousand men who'd been sent out to occupy an oasis in the desert. Never seen again either, not one of 'em.'

The Military Attaché coughed. 'They found this platoon of the East Calleshires all right, sir, but dead.

They'd suddenly moved out of range of the covering fire, but no one could say why.'

'Strange,' mused Heber-Hibbs.

'Wiped out to a man,' the Military Attaché said. 'At the time it was put down to lack of intelligence, but they weren't really sure.'

'Never a good thing,' agreed Heber-Hibbs gravely. 'Not having enough intelligence, I mean. Always makes for difficulties.'

'I was talking in the military sense, sir,' said Dunlop hastily. 'I meant a lack of good intelligence.'

'Ah . . .'

'There were plenty of well-trained brains about at the time,' Dunlop assured him. 'No doubt about that.'

'Which is something,' said Heber-Hibbs, who had served in several foreign stations where there hadn't been.

The Military Attaché forged on. 'It seems that the Colonel did all the right things – went by the book and all that – but he was blown up early on, visiting an observation post.'

'Did the wrong thing for the right reasons, I expect,' said Heber-Hibbs with a touch of melancholy.

'As did his successor after he'd been killed – an officer called Arkwright, I believe. He very bravely went off into the desert in an armoured car after the missing platoon.'

'The legion of the lost ones, the cohort of the damned,' said Heber Hibbs, misquoting Kipling, 'the poor little lambs who lost their way . . .'

'Ye-es, sir. I suppose you could put it like that. But I fear it didn't do any of them any good.'

'And I dare say,' sighed Heber-Hibbs, 'there were good reasons for our involvement in this débâcle?'

'Yes, sir.' The Military Attaché cleared his throat. 'As you know, sir, we have this long-standing defence treaty with the sheikhs of Lasserta . . .'

'A half-baked agreement,' responded Heber-Hibbs spiritedly, 'hatched up between Sheikh Ben Mirza Ibrahim Hajal Kisra's great-grandfather and Queen Victoria's ministers . . .'

'To come to the aid of the sheikhdom of Lasserta . . .'

'A benighted country that was only a half-baked protectorate at the time,' swept on Her Britannic Majesty's Ambassador to the state in question with some vigour.

'To come to their aid against their ancient tribal enemies if we deem it necessary,' finished the Military Attaché. 'I think that's the exact wording.'

'In exchange for what?' demanded Heber-Hibbs rhetorically. He, of all people, was well aware of there being no such thing as a free lunch, in the world of international diplomacy as everywhere else.

The Military Attaché took this question literally. 'In theory, sir, in exchange for the Lassertans permanently keeping the Sultan of Zonaras at bay.'

'Say no more,' growled the Ambassador.

There was, in fact, no need for either man to say anything. What had really been being defended at Bakhalla was the only known seam of queremitte ore in the free world. The hard-wearing qualities of this rare mineral had long been much prized by the armaments and space industries, as well as by more ordinary manufacturers. The Sultan of Zonaras was by no means the only man who would have liked to get his hands on queremitte twenty years ago – or now.

'Not so much a case, sir, of trade following the flag,' ventured the Military Attaché with an ironic smile, 'as of the flag following trade.'

'But we still don't really know what made the Engagement at Bakhalla such a disaster, then?' persisted the Ambassador.

'No, sir.'

'I suppose I should have known myself, but I was Third Secretary in Chile at the time, with other things on my plate, and anyway Lasserta was a long way away.' He frowned. 'Surely, man, it shouldn't have been too difficult to see off the Zonarans?'

'It shouldn't,' replied Christopher Dunlop cautiously, 'but it was.'

'Well, let me tell you, Christopher, that there's a cocky little lad staying at the Coningsby Hotel who intends to find out why it was.' The Ambassador stroked his chin. 'That is, if he doesn't know already.'

Colin Stubbings didn't know.

But as a student of military history he did know that time spent in reconnaissance is seldom wasted. While the remainder of the party from Calleshire was bathing and resting, he slipped out of the Coningsby Hotel and made his way to Bakhalla in one of the battered vehicles that in the town of Gatt-el-Abbas constituted cars for hire.

He found the site of the battle easily enough – a stretch of desert leading towards the Kisra Pass. It was this which had had to be held against the warring Zonarans in their advance southwards if Lasserta was to be saved. Tidily to one side lay the white-walled military cemetery, its occupants as neatly ordered as on the parade ground, but he would pay his respects there later – after he had found out what had gone wrong at the Engagement at Bakhalla.

All he had to go on was what a surviving mate of his father had told him. 'I couldn't see what happened all that well, lad,' the old soldier had said, 'because I was over on the west flank with a bunch of Lassertans – not that they were up to much. Couldn't really call 'em fighters. That's why we were there, I suppose.'

'Dad's lot . . .' Colin had prompted him.

'It was a funny thing.' The man had frowned. 'Suddenly your dad's platoon just wheeled away from the main advance and set off into the desert to the east, your dad leading. For no reason at all that anyone could see.'

'But under orders surely?' Colin had said, mindful too of *The Charge of the Light Brigade* and the disputed blame for giving the orders there.

'Not that anyone would admit to giving,' the old soldier had said carefully. 'Proper Valley of Death it looked from where I was, and hellish hot. Didn't stop the Adjutant going after them in an armoured car to see what they were up to.'

'Leading from behind, I suppose.' Colin Stubbings hadn't forgotten 'the sneer of cold command' either.

He'd got the shake of a grizzled head for an answer. 'He bought it too.'

'Communications all gone?'

'There was strict radio silence. We'd got orders to advance and take up our positions behind a good layer of trees and scrub well up the wadi to the north – that's where the blighters were coming from. There was nothing to the east but open ground. "B" platoon must have been a sitting target out there.'

Stubbings could see the scrubland himself now. It constituted a broad band of low but thick growth to the north. He turned his head and looked east, and rubbed his eyes . . . To the east there was rather more in the way of trees, and much better cover than ahead. No wonder his father had led his men that way . . . it must have seemed like Sanctuary Wood in a wilderness.

Puzzled, he went forward.

His father's friend had said there had been nothing to the east but he could see trees in plenty, and established scrub vegetation much more than – as the boys' book had it – 'twenty years a'growing'. Tall, well-grown trees . . .

It was nearing noon now and the desert was at its hottest, shimmering in the heat of the midday sun. He advanced over the rough ground as quickly as he could in that oven-like temperature but seemed to get no nearer to the trees. Muttering under his breath something about mad dogs and Englishmen, he forged on. He got no nearer, though, to the thick band of growth to the east.

Perspiring heavily, he was aware that the ground was falling away a little now, giving a better view of the heights of the Kisra Pass. That meant that 'B' platoon would have been especially vulnerable to fire from the north . . . 'If you can see them, they can see you' was a hard lesson learned in the First World War.

So was 'Know Thine Enemy.'

He was still no nearer the trees.

He stumbled on, weary now and more than a little thirsty. There was a disturbing heat haze coming off the desert and soon the broad swathe of trees ahead began to dance before his eyes. He would go as far as the trees and then turn back.

But walk as far and as fast as he could, he couldn't get to them.

It was then that he stumbled and almost fell. That stopped him for a moment, and when he looked up again the trees had gone.

All of them.

He rubbed his eyes.

There was nothing ahead but sand and desert.

Nothing at all.

Yet he hadn't been dreaming.

He was quite sure about that.

He stood stock still while he gave the matter thought.

His father – that unknown figure in a hallowed photograph, and dead before his son was born – could well have led his platoon to their deaths because of a mirage.

Probably had.

'Sorry, Mum,' he said later that night. 'I don't think the desert's going to give up its secrets.'

'There was no harm in hoping,' she said.

'Not after all this time,' he said.

'Your dad would have done what he thought was right at the time,' said Mrs Stubbings confidently.

'That's what you've always said,' said her son, nodding. 'All you can ever do, really, isn't it, if you've got to live with it afterwards?'

'Which is something he didn't have to do,' she reminded him, 'not coming back.'

'True.' It was something he hadn't thought about until now: the burden of living with military mistakes.

'Always knew his own mind, did your father,' she said.

'A complete mystery,' he announced to the East Calleshire Regimental Association at dinner on their last evening in Lasserta.

'We may never know what really happened.' He paused and gave a little, rather patronizing, smile. 'I'm afraid that war's like that – full of unsolved enigmas that have to be lived with.'

'And Anthony Eden?' enquired the Ambassador with genuine interest. 'What action did you say he should have taken at Suez?'

'Done a deal with Nasser,' said Colin Stubbings unhesitatingly.

'Reached a compromise?' translated Heber-Hibbs.

'Bought into the action more like,' cackled Stubbings. 'Saved a lot of trouble. If you can't beat 'em, join 'em.'

'Ah . . .' said the Ambassador.

'Costs less,' said the representative of the new

generation. 'Nothing wrong with a bit of baksheesh anyway, is there?'

'Well . . .' temporized the diplomat.

Stubbings smirked at Heber-Hibbs. 'As long as you keep it secret. That's what's important.' He winked and added, 'For more than thirty years, mind you . . .'

Handsel Monday

Sixteenth-century Scotland

The little girl lay motionless at the foot of the east turnpike stair. She was sprawled, head downwards, just where the bottom step fanned out into the great hall of the castle. How long she had been lying there, tumbling athwart the first three steps, the Sheriff of Fearnshire did not yet know. All he knew so far was that the child's cheek felt cold to the touch of his ungloved hand.

Quite cold. She was dead.

The air too was cold, bitterly cold, just as cold as it had been the last time that Sheriff Rhuaraidh Macmillan had come to Castle Balgalkin. To make matters worse – if they could be any worse than they already were, that is – it was snowing hard today as well. The cold, though, was the only thing that Sheriff Macmillan had so far found that was the same on this visit as it had been the last time he was at the castle.

Then – it had only been the Monday of last week, although now it seemed much longer ago – the whole of Fearnshire had been *en fête* for the feast of hogmanay. Or should, he mused as he took off his other glove, he start thinking of hogmanay by its French name of *hoguinane* now that everything in Scotland was being influenced by a queen from France?

That day – Hogmanay, he decided obstinately – there had been, as there was every year at Castle Balgalkin, a great ceilidh – and he wasn't going to change that good old Gaelic word for any French one – to celebrate the ending of the old year and the coming in of the new one. And that night, in the best Fearnshire tradition, the Laird of Balgalkin himself had answered the door to the first-footers.

Rhuaraidh Macmillan moved his hand from a cold cheek to the girl's outflung arms, the better to see her hands.

Today it was all very, very different. For one thing, when the Sheriff had arrived there had been no welcoming Laird at the door of the Castle Balgalkin. 'The ancient place of the stag with the white head' was what the desmesne had been called in olden times – Scottish times, not French ones. He wasn't surprised: this winter alone had been hard enough to bring any number of stags down off the hills in search of forage.

Macmillan lifted a limp little hand and started to examine small fingers with surprising tenderness.

On New Year's Eve, only the week before, Sheriff Macmillan and his lady wife had been acclaimed as they had arrived from Drummondreach by a piper who had taken up his bagpipes as soon as he saw the couple get near to the castle. There had been no piper at Castle Balgalkin today and no pibroch heralding his approach with ancient tune. Instead there had been only a distraught servant waiting at the gate, anxiously watching out for the coming of himself and his little entourage.

The child's fingers didn't seem broken to him. And the fingernails definitely weren't.

At the first sight of the Sheriff, the retainer had turned and run back inside the fortillage in a great hurry. Macmillan had heard quite clearly his urgent shout apprising his master of the Sheriff's arrival. His voice had echoed round the castle's sandstone walls with a diminishing resonance, but any sound made by the Laird as he crossed the great hall towards the Sheriff and his clerk had been muffled by the reeds and the rushes that were strewn about the floor.

Those same rushes, deep as they were, noted the Sheriff automatically, had not been deep and soft enough to save the girl as she fell. Even though her head was half covered by them, he could see from where he was standing that her face was badly discoloured by both blood and bruise on the left-hand side.

'It's a bad business, Rhuaraidh . . .' The servant's call had produced the man himself – Hector Leanaig, Laird of Balgalkin. He too had presented a very different picture from the genial host of the week before. A veritable giant of a man, he was sufficiently black-avised to have gone first-footing himself on New Year's Eve. He had come forward to meet the Sheriff, shaking his head sadly. 'A bad, bad business . . .'

'Tell me, Hector.' Macmillan had inclined his head attentively towards Hector Leanaig and waited. It would have been quite impossible to discern from the Sheriff's tone whether this was an invitation or a command.

'My Jeannie's dead,' the Laird had blurted out. Big and strong though he was, nevertheless the man looked shaken to his wattles now. There was an unhealthy pallor about him too, contrasting sharply with his raven-coloured hair. 'My poor, wee bairn.'

The Sheriff nodded. This was what he had been told.

'She's just where we found her,' Leanaig had struggled for speech but only achieved a rather tremulous croak. 'This way . . .'

Although at first the Laird had taken the lead through the castle, he fell back as soon as they neared the broken figure spread-eagled across the bottom three steps of the stair. The Sheriff had advanced alone, his clerk and the Laird lagging behind.

And now Rhuaraidh Macmillan was gently turning the girl's hands over and taking a long look at their outer aspects. There were grazes here and there on both and some dried blood over the back of the knuckles of her left hand.

'Poor wee Jeannie,' repeated the Laird brokenly.

'Aye, Hector,' agreed the Sheriff noncommittally. That, at least, was true enough, whatever had happened to her. He straightened up and changed his stance, the better to take a look at her head.

Seemingly Hector Leanaig could not bear to watch him going about his business, because he took a step back and averted his gaze from the sad scene.

The child was in her nightclothes, her gown rucked up on one side. A dreadful bruise disfigured the left-hand side of her face and, even without stooping, the Sheriff could see that her cheek was broken on that side. He dropped on one knee and, with great care, put his hand to her skull. That too might be broken. It was certainly cold to the touch and what blood was visible there was brown and dried: the girl, he concluded, must have been dead for several hours.

Hector Leanaig licked dry lips. 'She's just where we found her.'

'We?' queried Rhuaraidh Macmillan sharply. 'Who was it exactly who found her, then?'

'One of the women,' said Leanaig, jerking his head roughly over his shoulder but not turning round.

The Sheriff's gaze followed the direction of his gesture. In the far corner of the hall a buxom young woman was lurking in the shadows. She was weeping, stifling her sobs as best she could. Her face was almost invisible under a woven kirtle, but what he could see of her visage was swollen by tears. Here and there strands of blonde hair extruded from under the woollen garment. She would have been comely enough, he thought, had it not been for her obvious distress.

'Morag,' amplified the Laird, still not letting his gaze fall on her. 'Jeannie's nurse.'

Rhuaraidh Macmillan, though, took a good look at the weeping woman. Irony of ironies, she was standing under the traditional Christmas osier and evergreen kissing bough – the ivy and the holly there to ensure new growth in the spring to come. This had been suspended from a handy rafter – not too low to kiss under, not too high to be too difficult to secure. The apples and mistletoe in the kissing bough would have been an important part of the hogmanay festivities until those had come to an end the night before – Handsel Monday, as ever was. The kissing bough would have been fixed firmly enough for sure: it was considered very bad luck if it were to touch the ground, because in nature the parasitic mistletoe plant always hung downwards . . .

Perhaps, he thought, that was what had happened at Castle Balgalkin, because there was 'nae luck aboot this house, nae luck at a'. That was beyond doubt, whatever had befallen the girl.

The young woman under the kissing bough let forth a loud sob as she saw the Sheriff's eye rest upon her. Wrapped tightly round her shapely shoulders was a shawl; this she held with its edges closed together, as if for greater protection against the outside world. Rhuaraidh Macmillan, no amateur in these matters, was well aware of how frightened she was. And no wonder, if the dead child had been left in her charge.

'Morag Munro,' said Hector Leanaig roughly. 'She'll tell you herself . . .'

'The bairn wasna' there in her bed when I woke up,' said the young woman between chattering teeth. 'Handsel Monday or no'.' She stared wildly at the Sheriff. 'And I'd warned her . . .'

'What about?' asked Macmillan mildly. No good ever came of frightening witnesses too soon. He'd learned that a long time ago.

'Handsel Monday, of course,' said Morag, visibly surprised. 'Did ye not mind that yestre'en was Handsel Monday?'

'Tell me,' he invited her. Nothing was to be assumed when Sheriff Macmillan was going about his business of law and justice, nothing taken for granted. Not even the ancient customs attached to Handsel Monday.

' "When all people are to stay in bed until after sunrise",' she quoted, ' "so as not to be meeting fairies or witches".'

Hector Leanaig said dully, 'The first Monday in January, that's Handsel Monday. You know that, Rhuaraidh Macmillan, as well as I do.'

'Jeannie knew it,' Morag Munro gulped. 'And I told her she wasna' to leave her bed until I came for her in the morning.' The young woman dissolved into tears again. 'And when I did, her bed was empty.' Her shoulders shook as her sobs rang round the hall. 'She was gone.'

'And Mistress Leanaig?' asked Sheriff Macmillan, suddenly realizing what it was that was missing from the *mise-en-scène* and what it was that he had been subconsciously expecting as a backdrop to this tragedy: the unique and quite dreadful wailing of a mother suddenly bereft of one of her children.

'She's away over at Alcaig's,' said Leanaig thickly. He jerked a shoulder northwards in the direction of the firth. 'They say her father's a-dying.'

Macmillan nodded his ready comprehension. Mistress Leanaig, he knew, was the only daughter of the Lord of Alcaig's Isle.

'Her brothers came for her yesterday afternoon,' said Hector. 'She went at once.'

'In her condition?' asked Macmillan. If he remembered rightly, Mistress Leanaig was in the 'interesting condition' that the French called *enceinte*. At least, that was the reason the other guests had been given for

Hector Leanaig spending most of New Year's Eve dancing with a high-spirited young woman called Jemima from Balblair. There had been a memorable Orcadian version of Strip the Willow which no pregnant woman could have danced with safety. And which he, Rhuaraidh Macmillan, for one, wouldn't forget in a hurry – even though he himself had danced it featly with his own lady wife. Nor, he thought judiciously, would the fair-haired young woman from Balblair called Jemima, with whom Hector Leanaig had danced most of that evening, be likely to forget it soon either.

'Old man Alcaig was asking for her.' The Laird pointed up through a gun loop at the leaden sky. 'We could see that there was snow on the way and they were anxious to be well beyond Torgorm in daylight.'

'So . . .' invited the Sheriff, bringing his gaze back to the pathetic little form at his feet. He had no need to ask why Leanaig hadn't gone with his wife to her dying father's the day before. It was no secret in Fearnshire that old Alcaig and his fine sons didn't like the Laird of Balgalkin. And never had.

'So she went with them,' said Leanaig.

'Leaving the bairn with you . . .' If the Sheriff had remembered rightly, old Alcaig had quibbled for a long time over his daughter's tocher going with her to Leanaig. That it had gone there in the end was a triumph of tradition and usage over personal inclination.

'She said Jeannie was too young to be crossing the water on a night like last night.' Hector Leanaig ran a hand over his eyes. 'God!' he said distractedly, 'she'd have been safer with her mother . . .'

The Sheriff didn't answer this. Instead he started to examine the child's clothing. Though her nightgown was caught up under one knee, it did not look to him as if it had been really disarranged other than by the tumble down the stairs. Then he started to pull it to one side, lifting it clear of her piteous body.

A hectic choler took over Hector Leanaig's pale visage. 'Rhuaraidh, I swear by all that's holy that if there's a man in this place who's laid so much as a finger on her, I'll kill him myself with my bare hands, kinsman or not.'

'Whisht, man,' said the Sheriff soothingly. 'There's no call for that. No one's been near her in that way. Her goonie's quite clean and there's no sign of interference.'

A low moan escaped Morag, the nurse. 'The poor mite . . .'

'And there's no sign of a struggle,' added Rhuaraidh Macmillan, turning his attention to the turnpike stair, which curled up clock-wise from the hall on their left. He put his foot on the bottom step and peered up. The stone steps curled away out of his sight in an endless spiral. Above them, the turret tower was capped by a conical wooden roof. The stonework and wood of the turret, he noted, looked in reasonable condition. Some of the dowry which had come with Alcaig's daughter in the end had no doubt been spent on her new home, the castle at Balgalkin.

'Wait you here,' the Sheriff commanded, motioning to his clerk to keep everyone where they were. 'All of you,' he added firmly as Leanaig started forward to join him.

The Sheriff stepped delicately round the inert

figure on the lower steps and started to climb the round stair tower. In the first instance it took him up from the great hall to the second floor of the castle, but he could see that it went further up and beyond still. As he mounted the stair, he ran his left hand over the wall, but only a fine red sandstone dust marked his fingers.

He took his bearings afresh when he stepped off the stair at the first landing and reached the rooms above.

He came first to a little room hung about with fine linens and women's things which he took to be Mistress Leanaig's retiring room. The French fashion these days was to call a lady's place something quite different – by a new French word which he couldn't call to mind just this minute. His wife would know the name of it – and would be wanting one herself at Drummondreach soon too, he'd be bound.

He came next to the nursery. Here, against the longest wall of the room, was the child's bed and, over in the corner, a little truckle bed where he supposed the nurse, Morag Munro, slept. Macmillan took a careful look at both. Neither showed any sign of great disturbance. The bedding on the child's bed had been turned back as by its occupant slipping out of it quite normally.

There was nothing unusual about the other one either. He put a hand in the child's bed and then did the same between the rugs on the servant's one. There was no residual warmth to be felt now in either sleeping place.

Leaving the nursery he went to the master

bedroom, where the Laird and his lady slept – when she was at Balgalkin, that is. He paused on the threshold, the French name of Mistress Leanaig's own room having suddenly come to him after all. Boudoir – that was it.

The room here was a much grander affair than the others. Not only were there a great bed against the further wall and a garderobe, but there were hangings on all the walls and in the corner a small privy stair which did not climb to the upper floors like the turnpike one. Instead, it descended in a clock-wise spiral from the main bedroom to the great hall. This west turret, he deduced, was the Laird and his lady's stair and theirs alone.

The Sheriff advanced on the bed and pulled aside the curtains hanging from the tester – and found another bed covered in thick rugs from which all interior heat had gone. This one, though, did show signs of someone in it having had a rude awakening. To him, the bed coverings had all the look of having been thrust aside in great haste by its occupant.

Rhuaraidh Macmillan walked across to the window. To the north, under a lowering sky, lay a snow-clad Fearnshire and somewhere in that wilderness was a woman whose young daughter was unaccountably dead at the foot of the other stair with her skull broken.

Unaccountably to him, that is.

So far.

Taking his time, Rhuaraidh Macmillan went round the second floor all over again, and then climbed up to the top level by the turnpike stair. Here, without any refinements at all, slept the other retainers of

Castle Balgalkin. A persistent curious flapping sound he traced not to pigeons but to an old flagstaff from which was already flying the flag of the Leanaigs at half-mast.

He felt a spasm of pity for Mistress Leanaig, who from all accounts would be leaving one deathbed only to find another. And unless Hector had sent a messenger to Alcaig's Isle, she would read the flag's message as she neared Torgorm but not know for whom it was flying so low.

Macmillan came down to the main bedroom again and stood there thoughtfully before making for the privy stair. Again he put his left hand out and ran it over the wall, this time as he went down rather than up the stair. This time too a fine red sandstone dust marked his fingers.

But so did something else.

He paused and considered his hand. There was no doubt about it. He was looking at blood. Not a lot, but blood for all that. Macmillan stood for a long quiet minute on a step just above the last turn of the stair but still out of sight of those waiting at the foot of the other stair at the east end of the great hall.

Where the body lay.

Then the Sheriff put his hand down again on the wall of the privy stair.

Low down.

The sandstone felt slightly damp to his touch. He would have been the first to admit that the walls of Castle Balgalkin probably always felt slightly damp to the touch in winter – it was no wonder that the Queen from France was finding Scotland not to her liking after warmer climes. But this dampness was different. He crouched down to consider the patch. Unless he was very much mistaken, someone had taken a wet cloutie to the stone and rubbed it as clean as they could before he reached the castle.

Rhuaraidh Macmillan straightened up and turned silently back up the privy stair. He then walked through the master bedroom, and past the nursery and Mistress Leanaig's boudoir to the main east turnpike stair. He descended this and rejoined the dejected group waiting beside the distressful body at the bottom of the stairway.

Hector Leanaig was standing where he had left him, although his head was now sunk on his chest as if he was afraid to look up. The child's nurse, Morag Munro, was still standing under the kissing bough, well away from the others. As the Sheriff appeared down the turnpike stair, her weeping changed to a more primitive keening.

'It wasn't only me,' she said when she managed to speak. 'The mistress warned her about Handsel Monday too. She told her that on Handsel Monday night everyone has to keep to their beds until sunrise. Made her promise her mother she would stay there.' She gulped. 'I heard her say that myself.'

'I wonder why the child didn't stay in her own bed then,' mused Sheriff Macmillan aloud, addressing nobody in the great hall in particular.

'It's a dangerous night, Handsel Monday,' growled Hector Leanaig.

'I ken that right enough, Hector,' agreed Macmillan.

'But I don't believe in the fairies and witches myself, that's all.'

'Not believe?' echoed the Laird of Balgalkin, astonished.

'No, Hector.' The Sheriff shook his head. 'I'm afraid Handsel Monday is just an ancient way of putting an end to the feasting of hogmanay, that's all.'

Hector Leanaig said obstinately, 'Jeannie believed in it.'

'The English,' remarked the Sheriff, ignoring this, 'call the time when the kissing has to stop by the name of Twelfth Night.'

'Oh, the English,' said Leanaig dismissively. 'They're not right-minded folk at all.'

'But it's still when the kissing has to stop,' said the Sheriff, adding meaningfully, 'all the kissing, Hector . . .'

The Laird of Balgalkin stared at him, a flush mounting his cheek.

Rhuaraidh Macmillan stared down at the pitiable figure on the floor. 'What, Hector, do you think it could be that would make a wee girlie like this so disobedient?'

'I canna' think, man, of anything at all.'

'And I can only think of one thing myself,' said the Sheriff.

The Laird jerked his head up, the flush suffusing his whole face now. He searched the Sheriff's face. 'You can?'

'I'm afraid so,' said Macmillan very quietly. 'I think that Jeannie woke up in the night and found her nurse gone from her bed.'

Hector Leanaig said nothing while Morag Munro clutched her kirtle round her head even more tightly.

'And,' said the Sheriff evenly, 'I think when that happened, Jeannie was naturally frightened that the fairies or the witches must have spirited away her nurse, Morag.'

The wailing under the kissing bough stopped abruptly and a palpable silence fell in the great hall of Castle Balgalkin.

'But,' continued Rhuaraidh Macmillan in a steely voice, 'I don't think they had.'

'No?' said the Laird hoarsely.

'No, Hector. I think that something much worse than fairies or witches had taken Jeannie's nurse away from her bed in Jeannie's room.'

The Laird moistened his lips. 'Something much worse?'

'You, Hector,' said the Sheriff.

'Me?' spluttered the Laird of Balgalkin.

'I think,' maintained Macmillan unperturbed, 'that when little Jeannie woke up and saw Morag Munro was not in her bed in the nursery, her next thought – her very natural thought – was to find you, her father.'

'Well, that would be understandable, right enough,' responded Leanaig non-committally. 'If she did,' he added lamely.

'Don't forget,' carried on the Sheriff ineluctably, 'that last night – Handsel Monday – was one your daughter had been told on all sides by people she trusted to be very afraid of indeed.'

'Aye,' admitted Leanaig, 'that's true.'

'I think,' resumed Macmillan, 'Jeannie was very

frightened and did come looking for you – after all, you were only in your own bed in the next room, weren't you, Hector?'

Hector Leanaig said nothing.

'You either were or you weren't in your own bed, Hector,' said Rhuaraidh Macmillan without impatience. 'Which was it?'

'I was,' said Hector Leanaig gruffly.

'The trouble was,' said the Sheriff almost conversationally, 'that though you were in your own bed, I think you were not alone in it.'

Hector Leanaig's face told its own story. The flush on it slowly drained away before the Sheriff's eyes, to be replaced by a marked pallor. The man of law pointed to the pathetic bundle at their feet and said, 'Your Jeannie was young all right, but not too young to know what makes the beast with two backs . . .'

The woman under the kissing bough screamed. 'We didna' kill her. I tell you, we didna' kill her. She ran away.'

'And her father ran after her,' said the Sheriff calmly.

'To try to explain,' jerked out Hector. 'I swear that's all I did . . . I swear.'

'I know,' said Rhuaraidh Macmillan imperturbably. 'But Jeannie ran away down the stair before you could catch up with her.'

'She fell,' said Hector. 'Before I could catch her and explain.'

Morag Munro ran across the great hall and flung herself at the Sheriff's feet. 'Believe us,' she pleaded. 'We didna' touch her. It's true.'

'Partly true,' responded Macmillan. He pointed diagonally across the hall. 'But it was the other stair that she ran down. You didn't want anyone to guess she'd come from your room.'

Leanaig brushed his hair away from his eyes. 'How do you know that?'

'How else do you account for the crack on her head being on the left of her skull? This is a clockwise stair going up and a left-hand one coming down. If she'd tumbled down this turnpike stair here, her head would have hit the right-hand side of the stairway.' He looked down at the child and then at the step tapering to the apex of its triangle as it became the central pillar of the stair. 'There's nothing to catch her head on coming down on the left in this turnpike. She would have fallen to the right . . . and it's the left of her head that's stove in.'

The only sound in the great hall now was the heavy breathing of the Laird of Balgalkin as he struggled to control himself.

'And the privy stair,' whispered Hector Leanaig, as one making a great discovery, 'comes down the other way.'

'Clockwise from the top,' agreed the Sheriff.

'It's a stair that could be defended by a left-handed swordsman,' said the Laird almost absently.

'Jeannie hit her head on the left-hand side of the privy stair as she ran down it, away from you.' The Sheriff looked across at Morag Munro. 'From you both. And the pair of you hoped to get away with blaming Handsel Monday.'

Hector Leanaig sagged like a man stuffed with

straw reeling from a punch in the solar plexus. 'I may have killed my daughter, Rhuariadh, but I didn't murder her.'

'But she's as dead,' said the Sheriff bleakly, 'as if you had.'

The Laird made a visible effort to straighten himself up. 'What are you going to do?'

'Me?' Rhuariadh Macmillan gave a mirthless laugh. 'I'm not going to do anything, Hector Leanaig. No, I'm going to leave that to poor wee Jeannie here . . .'

'Jeannie?'

'Aye, man. She's going to haunt you here for the rest of your life.'

Preyed in Aid

'You're wanted, Seedy.' Inspector Harpe greeted his old friend Detective Inspector C. D. Sloan with the unwelcome message as he crossed the threshold of Berebury police station ready to report for duty.

'Who by?' asked Sloan cautiously. He was head of the tiny Criminal Intelligence Department of 'F' Division of the Calleshire force and a naturally careful man. Actually he thought he could guess who wanted him.

'Him upstairs, of course,' replied Harpe.

Sloan's step very nearly faltered. A request for attendance from his superior officer, Superintendent Leeyes, was never a good sign. Least of all did it cheer first thing in the morning on a dreary January day, the more especially when it was a day which fell at that low point towards the end of the month when memories of festive cheer had faded and the office Christmas decorations had been taken down but not yet decently put away for another year.

'How is he today?' he asked Harpe warily. The barometer outside the police station measured the ambient temperature and pressure of the county of Calleshire. The atmosphere inside the police station, on the other hand, tended to be calibrated against the current state of the Superintendent's temper.

Inspector Harpe gave this question some thought before he replied. 'Quiet.'

That, thought Sloan, could be good or bad.

'Very quiet,' added Harpe judiciously.

'Too quiet?'

'Could be.'

'Did he say what . . .'

'He wants to know all that you can tell him about the Reverend Christopher Carstairs.'

'The Vicar of St Leonard's?'

'None other.'

Detective Inspector Sloan drew breath and tried his best not to damn with faint praise. 'I should say he's well meaning, always trying to do his best, but more than a bit on the naïve side.'

'Gullible,' translated Harpe.

'And too compassionate by half,' finished Sloan.

'Always takes the side of the underdog.'

'That's exactly what I told the Super too.'

'And?'

'He wants you to see if there's anything known against.'

Sloan raised his eyebrows. 'Wouldn't have thought so myself for a moment, but I'll run a check.'

A few minutes later he was in his superior's office and saying, 'No, sir. Not a thing. Nothing known at all against Mr Carstairs. I've double-checked.' He coughed and enquired delicately, 'Were you expecting there to have been, then?'

'There was always the off chance,' said Superintendent Leeyes, not lifting his eyes from a sheet of paper on his desk, 'that the man might have plenty of previous and it's always just as well to make sure first.'

'No form of any sort,' insisted Detective Inspector Sloan firmly.

'It was just a thought, Sloan, that's all.' The Superintendent sounded almost wistful.

'Clean as a whistle,' said the Inspector, mystified.

The Superintendent essayed a little laugh. 'We can't say the same about Matthew Steele, though, can we?'

'Matthew Steele?' echoed Sloan, even more puzzled. Actually, he would have said that Matthew Steele didn't have one single thing in common with the Vicar of St Leonard's Church in Berebury, except, perhaps now he came to think about it, a well-developed way with words. 'No, sir. Record as long as your arm. You name it and Steele's done it. Done quite a lot of time for some of it too.' He paused. 'But not for all of it,' he added with heavy significance. 'Oh, no, not for all of it by any means.'

'And more talkative than a murmuration of starlings,' groaned Leeyes.

'But never a canary, sir,' pointed out Sloan.

'Steele never sings about anything,' snorted Leeyes. 'You don't have to tell me.'

'Always plenty to say for himself, though, when we take him in, has our Matthew Steele . . .'

'Talk the hind leg off a donkey.'

'He'll argue the toss with anyone,' agreed Sloan, 'but it doesn't usually amount to much.'

'That's not going to be a lot of help to me,' complained Leeyes.

'Should have been a lawyer,' said Sloan, wondering where all this was leading.

'Or in the pulpit,' suggested Leeyes unexpectedly.

'Not with his lack of principles,' said Sloan, realizing too late that, in standing up for men of the cloth, he'd inadvertently impugned the whole legal profession in passing.

With wholly uncharacteristic passivity, Superintendent Leeyes let this go by. Instead he went off at a tangent and asked if Sloan could tell him exactly when Ash Wednesday was.

'Not offhand, sir, but I'll look it up for you,' promised the Detective Inspector, even more puzzled.

'Do.' The Superintendent waved his hand. 'It's quite soon, isn't it?'

'A couple of weeks, at least . . .' Sloan's mother would know. She was a great churchwoman and would have the date at her fingertips. Bound to . . .

'That's what I meant, Sloan. Soon . . .'

'Easter's a movable feast, of course, sir, which is why the date varies from year to year,' murmured Sloan, mentally trying to connect Matthew Steele, con man and common thief, with any religious festival at all. He found it was just as difficult to equate 'a couple of weeks' with 'soon'. In Superintendent Leeyes's terminology, 'soon' usually meant within the hour at the very latest.

'Of course,' said Leeyes humbly. 'I'd quite forgotten that the date isn't always the same.'

'That's why, sir, I can't tell you straight away when

it will be.' On the other hand, unlike Matthew Steele, the Reverend Christopher Carstairs would obviously have a simple and straightforward link with Ash Wednesday on whatever date it happened to fall this year.

'Yes, of course,' said Leeyes, again unnaturally in agreement.

Sloan cleared his throat and asked, 'Has Steele been up to something again, then, sir?'

'Not that I know of,' said Leeyes.

Detective Inspector Sloan took a deep breath and said, 'Actually, sir, we think he may have been on the Tilson Street job.'

'The Calleshire and Counties Bank one?'

Detective Inspector Sloan nodded.

Superintendent Leeyes cocked his head to one side. 'Robbery with violence, wasn't it?'

'One of the girl tellers was hit over the head and the Bank Manager threatened. But it's only a hunch, sir, that Steele was involved. There's no way we can prove it. Not yet, anyway. Probably not until we can find the proceeds. We're doing all we can, of course, but it hasn't amounted to much so far. Is that the problem?'

The Superintendent shook his head. 'No, no, Sloan, it's not that. It's just that he and I are both in this church business at St Leonard's together.'

Sloan raised his eyebrows. 'You and Steele, sir?' Privately he was absolutely certain that Matthew Steele had orchestrated the Tilson Street bank job. All the Berebury CID needed now was hard evidence to prove it, but Sloan didn't want to say so. Not just now. Not until he knew what all this peculiar prevarication was about.

'Him and me,' said his superior officer regretfully.

'Sir?' If he couldn't finger Steele, then finding what had been stolen would be the next best thing . . .

'The two of us.' Leeyes grimaced. 'That's the trouble – or, rather, part of the trouble.'

Sloan frowned. This could be serious. In the police book, the Superintendent's consorting with known criminals would be considered a bad thing. Having anything to do with the likes of Matthew Steele – as opposed to actually having him on a charge for anything that could be considered wrong doing – would be a risky business for any policeman, let alone a full-blown Superintendent. 'Where, sir,' he asked tentatively, 'does Mr Carstairs come in, then?'

'It was all the Vicar's idea in the first place,' said Leeyes, his eyes still cast down on the paper lying on his desk. 'He's asked Steele too – not that he wanted to do it either, I gather, but the Vicar's a persuasive sort.'

'And what's Steele got to do with the Vicar?' asked Sloan pertinently.

'Steele's been repairing the church tower of St Leonard's for weeks now,' said Leeyes.

'He has, has he? I didn't know that.'

'I expect that's how the Vicar got to know him – and, come to that, it's probably why Steele didn't like to refuse to do it.'

'And does the Vicar know that Steele's got a bad record?' asked Sloan, still in a verbal fog.

'I shouldn't think so for a moment,' said Leeyes.

'But they've got trouble in their belfry. And before you ask, not bats.'

'At least there's not a lot Steele can nick in a church tower,' said Sloan, 'though we decided long ago that you couldn't ask for better cover for burglary than a builder's business. A covered van, ladders and a good excuse for going equipped with as many tools as you like . . .'

'And for parking in odd places,' contributed Leeyes.

Sloan hesitated. 'But I still don't see where you come in, sir.'

'I think,' the Superintendent grunted, 'that my wife may have had a hand in it.'

'Ah . . .' Sloan made a non-committal sound deep down in his throat.

'Only,' put in Leeyes with haste, 'because she was trying to be helpful, of course.'

'Of course,' agreed Sloan guardedly. By all accounts, the Superintendent's wife was a force to be reckoned with. Both at home and away, so to speak.

'You see, Sloan,' said the Superintendent, waving a hand, 'she's one of Mr Carstairs's flock – that's what you call it, isn't it?'

'A member of his congregation,' translated Sloan.

'That's it, Sloan, exactly. Mrs Leeyes attends St Leonard's Church every Sunday without fail.'

'And?' Sloan still couldn't see yet where all this was getting them.

'And,' said Leeyes hollowly, 'she went and volunteered me to take part in one of their Lent debates at the church.'

Sloan smothered a promising remark about it being

very good for the Superintendent's sins. This was only partly because his superior officer had never been known to admit to having transgressed in any way. Self-preservation came into it too. He said instead, 'I think I'm beginning to get the picture, sir.'

'I knew you would,' Leeyes said, seizing on this and pushing the sheet of paper on his desk over in Sloan's direction. 'Look. It's all here on this.'

Detective Inspector Sloan picked the paper up and read it. It was a letter from the Reverend Christopher Carstairs, Vicar of St Leonard's Church, Berebury, saying how much they were all looking forward to the participation of Police Superintendent Leeyes in an active debate with Matthew Steele at the church as part of their Lent Awareness Programme and enclosing a copy of a poster advertising it.

The Superintendent pointed a stubby finger at this. 'Have you got to the bottom line yet, Sloan?'

'Yes, sir,' said Sloan, hoping his lips hadn't been visibly twitching as he read that the subject of the debate was 'Original Sin'. 'I see what you mean now, sir.'

'But have you got to the very bottom, Sloan?'

Sloan ran his eye further down the poster until it lit upon the debate's subtitle: 'Would You Adam and Eve It?' This example of Cockney rhyming slang was displayed in eye-catching capital letters.

'What do you think of that, Sloan, eh?'

'Very trendy, sir.'

The Superintendent nodded dispiritedly. 'That's what I thought too.'

'And you, sir, I take it,' murmured Sloan, 'will be

there to put forward one view . . .' He scanned the rest of the letter, struggling not to let his voice quaver.

'That's part of the trouble.'

'And – ' Sloan took a very firm hold too of his facial expression, reducing it to the deadpan rigidity required of a public servant on distasteful duty – 'sir, have I got this right? Matthew Steele will be taking the opposite one.'

'Exactly, Sloan.'

'For or against original sin existing?'

'That's what it's all about,' said Leeyes tightly.

'Did you get to choose which, sir?' enquired Sloan diplomatically.

'The Vicar,' ground out Leeyes between clenched teeth, 'decided that I would want to take the orthodox police view.'

'Well, that's all right, then, sir, isn't it?' said Sloan.

'No, it isn't!' howled Leeyes.

'Sir?' Sloan decided he really should have paid more attention at his Sunday School classes. He hadn't known at the time, of course, that he was going to be a policeman.

'I've got to argue that man is equally ready to do either good or evil and has the freedom of will to choose between the two,' said the Superintendent.

'Ye-es,' said Sloan uncertainly. 'Well . . .'

'And Matthew Steele,' snarled Leeyes, 'gets to take the Vicar's personal theological stance. He's even given him a text.' He looked down. 'Romans chapter 7, verse 19: "For the good that I would I do not: but the evil which I would not, that I do." ' He snorted. 'I ask you, Matthew Steele!'

'That must be a first,' said Sloan sourly.

'It means that he's going to be able to argue that he doesn't have any choice whether he commits crimes . . .'

'Now I've heard everything,' said Sloan.

'Me too.'

'It's a new way of a villain saying he's got right on his side, sir,' observed Sloan after a moment's thought.

'It's what defence counsel are always on about,' said Leeyes grimly. 'The Vicar, you see, says that in the beginning – that is, when all this business about original sin first cropped up . . .'

'In the Garden of Eden?' suggested Sloan helpfully.

'No, no, Sloan. The Vicar says it was in AD four hundred and something when there was a famous dialogue on the subject with a man called Pelagius.'

'Pelagius?' Sloan sat up. 'Wait a minute, sir, wait a minute . . .'

'An English monk who got done for heresy when he went to Rome,' sniffed Leeyes. 'Makes a change that, for a God-botherer, doesn't it? Going from England to Rome.'

'The traffic's usually all the other way,' conceded Sloan. He frowned. 'But I do remember learning something about a man called Pelagius at school.'

'More than I ever did,' said Leeyes robustly.

'And a bishop called Germanus . . .'

'You've always had a police memory for names, Sloan,' admitted Leeyes grudgingly.

'In Religious Education, it was.' Detective Inspector Sloan metaphorically scratched his head. 'The teacher thought verses might stick in our minds better than talk.'

'And did they?' asked Superintendent Leeyes, never one to beat about the bush.

'I know it was someone called Hilaire Belloc who wrote them,'* said Sloan obliquely, giving himself time to think, 'because we all thought Hilaire was a funny name for a man.' The class comic, he remembered, had famously gone on a bit about it being very 'hilarious'. They'd all laughed uproariously at this, prolonged amusement being one of the tried and tested ways of cutting down teaching time.

'French, I expect, a name like that,' said Leeyes dismissively.

Sloan shut his eyes and concentrated hard. 'I don't know if I can remember the poem now.'

'Try,' commanded Leeyes.

' "Pelagius lived in Kardanoel," ' quoted the Detective Inspector, quondam schoolboy,

> ' "And taught a doctrine there,
> How whether you went to Heaven or Hell,
> It was your own affair." '

'I don't know where Kardanoel is, sir,' added Sloan, aware that this was unimportant. If it wasn't in 'F' Division in the county of Calleshire, the Superintendent didn't care.

'What matters more,' said Leeyes grandly, 'is that the Vicar of St Leonard's has asked me to argue the toss with Matthew Steele of all people.'

* Hilaire Belloc, *The Four Men: A Farrago* (London: Nelson, 1912).

'On the side of law and order, though,' offered Sloan by way of comfort.

'Naturally,' snapped Leeyes.

Greatly daring, Sloan went on, 'Against there being original sin, though, sir.' His own old Station Sergeant had believed that original sin was always there, lurking in the woodwork, so to speak. Their tutor at the police training college, on the other hand, had made them write down a quotation from someone called Clive Kluckholm: 'Nature provides potentialities which culture neglects or elaborates.' He wasn't sure if he understood that either.

Leeyes looked pained. 'It's not as easy as that, Sloan.'

'No, sir.' Sloan hadn't thought for one moment that it would be. Outside of the Ten Commandments, theology was never that simple.

'The Vicar – are you sure the Vicar's straight up, Sloan?'

'Quite sure, sir . . . except that he believes the best of everyone.' This, he appreciated, was a considerable failing in the Superintendent's book.

'The Vicar tells me that Steele is going to argue that he is as he is – he called him Common Man – because of there being such a thing as original sin . . . it being in the genes and all that.'

'I can see that he might want to argue that way,' said Sloan moderately.

'And that the world therefore has him as it made him.'

'Then all I can say,' said Sloan warmly, 'is that the world didn't make a very good job of him.'

'What I want to know,' said Leeyes belligerently, 'is how come Matthew Steele gets to argue on the side of the angels and I don't?'

'Perhaps,' suggested Sloan, one at least of his Sunday School lessons coming back to him, 'the Vicar did it on the principle that there is more joy in Heaven over one sinner who has repented than over ninety-nine who haven't sinned.' He was going to get Steele for leading the Tilson Street job if it was the last thing he did, debate or no debate. In his canon, hitting young women bank clerks over the head with baseball bats was just not on.

'And has he repented,' enquired Leeyes with real interest, 'since we're sure he's sinned?'

'Not that I know of, sir.'

'But the Vicar's still going to let him have his twopenn'orth on the subject.' Leeyes sighed. 'And I've been landed with having to argue the other way – for there being no such thing as original sin.'

'Only free will,' said Sloan thoughtfully.

'I don't like it, Sloan. Not one little bit.'

'It's only for the sake of argument, sir. Don't forget that.'

'It's all very well, Sloan, but I don't believe that people such as Steele can stay on the straight and narrow if they just put their minds to it, but this old monk Pelagius did.'

Since the view of most magistrates and all the do-gooders Sloan had ever known was that all malefactors and most recidivists could do just that, the detective inspector nodded not unsympathetically. 'The Devil's got the best tune there, all right.'

'And Steele's a proper limb of Satan to match,' the Superintendent came back smartly.

'I'm not sure you should be bringing Satan into this, sir.'

'Enemy territory, eh?' said Leeyes unexpectedly. 'You could be right.'

'Confusing the issue was what I had meant,' murmured Sloan.

'What I want, Sloan, are solid arguments,' said Leeyes, not listening.

'Did the Vicar give you any to be going on with?' asked Sloan, playing for time.

'No.' Superintendent Leeyes consulted a tattered notebook which, from the look of its cover, hadn't been produced in evidence since he had last been walking the beat. 'But he did warn me about one of their clever old churchwardens who likes catching speakers out with a trick question.'

'Forewarned is forearmed,' said Sloan sententiously.

Leeyes squinted down at his notebook. 'Something to do with St Thomas Aquinas and the number of angels who can dance on the head of a pin. That mean anything to you, Sloan?'

Sloan struggled with his memory. 'I think it's as many as want to, sir, seeing as angels don't take up any room.'

'So where's the trick, then?' asked Leeyes suspiciously.

'If you were to say a specific number, sir, it would have meant that you didn't know that angels were – er – I think it's called "non-corporeal".'

'I never thought they weren't,' said Leeyes indignantly. 'And I've never thought Steele was an angel either.'

'Nor me, sir,' said Sloan. The bank robbers had worn Mickey Mouse headpieces and carried something that might at first sight have been charity collecting boxes on poles but weren't. 'The Vicar might, of course.'

'Oh, and the Vicar said,' went on Leeyes, suddenly recollecting something else, 'to leave the Manichaeans and St Augustine out of it, because another couple of his parishioners were going to debate the struggle between Good and Evil the week after us.'

'Pity, that,' said Sloan reflectively. 'I should have said that that was much more our line of country than whether or not what you made of yourself is your own affair or in-built. After all, sir, we're part of the good versus evil struggle here, aren't we?'

'We're here to uphold the law, Sloan,' declared Leeyes heavily, 'and that's all. And we know, don't we, which side Steele would be on in that one. How much did they get away with at Tilson Street?'

'Best part of half a million pounds in used small-denomination notes – they made the staff give them the safe keys or else.' It was the 'or else' that had lifted the Calleshire and Counties Bank job out of the ordinary ruck of robberies and made Sloan so determined to catch the perpetrators. 'And a load of boxes from their safe deposit, although no one knows what's in them.'

Leeyes grunted. 'Ill-gotten gains, I expect.'

'Take a bit of stashing away, that lot, sir. But none

of it's at Steele's house or his yard, because we got a warrant and had a look-see.'

Superintendent Leeyes jerked his head. 'We'll get the whole crew somehow.'

'Yes, sir. In time.' They weren't talking about a nice ethical and theoretical discussion now. This was proper police business, not about scoring debating points for the edification of the converted.

'Sooner or later one of the gang will slip up,' he forecast.

'Like Adam and Eve,' ventured Sloan.

'That's what the ACC thinks too.' Leeyes waved the poster in his hand. 'I happened to mention this debate to him, in case there was any comeback . . .'

'One can't be too careful.'

'And seeing how he was a college man and would understand.'

'Ah . . .' The Assistant Chief Constable had had a classical education and had a reputation for being able to put a scholarly slant on most police problems.

'He said that we are all sons of Adam . . .'

'Especially Matthew Steele,' said Sloan.

'And daughters of Adam too, I suppose,' said Leeyes, who much disliked the recent rise in female convictions. 'The ACC did say, though, to watch out for Steele talking *digitis evidenter traiectis*.' The Superintendent grimaced. 'Taking the mickey, that's what he was doing. As usual.'

'He's always a great one for the Latin, the ACC.'

'I had to ask him what it meant,' admitted Leeyes unwillingly.

Detective Inspector Sloan decided against saying

anything to this. He had his pension to think of. Besides, the ACC was the only person at Berebury police station capable of cutting the Superintendent down to size.

'I suppose I ought to have guessed,' sniffed Leeyes.

'Sir?'

'I don't know where he went to school . . .'

'Eton.'

'It means that when you keep your fingers crossed you don't mean to keep a promise.'

Sloan said that he knew that even though he hadn't been to Eton.

'But it's only if people can't see that they're crossed that it's not cricket.'

Sloan said that he knew that too, but that he didn't think Matthew Steele or his associates played any of their little games according to the rules of cricket. 'Poker, more like.'

'The ACC also mentioned something about some people called the Prelapsarians as well,' went on Leeyes, adding shamelessly, 'but I didn't quite catch what he said. Mean anything to you?'

'No, sir. 'Fraid not.' He brightened. 'But I do know a joke about the Garden of Eden and evidence which might be useful.' All they needed to arrest Matthew Steele was evidence. The bank robbers hadn't left a shred of it behind at Tilson Street. They'd worn gloves as well as Mickey Mouse masks and had touched nothing in passing. Their getaway car had been stolen minutes before the robbery and left abandoned minutes afterwards. Of the money and the safe-deposit boxes, there was no sign at all.

'Let's be having it, then, Sloan,' said Leeyes sourly. 'You never know what'll come in handy when you're on your feet. Especially a joke.'

'It goes like this, sir. God said to Adam, "Adam, did you eat that there apple?" and Adam said, "No, God." '

'I've just worked it out,' Leeyes interrupted him. 'Prelapsarian must mean before the Fall of Man.'

'Quite so, sir. Anyway, then God said to Eve, "Eve, did you eat that there apple?" and Eve said, "No, God." '

'Have a word with the serpent, after that, did he?' enquired Leeyes. 'If you ask me, that's when the trouble started.'

'No, sir.' Sloan drew breath and heroically carried on. He was going to finish his story, come what may. 'So God said, "What about them two cores, then?" '

'And I take it what you haven't got at Tilson Street, Sloan, are any cores?'

'Not a thing, sir,' said Sloan bitterly. 'Not a single scrap of anything that the Crown Prosecution Service would call reliable evidence.'

'Or even what we would call evidence,' said Leeyes magisterially, having no very high opinion of the CPS. 'That matters too.'

'I know, sir,' murmured Sloan.

'What about the bank's security cameras?'

'One Mickey Mouse looks very like another.'

'And in the meantime,' he snorted, 'the Vicar wants me to debate original sin with Matthew Steele . . .'

'The Vicar doesn't know it's in the meantime,' pointed out Sloan. 'Doesn't even know he's got a record, I dare say. He's probably just chosen Steele because he's been around doing some building work in the church and because he's got a good debating manner.'

'Plausible is what I would call it . . .'

'That's what the Judge said too, when we got him last time.' Sloan paused. 'I suppose he thinks that appearing in public against you would be a bit of a lark.'

'Unless the Vicar has fed him some nonsense about sanctuary.'

'If you ask me, sir, what it does is confirm either that Steele is as cocky as ever and doesn't think we're going to make a charge stick or that for some reason he doesn't want to upset the Vicar. Or both.'

'Huh . . .' Police Superintendent Leeyes, Berebury's thief taker-in-chief, gave it as his considered opinion that Matthew Steele shouldn't be allowed to get away with a child's lolly, let alone a king's ransom.

'If it's not bats in the belfry, sir,' asked Sloan suddenly, 'what exactly is the trouble up there?'

'Search me, Sloan.'

'I was wondering, sir,' said Sloan slowly, 'whether we should search the church tower instead . . .'

Leeyes shot him a look.

'Anyone could bang about up there opening safe-deposit boxes without being heard.' Sloan got out his own notebook. 'I bet you he's been hauling bucket-loads of cement and anything else you care to name up there too.'

'If you ask me,' said Leeyes, 'that Vicar is daft enough to have given him a key to the tower.'

'I shouldn't be surprised, sir. Ingenuous is the word that comes to mind as far as Mr Carstairs is concerned.'

'The Vicar did say something about original sin and the Age of Enlightenment and as well,' began the Superintendent, but Sloan was already on his feet.

'I've gone in for a bit of enlightenment on my own, sir,' he said. 'If what's in the church tower is what I think might be hidden up there, then you may just be off the hook in Lent.' He got to the door and turned. 'Keep your fingers crossed.'

A Different Cast of Mind

The moment he stepped inside the door of the inn, Christopher Helmsdale knew for certain that he was wrongly dressed for the place. In spite of conscientiously wearing his usual weekend clothes, he stood out like a sore thumb among the men there. His trousers and roll-neck jersey were neither old enough nor shabby enough to melt into the background at the Fisherman's Arms at Almstone. And his shoes were a mite too clean.

It wasn't that he hadn't suspected this before leaving London for rural Calleshire; he had recollected the ambience of the place well enough. The trouble was that any clothes he might once have had that would have been halfway suitable had been thrown away by his wife long ago. Strolling in Richmond Park on Sundays made different – though no less exacting – sartorial demands on a man.

He laid his overcoat on a dark wooden settle situated under an oil painting of dead fur and feather – a still life of the chase – and beside an ancient metal spring balance that measured weight only in pounds and ounces. He'd almost forgotten that, but he remembered the stuffed champion trout in its glass case fixed to the opposite wall well enough. As far as Christopher was concerned, it had been there for ever. Caught by Sir Coningsby Falconer in 1865, it was still the heaviest trout to come out of the River Alm to date – and that in spite of the best efforts of the present baronet (another Sir Coningsby Falconer), Christopher Helmsdale's own father and all his cronies to do better.

Under the trout was the hotel's game book, in which the day's catches were duly recorded before being hastened – the way of all flesh – to the kitchen.

Christopher made a move to open the game book, but suddenly changed his mind and made for the bar instead. Although the bar was crowded, he was instantly recognized by an elderly man and offered a drink.

'Come away in, man,' said Peter Heath hospitably. 'Good to see you. Now, what'll you have?'

Sitting comfortably in a corner of the bar, Christopher searched his memory for the right questions to ask an old angler. 'The Alm running well?'

'Not too badly,' said Peter Heath, sipping slowly. 'Not too badly at all, all things considered.'

'And are the fish taking just now?'

'Aye, sometimes.' The fisherman gave a small smile. 'Not often enough, of course.'

'They never do,' agreed Christopher.

The two men drank companionably in silence for a while and then the older man asked which part of the river he proposed to visit the next morning.

'I haven't decided yet,' said Christopher. 'I came here straight from the office and Fridays are always too busy to think of anything else, more's the pity.'

'Of course.' The countryman nodded. 'I quite understand.'

'London's like that,' said the man from the City, sounding apologetic.

'Not to worry. Plenty of good places to choose from,' observed Peter Heath, who had been retired long enough for all the days of the week to feel the same. 'And there'll be no problem with the light at this time of year.'

Christopher took another taste of his whisky. 'I plan to have a look at one or two possible spots before I really make up my mind.'

'Good idea,' nodded the old fisherman, adding, 'we'll make a fisherman of you yet.'

In the event Christopher Helmsdale realized it hadn't been such a good idea after all. The trouble was that he wasn't nearly as skilled a fisherman as his father. And having a case of hand-tied dry flies in one pocket and a small screw-topped flask in the other wasn't going to turn him into one overnight either.

He paused first by the humpbacked bridge near the hotel, because, although his father had specified the River Alm, he hadn't said exactly which pool he was supposed to be heading for now. As he rested his elbows on the parapet, he considered three distinct possibilities, just as at his work he would have carefully listed all the possible alternatives before taking any action.

The first of these was the deep pool just below the bridge. This was the spot where, years and years ago, his father had caught his best-ever brown trout. That trout, whose exact weight was lost in the mists of time – his mother had always declared it gained an ounce a year – had entered into family legend. In the way of fishermen, all his father's subsequent catches had been measured against 'the trout from the pool below the bridge'.

He dallied there for a few more minutes, though, before he turned and walked along the south bank, heading downstream. He was making for that stretch of the River Alm which had always been his father's favourite place for the dry fly – the hand-tied dry fly. This was known as the Ornum Stretch and it was here, before his arthritic hip had started to give trouble, that his father had spent most of his fishing time.

Christopher grinned to himself and decided that this was probably the place on the Alm that his father had had in mind when he had written his instructions out for him.

It was therefore only an innate conscientiousness that made Christopher turn his steps still further downstream. He tramped along the river bank until he got to that stretch of water known as Almstone Reach. It was a goodish walk but one that Helmsdale *père* had taken often enough until his health had begun to fail.

The Almstone Reach had never been his father's favourite place for fishing – on the contrary, he was wont to refer to it as 'The Challenge of the Alm'. The challenge arose because his father had never ever succeeded in landing a trout from this stretch of the river – and that certainly wasn't for want of trying either.

Christopher Helmsdale stood now beside the Alm

and tried to decide which of the three places on the river would be the best: the Bridge Pool, the Ornum Stretch or the Almstone Reach . . . He could have tossed a coin to decide if there had been only two alternatives. Having three put that out of court. He would just have to make up his own mind . . .

He put his hand into his pocket, took out the flask and grinned to himself.

The Almstone Reach – challenge and all – it would be. He'd see that his father got to the fish there in the end.

He unscrewed the top of the flask and slowly tipped his father's cremated ashes into the water. Out of his other pocket he took his father's little case of home-tied flies that he had intended to cast into the river after the ashes – but something stayed his hand.

Perhaps he'd just see what he could do with them there himself one day . . .

Examination Results

'What you need to do, Sloan,' said Superintendent Leeyes testily, 'is to teach that young Constable of yours exactly what constitutes evidence and what doesn't.'

'Yes, sir,' responded Detective Inspector C. D. Sloan in as neutral tones as he could manage.

'Hard evidence,' emphasized the Superintendent. He was still smarting from having the police case against one of their most persistent offenders dismissed at the Berebury magistrates' court for lack of evidence. 'Your Detective Constable Crosby needs to get into that thick head of his the difference between hearsay and a signed witness statement.'

'Yes, sir,' said Detective Inspector Sloan, heroically resisting the temptation to disclaim Crosby as his Detective Constable. Had he, Sloan, been given the slightest choice in the matter – which he hadn't – Detective Constable William Edward Crosby would not have been the man by his side in any police investigation whatsoever, let alone one brought against the most plausible rogue in the whole county of Calleshire.

'Telling the Bench what someone else had said about the accused as if that would do instead of finding out for himself,' snorted Leeyes. 'The very idea . . . quite apart from the fact that it showed to all and sundry that he didn't know the first thing about what constituted inadmissible evidence.'

'Yes, sir.' Come to that, thought Sloan to himself, Crosby wasn't someone you'd want with you in an open boat after a shipwreck either . . .

'The magistrates aren't all that bright,' grumbled Leeyes, 'but even they can tell the difference between reported speech and recorded speech. First thing they were taught, I expect.'

'Yes, sir.' Sloan wouldn't have wanted Superintendent Leeyes with him in an open boat instead of Crosby, but for quite different reasons. Ten to one, if shipwrecked, the Superintendent would be following his usual practice of making waves rather than calming the waters – and as for going with the flow, well, that had never ever been his way.

Quite the contrary, in fact.

'If there's one thing I don't ever like to see,' rumbled on his superior officer, still disgruntled, 'it's a real villain getting off a charge on a mere technicality.'

'No, sir.' Sloan was with him there.

'Doesn't do the force any good at all, that.' Leeyes sniffed. 'The only people who enjoy it are those who read certain newspapers.'

'I take your point, sir,' said Sloan, even though the Superintendent's description of what had constituted a mere technicality enshrined one of the most fundamental principles of English criminal law. From where he stood, that meant that neither the Superintendent nor the errant Crosby had understood the enormity, and that the Bench did, but he wasn't going to say this. He, Sloan, had his pension to think of.

Superintendent Leeyes was still worrying at the same bone. 'Next time, Sloan, I want nothing but hard evidence presented in court. Is that understood?'

'Yes, sir.' He suppressed a sigh. 'I'll have a word . . .'

'Do that,' said Leeyes. 'And you can start over at the Ornum Arms at Almstone.'

'Sir?'

'Thief in the place,' said the Superintendent. 'Or so the landlord says.'

'Johnny Hedger,' supplied Sloan.

'Oh, you know him, do you?'

'Been there since Nelson lost his eye,' said Sloan.

'But nothing known?'

'No, sir.' This was police-speak for having a criminal record and Sloan knew that Johnny Hedger didn't have one. 'Clean as a whistle. He doesn't stand any nonsense from anyone in his house either.'

'If what the landlord is saying is true,' prophesied Leeyes, 'someone at the Ornum Arms is going to have a police record sooner or later. Sooner, I hope,' he added meaningfully.

Detective Inspector Sloan took out his notebook.

'And the sooner or later bit,' added Leeyes waspishly, 'depends on whether your Detective Constable can make a better fist of producing his evidence next time than he did yesterday.'

Sloan suppressed a strong temptation to say something about Crosby first having to find the aforementioned evidence before he could present it, like that famous lady cook saying 'First catch your hare' when advising on the making of hare pie. Instead, he murmured that he and the Detective Constable would start their investigation out at Almstone first thing Monday morning.

The Ornum Arms in the village of Almstone was an old public house that had begun life as a coaching inn – a hostelry in the true meaning of the term. The old courtyard into which the daily stagecoach from Calleford used to be driven had been glassed over now and the ostlers' quarters turned into residents' bedrooms, but there was still that about the place redolent of journey's end after a hard ride.

The two detectives found Johnny Hedger behind his bar but far from his usual self. There was no trace in his manner today of the customary professional bonhomie for which the landlord was celebrated along the whole Alm valley. Instead, the normally jovial man looked pale and shaken, and when he moved, he did so with exquisite care. He seemed too to be needing the public bar for physical support – something quite at odds with his large frame and renowned vigour.

'I'm glad you've come, gentlemen,' he said, waving them to a table, 'though I'm afraid, as you can see, you've caught us at rather a bad moment.' He grimaced as he pointed at a white-coated woman who was striding purposefully about the public bar with some glass specimen bottles and a clinical-looking case.

'Don't say that forensics have beaten us to it, Johnny,' said Sloan, puzzled. 'Or has something else happened that we haven't been told about?'

'We've got the food police here,' sighed the publican. 'They're swarming all over the place . . .'

Detective Constable Crosby said, 'Are they looking for a thief too?'

The burly landlord shook his head. 'Nay, lad. I only wish they were. They're here because we had a right disaster at the place on Saturday afternoon.' He straightened up painfully. 'That is, it must have happened on Saturday afternoon but we didn't know it was a disaster until early Sunday morning.' He shuddered at the memory. 'Or how big a one . . .'

Detective Inspector Sloan murmured something anodyne but sympathetic about troubles never coming singly.

'Singly!' echoed Johnny Hedger bitterly. 'If only they'd come singly it would have been all right.'

'Battalions?' suggested Sloan, a latent memory of his schoolday Shakespeare lessons coming back to him.

Johnny Hedger looked puzzled. 'No. It was a cricket club party that we had in the functions room.'

'Ah . . .'

'We catered for a hundred and fifty – popular local team, you know. Valuable booking too, but I wish now we'd never taken it. So does the wife . . .' He glanced in the direction of the stairs. 'I had to get the doctor to her in the night. It didn't surprise him, because he'd been called out a dozen times already by other people who'd eaten here. And he said he was sorry but that he would have to tell the authorities about it because food poisoning is a notifiable medical condition under some Public Health Act or other.'

'Bad luck,' said Sloan sympathetically.

'She's still proper poorly. Says she doesn't want to face food or drink ever again.'

'Food poisoning,' opined Sloan, 'leaves you like that.'

'Too right, Inspector.' Hedger acknowledged this with a jerk of his head in the direction of the kitchen. 'They say it was the Queen of Puddings that did it.' He passed a hand over his damp brow. 'Don't ask me to tell you how they found that out, but everyone who chose it was ill.'

'They have their methods,' said Sloan. He very nearly brought in a neat reference to Sherlock Holmes and Dr Watson but thought better of it. Johnny Hedger was in no mood today for light relief.

The landlord glanced down at something written on the back of an envelope and frowned. 'The pathologist called it *Typhimurium*, if that makes any sense to you.'

'No,' said Sloan comfortably, 'but doctors like to use words that no one else understands. Makes them feel more in control.'

'One of our lecturers,' offered Detective Constable Crosby, not long out of the police training college, 'called the using of words that only an in-group could understand "Badges of Belonging".'

Johnny Hedger was not interested in either psychology or semantics. 'These people say they think whatever it was that did it was in the duck eggs used in the pudding topping. We get the eggs from the farm up the road, you know . . .'

'Ah . . .'

'They gave the soup and the turkey salad a clean

bill of health – which is more,' added Hedger spiritedly, 'than the Health and Safety people will give the Ornum Arms until we've been practically taken to pieces and fumigated.'

'Dangerous things, duck eggs,' observed Sloan sapiently. 'Salmonella bacilli like living in them.'

'You're telling me,' said Johnny Hedger.

'Especially when they're not hard-boiled . . .' The working knowledge required by a Detective Inspector had always bordered on the arcane, but there was one thing he did remember about Queen of Puddings from his childhood that might be relevant. 'Meringue, made from white of egg, whipped on top?'

'And raspberry jam,' put in Detective Constable Crosby, anxious to help.

'But not in the oven for very long?' There was the rub, Sloan thought.

'That's the one,' sighed the landlord heavily. 'Not that we can do anything about it now. The Health and Safety people have closed us down until further notice.'

'There's no arguing with that lot,' said Crosby, still a little unsure of his own authority as an officer of the law but aware of others in the wider world who had even greater powers – powers against which there was no appeal.

Hedger winced as he shifted his bulk in response to a twinge of pain. 'I've had to send all the domestic staff home this morning.'

'You wouldn't have had many customers anyway,' said Sloan, 'not with Environmental Health around.'

'They've been crawling everywhere since first thing.' Hedger gave a melancholy smile. 'It's just as well that the chef's off sick too. He wouldn't like to see them there, poking into everything. Very territorial about his kitchen is our Melvyn.'

'It's your kitchen we've come about,' Sloan reminded him. 'Or, rather, goods continually stolen therefrom . . .'

'I could wish now that someone had taken those duck eggs,' said the landlord feelingly, 'never mind the ham and cheese that's always going missing.'

'The high-value items,' observed Sloan.

'To say nothing of the meat,' said Mine Host.

Detective Inspector Sloan pointed to the array of bottles behind the bar. 'But not the wines and spirits?'

'Not a drop,' said Johnny Hedger. 'Mind you, it's under lock and key when the bar's closed and there's always someone here when it isn't.'

'But kitchen's aren't usually secure,' murmured Sloan.

'No, and my accountant says that, according to the figures for the provisions we buy in, we should be making much more profit on the catering side than we do.' Hedger sighed. 'How he knows beats me, but there you are.'

'Clever chaps, accountants,' said Sloan. It was a view endorsed time and time again by his colleagues in the Fraud Squad.

'I suppose they know all the wrinkles,' said Detective Constable Crosby naïvely.

'Nearly all of them,' remarked Sloan. The Fraud Squad had one or two up their sleeves too, but this wasn't the time or place to say so. He got back to the matter in hand. 'What does your chef say – assuming it isn't him that's half-inching the goods, of course.'

Johnny Hedger frowned. 'Melvyn says it could be any of the kitchen staff. Or all of them. And that *I* can look into their handbags when they go home if I like, but he's not going to.'

'Chicken, isn't he!' pronounced Crosby, who had yet to encounter a really cross middle-aged woman with a genuine grievance.

'He says he's too young to die,' said the landlord.

'They'd take umbrage as quickly as they'd take a joint of beef, I suppose?' said Sloan more realistically.

'Quicker,' said the landlord gloomily. 'And take themselves off too, I dare say.'

'As good cooks go,' murmured Sloan.

Hedger rolled his eyes. 'They very nearly walked out on me when I stopped them eating when they were working here.'

'Even the leftovers?' asked Crosby.

'What's a leftover?' demanded Hedger rhetorically.

'Ah . . .' said Sloan, a man who in his day had spent a lot of time in court listening to lawyers splitting hairs. 'That's a point.'

'At least the accountant saved me from that one,' said Hedger. He sniffed. 'Makes a change from him costing me, which he does. An arm and a leg, usually.'

'How come?' enquired Crosby, evincing some interest at last.

'Said if I fed the staff here – that is, allowed them to eat my food on my premises while they were working here without charging them the going rate – then it would have to show in the books.'

'Which shut them up pretty quickly, I expect,' said Sloan, who knew a thing or two about mixing human nature with money both not in hand and taxable to boot.

'I'll say,' said Johnny, with something of his old energy returning. 'They didn't like that one little bit.'

'So if they want it, the staff have to steal the food rather than eat it here,' concluded Crosby simply.

'But it doesn't apply to you,' pointed out Sloan to the landlord. 'You must have eaten some of the pudding . . .'

'The accountant allows in the books for the wife and me consuming the restaurant food whether we do or not,' agreed Johnny, 'it not being considered natural that it should be otherwise.'

'Or,' persisted Sloan, 'you wouldn't both have been ill too.'

'That's true,' said Johnny uneasily.

'There's a thief in the house, all the same,' said Crosby.

'You find him, then,' said the landlord wearily. 'Or her. You're the detectives. Not me.'

'Someone must be taking the goods,' said Sloan, briskly, 'if there's food missing from the place on a regular basis.' Somewhere at the back of his mind was lurking the proper distinction between groceries and provisions, but this was not the moment either for such verbal niceties. The all-embracing word 'goods' would have to do.

'But how to find out who?' asked Hedger.

'And how to prove it,' added Detective Inspector Sloan. The trouble with all the animadversions of

Superintendent Leeyes was that they stuck in the mind. As he had said, identifying the guilty was only half the problem these days . . . Evidence – preferably of the watertight variety – came into it as well.

'I just want the losses stopped.' Hedger shrugged. 'It's quite difficult enough making a place like this pay without having the ground cut from under your feet by thieves in the night.'

'Not in the night,' put in Detective Constable Crosby, who was of a literal turn of mind. 'In the day.'

'You're right there,' admitted Johnny Hedger. 'It must be in the day. The deep freezers and the refrigerator are all locked when Melvyn goes home to Luston. He gives me the keys.'

'Melvyn's off sick too, you said,' remarked Sloan casually.

'Can't keep a thing down, his family say,' said Hedger with patent sympathy. 'None of them can. They've had to have the doctor to him. Just like me and the wife . . .' His voice trailed away as he was struck by the significance of the words he had uttered.

'Just so,' said Detective Inspector Sloan sedately.

'I think I see your drift,' Hedger went on lamely.

'I don't,' began Crosby, then he stopped. 'Oh, yes, I do.'

'Good,' said Sloan drily.

The Detective Constable said, 'Your chef could be suffering from half-baked duck eggs too, Johnny.'

Sloan pointed to the envelope which Hedger had shown them. 'Yes, or more accurately what the doctors have called whatever it is that caused the food poisoning. *Typhimurium*, did you say it was?'

'Which he must have got from pinching the duck eggs,' deduced the Detective Constable, a trifle belatedly.

'Well, I can tell you he didn't buy them from the farmer,' said Johnny Hedger. 'The Health and Safety people have checked on all the customers who've bought eggs from him. First thing they did.'

'Though whether Melvyn got his food poisoning from pinching the duck eggs,' amended Sloan. 'is something which remains to be proved . . .'

'Beyond reasonable doubt,' put in Johnny Hedger, veteran of the odd pub fracas and therefore no stranger to the magistrates' court. He looked up as a pleasant-faced middle-aged woman came in, her coat over her arm. 'Thank goodness you've arrived, Margaret,' he said to her. 'You can take over the bar – drinks only to be served today – and I can put my feet up for a bit.' He gave the two policemen a strained smile. 'Excuse me, gentlemen, I must take a look at the wife too.'

Detective Constable Crosby turned to Sloan and said, 'Can we go over to Luston now, sir, and finger the chef – this Melvyn fellow?'

'On what charge?' asked Sloan mildly. Luston was right over the other side of the county and he was well aware that the constable liked driving fast cars fast.

'Theft,' said Crosby promptly. 'He didn't just take a bite while he was here, because his whole family is ill. He must have taken either a load of the eggs or enough of the pudding for the lot of them.'

'Very probably. But what are you going to use for evidence? Real evidence, Crosby – the sort that the Superintendent likes, not the circumstantial variety.'

'The eggshells?'

'Gone long ago, I'll be bound.'

He frowned. 'What you said, sir? The *Typhimurium?*'

'And how are you going to prove that?'

Crosby's face fell.

'Think, man,' adjured Sloan. 'Think.'

Crosby scratched his head. 'Send in the food police?'

'Better than that. Try again.'

The Detective Constable's face looked quite blank.

'Shall we assume,' said Sloan patiently, 'that Melvyn's doctor has also diagnosed food poisoning and . . .'

'And notified it!' Crosby's hand smacked down on the table. 'Like the doctor here did.'

'Exactly. A different doctor in a different part of the county certifying that Melvyn and his family are suffering from the identical strain of the bacillus present in the food causing the trouble here should help your case no end.'

'My case, sir?' the Detective Constable's face turned pink with pleasure. 'Thank you, sir.'

'After all,' said Sloan, since food was the essence of the case here, 'dog doesn't eat dog.'

Child's Play

Henry Tyler wouldn't admit it, even to himself, but he was – there was no doubt about it – panting ever so slightly as he approached the Beacon Hotel. But he wasn't disappointed with what he found. He'd been drawn to the place in the first instance by its address – the sound of Tea Garden Lane had an attractive ring to any walker. So did the name of the area where it was situated – Happy Valley.

And then he'd spotted the building itself from halfway across the opposite hillside and immediately realized that the view from its terrace would be well worth the climb up. In theory, visiting High Rocks had been next on his agenda, but the hotel and luncheon called. High Rocks would have to wait.

He paused on the hill just below the hotel itself, ostensibly to admire that selfsame view but actually to get his breath back properly before he presented himself at the bar. A walking tour was all very well in its way, but it came hard to a civil servant who normally spent his working days at a desk in Whitehall.

Henry had passed the weekend before with his married sister, her husband and their two children in the small market town of Berebury, in rural Calleshire, by way of both winding down from the cares of state and limbering up for his break from routine. This plan had worked up to a point, even though the children had clamoured for his attention almost all the time they were awake. But meeting their demands had not exactly been preparation for striding through the steep lanes of the delightful border country of Kent and Sussex round Tunbridge Wells in high summer.

His nephew and niece, after all, had only required him to play pen and paper games with them. As far as more active pastimes were concerned, they were united in being against them, smacking as they did, they insisted, of compulsory games at school. Their doting uncle had ruefully concluded that the children of today were totally opposed to any activity that involved them in making any move that required more physical effort than tearing open a packet of crisps.

His breath recovered, Henry clambered up onto the hotel terrace and acknowledged that the view was memorable. He stood looking south until a more urgent need made itself felt. After all, even Goethe had said that no man could enjoy a view for more than fifteen minutes. As far as Henry was concerned at this moment, the bodily requirement of a long cold drink displaced the soul's drinking in of beauty in less than five.

He made his way inside what must have once served as the ground floor of a rather grand private house and was now a welcoming bar. A Foreign Office man himself, he was naturally interested in architecture. The place must be late Victorian, he decided, but nicely shorn of Victorian excess. There was already the feel of forthcoming Edwardian comfort and amplitude about it.

Henry collected something with which to slake his immediate thirst but resisted pausing overlong at the bar on the illogical grounds that he was too hungry and too thirsty. He'd need to forgo wine with his meal if he was to tackle High Rocks that afternoon.

He climbed a flight of stairs and found himself faced with a choice of rooms in which to eat. There was a dining room on his right set for a formal luncheon which he shied away from like a nervous horse. Formal luncheons were the bane of his working life in the Foreign Office. Some important guest invariably said something very undiplomatic, no matter how much time had been spent on the *placement*. Attempting to retrieve the situation usually spoilt Henry's afternoon and evening.

Beyond that he spotted a small room, ideal for the intimate exchange, but long experience had taught Henry to be as wary of private encounters as of formal luncheons. These were the rooms that were the first to be bugged. They were also the ones whose comings and goings were the first to be noted by interested observers. Moreover, who could say afterwards with any certainty what had or had not been said in a private room? In an uncertain world, civil servants liked certainty.

He moved forward carefully, spotting an inviting table in the window which must enjoy a splendid view, but he stopped when he saw that there was already someone sitting there. In a way this was a help, as his first instinct – being a Foriegn Office man to his fingertips – would have been to avoid such an exposed position. He was just reminding himself that he was off duty and it didn't matter where he sat when the figure at the table turned and said, 'Hello, Tyler.'

'Good Lord, Venables . . . What on earth are you doing here?'

'You wouldn't believe me if I told you,' said the other man morosely. He was sitting with his shoulders hunched forward, his hands cradling the bowl of a wine glass.

'Perhaps not,' agreed Henry.

He had some justification for this response. Malcolm Venables was known to work for one of the obscurer branches of what used to be called – before the advent of tabloid newspapers and their investigative journalism – as the secret service.

'I'm damned if I believe it myself,' said Venables testily. 'Never thought I'd find myself in Tunbridge Wells of all places.'

'In the way of work, you mean?' asked Henry cautiously, taking a second look at the man. Downcast was the only way of describing those drooping shoulders and sunken head.

Always alert on behalf of the needs of his own great department of state, Henry Tyler started to run through in his mind the circumstances that might have brought Venables to these parts in such a state of obvious depression.

'Yes, worse luck,' grumbled Venables.

'I see,' said Henry. This could be serious. The interaction between the Foreign Office and Malcolm Venables's own particular division of the secret service (which rejoiced in the name of Mercantile and Persuasion) was a very delicate matter indeed; so delicate, in fact, that otherwise honourable – and sometimes even Right Honourable – gentlemen had been known to stand up in high places and declare that no links existed.

Venables indicated the chair opposite him. 'Are you going to join me, Tyler? I'm alone. Absolutely alone,' he muttered. 'And likely to be out on a limb into the bargain before very long.'

'I don't suppose things are as bad as that,' said Henry, with the detachment of a man safely out of reach of his own office. He could see, though, that something had seriously upset Venables this Monday morning.

Henry cast his mind rapidly back over the news items in the papers. There had been nothing in them which had caught his attention today, and in spite of the pen and paper games with his nephew and niece, he had taken care to study the weekend papers as thoroughly as usual.

'They are,' said Venables, waving to the waiter to bring another glass. 'And I just must talk to somebody . . .'

'Problems?' Henry enquired delicately, taking the proffered chair and pulling it up at the table in the window opposite him.

'Just the one,' said Venables, taking a long sip from his glass. 'But it's a big one.'

'Swans singing before they die?' suggested Henry lightly, since this was an increasing problem in all government departments.

'No,' said Venables rather shortly. 'Not that.'

'Certain persons dying before they've sung?' This, thought Henry from long experience, was less of a worry, but you never knew . . .

'It's not a laughing matter, Tyler. This is serious.'

'Matter of life and death, then?' hazarded Henry a little unfairly. Unfairly, because he already knew that it wouldn't be death that worried the man from the Mercantile and Persuasion Division – an outfit known affectionately throughout the corridors of power as 'Markets and Perks'. Death was always the least of their troubles in that department – it was a number of other words beginning with 'D' which were the Four Horsemen of their particular Apocalypse. Henry was all too aware that Disclosure, Débâcle, Dishonour and Double-dealing ranked far higher on the danger list of M and P than mere death.

'Well, not quite life and death,' admitted Malcolm Venables grudgingly. 'Not for us, anyway. It might very well be for other people. Who can say?'

'Tell me what you can,' invited Tyler, mindful of constraints to do with the Official Secrets Act, D Notices, the need-to-know basis and plain common sense. There was, though, behind these the inviolable tradition of their respective services that that which was revealed between the two of them would not be spoken of to others. Ever.

Venables pointed to a row of venerable – if not yet quite antique – wireless receivers arrayed on a shelf above them by way of ornament. 'Would you say they were safe?'

'Valves worn out long ago,' said Henry briskly. 'Not a bug between them, I'm sure. Carry on . . .'

'I must say it'll be a relief to talk to somebody sane,' admitted Venables.

Tyler did his best to project sanity.

'Coming down to Tunbridge Wells has made me realize that there are no sane cryptographers. Did you know that, Tyler?'

'I've always had doubts about all experts,' said Henry Tyler mildly. 'Obsessive, conceited, compulsive, opinionated . . .'

'Paranoic . . . Oh, thank you.' This last was to the waiter who had brought more cutlery, a table mat and a napkin for Henry.

'Monomaniac too, most experts,' added Henry. 'Only about their own thing, of course.'

'Exactly,' agreed Venables, slightly more cheerfully. 'And that's the trouble. By the way, the wine here isn't at all bad . . .'

As he partook of an excellent white Macon Villages, Henry mentally struck High Rocks off his programme for the afternoon.

'Another thing about experts, Tyler . . .'

'Yes?'

'They just won't admit defeat.'

'Now that's your true specialist – totally unrealistic,' said Henry judicially. 'I've always found them more inclined to worry at problems long after the moment has passed.' Life at the Foreign Office could sometimes move on with surprising speed.

'They go on like a dog at a bone.' Malcolm Venables nodded and slid a piece of paper out of his pocket and slipped it inside the menu with a skill born of much practice at the ancient art of legerdemain. He handed the menu concealing the paper to Henry and said, 'What do you make of that, Tyler?'

It was a single sheet on which was written a series of apparently meaningless sentences.

'Well,' said Henry, after studying the paper for a long moment, 'I can see that there are – er – very definite overtones of *Alice in Wonderland* there.'

'That,' groaned Venables, 'is part of the problem. My boss thinks that my contact – I think we'd better call him my informant, my overseas informant, if you take my meaning – is having me on.'

'It has been known . . .'

'And our cryptographic department says it's one of the most interesting ciphers they've seen in many a long year and would I give them more time.'

'Which means they can't solve it,' Henry translated without difficulty.

'Exactly and, for reasons which I can't go into, I just can't give them more time . . .' He twisted in his seat and snatched the menu back as the waiter hove into view.

'Are you ready to order, gentlemen?' The man hovered, order pad in hand.

'We'll have the fish,' said Venables swiftly.

'Two fish . . .' The waiter melted away again.

'So urgent,' said Venables, handing the menu back to Henry, 'that if we fail, the problem'll probably end up on somebody's plate in your department, my friend, and nobody's going to like that.'

Henry, who could take a hint even better than the

next man – since hints, rather than plain English, were part of the currency of the Foreign Office – turned his attention back to the paper lurking inside the menu.

Venables leaned across the table and pointed to the words on the sheet. 'You'll see, Tyler, that each sentence contains a number incorporated in the text . . .'

'A written number,' murmured Henry, his eye running along a line which read, 'Beautiful Soup, so rich and green, Waiting in twelve hot tureens.' 'By the way, Venables,' he added plaintively, 'I mightn't have wanted the fish.'

The man from Mercantile and Persuasion ignored this last. 'What strikes you about those lines?'

Henry, who had been properly educated even at nursery level, searched for a childhood memory. 'Unless I am mistaken, the original text doesn't mention the exact number of tureens.'

'Precisely!' In his eagerness, Venables leaned across the table again and tapped the paper inside the menu. 'Here it says, "Who would not give all else for ten pennyworth only of beautiful soup?" '

'Soup?' The waiter materialized at their table. 'Do you want the soup as well?'

'No,' said Venables sharply.

The waiter put out a practised hand and started to tweak the menu from between Henry's fingers.

'I'm thinking about the soup,' said Henry with perfect truth, firmly hanging on to the menu.

'Very well, sir.' The man withdrew.

'What I'm thinking about the soup,' said Henry, as soon as he had gone, 'is that in Lewis Carroll's poem "Turtle Soup" it says two pennyworth not ten.'

'That's why I'm here in Tunbridge Wells,' said Malcolm Venables. 'I've been getting a world authority on the works of Lewis Carroll to take a look at it.'

'And?'

'And he says that while all the contexts on this paper here are textually correct, all the numbers that have been added or changed are meaningless to him.' Venables paused and added thoughtfully, 'Fancy devoting your working life to studying *Alice in Wonderland* . . .'

'No funnier than what you're doing,' said Henry.

'What do you mean?' responded Venables indignantly. 'I'm trying to save the nation from its actual and its commercial enemies . . .'

'One and the same from our perspective,' said Henry cynically.

'Could be,' admitted Venables. 'Well, this coded message is from one of our best men . . .'

'So . . .'

'And is meant to tell us the exact design of a new uranium-assisted gun hatched up behind the Net Curtain . . .'

Henry Tyler suddenly sat up very straight.

' . . . and moreover, one,' added Malcolm Venables meaningfully, 'which is remarkably like a new one of ours.'

'One of ours that no one was supposed to know about?' hazarded Henry intelligently. There, presumably, was the rub.

'Got it in one,' said Venables, his appetite reviving sufficiently for him to reach for a bread roll.

'And you need to know not only whether they –

whoever they are – have actually got it but who it was that gave it to them, if they did?'

'Precisely,' said the man from Mercantile and Persuasion, warming under this ready understanding. 'And preferably without anyone knowing that we know anything about anything at all.'

Henry Tyler was at one with him there. While, when there was cloak and dagger work about, he was quite content to leave the dagger side to the Ministry of Defence, he spent a lot of his own working life concentrating on keeping a number of cloaks tightly wrapped.

'But what forty-two walruses and seventy-two carpenters have to do with it, I can't begin to say,' the Foreign Office man admitted. Struck by a sudden thought, he said, 'Wasn't Lewis Carroll a mathematician in his private life?'

'He was and I've had one of them working on it as well,' said the man from Markets and Perks with a certain melancholy satisfaction, 'and all he said too was that it was interesting, very interesting.'

'Hang it all, Venables, it must mean something . . .'

'That's what my Minister thinks.'

'There's quite a lot hanging on it, isn't there?' deduced Henry realistically.

'You can say that again, Tyler. My 'K' for a start . . .'

'Quite, quite,' said Henry soothingly. Malcolm Venables was well known in the corridors of power to be suffering from 'Knight starvation'.

'Another odd thing about this message is that it's composed in words at all . . . Hang on, the waiter's coming back again.'

Henry exercised his own prestidigitatory skills by extricating the paper from the menu under cover of his napkin and slipping it beneath his table mat.

'Two fish,' announced the waiter, setting down a pair of substantial platters. 'Chef says to mind the plates. They're very hot.'

'They're not the only things at the table too hot to handle,' said Henry when the waiter had withdrawn to a safe distance and he'd retrieved the paper. 'I should think this *billet-doux* of yours is too.'

'What we were hoping for,' persisted Venables, 'was a drawing of the weaponry in question. We badly need to know if it's ours or theirs. A description wouldn't be half as good as a picture even if we could understand it, but we can't.'

'So the numbers aren't measurements?' said Henry, picking up his fish knife and fork.

'We've tried them every way we can – with and without computers – and no matter which way we hold them up to the light, they don't produce a measured drawing of any sort.'

'There is one thing about the numbers, though, isn't there,' observed Henry diffidently. 'Oh, yes, thank you, a little more of the Macon would go down very well.'

'What's that?' Venables paused, the bottle suspended over Henry's glass.

'There are no two the same.'

'Oh, that,' said Venables dismissively. 'Yes, the boffins pointed that out first before they really got to work. All the numbers between one and eighty-seven, none recurring. It didn't help, actually . . .'

Henry took another look at the text. 'I wouldn't say that, old man. Lend me a pencil, will you?'

'Here you are.' Malcolm Venables produced one with a chewed end from about his person.

'Thanks. Now, give me a minute, will you? And don't you let your fish get cold. This'll take a minute or two . . .'

'I say, what are you doing, Tyler?'

Henry pushed his own fish to one side and laid the paper flat on the table. He began to apply the pencil to the message. 'Give me half a minute and I'll tell you.'

'I hope you know what you're doing,' said Venables anxiously. 'You do realize that I'll be done for if anything goes wrong with that message?'

'Would the barrel of this gun of yours happen to look like this?' enquired Henry, a design beginning to take shape under the pencil.

'Good God!' Venables sat up, his fish forgotten. 'How did you work that out?'

'And the sights like this?' What was even more clearly a very formidable piece of armoury emerged as Henry drew lightly over the written words.

'I don't believe it . . .' breathed Venables. 'I just don't believe it.'

'I think you'll just have to,' said Henry bracingly as the final details of a horrendous weapon grew before their eyes. Realism was prized very highly at the Foreign Office.

'That's it, all right,' said Venables with barely suppressed excitement. 'How did you do it, Tyler?'

'I joined up the full stops at the end of every sentence in order,' explained Henry modestly.

'You did what?' spluttered the man from Mercantile and Persuasion.

'Starting,' said Henry Tyler, 'with the one that mentioned the figure one and going on to the one which talked about eighty-seven lobsters.'

'I don't believe it,' said Venables.

'It's called "Dot-to-Dot" and my niece does it rather well. She's seven, you know.'

Malcolm Venables wasn't listening. He was gazing out of the window. 'Do you realize, Tyler, that we can come back here each year for the rest of time and sit at this table and spout Tennyson to each other?'

'Tennyson?'

Venables nodded 'You remember . . .'

'No,' said Henry, who was getting really hungry now.

' "And," ' quoted Venables dreamily, ' "gazing from this height alone, We spoke of what had been." '

Like to Die

'The law,' pronounced Superintendent Leeyes heavily, 'is an ass.'

'Sir?' Detective Inspector C. D. Sloan raised an enquiring eyebrow but didn't commit himself to the general proposition. However much he agreed privately with any sentiment of his superior officer's, he had always found it prudent to wait to hear first exactly what it was that had provoked the Superintendent into generalization. He wondered what it was going to be this time.

'A total ass,' repeated the Superintendent, pushing about some papers on his desk in a fretful manner. 'Doesn't the man know we've got better things to do?'

'Which man?' asked Sloan very tentatively. In Leeyes's present mood, it might even have been better not to have put the question at all.

'The Coroner, of course,' snarled Leeyes.

'Ah . . .' Now Sloan understood. Mr Locombe-Stableford, Her Majesty's Coroner for the town of Berebury in the county of Calleshire, was an old sparring partner – not to say arch-enemy – of the Superintendent. This was because he was one of the few people in the world whose authority exceeded his own.

'It isn't even as if he doesn't know that we've got more than enough other things on our plate,' carried on the Superintendent in aggrieved tones. 'Much more important ones than this potty little case . . .'

'What case might that be, sir?'

Leeyes ignored this. 'There's that road traffic fatality over at Cullingoak, for instance.'

'Hit-and-run killers are very hard to find,' put in Sloan by way of apology. 'Everyone's working on that one flat out.'

'Just what I mean, Sloan,' said Leeyes sturdily. 'And I told him so.'

'The Coroner, sir.' Sloan came back to the matter in hand. 'What exactly is it that he – er – wants us to do?' The Detective Inspector knew one thing about Mr Locombe-Stableford and that was – like it or not – his writ ran throughout the patch covered by 'F' Division of the county constabulary.

'The Coroner,' said Leeyes flatly, 'has decided for reasons best known to himself to hold an inquest on a Mr Thomas Lean, a wealthy retired businessman . . .'

Since this action was totally within that august official's prerogative, Sloan waited.

' . . . who died yesterday in a nursing home.' Leeyes tapped his desk and added meaningfully, 'The Berebury Nursing Home.'

'Ah . . .' said Sloan.

The Berebury Nursing Home was considered one of the best in the whole county. Only the well connected and the well off went there; Sloan promptly amended the thought – well, the well off anyway. It was no use being well connected unless you were also well off if you wanted to be treated at the Berebury Nursing Home. He'd heard that the fees were monstrously steep.

'And they don't like it,' said Leeyes.

'The nursing home, you mean, sir?'

'Naturally.'

'Not good for business,' agreed Sloan.

'The Matron's in a proper taking about there being a post-mortem. Dr Dabbe's doing it now.'

'I can see that she might be,' said Sloan, frowning at an elusive memory. 'Isn't that where the Earl of Ornum's dotty old aunt is? Lady Alice . . .'

'Shouldn't be surprised,' said Leeyes. 'Now, this Thomas Lean hadn't been in there very long. He'd been pretty dicky for months and just got too ill to be nursed at home.'

'So why the inquest?' Sloan was beginning to see why the Superintendent thought the Coroner was being perverse and making more work for the Consultant Pathologist at the Berebury District Hospital Trust, into the bargain.

'Because his illness didn't kill him,' came back Leeyes smartly, 'that's why.'

'I see, sir.' Sloan reached for his notebook. That did sound more like work for the head of Berebury's tiny Criminal Investigation Department.

'It was food poisoning. Or so the patient's doctor says.' The Superintendent sniffed. He didn't like giving medical opinion any more credence than was absolutely necessary.

'And what have the family got to say?' Their views, thought Sloan, might be just as relevant as those of the Matron.

'We don't know yet,' said Leeyes. 'They were away on holiday when Thomas Lean died. They're on their way home from France now.'

Detective Inspector Sloan opened his notebook at a new page. 'This old gentleman, sir . . .'

'He wasn't all that old,' said Leeyes briskly. The Superintendent was getting towards retirement age himself and had turned against ageism. 'He was just coming up to seventy-five and that's not old these days.'

'No, sir,' agreed Sloan hastily. 'No age at all.'

Leeyes pulled one of the pieces of paper on his desk towards him. 'That's right. Seventy-four and eleven months. His birthday . . . oh, his birthday would have been tomorrow.'

The Matron of the Berebury Nursing Home seemed as upset about that as she was about everything else. 'You see, gentlemen, we always try to celebrate the birthdays of all of our patients . . . poor dears. Nothing elaborate, naturally.'

'Naturally,' agreed Detective Inspector Sloan.

'Not in their state of health,' chimed in Detective Constable Crosby. Because they were so busy down at the police station, Sloan had taken the detective constable with him to the nursing home as being better than nobody. Now he wasn't so sure that Crosby was better than nobody.

The Matron, who looked more than a little wan

herself, waved a hand. 'You know the sort of thing, a glass of sherry and a special cake and so forth – not that poor Mr Lean would have been fit to join in anything approaching a celebration today.'

'No?'

'And, as it happened, none of us would have felt like eating. Not after yesterday.' She shook her head sadly. 'And this would have been his last birthday, you know. He wasn't going to get better.'

Detective Constable Crosby looked interested.

'He'd come in here to die,' explained the Matron. 'He'd been going slowly downhill with cancer for a long time, but the chemotherapy was keeping him going – and the painkillers, of course. Then it got that the family couldn't manage any more.'

'I see,' said Sloan carefully. There were some homes, the police knew only too well, where the pain-killers killed more than the pain, but this hadn't been what had alerted the Coroner about this death.

'And,' she said, 'they were certainly helping him to hold his own.' She made a gesture of despair with her hands. 'If it hadn't been for this terrible food poisoning, we might have had him with us yet for weeks – perhaps months . . .'

It began to sound as if the Coroner was being pedantic to a fault and that the Superintendent was right after all. Mr Locombe-Stableford had dug his heels in over a legal nicety: a verdict of misadventure, perhaps, rather than natural causes.

'Tell me about yesterday,' invited Sloan.

'Everyone was very, very ill.' She shuddered at the memory. 'But everyone . . . staff and patients.'

'And especially Mr Lean . . .'

'Well, no . . . not at first anyway,' she said, drawing her brows together. 'That was the funny thing.'

'Funny peculiar or funny ha-ha?' asked Crosby.

She stared at him and said repressively, 'It was thought strange that he should appear to be less ill than everyone else and yet be the one to die.'

Detective Inspector Sloan leaned forward. He would deal with Crosby later, but all policemen were professionally interested in things that were funny peculiar. 'Go on . . .'

She winced. 'I – we – that is, everyone else started off with some dizziness and then abdominal pain . . .'

'Quite so,' said Sloan, making a note.

'And then there was nausea followed by severe vomiting.' The Matron obviously found reporting in the third person easier and went on in a more detached way: 'Several staff and patients collapsed and some of them then had diarrhoea . . .'

'But only Thomas Lean died,' said Crosby insouciantly.

She inclined her head.

'How did you manage?' asked Sloan. Perhaps the Coroner wasn't just being difficult . . .

'Dr Browne was very good. He came at once and saw everyone and took away specimens and so forth.'

Sloan nodded. He knew Dr Angus Browne – a family doctor of the old school. He was forthright but kind – and careful.

'He sent for the Environmental Health people or whatever it is they call themselves these days too.'

Very careful then, Dr Browne had been. Which was interesting.

'Food poisoning, you see, being a notifiable condition . . .'

'And then?'

'I can't really tell you that.' The Matron looked embarrassed and murmured apologetically, 'You see, I was one of the casualties myself at the time.'

'I understand.' Sloan turned over a page in his notebook. 'So . . .'

'So we had to call in extra staff.'

He looked up quizzically.

'Anyone,' she amplifed this, 'who hadn't eaten luncheon here on Thursday – night staff, people on stand-by and some agency nurses.'

'And then . . .'

'People started to recover later that night and by the next morning everyone was all right again.'

'Except Thomas Lean,' said Crosby mordantly.

'We – that is, the substitute staff alerted by Lady Alice – sent for Dr Browne again when they saw how poorly he had become.'

'Lady Alice . . .'

'She,' said the matron faintly, 'was the only person in the whole establishment not taken ill and spent her time wandering around, seeing how people were.'

'And she, I take it, was the only person not to have partaken of whatever it was that caused the food poisoning?' deduced Sloan, since not even *noblesse oblige* protected one against tainted food.

'Casseroled beef,' said the Matron with a certain melancholy. 'Dr Browne'll be here as soon as he's heard from the laboratory to explain to us exactly what was wrong with it. It was the only thing that everyone who was ill had eaten and everyone who had eaten it was ill.'

'But Mr Lean had it too,' said Crosby.

'Oh, yes,' said the Matron wearily, 'Mr Lean had the beef casserole.'

'He had his chips too,' said Crosby almost – but not quite – *sotto voce.*

The Matron, who still looked a trifle frayed at the edges, had too many other things on her mind to object to unseemly levity. 'By the time Dr Browne got back here, Mr Lean was having trembling convulsions and he died very soon after that.'

'We'll be talking to Dr Browne,' said Sloan, 'as soon as he arrives.'

'How long would the old boy have lasted otherwise?' enquired Crosby irrepressibly.

'Dr Browne wasn't sure and he didn't want to commit himself anyway. Not even when the family talked to him . . .'

'I was going to ask about them,' went on Sloan smoothly.

'Mr and Mrs Alan Lean – he's the son – had the chance of a few days' holiday in France.' She took a deep breath. 'I said to go if they wanted to. It wasn't as if there was anything more that anyone could do for his father and both he and his wife had been most attentive since Mr Lean had been here.'

Sloan made another note.

'We – that is, I – said they would have nothing to blame themselves for if he died while they were away.

Obviously,' the Matron expanded on what was clearly a well-worn theme, 'it is – er – more satisfactory if the family can take their farewells here, but – ' She paused for breath. Unwisely, as it turned out.

'All part of the service?' suggested Crosby, filling the conversational gap.

'But,' she rallied, 'I told them that if he were to die while they were away, we could always cope – do what was necessary and . . .'

'And put things on ice,' contributed Crosby helpfully.

'After all,' she said firmly, 'as Dr Browne has been kind enough to say more than once, some of our patients – like Lady Alice, for instance – come here and forget to die.'

'Except Thomas Lean,' remarked Crosby inevitably.

'We'd like to see Lady Alice,' said Sloan. What he would also like to do was to deal with Crosby. But not here and not now. Later, in the privacy of the police station.

Lady Alice might have forgotten to die; she hadn't forgotten Thursday's excitements. It seemed that people vomiting all over the place had brought back the dear old days during the war when she had served in the Women's Royal Naval Service. Until stemmed, she was inclined to reminiscence about the Bay of Biscay in winter in wartime.

'But you were all right,' said Sloan, getting a word in edgeways. 'Yesterday, I mean.' She had probably, he decided, been all right in the Bay of Biscay on a troopship too, submarines or no.

'Never have liked onions,' she cackled. 'They don't agree with me. So I don't eat 'em.'

'Very sensible,' said Sloan.

'They do me an omelette when there's onions about,' said the old lady.

'And I understand you saw Mr Thomas Lean . . .'

'He was like to die,' said Lady Alice.

'Like to die?' echoed Sloan.

'What they used to put first when they wrote their wills in the old days. They'd begin with "Like to die" and then you'd know they were making it on their deathbed.' She looked at him and said sadly, 'That's the worst of having ancestors . . . there's nothing new.'

'But Thomas Lean ate some of the casserole?' said the Detective Inspector, struggling back to the point.

'As to that,' responded Lady Alice, 'I couldn't say.'

'He was taken ill . . .'

'Oh, yes. But he hadn't been sick.' She looked at Sloan suspiciously. 'Did you say you were both policemen?'

'That's right, your ladyship.'

'St Michael types in disguise . . .'

'Not really.' It was Sloan's mother who was the churchgoer of the family; he didn't know the connection. 'At least, I don't think so.'

'He saved three people from wrongful execution,' said Lady Alice. 'We had a painting at home of him doing it. Never liked it. It went for death duties.'

'I don't think that in this case there will be an execution.'

'Pity.' Lady Alice looked Crosby up and down. 'Did you know that one of my ancestors who was the Bishop of Calleford used to hang people in the days when he had temporal powers as well as spiritual ones?'

Sloan thought it was safe to say that things weren't what they used to be, while Crosby hastened to tell her that he'd always gone to Sunday School when a lad.

'You were very lucky to escape the outbreak, Lady Alice,' said Sloan, adding persuasively, 'Tell me, did you notice anything out of the ordinary yesterday?'

'Only in the kitchen,' she said. 'I went down there for more water jugs. Dash of salt and plenty of cold water's what you need when—'

'What was out of the ordinary?' asked Sloan.

'They weren't shallots,' she said.

'What weren't?'

'I may not like 'em,' she said enigmatically, giving a high laugh, 'but I know my alliaceous vegetables, all right.'

'I'm sure,' he said pacifically. 'So?'

'They were daffodil bulbs not onions. That dim girl who does the vegetables still had some on the side-board. Saw 'em myself.'

Dr Angus Browne said the same thing but more scientifically twenty minutes later. 'The lab found the alkaloids narcissine – otherwise known as lycorine – and galantamine and scillotoxin – that's one of the glycoside scillamines – in the vomit and in the remains of the casserole.'

'And we found some *Narcissus pseudonarcissus* bulbs in the kitchen,' said Detective Inspector Sloan, not to be outdone in the matter of a 'little Latin and less Greek'.

'Easily enough mistaken, I suppose,' grunted the doctor, who was neither a gardener nor a cook.

'Animals seem to know the difference,' said Crosby, adding brightly, 'If they couldn't tell them apart, then they'd be dead, wouldn't they?'

'Just so.' The doctor looked at the constable and said, 'Anyway, the lab people have sent a copy of their findings over to Dabbe at the mortuary.'

'We've been on to the Environmental Health people and they tell us they've taken the wholesale greengrocers apart without finding anything wrong,' said Sloan, 'but we're going over there all the same.'

'They say they haven't found anything but onions in their onion sacks so far,' chimed in Crosby. 'They come in those string-bag affairs so you can see what you're getting.'

'There's one thing that's bothering me, doctor,' said Sloan. 'What I want to know is, if everyone else who had that casserole was promptly sick, why wasn't the deceased sick as well?'

'Easy,' the doctor said. 'He was on a whole raft of powerful anti-emetic tablets to stop him being sick. Vomiting is an established side effect of all his medication. He wasn't sick because he was on them and because he wasn't sick, he didn't get rid of the toxic substances as everyone else did.'

'It's a bit like a selective weedkiller, isn't it?' offered Crosby cheerfully.

Sloan stared at Crosby, struck by a new thought. 'I must say, Doctor, I find all that very interesting. Very interesting indeed. But not as interesting as something my constable has just said. Crosby, let us now go the way of all flesh . . .'

'Sir?' The constable looked quite alarmed.

'To the kitchen.'

The vegetable cook, her colour still not quite returned to normal, did her best to be helpful. Her job was to take what was needed from the cold store outside, weigh up what was needed for the day, and wash and prepare it ready for the cook, who came in later.

And if she had done anything wrong yesterday she would like to know what it was, if they didn't mind, and they might like to know that they'd been asking her to come and work at the Red Lion Hotel if she ever felt like leaving the nursing home. Very friendly, they were, at the Red Lion. Not like some places she could mention.

'I'm sure they are,' said Sloan pleasantly. 'Now, will you just show us over the cold store again. There was something I forgot to look at before. The lock . . .'

'A warrant?' echoed Leeyes back at the police station. 'Who for?'

'The son of the deceased,' said Sloan. 'On a charge of murder. Cleverest job I've come across in many a long day. Make everybody ill but just kill the one person who won't be sick when he's poisoned. All the son had to do was substitute the daffodil bulbs for the shallots in the cold store – you can see where he worked on the lock – and go away. I thought it was strange that he and his wife went abroad for the old boy's birthday.'

'What was so important about that? Couldn't it have waited?'

'Not if his father had written his pension funds in trust for him,' said Sloan. 'Thomas Lean would have had to die before he was seventy-five or take the pension himself. He left it as late as he dared because his father was so ill anyway.'

'I think,' said the Superintendent loftily, 'that I shall tell the Coroner that some new evidence came to light.'

Dead Letters

Sixteenth-century Scotland

The Sheriff of Fearnshire was definitely feeling his age. He was quite convinced too that winters were colder and lasting longer than they used to. And equally sure that summers were getting shorter and shorter every year. That Sheriff Rhuaraidh Macmillan's joints were a good deal stiffer than they had been when he was a young man was beyond doubt. There was, however, nothing at all wrong with his brain – even when he had just, as now, been abruptly awakened from a fitful doze in his chair.

This was why he was immediately alert when the youngest and smallest maid in his establishment suddenly staggered into his room heavily burdened with a pile of peats for the fire. For one thing, the fire was burning well and patently had no need at all of more peats until it was time to bank it up for the night. Another incongruity he noted was that it was not usually a maidservant who brought them into his sitting room, and certainly never this little one. Working at the peat hags and hauling their fuel about afterwards were considered to be man's work even though the peats did get lighter as they dried out.

The girl set the peats down by the fireside and came straight across to his side, standing close to his chair.

'There's a wee mannie that's after wanting to talk to you, sir,' she began timidly, sketching a token curtsy in his direction.

'Who are you?' he asked.

'Please, sir – ' the curtsy was deeper this time – 'I'm Elspeth from the kitchen.' That she was not familiar with the room was evident from the way in which she stared round at it.

'I didn't hear the pipes,' the Sheriff said. The house at Drummondreach had a hall-boy whose sole duty it was to herald equally the approach of friend and stranger with a fanfare of welcome on his uillean pipes. And set the bagpipes to sound the tocsin of warning too, should a known foe be sighted in the distance.

'Please, sir, the wee mannie wasn't at the door . . .' The girl was no height at all herself but she had a bright look. 'And I didn't see anyone coming up the brae either . . .'

One of the many things that being Sheriff of Fearnshire had taught Rhuaraidh Macmillan over the years was that a man could not be too careful to whom – and of whom – he spoke. Unknown men at his door very much came into this category: they could spell danger.

'He dinna' come by the high road, sir,' she said.

'So?' he barked crisply.

'Please, sir, he came out of the wood at the back.'

'Ah . . .' The Forest of Ard Meanach came right up to the very edge of the Drummondreach policies. A man could come out of the trees there without being observed from afar.

'I saw him in the steading when I was after getting the eggs from the nests.'

'You did, did you?' mused the Sheriff, thinking quickly. Back-door visitors could be very dangerous. It wasn't so much who came out of the wood that was a worry these days as what was liable to crawl out of the woodwork afterwards. And there was no knowing in the Scotland of today what exactly that might be – or where it might lead. He sighed and started to climb stiffly out of his chair. 'Well, then, Elspeth, you had better send my clerk to me at once and then go and bring the man in here.'

'He'd no' come in,' responded the girl. 'He said to say to you that he couldn'a.'

'He couldn'a?'

'And that he wouldn'a anyway, even if he could.'

The Sheriff, on his feet now, looked down at her. She was scarcely more than a child. But a bright child, for all that. 'Why not?'

'He says he needs must talk to the Sheriff privately.'

Rhuaraidh Macmillan frowned and said, 'I see.' These were difficult times in Scotland and a man in a position of authority such as the Sheriff of Fearnshire had to be careful, very careful. Actually, all men in Scotland now had to be very careful; and some women too, even more so. There was one woman in particular who should have been more so. A royal one, not noted for her wisdom . . .

'He's still outside,' she said, pointing over her shoulder in the direction of the wood behind the house.

'He called out to me on my way across the steading, but aye softly . . . and only after he'd seen I was alone.'

Sheriff Macmillan shot her a keen glance. 'And where exactly is he now?'

'In the little bothy behind the steading, sir.'

'Alone?' Men had been known to have been ambushed before now by messages such as these. Good men and true . . .

'Yes, sir.' She curtsied again. 'There's just himself.'

'How can you be so sure?'

'Please, sir, I looked specially when I went back to get the peats for the fire.'

'And did you ask him who he was?' If there was ever to be 'a chiel among them, taking notes' it had better not be this sharp-witted youngster or they would all be doomed.

'Yes, sir, but he wouldn't be after telling me his name.'

'Ah . . .' The Sheriff of Fearnshire was not totally surprised at this; only that whoever it was who wanted such secrecy had risked coming to Drummondreach in daylight in the first place. The burden of his spiel must be important, that was for sure. And urgent too.

'And he had his face hidden by his plaid,' she said, as if she had read his mind. 'But – ' she gave him a mischievous sideways glance – 'I ken't well enough who it was anyway.'

'Tell me,' he commanded her.

'It's Murdo Macrae from Balblair, sir.'

'And how did you know that?' Sheriff Macmillan knew Murdo Macrae all right. Murdo had always been a sound man, in favour of the rule of law and order even in distinctly shaky times: unhappy times, such as they were in just now, when no man knew who was his friend and who was his foe; and, more worryingly, knew who was a government spy – or, even worse, a double agent – whose aims and objects were not the administration of justice but the furtherance of the power of his political masters. He knew without being told that if Murdo Macrae had something to say then that something would be important, more important still if he deemed it to be a clandestine matter.

'Please, sir,' the girl was answering him, 'Dougal, the ferryman, brought Murdo Macrae over the firth last night.' Her gaze was resting in wonder on the wall hangings in the room as she spoke. She was looking at them as if she hadn't seen tapestries before. 'He'd come from the west . . .'

'Well?' Now that the Sheriff came to think of it, little Elspeth from the kitchen probably hadn't ever been in his private sanctum before, let alone seen a minor work from Angers. She might not have even been in this part of the house at all until now.

'Dougal, the ferryman, knew who he was and he told Fergus Macpherson and Fergus was at the house this morning with fish and Fergus told us . . .' She paused to take breath.

'It doesn't follow that Murdo Macrae is the man in the bothy,' objected the Sheriff sternly, quite forgetting that he was talking to a mere girl – and a kitchenmaid at that – and not addressing learned men in a court of law.

Quite unfazed by his words, Elspeth from the kitchen held out her own thin right hand. 'Dougal told

Fergus that his passenger had a bloody bandage on his right hand and Fergus, he told us in the kitchen.'

'So?'

'The man in the bothy has a wound on his right hand too, sir. I saw it when he was holding his plaid tight against his face.'

The Sheriff gave the girl a quizzical look. At this rate he would soon have to look to his own laurels – she hadn't missed a single thing that should be marked by a sheriff too.

Elspeth was still speaking. 'And the mannie outside said I wasna' to tell anyone but the Sheriff himself that he was there in the bothy. That was very important, he said.'

Rhuaraidh Macmillan gestured towards the hearth. 'So that's why you brought in the peats that the fire didn't need.'

She bobbed up and down. 'I don't ordinarily get to come in here, sir, and I thought if anyone saw me coming this way . . .'

'Quite right, Elspeth,' he said gravely. He would have to consider how he himself could best cross the steading to the bothy behind without causing comment. Scotland wasn't what it was. Or rather, perhaps, what it had been. And there might be men watching him too, as they watched others in these troubled times. He knew well enough that Drummondreach was no safer than anywhere else in Fearnshire these days. He waved a hand. 'Now, away with you, lassie, while I think. Keep your tongue to yourself, mind.'

She didn't make any effort to take her leave.

Instead, she stood uncertainly between the fire and the door while the Sheriff looked up at the sky and tried to calculate how long it would be before the darkness was deep enough to allow him to slip out to Murdo Macrae unseen.

'Sir,' she began tentatively.

He turned. 'Yes?'

'Calum Beg will be after bringing the horses back soon from the fields.'

'What about it?' The girl should know that such mundane matters were outwith the concern of the Sheriff of Fearnshire.

'They have to go across the steading for their feed.'

'You're not wanting me to ride to the bothy, surely?'

'No, sir.' She bobbed again. 'But if we were to stop Calum on the road in front and you were to take the horses in instead of him . . .'

'Then I could lead the horses round towards the steading and into the bothy in his coat without being recognized,' finished Rhuaraidh Macmillan, appreciative of her use of the royal 'we'. If only the daughter of James V had had half as much sense – no, there was a better word for what he was thinking of, a Greek word 'nous', that was it – as this youngster had, then Scotland – and probably England too, for that matter – wouldn't be in half the turmoil that it was now.

Calum Beg's coat was old and dirty but it covered Rhuaraidh Macmillan well enough. The Sheriff didn't have Calum Beg's accomplished way with his equine team but somehow he got the pair round the front of the demesne and into the steading behind. He hitched the horses to their post and slipped first into the steading. He came out with an old bucket and then, thus laden with this unsavoury touch of verisimilitude, went into the bothy.

'Thank God you've come, Sheriff,' said a voice out of the darkness at the back of the unlit building. The bedraggled figure of Murdo Macrae emerged from the shadows. 'Macmillan, we need your help ower badly.'

'We?'

'There's a great trouble brewing over Loch a'Ch-roisg way.' Macrae didn't answer him directly. 'I got away yestre'en, but it was a near thing . . .'

'And sore wounded . . .' observed the Sheriff, pointing to Macrae's blood-caked hand.

The man winced as he moved forward. 'This wound, Sheriff, is why we need your help. I'm a marked man now.'

'And you can't go back without a working sword arm anyway,' observed the Sheriff, ever the realist. 'You'd no' be able to defend yoursel'. You'd be cut down in an instant.'

Macrae acknowledged the truth of this with a jerk of his head. 'You need to know that the blackguards are laying siege to the house by the loch.'

'The Rogart rebels?' Sheriff Macmillan didn't really, need to ask. That band was only one of those roaming the Highlands bent on causing trouble for the forces of law and order, but its men were the most prominent of the marauders presently terrorizing Fearnshire. And the best armed.

'Aye, and that's not the worst of it.' Murdo Macrae's

face twisted into a grimace of pain quite separate from that caused by his injured hand. 'There's women and children in the house without men there able enough to guard them. The doors'll no' last much longer. They've taken a deal of battering already.'

The Sheriff nodded. It was a tale he had heard many times before over the county.

Murdo Macrae's voice dropped to a whisper. 'And,' he said hollowly, 'a rowan tree by the track here has been set about.'

Rhuaraidh Macmillan acknowledged the seriousness of this. A rowan tree by the track roughly hacked down was an old Highland indication of trouble to come nearby and soon. 'They've taken the cattle, no doubt . . .'

'And torched the hay . . .' His shoulders sagged. 'Sheriff, I'm sure they're bent on laying waste to the whole strath and there'll be no stopping them unless we get help.'

Rhuaraidh Macmillan said in his measured way, 'There's no enemy like an auld enemy . . .' Highland memories went back a long way but he had no need to remind Murdo Macrae of Balblair of that. 'And the men of Rogart are auld enemies with the people from Loch a'Chroisg, right enough.'

'That's half the trouble,' said Macrae.

'And the other half?' asked the Sheriff, although he was sure he already knew the cause of the present troubles at Loch a'Chroisg.

Murdo Macrae lifted his shoulder in something like a shrug of despair. 'That there's still some for the Queen and some that are not.'

'That leddie'd not be wanting bairns starved out,' said the Sheriff firmly, 'whoever they're fighting for. She had one of her own, remember . . .'

'Not that she ever got to see him over much from all accounts.' Murdo Macrae grimaced. 'And that's not natural for a mother or her wean.'

'Aye.'

There was no denying that the Crown that had come in with a lass and was well on its way to going out with a lass – or even two, if rumours about the health of the Queen of England were true – was not what it had once been. Rhuaraidh Macmillan was profoundly grateful for one thing, though, and that was that the county of Fearnshire was a long way from Edinburgh and even further from Fotheringhay Castle, where he'd heard Mary Queen of Scots was presently imprisoned.

'So it is said,' he murmured noncommittally.

There was an even older Highland tradition than a savaged rowan tree: one that went, 'A silent tongue got no one hung.' He knew well enough that words could be as dangerous as swords; would that the Queen had known it too. But earlier.

Murdo Macrae said eagerly, 'If, Sheriff, we could get word to the Lord of Alcaig's Isle, I know he'd take up his men to Loch a'Chroisg and see the men from Rogart off . . .'

'Aye, Murdo, that's true. Old Duncan Alcaig would deal with them right enough,' agreed Rhuaraidh Macmillan, adding thoughtfully, 'And he has sons, too. Big men now.'

'But he's an aye careful body,' Macrae pointed out.

He sounded rueful. 'He'd no' trust any messenger, any more than I would myself . . . not these days.'

The Sheriff acknowledged the truth of this. Old Alcaig was nobody's fool. 'Messengers are not always what they seem,' he conceded.

Nothing, you could be sure, he thought to himself, was what it seemed these days. There had been those letters famously found in a casket first and now, he'd heard, letters concealed in a firkin of beer. None of those letters had been what they had seemed either. And all of them had caused a deal of trouble for a certain Queen – enough trouble to dissuade any man from trusting that any missive sent off into the blue would reach its destination without being tampered with and reported on to the man's – or the woman's – enemies. Moreover, no man could rest assured that, even if letters did reach the right reader, they would be seen only by the eyes of the man to whom they had been addressed. Not any longer.

Murdo Macrae struggled to get his good hand inside his torn jerkin. 'I have letters for the Lord of Alcaig's Isle here, but I'd need to know that they will get to him and him alone, mind you, otherwise . . .' His voice trailed away and there was a moment's silence in the bothy, broken only by the stamping of the hooves of one of the horses in the steading. 'Otherwise, Sheriff,' he went on hoarsely, 'I'm worse than a dead man.'

Rhuaraidh Macmillan did not attempt to contradict him. The slashed rowan tree was evidence enough that Macrae spoke the truth there.

'Wait you, man,' he said, 'while I think . . .'

The wounded fighter stood in front of him, anxiously scanning the Sheriff's face. 'There's men hiding up in the wood,' he said, 'who'll take letters to Alcaig, right enough, but he'll not know they're safe to act on and not a trap.'

Rhuaraidh Macmillan didn't need reminding of the dangers of a trap. Fearnshire might be a long way from London, but even they had heard about the uncovering of the Babington plot.

'I have a small chest indoors,' the Sheriff began slowly, 'with a good lock on it . . .'

Murdo Macrae's shoulders promptly sagged in despair. 'Locks need keys, Sheriff, and keys are no more safe than messengers these days.'

'Aye, man, I know that fine . . .' All Scotland knew that. The boy William Douglas had obtained the key to Loch Leven Castle when he had released Mary Queen of Scots. He had thrown the key into the loch as he rowed her and her maid across the water. 'But I wasn't thinking of your parting with the key of the casket . . .'

Murdo Macrae stared at him, nursing his blood-stained hand. 'Is Alcaig meant to break the casket open, then?' He looked even more weary now. 'And if so, how's Alcaig to know that that isn'a a trap too?'

Sheriff Macmillan stroked his chin. 'The messenger that takes the casket is to tell him to put his own lock on it too – a barrel padlock – and keep the key of that himsel'.'

The wounded man looked at him uncomprehendingly. 'Why is that, Sheriff?'

'And when Alcaig has done that, he's to send the casket back to you.'

'Without his key?' asked Macrae dully, moving over to the bothy wall for support, clearly now beyond thought.

'That's right,' said the Sheriff briskly. 'Then all you have to do is to unlock your lock with your key and send the casket back to him with his own lock still on it . . .'

'So that he can open it with his own key,' said Murdo Macrae, his mud-bespattered face clearing and some of his weariness dropping from him.

'And only him,' said the Sheriff.

'I think I understand,' said the wounded man, passing his good hand over his brow. He was sweating now. 'But why . . .'

'Knowing that no one else can have got into it because only he has the key,' finished the Sheriff of Fearnshire. He stopped and picked up the noisome old bucket. 'Now, wait you while I send Elspeth from the kitchen and her egg basket out here. The casket and the key'll be in there under some food and drink.' He paused at the door and added drily, 'If you haven't got that business with the keys straight in your mind, Macrae, ask her to explain it to you. She'll tell you, right enough.'

Gold, Frankincense and Murder

'Christmas!' said Henry Tyler. 'Bah!'

'And we're expecting you on Christmas Eve as usual,' went on his sister Wendy placidly.

'But . . .' He was speaking on the telephone from London, 'but, Wen—'

'Now it's no use your pretending to be Ebenezer Scrooge in disguise, Henry.'

'Humbug,' exclaimed Henry more firmly.

'Nonsense,' declared his sister, quite unmoved. 'You enjoy Christmas just as much as the children. You know you do.'

'Ah, but this year I may just have to stay on in London over the holiday . . .' Henry Tyler spent his working days – and, in these troubled times, quite a lot of his working nights as well – at the Foreign Office in Whitehall.

What he was doing now to his sister would have been immediately recognized in ambassadorial circles as 'testing the reaction'. In the lower echelons of his department, it was known more simply as 'flying a kite'. Whatever you called it, Henry Tyler was an expert.

'And it's no use your saying there's trouble in the Baltic either,' countered Wendy Witherington warmly.

'Actually,' said Henry, 'it's the Balkans which are giving us a bit of a headache just now.'

'The children would never forgive you if you weren't there,' said Wendy, playing a trump card, although it wasn't really necessary. She knew that nothing short of an international crisis would keep Henry away from her home in the little market town of Berebury, in the heart of rural Calleshire, at Christmas time. The trouble was that these days international crises were not nearly so rare as they used to be.

'Ah, the children,' said their doting uncle. 'And what is it that they want Father Christmas to bring this year?'

'Edward wants a model railway engine for his set.'

'Does he indeed?'

'A Hornby LMS red engine called "Princess Elizabeth",' said Wendy Witherington readily. 'It's a 4–6–2.'

Henry made a note, marvelling that his sister, who seemed totally unable to differentiate between the Baltic and the Balkans – and quite probably the Balearics as well – had the details of a child's model train absolutely at her fingertips.

'And Jennifer?' he asked.

Wendy sighed. 'The Good Ship Lollipop jigsaw. Oh, and when you come, Henry, you'd better be able to explain to her how it is that while she could see Shirley Temple at the pictures – we took her last week – Shirley Temple couldn't see her.'

Henry, who had devoted a great deal of time in the last ten days trying to explain to a minister in His Majesty's Government exactly what Monsieur Pierre

Laval might have in mind for the future of France, said he would do his best.

'Who else will be staying, Wen?'

'Our old friends Peter and Dora Watkins – you remember them, don't you?'

'He's something in the bank, isn't he?' said Henry.

'Nearly a manager,' replied Wendy. 'Then there'll be Tom's old Uncle George.'

'I hope,' groaned Henry, 'that your barometer's up to it. It had a hard time last year.' Tom's Uncle George had been a renowned maker of scientific instruments in his day. 'He nearly tapped it to death.'

Wendy's mind was still on her house guests. 'Oh, and there'll be two refugees.'

'Two refugees?' Henry frowned even though he was alone in his room at the Foreign Office. They were beginning to be very careful there about some refugees.

'Yes, the Rector has asked us each to invite two refugees from the camp on the Calleford road to stay for Christmas this year. You remember our Mr Wallis, don't you, Henry?'

'Long sermons?' hazarded Henry.

'Then you do remember him,' said Wendy without irony. 'Well, he's arranged it all through some church organization. We've got to be very kind to them because they've lost everything.'

'Give them useful presents, you mean,' said Henry, decoding this last without difficulty.

'Warm socks and scarves and things,' agreed Wendy Witherington vaguely. 'And then we've got some people coming to dinner here on Christmas Eve.'

'Oh, yes?'

'Our doctor and his wife. Friar's their name. She's a bit heavy in the hand but he's quite good company. And,' said Wendy, drawing breath, 'our new next-door neighbours – they're called Steele – are coming too. He bought the pharmacy in the square last summer. We don't know them very well – I think he married one of his assistants – but it seemed the right thing to invite them at Christmas.'

'Quite so,' said Henry. 'That all?'

'Oh, and little Miss Hooper.'

'Sent her measurements, did she?'

'You know what I mean,' said his sister, unperturbed. 'She always comes then. Besides, I expect she'll know the refugees. She does a lot of church work.'

'What sort of refugees are they?' asked Henry cautiously.

But that Wendy did not know.

Henry himself wasn't sure, even after he'd first met them, and his brother-in-law was no help.

'Sorry, old man,' said that worthy as they foregathered in the drawing room, awaiting the arrival of the rest of the dinner guests on Christmas Eve. 'All I know is that this pair arrived from somewhere in Mitteleuropa last month with only what they stood up in.'

'Better out than in,' contributed Gordon Friar, the doctor, adding an old medical aphorism, 'like laudable pus.'

'I understand,' said Tom Witherington, 'that they only just got out too. Skin of their teeth and all that.'

'As the poet so wisely said,' murmured Henry, ' "The only certain freedom's in departure." '

'If you ask me,' said old Uncle George, a veteran of the Boer War, 'they did well to go while the going was good.'

'It's the sort of thing you can leave too late,' pronounced Dr Friar weightily. Leaving things too late was every doctor's nightmare.

'I don't envy 'em being where they are now,' said Tom. 'That camp they're in is pretty bleak, especially in the winter.'

This was immediately confirmed by Mrs Godiesky the moment she entered the room. She regarded the Witheringtons' glowing fire with deep appreciation. 'We 'ave been so cooald, so cooaald,' she said as she stared hungrily at the logs stacked by the open fireside. 'So very cooald . . .'

Her husband's English was slightly better, although also heavily accented. 'If we had not left when we did – ' he opened his hands expressively – 'then who knows what would have become of us?'

'Who, indeed?' echoed Henry, who actually had a very much better idea than anyone else present of what might have become of the Godieskys had they not left their native heath when they did. Reports reaching the Foreign Office were very, very discouraging.

'They closed my university department down overnight,' explained Professor Hans Godiesky. 'Without any warning at all.'

'It was very terrrrrible,' said Mrs Godiesky, holding

her hands out to the fire as if she could never be warm again.

'What sort of a department was it, sir?' enquired Henry casually of the professor.

'Chemistry,' said the refugee, just as the two Watkins came in and the hanging mistletoe was put to good use. They were followed fairly quickly by Robert and Lorraine Steele from next door. The introductions in their case were more formal. Robert Steele was a good bit older than his wife, who was dressed in a very becoming mixture of red and dark green, though with a skirt that was rather shorter than either Wendy's or Dora's and even more noticeably so than that of Marjorie Friar, who was clearly no dresser.

'We're so glad you could get away in time,' exclaimed Wendy, while Tom busied himself with furnishing everyone with sherry. 'It must be difficult if there's late dispensing to be done.'

'No trouble these days,' boomed Robert Steele. 'I've got a young assistant now. He's a great help.'

Then Miss Hooper, whose skirt was longest of all, was shown in. She was out of breath and full of apology for being late. 'Wendy, dear, I am so very sorry,' she fluttered. 'I'm afraid, the waits will be here in no time at all . . .'

'And they won't wait,' said Henry guilelessly, 'will they?'

'If you ask me,' opined Tom Witherington, 'they won't get past the Royal Oak in a hurry.'

'The children are coming down in their dressing gowns to listen to the carols,' said Wendy, rightly ignoring both remarks. 'And I don't mind how tired they get tonight.'

'Who's playing Father Christmas?' asked Robert Steele jovially. He was a plump fellow, whose gaze rested fondly on his young wife most of the time.

'Not me,' said Tom Witherington.

'I am,' declared Henry. 'For my sins.'

'Then when I am tackled on the matter,' said the children's father piously, 'I can put my hand on my heart and swear total innocence.'

'And how will you get out of giving an honest answer, Henry?' enquired Dora Watkins playfully.

'I shall hope,' replied Henry, 'to remain true to the traditions of the Foreign Service and give an answer that is at one and the same time absolutely correct and totally meaningless . . .'

At which moment the sound of the dinner gong being struck came from the hall and presently the whole party moved through to the dining room, Uncle George giving the barometer a surreptitious tap on the way.

Henry Tyler studied the members of the party under cover of a certain amount of merry chat. It was part and parcel of his training that he could at one and the same time discuss Christmas festivities in England with poor Mrs Godiesky while covertly observing the other guests. Lorraine Steele was clearly the apple of her husband's eye but he wasn't sure that the same could be said for Marjorie Friar, who emerged as a complainer and sounded – and looked – quite aggrieved with life.

Lorraine Steele, though, was anything but dowdy. Henry decided her choice of red and green – Christmas colours – was a sign of a new outfit for Yuletide.

He was also listening for useful clues about their homeland in the Professor's conversation, while becoming aware that Tom's old Uncle George really was getting quite senile now and learning that the latest of Mrs Friar's succession of housemaids had given in her notice.

'And at Christmas too,' she complained. 'So inconsiderate.'

Peter Watkins was displaying a modest pride in his Christmas present to his wife.

'Well,' he said in the measured tones of his profession of banking, 'personally, I'm sure that refrigerators are going to be the thing of the future.'

'There's nothing wrong with a good old-fashioned larder,' said Wendy stoutly, like the good wife she was. There was little chance of Tom Witherington being able to afford a luxury like a refrigerator for a very long time. 'Besides, I don't think Cook would want to change her ways now. She's quite set in them, you know.'

'But think of the food we'll save,' said Dora. 'It'll never go bad now.'

' "Use it up, wear it out." ' Something had stirred in old Uncle George's memory. ' "Make it do, do without or we'll send it to Belgium." '

'And you'll be more likely to avoid food poisoning too,' said Robert Steele earnestly. 'Won't they, Dr Friar?'

'Yes, indeed,' the medical man agreed at once. 'There's always too much of that about and it can be very dangerous.'

The pharmacist looked at both the Watkins and said gallantly, 'I can't think of a better present.'

'But you did, darling,' chipped in Lorraine Steele brightly, 'didn't you?'

Henry was aware of an unspoken communication passing between the two Steeles; and then Lorraine Steele allowed her left hand casually to appear above the table. Her fourth finger was adorned with both a broad gold wedding ring and a ring on which was set a beautiful solitaire diamond.

'Robert's present,' she said rather complacently, patting her blonde Marcel-waved hair and twisting the diamond ring round. 'Isn't it lovely?'

'I wanted her to wear it on her right hand,' put in Robert Steele, 'because she's left-handed, but she won't hear of it.'

'I should think not,' said Dora Watkins at once. 'The gold wedding ring sets it off so nicely.'

'That's what I say too,' said Mrs Steele prettily, lowering her beringed hand out of sight again.

'Listen!' cried Wendy suddenly. 'It's the waits. I can hear them now. Come along, everyone. It's mince pies and coffee all round in the hall afterwards.'

The Berebury carol singers parked their lanterns outside the front door and crowded round the Christmas tree in the Witheringtons' entrance hall, their sheets of music held at the ready.

'Right,' called out their leader, a young man with a

rather prominent Adam's apple. He began waving a little baton. 'All together now . . .'

The familiar words of 'Once in Royal David's City' soon rang out through the house, filling it with joyous sound. Henry caught a glimpse of a tear in Mrs Godiesky's eye and noted a look of great nostalgia in little Miss Hooper's earnest expression. There must have been ghosts of Christmases past in the scene for her too.

Afterwards, when it became important to re-create the scene in his mind for the police, Henry could place only the Steeles at the back of the entrance hall, with Dr Friar and Uncle George beside them. Peter and Dora Watkins had opted to stand a few steps up the stairs to the first-floor landing, slightly out of the press of people but giving them a good view. Mrs Friar was standing awkwardly in front of the leader of the choir. Of Professor Hans Godiesky there was no sign whatsoever while the carols were being sung.

Henry remembered noticing suppressed excitement in the faces of his niece and nephew perched at the top of the stairs and hoping it was the music that they had found entrancing and not the piles of mince pies awaiting them among the decorative smilax on the credenza at the back of the hall.

They – and everyone else – fell upon them nonetheless as soon as the last carol had been sung. There was a hot punch too, carefully mulled to just the right temperature by Tom Witherington for those old enough to partake of it, and homemade lemonade for the young.

Almost before the last choirboy had scoffed the last mince pie, the party at the Witheringtons' broke up.

The pharmacist and his wife were the first to leave. They shook hands all round.

'I know it's early,' said Lorraine Steele apologetically, 'but I'm afraid Robert's poor old tummy's playing him up again.'

Henry, who had been expecting a rather limp paw, was surprised to find how firm her handshake was.

'If you'll forgive us,' said Lorraine's husband to Wendy, 'I think we'd better be on our way now.'

Robert Steele essayed a glassy, strained smile, but to Henry's eye he looked more than a little white at the gills. Perhaps he too had spotted that the ring that was his Christmas present to his wife had got a nasty stain on the inner side of it.

The pair hurried off together in a flurry of farewells. Then the wispy Miss Hooper declared the evening a great success but said she wanted to check everything at St Faith's before the midnight service and she too slipped away.

'What I want to know,' said Dora Watkins provocatively when the rest of the guests had reassembled in the drawing room and Edward and Jennifer had been sent back – very unwillingly – to bed, 'is whether it's better to be an old man's darling or a young man's slave?'

A frown crossed Wendy's face. 'I'm not sure,' she said seriously.

'I reckon our Mrs Steele's got her husband where she wants him, all right,' said Peter Watkins, 'don't you?'

'Come back, William Wilberforce, there's more work on slavery still to be done,' said Tom Witherington lightly. 'What about a nightcap, anyone?'

But there were no takers and in a few moments the Friars too had left.

Wendy suddenly said she had decided against going to the midnight service after all and would see everyone in the morning. The rest of the household also opted for an early night and in the event Henry Tyler was the only one of the party to attend the midnight service at St Faith's Church that night.

The words of the last carol, 'We Three Kings of Orient are . . .', were still ringing in his ears as he crossed the market square to the church. Henry wished that the Foreign Office had only kings to deal with: life would be simpler then. Dictators – and Presidents, particularly one President not so very many miles from 'perfidious Albion' – were much more unpredictable.

He sang the words of the last verse of the carol as he climbed the church steps:

> 'Myrrh is mine; it's bitter perfume
> Breathes a life of gathering gloom;
> Sorrowing, sighing, bleeding, dying,
> Sealed in the stone-cold tomb.'

Perhaps, he thought, as he sought a back pew and his nostrils caught the inimical odour of a mixture of burning candles and church flowers, he should have been thinking of frankincense or even – when he saw the burnished candlesticks and altar cross – Melchior's gold . . .

His private orisons were interrupted a few minutes later by a sudden flurry of activity near the front of the church and he looked up in time to see little Miss Hooper being helped out by the two churchwardens.

'If I might just have a drink of water,' he heard her say before she was borne off to the vestry. 'I'll be all right in a minute. So sorry to make a fuss. So very sorry . . .'

The Rector's sermon was its usual interminable length and he was able to wish his congregation a happy Christmas as they left the church. As Henry walked back across the square he met Dr Friar coming out of the Steeles' house.

'Chap's collapsed,' he murmured. 'Severe epigastric pain and vomiting. Mrs Steele came round to ask me if I would go and see him. There was blood in the vomit and that frightened her.'

'It would,' said Henry.

'He's pretty ill,' said the doctor. 'I'm getting him into hospital as soon as possible.'

'Could it have been something he ate here?' said Henry, telling him about little Miss Hooper.

'Too soon to tell, but quite possible,' said the doctor gruffly. 'You'd better check how the others are when you get in. I rather think Wendy might be ill too, from the look of her when we left, and I must say my wife wasn't feeling too grand when I went out. Ring me if you need me.'

Henry came back to a very disturbed house indeed, with several bedroom lights on. No one was very ill, but Wendy and Mrs Godiesky were distinctly unwell. Dora Watkins was perfectly all right and was busy ministering to those who weren't.

Happily, there was no sound from the children's room and he crept in there to place a full stocking beside each of their beds. As he came back downstairs to the hall, he thought he heard an ambulance bell next door.

'The position will be clearer in the morning,' he said to himself, a Foreign Office man to the end of his fingertips.

It was.

Half the Witherington household had had a severe gastrointestinal upset during the night and Robert Steele had died in the Berebury Royal Infirmary at about two o'clock in the morning.

When Henry met his sister on Christmas morning she had a very wan face indeed.

'Oh, Henry,' she cried, 'isn't it terrible about Robert Steele? And the rector says half the young waits were ill in the night too, and poor little Miss Hooper as well!'

'That lets the punch out, doesn't it,' said Henry thoughtfully, 'seeing as the youngsters weren't supposed to have any.'

'Cook says—'

'Is she all right?' enquired Henry curiously.

'She hasn't been ill, if that's what you mean, but

she's very upset.' Wendy sounded quite nervous. 'Cook says nothing like this has ever happened to her before.'

'It hasn't happened to her now,' pointed out Henry unkindly, but Wendy wasn't listening.

'And Edward and Jennifer are all right, thank goodness,' said Wendy a little tearfully. 'Tom's beginning to feel better but I hear Mrs Friar's pretty ill still and poor Mrs Godiesky is feeling terrible. And as for Robert Steele . . . I just don't know what to think. Oh, Henry, I feel it's all my fault.'

'Well, it wasn't the lemonade,' deduced Henry. 'Both children had lots. I saw them drinking it.'

'They had a mince pie each too,' said their mother. 'I noticed. But some people who had them have been very ill since . . .'

'Exactly, my dear. Some, but not all.'

'But what could it have been, then?' quavered Wendy. 'Cook is quite sure she used only the best of everything. And it stands to reason it was something that they ate here.' She struggled to put her fears into words. 'Here was the only place they all were.'

'It stands to reason that it was something they were given here,' agreed Henry, whom more than one ambassador had accused of pedantry, 'which is not quite the same thing.'

She stared at him. 'Henry, what do you mean?'

Inspector Milsom knew what he meant.

It was the evening of Boxing Day when he and Constable Bewman came to the Witheringtons' house.

'A number of people would appear to have suffered

from the effects of ingesting a small quantity of a dangerous substance at this address,' Milsom announced to the company assembled at his behest. 'One with fatal results.'

Mrs Godiesky shuddered. 'Me, I suffer a lot.'

'Me too,' Peter Watkins chimed in.

'But not, I think, sir, your wife?' Inspector Milsom looked interrogatively at Dora Watkins.

'No, Inspector,' said Dora. 'I was quite all right.'

'Just as well,' said Tom Witherington. He still looked pale. 'We needed her to look after us.'

'Quite so,' said the Inspector.

'It wasn't food poisoning, then?' said Wendy eagerly. 'Cook will be very pleased . . .'

'It would be more accurate, madam,' said Inspector Milsom, who didn't have a cook to be in awe of, 'to say that there was poison in the food.'

Wendy paled. 'Oh . . .'

'This dangerous substance of which you speak,' enquired Professor Godiesky with interest, 'is its nature known?'

'In England,' said the Inspector, 'we call it corrosive sublimate . . .'

'Mercury? Ah . . .' The refugee nodded sagely. 'That would explain everything.'

'Not quite everything, sir,' said the Inspector mildly. 'Now, if we might see you one at a time, please.'

'This poison, Inspector,' said Henry after he had given his account of the carol-singing to the two policemen, 'I take it that it is not easily available?'

'That is correct, sir. But specific groups of people can obtain it.'

'Doctors and pharmacists?' hazarded Henry.

'And certain manufacturers . . .'

'Certain . . . Oh, Uncle George?' said Henry. 'Of course. There's plenty of mercury in thermometers.'

'The old gentleman is definitely a little confused, sir.'

'And professors of chemistry?' said Henry.

'In his position,' said the Inspector judiciously, 'I should myself have considered having something with me just in case.'

'There being a fate worse than death,' agreed Henry swiftly, 'such as life in some places in Europe today. Inspector, might I ask what form this poison takes?'

'It's a white crystalline substance.'

'Easily confused with sugar?'

'It would seem easily enough,' said the policeman drily.

'And what you don't know, Inspector,' deduced Henry intelligently, 'is whether it was scattered on the mince pies . . . I take it was on the mince pies?'

'They were the most likely vehicle,' conceded the policeman.

'By accident or whether it was meant to make a number of people slightly ill or . . .'

'Or,' put in Constable Bewman keenly, 'one person very ill indeed?'

'Or,' persisted Henry quietly, 'both.'

'That is so.' He gave a dry cough. 'As it happens, it did both make several people ill and one fatally so.'

'Which also might have been intended?' Nobody had ever called Henry slow.

'From all accounts,' said Milson obliquely, 'Mr

Steele had a weak tummy before he ingested the corrosive sublimate of mercury.'

'Uncle George wasn't ill, was he?'

'No, sir, nor Dr Friar.' He gave his dry cough. 'I am told that Dr Friar never partakes of pastry.'

'Mrs Steele?'

'Slightly ill. She says she just had one mince pie. Mrs Watkins didn't have any. Nor did the professor.'

' "The one without the parsley," ' quoted Henry, ' "is the one without the poison." '

'Just so, sir. It would appear at first sight from our immediate calculations quite possible that—'

'Inspector, if you can hedge your bets as well as that before you say anything, we could find you a job in the Foreign Office.'

'Thank you, sir. As I was saying, sir, it is possible that the poison was only in the mince pies furthest from the staircase. Bewman here has done a chart of where the victims took their pies from.'

'Which would explain why some people were unaffected,' said Henry.

'Which might explain it, sir.' The Inspector clearly rivalled Henry in his precision. 'The Professor just wasn't there to take one at all. He says he went to his room to finish a present for his wife. He was carving something for her out of a piece of old wood.'

'Needs must when the Devil drives,' responded Henry absently. He was still thinking. 'It's a pretty little problem, as they say.'

'Means and opportunity would seem to be present,' murmured Milsom.

'That leaves motive, doesn't it?' said Henry.

'The old gentleman mightn't have had one, seeing he's as he is, sir, if you take my meaning, and of course we don't know anything about the professor and his wife, do we sir? Not yet.'

'Not a thing.'

'That leaves the doctor . . .'

'I'd've murdered Mrs Friar years ago,' announced Henry cheerfully, 'if she had been my wife.'

'And Mrs Steele.' There was a little pause and then Inspector Milsom said, 'I understand the new young assistant at the pharmacy is more what you might call a contemporary of Mrs Steele.'

'Ah, so that's the way the wind's blowing, is it?'

'And then, sir,' said the policeman, 'after motive there's still what we always call down at the station the fourth dimension of crime . . .'

'And what might that be, Inspector?'

'Proof.' He got up to go. 'Thank you for your help, sir.'

Henry sat quite still after the two policemen had gone, his memory teasing him. Someone he knew had been poisoned with corrosive sublimate of mercury, served to him in tarts. By a tart too, if history was to be believed.

No, not someone he knew.

Someone he knew of.

Someone they knew about at the Foreign Office because it had been a political murder, a famous political murder set round an eternal triangle . . .

Henry Tyler sought out Professor Godiesky and explained.

'It was recorded by contemporary authors,' Henry

said, 'that when the tarts poisoned with mercury were delivered to the Tower of London for Sir Thomas Overbury, the fingernail of the woman delivering them had accidentally been poked through the pastry . . .'

The Professor nodded sapiently. 'And it was stained black?'

'That's right,' said Henry. History did have some lessons to teach, in spite of what Henry Ford had said. 'But it would wash off?'

'Yes,' said Hans Godiesky simply.

'So I'm afraid that doesn't get us anywhere, does it?'

The academic leaned forward slightly, as if addressing a tutorial. 'There is, however, one substance on which mercury always leaves its mark.'

'There is?' said Henry.

'Its – how do you say it in English? – its ineradicable mark.'

'That's how we say it,' said Henry slowly. 'And which substance, sir, would that be?'

'Gold, Mr Tyler. Mercury stains gold.'

'For ever?'

'For ever.' He waved a hand. 'An amalgam is created.'

'And I,' Henry gave a faint smile, 'I was foolish enough to think it was diamonds that were for ever.'

'Pardon?'

'Nothing, Professor. Nothing at all. Forgive me, but I think I may be able to catch the Inspector and tell him to look to the lady. And her gold wedding ring.'

'Look to the lady?' The refugee was now totally bewildered. 'I do not understand . . .'

'It's a quotation.'

'Ach, sir, I fear I am only a scientist.'

'There's a better quotation,' said Henry, 'about looking to science for the righting of wrongs. I rather think Mrs Steele may have looked to science too, to – er – improve her lot. And if she carefully scattered the corrosive sublimate over some mince pies and not others, it would have been with her left hand . . .'

'Because she was left-handed,' said the Professor immediately. 'That I remember. And you think one mince pie would have had – I know the English think this important – more than its fair share?'

'I do. Then all she had to do was to give her husband that one and Bob's your uncle. Clever of her to do it in someone else's house.'

Hans Godiesky looked totally mystified. 'And who was Bob?'

'Don't worry about Bob,' said Henry from the door. 'Think about Melchior and his gold instead.'

The Trouble and Strife

Detective Inspector C. D. Sloan sighed deeply and started to explain all over again to the woman sitting in front of him that people may go missing of their own accord at any time if they so wished. What they called it these days was 'dropping out', but he didn't suppose that the aggressive woman before him would want him to use the term about her daughter.

'Not my Susan,' declared Mrs Briggs firmly, 'whatever you're going to try to tell me about it being a free country.'

'Anyone,' stated the policeman, who hadn't been going to say anything about it being a free country. He also forbore to explain that Susan Cavendish wasn't 'her' Susan any more but had apparently been a married woman in her own right for nearly three years now. She should have been her own woman long ago.

'She's not been in touch for a full month,' said Mrs Briggs, ignoring this, 'and that's not right, is it?'

'She doesn't have to be in touch if she doesn't want to be,' repeated Sloan patiently. 'She is, after all, of full age.'

'And I may say, officer, she is also an Englishwoman born in wedlock and had her feet on dry land when I last saw her,' Mrs Briggs completed the adage tartly, 'but she's still missing.'

'Which she has every right to be if she so wishes,' pointed out the Detective Inspector. With a mother like Mrs Briggs, he might very well have opted to go missing himself.

'And that's never happened before,' insisted Susan's mother, ignoring this last remark of his too. 'They used to come in to see me every weekend without fail. Susan did my shopping while that no good husband of hers did any odd jobs about the house I needed doing.'

'I see.' Sloan had known a good few sons-in-law who never did a hand's turn in their wife's mother's house but this didn't seem the moment to say so.

'And I'm just not satisfied that she's all right,' said Mrs Briggs belligerently. 'So I'm reporting her missing here and now whatever you say.'

'Was your daughter all right when you last saw her?' parried Sloan.

'It depends what you mean by all right,' responded Mrs Briggs. 'Physically she was as fit as the butcher's dog . . .'

'That's something,' put in Detective Constable Crosby from the sidelines.

Mrs Briggs favoured him with a baleful stare and turned back to Sloan. 'But she wasn't happy in herself, even though she said the divorce was working its way through – and not before time too, if you ask me.'

'Divorce?' said Sloan, the policeman in him automatically pricking up his ears.

'She'd decided to leave him at last,' said Mrs Briggs.

'Nasty piece of work, I always said, that Christopher Cavendish, for all that he's done well at his job.'

'And what was that?' enquired Sloan, pulling a piece of paper towards him.

'He was one of those computer people,' she said, sniffing. 'You know – the sort who sit at home all day in front of a screen and call it working. How does anyone know whether you're working or not, that's what I want to know?'

'I dare say the usual yardsticks apply,' murmured Sloan.

'Come again?'

'The making of money,' said Sloan smoothly.

'He did that,' she admitted grudgingly. 'They had a lovely old house, though a bit on the small side if they'd wanted to start a family . . .'

'Ah, I was going to ask about—'

'Which mercifully, the way things have turned out, they hadn't done.' She sniffed. 'Susan wanted a baby – don't ask me why. Nothing but trouble, children. I was always telling her that.'

Detective Inspector Sloan made a note.

'Of course, half of the house will be my Susan's when they settle up – half of everything, come to that – so she won't come out of it too badly.' She glared at Sloan. 'If she's all right, that is.'

'Tell me, have you approached the husband . . .' Sloan paused and looked down at his notes. 'Yes, he is the husband still, isn't he, if the divorce hasn't come through yet? Have you asked him where she might be? He at least might have some idea, even if they have parted, as you say they have.'

'That's the trouble,' Mrs Briggs said instantly. 'I don't know where he is either.'

'So the husband is missing too, is he?' asked Sloan with interest.

'Well, I never,' remarked Detective Constable Crosby.

Mrs Briggs bridled. 'I wouldn't know about him being missing, but the house has been sold – I do know that – and he's gone too, but where I don't know. Good riddance for Susan, if you ask me.' She gave a self-satisfied smirk. 'I always said she should never have married him in the first place. If I told her that once, I told her so a dozen times.'

'Not good enough?' put in Detective Constable Crosby helpfully. He was still a bachelor himself.

'Not by a long chalk,' said Mrs Briggs, taking a deep breath preparatory to enlarging on this at length.

Detective Inspector Sloan forestalled her. 'And have you made enquiries at her place of work?'

'In a manner of speaking,' conceded Mrs Briggs. 'Not that I got very far.'

'How come?' asked Detective Constable Crosby, in whom his superiors had so far failed to instil any proper sense of formality when dealing with members of the public.

'Susan worked for a temping agency in Berebury and they say that someone just rang in one day to say she wouldn't be available for work any more.'

'Someone?' pounced Sloan.

'They couldn't swear it was her,' said Mrs Briggs. 'In fact, they couldn't even be sure that it was a woman who had rung.' She suddenly became a little more human and admitted, 'That's when I began to get really worried.'

'I see, madam.' He did too. 'You say their marital home has been sold?'

'The house agents' sale board has come down and Wetherspoons cleared the furniture at the end of last week.' She pursed her lips. 'Sid Wetherspoon wouldn't tell me where they were taking it. Commercially sensitive information, he called it.'

Detective Inspector Sloan made a note. He'd have a word with the house agents and the removal people himself.

'And their solicitors won't tell me either,' she went on in aggrieved tones. 'Client confidentiality was what they said.'

'Quite so,' murmured Sloan.

'There was something else.'

'What was that, madam?'

'All Susan's stuff was in that van that went along with Christopher's.'

'Not just his?' asked Detective Constable Crosby, patently puzzled.

'No, and I do know that because I watched it go.' She snorted gently. 'It was just as well she wasn't pregnant after all . . .'

'After all?' prompted Sloan, leaving aside for the time being the more germane matter of all the furniture going from the house together.

'She'd wanted a baby at first but one didn't come along,' said Mrs Briggs. 'And before you ask, the doctor wouldn't tell me anything either. Said he'd be struck off the register or something like that. Excuses,' she said richly, 'all of them.'

'That'd be because of that chap Hippocrates,' put in Crosby. 'He's the one the doctors swear by.' He frowned. 'Funny that, since he wasn't a Christian.'

'At least,' said Mrs Briggs, ignoring this, 'there being no baby on the way will have made the divorce simpler, which is something to be thankful for.'

'Quite so,' said Detective Inspector Sloan, rising to his feet. 'Well, thank you, Mrs Briggs. We'll be looking into the matter for you.'

'Then there's the question of her car,' said the woman, not making a move. 'That's worrying, too.'

Detective Constable Crosby's face brightened. 'Do you know the number?'

'Course, I do,' she came back at him on the instant. 'And the make.'

'What's so worrying about her car?' asked Detective Inspector Sloan quickly.

'She sold it before she disappeared. At least,' she said meaningfully, 'someone did. Took it into that big dealers down by the river and sold it.'

'For cash or a trade-in?' asked Crosby.

'Cash,' said Mrs Briggs promptly.

'How do you know that?' said Sloan.

'I saw it in their showroom.' She twisted her lips. 'Besides, car dealers don't have funny ideas about what's commercially sensitive information.'

'Except the real second-hand value,' muttered Crosby. 'They'll never tell you that about any car you're trading in.'

'That I wouldn't know, never having been a driver

myself,' she said, reminded of another grievance. 'At least their old house was on an easy bus route for me. It suited me nicely being where it was – I could get there whenever I wanted.'

'And what car does your son-in-law drive, madam?' enquired Sloan as casually as he could. These days owners of cars and their addresses could be traced by police authorities with the speed of light.

'Christopher?' she said scornfully. 'Oh, he didn't have a car. Only Susan did. Said he didn't need one, working from home like he did.' She screwed up her face. 'And anyway he'd got some potty idea about not adding to the world's pollution problems. What he thinks he could do about global warming beats me.'

'I think,' said Detective Inspector Sloan a trifle portentously, 'you'd better leave things as they are at present, madam. We'll be in touch in – er – in due course.'

'I'm sure I hope so,' said Mrs Briggs, 'but if you ask me, he's made away with her and made off with all the money.'

'Have you any particular basis for making these allegations, madam?' asked Sloan wearily. He was beginning to feel quite sorry for both her daughter and her son-in-law.

'I thought you'd never ask,' she said acidly.

'Well?'

Mrs Briggs dived into her handbag, retrieved a glossy sheet of paper and waved it before his eyes. 'This.'

'The estate agents' sale particulars of their house?' said Sloan.

'That's right,' she said.

'What about it?'

'Read it,' she commanded. 'Especially the bit about the garage.'

' "Detached garage, brick with slate roof," ' he quoted, ' "well equipped with workbench, tool cupboard and two electrical points." ' He lifted his gaze. 'Sounds very nice. What's wrong with it?'

'There's something missing from the description,' she said stubbornly.

'What?' asked Sloan.

'Inspection pit,' she said. 'There always used to be one there and it isn't mentioned in this.'

'And you think,' began Crosby incautiously.

'Yes,' she said. 'I do.'

Detective Inspector Sloan got rid of Mrs Briggs by falling back on an age-old police formula that comprised thanking her for coming in and promising to keep in touch with her to let her know how their enquiries were progressing.

He was nothing like as circumspect when talking to his Superintendent.

'I don't like it, sir. I've had a look at it and the inspection pit in the garage at the Cavendishs' old home has obviously been filled in very recently.'

'Go on,' said Superintendent Leeyes gruffly.

'The house agents say that they paid the cheque from the sale of the house direct to the bank as agreed. It was made out to both Christopher and Susan

Cavendish and their instructions were that it was to go into the couple's joint account there.'

'Which said joint account could still be functioning,' said the superintendent heavily, 'if either had power to draw on it.'

'Exactly, sir.' He cleared his throat. 'In fact, since then all the withdrawals have been made by Christopher Cavendish.'

'I don't like that,' said Leeyes.

'I also had a word with Sid Wetherspoon, the removals man,' continued Sloan. 'He took all the furniture over to a house right out in the country behind Almstone, but Christopher Cavendish had asked him particularly not to disclose where it was to anyone . . . He stressed that bit very heavily to Sid. Said there was woman trouble and he was sure Sid – man to man – would understand.'

'Well, then,' said Leeyes.

'Very nice place, actually, sir, that house, but empty except for the furniture that Sid had delivered there.'

'The neighbours?' Superintendent Leeyes always insisted that inquisitive neighbours were worth their weight in gold to an overworked police force.

'The woman next door had seen a man and a young woman arrive there a week or so ago. She'd offered them the proverbial cup of tea over the garden fence but they said they had a plane to catch and wouldn't be back until they'd had a long holiday.'

'That's a good one,' snorted Leeyes.

'The neighbour said the pair were collected by hire car and haven't been seen since.'

The Superintendent tapped his desk with his

pencil. 'I don't like it at all, Sloan. I'm afraid that in the first place you're going to have to open up that inspection pit.'

'That's what I thought too, sir.'

'Then get a warrant.'

It was half an hour before the spades of the sweating diggers who were working in the garage struck anything.

'It's metal from the sound of it,' called out Detective Constable Crosby.

'Keep going,' commanded Sloan.

'Looks like a small strong box,' said Crosby, while his fellow Constable scraped away the mixture of sand and aggregate that was covering a square metal edge.

'A little water and cement in there,' observed Sloan, 'and that lot would have set into concrete overnight.'

'Perhaps it was something he meant to do,' said Crosby, straightening up. 'And didn't get round to.' The Constable himself was a great procrastinator.

'Criminals usually make mistakes,' said Sloan. 'Can you get a grip on it?'

In the event the metal box came out quite easily.

'It's not even locked,' said Crosby, surprised and somehow disappointed.

Detective Inspector Sloan lifted the lid. The box contained nothing but a plastic bag. Inside it was a conventional Change of Address card of the variety bought at any stationer's shop. The details had been completed with a waterproof pen and spelled out the address of a house.

'But that's where Sid Wetherspoon delivered the furniture,' said Crosby.

'It is indeed,' agreed Sloan. 'Read on, Crosby.'

The Detective Constable peered over Sloan's shoulder and read out aloud, ' "To Whom It May Concern" . . . I don't get it, sir. Who does It concern?'

'Us,' said Sloan pithily. 'Keep going.'

'It says "Strictly Confidential",' said Crosby.

Detective Inspector Sloan tapped the card. 'Don't forget this last message.'

At the bottom of the card was written 'Important. We don't want Mum to know where we are until after the baby's arrived.'

'Christopher Cavendish was right when he told Sid Wetherspoon that he'd got woman trouble, sir,' explained Sloan to Superintendent Leeyes later. 'He had. We just thought of the wrong woman, that's all.'

Losing the Plot

'What a truly magnificent view!' exclaimed Marion Carstairs. Like everyone else who entered the sitting room of the house on the hill at Almstone known as the Toft for the first time, she had crossed straight to the bay window and gazed out.

'It is indeed,' agreed Kenneth Marsden of Messrs Crombie and Marsden, Estate Agents and Valuers, of Berebury, 'although, as I am sure you already know, Miss Carstairs, you don't own the view from your windows unless, that is,' he added, 'you own that land as well.'

'Like dukes,' murmured Marion absently. 'They always made sure that they possessed all the land that could be seen from their mansions. After all, Capability Brown expected it of them.'

'Really?' said Kenneth Marsden politely. 'How interesting.'

'But this panorama is quite exceptional.'

'That's what everyone to whom I've shown the property says,' murmured the estate agent, finding that there was something about this lean, intelligent woman that made him pay more than usual attention to his grammar.

'You know, Mr Marsden, I do believe you can see the whole of the Alm valley from here.' Marion scanned the horizon. 'Isn't that Billing Bridge over there? I'm sure I came over the river that way.'

'It is,' said the estate agent, adding with professional caution, 'I am told that on a clear day you can see the spire of Calleford Minster.' He was well aware that those now following his calling had to be so much more circumspect in what they said in these days of rules and regulation than hitherto.

She was still looking eagerly out of the window. 'South, south-west – the sunsets must be a real joy up here too.'

'I'm sure,' said Kenneth Marsden quickly, 'but as it happens I haven't ever been here in the evening to see.'

She smiled. 'And I am hoping that I shall be here quite soon to do just that. You've got the address of my solicitors, haven't you?'

'There are, of course, other prospective purchasers who wish to see over the property.' He said this quite automatically, although in fact there had been very few and none of those were local. Miss Carstairs had come from London.

'Naturally. I quite understand that.' She turned back and said, 'Tell me, how could Mr and Mrs Boness have borne to move away from here?'

'Well, in a manner of speaking they haven't.' Kenneth Marsden pointed out of the window. 'Do you see that little building down there to the left under the slope? It's called the Croft . . .'

'Toft and Croft!' exclaimed Marion Carstairs, clapping her hands. 'Of course! Toft and croft – that means the house and land on a hill in both Old English and Old Norse.'

'Well, they just moved into the Croft,' said Marsden, skating over the etymology.

'Keeping the view.'

'Exactly.'

'But,' she observed, pointing out of the window, 'if that wire fence over there is anything to go by, they've also kept the land right up to just in front of the Toft.'

'I am given to understand,' said the estate agent carefully, 'that Mrs Boness is quite a gardener and wished to retain as much of the original ground as possible.'

'Ah, I see . . .' All she could actually see were a few straggly wallflowers and an old felled birch tree.

'In fact, Miss Carstairs, as you will note from the title deeds, they did move their boundary back a little for the previous owners – the Mullens, they were called.'

'Oh, was there some trouble over it, then?' she asked swiftly.

'Mr Boness told me that it was to oblige the Mullens over some trees,' said the estate agent. 'They wanted them in their garden, not his. I believe, though, that Mr Boness had them cut down himself after the Mullens left.'

'But – ' Marion Carstairs's eyebrows came up – 'I thought it was Mr Boness who is selling this house now. You hadn't told me that there had been someone else occupying it after them.'

'Oh, yes, but they were here only for four or five

years. Michael Boness actually bought the place back from the new people, thinking he and his wife would move in again themselves.'

'But they didn't?'

'No. I was advised that in the end Mrs Boness decided she was quite happy where she was down in the Croft, and that's why they put the property back on the market.'

'Some gardeners like making new gardens and some don't,' observed Marion Carstairs. From what she could see of it, the garden of the house below had little to commend it besides the wallflowers but she did not say so. 'We're all different. That's the joy of being a gardener.'

The estate agent nodded. 'And, as you will have seen on your way in, there is still plenty of land with the property. It's just that it's on both sides of the house rather than in the front of it.'

'Oh, it's quite enough for my wants, Mr Marsden, I do assure you,' responded Marion Carstairs truthfully. 'Quite enough. And it's an alkaline soil, which is exactly what I am looking for.'

'Good. Now, if you'd like to see the other rooms . . .'

It was early autumn by the time Marion Carstairs moved in to the Toft and was able to explore the garden properly for the first time. It was then that she took a really good look at the stretch of ground on her side of the wire fence opposite the bay window. What she saw was a row of sawn-off tree stumps, their remains now hardly visible above the grass. This had lain unmown through the summer months that the house had been on the market and it was now long and untidy.

On Michael Boness's side of the fence was a row of newly planted small young trees that had not been there when she had agreed to buy the Toft. The bed of the new trees extended almost exactly the length of her bay window.

'Leyland cypress, unless I'm very much mistaken,' she said to herself.

She said nothing to Michael Boness, though, when she met him in the village store, accepting his welcome to the Toft and Almstone with her customary reserved politeness.

It's *Cupressocyparis leylandii*, Jean,' she told her sister later that week, when she telephoned her to report that she was settled in at the Toft. 'It'll grow a good three feet a year. What's that? Oh, yes, it'll be up to the level of the bay window in no time at all. And it's planted as densely as possible too. Just like the hedge that was here before. I reckon that he moved the boundary back when he got possession so that the stumps wouldn't be in the way of this new hedge.'

'Naughty,' said her sister.

'Clever,' said Marion.

She spent the winter preparing the ground for a spring planting of little Christmas trees. These she installed in the ground to the sides of the house and adjacent to the boundary fence, tending them carefully until they were properly established. A good horticultural specialist might have considered her a little unwise to put them in ground so very near a rapidly growing hedge of leylandii since this would all too soon take both light and moisture from the infant Christmas trees, but this factor did not seem to have occurred to Marion Carstairs.

Instead she seemed to be concentrating all her attention on the tree stumps.

'Now that I've had the stumps freshly cut I'll be able to kill them off before I have them taken out,' she called cheerfully across to Michael Boness when he appeared near her boundary one day when she was in the garden, carefully painting the fresh surface of each stump with a clear liquid. 'I'm sure they'll be so much easier to lift when they've died off completely, aren't you?'

'If anything you're using in the way of poison gets to the hedge on my side and damages it,' her neighbour began belligerently, 'you'll be in trouble, I can tell you.'

Marion Carstairs looked quite shocked. 'I shouldn't dream of letting that happen, Mr Boness. I promise you, I'll be very careful.'

'That's all very well,' Boness grunted, 'but I'll have you know that that hedge stays where it is, no matter what you say.'

'I shouldn't dream of saying anything, Mr Boness,' said Marion Carstairs in dulcet tones. 'Why should I? It's your hedge.'

'Because if,' he began heatedly and then fell suddenly silent.

'Your hedge is nothing to do with me,' went on Marion, still sweetly reasonable. 'The very idea . . .'

At the end of her first year at the house, the leylandii was growing fast and thickening up well. All that Marion Carstairs had seen of Mr and Mrs Boness had been when she had called with the church choir singing Christmas carols. 'God rest you merry,' she had sung with the rest of the choir at their door. 'Let nothing you dismay . . .'

By the end of Marion's second summer at the Toft Mike Boness's new leylandii hedge was beginning to show signs of interfering with the splendid view of the valley from her sitting room.

'I'm planning on having these old stumps out in the spring, Mr Boness,' she said one day when he was up near her boundary, examining his leylandii hedge.

'You'd better not disturb any roots on my side,' he said gruffly, 'or there'll be real trouble. That hedge stays.'

'Oh, I think we'll be able to get them out all right without doing any damage to your garden or mine,' she said.

'They're coming along very well now, these trees of mine are,' he said.

'They are indeed,' she said warmly.

'They're going to be fine, tall trees in no time at all.'

'I'm sure,' said Marion agreeably.

'Give me and the missus a bit of privacy in our old age, they will,' he went on, puzzled by her lack of reaction.

'They will indeed,' she said immediately. 'Just what you want as time goes by.'

'Doesn't help your view much though, does it?' Boness ventured slyly, watching her face.

'True,' admitted Marion Carstairs, 'but then I've always thought Goethe got it right.'

'Who?' he asked suspiciously.

'Goethe. A German poet.' Marion waved an arm over the valley. 'He said that no one could look at the view for more than fifteen minutes.'

'Did he?' Michael Boness sounded baffled. 'You do know these trees could get to more than a hundred feet if they're not trimmed?'

'Really? Do take care, won't you?' said Marion solicitously. 'You wouldn't want to fall off a ladder . . .'

'I'm not going to fall off a ladder,' he said crossly, 'because I'm not going to trim them.'

'Ah, then you won't need to worry about falling, will you?' she said.

She duly recounted the conversation to her sister, Jean, over the telephone that evening. 'Poor man,' she laughed. 'He doesn't know what to make of me.'

'Poor nothing,' snorted Jean. 'He's waiting for you to go down on bended knee and beg him to cut the leylandii down so that you can have your lovely view back.'

'He's going to be disappointed, then,' said Marion Carstairs. 'I will ask him, of course, but not just yet.'

'So how are your Christmas trees coming along?' asked her sister.

'Slowly but well,' said Marion. 'Another twelve months should see them just right.'

'And his leylandii?'

'Just wrong,' said Marion. 'For him, I mean. Fomes spreads underground along the roots at about a yard a year.'

'I'm very happy to hear it . . .' She stopped. 'But, Marion, won't it look very odd if the whole of his hedge is attacked by it at once?'

'Ah,' said Marion mysteriously, 'I've thought of that. And about what to do if he gets on to someone about the fomes, as I'm sure he will.'

'I hope you have. After all, dear, fungi – what did you say the Latin name for fomes was?'

'*Heterobasidin annosum* . . .'

'Even ones with outlandish names like – er – that don't usually travel in straight lines – and you know that, even if Mike Boness doesn't.'

'Ah,' she said, 'don't forget that the source of the infection – the old tree stumps – is in a straight line too.'

'But surely you don't want him ever to know that that's where it's come from.'

'No, of course not. That's why I had the stumps out and the ground grassed over . . . Nobody will know they were ever there and as sure as eggs Michael Boness isn't going to tell anyone.'

'Why not?'

'For one thing, when he's had it spelled out to him, his estate agent won't like to hear what his client has been up to.'

'Go on . . .'

'But it could be argued,' Marion said cogently, 'that

recently planted trees such as his leylandii are unusually susceptible to that sort of infestation.'

'I do hope,' said Jean piously, 'that you don't have to argue anything.'

The next winter passed. This Christmas-tide the church choir sang the carol 'The Holly and the Ivy' at the front door of the Croft. When the choir came to the line 'When they are both full-grown' Michael Boness managed not to meet Marion Carstairs's eye.

It was high summer when Marion started to see early signs of disease in the leylandii hedge, which was now both thick and tall. That was when Marion first asked Mike Boness if he would consider lowering his trees so that she could have her view back.

'I thought you'd ask one day,' he said, grinning unpleasantly. 'All that talk about not minding what you looked at was hot air.'

'It's making my sitting room quite dark too,' she said meekly.

'That's your problem,' he said.

'Oh, dear.' Marion gave what she hoped was a womanly sigh. 'I really don't know what to do next.'

'You can't do anything,' he said roughly. 'It's my hedge, not yours. I can plant it wherever I like and let it get as high as I like, and neither you nor anyone else can stop me, no matter what you say.'

'But . . .'

'And,' he added, 'since you've probably already

thought about asking him, neither can your solicitor. They're clever, all right, but not that clever.'

'No.' She sighed again. 'I suppose not . . .'

'So you might as well save your breath and your money.'

'And that's your last word, is it?' she asked.

Mike Boness paused and seemed to consider this. 'Well,' he drawled eventually, 'I dare say I could buy the Toft back from you if I had a mind to.'

'Buy it back?'

'That's if you were prepared to agree to my price, of course.'

'You mean you would really like to have it back again?'

'Only if the price was right, naturally.' He sniffed. 'It's not worth anything like what you gave for it, I can tell you.'

'Really?' she said.

'Not without the view.'

'I suppose you're right.'

He waved an arm over the valley. 'But with it . . . then, that's different, isn't it?'

'Very,' said Marion Carstairs drily.

'Think about it,' he said.

'I will,' she promised.

'Mind you, I won't pay a lot.' He twisted his lips. 'But you're not going to get too many people willing to take the Toft off your hands now.'

'Not without the view,' she conceded gravely.

*

She was highly amused, though, when she described the encounter to her sister. 'What? No, we didn't talk money. It's a bit soon.'

'Soon for what?' enquired Jean.

'My Christmas trees. I'm waiting for the valuable seasonal trade, remember . . .'

'Of course.'

'And for the damage from the fomes to be quite apparent.'

Marion Carstairs was all sympathy the next time she saw Mike Boness. 'Your poor hedge, Mr Boness. It has got something nasty, hasn't it? I do hope you weren't hoping to use it for timber.'

'I've got an expert coming to see it,' he said thickly, 'and if he tells me that it's anything you've done to it, then I'll be taking the matter further.'

'Me?' protested Marion. 'I haven't been near your hedge.'

'He's a proper tree specialist.'

'Just what you need,' she said.

'He'll know, and then watch out.'

'If I've done anything,' she corrected him.

'We'll see about that,' he said, storming away, red-faced. 'For my money, you'll be hearing more about this.'

Marion watched the arboriculturist come and go from behind her bedroom curtain. The one thing she didn't want at this stage was to be recognized. She was pleased, though, to see the expert look long and hard over the fence into her garden and then go over to peer equally hard at and dig round the remains of a felled birch tree on Mike Boness's land. That was after he had taken some samples of soil and of a fungus that had made its appearance on some of the leylandii roots. He took a core sample too from the stem of one of the dying leylandii trees.

'A textbook examination,' she reported to her sister, metaphorically rubbing her hands. 'Any minute now he'll be telling Boness about the fomes and that the spore could have come from that old birch of his. Birches are very susceptible to fomes too.'

'Like leylandii and Christmas trees,' observed her sister happily.

'Exactly. Now, I think our time has come . . . How much did you say you and Paul lost when you sold the house back to Boness, Jean?'

The sum of money named by Jean Mullen formed the basis of a claim by Marion Carstairs, the retired professor of plant biology at the Toft, against Michael Boness, the owner of the Croft, for damage to a substantial crop of *Picea abies* – otherwise known as Christmas tree – by a fungus called fomes, caught from his leylandii trees.

It was successful.

And without coming to court either.

A Soldier of the Queen

Private Saffery was quite surprised at the extent of his own fear. Nothing he had ever experienced in his time in the army so far had been quite as frightening as this. He shivered, clutched his gun even more tightly and nerved himself to a total and unnatural stillness.

Worst of all was the waiting.

His ordeal had begun on the Friday morning when the next week's roster had been pinned up in the barracks which were presently being occupied by the 2nd Battalion of the East Calleshire Regiment.

'Sentry duty?' said his oppo, Mike Clarkson. 'Nothing to it, mate. Did my stint last month and not a thing happened.'

'As I remember,' Saffery remarked sturdily, 'you didn't enjoy it and said so quite a lot.'

'No. . . Well, not at the time, maybe,' agreed Clarkson. 'But it was all right afterwards.'

'So's having a baby, my mother says,' retorted Saffery.

'I wouldn't know about that,' conceded Clarkson, 'but all I can say, Kev, is that though I admit sentry duty is no picnic at the time, it's no problem after you've done it once. Honest.'

'Like having a baby, I suppose,' said Kevin Saffery, who at the time hadn't known all that much about either process.

He did now.

About the preparations for sentry duty, anyway. And just at this moment Private Kevin Saffery heartily wished it was already afterwards for him too, just like it was for Mike Clarkson.

Even so, his friend Private Clarkson had been more encouraging than some of his other mates. They seemed inclined to regard a turn of sentry duty in this day and age, let alone in this place, as something of an initiation rite.

'After which I'll be a real soldier, I suppose,' Kevin had said bitterly in response to this. He came from an old army family where the expression 'being a real soldier' didn't just mean not crying when you grazed your knee falling off your bike. It meant the same as 'being blooded' in other fields – notably the hunting ones – as well as most probably literally becoming 'bloodied' into the bargain.

'Well, you'll be different anyway,' Clarkson had mumbled inarticulately. 'And you'll feel different somehow. Bit difficult to explain . . .'

Now, out of the barracks and – except for one other soldier in sight – to all intents and purposes entirely on his own, Kevin Saffery knew what Clarkson had meant. He shivered again. And not from cold.

'Watch out for the kids,' Clarkson had warned him too. 'They're worse than the adults. Much worse.'

It was something Private Saffery had already heard on all sides and he had said so.

'When I have kids,' said Private Clarkson feelingly, 'I shall lock 'em up indoors when they're not in school. All the time.'

On the other hand, Private Milligan's advice had been strictly practical. 'When you see them getting ready to shoot . . .'

'Yes?' he had asked urgently.

'Freeze, man, freeze, or you'll never hear the end of it.'

'Thanks a lot, mate.'

For nothing, he nearly added. Not being able to keep absolutely still was the one thing Private Kevin Saffery feared most of all.

As usual, the Corporal had managed to be his customary nasty little self at the same time as being strictly practical. 'Your main problem, all of you lot,' he had said, when addressing the next week's roster of raw duty men in the barrack room, 'will be cramp. Simple but painful. And sleeping with corks in your bed like your granny does won't help.'

There was a dutiful snigger.

'The 'uman body,' he went on, 'wasn't meant for keeping really still for as long as you've got to do it for.' He sneered. 'Now, if you was cats it would come easy. But you're not cats, are you?' He glared at them. 'Well, are you cats?'

'No, Corporal,' they had chorused. Kevin had heard some reservation about this on his left, but fortunately the words 'It's that ginger tom from next door' and a veiled reference to an overseas cathouse had not reached the Corporal. There would have been trouble if they had.

Big trouble.

'Cats can watch mice for hours without twitching a whisker,' declared the little corporal, 'and if I catch any of you shower twitching whiskers while you're on sentry go you're on a charge. Understood?'

'Understood,' they had all echoed dutifully, murder in their hearts. The name of the murder was 'fragging' and Private Saffery had learned the word at his grandfather's knee.

'Saw a bit of it done once,' the old man had once told him, still too much of an old soldier and thus too wise to say right out whether or not he'd been the one to do it. 'On the road to Mersa Matruh.'

'But what is it, Grandad?' a younger and more innocent Kevin had wanted to know. He'd been of an age then when new words – especially the dubious-sounding ones which his grandfather used – were suddenly interesting. He'd only just been clouted by his mother for saying 'frigging' and to a lad of his age the word 'fragging' seemed deliciously dangerous-sounding too.

'Dangerous?' his grandfather had growled. 'Of course it was dangerous. To both sides, you might say.'

'But what does "fragging" mean, Grandad?'

Any resemblance of the tableau the two of them made, talking at his grandfather's gate, to the famous picture of little Peterkin asking old Kaspar about a certain famous victory at Blenheim was purely coincidental.

'Theoretically,' said old grandfather Saffery, a faraway look in his rheumy eyes, 'fragging is when you kill the man who leads you into danger in war.'

'Yes, but what is it really?' The word 'theoretically' was one that a young Kevin already knew and did not like. 'Can't you give me a f'rinstance, Grandad? Please . . .'

The old man had gone on staring into the distance. 'It's when you take the opportunity to shoot some bastard of a Corporal in the back of his head on the only occasion when you've got half a chance of doing it without being caught in the act – which is when you're going into action behind him. Now, be off with you, boy, before it happens to you.'

Kevin had got halfway down the path before he heard his grandfather shout after him. He turned back. 'What is it, Grandad?'

'I said that corporals are dangerous and don't you ever forget it.'

'No, Grandad. I won't.'

'Especially little ones . . .'

The person who looked most dangerous of all while the Corporal was going through his spiel was Private 'Edge' Bates. Edge wasn't his real name. Private Bates was called this because of the time he spent sharpening his bayonet. No one, declared Edge Bates with monotonous frequency, was going to creep up behind him on a dark night without feeling the specially sharpened blade.

The Sergeant had been as full of dire warnings as the Corporal in what passed as his pep talk. 'And remember, all of you, that should you happen to fall while you're on sentry go – ' here he glared at them all in such a way as to make it quite clear that if they did fall to the ground it would be considered to be their own fault – 'we shan't come and get you.' The Sergeant's eye travelled balefully up and down the serried ranks of men. 'That clearly understood?'

Kevin's great-grandfather had been a stretcher bearer in France in 1915 at the bloody cock-up called Loos. He'd – if family legend was to be believed – always got his wounded man whatever the danger. It seemed a bit hard that, if Kevin was to fall at his post, he'd just be left there until the guard was changed.

Kevin didn't remember the stretcher bearer in the family himself because, although he'd survived the Battle of Loos, a German shell had had his name on it at the mudbath that became the bloodbath of Passchendaele.

Private Saffery's hands were already clammy now where he clutched his rifle. He concentrated on thinking about his name – their name. Saffery, his father said, came from the Arabic for sword – at least the first part, '*saifer*', did. That meant '*sword of*' and '*rey*' was Spanish for 'king'.

'So Saffery means "sword of the king",' explained his father, whose own army service had been in the dull and disappointing years of peace. 'Only in our case, we have queens.'

'Yes, Dad.'

Saffery *père* had served his time in the army uneventfully and then taken a pub in the country. He was still a disappointed man, having learned to his cost that Mine Host cannot afford to voice opinions of his own, still less express them with real feeling – not and keep the inn's customers, anyway. He could – and would – though, presently tell all and sundry about his son's sentry duty.

And be proud of it.

The accent had been on pride too, when their officer had addressed them that morning, but Kevin, who had been up since before dawn ready for a full inspection and had not in any case slept well, scarcely listened to him. The officer had been talking about the Battle of Talavera, in which the alertness and devotion to duty of a sentry had apparently saved the East Calleshire Regiment from either the enemy or the wrath of the Duke of Wellington – Kevin wasn't sure which – and in any case thought those geese whose alarm call had saved Rome would probably have done the job just as well at the time.

And, whatever the officer had in his mind, talk of a soldier's duty conjured up only one picture in Kevin's mind. It was of an ancient painting, a copy of which had hung in the miserable church hall where he'd been sent to Sunday School as a child. The picture had been of a dismayed Roman soldier at Pompeii, watching the remorseless advance of burning lava from Mount Vesuvius heading in his direction. The caption had stayed with Kevin longer than any text or regulation. He could see it now: 'Faithful unto death'.

His fingers were too slippery now to work properly should they need to, but that worry was succeeded by an even greater horror – he wanted to cough. A tickle somewhere at the back of his throat became a real threat to his stillness. He clamped his jaws shut and soon felt his eyes begin to bulge like a frog's. He would choke to death if he didn't open his mouth and cough soon . . .

It was then that he heard a whisper from the sentry on his right. Strictly forbidden, of course. The man would have been put on a charge if anyone had heard his warning.

'Watch it. Here they come . . .'

And Private Kevin Saffery of the 2nd Battalion, the East Calleshire Regiment, froze as still as Niobe herself as the day's first coachload of foreign tourists spilled out into Whitehall, directly in front of the entrance to Horseguards' Parade, cameras at the ready.

Touch Not the Cat

They said, of course, that she should have had a dog. Not a great big dog that she couldn't handle at her time of life, nor one which needed long walks night and morning whatever the weather, which she obviously couldn't have managed, and certainly not the size of dog that ate a lot, things being what they were.

Or, at least, as they thought things were.

No, what the old lady could have done with, they said – afterwards, of course – was a small dog that barked. A barking dog, they thought, would have protected her in a way that a cat never could. They said – afterwards, of course – that having a dog might have saved her.

Well, someone modified this, at the very least it might have raised the alarm. That would have been something. Somebody, they said, might just have heard a dog barking in her cottage and gone to see what the trouble was. A small dog like a chihuahua, say, or a little terrier. Everyone else's small dogs always seemed to be barking when anyone came to the door. Why hadn't she had one too, just to be on the safe side? After all, Almstone was a pretty remote little village and there weren't all that many people about there after dark these days.

They all knew the answer to why she hadn't had a dog, of course. Mrs Doughty had a cat.

But a dog would have helped.

And Mr Mackenzie next door, although both very deaf and very Scottish, might have heard a dog barking. In the event – the sad event – it had been Mr Mackenzie who had found her afterwards. On account of the milk bottles not having been taken in, that was, and very upset about it, he had been.

Old Mrs Doughty hadn't had a dog not only because she had a cat but also because she had always insisted that her cat would take care of her.

'Pusskins will look after me,' the old lady had said time and again, stroking the rather bad-tempered black and white moggie. 'Won't you, my lovely?'

Pusskins, who never miaowed except at mealtimes, would arch his back and allow her to rub behind his good ear. (The other had come to grief in a memorable encounter with a ginger tom in the alley on the other side of the cottage.)

It was a great-nephew, full of undesirable book learning, who had first said that Pusskins was the old lady's familiar. He'd always thought of his great-aunt as a witch anyway, probably because she didn't wash overmuch.

His mother, who hadn't quite understood his meaning, told him not to be so forward. At the time she had had high hopes of a bracket clock that had stood on the cottage mantelpiece (without going) for as long as she could remember. As she was to tell the other relations again and again, the clock had been promised . . .

Familiar or not, Pusskins was therefore eyed warily while Mrs Doughty's relations consoled themselves in the way that relations will – afterwards, of course – with saying things to each other such as, 'You didn't get to her age and go on living alone without having a mind of your own,' and, 'If she didn't want a dog on account of having that mangy old cat, then that was that, wasn't it?'

That had certainly been that in the old lady's cottage when the burglar had come and gone. That is, the police were fairly sure that he had come only as a burglar. What was unfortunately undeniable was that, though he might have come only as burglar, he had indubitably left as a murderer as well.

What was equally obvious was that the cat had not been able to protect his mistress after all. The police as well as the relations knew Pusskins had done his best, of course, because not only was there the old lady's blood everywhere in the little cottage but, most interestingly, the police said, there was also blood – human blood, that wasn't hers – on Pusskins's claws as well.

It was a young detective constable from Berebury called Crosby, who manifestly hadn't enjoyed the sight of an elderly bludgeoned head, who had first turned his wayward attention to the cat and noticed some blood there. He had even managed to get a sample of it before Pusskins – a preternaturally clean member of his species, in spite of his battered appearance – could lick it off his paws.

Which the cat had promptly tried to do.

'Be careful, Crosby,' Detective Inspector C. D. Sloan had adjured, seeing him with the cat. 'It might turn nasty.' It was he who, for his sins, was in charge of the murder inquiry.

'Yes, sir,' the young Constable had said, promising to take every precaution, while remarking inconsequentially that Captain Hook had killed himself by scratching behind his ear with the wrong hand.

'Nature red in tooth and claw,' was what the clever great-nephew had said when he heard about it.

His mother hadn't liked that remark either.

'And when you've finished with the animal welfare side,' the senior policeman had said to Detective Constable Crosby with some asperity, 'you can come and give me a hand over here while we establish a common entrance.'

Common entrance, Detective Constable Crosby had learned early on, was not only an entrance examination for children going to public schools but a safe route established by the police at a murder scene for all those professionals in homicide who have to approach the body, and, having their lawful business there, mustn't accidentally destroy important evidence in the process.

'And you'd better look sharp, Crosby,' said Detective Inspector Sloan. 'The photograph boys'll be here any minute now and Dr Dabbe doesn't hang about when he's at the wheel either.'

*

Dr Dabbe, the Consultant Pathologist to the Berebury Hospitals Trust, readily gave it as his considered opinion that the cause of Mrs Doughty's death was a fracture of the base of the skull brought about by the application of a blunt instrument from above and behind.

'A heavy blunt instrument,' he added after a closer examination of Mrs Doughty's head.

'Anything you can tell us about the person who used it, doctor?' asked Detective Inspector Sloan carefully. When he was a lad, the use of heavy blunt instruments as murder weapons had been thought to be an exclusively male province, but you could never tell these days.

'Anyone with the ability to lift a club hammer,' said the pathologist briefly.

Sloan just managed not to remark that that narrowed the field nicely and asked the doctor a few questions on haematology instead.

But, as Detective Inspector Sloan presently explained to the family, who, though they might have been a bit slow to visit while the old lady was alive, had assembled quickly enough when they heard that she was dead, what help was a cat's scratch on a man unless it happened to be on his face and needed explaining away?

The blood sample, the Inspector explained to them and to a slightly crestfallen Detective Constable Crosby, would become important only if they were able to catch the man from whom it had come – and that, he had to remind them, was not necessarily going to be easy. Blood there was, and that in plenty; other clues there were not. Someone had come and robbed and killed and gone, and that was all anyone in authority could tell them at this stage.

As well as the relatives, there had also been the next-door neighbour, Mr Mackenzie, to question, comfort, inform, pacify . . . and take a statement from. Detective Inspector Sloan was never entirely clear about the actual role of a police officer in these circumstances. He knew the theoretical one backwards. Members of the Criminal Investigation Department of every constabulary were there to investigate criminal occurrences, but, like a lot of life, it seldom worked out quite as simply as that. He'd long ago come to terms with the fact that a policeman had nearly as many parts to play in life as the seven ages of Shakespeare's man.

And some of them were not so easy.

What did you say to an apparently rational neighbour at a murder scene whose main concern was an archaic, not to say primitive, belief that it portended misfortune if a cat were permitted to leap over a corpse?

'I think, sir,' he said to Mr Mackenzie as kindly as he could, 'that these days that is just felt to be superstition. I can't see what further injury a cat could possibly do to a dead body already damaged almost beyond recognition.'

Sloan knew, of course, as well as everyone else, of the hundred and one uses of a dead cat, but that was something quite different.

Mr Mackenzie insisted that this fear was a real one and not just what he had the honesty to call a 'fret' on his part. 'Why, man, do ye no' realize that a watch was kept over a corp' in Scotland in the old days expressly to stop something like that happening?'

'No, sir.'

'Funny things, cats,' mused Mr Mackenzie. 'You never know what they're thinking.'

'Just so,' agreed Sloan, meticulously making another point, 'but we don't know for certain whether – er – the animal in question did actually jump over the late Mrs Doughty, do we, sir?'

All Sloan hoped was that this subject never ever came up in Superintendent Leeyes's presence. Ever since the Superintendent had attended an evening class on 'Physics for Everyman' he had been trying to explain something called 'Dead Cat Bounce' to the entire constabulary.

Without success.

Pusskins, his paws now decently clean, was present at this family and friends conference. In fact, he stared at Mr Mackenzie as balefully as Detective Inspector Sloan would have liked to have done, but the latter had his pension to think of.

It soon emerged that Pusskins might have his pension to think of too.

Therefore the cat was also present at the subsequent meeting at which his own immediate future was decided. There was a surprising amount of competition to give him a new home. This had more to do with having an eye to the future than any concern for animal rights – it not yet being known how the old lady might have provided for him. There was a very real fear in the family that Pusskins might be the residuary legatee . . .

Something else that was troubling to the – by now very – extended family was whether Mrs Doughty had had money or not. (The bracket clock had been stolen but no one knew exactly what else.) Nobody else really knew what she had had in the way of assets, except perhaps now the burglar. The family, though, to be on the safe side, was taking a distinctly Morton's Fork view of her finances – she must have had money because she hadn't spent it – and, at least until the will was read, Pusskins was safe, not to say to be pampered.

In the end the old lady's niece took Pusskins home with her, her claim – as a blood relation – over that of a nephew on Mrs Doughty's late husband's side of the family being considered superior. This delicate matter was clinched by the said nephew's wife having in the past always used an allergy to cats as an excuse for not visiting the cottage at Almstone.

Once in the niece's home, Pusskins retreated to a south-facing windowsill, where he devoted his days to lying in the sun and attending to his personal hygiene in full view of the neighbours, which the old lady's niece didn't think was very nice.

The cat alternated his pose effortlessly between couchant and rampant as the fancy took him and, to the niece's despair, ate this but not that – and then that but not this. Moral ascendancy over the niece having thus been achieved, he just waited.

And waited.

He waited for exactly seventeen days.

Even when Detective Inspector Sloan and Detective

Constable Crosby – and a veterinary surgeon – came to the niece's house, Pusskins only evinced a rather languid interest in their tale of a man with some rather nasty scratches on his arms and legs who had had to consult his doctor because he had an indolent ulcer on his right leg and some very enlarged and suppurating lymph nodes.

'The doctor,' reported the police inspector with a pardonable touch of drama, it being something of a professional coup, 'diagnosed that the man was suffering from *Pasturella multicida*.'

The niece exclaimed, 'Lord, bless us, and whatever is that when it's at home?' having not yet caught up with the precise dangers of salmonella poisoning as presented by the popular press and vaguely associating the two.

'Moreover,' added Crosby, the detective constable accompanying Detective Inspector Sloan, who was determined to have his say too, 'the man had the same blood profile as the blood which the cat had on its claws.'

Even then Pusskins didn't stir. But when he heard the veterinary surgeon explain that a diagnosis of *Pasturella multicida* in the man meant that the old lady's murderer must have caught 'cat-scratch fever' from this particular member of the family *felix domesticus*, Pusskins twitched his whiskers in a very satisfied way indeed.

Exit Strategy

'There's nothing wrong with her heart,' said the doctor, folding his stethoscope and stuffing it back into his black bag. 'Sound as a bell.'

'Only her mind,' said Mrs Barker's daughter tightly.

'That means she could go on like this for a long time,' the doctor said. He paused. 'A very long time, I'm afraid.'

'I'm not so sure that I can,' said Mrs Barker's daughter, near to tears.

The doctor shot her a quick professional glance, taking in her slight tremor and quavering voice, as well as the imminence of a loss of self-control she might not welcome.

'I wouldn't mind so much, doctor,' she said with deep feeling, 'if it was her heart that was bad and her mind was all right.'

'The elderly mentally infirm are very difficult to deal with,' he said to her as he had said to so many adult sons and daughters in this painful situation in his time in general practice. 'There's no getting away from it. Very difficult indeed.'

'You don't need to tell me that,' she said, adding on a rising note of despair, 'Mother doesn't even know who I am any more. She doesn't recognize me, her own daughter!'

'It's not at all uncommon.' He nodded, and waved to Mrs Barker's medical record on the table. 'We agreed, didn't we, that she's been suffering from senile dementia for quite a while.' In the doctor's book this was preferable to hiding the patient away from society, concealing incontinence and pretending to the neighbours that there was nothing wrong, but not everyone, he knew, would agree with this. 'What is sadder,' he went on, 'is that your mother doesn't know who she is either.'

'And I shall be going the same way quite soon, I'm sure.' She managed a little laugh. 'The other day I caught myself putting the cat's dry food in my own cereal bowl. I'd even poured milk over it before I realized what I'd done.'

He smiled. 'Happens easily enough. We all do that sort of thing.' He was a busy man and went straight back to the point of the consultation. 'I'm only sorry that I can't promise you an early place in the right sort of nursing home for her. There are very long waiting lists for the good ones and – ' he hesitated – 'they are rather expensive.' Mrs Barker, he knew, had sold her bungalow when she came to live with her daughter, and so there would then be nursing home fees to be clawed back from her assets to pay for her long-term care. But her exhausted daughter was his patient too and so he asked, 'Is there any chance of your sharing the care or are you the only one?'

'I've got a sister over Calleford way,' said Mrs

Barker's daughter slowly. 'I might ask her if she'd do her stint for a while to give me a bit of a rest.'

'A little respite care can be a great help,' said the doctor, going on his way. 'Try her.'

Mrs Barker's daughter didn't allow herself the merest smirk of self-congratulation after she'd shown the doctor out of the house. Instead, she picked up the telephone and dialled her son in Luston. 'No problem, Martin,' she said. 'I think the doctor imagines I might be going to lose my Elgins soon too.'

'Good. Now when?'

'I thought you said Sunday morning's the busiest time over there.'

'I did. That'll do fine.'

'I've got her a costume.'

'No labels?'

'I'm not the one who's demented,' said his mother sharply.

'Only teasing,' chuckled the voice at the other end of the line. 'There's no inscription inside her wedding ring, is there, by any chance? You know, her and grandad's name or anything like that?'

'I got the nurse to take it off her finger months ago,' said his mother, 'because of granny's arthritis.'

'Ah, I thought you might have done,' said Martin drily. 'What about her dentures?'

'I thought we'd leave those behind here just in case,' said Mrs Barker's daughter. 'You never know . . .'

'What about her teeth? Dentists are very good at keeping records these days.'

'She hadn't been near one in years – besides, she's only got a couple left now.'

'That's good,' said the voice at the other end. 'And no distinguishing scars, you said?'

'None,' said Mrs Barker's daughter, adding almost absently, 'In her way she's always been very healthy.'

'Good,' said the voice in matter-of fact tones. 'I think that's everything, then.'

'I'll put the costume on under her ordinary clothes before we leave the house and I'll meet you in the car park there. When do you suggest?'

'Half past ten,' said her son briskly. 'Don't be late.'

'I won't,' promised Mrs Barker's daughter, putting down the telephone and heading to the kitchen to make some lunch. Nobody was going to be able to say that Mrs Barker wasn't well nourished or hadn't been properly looked after. She had. That was part of the trouble.

If old Mrs Barker thought there was anything out of the ordinary in being dressed in a swimming costume before putting on her outdoor clothes she did not say so. Indeed, she did no more than give her customary grunt and start to dribble. She trotted out to the car happily enough though – she liked being driven around. She even got out of the car when it stopped – which was something that did not always happen without a struggle.

Her daughter wiped Mrs Barker's face clean and took her by the arm. Her grandson sauntered across the swimming pool's car park and joined them. With the old lady between them, daughter and grandson strolled casually up to the entrance.

'You get the tickets, dear,' called out Mrs Barker's daughter cheerfully, 'and we'll see you in the water.'

'Righteo,' said Martin, approaching the booth, cash in hand.

He collected three tickets and handed two of them over to his mother. Much to her annoyance, the changing area at the swimming pool had recently become unisex. She had vociferously disapproved of this at the time but now she was grateful. It gave Martin a chance to be at his grandmother's other side, after she had been undressed, as they assisted her towards the swimming bath.

Martin had been right. On a Sunday morning the pool was indeed crowded. They helped Mrs Barker down the little flight of steps at the shallow end and stood with her there for a while. Then Martin swam away, while Mrs Barker's daughter gently folded her mother's stiff fingers round the safety bar. 'Stay there, Mother,' she said, 'and hold on until I come back. I'm just going for a swim.'

There was no change in Mrs Barker's customary expression of total bewilderment. It didn't noticeably alter when time went by; nor when one of the attendants came up to her to ask her if she was all right – or how long she had been there – or who she was – or where she lived – and, most importantly, who it was who had brought her there.

There was only one thing that was really certain

and that was that by nightfall Social Services had got her safely installed in a specialist care home in a strange town.

There, as a temporary measure, they named her Mary Celeste, because, as the care worker on duty that day said, 'She had been found adrift in the water and no one knew why.'

But they guessed.

The Wild Card

'Not another?'

'Two more actually, sir.'

'How many is that altogether now?'

'Six, sir.' Detective Inspector C. D. Sloan enjoyed practising what has come to be known as 'the discipline of curiosity' in its own right, but looking into this particular matter had been work: police work.

Superintendent Leeyes grunted. 'Doesn't make sense, Sloan, does it?'

'No, sir.'

'Who was it this time?'

'Gerald Ardingly . . .'

'Not the Chairman of our sainted bus outfit?' snorted the Superintendent.

'Him,' agreed Detective Inspector Sloan inelegantly.

'Can't be too sorry for either him or his Calleshire buses. Must be making a mint. And who else?'

'The editor of the *Luston News*.'

'Not he who will use his columns campaigning for a better police presence in the city?' said Leeyes sardonically.

'There's a mention of how ineffective we are most

weeks,' agreed Sloan uneasily, 'although I must say I didn't notice anything this week.'

'If I remember rightly,' said the Superintendent, 'he's always writing that we're wasting too much time these days on rural policing.'

'Crime does seem to have shifted out to the country and away from the city lately,' ventured Sloan tentatively. It was ironic that fictional crime seemed to have moved in the opposite direction at the same time. Country house robberies were for real these days.

'He will go on about what we haven't done rather than what we have,' persisted Leeyes.

Detective Inspector Sloan decided against saying anything about good news not selling newspapers.

'Who else?' asked Leeyes, coming back to the notes on his desk.

'Nigel Halesworth,' said Sloan.

'Huh.' Leeyes's snort was even more pronounced this time. 'He's the top bean counter over at United Mellemetics, isn't he?'

'Finance director,' said Sloan.

'Same thing,' said Leeyes robustly. 'He's a skinflint anyway. I heard that he wouldn't give the Mayoress anything at all for the charity of her choice for her year in office.'

'The children's hospice,' supplied Sloan, who had already made his own contribution. 'They need all the money that they can get.'

'He said, if I was told rightly,' growled Leeyes, 'that he didn't approve of handouts to help the health service.'

'Credit card stolen last week,' carried on Sloan stolidly, 'and the card company duly notified of the loss by Nigel Halesworth. Couldn't do it quickly enough actually. Tried to blame the police for not preventing the theft, let alone for not catching whoever took it, even though he'd been the one who'd been careless. Left it in his jacket pocket somewhere.'

'Wanted to know what he paid his taxes for, I dare say, as usual,' said the Superintendent placidly.

'Yes, sir.'

'Then?'

'Then the same evening his card was pushed back through the Halesworths' letter box.'

'Just like with all the others?'

'Yes, sir.' He cleared his throat. 'Wiped clean of fingerprints, of course.'

'It's not the wiping that matters,' barked Leeyes on the instant, 'it's the swiping that counts, let alone the skimming.'

Sloan frowned. 'There's no evidence of these cards being used to make counterfeits, sir. There's been only one withdrawal on each of them. And,' he added, 'you don't even need to have the card swiped these days, sir.'

'If you ask me, Sloan, there's far, far too much of that done over the telephone now – and without any checks.'

'And just as with all the others taken so far,' carried on Sloan, 'the credit card companies will confirm only that a large single withdrawal had been made just before the loss was notified and the account stopped.'

Superintendent Leeyes sat back in his chair and

stroked his chin in deep thought. 'We could be looking at a rather sophisticated form of blackmail, Sloan.'

'We could indeed, sir,' agreed Sloan warmly. 'No written demands, no muddled assignations, no handing over of actual cash – just a credit card stolen and returned to the owner's house almost immediately the unauthorized transaction has been made.'

'I don't like it,' said Leeyes.

'Just the one snag actually . . .'

'An audit trail,' said the Superintendent, simply.

'In theory the credit card company should be able to tell us where the payment has gone,' said Sloan, pausing.

'They should indeed,' Leeyes grunted. 'Save us a lot of bother.'

'And would be able to,' pointed out Detective Inspector Sloan, 'but they say they'll do it only if the customer queries the charge to the account and gives them their permission. They won't play ball otherwise. Not without a court order.'

Leeyes muttered something distinctly subversive about the Human Rights Act and its pernicious effect on the proper pursuit of enquiries by a beleaguered and overworked police force.

'And,' hurried on Sloan, 'I don't see us getting access to any of their accounts if the customers don't complain.'

'And you say the card holders won't do that?' said Leeyes. 'You're quite sure about that, Sloan, are you?'

'Not a single one of them,' insisted Sloan. 'Half a dozen of the richest businessmen in the town who have had a charge made on their account by the unauthorized use of their credit cards won't say a dicky bird about it . . . That's as far as we've got.'

'Large amounts,' declared Leeyes in a worldly-wise manner. 'Must be. We wouldn't have heard anything about it at all if it had been peanuts.'

'It seems,' said Sloan, 'that they all just say that nothing has been wrongly charged to them and pay up as if everything was hunky-dory and nothing out of the ordinary had happened.'

'Smells worse than dead fish,' pronounced the Superintendent.

'Even the chairman of the Chamber of Trade won't say a word,' said Sloan, 'and he's usually the first to make a fuss about anything.' He sniffed. 'Only, we are always given to understand, on behalf of one of his members, of course.'

'As usual.'

'Whenever he complains, he always insists it's never him personally.'

'Pompous ass,' said Leeyes succinctly.

'The head honcho at Calleshire Systems wouldn't even speak to us after his card came back. Made a terrific fuss to begin with when it was first stolen and then afterwards got his public relations lady to sweet-talk us into thinking that nothing noteworthy had happened and that everything in the garden was lovely.'

'Sounds like blackmail to me,' said Leeyes again. 'And now this business with the Dipper has come up.'

'Our Charlie, the town's lightest-fingered crook,' agreed Sloan.

'Now dead,' said the Superintendent without any noticeable regret.

'Totalled his car and himself on the Luston road last night,' said Sloan. 'Going faster than he should, of course, and then he hit a spot of black ice by the bridge and went into the river.'

'It's a tight corner at the best of times,' said the Superintendent.

'No one could've called last night the best of times on the road,' said Sloan. 'Car and Dipper both written off before any of the rescue services got there. Straightforward accident – Traffic Division are quite sure about that.'

'And after the Lord Mayor's Show, the dustcart,' observed the Superintendent.

'Beg pardon, sir . . . Oh, I see what you mean.' Sloan's face cleared. 'The Coroner's officer.'

'Constable Stuart,' agreed Leeyes. 'Go on.'

'He reported that a credit card was found on the Dipper's body that isn't – wasn't – the Dipper's,' said Sloan.

'Ah . . .' said Leeyes.

'It belongs to the chairman of the Luston Football Club.' He consulted his notebook. 'As well as finding the chairman's credit card,' he went on, 'Constable Stuart also reported that there was a note with it with the chairman's name and address on it and the exact time that the card had to be put through the owner's letter box last night.'

'Whose handwriting?' pounced Leeyes.

'The Dipper's,' replied Sloan regretfully. 'He must have been on his way over to Luston to deliver it when he hit the ice. The timing was quite tight – he'd have had to step on it.' He paused. 'Probably did, which would account for the skid.'

'We might get a "calls made" telephone printout,' said Leeyes who had lost interest in the Dipper's accident and was concentrating on the job in hand.

'But not calls received,' said Sloan pertinently. 'I think we would find that all the relevant calls were made to the Dipper and none by him.'

'Which means he might not have known who made them,' concluded Leeyes.

'I think that we'll find that will be the case,' said Sloan prosaically.

'That is,' growled Leeyes, 'when we find whoever made them.'

'If we ever do,' temporized Sloan. 'The Dipper might've been the best pickpocket in the business . . .'

'No doubt about that,' grunted Leeyes. 'Should have been on the stage.'

'But, although he certainly wasn't the brightest of the bright, even he wouldn't have been daft enough to ask questions when it was better not to do so.'

'It's all this new business of the "need-to-know" basis catching on,' grimaced the Superintendent, who resented being denied any information at all by anyone at any level at any time. 'It's all the fashion these days, more's the pity.'

'And the Dipper always knew what constituted evidence and what didn't,' sighed Sloan. 'I will say that for him.'

Superintendent Leeyes said something unflattering under his breath about wishing that the same could always be said of the Crown Prosecution Service.

'Quite so, sir,' he murmured. This, diplomatically, Sloan affected not to have heard. 'Petty crook the Dipper might have been, but he was no amateur at keeping out of real trouble.'

'And someone else knew that too,' said Leeyes.

'Oh, yes,' said Sloan at once. 'The Dipper'll have been hand-picked, you can be sure of that.'

'And paid in cash presumably.'

'Funny you should say that, sir . . .'

'Well?'

'PC Stuart's had a bit of a shufti round the Dipper's place, looking for relatives and so forth . . .'

'Loads of cash?'

'No, sir. Come to that, hardly any. All he found that could be called at all out of the ordinary was a cutting from this week's local paper . . .' He paused.

'Get on with it, man,' barked Leeyes.

'It was a published list of the latest donors to the Mayoress's appeal on behalf of the children's hospice.'

'Well, I never.' A beatific smile overtook Superintendent Leeyes's usually scowling features. 'And would, by any chance, any of the people on this list of ours here feature on it?'

'Prominently,' said Detective Inspector Sloan. 'All except the last one.'

'Which, I take it, will be on next week's list?'

'I shouldn't be at all surprised, sir.'

'Neither would I, Sloan.' He slapped the file on his desk shut and handed it back to the detective inspector. 'Neither would I.'

Coup de Grâce

'That you, Wendy? Henry here.' Henry Tyler, civil servant *extraordinaire*, was sitting at his desk in the Foreign Office in London. He was presently on the telephone to his sister in the little market town of Berebury. 'I thought you ought to know that I'm going to be coming down to Calleshire next weekend.'

'Darling, how lovely!'

'No, no . . .'

'But the children will be so pleased to see their favourite uncle again.'

'It's not quite like that . . .' He rattled the telephone cradle up and down. 'Operator! Operator! Don't cut us off, please . . . We haven't finished yet.'

'Henry,' he heard his sister say amidst crackles, 'this is a terrible line and I can't hear you properly. I said when may we expect you?'

'It's not quite like that, Wen,' he repeated hesitantly. 'I'm afraid I shan't be staying with you this time.'

'Work?'

'Only in a manner of speaking.'

Henry was staring out of his office window while he spoke to his sister. A busy London street scene was visible below, but he wasn't looking at the cabbies or the men and women hurrying along the pavements beneath him. It was the screaming headlines on the vendors' boards which had caught his attention. He could read the words 'Von Ribbentrop' and 'Herr Hitler' quite clearly even at a distance. One newspaper seller had obviously abandoned an attempt to fit in the name 'Chamberlain' as being too long a word for his news-stand.

Wendy Witherington said, 'I know I shouldn't ask . . .'

'I'm bidden to stay at Calle Castle for the weekend,' volunteered her brother. This statement could be fairly described as the truth but not by any means the whole truth.

'At the Duke of Calleshire's?' exclaimed his sister. 'How lovely for you, darling.'

'There's a hunt ball on the Saturday . . .'

He forbore to explain that he was going to Calle Castle because there would be others there who had also been invited on whom his political masters in Whitehall wished an eye kept. A wary eye. And those particular others were going to be there – and not perhaps, for instance, at Cliveden that weekend instead – because an invitation to Calle Castle from Her Grace, the Duchess of Calleshire, to stay there for the hunt ball was one that very few people would refuse. Actually, he mused, as he drew little pictures on his blotting paper, these particular others wouldn't have wanted to refuse the invitation anyway. Like himself, they would all have their own reasons for being at the castle, with European matters in the highly fragile state they were just now.

'Everybody'll be there, I suppose,' said his sister a little wistfully.

This, he knew, did not include Wendy and her husband, Tom Witherington, but did embrace everyone who was anyone in the mainly rural county of Calleshire and quite a number of luminaries from the outside world. The *haut-monde* as well as fashion and politics would be well represented there for sure and, more importantly, so would international affairs – which is where Henry Tyler's duties came in.

'Oh, how exciting for you,' continued Wendy.

'I very much hope not,' returned Henry Tyler vigorously, although he knew very well that some of the people who would be at Calle Castle at the weekend were not without a taste for danger and might not be too averse to a little action, as well – strictly in the interests of national security, of course. 'In my experience, my dear sister, a man can have a little too much excitement for his own good.'

'I'm sorry, darling,' said Wendy Witherington immediately. Apologetic she might be; deceived she was not. She was well aware that some of her brother's assignments on behalf of his employers had verged on the bizarre. 'I shouldn't have asked, I know, but do be extra careful, won't you?' She gave a sigh. 'Do you suppose it will be as splendid an occasion as the Duchess of Richmond's great ball before Waterloo?'

'I'll tell you whether it was next week,' Henry said lightly. The parallels were a mite too close for his liking – another war in Europe was undeniably in the offing, although with different enemies and different allies from those at Waterloo – but he did not say so. Wendy and her Tom would find that out for themselves soon enough. And be thankful that their son – his nephew – was too young for the coming conflict.

Wendy hesitated and then said, 'Of course you don't want anything to go wrong naturally, but if . . .'

'And neither does anyone else,' he finished firmly before she could say anything more, adding under his breath, 'especially my Minister.'

Henry's Minister was a man with so much on his mind at this defining moment in world history that he didn't need anything else to worry about. Which is where Henry Tyler and his watching brief came in.

'It won't go wrong if you've got anything to do with it,' Wendy said loyally, 'but I would like to know what the ball dresses are like, Henry. Especially if light green is still in – such a very flattering colour, I always think.'

'I'll make a note,' he promised gravely.

Not a hunting man himself – of foxes, that is – it was white tie and tails for him at Calle Castle, rather than hunting pink, when he ascended the magnificent staircase there on the night of the hunt ball.

He was received by the Duchess, resplendent in the famous Calleshire diamonds. 'I'm very glad you could come, Mr Tyler,' she murmured so graciously that Henry was quite left in the dark as to whether she knew there was a purpose to his visit. 'How nice to see you back in Calleshire,' she added, before handing him over to her husband at her side.

The Duke had probably guessed that he was here on duty.

'Good to see you, m'boy,' he boomed. 'Do you know the Ambassador here? Ambassador, this is Henry Tyler – an old friend. Henry, let me introduce His Excellency the Polish Ambassador to the sheikhdom of Lasserta . . .'

Henry bowed, concealing his inward amusement at the way in which the Duke – like everyone else – had ducked out of pronouncing the Ambassador's name. Fortunately an extensive training at the Foreign Office had encompassed practice with saying Polish titles out loud.

'Count Zeczenbroski,' said Henry, bowing again slightly whilst resisting the temptation to click his heels together as well. 'I don't know how long you've been in post there but I'm sure you'll know our man in Lasserta.'

'Indeed,' said the Count, shaking hands warmly. 'Your Mr Heber-Hibbs and I are old friends. In fact, his boy Anthony plays with my own son. A good man.'

'Who lies abroad for the good of his country,' Henry completed the definition of an Ambassador with practised ease. The sheikhdom of Lasserta was in theory not really big enough in size or history to merit an ambassador-in-residence from either Great Britain or Poland, or, for that matter, few of the other European countries who saw fit to be represented there at that diplomatic level. However, since the sheikhdom was sitting on the only known supply of queremitte ore on the planet outside the Soviet Union, they were all there all the same.

In strength.

This was understandable, since queremitte was an element of great value in the armaments world. It was thus much sought after by those nations who were arming – or rearming – as fast as they possibly could. Countries who had already put 'guns before butter', so to speak, had almost exhausted their stocks, while those nations that had only just come under starter's orders in the arms race were even more anxious to secure supplies of one of the hardest-wearing of all known metals to aid them in their hasty manufacture of new weapons.

'And you left the Sheikh well, I trust?' Henry enquired. Of one thing he could be quite sure and that was that the young son of Sheikh Ben Mugnal Mirza Ibrahim Hajal Kisra would not be mixing with the sons of any of the ambassadors at his court. The Sheikh played his cards far too close to his chest to risk anything being given away by childish babble. And there was also the very real fear of the kidnap and ransom of his heir.

'In great form, I assure you,' said the Count. He smiled politely as an overweight man with a red face overtook them on their way into the castle's ballroom.

'The Lord Lieutenant,' murmured Henry. 'A great man in the saddle in his day, I understand.'

The Count, whose own sport was duck-shooting on the Pripet Marshes, acknowledged this fact with a cursory nod before passing on to Henry some information of his own. 'I understand,' he said in a voice rather below that used in normal conversation, 'that your man in Lasserta has been beaten at the post by a very unfriendly power.'

Henry bent his head towards Count Zeczenbroski. 'Indeed?' he said, not showing by even the flicker of an eyelid that this fact was not only not news to him but the very reason for his own presence at the castle tonight.

'It is said that that young man over there – ' here the Count indicated a handsome blond man who was squiring a tall, elegant girl in a dress of deep electric blue – 'has obtained a verbal agreement to the assigning of the queremitte mining rights to his government.'

'He is their Military Attaché,' observed Henry mildly, 'so perhaps we shouldn't be too surprised.' The blond young man was one of the reasons that Henry was at the hunt ball, but he did not say so. Yet another reason was the well-built girl with whom the man was now starting to dance. She had a vaguely foreign look and a slightly old-fashioned evening bag on her arm. They were a well-matched pair – she was nearly as tall as the Military Attaché and was dancing with notable verve. 'Besides, what does a verbal agreement amount to in these modern times?'

'If it's from the Sheikh, everything,' the Polish Ambassador replied. 'It is said that the word of the Sheikh is his bond.'

'Tell me then, Count, how did that young man manage to persuade the Sheikh to part with his precious ore verbally?'

The Count raised his shoulders ever so slightly and opened his hands in an age-old gesture. 'My dear Mr

Tyler, who knows? There was some talk, I understand, of – what shall I call it? – leverage . . .'

'Really?' said Henry Tyler, feigning a well-bred astonishment. A man did not have to be a linguist to translate that word into the uglier one of 'blackmail'.

The Ambassador leaned forward and spoke in confidential tones. 'Something to do with a secret distillery having been found in the hills to the north was what I had heard,' volunteered Count Zeczenbroski after he had made sure no one was within earshot.

'A distillery,' concurred Henry Tyler, nodding sagely, 'would not have gone down very well in Gatt-el-Abbas.' In the capital of Lasserta, consumption of alcohol in any shape or form was deemed a flogging matter. If the Sheikh was known to have been guilty of this, then his throne would have been in very real danger.

The Count became even more confidential. 'I gather the Sheikh got quite fond of the stuff while a pupil at Sandhurst.'

'And that particular Military Attaché knew about it?' said Henry, looking across at the blond young man.

Had the Count had a fine waxed moustache he would undoubtedly have twirled the ends of it when he asked, 'About the fondness or the distillery?'

'Either, my dear Count,' said Henry smoothly, 'or both.'

There had been no need at all for him to pose the question since Henry already knew all about the Sheikh's weakness for a dram of whisky from His Britannic Majesty's Ambassador to the sheikhdom, Mr Godfrey Heber-Hibbs. His note to the Foreign Office had explained that there had been a batch of wild, hard-drinking Scots in the Sheikh's cohort during his terms at Sandhurst who had led him astray in the matter of that golden liquid which was so strictly forbidden in Lasserta. The distillery which had been 'discovered' many miles to the north of the Sheikh's palace at Bakhalla had, Henry also knew, been planted there by the aforementioned Military Attaché on behalf of his political masters. A promise to keep it secret in return for sole access to the queremitte would have been easy enough to extract from a Sheikh occupying a distinctly uncertain throne. Unlike the redoubtable Lion of Judah, Ben Mugnal Mirza Ibrahim Hajal Kisra did not, by any means, have all of his people behind him. And some of those who were behind him were there only for the purpose of trying to stab him in the back . . .

'I gather,' said the Polish Ambassador cautiously, 'that his having been led astray in the respect of alcohol at your military academy was not unknown among a certain group of his contemporaries.'

'Ah . . .' said Henry expressively.

What neither the Polish Ambassador nor, he hoped, anyone else knew was that the fake distillery in the desert had disappeared as secretly as it had arrived – thanks to the nifty overnight spadework of some active 'gardeners' temporarily on Mr Heber-Hibbs's staff in Lasserta. The odd mentions of the word 'mirages' in such local papers as there were had been dropped casually by the Ambassador's press attaché.

Henry looked up. 'You must excuse me now, Count. I see an old friend in need of a partner . . .'

Henry crossed the ballroom and soon was taking to the floor with the wife of the High Sheriff.

'George was never a dancer,' complained George's wife, Judy, allowing herself to be swept to her feet, 'and now he won't even try.'

'One of the delights of growing older,' said Henry diplomatically, 'is that one doesn't have to do what one doesn't like doing any longer.'

Judy, Henry knew, did like dancing and in a moment they were stepping it featly round the ballroom. This enabled Henry to keep an eye on the blond young man and his tall, elegant partner, who were doing much the same but considerably closer together.

This pattern was repeated after supper in the castle's famous dining room, a long saloon dedicated to trophies of the chase. To the outside observer, it seemed that a chase of an altogether different – but as old a – kind was going on between the Military Attaché and his lady companion. Their dancing was becoming wilder and wilder, and more and more intimate. The girl appeared almost abandoned in her gyrations, while the young man would seem to have too much drink taken.

After yet another turn of the ballroom, Henry saw him pulling the girl towards a door that Henry knew gave eventually on to a flight of stairs and thence to the upper storeys of the castle.

The girl appeared to stumble and then regained her balance. She let the man take her hand and they went off together through the door.

'What it is to be young!' said Judy, watching them go.

'I dare say they're going in search of a little night air,' murmured Henry. 'It's pretty warm in here.'

'It reminds me of the evening that George and I—'

'Judy, my dear,' he interrupted the Lord Lieutenant's wife suavely, steering her off the dance floor, 'I simply must return you to George now or he'll be after me for alienation of affection . . .'

This done, Henry began to make his way out of the ballroom himself.

Before he could do so, the girl from the dancing pair came rushing into the room in great distress, her electric blue dress all dishevelled. 'Monsieurs, help! Help!' she cried. 'Hans, he 'as gone and jumped out of the landing vindow . . .'

Henry strode towards the door.

'No, no, m'sieur,' she called out urgently, barring his way. 'Not up there. Down 'ere. He is lying outside on the ground.' She gave a great cry. 'He asked me to marry him, you see.'

'And?' barked the High Sheriff, who might not have been a dancer but was still quick on his feet. He had reached the girl nearly as quickly as Henry.

'And when I said I wouldn't, he opened the vindow and jumped out.' She gulped. 'It's all my fault. He always said 'e would kill himself if I wouldn't marry 'im.'

'He did, did he?' said the High Sheriff.

'But, moi, I didn't believe him.' She started to sob. 'He's dead! I know he's dead – it is such a long way down to the ground in this place.'

'This way,' said the Duke of Calleshire, making for

a different door, while Henry edged ahead of the Lord Lieutenant.

The girl continued her loud keening. 'Poor Hans, oh, poor Hans, but, m'sieur – ' this to the Lord Lieutenant, now an unhealthy shade of purple, and clearly wanting to follow the Duke – 'I can tell you, 'e was not ready for marriage. No, not yet, but 'e was much too young to die.'

Henry shot after the Duke, a man who presumably knew the quickest way to ground level. Spread-eagled on the drive before them lay the body of the blond young man. Even at a distance Henry could tell that the fellow was dead – it wasn't only vultures who could recognize absence of life from afar.

So could experienced men.

And women.

Henry reached the body and then turned and looked back at the castle.

There was something wrong, but he couldn't think for the moment what it was. He stood, taking in the scene as quickly as he could and concentrating furiously. Then it came to him.

He slipped quickly away from the men standing over the body of the blond young man and hastened back into the castle. As he shot up the stairs to the ballroom, he met the Lord Lieutenant, quite choleric now, hurrying down. 'I'm ringing for a doctor,' Henry said, dashing past the man.

He didn't do any such thing, but instead rushed up to the first-floor landing. There were three windows there, all closed, but only one unfastened. He flung it open just as the High Sheriff, nobody's fool, looked up. Henry waved at him. After the High Sheriff had turned his attention back to the body, Henry ran his finger along the underside of the sash window to make sure there was no blood there – the girl, well trained in unarmed combat as she had been, might, after all, have had to bring it down on the man's fingers before he would let go. What she had forgotten to do was open it again after she had pushed him out.

'And was it all very splendid?' asked his sister, Wendy, later when he did visit her. 'Apart from that poor young man's suicide, of course. Though I do understand if he was really in love . . . He wasn't English, was he?'

'No.'

'Ah, that explains it,' she said, adding rather complacently, 'Tom was beside himself until I said I'd marry him.'

'I remember.' He smiled.

'But what about the girl?' Wendy recollected herself. 'She was foreign too, wasn't she?'

'So it was said,' agreed Henry. 'She left the country before the inquest – though she'd given the police a statement, of course.'

'And you?' asked his sister anxiously. 'How did you get on?'

'Oh, I just had a watching brief, that's all. You might say that I did a bit of light dusting – a woman's work is never done, is it? By the way, Wendy.'

'Yes?'

'Light green is out this year.'

'Oh . . .' Her face fell. 'So what colour is in, then?'

'Electric blue. I noticed specially . . .'

Dummy Run

'I'm sorry to trouble you, Inspector Sloan.' The voice of the Station Sergeant on the internal telephone at the police station at Berebury interrupted the Detective Inspector while he was working in his office. 'But I'm afraid we've got a bit of a problem down here in the custody suite.'

'Who with?' enquired Sloan immediately, since it was unlikely that any problem arising in what he still thought of as the charge room would be of a vegetable or mineral nature, and cars came under Traffic Division anyway. At any police station the most probable problem would be animal – human animal, that is.

'An old sparring partner of yours and mine,' replied the Sergeant.

Sloan sighed. He had been attempting to tackle some paperwork that was too sensitive to be put on any computer – which was saying something about the security of computers – and too important to be left to Detective Constable Crosby. This said quite a lot about the skills of that junior officer, who was at this very moment waiting outside his door while Sloan thought of a job for him to do that was within his slender capabilities. The paperwork was long overdue in its rightful place in his locked filing cabinet which didn't help.

'All right,' he said to the Station Sergeant. 'Tell me . . .'

'Larky Nolson.'

'Oh, not him again!' Sloan exclaimed in pure exasperation. Not for nothing was Larky Nolson known throughout 'F' Division of the county of Calleshire constabulary as the Prince of Recidivists.

'None other.' The Station Sergeant coughed. 'He's asking for you particularly, sir. He says he won't deal with anyone else.' He paused and added significantly. 'Not even the ACC.'

'Where does the ACC come in?' asked Sloan warily. The Assistant Chief Constable was of the old school, not so much out of this world as a cut above it. The likes of Larky Nolson were usually kept at a respectable distance from police officers as senior as the Assistant Chief Constable.

'He just happened to be passing through our entrance and heard all the fuss,' the Station Sergeant said. 'He couldn't help hearing it, of course. We all know that Larky can be noisy if he thinks he isn't getting his rights. And naturally once Larky caught sight of the ACC, he had to have his say, didn't he?'

'Who? Larky?'

'No, the ACC.'

Detective Inspector Sloan sighed again. 'And what did the ACC say?'

'As far as I can remember, sir,' the Station Sergeant said, 'it sounded like *deprendi miserum est*.'

'Latin,' divined Sloan. The ACC was long on old and

outmoded languages; equally, he was a little short on experience of the beat.

'That's right, sir. I thought at first he was calling Larky a miserable so and so. Which he is, of course.'

'But he wasn't?'

'No, sir. The ACC said it meant "getting caught is no fun at all".'

'And what' enquired Detective Inspector Sloan with interest, 'did our Larky have to say to that?'

The Station Sergeant coughed. 'I didn't quite catch it sufficiently clearly to put it in the report book, sir.'

'I see.' The Station Sergeant was long on common sense. That went with the territory.

'But the gist of it was that Larky wanted you to come down to see him yourself, sir, and not to be fobbed off with some toffee-nosed cleverclogs . . . or words to that effect.'

'He's making a big mistake,' said Sloan vigorously, 'if he thinks that sort of flattery will get him anywhere.'

'I've already told him that,' said the Station Sergeant stolidly.

'And what did he say?'

'I thought it better that time not to have heard his comments at all, sir,' the Sergeant replied, demonstrating that at least one policeman had good judgement too.

'Demanding his rights as usual, I suppose,' grumbled Sloan. 'With knobs on.'

'Demanding his rights, yes,' responded the Station Sergeant, 'but as usual, no.'

'Well, lock him up and tell the custody officer that I'll be down presently.' He would see Detective

Constable Crosby first. The lad would still be waiting outside the office for his marching orders for the day.

'I don't think I can do that, sir,' said the voice at the other end of the line, adding regretfully, 'not with the law as it stands.'

'Why not? What's the charge?'

'The charge that Larky has come in about,' said the Station Sergeant, picking his words with unusual care, 'is one of common assault . . .'

'Well, I grant you it's not in his line,' conceded Sloan promptly. 'I've never known him violent when he's been on a job, although as I remember he has been known to have a nasty attack of "dock asthma" when the prosecution starts to get to him.'

'Larky isn't being charged,' said the Station Sergeant gently.

'So what's all this about, then?' demanded the Detective Inspector irritably.

'It's him that's bringing the charge.'

'Larky?' exclaimed Sloan. 'Are you sure?'

Larky Nolson's very considerable criminal reputation rested on his success in keeping a low profile when on the job. His hallmarks were a capacity to remain totally unmemorable and the ability to keep his every illegal action as unobtrusive as possible. In the event, few of his victims even noticed him, still less suspected him of criminal propensities.

'Dead sure, sir,' said the Station Sergeant. 'He alleges that he was attacked without provocation at two o'clock this morning in Acacia Avenue.'

'And did he happen to say what he was doing in Acacia Avenue at two o'clock this morning?'

'Taking a walk with his wife.'

'Tell him to pull the other one,' said Sloan wearily. 'And that I've got better things to do than come down and listen to some cock-and-bull story . . .'

'I'm afraid that the time and place are not in dispute, sir,' said the Station Sergeant.

'Not even the bit about him taking a walk with his wife?' asked Sloan acidly.

'I'm afraid that's true too, sir.'

'Sergeant, have you ever encountered Mrs Nolson?'

'Many times, sir,' sighed the voice at the other end of the telephone. 'She always comes in when we nick him.'

'Love's young dream, she isn't,' said Sloan flatly.

'No, sir,' the man agreed. 'More like "ill met by moonlight", you might say.' He paused. 'Actually, now I come to think of it, ill met by moonlight would go for the whole of this business.'

'So what exactly is the problem, then?' enquired Sloan briskly, hanging on to his patience with an effort. 'In a nutshell, if you can . . . I've got work to do, and Crosby needing to see me before he gets going . . . although on what I don't know, as he's pretty useless.'

'The problem, sir,' said the Station Sergeant heavily, 'is seeing that we don't conspire to pervert the course of justice.'

'That is not usually a problem . . .'

'It is now.'

'You'd better explain.'

'Larky insists that he was assaulted by a man called Bates . . .'

'At two o'clock this morning in Acacia Avenue when he wasn't robbing him?'

'You've got it in one, sir. This Bates – Herbert, I think he's called . . .'

'Hang on, Sergeant, hang on. I know a man who lives in Acacia Avenue called Herbert Bates, but he's an elderly man . . .'

'That's him, sir.'

'Can't be,' declared Sloan confidently. 'The Herbert Bates I know is an ancient little fellow and quiet with it. Wouldn't say "Boo" to a goose, let alone tackle Larky and his missus in the middle of the night.'

'Him,' repeated the Station Sergeant.

'Retired clerk,' mused Sloan. 'Took on the secretaryship of our horticultural society when the previous one died . . .'

'That's exactly what I meant by our having a problem, sir.'

'And a very good society secretary Herbert is . . . What did you say, Sergeant?'

'That's the problem, sir.'

'How come?'

'Herbert Bates did hit Larky and Larky wants Bates's guts for garters.'

'Herbert Bates? Are you trying to tell me that little old Herbert Bates fetched his fist to Larky Nolson? I don't believe it!'

'It's not me that's telling you, sir,' said the Station Sergeant, who had earned his spurs long ago in the magistrates' court and therefore knew all about the difference between the spoken word and reported speech. 'It's Larky that's telling us.'

'Then I definitely don't believe it.'

'No, sir.' The Station Sergeant coughed. 'I wouldn't have done so myself either, except that Mr Bates says not only that he did hit Larky but that given half a chance, he'd do it again.'

'See that he doesn't get half a chance,' Sloan instructed him automatically, his mind elsewhere. 'Tell me, Sergeant, what had Larky done?'

'Depends on who's telling you,' responded the Station Sergeant promptly.

'Frankly, I'd go for Herbert Bates's version first,' said Sloan. 'Any day. He's a good bloke. First-class secretary too . . . best we've ever had at the Horticultural society.'

'This case is all about gardens—' began the Sergeant.

'Herbert's a vegetable man,' Sloan interrupted him. The Detective Inspector himself was a noted rose grower. 'Prize vegetables,' he added with emphasis.

'That,' said the Sergeant drily, 'would appear to be the trouble.'

'But Larky Nolson isn't into flowers or vegetables.' He stopped. 'Unless he was trying to steal them, of course. I wouldn't put that past him, and old Herbert's cauliflowers would be worth stealing, no doubt about that.'

'That would seem to be Mr Bates's view too,' said the Sergeant. 'Beautiful, he said they were. The curd just right . . .'

'So,' divined Sloan, 'that was what Larky and his wife were up to, wasn't it?'

'Nearly, but not quite, sir.'

'Well, all I can say is that I don't blame Herbert if Larky was knocking off his vegetables . . .'

'I understand from Mr Bates,' reported the Station Sergeant cautiously, 'that some of his best cauliflowers had in fact been stolen from his garden by someone on three occasions in the past couple of weeks, one four days before.'

'Larky?'

'This has not yet been established,' said the voice down the telephone with even greater circumspection. 'It is, of course, a distinct possibility.'

'Vegetables don't come any better anywhere in Calleshire,' averred Sloan with all the enthusiasm of the true gardener.

'This is Mr Bates's opinion too,' said the Station Sergeant.

'And that of most show judges,' said Sloan warmly.

'Unfortunately, Larky was heard by Mr Bates to take another view . . .'

'At two o'clock in the morning?'

'Quite audible, Mr Bates says he was.'

'And what was Herbert Bates doing up and about then?' asked Sloan, although he thought now he could guess.

'Lying in wait for whoever was stealing his cauliflowers.'

'And who should come along but Larky and his missus?'

'That's right, sir. Mr Bates was hiding up in his shed for the third night running at the time.'

'And?' The old man must have been getting pretty tired and fractious by then.

'Larky and his wife came along and looked over Mr Bates's fence . . .'

'But didn't enter his garden?'

'Unfortunately not. I mean, no, sir.' The Station Sergeant hastily corrected himself on this important point of law. 'All Larky did was say very loudly and clearly that he didn't think Herbert Bates's cauliflowers were half as good as Stan Redden's down the road.'

'Stan is Herbert's great show rival,' said Sloan.

'Not worth stealing, were Larky's words, and I understand his wife agreed. Rather loudly, from what Mr Bates said.'

'Which, I take it,' concluded Sloan realistically, 'was why and when Herbert came out of his shed and went for Larky.'

'It was,' agreed the Station Sergeant. 'Mr Bates says that he was provoked beyond his powers of self-control.'

'I'm afraid, though, that Larky Nolson's a real barrack-room lawyer,' mused Sloan.

This sentiment was heartily endorsed. 'Everyone around here'll tell you that, sir.'

'Let me think this through, Sergeant. I'll come back to you as soon as I've sent Crosby on his way.'

Sloan put the telephone down and called the Detective Constable in. Before he could frame any orders for him, the telephone rang again. It was the Assistant Chief Constable.

'Ah, Sloan . . .'

'Sir?'

'This alleged assault case . . .'

'Yes, sir?'

'I don't like the sound of it at all.'

'No, sir.'

'Can't have grown men hitting each other like this in the middle of the night.'

'No, sir. Certainly not.'

'Gives the place a bad name.'

'Quite so, sir.'

'And we can't on any account be seen to condone that sort of behaviour.'

'No, sir,' agreed Sloan virtuously. 'Definitely not.'

'Nor, on the other hand, though,' said the ACC considеringly, 'does it do any good for a case to be laughed out of court. Or fail.'

'Never,' said Sloan with feeling.

'Can't have that, then, can we?'

'No, sir.'

'I ask you, Sloan, what sort of a *casus belli* are cauliflowers?'

'The press will like the cauliflowers,' forecast Sloan gloomily. 'Right up their street.'

'The Lord Chancellor won't,' responded the Assistant Chief Constable smartly.

'No.'

'Of course,' mused the ACC, 'the Crown Prosecution Service could always decide the case won't stand up in court.'

'The accused has admitted to the assault,' Sloan told him.

'Ah . . .' The ACC sounded as if he was tapping a pencil on his desk. 'I thought that might be the case. So we can't get away with *de minimus* . . .'

'Cabbages, perhaps, sir, assault no.' That the law did not concern itself with trifles was one of the ACC's favourite quotations. In Latin, of course. 'Although you never can tell with the CPS,' added Sloan feelingly.

'Very true, Inspector. Very true.' He coughed. 'It seems to me that their motto is "Evidence before justice".'

'Quite so, sir,' said Sloan, before the ACC put that into Latin too. 'Of course, sir, admitting guilt here and pleading guilty in court are not necessarily one and the same thing.' In his experience, nothing brought about a sea change in an accused person's stance quicker than a lawyer for the defence.

'Quite right, Sloan. Solicitors do have to earn their oats . . .'

'If you say so, sir.'

'So do policemen, Inspector.' The Assistant Chief Constable paused before adding, 'And young policemen have to learn their job first too, don't they?'

'Naturally, sir,' said Sloan stiffly, unsure of where this was leading.

'And they've all got to begin somewhere . . .'

'Of course . . .'

'Even the least promising.'

'Them, too,' said Sloan fervently.

Detective Constable Crosby, who was standing in front of him now, was a case in point. He was the least bright star in the detective firmament of 'F' Division, the police equivalent of being all fingers and thumbs in whatever he did.

'In my opinion,' said the ACC loftily, 'it's never a

bad idea for beginners to cut their teeth on something not too important.'

'Of course . . .'

'Cases where the outcome isn't vital to law and order.'

'I think I take your point, sir.'

'After all, he – I mean, any inexperienced young constable – could make mistakes in putting a case together.'

'Easily, sir.'

'And even accidentally let fall things he – or she, of course – shouldn't.'

'It has been known, sir.'

'And afterwards he – or she, of course – could be shown what he – or she, of course – had done shall we say less than well rather than wrong.'

'If they had,' pointed out Sloan.

'On the other hand, Inspector, no way must we fail to honour our obligations under paragraph forty of Magna Carta.'

'I can't quite recall . . .'

' "To no one will we sell, to no one deny or delay right or justice",' declared the ACC in ringing tones, thus clearing his own decks and handing the problem straight back to Sloan.

Sloan passed a modified version of this on to Detective Constable Crosby – jejune but eager – and sent him off to take statements all round and prepare the case against Herbert Bates.

'It's all yours, lad,' said Sloan basely. 'See how you get on for starters . . .'

Detective Inspector Sloan's highly confidential filing was almost finished by the time the young Detective Constable reported back the next day.

He looked crestfallen. 'I'm sorry, sir,' he mumbled, 'but there isn't going to be a case after all.'

'How come?'

'Larky Nolson has withdrawn the charge.'

'Tell me.'

'It's like this, sir,' said Crosby very apologetically, 'I took some of the soil off Larky's shoes and matched it with that in Mr Bates's garden, although I know that doesn't actually prove anything . . .'

'No.'

'And the shoe matched the footprints in Mr Bates's ground, although they are four days old and it's only circumstantial evidence anyway.'

An uneasy thought occurred to Sloan, as ever worried by possible allegations of police irregularities. 'How did you get Larky to take his shoe off?'

'I accidentally spilt some hot tea on his foot, sir. It didn't scald him,' he added hastily, on catching sight of his superior's expression.

'And?' Heroically, Sloan refrained from comment.

'I got the remains of some cooked cauliflower from Larky's dustbin.'

'Without his permission?'

'I got it from the corporation waste collection van. Yesterday was collection day.'

'You did, did you?'

'I understand, sir,' he said anxiously, 'that once the contents have been taken by the binmen, the owner has voluntarily surrendered his rights to them. I did check that with the council, sir.'

'That's not proof positive either.'

'No, sir. So I got a sample of the cauliflowers in the supermarket. It's the only place where you can buy them in the town.'

'Now that all the greengrocers have gone . . .' No shopper himself, Sloan knew this from his wife.

'You remember that bit in the local paper complaining that they mostly sell foreign greengrocery there, sir?'

'I'm beginning to get your drift, Crosby.'

'So I got Forensics to check, sir.'

'Different cauliflowers?' So vegetable as well as animal did come into the equation, after all.

'Very. And, sir, they could tell which had been treated with commercial chemicals and which hadn't.'

'Herbert Bates's?' Larky could have bought his cauliflowers outside the town, of course, but it wasn't all that likely.

'Yes, sir. He doesn't use chemicals.'

'Wonderful what scientists can do these days. Now, when I was first on the beat . . .' He stopped. The luxury of reminiscence could wait. 'Then what, Crosby?'

'I drew Larky Nolson's attention to my findings, sir, and he decided against proceeding with the charge against Herbert Bates.'

'And are we now faced with Herbert Bates bringing a counter-charge for theft against Larky Nolson?'

'No, sir.'

'How can you be so sure?'

'The Forensics people told me that Herbert Bates's cauliflowers were on the list of varieties that can no longer be marketed under European regulations, sir.' He looked at Sloan and asked anxiously, 'Do you want chapter and verse on that, sir?'

'Heaven forbid,' said Sloan speedily. 'But Herbert isn't into marketing, surely?'

'There was a board by his gate with a chalk message on it to the effect that cabbages could be bought . . .'

Sloan scratched his chin, a little puzzled. It was something he had never noticed himself.

Crosby put his notebook down on Sloan's desk. 'I'm very sorry, sir, but nobody seems to be charging anybody now. Is that all right?'

A Mother's Guide to Cheating

Also by Kate Long

The Bad Mother's Handbook

Swallowing Grandma

Queen Mum

The Daughter Game

Kate Long

A Mother's Guide to Cheating

SIMON & SCHUSTER

London · New York · Sydney · Toronto

A CBS COMPANY

First published in Great Britain by Simon & Schuster UK Ltd, 2010
A CBS COMPANY

3 5 7 9 10 8 6 4 2

Simon & Schuster UK Ltd
1st Floor
222 Gray's Inn Road
London WC1X 8HB

www.simonandschuster.co.uk

Simon & Schuster Australia
Sydney

A CIP catalogue record for this book
is available from the British Library

Hardback ISBN 978-1-84737-750-0
Trade Paperback ISBN 978-1-84737-751-7

Typeset by M Rules
Printed in the UK by CPI Mackays, Chatham ME5 8TD

For Alexandra WILLOW Lister

9 May 2005 – 15 June 2008

Thanks to the following for their help with research: John and Margaret Green, Kat Dibbits, Susan Donley, Joyce Carter, Judith Magill, Judy Strachan, Joan Turner, Anna Eveley, Joanne Ash, Tracey and Den Hartshorn, Ruth and David Riley, Amanda Dubicki, Reg Moorland, www.grandparentsapart.co.uk and Ben Long.

Also, thanks as ever to the WW girls for their excellent feedback, to Suzanne Baboneau, and to Peter Straus.

A Mother's Guide to Cheating

CHAPTER 1

Photograph 46, Album One

Location: the back garden at Pincroft, Bolton

Taken by: Dad

Subject: The rear of the house, flat and rendered, looks over a straight-sided lawn bordered by bare black earth. Can a garden look packed-away? This one does. The beds remain unfilled, and will stay that way till spring. Round the front, though, it's a whole different story: Carol's mother Frieda has planted blocks of purple and white pansies, there is an Alpine rockery and even a little sundial. But the front of the 1930s semi boasts a gable with a tile pattern, and a bay window, and a proper porch, and is on view to passers-by. This is 1963. Appearances matter.

At the top edge of the picture is Carol White, aged eight. She is raking up fallen beech leaves, as a punishment. She has on her black wellies, brown crimplene trews, a yellow jumper, and a face like thunder.

Asked, the day before, to go round and pick snails off the hedge, Carol instead attempted a rescue. She should have drowned the snails in her bucket, but when it came to turning on the outside tap, she couldn't bring herself to do it. They were, when she examined them, unexpectedly beautiful, the radiating flecks on their shells reminding her of the patterns in her own irises. Then there were the little jelly feelers, so friendly and sad. Nothing else to do but line an Oxo tin with leaves, and tumble the snails on top, with the lid open a crack for air.

For such slow creatures, snails (it turns out) can cover a lot of ground in six hours. The square of bedroom carpet has had to be scrubbed, the wallpaper wiped down and the candlewick bedspread put on a hot wash. There it hangs at the opposite edge of the picture, a soggy curtain in tufted salmon.

'What did you think you were doing?' cries Frieda, her voice shrill with martyrdom. 'As if I haven't enough on, trying to keep this place decent.'

No good trying to explain. In her mother's book, cleanliness will always trump invertebrate welfare. If it wasn't for Dad, Carol thinks, she'd pack her satchel and go live in the forest like the Babes in the Wood.

2007

Sometimes I think I had a premonition. That the moment I picked up the phone, I had this sense something was wrong. But more likely, it being a Wednesday evening, I'd have been rushing round trying to get washed up and cleared away before going to the gym, and not thinking about anything other than where I'd put my water bottle and whether it was too late to walk – in which case I needed to shift the wheelie-bin and get the car out of the garage.

I do remember I couldn't tell who was speaking at first, because Jaz was in such a state. Then I managed to make out 'Mum', and that's when I started to get frightened. I said, 'Jaz, love, what's the matter?' She just cried harder. I said, 'Jaz, are you all right?' which was a daft question because of course she wasn't all right, she was absolutely beside herself, incoherent. And she's normally so cool, so laid-back; that or in a temper about something. Not tears, though, she's never been one for tears.

So I said, 'What's happened? Whatever's the matter?'

She said, 'He told me, Mum, he told me straight out.' Which I couldn't make sense of. All I knew was that something was dreadfully wrong.

It's amazing how you can go from calm to terrified in a few seconds, like revving up a car. I made myself ask, 'Is it Matty?' Because that was the very worst scenario I could imagine; the call every grandparent dreads. I remember looking down at my hand where it was holding the edge of the chair and the knuckles were white, and at the back of my mind I was making all these mad bargains with heaven and fate – anything.

'It's not Matty,' I heard her say.

My legs nearly gave out with relief. Thank You, God, thank You, God, I was saying in my head. At least if Matty was all right, if my Matty was safe and sound, I could cope with whatever was coming.

'Tell me, love,' I said. 'Whatever is it? Surely we can sort it out?'

'No, Mum,' she said. 'It's all shattered, all of it.'

They say families follow certain patterns. Like, if you're knocked about as a kid, you might end up marrying someone who knocks you about, and if your mother's a cold fish, you're going to find it hard to bond with your own children. I'd have said that was phooey: thinking of my own mum Frieda, and how she was with me, and how I've been with Jaz, there's no comparison. But then, you don't know what children take in when they're young. You can run yourself ragged for them, and they'll still seize on the one thing you did wrong. Which in my case was to marry a cheat.

Which, it turned out, was what Jaz had done.

Normally it takes me fifteen minutes to get to the other side of Nantwich: I did it in eight. I don't know what I was expecting when I pulled up outside the house. Smashed windows, a pile of Ian's belongings on the front steps, maybe. Instead, everything looked normal: planters full of dead lobelia, plastic cart of Matty's in the middle of the drive, gate off its hinges. One day, I thought, Ian might actually get round to fixing the place up. Or not.

Jaz had left the door on the latch for me, so I went straight in. There's always a lot of clutter in Jaz and Ian's hall and it's narrow to begin with, so I had to go carefully, stepping over shoes and squeezing round the pushbikes and pausing to pick up clothes I'd dislodged from the radiator. Piles of stuff on the stairs, as usual; it would drive me round the bend if I lived here. I don't ever criticise, though. That would be asking for trouble.

As soon as I called her name she appeared in the kitchen doorway.

'Oh, love,' I said.

She's always been a beautiful girl. I've tried never to make a big deal of it, but other people would comment, especially when she was little. 'Child model,' Mrs Wynne next door used to say. 'You should send her photo off.' Even when she started with her piercings and her long clothes, my daughter still turned heads.

Now, though, standing in front of me in this gloomy hall, she just looked a mess. Her eyes were red and swollen, marked with tracks of mascara, and her long, thick hair was all over the place. The baggy black jumper made her seem much younger than her twenty-seven years.

I moved forward to give her a hug, but she started to talk in a way that kept me back.

'Complete fucking *bastard*,' she said. 'I can't believe what he's done. Just goes, "Yeah, I've slept with someone". Like it was nothing. Like it was *fucking nothing*.'

Even though there was no questioning her distress, I had some trouble taking in the image. Ian – casually announcing his infidelity? Surely not. One of us must have it wrong.

'Are you saying – he's admitted he's having an affair?'

'Of course he's *fucking* admitted it! That's what I've been *telling you*!' She struck the doorframe with the flat of her hand, and I saw tears drop off her chin.

So that was it. There didn't seem to be any doubt. Ian, the boy everyone liked: shyly spoken, posh, gawky. Decent, we'd thought. Straightforward. Good for Jaz. That big wedding four years ago, all for nothing. Marquee, open-topped car, special bamboo holders for the flowers. Dress that she wanted altering right at the last minute. I still had the pillars off the cake sitting on my kitchen shelf.

'Oh, love,' I said again.

'I hate him, Mum. I *hate him*. If he was here now, I swear I'd fucking kill him. I would, I swear. I'm not joking. I'd *fucking* kill him.'

'Where's Matty?' I asked cautiously.

Jaz looked at me as though I was mad. 'He's up-fucking-*stairs*. In his cot. Where did you think he was? On the *fucking moon*?'

I didn't dare ask if he was OK in case she took it the wrong way, but suddenly I was desperate to see. 'I thought I heard him calling,' I fibbed, and scooted back down the hall.

By the time I got to the top of the stairs, my blood was pounding. Matty's door was a few inches ajar and the night light showing. With extreme care I pushed the door open further, wincing at the shush-scrape of the carpet, and stuck my head round.

The sight of him asleep always makes me catch my breath. He was lying on his back with his fists balled, the way he used to when he was a tiny baby, and his lips were slightly parted. Dawg was underneath him, grey cloth tail poking out. 'You're going to have to get him one of those toddler beds soon,' I'd said to Jaz only the week before. 'And you reckon he'll stay there, do you?' had been her reply. 'You think he'll lie down, stick his thumb in his mouth, and that'll be it till the morning?' She said she wanted to wait till he could climb out of the cot unaided before letting him loose with a bed. So I went along with it. He's her child, after all.

I stood there in the calm dim glow of his moon-shaped lamp and watched his little chest move up and down, up and down, till I felt ready to go back downstairs. To be honest, I could have stayed there all night.

She was sitting at the kitchen table, head in hands, her coloured scarves draping down over plates and mugs and papers and books. When she heard me, she sat upright and I thought, At least she's stopped crying.

'Where's Ian?' I asked, drawing back a chair.

'Fuck knows.'

I waited for her to go on.

'It was a text.' Jaz looked as though she was about to spit. 'We were in here, talking about his day, everything normal. A bog-standard tea-time. Next thing his phone bleeps, but he doesn't open it, he takes it off into the lounge, really shifty. And you know that way he has of pushing his glasses up when he's nervous about something? It was such a weird reaction he might as well have waved a fucking flag, though I don't think he realised. Too much on his mind. When he went up to run Matty's bath, I got out the phone and checked.'

The lights on the baby monitor flickered briefly, settled.

'What did it say? Can you tell me?'

She shrugged as if she was past caring. 'It said: *What did you dream last night?*'

I was seeing it with her, imagining the letters on the screen.

'Well, perhaps it wasn't necessarily—'

'Then some kisses.'

'Oh.'

'Then a name.'

Without warning she got up, grabbed a mug off the table and slammed it onto the quarry tiles at her feet. It shattered like a bomb.

'Her fucking *name*. Now I'll always know it!'

'Good God, Jaz. You'll wake Matty.'

Her eyes, when she looked at me, were wild and stary, and for a moment I didn't know what to do. What *do* you do when everything you thought was safe is just falling apart?

Then I thought, Sod it, someone's got to get a grip.

I began to stack the dirty plates on the table, because I can't think straight when everywhere's untidy. While my daughter stood in the middle of the room grasping her own hair, I ferried crockery to the sink, ran the hot tap, and set to gathering pieces of broken cup. 'You can't leave it like this,' I said. 'If Matty walks in here with no slippers tomorrow morning—'

She bent and took a single sliver of white china between her finger and thumb.

'Come on, love,' I said. 'Let's clear away and then I'll make us a hot drink and we can go sit in the lounge. It'll be better there.'

I guided her to the bin, then handed her a damp cloth so she could wipe up all the very tiny fragments. As I washed and stacked, I kept an eye on her.

'Don't touch my papers,' she said at one point, when I reached across the table for a dirty spoon.

As if. Even when she lived under my roof I never dared interfere with her stuff.

Once I'd finished the dishes it was tempting to go through the whole kitchen, collect up all the books and toys and carry them next door, put away the pans and bowls that had been left out, stick the pot plants in for a good soak and wipe the soil off the windowsill. Some of her leaflets and postcards had fallen off the cork board; there was a pile of assorted boots on the doormat. I longed to put these small things right.

Instead I brewed two teas, picked up the baby monitor, and led Jaz through to the sofa. We sat for a while watching the television play mutely, pictures of a bossy-looking woman preparing vegetables in a low-beamed kitchen.

'Don't,' she said, when she saw me eyeing the hearth, and the tumbler containing six wax crayons in an inch of orange squash.

'It might tip over.'

'And you think I care?'

The woman on TV yanked a chicken open and paused, smugly. I wondered where Ian was and what he was doing right at this moment.

Jaz said: 'When I asked him about the text he looked – frozen. Like he had no idea what to say. I mean, he obviously wasn't expecting the question. So I asked him again and he came right out with it. I suppose he didn't have time to think up a story. No time to prepare a defence.' She laughed bitterly. 'He could have said it was a mistake. People get phone numbers wrong, don't they? Why didn't he go for straight denial? I might have bought it.'

'You wouldn't.'

'No, you're right, I wouldn't. *Fuck* him. Why didn't he *delete* it?'

I said, 'Did he tell you much else?'

'Only that he'd seen her twice. He met her in the pub near where he works. The first time they did anything, they only kissed. Apparently. The next time, he went back to hers. It was a lunchtime. So much more con*venient*.' She flopped back against the Indian throw. 'What I don't get, Mum, what I don't get is – you know, actually I don't get fucking *any* of it. It's so, it's out of the blue, I wasn't expecting it, I didn't think there was anything wrong. There's nothing wrong with me, is there?'

That made me want to cry. Really I needed to hold her, but she was still too spiky; she'd have pushed me away and I couldn't have stood that on top of everything else. I said, 'Jaz, there's nothing wrong with you. Ian must be having some kind of, I don't know, crisis.'

'I'll give him a fucking crisis,' she said.

By now the woman chef was sharing her chicken with some laughing friends at a pristine table. 'See my glorious world,' she was saying. I'd have turned the bloody TV off if I'd stood a chance of finding the remote.

'Did he say he was sorry?'

'Yeah. And that he'll never see her again, it meant nothing, one-off, blah blah. Like they do.'

'It's not always talk,' I said. 'Sometimes they mean it.'

Jaz gave me a withering look.

'I'm sure he'll come back.'

'He'd better not.'

'I don't mean straight away, obviously. When things have calmed down. Then you can talk, and try to get to the root of—'

She sat up and leaned towards me. 'You're not getting it, Mum. Ian's gone because I've thrown him out.'

'Well, yes, I see. And I know that just at this moment you'll be feeling—'

'Mum, read my lips,' she said. 'This marriage is over. Over. Ian's made his position clear. *I'm* not good enough – *this* isn't good enough for him.' She swung her arm round to take in the room with all its evidence of family life: the stack of toddler vests balanced on the chair arm, the tumbled Duplo, Ian's computer magazines mixed with her foreign language dictionaries, and cardboard wallets dumped all along the top of the sideboard and the coffee-table and the windowseat.

'Oh, I'm sure it is enough, love, it's—'

'The one thing I won't do,' she cut in, 'let's be totally clear on this, is live with a man who doesn't put his marriage first. A man who lies and cheats. A man who thinks he can get away with treating me like a fool because I'll always turn a blind eye, I'll always forgive him. Make like I'm a *fucking* door-mat. 'Cause that's not me and I won't have it; I've never taken shit from anyone and I'm not about to start now.' The baby monitor crackled and she nodded at it angrily. 'Plus, I'm not bringing Matty up in that kind of a household. No way. I'm not putting either of us through that pantomime. Damaging him. He doesn't need a childhood like *that*.'

And I thought, So here we go. I might have known it would come down to this. Somehow it turns out to be my fault, again.

CHAPTER 2

Photograph 294, Album Three

Location: Acton Scott Historic Working Farm, Shropshire

Taken by: Carol

Subject: Twelve-year-old Jaz stands within a semi-circle of interested geese and ducks, her back against the wall of a pigsty. She is wearing a frilly cap and an apron, and carrying a bucket of grain. If it weren't for the jeans and the trainers showing at the bottom, she could be a dairymaid from the 1800s – which is the general idea. She has already had a go at making butter pats, and been taught the correct way to hold a chick. She's watched a demonstration of spinning and carding, and how you'd saddle a carthorse. The sun is out and it should be a top day, except that Phil is AWOL again after a fight and Carol is as blue as a wife can be.

Not that she's letting on to Jaz. 'Dad's having to work extra hours,' she's told her, and so they make free in the gift shop and eat triple-scoop ice creams and hire a rowing boat and order a Victorian cream tea. Every ounce of Carol's strength goes into keeping that smile.

Meanwhile, Jaz plans what to do when they get home. She will run her own bath, put her nightie on, then attempt to make her mother a hot drink. Perhaps she can add a snack and bring a tray through, the way her mum does when anyone's ill. It is all Jaz can think to do in the face of her mother's despair, and even now she's guessing it's not enough.

The obvious course of action was to take Matty for a few days. 'Give you time to get yourself together,' I told Jaz, the morning after both our lives had caved in. 'He was due to come to me on Saturday, anyway. It's no trouble.'

'Would you?'

'Of course. You need some space.'

She nodded.

'And you need to speak to Ian,' I added unwisely.

'I'm never speaking to him again,' she snapped. 'So you can forget that idea.'

Don't be daft, I nearly said. There's all kinds of stuff you need to sort out. Even if you both decide the marriage is finished, there'll be maintenance and access and divvying up your assets, and you can't do all of it through a solicitor – well, you can, but it costs an arm and a leg. And, in any case, I don't believe the marriage is over: I think you'll get through this, maybe with some counselling, and come back together for the sake of little Matty. I think Ian's had a stupid bloody selfish slip, that's all it is, and after you've both done a lot of soul-searching, and he's apologised and you've had a good old shout, probably lots of shouting, you'll move on. It might take months, but you will get there.

I didn't say any of that, obviously. Sometimes I think my head'll explode, all the unspoken words in there.

I keep Matty's room ready, because not only is he with me most weekends for a stopover, give his mum and dad chance to have a lie-in, but you never know when there might be a crisis.

'Is that new?' Jaz asked, putting the changing bag down on the chest of drawers and pointing to a wall light in the shape of a gecko.

'It is. I meant to store it away for a Christmas present, but then I thought, well, it seems a shame not to have it out, let him have the enjoyment of it now.'

'You're hopeless.'

'I know.'

I straightened the cot cover and plugged the monitor in. Between our feet, Matty sat and rolled a wooden truck back and forth like someone planing floorboards.

'Car,' he said.

'And tonight,' I said, sinking to my haunches, 'you're going to stay with Nanna. Won't that be nice? We can read *Dear Zoo* and *On the Road.* And you can have a boiled egg.'

The truck crashed against the leg of the cot and Matty cackled.

'You're talking to yourself,' said Jaz.

'He has a special egg cup,' I said, hauling myself up again. 'Mrs Wynne brought it me back off holiday. It's shaped like a Highland cow.'

Jaz drew her hand over her face.

'Look,' I said, 'you need to go back home now and get some sleep. I bet you were up all night, yeah?' I'd sat up till 3 a.m. myself, watching the night sky from Jaz's old room, wondering who the hell my daughter had married. But there was nothing to be gained from sharing that. 'Stick the answerphone on and put your head down for a few hours. You're fit for nothing at the moment.'

'Yeah,' she said. 'I should be working. There's a translation I need to finish for Uniflect.'

'Can't it wait? Look, I'll make us a cup of tea.'

'I'm still drinking this one, Mum.'

'Can I get you something to eat?'

'I'm not hungry.'

'Syrupy porridge? I've got some in. Or I could do cheese on toast; Matty likes that.'

'Brrrm brrrm,' said Matty.

'I'm not hungry.'

'How about if I do some, and then you see how you feel?'

Jaz looked as if she was about to speak, then she turned away and began to tug at a lock of hair.

The problem, I felt like saying, is that I don't know what to do. I'm grown up, I'm the mum, I'm supposed to know. But I don't.

I bent down and picked up Matty's beaker. 'Cheese on toast it is, then. And an egg in the cow cup?'

'Egg,' said Matty.

Jaz turned back to me, her face pinched and white. 'Actually,' she said, 'there is something I'd like. Do you mind if I crash out upstairs for a while? I can't face driving back right now. I just want my old bed for a few hours.'

I tell you, I could have wept.

After we'd eaten – after Jaz had sat and stared at her food, and Matty had spread his over a wide area – I took her up and closed the curtains.

'Sit there while I make up the bed,' I told her, and she plonked herself in front of the dressing-table. I got fresh sheets from the airing cupboard and grabbed the pillows off my own bed because they're the decent ones.

'You've taken my posters down,' she said, as she watched me shake out the duvet cover.

'Well, yes. It's my guest room, now.'

I could see her eyes swivelling round, clocking all the changes. 'And you've repainted the ceiling. And the lampshade's new. And that's not my duvet.'

I said: 'Love, I couldn't leave it untouched for ever. If I have people to stay, they don't want to be looking at pictures of half-naked men waving guitars about or leaning on gravestones.' I tried a laugh. 'Could give them nightmares.'

'Well, I hope you haven't thrown them away.'

'Of course I haven't. They're on top of the wardrobe in Matty's room.'

'And what about my lampshade?'

I paused, pillowcase in hand. 'What about it?'

'Did you keep that?'

'No, it went to the tip. I didn't for one minute think you'd want it.'

'I customised it,' she said. 'I painted it myself.'

'Black, with crosses and roses. It didn't really go with anything any more. And it was very battered. You wouldn't have wanted it up in your house, would you?'

'Dunno. But you could have offered it to me before you chucked it out.'

I shook the pillow down and dropped it onto the bed.

'Did you keep my old curtains?'

'They're in the loft,' I said quickly. I didn't dare tell her I'd cut them up to make a garden kneeler.

'Good.' She continued to watch me in a glazed, spacey way. 'I suppose I should be helping with that.'

'You stay where you are. Just this duvet to sort out and we're done. Then you can put your head down. Matty and I might go for a walk so you can have total peace.'

'Yeah.'

'Do you want to borrow one of my nighties?'

For a moment she actually smiled. 'I'll give that one a miss,

Mum. I've got a T-shirt on under this jumper; I can sleep in that.'

I left her to get undressed, and when I came back she was under the covers. I drew the curtains closer to block out the little triangle of light at the top, and went to sit on the bed next to her. 'Can I get you anything? Cup of Horlicks? Do you want the radio out of my room?'

She shook her head and closed her eyes. 'Oh – you have still got Kitten?'

'Of course. I'd never throw Kitten out. He's in Matty's cot.'

'Can I have him?'

'Now?'

'Yeah.'

I stepped across the landing and retrieved the cat-doll from under a pile of bright, newer teddies. 'You're in demand again,' I told it. 'I hope you're more use than me.'

'Thanks,' she murmured, when I placed it in her hand. She never opened her eyes, and I think she was asleep two minutes after. You sod, Ian Reid, I thought as I closed the door on her quietly. You utter, utter sod.

Matty didn't want to go for a walk; he'd been watching a cookery programme on CBeebies, and it was baking or nothing.

'Shall we make rolls for tea, then?' I asked, because I knew I had a packet of bread mix in the cupboard, and all you do is add water and knead. Matty made a drilling noise which I took to mean yes, so I got down the big mixing bowl that was my mother's, and carried a chair in from the lounge for him to stand on.

'You'll need to let Nanna measure out the water,' I told him. I didn't want him near the tap. Laverne-next-door's cousin's little girl was very badly scalded with a hot tap last year. That story's haunted me ever since I heard it. Her mother was only in the next room, ironing.

I opened the packet, and a little bit of flour puffed up into the air. 'Oh,' said Matty, impressed. I patted the sides for fun and another tiny cloud rose up. Matty squealed. I slid the packet slightly over towards him, smiling, and without hesitation he stuck out his palm and walloped the side. Bread mix exploded out of the top and the packet fell over, spilling a long white plume across the kitchen surface.

'Oops,' I said.

'Oops,' echoed Matty.

'My fault,' I said. 'Nanna's fault. Silly Nanna. What was I thinking.'

I began to scrape the mix back up but, as I did so, Matty leaned in over my arm and sneezed spectacularly. The air in front of us became at once thick and misty. Flour hung in suspension, like smoke, like the pall after a bomb's gone off. 'Uh-oh,' he said.

'Uh-oh indeed. My goodness. What a mess.'

'All-gone.' He waved his arms.

'Not really, Matty. Not even slightly, in fact.'

While I wetted a piece of kitchen towel, he began to blow at the flour like a maniac, spreading it as far as his lungs could reach. I thought, I'm going to be cleaning this room till midnight.

'Gotcha,' I said, swooping in and lifting him off the chair, out of range of the bread mix. 'Now, mister, let's see if we can clean you up. Oh, good grief. It's all in your hair, down your T-shirt. You've even got it on your eyelashes. If your mummy sees you like this . . . Close your eyes. Close your eyes, Matty. No, don't wipe it on your trousers. I've got a cloth. Close your eyes while Nanna sorts you out.' As he twisted away from me I could see that my front was covered in streaks of flour too, and that a pale film had settled over everything even as far as the sink, which meant it must be on all the plates in the plate rack and the cups above and the storage jars, and the lot would need taking down and washing.

And at the same time I was thinking, His nails need a proper scrub with a brush if I'm going to let him help knead the dough, and is there enough mix left, should I weigh it out and scale down the amount of water, and when is he due a nappy change, and I was just asking him again to stop blowing at me when the phone rang.

It took me about twenty rings to brush the worst of the mess off myself, shepherd Matty into the living room and shut the kitchen door behind us, pull the toy box out again from under the coffee-table, and locate the phone. If it was Ian, I was going to tell him what I bloody well thought of him. No, I couldn't do that because Matty was at my elbow. I was going to be icily polite, then, and tell him Jaz would ring back when she was less upset, then hang up. No, I'd be better just hanging up, full stop. Unless that was too rude. Except he'd gone beyond rude with what he'd done, even if he was the father of my grandchild.

Then, as I reached for the handset, I had this flash that it might, in fact, be Phil, and I wondered what the hell to say to him, because Jaz had said to me twice now, *Don't tell Dad yet*. But if he asked after Jaz (and he always did), or if he heard Matty in the background, I wasn't going to lie. I wasn't going down that route. There'd been enough lies in our family.

So when I pressed the accept button, I was already worked up, and not fully on the ball. Which is why I made such a hash of it; why I managed to make everything a whole lot worse.

CHAPTER 3

Photograph 271, Album Two

Location: the hallway, Sunnybank, Shropshire

Taken by: Carol

Subject: Jaz, ten, in a blue sequinned party frock. She stands stiff and furious, the Deco glass of the front door fanning behind her in an accidental headdress. It's clothing that's the issue: Jaz would prefer to wear a black strapless top with jeans, and has stated this preference energetically for the last hour. But Phil says the outfit's too old for her and, just for once, Carol's backing him up. 'Nobody else'll be in a dress,' complains Jaz. 'Dresses are lame.' 'Then wear your jeans with a nice blouse,' says Carol. If looks could kill, Carol would be eviscerated on the spot.

But this is not actually the argument. This is an add-on, an extra layer on top of something else. What Jaz is really sulking about – has been for weeks – is that she's been banned from the travellers' camp that's appeared on the wasteground behind the local GP surgery. 'Why would you want to keep going there anyway?' asks Phil. 'Because they're interesting,*' says Jaz. And, when she catches him making faces behind her back, adds, 'More interesting than either of you, anyway.'*

Phil laughs his head off, but it's a line that cuts Carol to the quick.

'Hello? Am I speaking to Carol Morgan?'

The tone was formal, and I thought it might be a cold-caller. At the same time, Matty was holding up a pot of Play-Doh for me to unscrew, pushing it into my chest.

'Who is this?' I said crossly.

'David.'

I still wasn't with it.

'David Reid,' he said. 'Ian's father.'

There were, I saw now, white footprints across my blue carpet and a shower of white over the arm of the sofa. When I turned to look in the mirror, there was flour in my hair and also caught in the top folds of my blouse. A tilt of the head dislodged another flurry.

'We should talk,' went on David, his tone ultra-cool. I stopped seeing the marks on the furniture and pictured him instead at the wedding in his morning suit, and his snooty girlfriend buzzing around in the background as though it was her son getting married. *I've moved the flowers so they're in the centre of the table, Carol.*

'Talk?' I said.

'Nanna,' said Matty, thumping the pot against my breastbone. '*Nanna.*'

'Is Jasmine with you?' he said. 'Is she around? Because Ian's been trying to call her, and she won't answer. Is that Matty?'

'Jaz is with me, yes. But she's having a lie-down, I'm not disturbing her.'

'If you could. Ian needs to speak to her urgently.'

'He'll have to wait. She's not ready.'

'You should know, he's staying with me at the moment. He's very upset.'

I snatched at the Play-Doh pot and flung it at the hearth. The top pinged off, and Matty scrambled after it.

'Upset?' I said. 'Upset? I should damn well think he is. Jaz is pretty "upset", too. She's devastated. What Ian's done to her is –' I almost said 'unforgivable', but stopped myself in time – 'despicable. At the very least she needs some time to come to terms with it.'

'There's nothing to be gained from silence,' David was saying. 'The sooner they get together and talk it through, the better.'

'She needs *time*,' I repeated.

'I disagree. The longer she shuts him out, the harder it's going to be.'

'For who, exactly?'

There was a pause, then David spoke again. 'For everyone. Look, I've always had you down as a very reasonable person, Carol, so if the two of us could—'

'Oh, *reasonable*, is it? Depends what your definition of reasonable is, doesn't it? I suppose you want me to go upstairs, wake her and tell her it's all OK, Ian's sorry, and she should be a good girl and take him straight back. Four years they've been married, four years, and if he can't keep his hands to himself in that time then they've no chance. She might as well ditch him now. Everything on a golden plate, he's had, you've seen to that –'

'I resent the implication there.'

'– and it's still not good enough. I don't know who he thinks he is, what right he has to – That lovely girl up there – God, what's wrong with people that they can't *hold on to what they have and be grateful?*'

I realised I must have been shouting, because Matty had stopped playing and was looking at me. I put my hand against my mouth, ashamed, and at that moment the living-room door opened and Jaz walked in.

'What's going on?' she said. 'I could hear you on the stairs.'

I shushed her, but it was too late.

'Can I hear Jasmine?' came David's voice, thin and powerless out of the receiver. 'Jasmine? Jasmine?' I held the phone to my chest, muffling him.

Her face fell. 'Oh God, what have you been saying, Mum?'

'I don't know,' I said. 'It just came out.'

'Well, it shouldn't have. This is my crisis.' And she took the phone away from me and switched it off.

There've been several notable occasions when I've opened my mouth and come out with the opposite of what I wanted to say. Sometimes, if I can't sleep at night, I play those times back and then I have to get up and stick the radio on and have a milky drink or maybe do a few stretches. Must be nice to be one of those people who aren't bothered.

After Jaz had taken Matty upstairs to change him I felt the urge to haul out her wedding album, compound the misery of the moment. The album (hand-tooled, gilt-finished) lived in the space under the bureau, in a special white box. Last time it had an airing was the night Jaz came round to tell me she was pregnant.

I wiped the dust away with my sleeve and lifted the lid.

Inside, it smelled of the past. Leather, cream card, tissue paper edged in gold: all those layers protecting, and not one of them any use in the end. Here at the front was Phil – open-faced, amiable cheat. It's eight years since I finally threw him out – an age ago – yet if I look at his picture for too long, time's compressed to nothing. He was standing under the archway at the entrance to the church, Jaz clutching his arm. Later she'd told me she was so nervous she thought she might be sick, right there in the porch, but Phil had distracted her with a story about how he'd sneaked into the hotel earlier and drawn a penis on the inside of David's place-card. She'd been so busy being annoyed, she'd forgotten to be scared. So Phil had been some use. And at least he had turned up, without Penny in tow, and had given Jaz away properly. He even behaved himself at the reception, if you didn't count trying to kiss me at the end of the evening.

On the next page was the immaculate David with his lovely consort, Jacky, like a couple out of *Cheshire Life*. 'I tell you, I'd have sold my bloody flat to pay for this wedding if I'd known he'd be so up himself,' Phil said to me afterwards. 'Lording it over everyone.' I'd thought that was a bit unfair at the time; put simply, David had money, and we didn't.

I suppose you want me to go upstairs, wake her and tell her it's all OK, Ian's sorry, and she should be a good girl and take him straight back, I heard myself say again. Lord above, why had I come out with that, when ultimately I wanted them reconciled?

I turned the page quickly.

Now it was Dad's lost and vacant eyes staring back at me. We'd picked confetti off his front, lifting his arms out of the way to get at the little horseshoes. 'I think he enjoyed himself,' I remember saying to Jaz as we got him ready to wheel back. 'I'm sure he knew what was going on.' You tell yourself all sorts.

The next page was a close-up of the happy couple: Ian now, to my eye, slightly shifty behind his metal-framed glasses, as though he'd pulled off something that he didn't deserve, and Jaz tragically radiant beside him. Her long hair was drawn back at the temples, mediaeval-style, and she had a circlet of artificial daisies on her brow. 'We do some very nice tiaras,' the woman in the bridal shop had said. But Jaz wouldn't budge. 'I want it to look as though I've picked them fresh from the fields.' The shop woman wrinkling up her nose when she thought I wasn't looking. God knows what face she'd have made if she'd known we were having black ribbons too.

A memory came suddenly of a teenage Jaz getting ready to go out one night, popping her head round the living-room door and asking whether she could borrow my jacket, and me saying, 'Which one?' Jaz tilting further so her body was hidden by the jamb, mumbling, 'Oh, just that velvet one.' So I knew she already had it on. 'But you've got a velvet jacket of your own,' I'd said. 'Not like yours. Mine's a blazer-type. Yours is all silky and drapey.' She'd come in then and showed me, lifting up the tails, waggling the bell sleeves. I seem to recall her with crimped hair, or that may have been another time. 'That's because it was very expensive, Jaz. It's meant for special occasions.' Of course she won, beauty over age, and the jacket became hers. *You want to borrow it back from her*, I imagined Phil saying, and then David's voice sliced in again: *I resent the implication there*.

I let my gaze fall one last time, then closed the album against the brightness of her smile.

Thing about Matty is, he's at that terrifically portable stage. True, I can't take him to the gym, or when I do my swimming, or on any of the Beavers excursions (or to work, of course, which is another bone of contention with Jaz). But aside from that, as long as the place we're going to can supply him with a container plus some small objects to put in and take out, he's fine. Failing that, there's entertainment to be had from anything that can be rolled, anything that can be hidden under, any object that can be used to strike another object, and all pipework and cabling.

So when I go to see Dad, Matty makes himself at home wherever we're based. If we're in the central lounge, he'll explore the toy box they keep there for visiting grandchildren, and submit to being ruffled and cooed over by any number of elderly strangers. If he's in Dad's room, he'll make a bee-line for the yucca in the corner with its fascinating white gravel. As long as you check he's not putting any of it in his mouth, you can pretty much leave him be. Give him a mug to fill and he's occupied for half an hour.

These days, Sunday mornings are a good time to visit, because I always have Matty with me then; he's stayed over Saturday nights since he was weaned. I have him till tea-time, till *Songs of Praise* he's all mine. And visiting my dad is now part of the routine. What used to be a potentially upsetting part of the weekend is transformed, because I tell you, it's a heck of a lot easier to go along with Matty than it is to go on my own. He's a fresh, new thing in the land of the old. He's something to focus the conversation on, something to distract from the horribleness that is watching your father leave you by degrees.

This week we arrived to find Dad propped up in bed, having his tea out of a lidded cup. 'Well, I'm glad you're here,' went the hearty nursing assistant, 'because we're doing very nicely indeed today.'

'Yes?' I wondered whether Dad had done something remarkable.

'His chest's completely clear, what do you think about that? None of the nasty coughing that kept him awake before. He's had three really good nights, and today he's full of the joys of spring, aren't you?'

Dad, glassy-eyed and weary underneath her strong arms.

'Great,' I said.

Once she'd finished and left, the first job was to go round the room moving pills, pads, hearing-aid batteries, unsuitable sweets, coins, pen tops. I plonked Matty with his changing bag by the yucca and gave Dad a kiss, and then I sat down to assess the state of play.

She was right, I thought, when I got a proper look at him. He was a better colour, and he was sitting up straighter than last week. The blue shadows under his eyes had almost gone.

'I've brought Matty,' I announced brightly, as I always did. Matty paused at his name, then carried on shovelling stones with his fingers.

'He's staying with me for a few days,' I went on.

Dad blinked.

'So we're both enjoying that.'

'Bee,' said Matty, pointing at a fly on the wall above him.

'Not a bee,' I said. 'Just a fly. Dirty fly. Bleah.'

Dad cleared his throat, like someone about to speak.

I waited, but nothing came.

'Anyway, it's great to have him, but it is making life a bit tricky, because I'm having to take him to nursery the mornings I'm in the shop, and it's the wrong direction so that adds an extra half an hour to the journey. Cutting across from Nunheath isn't an option because I have to come back for Josh next door; I can't suddenly tell him to start taking the school bus. Although I suppose he could, but it's messing his mum about, and she's enough on. You remember Josh's mum? Laverne?'

We used to joke about Laverne, how thin she was. 'Not as far through as a tram ticket,' Dad used to say. 'She daresn't step over a grid in case she falls through.'

Matty laughed suddenly. 'All-gone,' he said.

'What has, sweetheart? Oh.'

He'd found a cup of cold tea I'd managed to miss on first inspection, had tipped it onto the floor in the space between his legs and was measuring the effect of liquid on nylon fibre. I took the cup off him and placed it out of reach. Then I dabbed up the pool with a handful of tissues. Not for nothing do they have mottled-pattern carpets here.

'Hey, I've got your Scooby car with me,' I told him. 'And let's see if Nanna doesn't have a packet of raisins for a good boy.' I extracted both items from my bag, then came and knelt beside him so I could lay the raisins out in a row across the little table. He likes it when I do that, and I needed him to be occupied, to let me think for a minute. There's a fine line between being a distraction and a nuisance.

Above me, Dad sighed. I got up and went back to the chair.

'I was thinking on the way here,' I said, leaning forward in the hope I might catch his interest, 'do you remember when Jaz was little, and you let her help make a bird scarer for your veg?'

For a second I thought he was nodding in acknowledgement, but it was just a wobble of the head.

'Do you remember,' I went on, 'all the milk bottle tops and foil pie cases and strips of tinsel she tied on? And there was a budgie bell and a couple of old forks, strung on about a mile of twine. How many pegs did you use in the end? I know it was more bird scarer than garden when she'd finished. I've a photo of it somewhere. And we were watching out the kitchen window, it had only been up an hour, and this jackdaw came down and started taking the tinsel off. Pulling away at it, like it was a worm. Do you remember, Dad? I thought she'd hurt herself with laughing so much. You said, "I reckon you've made a bird disco, Jaz". She thought that was fantastic.'

I paused, because you can do that with Dad. Silences are OK. Over in the corner Matty was busy squashing raisins under car wheels, but overlaid with that was an image of his mother, aged about nine, clapping her hands to her face with delight.

'It's different being a grandparent, isn't it?' I said. 'I know there were times, when she was growing up, Jaz would talk to you when she wouldn't to me. Not that I minded. What I say is, thank God there was someone she *would* talk to.'

Outside the room a trolley rattled; someone shouted a greeting. Matty's car fell off the table, scattering raisins.

'I went to a talk on nineteen thirties' suburban architecture last week,' I said, because as well as long silences, non-sequiturs are also fine when you're talking to Dad. Whatever pops into your head, really. 'Gwen from the gym invited me. It was good, you'd have loved it. All houses like Sunnybank, and Pincroft. The speaker was saying how few Thirties buildings still have their proper metal windowframes, and I felt like sticking my hand up and shouting, "Mine has!".'

Dad's eyes were empty, but I never let that put me off. Because it's like they say about comas: you can have someone lying there apparently unconscious, and then when they wake up they can tell you word for word what they've heard people saying around them. And Matty, months before he could speak, could point to all sorts. You'd go, 'Where's the light?' And his arm would ping straight up. 'Where's the car?' And he'd swivel to the window. So just because Dad's so quiet doesn't mean he's not still with us at some deep level. And the strange thing is, I can tell this dad things I would never have been able to before.

I reached out for his hand.

'Do you ever wonder,' I said, 'what would have happened if you'd taken different decisions in your life? I do. If I'd stuck with Phil, say, and made more of an effort to blot out what was going on, how Jaz would have turned out. Or should I have kicked him into touch right at the start, when I first found out? Would that have been better? I wish now I'd confided in you, but coping with someone else's upset on top of your own ... And Mum would have gone, "I told you so". Sometimes I used to imagine you coming round to our house and punching him in the face. I want to punch Ian. I want to sock him in the jaw.'

The shadows on the wall were focusing and unfocusing as the sunlight altered; Matty's fly crawled across the headboard.

'Jaz must think it's all men ever do. Sorry, sorry, Dad. Not you, obviously.'

Someone far off was playing Glenn Miller.

'Or David. Oh, did I tell you he'd rung? I made a hash of that, too. Typically. They'll put it on my headstone: *Tried Hard, Made Everything Worse.*'

And just as I was thinking I shouldn't have mentioned graves, the sun came out, making a tiny brilliant spotlight from my watch appear on the wall just by Dad's shoulder. Matty lifted his head, transfixed. 'That?' he said. For fun I jiggled my wrist so the spot danced about, and within seconds he'd left his pot of gravel and was up by the bedhead, tugging at the nearest pillow in an attempt to reach it.

'Careful,' I said, torn between delight and concern.

Matty slapped his palm against the wall. Slowly Dad turned his head, like a man trying to locate a sound in thick fog.

I made the beam slide down to the end of the bed, out of Dad's way, and Matty followed it, patting the bedcover. There I let the light play on his fingers and he stood still for a moment, puzzling. At the same time, Dad shifted so his right arm came out from under the covers, and now you could see both sets of flesh within touching distance: the chubby unblemished, and the freckled slack.

The scene held me. Were Dad's eyes watching Matty, or were they fixed on some point beyond him? If I had my camera, if I took a photo now, would the picture turn out happy or sad?

CHAPTER 4

Photograph: newspaper clipping between the pages of a Christmas 1967 Woman's Realm *inside Carol's bureau, Sunnybank.*

Location: the square outside the Red Lion, Tannerside

Taken by: the Bolton Evening News

Subject: The Big Switch-On *reads the caption.* Tannerside's Tree of Light is illuminated by councillors Bob White and Tommy Pharaoh.

At the base of this twenty-foot Douglas fir, the two men shake hands. There's been a good turn-out despite the drizzle – too many people for them all to fit into the shot. Carol, Councillor White's daughter, just squeezes in, though she's not actually that keen to appear in the local rag wearing this stupid tam o' shanter her mother forced over her ears before she was allowed out. 'You want to try looking smart, for once,' said Frieda.

For all the icy wind and headgear humiliation, Carol's enjoyed the walk up, just her and her dad together.

'How you doing?' he asks.

'Happy as a sandbag,' Carol says.

A standard and much-loved exchange.

When they draw near the cemetery and a car slooshes through a puddle, soaking them both, Bob goes, 'There's nowt like good manners, and that was nowt like it.' It's a turn of phrase which never fails to make Carol laugh.

He has dozens of these sayings. They are who he is. Every time she drops something, he chirps, 'Did it bite you?' If she complains that something's not fair, she gets, 'Neither are th' hairs on a black pig's bum.' Then there are his nicknames: people from Horwich are 'sleepers'; from Standish, 'pow-yeds'; from Bolton, 'trotters'; from Wigan 'purrers'. Purrers sounds nice, thinks Carol, the first time she hears it. She pictures Tenniel's drawing of the Cheshire Cat, perched on the gates of Mesnes Park. But 'purring', Bob enlightens her, means kicking someone with clogs on. It's all good fun.

The only saying she can think of that her mother uses is, 'Go rub it better with a brick.'

Ian caught up with us eventually. He was waiting for me one morning when I got to The Olive.

'Carol,' he said, pushing at the bridge of his glasses. 'I need to see you.'

'Not here, not now,' I said, fumbling with the keys in my eagerness to escape inside. What if Moira popped in to check a customer order or a delivery, walked through the door and found a family drama unfolding in the middle of her shop? Tears and accusations amid the wooden mushrooms.

'Carol,' he said.

'It's Jaz you should be talking to,' I told him. The key slid home and turned. 'Go round there. She's in.'

'No, she isn't.'

I was genuinely surprised. 'She was in an hour ago because I stopped off to pick up some more of Matty's clothes. She must have nipped out for something. I'd try again.'

And with that I slipped inside and locked the door against him.

He loitered for five minutes and then walked off. Good, I thought. I got on with my jobs: turning on the lights, the till, checking the post and answerphone, unpacking a load of cat-motif mugs for examination and then flattening the cardboard box ready to go in the bin out the back.

After that I flipped the sign round and opened the door. Ian was standing on the pavement opposite.

'You can't come in,' I called, stupidly.

'You can't stop me, I'm a customer,' he said, and walked straight over, crossed the threshold, installed himself by a display of slate clocks. No one else was around. We don't usually get anyone till ten at the earliest, so why Moira always wants the place open at nine-thirty sharp is beyond me.

Ian glanced at the shelf nearest, then picked up a marble egg and weighed it in his hand the way everyone does who touches them. 'I'm not hanging round there indefinitely, Carol. She's in but not answering the door, and she's got the deadbolts on. She won't pick up the phone either.'

'She will. I was chatting to her last night.'

'We've got caller display. She won't pick up when she knows it's me.'

'Ring from a friend's, use a different mobile.'

'I tried that. She hung up.'

'Can you blame her?' I said.

I watched his expression flicker for a moment. Ian isn't the kind of man who's built for deceit; he's nowhere near cool enough.

'No, of course I don't blame her. But we can't carry on like this. I have to explain.'

'To her, though, not to me.'

He put the egg down – I was relieved about that – and approached the counter.

'You need to hear, Carol. You need to help. You understand Jaz better than anyone.'

It was an astute compliment on his part. 'Well,' I said.

'I know what I've done, I know just how badly I've messed up. I love Jaz, and Matty; they're the only things I care about. Not that woman, she was nothing. What happened was a slip. It absolutely didn't mean anything. It'll never happen again.'

'Why did you do it, Ian?'

He shook his head. 'I don't know.' And he did look bewildered, as though he truly couldn't fathom it.

'You need to take responsibility,' I said.

'That's what I'm trying—'

'She's very, very upset.'

'Yes. She must be.'

'Devastated.'

'Tell me what I can do, Carol.'

I let myself imagine, for a moment, what might have happened if someone had taken Phil aside all those years ago and told him. Whether Phil could have been straightened out. I turned my head away from Ian, and across the floor of the shop, ground-in specks of glitter winked and sparkled at me; we'd had some frosted twigs in over Christmas and they'd shed like billy-o, we'd been hoovering every day. Christmas, when Matty wasn't even walking.

I had a chance to make things good.

'She is dreadfully hurt,' I said.

Ian hung his head. 'I feel terrible. Please, tell me what to do.'

'OK, then,' I said, sitting myself on the edge of the counter because by now my legs were trembling. 'Firstly, don't corner her. Don't stake out the house or ring every half-hour. She doesn't react well to being pursued. Send her a letter – I'll give it to her if you're worried she'll just stick it in the shredder, though I don't think she will. Give me a letter and I'll make sure she gets it. In it you say what you've told me: that you love her and Matty; that she's not done anything wrong, it's entirely your fault; that it was a stupid, joyless one-off and it will *never ever happen again.*' He was nodding emphatically. 'That last bit's really important. You must never let her down again, Ian. She won't give you a second chance.'

She might not even give you a first, I thought, but I kept that to myself.

'Will it work? Will she have me back?'

'I don't know.' In my head I saw Matty, pyjama-ed, rolling his toy car up and down the newel post in their hall. 'But you have to give it a try.'

After he'd gone I turned on the shop's CD-player and listened to some Celtic harp. I felt drained, as though I'd been doing some hard physical labour. The urge to ring Jaz was enormous, but I made myself stay off the phone because I knew I'd only blurt out something I wasn't supposed to. Though I did call the nursery and check on Matty. 'Is anything wrong?' the girl asked me when she came back from the toddler room. 'Nothing,' I said. Then, because I didn't want to sound weird, I said, 'He looked a bit flushed when I dropped him off this morning.' 'Well, he's fine now,' she said. 'He's playing Funky Footsteps.'

We had four paying customers all morning – you can see why Moira frets – so I had plenty of time to go over events. Mainly I thought about Ian: how much did we ever really know about him? The first time Jaz mentioned him was the Christmas after she started at the Rocket café. 'I met him on a protest, Mum,' she said, and when I told Phil he went, 'Of course she did.'

We thought we knew what was coming. The Sullen Boys, Phil used to call them, the thin, shifty youths who refused to meet your eye and slipped away upstairs the moment you paused to draw breath. The bedroom door would shut and you'd be crashing around in the kitchen, trying not to think about what was going on above. Couldn't believe it when Ian turned up in a shirt and tie, normal hair, voice like a BBC newsreader. His table manners were lovely. 'Were you protesting, too?' I asked him over the washing up. 'No, I was trying to get into my office,' he said. We were so busy admiring what he wasn't, we never thought to probe what he was.

And he seemed so kind. One time he came and dug out my pond while I was at work, for a surprise. I came back to find a moulded liner, like a giant tortoise shell, propped against the back fence. I love that pond. When I spied my first load of frogspawn a few months later, he was the person I rushed to tell.

Phil reckoned Jaz was the happiest she'd ever been, and we were happy for her. How much had we all invested in this charming, earnest, motherless young man, taking him into the family, knotting him into our hopes and dreams. The day Matty was born, I'd thought my world was complete, that everything was stable at last. Goes to show how wrong you can be.

Jaz had Matty that night, so it was a chance for me to catch up on jobs before I drove up to Chester library for a lecture on Clarice Cliff. The clematis wanted tying back before it snapped, and I'd some raffle ticket stubs to fill out and give back to Laverne, an outrageous estimated gas bill to chase up, plus my hair desperately needed a wash and blow-dry. I knew I'd have to scoot if I was going to make it out of the house for half-six.

The phone went while I was leaning over the bath side with my head under the shower.

I threw a towel round my sopping hair and ran to pick up.

'Carol?' It was David Reid.

'Yes; what?' I said abruptly, because once again he'd caught me on the hop.

There was a slight hesitation.

'Ian and I were talking at breakfast this morning. I gather you're acting as mediator.'

'Ahm, I suppose, yes.'

'He's very relieved. Jasmine's still not taking his calls.'

'No.'

'So what's been the reaction? Do you think we might be making progress?'

The towel was sliding to one side and cold water was trickling down the back of my neck. I said, 'I've not spoken to Jaz yet, but I'm seeing her for tea tomorrow and we'll talk then. To be honest, just at this—'

'Good,' he said, sounding like a headmaster. 'That's good. I'm so glad you decided to help.'

I felt a hot flare rise up inside my chest.

'*Well, someone's got to try and make something out of this mess,*' I said. Then I hung up and stood with my hand over my eyes for a moment. It wasn't David's fault; he hadn't deserved that. But then, what a bloody imperious thing for him to say. I was right, I was wrong. I was very hot, suddenly. When I looked across the room I could see myself in the mirror: *Middle-aged Woman in a Turban, Flushed.* You'd think I'd have learned by now to be wise and serene. I put my palms to the sides of my face and lifted the slack skin tauter.

The next second, the phone rang again.

I snatched at the receiver. '*Yes?*'

'God's sake,' said the voice of my ex-husband. 'No need to

be like that. I only wanted to ask what's going on with our Jaz.'

Too late now for Clarice Cliff, but I reckoned I could still make it to the gym if I put a spurt on. I needed to work out my temper on something. And to be with other women, have a giggle, listen to some music and get out from inside my own head.

Why didn't you tell me, Carol?

Because Jaz said she wanted a chance to think.

So how come she's just told me now?

I don't know, Phil. I don't know why Jaz would do that.

Upstairs, then, for my T-shirt and leggings. My trainers were supposed to be in the bottom of the wardrobe, but weren't. Were they by the back door? What was this? My top slipped off the hanger and crumpled to beggary—

Is she right?

What do you mean?

Has he been playing away?

Of course he has. He's confessed.

Fucking hell.

That about sums it up, yes.

A different top, then, with longer sleeves. That would be too warm, but no choice. At least the leggings were in an OK state.

What are we going to do?

I don't see what we can do. I'm looking after Matty.

You do that anyway.

Not this much. Everything else is on hold, I can't get on with my ordinary stuff. I'm not complaining, Phil, I love him being here. I just want it to go back to normal, for us all.

Answerphone on, trainers located and laced—

Have you talked to her?

Obviously I've talked to her, I've done nothing else for over a week. But she's confused at the moment. I think it has to come down to Jaz, whether she wants him back or not. Then we have to support her either way.

What do you reckon she should do?

Whatever she thinks is best for her and Matty.

Bottle of water, bottle of water, keys keys keys—

Ian's a shit.

Well, yes.

Keys. Coat—

And that's when the phone rang again, and it was Jaz on the machine, and this time I knew I wasn't going anywhere.

CHAPTER 5

Photograph 311, Album Three

Location: Chester Rows

Taken by: Carol

Subject: Jaz and Solange Moreau, school French exchange student, stand arm in arm, grinning. Solange is neat and minxy in her mini-skirt and boots: obviously French mothers are more liberal regarding their daughters' attire. Jaz is much more suitably kitted out in jeans, sweater and long, lime-green scarf. Next to them is Jaz's friend, Natalie, standing apart, looking suspicious. Behind them all is Phil. He's pulling the same stupid expression as the one in his school photograph of 1968.

Carol has enjoyed having Solange to stay: she is drawn by the girl's fractured English, and the fact that she's away from home at such a young age. And the attraction seems to be mutual. Not an hour ago, Solange produced from nowhere a lovely set of soaps bearing an impossibly expensive label, and handed them over. 'For my vacation mother,' she explains prettily. 'Well, aren't they beautiful?' says Carol, impressed. 'But you shouldn't have. However did you afford them?'

When Jaz translates, Solange laughs and laughs, as though it's the funniest line she's ever heard. Carol can't see the joke, and nor, judging by their expressions, can Jaz or Nat. Strange creatures, teenage girls. There's been a terrible atmosphere in the house for nearly two days now. She presumes they've had some kind of a fall-out. Whatever it is, it can't be Carol's fault, because she's bent over backwards to make the visit a success.

Not to worry. Solange returns to France tomorrow, and then everything will be back to normal.

Jaz said she'd gone to pick Matty up from nursery as usual, and he had not been there.

'It's all right,' she went on, before I could begin hyperventilating. 'I mean, he's with me now.'

She paused, and I could hear him chuntering in the background. 'Oh, God, love,' I said.

And she told me this: that while she stood shaking in the hallway, among all the little coats and bags, the nursery manager came with a message about Matty's daddy collecting him twenty minutes ago. No, he hadn't mentioned where they were headed. But Mr Reid had forgotten Matty's jumper, so maybe Mrs Reid could take it. Jaz hadn't waited to argue, she'd simply grabbed the jumper and dashed out onto the pavement, scanning up and down in case she could see Ian's car. For a few minutes she ran the length of the road and back again without knowing what she was doing. Then she gathered herself to ring Ian's number on her mobile. It took two goes before he answered, at which point he calmly told her to cross the street. So she did, and through the window of a grotty little café she saw them: Matty in a high chair eating a bowl of chips, Ian with a newspaper open in front of him. 'He *waved* at me, Mum, like it was no big deal.' When she went in, he invited her to stay and have a coffee with them. But she was too agitated to sit down. 'I didn't know where the hell you were!' she told him. 'You could have taken him anywhere.'

And Ian said simply, 'He's my son, Jaz. I can take him anywhere I want.'

My stomach flipped over when I heard that. Not just because I was annoyed with Ian for not waiting, for ignoring what I'd told him – *Don't confront her, don't corner her*, I'd said – but because of the implications. And I knew, before Jaz finished the story, exactly how she would have reacted. My throat got tighter and tighter as she told me what she'd said to him, there in the café while the other patrons sat and watched, while Matty played with his chips. All the words she'd been holding back, brooding over for the last few days, flooding out. Matty hearing it, breathing it in like poisonous smoke.

'What did Ian do?' I said at last.

'I didn't give him a chance to do anything. I picked up Matty and left.'

I saw in my mind's eye a howling toddler dragged from his chair and bundled into the car, Ian dashing outside, watching them drive off while Matty sobbed and kicked in his booster seat. It was unbearable.

'I was going to tell you, he came to the shop today.'

'That was bloody sneaky of him.'

'I don't think he knew what else to do. He was desperate to see you.'

'You sound like you feel sorry for him,' said Jaz, dangerously.

'I don't—'

There was a clattering noise in the background. 'Fucking hell,' Jaz said under her breath. 'Matty? Matty! Leave it. Come here. *Come here.*'

I said, 'Bring him round to mine, give yourself a bit of peace. Have a nice bath. Or I'll pop over now and pick him up. I can be with you in ten minutes. Yeah?'

Silence. I was picking up my keys again, ready.

'No,' she said. 'He's staying with me. From now on, I'm not letting him out of my sight.'

'Make the most of it while she's small,' people used to say to me when Jaz was young. 'The time goes by in a flash.' It's one of those mantras parents pass between themselves. I remember saying it to Laverne when her Josh was at primary school. I've come out with it in supermarket queues, to young mums waiting in the nursery foyer, to Mrs Wynne-on-the-other-side's granddaughter, to friends and acquaintances and strangers. I said it to Jaz and Ian six months in when they were beside themselves with lack of sleep. 'None of it lasts long,' I told them, 'none of these stages you're convinced will go on for ever. In the blink of an eye they're gone.' You get to my age, you suddenly feel the urge to warn everyone, to explain that you were there once, and you were left gaping at how quickly your children passed through. Even now I'll sometimes be clearing out a cupboard, or moving a piece of furniture, and I'll discover an object belonging to girl-Jaz. This can be an unexpected treasure, or an irritant, like the time a Kinder dragon got into the hoover and broke the roller mechanism. But other days such finds are a blade through the heart, and I could lie down and weep that this tiny sock no longer has an owner; that the milk teeth which made the marks on this discarded plastic spoon now live in my china cabinet inside a pot with a fairy on the lid. That moment when you go to take your child's hand, as you've done for years, and she shakes you off because she's too old: that's a killer.

Thank goodness for grandchildren, our second chances.

It was easier in the mornings without Matty, I had to admit. It wasn't just the dressing, the feeding, the clearing up – procedures which often had to be repeated, from scratch. It was the run to nursery that really stretched me. To get him there, settle him, unpack his stuff, come back, pick up Josh from next door, drop him outside the high school and be at the shop on time, I had to be out of the house by 7.45 at the latest. Any accidents, any tantrums or fevers or suspicious rashes, and we were all scuppered.

So although I missed him, it was certainly less complicated to have only myself to get ready. I got half an hour's lie-in, ate my breakfast at one sitting, listened to the news and managed a proper job with my make-up and curling tongs. Josh would be relieved too, I thought, to avoid all that last-minute rush. Or be forced to listen to Matty-anecdotes the whole journey.

He was sitting on the wall when I got outside.

'You should have rung the bell,' I said.

'Needed some fresh air.' He got to his feet and shouldered his sports bag.

Needed to get away from his mother, I guessed. Laverne was fine as a neighbour, but I shouldn't have liked to share a house with her. Small, stringy, artistic, over-attentive, she buzzed round her son's lumbering frame like a mosquito. Where was Josh's dad? I used to wonder. Not that I ever dared ask her. There was a brittleness there I didn't want to test.

'Mum OK to pick you up tonight?'

'Uh-huh.'

Laverne didn't want him going on the bus in case of what she called 'rough elements'. And since I drove past the school gates every morning, at exactly the right time, it was no bother to take him. He was a nice lad. Meanwhile Laverne would don a leotard and sweatpants and head in the opposite direction to teach dance at the Opel-Warner Studios. So I saw a fair bit of Josh, holed up as we were in my Micra every weekday morning, and I guessed he talked to me far more than he talked to his mum.

When he was twelve or thirteen he went through a phase of coming round a lot. He'd say he wanted to watch a particular programme but his mother had the TV on another station. Or he'd appear as I was cooking tea and cadge half a meal. At first I thought she wasn't feeding him properly – Laverne has a great horror of fat and fat people – but it wasn't always food he was after. Often he'd just sit in the living room with a drink of squash. 'You want to watch out,' Phil said when I told him. 'He's obviously got a crush on you.' 'Oh, obviously,' I remember saying. 'Because it's so normal for a twelve-year-old to fancy someone of forty-nine.'

It wasn't anything like that. The lad just wanted some peace. Which was fine by me, but I could tell Laverne wasn't suited, so in the end I knocked the visits on the head. He was all right about it; he knows his mother.

'What are you up to today, then?' I asked, as the car pulled out of the Close.

He pulled at his shirt where it had bunched under the seat belt. 'OK morning, triple-bad afternoon.'

'Not the Hungarian chemist?'

'Yup.'

'Is he really from Hungary?'

'Dunno. Round there. Transylvania, could be.'

'How are his teeth?'

'I try not to look.'

'Does he avoid mirrors?'

'I would if I had a face as ugly as his.'

'You really don't like him, do you?'

'Nope.'

We waited at the roundabout while a lorry carrying sheep crossed onto the Shrewsbury road.

'When I was at school,' I said, 'the teachers used to hit us over the knuckles with a ruler.'

'Oh, he'd use a ruler if he could get away with it.' Josh mimed a slashing action. 'He's bad enough as it is.'

We moved onto the bypass.

'Right, there was this one time, yeah, when he was showing us how we had to be careful with phosphorous. He had these tongs and gloves and he was making a big deal about how it burns your skin if you just touch it, like it's really corrosive. He got this kid he really hates to come up and pass him stuff, yeah, and then he asks him to hold his hand out and sticks this lump of phosphorous right in the middle of his palm.'

'Oh good God.'

'Except it wasn't phosphorous, it was something else, something that it didn't matter if you touched it, dunno what, but this boy didn't know. He just freaked: he was leaping about and screaming, shaking his hand, running to the sink, and the Hungarian was peeing himself laughing. He made all the other kids join in too.'

'That's appalling.'

'He said it was to make sure we remembered never to touch chemicals with our bare hands.'

'Well, I think that's disgraceful behaviour from a teacher. That boy's parents should complain.'

'It's not that easy, though. He'd just be even more of a git, I reckon.'

'Someone should say something.'

The traffic was getting heavier as we came into the middle of town. Knots of children in school blazers could be seen at intervals, crowding the footpath, calling to each other.

'We had to go in once and complain about a teacher,' I said. 'When Jaz was in Year Nine.'

'Yeah?'

'He tried to wriggle out of it, put the blame on her. But I knew.'

I clicked my indicator on and pulled into the side of the road, between two other parked cars. All Josh had to do from here was walk 400 yards and he'd be at the school gate.

'Never mind, hey.' He undid his seat belt and turned to reach for his bag. 'Come the revolution, they'll all be up against the wall.'

'Have a nice day,' I said to him as he climbed out.

'I won't.'

Which is how we always part. I watched him slouch away, then I stuck my indicator on, checked my mirror, and pulled out into the stream of traffic.

'I was thinking about Jasmine and Mr Woodhall,' I said to Dad. The room was so quiet that I could hear the ticking of the starburst clock above the door. Dad sat in a high-backed armchair, looking like a man who might be listening. Perhaps he'd noticed Matty wasn't there, perhaps he hadn't. 'Do you remember,' I said to him, 'that teacher who made her cry?'

I pictured a corridor on a darkening afternoon, harvest displays, a cleaner pulling a vac out from a cupboard, some of the classrooms unlit. *I have to ask*, Mr Woodhall had said, *is there anything going on at home we should know about? She seems like a very angry little girl at the moment*. And I went, *Well, of course she's angry! You made her share something you'd told her would be private*. He shook his head and pressed his lips together, slid Jaz's book across for me to read.

Dad gave a little cough, and at the same moment one of the care assistants appeared at the door to ask if I owned a V reg Astra. 'No,' I said. She went away.

I said to him, 'I feel as though I'm walking a tightrope. Ian's got every right to see his son, but it's saying that to Jaz. She's still beside herself, she can't think straight. I'm worried she'll set up a situation—'

Dad's fingers flexed briefly under mine.

'And you see, if I didn't work, I could have Matty for her all the time; she'd like that. She's always telling me about other people's parents who provide round-the-clock free childcare.'

I pictured the shop, and Moira. I loved driving into town every day, chatting to customers, Friday lunches at Healey's, going through the reps' catalogues. Then Mr Woodhall's face loomed across my memory again, triumphant: '*I take it you didn't really stab your husband to death and then take Jasmine to Disneyland afterwards?*'

I stood up quickly, still holding Dad's hand. He looked in my direction for a moment, as if to ask what I was doing.

'Breaking a dream,' I told him.

But the film played on. Mr Woodhall pushing the book across to me, the house point chart on the wall behind him a column of red stars, a jar of teasel heads on his desk.

'*How could you have made her read something like this out in front of everyone?*'

'*Oh, I can't make Jasmine do anything, Mrs Morgan. You should know that. No, she volunteered to share this.*'

I looked down at my father's scalp, the marked and uneven skin, the sparse grey hairs. If he would only talk to me, I'd not find myself falling into these thoughts. Don't pick up my gloom, I told him silently.

'Hey,' I said, sitting myself closer to him, 'remember how good our Jaz was that time I broke my arm? Wasn't she a love? Did all the shopping for me, came in from school every night and got straight on with tea. It brought out the best in her, being in charge like that. For that month she was smashing. It makes me wonder—'

'*What?*' another person would have said. '*What does it make you wonder?*'

And I'd have gone, '*Oh, nothing.*'

The clock ticked; Dad sighed. Jaz's childhood ran away before my eyes.

CHAPTER 6

Photograph 329, Album Three

Location: a fairground, Pwllheli

Taken by: Carol

Subject: a teenage Jaz swooping down in the seat of a ferris wheel, with Nat next to her, both mid-scream. Nat is leaning into Jaz and looks to be properly frightened; Carol guessed she didn't want to go on this ride but didn't dare back out. Jaz, on the other hand, knows no fear.

At the edge of the picture is the claw end of the giant inflatable hammer that Phil's been forced to carry all afternoon. Carol thinks she might wrench it from his grasp and club him with it, any minute now. Except that would be a comic gesture, and it is not a comic situation.

The whole holiday, they have been sniping at each other. The caravan they rented has acted like a microscope, hugely magnifying all that's wrong with their marriage. There somehow isn't the space to argue, and anyway, they can't in front of Nat.

Today has been the worst. Every time the wheel carries the two girls upwards, Carol and Phil start to row. By the time Jaz is at the zenith, they are all but spitting at each other. As she's lowered into view again, it's smiles all round.

As if their daughter's blind and stupid.

One day, Jaz thinks, she's going to meet someone to whom she can confide all this, someone she can totally trust. Someone who will never let her down.

I was going to dress up to see David: my blue skirt from Autograph and a cream blouse, heels. But then I thought, I can't be bothered with all that. I'm not being intimidated. Let him see me as I am.

Typically, the place he'd chosen turned out to be a hotel restaurant, not a pub. The waitress put us in a sort of conservatory, blond wood and sage fittings.

'I knew you'd wear a suit,' I said.

David looked surprised. 'I've come straight from work.'

'So have I.'

He made no comment. We can't all be property moguls, I felt like saying. Someone has to meet society's need for pot pourri and napkin rings.

'It's a tad pretentious here, but they do a decent lunch menu,' he said. 'Do you want to look at the wine list?'

'I'm not sure it's a good idea to add alcohol into the mix.'

'Why? You're not planning to shout at me again, are you?'

The moment teetered while I decided whether to take umbrage. That's why we've come to this place, then, I thought. Protective camouflage. I said: 'I didn't shout. Anyway, it depends.'

'On what?'

'On you.'

'I'll order mineral water.'

When it came, I let him pour. I asked the waitress for pasta, but I knew I was too worked up to eat.

'So,' he said, 'to business. What are we going to do, Carol? What practical steps can we take to help get Jaz and Ian back together? You are still agreed that's the way forward?'

'I think so. I don't know. Yes. In the long term.'

'OK.'

'No one can wave a magic wand here. He had an affair.'

'Not really an affair.'

'Yes, David. He slept with another woman. If you're not going to call a spade a spade, then we'll get nowhere. This is a complete waste of time.'

He looked down at his serviette. 'I'm sorry. That wasn't my intention.'

'You do believe it was a one-off?'

'God, yes. My son's not capable of any kind of sustained duplicity.' He made it sound almost like a failing.

'Do we know anything more about this girl?'

David shook his head. 'She's not important. Honestly. This – slip – was about a moment rather than an individual. We won't hear from her again.'

'Ian told you that?'

'He did, yes.'

'Forgive me,' I snapped, 'but it's a standard line. Adulterers tend not to go, "Oh, yeah, this is only the start, you ain't seen nothing yet".'

'All I can do is ask you to go with me on this.'

In the intervals between talking I could make out background music. 'Three Times a Lady'. *Love* stretched over five ludicrous syllables.

'I suppose,' said David, 'what I'm trying to avoid is any kind of hysterical reaction – no, listen a moment. It's important to keep a perspective.'

'Hard to have much sense of perspective when your husband's screwing around,' I said. 'I don't believe you have any idea how it's affected Jaz. She's absolutely crushed. Unless Ian understands what he's done—'

'Oh, he understands.'

'Does he? You don't seem to.'

The waitress came back and we both sat mutely while she moved cutlery around. Smile smile, we went, like a couple who'd come on a date or something.

When she'd gone, David said, 'All I'm trying to do is take the long view. After the immediate emotional reaction's died down there'll come a point where they see the bigger picture. When Ian's not consumed with guilt and fear, and Jaz isn't beside herself with anger.'

'And hurt.'

'And hurt. Then they'll start to see the shape of their marriage as a whole, and Matty's needs, and be able to weigh up the true impact of . . .' He faltered over the word.

'See? You can't even call it what it is,' I said. 'Who are you to start dictating the action?'

'For God's sake, Carol, haven't you been listening to a word I've said? I'm dictating nothing! That's why I'm here. So we can talk it through together, and agree. I want you on board with this. Without you, any reconciliation plan of mine simply will not work!'

The smart old lady at the next table looked across, and I felt ashamed.

It's your manner, I wanted to tell him. You sound like you're running an executive meeting.

'I appreciate you're feeling very let down,' he went on. 'Don't make the mistake of assuming I'm not. I know full well Ian's been a bloody fool.'

'Have you told him that?'

'Of course I have. He's under no illusions. I just don't think there's much to be gained from continuing to shout the odds. However natural recrimination might be, ultimately it's unproductive.'

'You're like a damn robot,' I blurted.

He blinked.

'Sorry,' I said.

Before he could reply, the waitress arrived and set our dinner down in front of us. I bent, shame-faced, over my cloggy pasta and wished I was back in Moira's shop. At all the tables around us, people ate and drank and had a nice time.

'If we can be practical for a moment.' David laid his fork down and looked at me. 'I'd say the most pressing issue's actually Matty.'

'Oh, it is.'

'He's really the prime consideration and, in a sense, our most useful bargaining tool. But we have to tread with extreme care.'

'Yes, I meant to say about that—'

'After the business at the nursery, Ian's very concerned about access.'

'Well, he shouldn't have wound Jaz up that way. It was asking for trouble. He was supposed to be waiting for me to have a word first.'

'He misses his son,' said David. Behind him, the window began to spot with rain.

'Yes, I can understand that. But he shouldn't have taken Matty with no word about where he was going. You hear about these men snatching their kids and emigrating with them. Or worse. Jaz was frightened. People react strongly when they're frightened.'

David shook his head. 'The way it happened was a mistake. He only went across the road. He was watching for her; when he saw her car he was going to step out and flag her down, but I think Matty needed his nappy changing at the crucial moment and he missed her arriving. I gather she was later than usual.'

'Don't make it sound like it was her fault.'

'I'm not. I'm explaining what happened.'

The waitress appeared, wanting to know if everything was all right. I could tell you a tale, I thought.

When she'd gone, I said, 'It was bad luck, then.'

'Yes. I think he had it in mind it was going to be a kind of reconciliation. Meeting on neutral territory, and with Matty there. She refuses to see him, you know; all Ian wants to do is apologise, but she won't let him. I don't see how they can move on.'

'You've already made that point,' I said.

It was getting Jaz to the state where she could talk rationally, make fair and sensible bargains. David hadn't a clue.

Afterwards we were ushered into a lounge area for coffee. We sat at opposite ends of a huge striped sofa, and I could tell from the way the waitress eyed me that she thought we were a couple: Love in the Middle Years. 'You're way off the mark there, pet,' I nearly said to her. Which started me thinking about Phil and trying to picture him in a place like this, how he'd stand out. Not because of his clothes or manners; he wasn't a yob. But he never picked up on atmosphere. He'd have been winking at the staff, asking for a diet water, sticking his forks into potatoes and pretending they were dancing feet.

'Did you know Matty's latest obsession?' I said, before my mind could get hijacked by unwanted images. 'His thing about doorbells?'

'Go on,' said David.

'Well, when you go to someone's house, he has to be lifted up to ring the bell. He gets very upset if you do it first.'

'What if there's no bell?'

'You have to pretend. He presses a moulding or something, and you have to go "ding dong" for him.'

'Thanks for the warning. I'll bear it in mind.'

'You get some funny looks.'

'I should imagine so.'

The coffee came in dolls' cups, together with a bowl of giant sugar crystals like shards of quartz.

'Do you take Matty out much?' I asked, picturing for a moment that suit in the muddy park, or under onslaught from an ice lolly.

'We've been out together, en famille. We generally go for a walk when I pop round to check the house.' He paused, frowning. 'You see, Carol, that's another issue: it's my house, I own it, and yet it's my son who's been kicked out. She's actually taken it upon herself to change the locks. I could be damned awkward about that, if I wanted to be.'

I took refuge in a sympathetic expression.

'Ian's very important to me,' he went on.

'Obviously.'

'I mean, having lost his mother—'

'Yes, I can see that.'

'For years it was just the two of us. A house of men. He's a good lad.'

'I think he does love Jaz.'

'Oh, he does, he does. If you can make her see that, Carol.'

'I'll do my level best.'

'Because this isn't a game. She really doesn't want to get into point-scoring. That's not meant in any way as a threat, I'm just stating facts. If Jaz starts being obstructive, she'll find Ian more than capable of matching her.'

I had to look away to stop myself saying, 'Why in God's name did he start all this, then?' What kind of men was I dealing with, in this father and son? How far could I trust either of them? Then again, what other choice was there? Across the room from us, on a matching sofa, was a smart elderly couple; he was fiddling with the clasp of her bracelet, and she was smiling over something he'd said. On our left two young businessmen studied a laptop. The tall windows sported swagged drapes; a chandelier hung from the centre of the ceiling. I really should have dressed up a bit more for this place. Had he meant me to feel outfaced?

'Anyway, to sum up,' said David's voice from a long, long way away, 'can I take it that you and I are, essentially, singing from the same hymnsheet? That you're willing to work with me in bringing about an eventual reconciliation? Would that be a fair assessment, Carol?'

'Yes,' I said faintly.

'Good.' He leaned forward and re-filled my coffee cup, even though I hadn't asked him to. 'Excellent. Because in that case, leave it with me. I think I might have an idea.'

CHAPTER 7

Photograph: unnumbered, loose in the back of Jaz and Ian's wedding album, Sunnybank.

Location: outside the church porch

Taken by: Carol

Subject: the bridal crowd, post-official photographs, but before everyone's gone in for the eats. Jaz is in the foreground, looking at Ian. Behind her is David, his eyes on Jaz, and in the opposite corner, Phil watches David. A fascinating range of expressions is covered in this string of vision.

Twenty minutes ago, Phil drew Jaz aside and told her a bald lie: that he overheard her new father-in-law say her dress looks cheap. Since the wedding dress is the only item funded exclusively by the bride's family, the slur is a double whammy. Where a different girl would have flounced off to tell her mother, or tackled David on the spot, Jaz absorbs the information into herself silently. That's always been her way. She internalises everything. The words spiral down through her consciousness like black ink dropped into a glass of clear water.

Why did you do it? Phil is already asking himself. He has no idea what prompted the invention, except that David's a smug bastard, and things have been so shitty lately with Penny sulking about him coming to the wedding, as if he wouldn't see his own daughter married, and bloody awful it was, too, leaving her this morning in floods of tears. Christ knows what she'll have done by the time he gets back. If he goes back. Funny, but living with someone turns out to be not at all the same as having an affair with them, and their flat's too cramped and none of his things are to hand. He misses his shed. And here's David swanking about with that smart bitch at his side.

He didn't mean to hurt Jaz. He never means to hurt anyone. Carol understands that. If he can find Carol, talk to her, it'll be OK. What he really needs at this moment is a pair of arms round him.

We always called it 'the shed', but it was almost the size of a garage, sturdy and brick-built and with a concrete floor. Phil used to reckon it had been a coal-hole-plus-lav, knocked through, but houses like Sunnybank came with internal bathrooms, so I think it was always a general outhouse.

Phil's kingdom, this had been, the place he retreated to when the atmosphere got too tense, or he felt outnumbered. When he reigned here, it was terrifically ordered: tools in one section, decorating materials in another, car stuff here, garden implements there. He installed metal shelves and kitchen base units, bought plastic boxes on wheels and racks that you screwed to the wall. The ceiling was high enough for him to board over half of it and use it to store miscellaneous junk, and woe betide anyone who ignored his system. Even his screwdrivers were lined up in order of size. 'I'll shift it all, I'll shift it,' he used to say. 'I'll come round and take my stuff away, just give us chance.' Eight years he'd been feeding me that line.

Since he'd gone, the place had become a dumping ground. Any item I was too unconfident to sling got shoved in the far corner with the rolls of wallpaper and paint trays. Then having to clear Pincroft generated a load more bags and boxes I couldn't part with, and that I didn't have the time or courage to sort properly. For months I'd been setting myself targets – a box a week, say – and then, at the last minute, I'd find myself putting the job off, casting about for something easier to do. Because the idea of getting rid of anything without Dad's permission seemed like the grossest act of betrayal. Breaking up your parents' home: it's a job that comes to us all, one of those rites of passage, and it's just horrid.

But today I was going to roll up my sleeves and make a start. Here was one area of my life over which I had some control.

I dragged in a patio chair to work on, unfurled three bin bags (Keep, Throw, Charity Shop), and set to on the first box. On the top were bundles of bone-handled cutlery wrapped in my mother's fancy tablecloths. I thought how many hours she'd worked at those cloths, how she'd taught me all the stitches one after another, stem-stitch and satin- and chain-stitch and French knots, separating lengths of embroidery thread and laying them across the arm of the sofa. Her Singer box of trimmings, braid and ribbon was in the second layer down, along with a Tupperware container of sewing-machine accessories, and her embroidery hoops I was always so afraid of cracking. Two nickel-plated candlesticks in the shape of leaping deer were next – they'd sat on the box-room mantel for as many years as I could remember – and then a plastic bag of recipe books, most of them fat with clippings from magazines and packet-sides. I let a page fall open at random: *Date Delights* said the article heading, above a marginal advert for Nostroline nasal spray. Might I, one day, be moved to cook a Date Delight? Or Cornflour Foam, Cheese-and-Rice Shape? It seemed unlikely. But to consign all her work to the wheelie-bin was unthinkable.

Further down the box there was a green dragon tea service, incomplete but lovely to see again, and also a Lustreware fruit bowl with a great crack through the centre. I held the bowl in my hands for a while, turning it this way and that to gauge how visible the damage really was. Too visible, I decided, but even then I couldn't bring myself to put it in the throwaway pile. That bowl had been on our sideboard throughout my childhood. I could see my mother dusting it now.

And then, towards the bottom of the box, was real treasure: two yellow Kodak envelopes. That meant two virgin batches of photographs, unviewed and uncatalogued. My heart gave a little jolt of anticipation. Another night where I'd be able to get the albums out and go through them, refining our family story.

The prints, when I opened the flap, were an out-of-fashion size, mean and small by today's standards. They weren't especially old ones, but then I wouldn't have expected them to be. Pictures of my girlhood were few and far between.

This first set seemed to be of a family barbecue in the garden here, with another, more random selection towards the back of the pile. Eagerly I pushed the shed door further open to let more light in, and settled myself against the work bench.

Phil's picture was at the front, a Phil with thicker hair and a sharper jaw-line, but the same easy, charming smile. 'Git,' I told him, and the word hung satisfyingly in the air for a moment. But even just speaking that one syllable started a little hot fizz in the middle of my chest. Thinking of your ex is like scratching eczema, a woman on *Oprah* once said. Let yourself get started, and you'll end up a terrible mess.

I slid the picture away to uncover instead a bright-eyed Dad with a very young Jaz perched on his knee. What age was she there? I could only dimly remember the hair-in-plaits phase; she was usually too impatient for anything other than a light brushing. Knowing Jaz, she'd have had those ribbons off minutes after the picture was taken.

The next photograph fixed the date more clearly, because it was of Mum, which had to mean pre-1986. And then it clicked: my thirtieth birthday. Which made Jaz five, Mum about to be diagnosed. Another year on and she'd be dead. I held the photo up to peer more closely. What I was looking for, I suppose, was whether there was anything in her face to show that she knew. Her eyes were slits against the sun, her mouth turned down at the corners. There was still no getting past that expression.

I put her picture to the back and carried on. More pictures of the party, the lawn in its pre-pond days, the kitchen before we had it extended, Dad actually lifting Jaz right up and swinging her round. And here was my very best friend Eileen – good God, Eileen! – raising a glass and obviously in the middle of saying something. 'Oh, I miss you,' I said, 'like you wouldn't believe. What I could tell you if you were still here.' *I know*, she went. *It's a bugger*.

I sat for a minute, holding the pack and thinking how fast twenty years can go. Some days I feel all ages and no age, as though I'm hovering over time, somehow. I can be back at school in a blink, with everyone I knew and all the same jokes and worries and obsessions. Astonishing how you can be the girl at the leavers' assembly – winking at your pals while the Headmistress drones on about the world awaiting you – and also the grandmother sitting on your own in a cramped shed sorting through the dregs of your dad's life. *Failure is a natural part of existence* (I could actually hear old Miss Wilson saying it, see the rope of beads swinging from her bosom), *but it's how we deal with failure that matters*. It's the only line of hers that's stuck; that and the one about strangers judging you by your fingernails. I always hear her voice when I'm rooting for an emery board. Eileen used to do a very good impression of Miss Wilson.

The packet began to slide off my knee, and that brought me back to myself. *Get your skates on*, said Eileen.

The last photo of the batch was me with Phil, our arms round each other. I had my hair in a bob with a side-swept fringe, and I was wearing extraordinary blue eye-shadow. Phil was puckering his lips as if for a kiss.

A slight surface unevenness caught the light and made me turn the print over: *Pretty Woman*, my dad had written, in his loopy hand. I never labelled my photographs, so seeing Dad's caption was a shock, like suddenly hearing his voice in the shed with me. Hastily I went back and flicked through to check for other hidden messages, but there was nothing more, which left me feeling both disappointed and relieved. What might he have written on the back of Phil's? I didn't want to imagine.

The next batch proved to be a strange selection: Jaz, older, about ten, on a grey horse (when had Jaz ever been on a horse?); two shots of a frog out of focus; a sunset; Jaz's best friend Natalie astride a gate, balancing on a milestone, hanging by her hands from a tree, pulling a nasty face; Jaz throwing herself about in a field; a black dog tied to the post of a rotary clothes-line; a yellow toadstool. 'Funny girl,' I said to the one of her dancing. 'What were you up to there?' As I went through the set again, I wondered whether Jaz had ever felt the way I did about growing up, or whether she saw her childhood as a distinct period which was now closed, a life compartmentalised into School, University, Before Matty and after. Pre-Infidelity, Post-Infidelity.

It struck me that I could call Jaz this evening and tell her about finding them. 'Shall I bring them round?' I could say. Or, 'Do you fancy popping over?' Important, this, because since the nursery incident she'd been too busy to see me. I knew the drill: left her alone, stayed occupied, kept off the phone, even though I missed Matty like hell. You have to give Jaz space, and then you have to supply her with an opening. It's the way she's always been.

I slid the photos back, put the envelope to one side, and carried on sorting.

The banging started as I was unrolling a teacloth of spoons. It wasn't clear at first what the noise was or even where it was happening. Only when I stepped out of the shed did I understand it was coming from the front of my own house. Thumping, violent thumping, as though someone was trying to break in. What the hell was going on? I ran up the path, rounded the corner, then stood and stared.

A big fat woman was kicking the bottom panel of my door.

No, not a fat woman: a pregnant one. Dorothy Wynne's grand-daughter, Alice.

Kicking because her arms were full of a limp child.

'It's Libby!' she shouted when she saw me. 'Something's wrong.'

I ran to open up, and she stumbled over the threshold and laid the infant girl down in the middle of the hall carpet.

'What's happened?'

'I don't know what to do,' she said in a rush. 'I went to wake her up from her nap two minutes ago and she wouldn't come round; she was all, like she is now, floppy, wouldn't open her eyes, and she's so hot. Look at her, she's burning up, she's red.'

The little girl's lips were parted and her eyelids closed but fluttery. Her cheeks were scarlet patches, as though someone had slapped her.

'Get her top off,' I said. I was thinking, We need to look for a rash.

Alice unzipped the little fleece and dragged it, with T-shirt and vest, up over Libby's face while I fed her arms through the sleeves. The child was completely unresisting. Her head lolled back like a baby's. 'How long's she been like this?'

'She was like it when I went to wake her. I went up and she was . . . her eyelids were all fluttery.'

'What about before?'

'Fine, OK, just normal.'

'Strip her completely,' I said. 'Underwear and all.'

There was a clattering on the step. When I looked up it was Mrs Wynne, leaning against the jamb with her stick. She was trembling and panting, and normally I'd have leaped up to usher her onto a seat. But not right now. Instead I bolted upstairs for Matty's ear thermometer. *Be working*, I told it, *be working*. The relief when I heard it beep and the digital panel lit up.

When I got back down, Alice had started to weep with fright. I could see at once, though, that the little girl's limbs and torso were white and unmarked. 'Shut the front door and take your grandma through to the lounge,' I said, because I could see Alice was in no state to hold a thermometer steady.

I helped her to her feet, and in the brief space the two women were out of the hall, I managed to take a reading. Libby's temperature was high, but not dramatically. I felt her tummy, and it was soft.

'What do you think?' said Alice from behind me.

'I think I've been here before. How old's Libby?'

'Five.'

'Jaz was younger, but I'm pretty sure it's the same. Listen, was Libby maybe a bit cooked? She'd plenty of layers on. Was her room very warm? I know your grandma likes the heating high.'

Alice gave a nervous giggle. 'Sweltering.'

'Then I suspect,' I said cautiously, 'it's what they call a febrile convulsion. If young children get too hot they can have these mini-fits; Jaz had a couple of similar dos when she was tiny. It looks scary, but it soon passes off.'

'Does that mean she's going to be OK?'

'You stay with her and talk to her while I get some warm water.'

I brought back two clean towels, plus a plastic bucket of Matty's which had been the first container to hand, and set to work wiping Libby down. 'You too,' I said to Alice. 'It'll cool her gently.'

Within moments, Libby had started to whimper, and then cry, a normal, blessed noise. Her mother's face crumpled with relief. 'Oh, sweetheart, sweetheart, shush shush, Mummy's here. I'm here, you're all right.' She scooped the naked child up and started to rock her.

'Obviously she still needs checking over, for your peace of mind as much as anything.'

'Yes, yes,' said Alice.

'Shall I call the surgery for you? I can run you down there, too, although actually a walk in the fresh air might perk her up. Do you want to pop her vest back on now? I'll go call the doctor's, and have a word with your grandma—'

'I'll do anything,' Alice broke in, 'if she's OK. Anything, do you know what I mean? If she's all right, if she's just all right.'

'Yes,' I said.

I left her rocking and went to phone the GP.

It was dropping dark by the time I got back from the surgery. It hadn't seemed right to send Alice on her own, and Mrs Wynne wasn't up to the job. 'Thank you, oh, thank you,' Alice kept saying, the way you do when you've been frightened out of your wits and then someone gives you the all-clear.

I stepped into the hall but I didn't switch the light on. I went and sat on the stairs and contemplated the stained-glass panels in the door. The colours at this time of day were muted and dusky, the dimples and surface imperfections highlighted silver by a porch lamp on the house opposite. Jaz used to trace the lines of lead with her fingertips while I was doing her coat up, handing over her schoolbag, nagging her to be careful crossing the road. A hundred thousand years ago.

'You were so calm,' Alice had said afterwards. And she'd put her hand to her pregnant belly and sighed, as though the weight of the world was across her young frame. 'You just knew what to do, and there I was flapping about in a panic. I suppose it gets easier, does it?'

In the gloom of the hallway I leaned my arm against the stair-gate and remembered the other times Jaz was ill: a dash up to hospital when she caught a chest infection at four weeks; chicken pox that revealed itself on the first day of a holiday; nights up with croup; a gash from a knife we'd told her not to touch; the Bad Time. I thought of a moment during delivery when the midwife announced the baby was in distress and they'd have to induce. And years later, that awful morning I went into her bedroom to wake her and she wasn't there.

Which was when the phone rang, out of the gloom. I got down off the step and picked up the receiver. It was Jaz.

'I tried calling earlier.'

'Ah.'

'But you were out,' she said, her tone accusing.

'That's right.'

'It was your afternoon off. I thought you'd be home.'

Headlamps passed. I thought of Alice, crouched here in this hall, rocking. 'There was a mini-crisis next door and I got involved.'

'Trust you, Mum.'

'Can I help it if people see me as calm and competent?'

She laughed, but not unkindly. 'Talking of crises,' she said.

'Do you want me to look after Matty?' I asked, my heart doing a giant leap.

'Yeah, if you could. I've lost a bloody filling and I need to get it sorted quick, but there aren't any spaces at nursery. They're so inflexible at that place, which is ridiculous when you think how much it costs.'

'Tell me when.'

'Tomorrow afternoon. Can you sort something with Moira?'

'I can swap a Saturday, probably. I'll give her a ring now but I shouldn't think there'll be a problem.'

'Thank God. This tooth's driving me nuts. I can't stop poking at it, even though it hurts like fuck. And coming on top of everything else—'

'I know.'

'Sometimes it's the little things that finish you off.'

'Don't worry,' I said. 'It'll be fine.' I closed my eyes and became part of the darkness. 'I'm always here if you need me.'

CHAPTER 8

Photograph: unnumbered, loose inside an old Bunny-Bons toffee tin, the shed, Sunnybank.

Location: the swimming pool, Stackholme Grammar, Bolton, 1968

Taken by: Mr Soper (Physics)

Subject: The swimsuited girls of 2A stand in a double row against a wall of mustard-coloured tiles. They have been told, time without number, how lucky they are to have their own pool on the premises; the poor children of St Joseph's have to be bussed all the way across town to the municipal baths. But the municipal baths are clean and modern, whereas Stackholme pool was built in 1912, looks like the annexe of a museum and feels, to those girls shivering in their navy costumes, like a walk-in refrigerator. Painted iron pillars ending in scrolled acanthus leaves hold up the ceiling, polished wooden benches line the sides. In the foyer, pictures of teams long dead hang on fraying string, behind speckled glass.

Rumour has it that their swimming teacher is really a man. Certainly Mrs Monks' arms are thick and beefy, and she has no obvious waist, but whether she shaves her chin every morning has never been established. Male or female, she's a bastard. Another rumour says she can't actually swim herself, but this turns out to be wrong.

One month before this photo is taken, Carol and her best friend Eileen's class is getting ready to practise crouching dives. There are twenty-five girls lined up along the length of the pool, and Carol is the last on the right, near the shallow-end steps. Mrs Monks' whistle shrills, echoes, and the row of navy swimsuits topples in like a Busby Berkeley routine.

It is Eileen, emerging further up the pool, who spots something is wrong.

'You should never have made her dive past the five-foot mark!' she says, as a dripping Mrs Monks lays Carol out on the side. The girls watch fascinated as bloody saliva spools from Carol's mouth and settles into the grooves between the tiles.

'She's fine,' snaps Mrs Monks. 'Go and get me some tissues.'

And Carol is fine, of course she is, good heavens. She's bitten her tongue so badly she won't be able to talk for a week, and one of her bottom front teeth is loose, but that's nothing, really. She needs to pull herself together. Wasn't she watching where she was going? There's no apology, no letter home to Bob and Frieda White to warn them of the possible after-effects of a blow to the chin. The only concession Mrs Monks makes is to allow Eileen to wait behind while they tidy Carol up.

'Cow,' says Eileen as they trudge across the rec together. 'If I hadn't been watching, you could have died.'

'Ugh,' says Carol.

'We should go see the Headmistress about it.'

'Gugh,' says Carol.

'Don't worry, though,' says Eileen. 'I'll always look out for

you, you can be sure of that. If you ever go under again, I'll know.'

All Carol can do is hold the paper towel to her lip.

It being a sunny day, I had Matty out in the garden with a washing-up bowl full of water and a selection of containers. Laverne's back door was open and she was playing some classical music – piano, very clean and sharp – which kind of went with the afternoon. Meanwhile Matty filled a margarine tub, poured it first into a roseless watering can, and from there into a colander. I stalked around him with my camera, crouching and rising by turns to catch the moment the silver stream fell, and playing with the shutter speed so that sometimes it was the water in focus and sometimes his face. His concentration was impressive; a Nobel physicist couldn't have been studying harder.

'Wish I was doing that,' said Josh's voice from behind me.

I took the viewfinder away from my eye and turned. He was leaning against the fence, looking like a boy with nothing to do.

'Be my guest,' I said. 'Matty won't mind.'

Josh's mouth twisted into something like a smile. 'I don't mean literally, like, on my knees with my hands in the water, yeah?'

'What do you mean, then?'

'I mean, I wish I was that age again. Sometimes. Like, when you've got no cares and everything's done for you, life's a doss.'

He stroked his smooth chin. Yes, I thought, I bet it's tough being a teenage boy these days.

'Not much freedom, though, Josh; that's the pay-off. He has to go wherever we go, eat what we put in front of him, stay in his cot till we lift him out.'

'Yeah, but. Freedom's overrated.'

'You only say that because you've got it.' Yet even as I spoke I pictured Laverne and the way she hung on him all the time, and how he didn't actually have much freedom at all, which meant that once again I was talking rubbish. *Mum doesn't say right out I can't do stuff*, Josh once told me. *She just makes me feel so guilty, I go off the idea*.

We watched Matty tip liquid from a height like a fancy Spanish wine waiter, then open his hand and drop the watering can in the bowl. Waves slopped over the plastic sides, and the paving stones around the base were stained in a jagged fan shape.

'What they do at school,' said Josh, 'is they try and splash your trousers while you're in the bogs, you know, at the front, then they can go round saying you've peed yourself.'

'Charming.'

'Have you got any washing-up liquid?'

'Why?'

''Cause you can put some in the bowl and give Matty a straw, yeah, and let him blow a load of bubbles. It's good, that. They go everywhere, you get like a mountain.'

'Nice idea, but he's too young.'

'It's not difficult. You only have to blow.'

'There's a good chance he'd suck, and then we'd all be in a mess.'

The image amused Josh, and he snorted with laughter. Before he could object, I'd brought up my camera and snapped him.

'Oy!' he said, shielding his face too late.

'Sorry. I couldn't resist.' I pressed review and brought up the picture on the screen for him. 'It's a nice one. I'll delete it if you want, though.'

He craned his neck. 'God. Do I look like that?'

'Like what?'

'Shrek.'

'You do *not* look like Shrek.'

'Colour me in with a green felt tip.'

I took the camera back. 'I'm not rising to the bait.'

At which point Laverne swept out. 'What bait would that be?' she said. She's got this way of holding her head up – a dancer's posture, I suppose. You could mistake it for snootiness. I know it's just tense muscles.

'Josh doesn't like having his picture taken.' I passed the camera across again. 'But I think he takes a good portrait.'

Laverne clutched the camera and stared at the screen for several seconds. After a moment she took a deep, intense breath. 'Oh, Carol, yes.' Behind her, Josh made a strangling gesture on his own neck.

'Shall I do you a copy?'

'Please, no,' said Josh.

'That would be lovely.'

'Uh-oh,' said Matty suddenly. 'Nanna, uh-oh.'

While we were admiring my composition, he'd taken the car sponge and held it above his head so that half a pint of water had streamed down his arm and soaked into his navy T-shirt. His torso gleamed like a sealion; he was sodden.

'Oops,' said Josh, and there was glee in his tone. I think he might have been expecting me to shout.

'Uh-oh indeed,' I said, looping my camera strap over a fencepost and going to inspect the damage. 'Good heavens. Where's all this water come from? Whatever are we going to do?'

Matty did his shrug sign, palms spread.

'His mum's going to be a bit fed up,' I heard Laverne say.

'Children should get messy sometimes,' I said over my shoulder.

'But he's drenched!'

'I've got spare clothes.'

'You think of everything.' Laverne sounded unconvinced by the argument.

'Of course. That's a grandma's job.'

I knelt down on the film of spilled water and began to peel away Matty's shirt, exposing his pale, rounded tummy. It didn't seem any time since Jaz had brought him home from hospital with the clip still on his umbilical stump; now his belly button was a smooth neat hole. Months passed like minutes.

'I remember when Josh was that age,' said Laverne.

I tugged at the waistband of Matty's trousers. 'How's that nappy going on, while we're at it?'

In the background, Josh made a disgusted noise, and a second or two later I heard their back door click shut.

I felt Laverne's eyes. 'Matty means the world to you, doesn't he?'

'Yes,' I said. 'He does.'

The garden seemed full of Laverne's presence, and for a moment I had the strongest impression it was Jaz whose eyes burned into me, observing, appraising.

I don't know why you clean the house more thoroughly for people you hardly ever see. Maybe it's because there's more chance of fooling them into thinking you lead a life of poise and order, whereas your regular visitors are too familiar with the truth. Whatever, I was burning round the house like a madwoman, shifting pockets of dust that had lain inoffensively for months. And as I went along, I thought of David's high-arched Victorian hallway with its parquet floor, wondered who it was got down on their hands and knees with a tub of polish every week to bring a shine to that. Then the picture became Mum and the way she used to clean at Pincroft: unnecessarily, in ways you'd laugh at nowadays. Every morning, all cushions taken outside and beaten, every door handle polished religiously, the front step edge chalked white with a donkey stone. When she dusted pictures, she'd to take them off the walls and do the backs as well. Beds were stripped to air daily, and each week she'd haul the mattress off its iron frame for brushing and turning. Up at six in winter darkness to clear out the grate, dragging sodden freezing sheets out of the top-loader and feeding them through the electric mangle; you could see why she was always tired. Then again, it's only what her own mother had to do.

I lifted the ornaments off the mantelpiece one by one: Matty's baby photo, Jaz's clay pot, Mum's Sylvac vase, Mum's Beswick budgie, the cigarette-and-match dispenser Dad had made himself out of oak in the days when he smoked. Always good with his hands, my dad. Then I ran the cloth over the buff tiles that Jaz hated so much (she'd cheered that time I dropped the poker and chipped the corner off the hearth, as if for one minute that would've meant getting new). Finally I put everything back again, remembering how there used to be a set of teardrop-shaped wooden mice at the window end that Phil had brought back from a so-called sales trip. They'd gone in the fire when I found out where he'd really been. All my life spread out on this bloody mantelpiece.

The duster I threw in the washing machine, then I went upstairs to make myself presentable. There was still an hour to go, so no point getting jittery. Except I was beyond jittery, already.

When I glanced out of the bedroom window I could see Josh and Matty on Laverne's neat back lawn. Matty was chipping at the grass with a teaspoon, and Josh was standing at the far end, running a remote-controlled jeep backwards and forwards. I leaned against the curtain for a minute and watched them, trying to slow my breathing and not think too much about the fact that Ian and David and Jaz were on their way here. 'They can sit down and talk things through; we can act as referees,' David had said. But 'referee' implied impartiality. I put my fingertips to my forehead and closed my eyes.

The doorbell rang.

'An hour, there's another hour to go,' I muttered as I ran down the stairs. A tall shape moved behind the coloured glass.

'I thought,' said David as he stepped inside, 'that if I got here early, we could go through our strategy together. Compare notes.'

'Oh, right,' I said. 'You'll have to give me a minute.' Then I fled back upstairs, leaving him standing there in the hallway. I'm not normally so rude; it must have been the shock.

In front of the dressing-table I rubbed foundation in at top speed, drew on my lipstick in a panicky sweep and dragged a comb through my hair. 'Referee,' I said experimentally into the mirror. 'Refereeing.' It sounded an odd word when you said it aloud.

When I came back down he'd taken himself into the lounge and was on his mobile. 'If you want,' he was saying, without enthusiasm. 'Not really. OK, then, whenever.'

He snapped the phone shut as I walked in.

'Clinching another property deal?' I'd spoken before I could stop myself. 'Sorry, ignore me.'

But he shook his head mildly. 'Just a friend. A complicated friend.' While I dithered over whether to ask, he turned and pointed to my gallery of Jaz photos above the bureau. 'That one's interesting,' he said, indicating the one of her peering through leaves, her hair hanging down, sunlight needling the green canopy behind her head. 'Was she an expert tree-climber, by any chance?'

'She was. Like a fearless monkey. I used to die a thousand deaths watching her.'

'You've got a good eye for composition.'

'I used to go to classes, up at the high school.'

He faced me again. 'Could I possibly have a drink, Carol?'

'Oh, of course. Yes. I should have asked. Tea? Coffee?'

David raised his eyebrows at me.

'I might have some red wine in the larder.'

'That would do it,' he said.

'I'll get a glass.'

'Aren't you having any?'

My first instinct was to say no, and then I realised I did want some wine, very much.

We sat in opposite armchairs with the buff-tiled fireplace between us and the bottle on the cold hearth. I noticed the way he leaned back, relaxed: a man at ease with himself. Meanwhile I could have run up the walls. 'You're wearing a suit again,' I said.

'Possibly more appropriate than an apron.'

'Bloody hell.' I dropped my gaze to my lap and saw gingham. 'You could have said.'

'I just have.'

I put my glass down and untied the apron strings.

'So,' he said. 'How are things with you?'

'Well, Jaz is still all over the place, but Matty's on good form. He's discovered the birdfeeder and he likes nothing better than to put bread out and watch the jackdaws squabble.'

'What about yourself, Carol? How are you doing?'

'Me? Gosh. You know! Staggering along.' I gave a nervous laugh, and reached for the first thing I could think of. 'In desperate need of a lawnmower, actually.'

'Oh?'

'Phil's taken mine – to fix, he claims – and shows no sign of bringing it back. But that's standard. I don't know why I expected anything else.'

'You seem to get on with him pretty well, though.'

What mad gremlin had made me bring my ex into the conversation? 'It depends what you mean by pretty well. You know how things were at the wedding. We're civil. We don't throw things at each other.'

'Better than me and Jacky, then,' he said. 'I lost a few plates to her before she left.'

Jacky gone? That was a turn-up for the books.

'I didn't realise.'

'About six months ago, now.'

'I always had you two down as suited.'

'Apparently not.' David raised his glass and stared through the wine, like a mystic. 'She said she wasn't happy, and then she went.'

'I'm sorry.'

'There's no need to be. I'm—'

'Seeing someone else?' I don't know what made me cut in like that. Nerves, probably.

'Well, I suppose.'

'Oh, great.'

'I don't know if it's that,' he said, oddly.

I imagined him at some dinner-party, surrounded by other suits and Jacky-lookalikes. Luckily his phone beeped as I was wracking my brains for an appropriate reply. He took the mobile out again, checked the screen, sighed, and switched it off.

'Anyway,' he went on, shifting forward in his seat. 'To the matter in hand.'

'Yes.'

'Starting from the point,' he said, 'that basically we want Ian and Jaz back together.'

'With the proviso he apologises, and that he never ever strays again.'

'Strays,' David repeated.

'What?'

'It's rather an old-fashioned word.'

I didn't like to say it was what Phil always used.

'But yes, obviously,' he went on, 'Ian's got to give. So has Jaz. Important, I think, for her not to end up using it as a stick to beat him with later on. Forgiving someone entails moving on.'

'Except it'll take time to get over.'

'Understood.' He put his fingertips together.

'The person who's most important here,' I said, 'is Matty. He's at the centre of all this, he's the one caught up in the middle. Matty changes everything. If it weren't for Matty—'

If it weren't for Matty I'd say to Jaz, 'Kick the bugger into touch. You don't want to waste your life on a cheat. Find someone who deserves you, or it'll eat up your self-esteem to nothing. Life's hard enough without being taken for a fool by the person who's supposed to be your number-one support.'

David nodded once, but I didn't know if it was in sympathy, or to check me. 'It seems to me, then, that if we can keep the discussion from getting too heated, and we can keep stressing the positives of staying together, then we should be able to make a little headway.' He paused. 'I know what you're thinking: easier said than done.'

'They're not going to walk out of here hand-in-hand, are they?'

'I never said they were. But maybe we can point them in the right general direction, or at least plant the possibility in their minds. You look doubtful, Carol. Don't be. We have to try. Someone has to get them off the starting blocks.'

'But what if we do more harm than good? Maybe we shouldn't be interfering. They're adults, after all.'

'Adults who've backed themselves into a corner and don't know how to get out. Adults who need our help.'

'Will it help, though? You don't know Jaz like I do; if you try to pressure her, she might go the other way out of sheer cussedness.'

'I think you're underestimating her.'

Underestimating my daughter? Mild as it was, the accusation sent me into a flurry of panic. What kind of a mother made such disparaging claims? Whose side was I supposed to be on? Appalling. And yet, Jaz *did* sometimes behave that way, and David needed to be aware of that. Was I wrong to warn him? For all he'd set this meeting up, had he really grasped the situation? Why should his approach be any better than mine?

From the garden came the sounds of Matty's squeals, Laverne's bright tones, faint saxophone music. Jaz would be taking Matty back home after this, whatever the result. His bag was packed and on the stairs.

'See, I believe Jasmine has more about her than that,' David went on. 'I've always had a lot of time for her. I like people who have something a bit unusual about them, not-your-average. She's clever, and she thinks for herself. It was a great shame she didn't get her degree in the end. She told me she was predicted a First.'

'That's right.'

'I'm not surprised. How long was she ill?'

I took a deep breath, because this was always a tricky question to answer. To measure the exact length of Jaz's depression, I'd have to be clear on when it began, and I've never got to the bottom of that. Sometimes I think it started before she went to university, in that lead-up to A-levels when I worried myself sick in case she was taking drugs, and Phil claimed it was hormones, or my fault, depending how well the divorce negotiations were going. At what point does moping about and general moodiness become a clinical condition? And, do you know, no one's ever been able to answer that for me.

I said, 'She came home from Leeds – she'd just started in her second year – because she said she wanted to change courses and they wouldn't let her, she was too far along. I can see her now: her face was grey and she had this awful rash round her chin. All she did for that first week was lie in bed. I didn't know what to do. It was the worst time, actually, because my dad had just been diagnosed with dementia and, to be honest, I was more focused on that. I thought Jaz was just a bit down.' *I thought Jaz was being self-dramatising and lazy, and heaping pressure on me for the hell of it.*

David was watching me closely, as though he could see the big cloud of guilt gathering over my head.

'But she was officially diagnosed?'

I nodded. 'Not for a while, though.' I'd stood in her bedroom doorway and yelled at her to get up and shape herself. Me, her mother. 'If she'd got help sooner . . .'

'She was recovered by the time she met Ian.'

'Oh, yes. She was working, in the Rocket café. Now a tanning salon.'

'I dimly remember it.'

'It only lasted two years. Too far off the High Street, and vegetarian wholefood's a niche market round here anyway. But she did like the place, she got on well with her colleagues. Then again, she enjoys being a freelance translator; she can pick her own hours, take on as much as she feels she can cope with. It leaves her more time to do other things.'

'She has a lot of friends?'

Again I hesitated. Jaz's friends. I wasn't about to go into that business during her teens when she claimed she was being bullied, and Phil and I marched round to the school only to be told that Jaz herself was one of the perpetrators. 'Six of one,' the Headmistress had said, 'and half a dozen of the other. A – well, a boy – some silly gossip, I'm not entirely clear what kicked it off, but I'm not taking any action against individuals. In my experience, these things usually work themselves through without too much adult intervention.' After that, Jaz didn't go out so much, and you'd not to mention certain names in her hearing. Nights I lay awake, worrying. 'I thought you wanted her to stay in more,' Phil had said. Which shows his grasp of the situation.

'Her best friend's Natalie,' I said to David. 'Nat. The one who was chief bridesmaid.'

'Ah yes.'

The sort of girl who's pleasant to your face and flicks Vs behind your back, I could have added. Who'd laugh if you fell over and hurt yourself. Who – and I'll never ever forgive her for it – played dumb the time my daughter ran away. Standing there in her school uniform, shrugging at me, looking at the floor.

I said, 'She's quite different from Jaz, but they got together at primary school and they've been pals ever since. So I suppose you could say she's a loyal girl. She works as a receptionist at a garage on the industrial estate.'

'It bothers me sometimes,' David broke in, in a way that made me realise he hadn't been with me for the last few seconds, 'that Ian's rather isolated. He didn't keep in touch with his schoolfriends when he went to Bristol, and then he didn't keep up with the Bristol lot either. He socialises with people from the office. I've told him, it's not ideal.'

Blimey, speak your mind, I thought. I'd never dare say that kind of thing to Jaz.

'Well,' I said, 'I do think you need a best mate. It's part of who you are.'

Then I heard Eileen's voice going, *Remember Bentham's Outfitters?* and I was back there with her, standing by the changing rooms in our school uniforms, and making faces at the ladies as they peered out. Our rule was, all the ones who looked a sight, we gave the thumbs up, big smiles, encouraging nods. To all the ones who looked nice, we'd fake dismay or horror. Eileen had gone so far as to imitate being strangled. One giant woman in purple satin we wolf-whistled. It took an elderly lady in a neckbrace to stop us. 'Who do you think you are?' she hissed. 'You should know, that lady you're laughing at has a degree in Biochemistry.' 'Yes,' said Eileen, 'but she also has a moustache.' Then we'd legged it. Your friends aren't just important for now. They validate your past.

'But it's harder for young people today,' I said. 'Making proper friends. Somehow they don't want to lose face, they take themselves so much more seriously. Get to my age and it doesn't matter as much. You don't care. I'll talk to anyone, me.'

'That's because you've got natural warmth.'

The compliment, coming out of nowhere, caught me on the hop, and I felt myself blush. But before I could flounder, David stood up.

'On your marks,' he said. 'That's Jasmine's car. They're here.'

CHAPTER 9

Photograph 290, Album Two

Location: Jaz's bedroom

Taken by: Jaz

Subject: hamster Mojo's monument, restored after some nocturnal disruption by cats or foxes. Carol has donated a clump of snowdrops, together with a sneaky clove of garlic pushed into the soil, which she hopes will deter grave robbers.

The day Mojo dies, Jaz, ten, announces, 'I'll never smile again.' And for a week afterwards, Carol fears it might be true. Never has a rodent been so mourned. At the weekend, in desperation, Phil marches to the pet shop in town and buys a new hamster, a baby Russian Dwarf the size of a kumquat and almost obscenely cute. Even the woman behind the counter clucks and coos as she pops him in his little carrier. Jaz will be delirious. What child wouldn't be?

When Phil and Carol call her down to see, they are united in confident anticipation. The tiny creature is sitting in his dish, quivering.

Jaz stalks over, takes one look, turns and flees back upstairs. When her mother goes to investigate, all Jaz will say is, 'It's not Mojo.' 'Mojo wouldn't mind,' says Carol. But Jaz isn't for budging. There's only room for one hamster in her heart. Mojo was the one, and no other will do.

To say the pet shop is not keen on returns is an understatement, but when Phil threatens to set the animal loose in the precinct, and Carol explains they aren't after their money back, the owner relents.

'Any normal kid would give their eye teeth for one of them little furry buggers,' says Phil as they trudge back home. 'Not our Jaz, though, oh no. Nothing so straightforward. You wouldn't credit it, would you?'

I would, actually, thinks Carol, but sensibly decides to keep her mouth shut.

'Come in, come in,' David went, sweeping the door open. I felt a little flash of irritation as he nodded them past, into the hall: whose house was this?

'We're in the lounge,' I added.

Jaz was looking better than I'd seen her for a while. She'd tied her hair back and put a skirt and jacket on, almost like someone attending a job interview. Ian, on the other hand, looked ill. 'Carol,' he muttered as I took his coat from his thin shoulders. I touched his arm briefly, furtively, then moved away before he could show any kind of reaction.

'Can I get anybody anything?' I said.

'We're fine,' said Ian.

'Drink? Tea, coffee, glass of Merlot?'

'No, we're fine.'

'Something to eat?' I couldn't seem to stop myself.

'Mum,' said Jaz.

We positioned ourselves round the room like the Stations of the Cross.

'So the reason we're here,' said David, compère for the

afternoon, 'is to talk through how you move forward from this – from this. Whether or not you decide you want to stay together, or part, we want to provide an opportunity for you both to have your say. So you know where you stand.'

Ian's face was set and pinched with acceptance, but Jaz sprang up out of her seat, immediately on the defensive. 'I thought we were just here to discuss access rights,' she said, looking from one of us to the other. 'I'm sorry, that's the only reason I'm here. Not for any kind of reconciliation. Mum?'

'Well,' I said. 'It can't do any harm. Since you're here.'

Can't it, said the expression on her face.

'Please,' said Ian. 'Please, Jaz, just let me talk to you.'

I wondered what the three of us looked like, poised on the edge of hope, while we waited for her to deliver her verdict.

David said: 'Don't you want the chance to tell Ian exactly what he's put you through? Don't you think he should hear it?'

Her face worked as she considered. After a few moments, she sat, but grudgingly. 'He knows,' she said.

'I don't believe he does,' said David. 'Not really. Only you can tell him that. Isn't there anything you want to ask him?'

When she didn't reply, he carried on.

'My plan was to create a safe forum, if you like. To let each of you speak for two minutes, uninterrupted, and say what you feel most needs saying. And have us here for back-up.'

Let each of you speak? I was thinking. It sounds like bloody speed-dating. She'll never buy that. Any second now, she's going to swear in his face.

'Neither of you must interrupt the other,' he said. 'That's essential. The person speaking has the floor, but for two minutes only. That should mean the most important things rise to the top – all the rest of it, you can deal with in your own time. But it's the most productive starting-point, trust me.'

To my utter amazement, she did.

'So you mean, get him to face up to what he's done.'

'I have faced—' Ian began, but David waved his hand.

'Just give it a shot.'

Something passed between them, which Jaz missed because she'd closed her eyes and was pulling her hands through her hair. I knew she was gearing up for an outburst. David had no idea what he was about to unleash.

'Jaz?'

'Is it my "go", then?'

'It is.'

'Right,' she began, her hands still busy. 'Right. OK, OK. I can't *get* why you did it. I mean, I *can't get* it. What in God's name did you think you were doing? When you had everything you wanted, I can't— Was she pretty? Was she worth it? Was she a *good fuck*? Because, you know, everything's ruined now, everything's gone, you've thrown everything away so I fucking hope she was worth it, and I swear to God if I ever *ever* meet that bitch I'll tear her fucking face off, then we'll see how she does stealing other people's husbands, sad fucking *cow* who can't get a proper boyfriend of her own.

'Did you not think? Did you not stop for one minute and think about me? About Matty? Everything we've been through together, that time you had those chest pains and you thought you were fucking dying, and I was running you up to hospital and you were practically making your fucking will in the car. And when I told you I was pregnant, and you *cried* because you were so blown away by it, and you said how you'd never truly been happy till you met me.

'And I could understand it – no, I couldn't understand it, but I could maybe get my head round it more if it was definitely just the once, just a complete one-off, but *how do I know?* Oh, I know what you *said*, but that counts for nothing, does it? Fucking damage limitation's all you're concerned with now.

Trouble is, as soon as you start lying to people, they stop trusting you, yeah? I'll never be able to believe another fucking thing you say. Any time you're late home, any time you're – anywhere. How could you not have thought that through? And me and Matty, and everything we had – how could you have blanked it? Was she so fucking fantastic that *the whole of the rest of your life went out of your head?*'

Ian had his fist against his mouth, and at that point he took his knuckles away and made as if to speak, but Jaz carried on.

'Do you not think *I've* had offers? Look at me. Look at me! Men are always coming on to me. That bloke at the garden centre who delivered the planters, I virtually had to push him out the door, he left his number and everything. The guy at the garage with the earring, he always chats me up. I could have an affair tomorrow if I wanted. But I wouldn't. See, that's the difference. I took my wedding vows seriously.'

'*I* did,' Ian began. 'It's—'

David's hand came up, warning. 'Let her finish.'

For a moment Jaz sat with her head bowed, hands clasped in her lap. Then she said in a flat, soft voice, 'I can talk for ever, but it won't change anything. You've ruined us. We can never go back. You know that, don't you? It's over, and it's your fault.'

After that there was a horrible silence. I could hear my heart thudding in my ears, so loud it must have been audible to everyone else.

'Can I speak now?' said Ian.

Jaz shrugged. 'I've nothing more to say.'

'Go on,' said David.

Ian shifted, cleared his throat, ran his hand across his brow. 'I'm not sure I can do this,' he said at last.

'Oh, get on with it,' said Jaz.

He held his palms upwards, defeated.

'I've gone over and over it in my mind, all the time you

wouldn't speak to me. Sitting there in the car with you, trying to hold it all back, and now I don't know where to begin. What can I say?'

'Sorry would be a start.'

'Of *course* I'm sorry!' The words exploded out of him. 'How could you think anything else! Sorry? There's not one minute goes past, not one second when I don't wish like mad it hadn't happened. I know I've done wrong! I know how hurt you are! God, if I could turn the clock back, I would do anything, anything for it not to—'

'That makes two of us, then.'

'—been trying and trying for weeks to apologise and make things right again but you wouldn't let me.'

'Because what is there you can say, Ian? How can you possibly make it OK again? That's what I've been telling you.'

'Then I might as well give up now.'

It was shocking to see this white-faced young man staring at Jaz with his jaw clenched and his breathing fast. A stranger in my house.

'No,' said Jaz. 'I want to hear anyway. *Explain to me* what you thought you were doing. I want to hear *every* detail, *every* step. I have to hear it.'

Oh, love, I thought. You don't.

Ian swallowed. 'It was nothing. It meant nothing. She was nothing. She is nothing.'

'So *why*?'

'Because. Because. What it was – she – it's hard to know how to—'

'Jesus!'

'Let him speak, Jasmine.' David twisted at his cuff. 'Two minutes. You had your time, now let him.'

'Fuck your two minutes,' muttered Jaz, but David ignored her.

'I will explain,' said Ian. 'But I can't do it in front of everyone. It has to be in private.'

I was on my feet in an instant, ready to leave them to it. David, though, stayed where he was. 'As long as you get your say.'

When no one spoke, he stood up, unfastened his watch and handed it to Jaz.

'Here,' he said. 'You'll need this. It's got a second hand.'

I couldn't believe the boldness of the gesture, but she took it from him.

We left the room as swiftly as we could, and closed the door behind us.

From the kitchen we could see Laverne hanging out her washing, and further down the garden, the top of Josh's head. I guessed by Matty's shrieks that the remote-controlled jeep was still in play.

David came to stand next to me at the window.

Without looking at him I said: 'It really is no good pushing Jaz into anything. If she feels cornered, she becomes very unpredictable. Softly softly catchee monkey, it has to be with her. She's been that way pretty much since she was a girl.'

He nodded. 'And my son's always been – what do they call certain metals? – ductile. Does as he's told. Just as well, given the circumstances of his upbringing.'

A sudden breeze flapped Laverne's sheets. I watched the surface of my pond shiver and tried to picture Ian as a boy.

'Has he told you why, yet?'

'Why this other woman?'

'Yes.'

'Not really.'

'Have you asked?'

'Of course. But it's difficult for him. I'm not sure he can

articulate it properly. I suspect simple opportunity played a part—'

'For God's sake! Are all men like that?' I snapped.

David moved away from me and sat down at the table. 'Well, I was never unfaithful to my wife, if that's what you mean.'

Bloody hell. 'I didn't mean you, I wasn't thinking of you. The way it came out was wrong.'

'Forget it. Really. I think we're all pretty wound up, aren't we? How about putting the kettle on? I could do with a very strong coffee.'

It was good to be given an everyday task. As I got the cups down, fetched out teaspoons, filled the sugar bowl, I tried to listen for any sounds from the living room. If Jaz and Ian were arguing, their voices would carry. But there was nothing. I flicked the water on to boil.

'Busy lady.' David pointed at the wall calendar hanging up on the larder door.

'You don't have to tell me.'

'Beavers is for, remind me?'

'Six-to-eights. Cubs eight to ten. Scouts after that.'

'Are you an Akela, then, or whatever they call it?'

'No, just general dogsbody. Orange squash-pourer, provider of fairy cakes, that sort of lark. They have so many rules now about adult-to-child ratios. I step in when they need an extra body.'

'Woggle at the ready?'

'I don't qualify for a woggle.'

'Bad luck. How did you get involved? Jaz wasn't a Beaver, was she?'

'Can you imagine Jaz joining any sort of organised brigade? No, it was the lad next door.' I came over and set the mugs down in front of him, and that's when I saw he was smirking.

'Well, actually, the joke's on you, David Reid, because these days girls can join Beavers if they want to. It's equal rights.'

'What – and boys Brownies?'

'I suppose so. Though I'm not sure there's a vast take-up.'

'Strange times we live in.' He lifted his coffee to sip, and paused.

'What?' I prompted him.

'Occasionally I have trouble negotiating this modern world of ours. I don't know if you ever feel that way, Carol.'

Just lately, all the time, I thought. David, there are mornings I wake up and I hardly dare get out of bed for fear of what the day holds. But I could tell he was trying to keep it light, so I said: 'Josh next door's always having to explain things to me. He comes out with all this stuff, and I'm sitting there trying to make sense of it. Once he said he was having a Wii for his birthday and I almost crashed the car. Because when words change their meaning, no one tells you, do they? They should have it on public information films, stop you getting yourself into bother. Mind you, at least I never went round calling people a wanker like my mother used to do. She thought it was a pet term, like "little tinker".'

'Good God. What did she say when you told her?'

'We never dared. The shock would have killed her.'

David drank his coffee and we both strained our ears for the sound of shouting. The longer this lull went on, we were thinking, the more hopeful it was.

'I do worry about what sort of world Matty's growing up into, though,' I said. 'When I was young – and I know that makes me sound about ninety – people knew where they were, somehow. The lines were drawn and you hadn't to cross them, and everyone benefited from that. Or so it seems to me.'

'I agree.'

'There are too many choices these days. I think that's at the root of it. People think they want choice, but if they have too much it can make life over-complicated. And then they're always looking over their shoulder, thinking should they have done this or that, and comparing other folk with where they are, what they've got. Which makes them dissatisfied and restless. Sometimes it's good just to be told what to do.'

'Well, it's human instinct to strive for freedom,' said David. 'But I know what you're saying. Somewhere there's a golden land between PC madness and the bad old days of forelock-tugging and trial by community.'

'I think we had it. I think that was our youth.'

There followed a silence which, under different circumstances, might have been companionable, but we were both too keyed up. I opened my mouth to speak – not sure what I would have said – but as I did so I saw something through the window that made me turn and look out. I was just in time to see my clothes prop, swayed by a powerful blast of wind, slide away from the washing line and fall with a metallic clatter across the pond. The top section struck a plastic planter which would normally have been stable enough, only I'd propped it up on a couple of bricks so the rim showed above the tops of the reeds. The planter toppled sideways, and lodged against a stone pot, spilling soil into the water.

'Timber,' said David, following my gaze.

All my mind could see for a few seconds was a sequence where it was Matty beneath the pole. If Matty had been in the garden then, if he'd been playing in the reeds just there . . . I stood and stared at the spot.

'Are you all right, Carol? I don't think there's too much damage. Shall we go and see?'

I took myself over to the door and opened it. The air was fresh and clean on my face, but the vision lingered.

'Do you want a hand?' asked David.

'No. I'll just go and right that planter. Won't be a mo.'

As soon as I was outside, my hair whipped around my face and my blouse flapped against my sides. The leaves of Laverne's aspen shimmered above the fence like fish scales. I picked my way across the long lawn and walked round the path to where the damage was. When I got close I could see the planter had cracked at the rim, creating a lip through which dark compost trickled, but was otherwise intact. No stems were broken, no flowers had come off. So I bent down and pulled the pot upright, patted the lobelias in securely, then set it back on its bricks. Then I knelt to sweep up the crumbs of earth. The water in front of me was cloudy with a film of particles across the surface, but that would soon break up.

I stood again and looked back at the house. Through the patio doors I could see Jaz and Ian; I didn't mean to spy, but I couldn't help myself. Jaz I made out fairly easily. She'd changed seats, and was now opposite the fireplace. I couldn't see Ian at all. Suddenly he moved and I realised he was crouched at Jaz's feet, like a man about to propose. They were too far away for me to make out any detail.

My chest went tight with hope and anxiety. So much hung on this afternoon, more than I thought I could bear. I flicked my gaze across to Laverne's, but her lawn was now deserted and her windows were dark. I knew they sat in the front to watch TV, and that's probably where Matty had gone. Back in my kitchen, David got up and began to pace about, his hand to his ear, his head cocked. Man on mobile. All of them seemed very far away. I knew I ought to go in, but I couldn't do it. Instead I stepped up to the fence and leaned against it, not caring about mildew marks or splinters.

'Come on, love,' I whispered. 'Come on, Jaz. Move it forward. Be brave.'

The light was changing around me, the afternoon turning

towards evening, and everything in the garden seemed very sharp and clear: the rags of dandelion leaves at my feet, the shrivelled heads of last year's lilac, the yellow-brown knuckles on the horsetail stalks. Once Jaz built a den in this section, resting the back panel of a wardrobe against the post and incorporating the side of the shed as one wall. I remembered her ferrying picnic cutlery and paper plates across the grass, and later having a major sulk at me because I'd said she couldn't use one of my pillows outside. It didn't feel like that long ago, but it was almost two decades.

Which made me think of what David and I had been discussing, about our generation having had the best of it, and that started a series of images falling like dominoes. Grass-sledging on an old door down Latimer's Bank; Eileen secretly drawing faces on the bananas in the school Harvest display; a yellow skirt of mine with white ric rac braid round the hem; Phil in his first work suit, a brown creation with huge lapels. I thought of the first time Phil asked me out, how he'd leaned against our gate at Pincroft whistling 'Maggie May'. How had I got here, to this point? Standing in my own garden, afraid to go in. And I wondered what David's youth had been like in comparison, and whether he'd always been so self-assured, and how we'd have got along if we'd known each other then. I was just trying to imagine what his wife might have been like, when the scene in the living room changed.

David took his hand away from his ear and looked round, as though distracted by a noise. Seconds later, Jaz was on her feet, Ian leaning sharply backwards to get out of the way and then he was up too, and both of them were waving their arms. I saw David slide his hand into his pocket, glance towards the living-room door and then turn to face the garden, searching for me.

I came out from the shelter of the fence and hurried back along the path. As I drew nearer I could make out Jaz's face; it had that chiselled look she gets when she's beyond all that's rational, and my heart sank. Ian had his back to me by then, but his gestures looked like pleading ones.

I wrenched at the door handle and slipped back inside the kitchen. There was no need to say anything. David shook his head at me and we both stood there listening to the row. After a while he walked across and put his hand on my shoulder, and the gesture brought tears to my eyes.

'Should we go through?' he said. 'I think we should go through.' Then he looked down at my face. 'Oh, Carol,' he said, and I let myself fall towards him to be held, just for a second.

That's when the living-room door burst open and Jaz flew in.

'Get him out!' she was shouting. 'Get him out of here! Get him out of this house!'

'Right, now, come on, calm down. There's nothing to be gained by all this shouting,' David began, letting me loose. I saw his chin go up assertively, and thought even through the chaos, Here's a man who's used to people listening to him. But I knew that tone wouldn't work with Jaz.

'Hey, love,' I said.

'Get him out!'

Ian appeared behind her. 'I didn't mean it like that,' he was saying. 'Please, Jaz, you know that's not what I meant.'

'*Get him out!*' She put her hands over her ears and screwed her eyes shut.

'Let's all take a short break,' said David.

'No,' I said. 'I'm sorry, David, that won't do it.'

'What, then?'

'I think Ian had better go. For now. We can re-group later.'

'Please, oh, God,' said Ian, though it wasn't clear who he was addressing. It wrung me out to hear him.

I went to put my arms round Jaz and she was stiff as a board. 'Sorry,' I mouthed to the others.

David stood for a few seconds, then nodded at his son. 'Get your coat.'

They shuffled round us into the hallway, David steering Ian as though he was dealing with an invalid. Over the top of Jaz's head I watched the two men, one tall and skinny, the other slightly shorter and thicker-set, and it reminded me of a war film I'd caught on TV a week ago, where the Captain led his shattered men to safety. David hauled their coats off the newel post and opened the front door. I was waiting for him to turn and say goodbye, but he didn't.

CHAPTER 10

Photograph 337, Album Three

Location: the hallway, Sunnybank, Shropshire

Taken by: Carol

Subject: Jaz, the evening she turns fourteen, with Nat. Carol's driven them to Manchester and back, because this is the birthday treat Jaz requested months ago. She wanted to go clothes shopping with her best friend, asked for no presents but money.

Initially the girls' plan is to go alone, on the train, but Carol puts her foot down. It's too far, they're too young. 'Quicker if you go by car,' she says. 'More time for the shops.'

A good argument, that, and the girls concede the point. It's not like they have to go round with her. Mrs Morgan can look in Lakeland or something, while they buzz off and have fun.

When they get to the Arndale, though, it becomes clear that Nat at least wants to stick by Carol's side. 'What do you think of this, Mrs Morgan?' she keeps saying, riffling through one clothes rail after another. 'Do you like that?' Carol can't see any of the garments suiting either of them: a baby pink cardigan with pom poms at the neck; tweed jodhpurs; a fringed velvet cap. Meanwhile Jaz casts longing looks across the atrium and sighs loudly.

When at last Jaz says, 'Are you coming, or what?' Nat claims to have period pain, and says that she must go somewhere she can sit down. Carol spots her cue. 'We'll meet you in River Island at twelve,' she tells her daughter. Then she takes Nat to a café, installs her behind a hot chocolate, and asks her what's going on.

Nat's sulky little mouth turns down even further.

'Come on,' says Carol, trying not to be irritated.

'She hates me and I don't know what to do,' says Nat.

'She doesn't hate you,' says Carol.

'She does,' says Nat.

It transpires that the casting list went up yesterday for the school play, and Nat's been the bearer of bad news. Jaz is not to be Eliza, nor even Mrs Higgins or Mrs Pearce. She's an Ascot lady – one of the crowd, merely.

'Did you get a bigger part than her?' asks Carol. But no, that's not it. Nat isn't even in the play.

'She really, really wanted to be Eliza,' says Nat. 'I think she's cross with me because I was the one who told her.'

'But that wouldn't make sense,' says Carol.

Nat gives her a look that says, Boy, you can be thick at times.

'Well. She'll get over it. Don't fret. You're her best friend,' says Carol.

'The problem is, I like Jaz more than she likes me,' says Nat, with a rare flash of perception.

'Nonsense,' lies Carol.

On the drive home, the atmosphere is better. Her lap laden with carrier bags, Jaz is starting to thaw. By the time they're on the motorway, it's grins all round. Carol glances from time to time in the mirror. Every day, it seems, her daughter becomes another degree less fathomable.

*

We'd taken a jigsaw with us this time to keep Matty occupied: coloured dogs that fit into matching slots on a board. Each dog had a wooden peg through its middle and an expression of injured surprise on its face.

I put Matty down on the carpet, Jaz unloaded his kit, and the nursing assistant cranked Dad's bed up into a sitting position.

'Now then, how are you?' I said, bending to kiss him. His cheek was cool and dry, slightly stubbly.

The nurse was ahead of me. 'He's had some disturbed nights lately so we've been letting him lie in. He missed his shave this week.'

'I can do it,' I said.

Jaz gave me a funny look. 'You're going to shave Grandad?'

'It's no bother. I've done it before.'

Eew, said her expression. I ignored it.

'Jaz has come to see you, Dad. And she's brought Matty. We think he might be cutting a tooth.'

Matty sat on the carpet, gnawing hard at one of the wooden dogs and drooling onto his T-shirt.

'Yeah, great timing, Matts,' said Jaz. 'Just what I need at the moment.'

In the locker next to Dad's bed I located his electric razor and some moisturizer.

'I don't know how you come here week after week,' Jaz had said on the way in.

'I come to see your grandad.'

'I know. But it's so depressing. The place, I mean.'

'Not really.'

The razor buzzed in my fingers and I turned Dad's face gently towards me. 'Just tidying you up,' I told him. 'Hold still.'

Close to, I could see all the damage that age does: the liver spots, the detail of loose skin over bone, the criss-cross of lines under his eyes. There was a little cyst on his upper lid, and his eyebrows were shaggy and needing a trim. A huge sense of protectiveness welled up in my chest, and I wanted to hug him to me. Jaz's presence held me back, though. When the razor made contact with his chin he flinched. I made a soothing sound, and slowly moved the foil up and down, around the moulding of his face.

'When you were little,' I said over my shoulder, 'Grandad let you make a perfume shop in his shed. Do you remember, Jaz?'

'No.'

'He saved you all his jam jars, cleared a shelf and helped you make labels.'

'Perfume?'

'Out of rose petals. He let you take half his best roses. You used to mash them up in water.'

'Oh, yeah.'

When I turned round, she was stretched out on the floor next to Matty, twirling a wooden dog by its peg.

'And you used to sell them to us for twenty pence a jar.'

'Yeah, they used to go all stinky in a day or two. I never learned, it was always a disappointment. I'd go, "Smell this beautiful scent" – then *ugh*.'

I smiled at her. Underneath my fingers, Dad shuddered.

'You used to spend hours together, you and your grandad. Hours and hours, nattering away. I think there were things you'd tell him that you wouldn't tell me or your dad.'

Jaz rolled over and sat up. 'What was Grandma like? I don't really remember her.'

A shrew, I thought. That's the word you'd use. Critical, negative, pessimistic. Must have made Dad's life grim. Didn't do much for mine either.

'She was very fond of you,' I said. Which was getting on for the truth. Once we'd gone to see her in the convalescent home and without even a word she'd taken toddler Jaz off into the grounds, leaving Dad and me sitting by the bed like fools for half an hour. Certainly she'd been more tolerant of Jaz than she ever was of us.

'Did Grandad miss her when she died?'

'He was devastated.'

I shifted round so I could get at Dad's other side. He blinked mildly at me, as though he knew I was there to do him a service even if he wasn't sure what that service was. 'Soon have you looking tip-top,' I told him.

'Can he hear you, though?' asked Jaz.

'Of course he can.'

She looked at me pityingly. Meanwhile Matty had been ferrying fistfuls of gravel from the yucca and was using them to fill the slots in his jigsaw, crouching intently. Small white stones trickled from his grasp and bounce-scattered across the floor.

Jaz turned back and assessed the scope of the operation. Then she pushed her hair back behind her ears and joined in, smoothing out the piles of gravel with her finger for him, patting them into place, picking at the ones that had bedded down in the carpet fibres. It was nice to watch, their two heads bobbing next to each other.

When all the holes were filled to his satisfaction, Matty began trying to force each dog on top. His small fingers pressed against the varnish so hard the skin turned white. Getting no result, he swapped dogs and pushed again. 'Gone,' he said. 'Gone, gone.'

'Will they not go in?' I said. 'Naughty doggies.'

'Gone!' He lifted up the jigsaw piece and banged it down.

'Nanna'll help,' I said, switching the shaver off. Jaz shook her head.

'Let him work it out for himself, Mum.'

Matty slammed the board a few more times, then drew his

arm back and flung his dog across the room. It landed near my feet, so I reached down and rescued it. 'Bad dog,' I said.

But when I raised my head, Matty was picking at the stones with his index finger and pushing them away, out of the hole. Jaz reached over and took the dog off me, and put it down next to him. When the slot was clear, he tried again, only with the wrong dog. I could see his frustration mounting and it was twisting me up inside.

'Matty,' I began.

'Look,' announced Jaz in the tone of a children's TV presenter. 'Look who's coming.' And she walked the right dog, the blue dog, along the edge of the board and onto his hand. His frown disappeared instantly, and where I'd have held the piece ready for him to slot in, she just passed it across, then waited till he'd worked out which was the right way round and we could give him a cheer.

'You're very good with him,' I said. Jaz shrugged. I was thinking, If only my mother had had a tenth of that patience.

Dad cleared his throat suddenly, then leaned forward as if to get a better view of his great-grandson. I got up off the bed and went to put the shaver away, keeping my eyes on him all the time. It seemed that, at any minute, he would speak.

'Ta,' said Matty. 'Ta, doggy.'

Jaz said: 'It's trying to give him the attention of two people, you know?' She handed another piece over.

'Grandad's watching you,' I said. 'Matty, can you wave at Great-Grandad? Say "hiya".'

'Hiya.'

'Because I don't think Ian's really sorry,' she went on. 'Sorry he's been caught, that's all. That's what I told him: "If you were bothered about your wife and child, you'd never have done it in the first place".'

I stroked Matty's head, for comfort.

'What gets me, Mum, is how he tried to make it sound like I had something to do with it.'

'I'm sure he didn't exactly mean that—'

'You weren't there!'

'All I'm saying is, some men aren't very good at coping when children are young. They can feel shut out. Maybe that's what he was—'

'So instead they go and jump on the first bit of skirt that comes their way.'

'I'm not saying it's right, I'm not making excuses for him.'

'Not much.'

A memory of Phil with his head in his hands, sitting on the stairs, weeping.

'I'm really not, Jaz. Only trying to explain what might have gone through his mind.'

'As though his *mind* had anything to do with it,' she snapped, pushing the jigsaw away and struggling to her feet.

'Will you try talking to him again? David would come over.'

'Oh, I'm quite sure he would,' she said in a tone I didn't much like. 'No, that's it. In fact, all Ian's speech-making did was make it clearer to me. I'm definitely getting a divorce. Definitely. It's over.'

I glanced across at Dad to see if anything had registered. He looked anxious, but probably not more than usual. I'd talk to him some more about Jaz next time, when I was on my own. Reassure him, explain.

'So,' I said cautiously. 'How are you going to arrange things with Matty?'

She didn't acknowledge me in any way. I might as well not have spoken. I could feel the fury sparking off her.

The sunburst clock ticked on, and we sat there watching Matty trying to force a green dog into a white hole, three adults playing mute: Dad because he couldn't speak, Jaz because she wouldn't, and me because I didn't dare.

The bouquet was waiting for me when I got home. It was propped against the front door, which meant Jaz spotted it immediately.

'What's that?' she said, even though it was perfectly obvious.

I got out of the car and hurried over to see. The card was inside a miniature envelope; on an instinct I whipped it out and stuck it in my pocket. The plastic holder I dropped deftly behind a bush. Jaz didn't see because she was checking Matty's straps.

'My God,' she said, when she got close. 'I bet those cost a bit.'

'Yes,' I said. I turned the key and stepped into the hall.

'Who are they from?'

'I don't know,' I said truthfully.

'Is there no card?'

'Can't see one. Are you having a drink?'

She was peering around the sides of the bouquet. Any minute now, I thought, she's going to stick her hands inside and begin parting the stems.

Eventually she gave up. 'No, I won't, thanks, because if I leave it any later Matty'll have his nap too late on and then I won't be able to get him off at bedtime.'

'OK, then. Well, drive safely and I'll see you Wednesday.'

'Yeah.' She paused in the doorway. 'It's not Dad, after a reconciliation, is it?'

I smiled. 'The flowers? Could be.'

She huffed, and left.

I walked through to the kitchen, holding the flowers ahead of me like an Olympic torch. Vases were in the base unit next to the cooker, so I laid the bouquet in the sink and squatted down to search. All my mother's crockery was stashed in here: her big blue and white serving dishes, her Lustreware tea set, her pressed glass bowls, and at the very back, her Crown Devon vases. I drew out the tallest, a pale blue ribbed funnel, and as I did so I could hear Phil go, *You're turning this house into Pincroft, that's what you're doing*. Because he'd hated the antimacassars with their embroidered peonies, and the uranium glass dressing-table set, and the ebony brush and mirror set that hung in the hallway. 'This old tat,' he used to say. Left to himself we'd have had a palace of vinyl and brushed steel.

I put everything back carefully in its proper place, and carried the vase over to the drainer. Then I set about unravelling the cellophane. Little sachet of plant food to make up, stem bases to cut or split, and all the time I still had my coat on and the card was burning a hole in the pocket. Dorothy Wynne's grand-daughter, the flowers might be from, although I'd already had a thank you card after the business with little Libby. Or Moira, as a pick-me-up because she knew I was having a difficult time. I positioned the gypsophila and ferns, and fed each bloom in one by one: yellow dahlias, yellow and white asters, a lily, white carnations. I coaxed them into place, then stepped back to consider the effect. Finally I topped up the water level and slid the vase onto the windowsill. Only then did I reach into my pockets and bring out the card.

My turn to apologise, I think. Onwards and upwards. David. X

I was touched by this little act of thoughtfulness. We'd not spoken since the fall-out – I'd wanted to ring, but hadn't dared in case he somehow blamed me for what had happened. But perhaps he now understood how little control I had over Jaz.

Relief made me suddenly exhausted, and I had to sit down.

A bouquet of flowers. What would Phil think if he came

round with the lawnmower and saw them? He'd be shocked to find they were from a man, that was certain. His ex-wife didn't have boyfriends. No subterfuge, either; I really didn't. When the girls at the gym joked or moaned about their partners, I laughed or frowned along with them. When they turned their attention to my love-life I always responded straight away with another question. Amazing how easy it is to divert someone straight back onto the topic of themselves. Jaz (drunk) asked me once why I'd never dated after Phil and, unable to break the habit of a lifetime, I'd gone, 'Would you like me to?' 'No,' she'd said. 'Too complicated. Too weird.' And that was the topic closed. But it wasn't Jaz who stopped me from dating, or even Phil. It was me.

I used to pick up magazines packed with true-life stories suggesting lovers were waiting to ambush you on every corner. *Crash Course in Romance – how a bump in the car led to a ring on my finger! He came to fix my burglar alarm – now it's wedding bells I'm hearing!* And probably if you put yourself about a bit, as my mother would say, you would find someone who wasn't revolting.

I wasn't in bad shape. Nor did I move in a world entirely of women. Men came into the shop sometimes, occasionally eyed me up. There was the haberdasher, Gavin, who used to flirt with me a little; he was nice, but he was married. Launce, who ran the photography class, had made several comments that might have been taken as overtures, but he was a lot older than me and anyway, it's possible he was only being friendly. One time I'd been asked out for a drink by Dorothy Wynne's gardener, a sharp-nosed Celt with sandy lashes and a bulging Adam's apple, not my type at all. So that had made me wary for a while of engaging in any ordinary polite chat, because the embarrassment of rejecting even virtual strangers was too distressing. I hate upsetting people.

But you did have to want to get out there, throw yourself into the hurly-burly. I found that hard. Even when we were teenagers, Eileen would be walking up to boys and chatting like it was no bother, while I'd be observing from a safe distance. 'Stop studying the ground all the time,' she'd say to me sometimes. 'Put your head up. Smile.' So I did, and look who I caught.

Now I found myself thinking about fluff-haired Derek, the first boy I ever kissed, how he danced with me at Pamela Martin's fourteenth birthday party, and how nothing had come of it afterwards because he was too shy to seek me out and I was too shy to put myself in his way. I remembered the brief crush I'd had on Tom Street, school football captain and future head boy, after he mended my locker door for me and commented how tidy I kept my books. But it was Phil, always Phil hanging about on the edges of my teenage consciousness, so that even when I was going out with Peter Robbins, who was decent and bright and not bad-looking, I couldn't help but keep a watch on Phil and secretly rejoice when he broke up with Margaret Hodgkiss.

For our first date he took me to the motorway bridge – it sounds so dull but it wasn't – and we watched traffic and talked. I remember saying to him, 'You're more serious when you're on your own.' I don't know what he said back, but I do recall him taking off my scarf and dangling it over the parapet, and laughing at my protests. I thought I'd die of happiness.

I could see him now, perched on our coping stones, swinging his legs. Mum never liked him but then, she liked nobody. Dad kept his mouth shut. *It's this other woman*, said Eileen, from thirty years ago. *That's who you should be angry with.*

On the windowsill, my flowers shone.

CHAPTER 11

Photograph 39, Album One

Location: Longleat Manor, Wiltshire

Taken by: Bob

Subject: the Knot Garden. Although the spectacular colours here won't show up on black and white film, he'll remember them, he thinks.

It's been a grand day out so far, in his new Austin 30 with its cream wheel trims, its rounded rear windscreen, the smart blue and black dashboard. The kind of car you want to take on a decent run. 'And what makes you think I've got time to swan off on a great long trip?' was Frieda's response when he first suggested the drive, but she's come anyway.

Inside, the house was like nothing you could dream of: great long galleries hung with tapestries, a staircase like the one Vivien Leigh fell down in Gone With the Wind*, a twenty-seat table, ceilings so elaborately decorated it hurts your neck to take in all the detail. 'Have you seen?' he keeps asking Frieda. He's like a boy in his enthusiasm. 'Think of the dusting,' she says, shuddering. But he doesn't let that put him off his stride. What riches, what grandeur. It's overwhelming, the idea that anyone could live here, day to day.*

Now they're out in the grounds and he's imagining what it must be like to be a lord. 'Who would you have wanted to be, if you could be anyone in history?' he asks Frieda.

'A man,' she says.

'What man?' he says.

'Any man,' she replies, and strides off, leaving him among the flowers. What's that supposed to mean? He's a patient bloke, but there are times he could go and sit in the driver's seat and lean his head against the Austin's horn.

Perhaps she'll be happier when the baby arrives. God help them both if she isn't.

We took the Beavers down to Blakemere Moss every year for orienteering and mapwork practice, but it meant an afternoon preparing the ground. This was my fourth year tying ribbons to saplings and laying twigs on the grass to make arrow shapes; the first time I'd ever carried out the task assisted by David and Matty.

The afternoon was damp and cool. By evening there would be a mist over the lake.

'Were you a Girl Scout?' asked David.

'Nope. My best friend spat on Brownies and Guides, so I never pursued it. Were you ever a Cub?'

He shook his head. 'I was a school prefect, briefly. Till I got demoted. Look, I'll do the ribbons if you like. It's easier for me to reach.'

'No, you hang onto Matty for me. I can't tie them very high or the Beavers won't be able to spot them.'

On the end of his toddler reins my grandson strained after ducks, water, freedom. I cleared a space of leaves till the soil showed, and aligned my lengths of wood so they pointed down the right path.

I said, 'It worries me she has no pattern, no model for a good marriage.'

David reached out a hand to help me up. 'For that matter, neither does Ian. It wasn't something either you or I chose, or can go back and change. Shouldering extra blame's not going to help anyone. I'm sure you did your best.'

'I tried.'

'Well, then. And Ian wasn't without maternal figures when he was growing up. He was very close to my sister at one time, before she moved to the States. I've had partners he's been fond of. Not so much Jacky, they never really hit it off, but some of the others. He still gets birthday cards from a couple. Here, let me hold that while you sort out your ribbon.' He took the clipboard from me and brought the map into focus, squinting. 'We're going round as far as the car park?'

'That's right.'

Matty pulled towards the lake, attracted by the swaying bulrush heads. I snapped a length of juncus for him and put it into his hand, and he was instantly satisfied.

'Does Ian get on well with – your new girlfriend?' I ventured.

'She isn't really a girlfriend, and they've not met,' said David. 'Did your flowers last?'

'Flowers? Oh, ages. In fact, I only threw the last ones away yesterday.'

'It's a decent florist. I've used them a few times.'

My spirits dipped a little. No woman likes to feel she's part of a bulk order.

We moved on, Matty stumbling between us on the ridgy mud. His frog wellies were already caked. They'd need sluicing before I handed them back.

'How's Ian managing?'

David clasped the reins more tightly and frowned. 'Doesn't talk much. Stays up late because he can't sleep, watches TV till the small hours. He's been very forgetful, forgot his coat one day, his briefcase this morning. Lost his watch last week and couldn't remember where he'd left it. He was like that after his mother died. Without being overdramatic, I think I can say my son's in real distress. But you perhaps wouldn't pick up on those things if you didn't know him. He's like me in a lot of ways. Doesn't make a show of his feelings. Jaz is like you?'

'God, no. She's just herself.'

For a while we walked in silence. The sky above the treeline was milky-blank and the vegetation on the far bank washed out and pale. We were coming to the timber bridge where the cotton grass grew; once Jaz had turned over a chunk of dead wood on this stretch and found a clutch of baby newts huddled underneath. When she'd touched them, they'd lain inert, like rubber animals. She wanted to take them home but I'd stood my ground that time. I didn't want their tiny amphibian deaths on my conscience.

'We'd to come to the Moss every few weeks when Jaz was a girl,' I said, sliding my secateurs into my pocket. 'For picnics, all sorts. Jaz used to love scrambling around and investigating.'

'Ian used to like Delamere Forest. We went camping there on a couple of occasions.'

I couldn't stop myself. 'You, in a tent?'

'Why ever not?'

'You're always so smart. I can't imagine you roughing it. This is the first time I've seen you not wearing a suit.'

David looked at me in mild surprise, then down at his jeans and walking boots. 'I'm sure it isn't.'

'It is. You think: the wedding, Matty's naming ceremony, the two or three meals we met up for to celebrate the engagement and make arrangements for the reception. I'm only saying, it's not a criticism.'

'Oh good.'

'Hang on, I need to post another marker.'

I spooled out more ribbon and clipped it to the right length.

The tree I'd lighted on was a rowan with thin, shivering leaves. In the autumn, Jaz used to pick the berries and wear them like earrings.

'We really don't know each other very well, do we?' said David from behind me.

'I know we're of the same mind. I know we both want to help.'

When I turned he was standing under a silver birch, his grey hair slightly dishevelled and the hems of his jeans flecked with mud, while my grandson – *his* grandson – poked at a puddle with his length of reed.

'Ian's desperate to see Matty. This situation can't go on indefinitely.'

'No, I know. She just needs a little bit of space. It's only till she's come to terms—'

'How long will that be, though, Carol?' At the lake's end a flock of gulls took off, slopping waves against the banks, disturbing the peace. 'I haven't told Ian where I am this afternoon. I did think about bringing him, just to meet up for half an hour, but . . .' He let the sentence hang.

I fixed my gaze on a ripple and followed it to the shore where ghost-Jaz crouched, skimming stone after stone across the water.

'So the Hungarian, right, he's explaining these three states of matter, yeah? How you've got your solids, your liquids and your gas.' Josh's voice was full of enthusiasm as I negotiated the Blakemere roundabout.

'Uh-huh. I know about those.'

'Yeah, and he's talking about how the molecules are packed together, and then he drags out this swivel chair he always sits on, and he goes: "*This is a chair*." And straight away the boy he really hates, he stands up and starts applauding.'

'Ouch.'

'It was brilliant, 'cause after a second or two some of the others did the same, and soon the whole class was on their feet, clapping. All clapping the Hungarian's genius in being able to correctly identify a piece of furniture.'

'How did he react?'

'Aw, he just totally lost it. His head exploded. There were literally brains everywhere.'

'What, literally?' I indicated right and moved into the outside lane, ready for the traffic lights. 'Was the boy all right, though?' I said while we waited for green. 'Because the Hungarian can be vicious, can't he?'

Josh shrugged. 'It was worth it. It was a blast.'

'When I was at school we had a foreign teacher who could never keep control. Mr de Silva, his name was. Taught music. Don't know what he was doing in Bolton. The boys used to make his life hell.'

'What did they do?'

'Well, we had our singing in the hall, and it was a room with huge floor-length curtains down one side. The boys used to spend half of every lesson hiding behind these curtains. They'd wait till he turned to the piano, and then they'd sneak across, one by one, till there was hardly anyone left singing, just the girls. Mr de Silva must have noticed but I suppose he was too frightened to tackle us. Poor man. You'd see all these shoes sticking out from under the hem.'

'Smart.'

'Not that I'm giving you ideas.'

We pulled onto the main road; another minute and we'd be at the school.

'Can you let me out here?' Josh said suddenly.

'Here?'

'There's someone I need to talk to.'

I took my eyes off the road for a second to glance across at him, and he was leaning forward urgently. When I scanned up and down the pavement, the only likely people I could see were a pair of girls far up ahead.

'Ah,' I said.

'So if you could?'

'All right. Hang on.'

He was pawing at the door even as I was pulling in.

'Man with a mission,' I said, smiling.

'Something like that.' He reached for his bag.

'Have a nice day.'

'I won't.'

He set off walking fast. It wouldn't be fair to spy on him, but I let myself watch for twenty paces. His chin was set, his bag swung as he strode into the brightness of a new school day, and his loping, vulnerable gait reminded me painfully of Ian.

Which might have been what tipped me into action.

Matty concentrated as his father slotted two pieces of blue track together and hitched them to the existing layout. Thomas the Tank Engine's route would take him past the fireplace, under the coffee-table, across the carpet to the display cabinet and then alongside the radiator, where there was a junction that would either bring him back round to the hearth or up against a buffer. A plastic tunnel lay on its back like a giant green woodlouse, and next to Ian's feet was a polythene box of die-cast vehicles, ready for dispersal. Matty held the train.

'This is not taking sides. This is not condoning what he's done. I can't stress enough how important it is that Jaz doesn't get to hear about it,' I said to David, who was standing with me in the living-room doorway.

'I know. It's very good of you.'

Our eyes met and I could see at once he knew the score: if Ian was allowed to see his son, he was less likely to make some gesture motivated by spite. Desperate people sometimes did desperate things. The arrangement was about self-preservation, not charity.

That said, it felt nice to watch them together.

'Don't they have some great toys nowadays?' I said, as Ian took Matty's finger and showed him how to push the start lever.

'I'll say. I had a Hornby 00 gauge when I was a boy, but not till I was a lot older. This stuff's good. Chunky. Solid.'

'I got the metal ones at a boot sale, thought I'd been very clever but they're the wrong scale, of course. I'm always doing things like that.'

'You do very well, as far as I can see,' said David.

The train shirred past our feet. 'Watch out, Thomas!' I called after it.

'Gordon,' corrected the men in unison.

'Gordon's an LNER A3. Thomas is a Brighton Line E2,' added David helpfully.

At the opposite corner of the room, Matty piled cars, a bus and a steamroller onto the track, then sat back to wait for the crash.

'Catastrophe, that's what he enjoys best,' I said, as my grandson rocked himself with anticipation.

'Not that we had a lot of toys back then,' said David. 'We used to spend most of our time outdoors. Up trees, building dens, down the canal, wherever we fancied. I'd go out in a morning and I wouldn't come back for hours. We were never bored, I'll tell you.'

'You couldn't do that now, though.'

'Why not? Ian used to.'

'Did he?'

'Of course. I couldn't be watching him every minute of the day.'

The Gordon-train rounded the corner, trundled into the tunnel, emerged, and smashed into the roadblock. Matty's hands flew to his cheeks in mock horror. 'Uh-oh,' he said. The engine lay on its side, pistons working busily. 'Uh-oh!'

'Emergency,' cried Ian, and leaned over to fish an ambulance out of the box. Their heads bent together.

I thought I might feel less complicit if I took myself into another room.

'Let's leave them to it, shall we?' I said, detaching myself from the doorframe and stepping backwards into the hall. 'Come through. We'll swap news.'

David settled himself at the kitchen table and folded his hands like a man about to say grace.

'So, any movement at all from Jasmine yet?'

I flicked on the kettle and shook my head. 'But it's good she hasn't mentioned solicitors or anything like that for a bit. I think she's keeping her options open.'

'I'm quite sure she is,' replied David, rather acidly, and I realised how I'd sounded.

'What I mean is, if she doesn't want to start legal proceedings, then it must be because she doesn't think the marriage is necessarily over. Which is good. At the moment she seems to want to keep the status quo.'

'All right for her.'

'I do appreciate that.' The kettle clicked off, and I turned away from him to pour the water. 'It's not nice going behind your daughter's back, you know.'

Steam rose up around my face in a hot flush.

'Carol?' said Ian from the hallway. 'Carol, where do you keep Matty's changing stuff?'

'In his room, under the cot. But look, I'll do it.'

'No, you're fine. Stay where you are.' Ian was through the stair gate before I could argue.

I slotted the kettle back onto its stand and brought the cups across. 'He's good that way, isn't he? A real hands-on dad.'

When he's allowed to be, said David's expression.

The sun came out and lit up the kitchen. Twenty feet from the kitchen window, Mrs Wynne's cat leaped onto our fence and began to pick its way along the top.

'Phil was useless, nappy-wise. He never soiled his fingers with anything so basic.'

David shrugged. 'Different days, though, weren't they? I never changed a nappy either. Then again, I had my share of mopping up bodily fluids later on, with Jeanette.'

'Yes, of course.'

Ian thumped back down with the changing mat under his arm and disappeared into the lounge.

'He is a good father,' said David. 'Whatever else he's done.'

I had a sudden memory of Bolton Central Library as it was when I was a child, and me weaving between the rows of towering shelves to find Dad. His face lighting up when he saw me, holding his hand out for the book I was carrying. *Now, what have you got there?*

'I do think children need a father figure.'

'Glad to hear you say so.'

'It's true. Mine had more to do with bringing me up than my mother ever did.'

'How was that? Was she ill?'

'No, just nowty. You know, peevish, perpetually bad-tempered. Don't get me wrong, she did all the practical side, the washing and the meals. But it was Dad who made the time. He was marvellous with Jaz when she was little. Nowadays it's obviously different, because of his—'

'Watch out, gas masks at the ready, folks.' Ian was standing in the doorway swinging a nappy sack on his finger. 'Where do you want this, Carol?'

'Straight outside, black bin. Thanks.'

When he'd gone, David said, 'How often do you see your father?'

'I usually go Sunday mornings. The year he first went into Willowbrook I visited most evenings, but as time went on he got, I don't know, lost in himself. And it's hard to sit there, watching him decline.'

'I imagine it is.'

'So now it's once a week, and my evenings are spent at the pool or the Scout hut or the gym.'

'Ah, yes, your women's gym.' He raised his eyebrows. 'And what goes on there?'

'What do you think goes on? We do circuits—'

'Just women?'

'Just women.'

'I couldn't join, then?'

'I wouldn't have thought so.'

'That's discrimination.'

'Not really. It's not as though you're denied the opportunity to exercise somewhere else. Anyway, if you were prepared to stick on a pink leotard, we might have you.'

The back door flew open and Ian blundered in. 'I don't know what that child's been eating,' he complained, positioning himself at the sink and squirting soap into his palm. 'You could strip paint with the fumes.'

From the next room we could hear the sound of engine clashing with engine.

'The joys of fatherhood,' I nearly said. But just in time I realised I hadn't the confidence to make that sort of joke. We weren't on those terms any longer, probably never would be again.

Something else he'd fractured with his infidelity.

CHAPTER 12

Photograph: newspaper clipping, loose between the pages of The Marvellous Stories of Jesus *from the bureau, Sunnybank*

Location: Tannerside church hall

Taken by: the Wigan Observer

Subject: Carol, aged about ten, sits with her mother and six other women at a decorator's table covered in 1,200 palm crosses. Every single one has been hand-made; Carol thinks she could construct a palm cross in her sleep. The hallway at Pincroft has been full of bundles of unsplit reeds that need separating, trimming and folding to make a loopy, top-heavy crucifix. Palm reeds dry your fingers and leave the skin powdery, a sensation Carol hates, though it's satisfying to watch the pile of squashy crosses grow. She likes to arrange them by size, compare the biggest with the smallest. 'Why can't we ask people to keep the ones they had last year?' she enquires of her mother. 'Because you can't,' snaps Frieda. 'Because it's about renewal,' explains the vicar. Carol's crosses will end up in hospices and old folk's homes, as well as with parishioners like bow-legged Mrs Greenhalgh. For the next twelve months those wispy tokens will be tucked behind calendars or picture-

frames, pressed into Bibles, or drawing-pinned to chimney-breasts. It's a pleasing thought.

Meanwhile Frieda surveys the table, her Passiontide labours complete, and hums to herself. Lent's the time of year she likes best, that period of contemplation and denial before the brashness of Easter. Her favourite hymns deal with blood, thorns, decay, scaffolds, toil, chariots of wrath, encircling gloom and Herod.

It occurs to Carol that her mother would probably like a full-size cross of her own; would bang in three of the nails herself.

After David and Ian had gone, I put Matty down for his nap, cleared away the train track, then went and lay on my own bed for a while. The house felt very empty. It reminded me of that first week Jaz left for Leeds and how I'd kept every radio in the house turned on, singing along to the music, answering the presenters back. Not that I ever saw a huge amount of Jaz in those days, even when she lived in the bedroom next door to mine. I'd hear her music, though, and smell her incense; her clothes were in the washing basket and her little pots in the fridge. All those years of nagging people to clear up after themselves, and suddenly tidiness equalled absence. The coat hooks by the front door laid bare after a lifetime undercover, the newel post naked at last. I was able to stand in my own hallway and hear the tap dripping in the kitchen, Laverne's wind chimes on the back porch, my own breath.

And without warning, my memory flicked to Phil, and the week of his leaving. I could see him now, standing in the kitchen with his car keys in his hand, while his suitcases waited at the bottom of the stairs. *Please, I'm so sorry. Can we not talk it through one more time?* Me, still in my slippers, commanding him from my threshold with the towering strength of the righteous.

He'd gone straight from me to Penny, and he'd been there ever since. Not so sorry after all, then.

A glow of outrage started up in my chest as I remembered snippets from afterwards: the call from the ironmongers telling me my wallpaper was in, when in fact Phil had placed the order for Penny; replying to all the Phil-and-Carol Christmas cards that year; discovering Mrs Wynne had told everyone it was Phil who'd left me. The wearying, wearying round of explanation, for months afterwards. Fielding other people's embarrassment and, worse, their pity.

Damn him to hell and back. Eight years gone, and he still had the ability to wind me up.

On the bedside table Matty's monitor made a rustling sound, and over the airwaves I heard him sigh. Then more silence.

I slowed my breathing deliberately, relaxed my muscles, and found myself wondering about David's not-girlfriend. At first I could only conjure up Jacky, complete with wedding hat. But then I thought of that advert for Sandals holiday resorts, and the mature couple who run through the waves, and I thought, Yes, that'll be her. Superior, upgraded, glossy. The sort of woman you'd never find travelling with a coachload of Beavers, singing 'A sailor went to sea sea sea'.

There it came again: Phil's face as I shut the door on him – his face the first time I asked him who Penny was – his face as Jaz got in the car to go to Nat's for a sleepover and I turned to him on the doorstep and said, 'We need to talk.'

Then the bell rang for real, and Matty woke and started crying and I ran to get him and staggered downstairs with my hair still messed up from the pillow and it was the man himself, bloody Phil at the bloody door.

We stood and stared at each other.

'You!' I said.

'I've got your lawnmower,' he said. 'What? What have I done now?'

I let him in anyway.

When he'd carried the lawnmower through to the shed he stood for a while on the patio, considering. Meanwhile I strapped Matty into his high chair, warmed a bowl of mash and mince and watched through the kitchen window as my ex-husband squatted down by the pond and poked at the reeds, got to his feet, strolled to the fence and peered into Laverne's garden. I was on the verge of going out to ask what the hell he thought he was doing when he started back up the path. But even then he seemed to be studying the paving slabs as he went, pausing to nudge with his toe at some unevenness, pressing down a bit of moss further on.

Finally he reached the back door.

'When you've quite finished,' I said.

'You've a slate missing off your roof.'

'Yes,' I said, though it was news to me.

'By the chimney.'

'I know.'

'Best get it seen to while the weather's fine.' He saw my expression. 'All right, I'm only trying to be helpful.'

'If you want to help, you can supervise your grandson while I clear away.'

'Okey-dokey.' He settled himself at the table, grinning. I passed over the bowl and Phil set it down on the tray. 'Chow-time, old chap.'

Matty looked at him indifferently, then picked up his spoon and began to bite the handle end.

'And here's his drink,' I said, holding out the beaker.

'Lucky Matty.' Phil looked hopefully in the direction of the kettle, but I ignored him.

'Don't let him bang it around or the lid comes off.'

'No, Miss.'

'And pull his bib back down, will you? It's all round his throat.' I turned away and began to tidy round the sink.

'So,' I heard him say, 'everything all right with you?'

'As much as it can be,' I said. Stupid question.

Matty gave a little yelp that turned into a giggle. When I looked round, Phil was pulling some kind of comedy face. Dinner sat untouched.

'Oops,' he said. 'Come on, Matt, let's get this show on the road.' He guided the spoon into the food and loaded it up.

'Matty can do that himself. I just need you to supervise.' I went back to wiping down the drainer.

'Any sign of Jaz and Ian getting themselves sorted?'

'Not yet.'

Just for a second I imagined telling him exactly who'd been here an hour before, what secret deals I'd been working.

'Oh well, probably best leave them to it. They're adults.'

'Yes.'

'But you're OK in yourself?'

'Why wouldn't I be?'

'Jesus, Carol, I'm only asking.'

'Watch your language,' I said. 'Little pitchers, big ears.'

The waggling zip pull on Phil's pocket had caught Matty's attention and he'd stopped eating. I put my dishcloth down, ready to take over.

'It's all right, I can manage,' said Phil. 'Come on, lad, chop chop.'

When he failed to get any reaction, he took the spoon himself and started making energetic scooping movements with it. Any minute now, I thought, he's going to pretend to eat it himself. And yes, there he was, smacking his lips half an inch above the spoon end with the hyperactive glee of a children's entertainer.

'Marcel Marceau would be proud.'

'I've got his interest, though.' Without warning Phil opened his mouth wide, bared his teeth, and lunged at the bowl, snapping his jaws. 'Mr Crocodile's after your stew.'

'He doesn't like it. Phil, look, you're frightening him.'

'Rubbish. He's laughing.'

'That's fear.'

As if to make some sort of statement, Matty took the spoon back and dropped it over the side.

'I'll get it,' said Phil. He bent down, reached in between the metal legs of the high chair, got a purchase on the smeary spoon handle, and retreated. Only, in levering himself back up again, he caught the tray with his shoulder and tipped it up. The bowl of cold mash slid backwards, caught against the lip, flipped up and emptied itself down Matty's front, before slipping off his lap and bouncing onto the lino.

'Oh, for *goodness* sake.'

'Give us a break, Carol. I'm doing my best.'

That's half the trouble, I nearly said. Even your best is bloody useless.

I picked up the roll of kitchen towel and started to unravel it. *You're just not comfortable in the role of Grandad, are you?* went my head. *Like you weren't comfortable in the role of Dad.*

'I'll get Matty down for you, shall I?'

'No. Leave him there till I've wiped this mess off the floor. And mind your feet; you're treading in it.'

You were nervous of Jaz, I told him silently, *from the word go, and the bigger she got, the worse it became. And your approach to nerves is to go into joker mode, whether it's appropriate or not. I can still remember passing that girl in the hall at one of Jaz's birthday parties, and her saying, 'Mr Morgan's weird.' And I'd gone in and there you were, prancing round the table, wearing false teeth made out of orange peel and a party ring as a monocle. The only people laughing were the mums.*

The stew had splashed further than I could have imagined. There was a great streak of it up the cupboard door below the sink, and blobs of pale mash across the tiles as far as the cooker.

And don't get me started on Mr Sock; you never knew when a joke was over. Asking her friends to park their broomsticks by the door, calling Natalie 'Miss Sunshine' to her face. That time Nat turned up crying and you asked if it was because she'd bought the wrong shade of nail polish again. Trust me, they didn't see the funny side. No one 'lightened up'.

Phil had sat down again, and Matty was throwing himself from side to side with a violence that made me glad the high chair had wide legs. I placed the bowl in the sink and turned on the tap. 'Get some spaghetti hoops out of the cupboard, will you, while I sponge his trousers. We'll start again.'

For a few minutes it was almost like old times, buzzing about the kitchen, getting in each other's way. Phil always did want to open the cutlery drawer at the exact same moment I was reaching over it to the toaster. But now he was asking questions all the time: 'The whole tin? Is a teaspoon OK? Does his cup need a wipe?' Then, as I was chopping toast into strips, he said, 'Penny's not been well.'

I tried not to pause, to keep the knife going while I considered how on earth to respond. Your ex-husband confides that his new partner is feeling under the weather. Do you a) punch the air and say *Serves the bitch right!* b) give him the long, cool look of someone who doesn't give a damn, or c) express polite sympathy. I carried on chopping, even though the toast fingers were now of julienne dimensions. What did he mean, 'not well'? Were we talking a nasty cold, or cancer? If I stood here biting the inside of my cheek and said absolutely nothing, would he elaborate?

Then the phone rang next to me, and the knife skittered out of my grasp and twirled across the work surface.

'Excuse me,' I said, and snatched up the receiver.

It was Jaz.

'Mum?'

'Yes. Hang on while I—' The back door was ajar and I slipped through it, closing it behind me, leaving Phil to play Grandad. The air on the patio was balmy. A wood pigeon cooed from the top of the shed. 'Everything all right, love?'

'Yeah, all it was, would you mind if I picked up Matty a bit late? This document's taking me longer than I thought. There's loads of legal jargon in it I keep having to look up.'

'No bother. Give me a call when you're near finishing and I'll bob him over. What's that I can hear in the background, by the way?'

'Tchaikovsky Piano Concerto. It helps me concentrate. Why?'

I smiled, even though she couldn't see me. 'I remember when it was nothing but thumping rock music with you. Thud thud thud through the floor.'

'I've always liked classical.'

'Have you?'

'Yeah.'

A skein of geese pulled across the sky, and I flew with them for a moment.

'Have you heard from Ian?' she said.

'No. Have you?'

A snort. 'Nothing. It's like he's not interested. Not interested in his own child. Can you believe it, after all that fuss?'

'Your dad's here,' I blurted.

'What's he want?'

'I don't think he knows himself. Look, I've got to go, Jaz. I left him in charge and he's bound to be making a hash of things. Lord knows what kind of a mess I'll find when I go back in.'

I pressed End Call and stepped back inside. The high chair was empty, Matty's bowl of spaghetti untouched.

'Phil? Phil?'

I hurried through to the living room. And there they were, Matty lying across the changing mat Ian had left out, bare legs kicking, and Phil unfurling a clean nappy with the flourish of a magician.

'What are you doing?'

'What's it look like? You were busy, Mr Stinky here needed sorting.'

'But you've never changed a nappy in your life.'

'I used to do Jaz's.'

'You didn't.'

'I bloody did, Carol. Christ, you've got a selective memory.'

'Watch your language,' I said, staring at the way he hoisted Matty's hips, slid the nappy under, pulled the side tabs clear, wrapped them neatly round the front.

'The old one's over there,' he said. 'I don't know where you want it putting.'

Which goes to show, you can be wrong about people, even those you think you know inside out.

CHAPTER 13

Photograph 279, Album Two

Location: Chester Zoo

Taken by: Carol

Subject: Jaz, eleven, stands in front of a wire-link fence, a toy snake draped round her neck. Phil's half-in, half-out of the photograph, which happens to be a good representation of how he is with the family these days. Earlier he tried to enliven the trip by breaking suddenly into a sprint, waving his arms and crying, 'They're loose! They're loose!'

After the panic has subsided, he is invited to the manager's office to explain himself. There is no explanation for Phil, thinks Carol. She has only recently trained him out of shouting, 'I've won!' every time he visits a cash machine, and writing For smuggling diamonds *on all her chequebook stubs. Really, it wears you down.*

So Phil skulks on the periphery of the picture, neither use nor ornament. Nobody takes any notice of him, that's the trouble; nobody understands his sense of humour. Well, there is one person he can make laugh, but she's not here.

*

'Sometimes,' I confided to Josh as we came into the outskirts of town, 'when I'm on a short journey, I get this mad impulse to keep going and not stop, drive and drive, and see where the road takes me.'

'Mum comes out with stuff like that,' he said.

'Maybe all mothers feel the same way.'

'Not just mums. If I could drive . . .'

'Another couple of years and you'll be old enough to learn.'

'Yeah, right, like Mum's ever going to let me loose behind a steering wheel.'

I knew what he meant: I couldn't picture it either.

'If I could,' he went on, 'I'd get on a plane this afternoon. If I was old enough, and I had a passport. And a stack of money.'

'And your mother would have a nervous breakdown. We'd be sweeping up the pieces even before you'd got to the departure lounge.'

'Yeah.' He picked at the skin around his thumbnail. 'Best stay at home and practise staring at the wallpaper.'

There were so many activities Laverne vetoed: she didn't want Josh travelling fifteen miles to spend the day in Chester on his own, or surfing the net unsupervised, wearing low-slung jeans, sticking posters in his room, listening to music with unsound lyrics, watching the catchphrase comedy he needed to be in the social loop. Laverne's list of prohibiteds was long and broad-ranging. She'd have had him in short trousers if she could.

'Well. It's hard being a mum,' I said non-committally.

'Harder being a teenager.'

'I expect it is these days, yes.'

He reached over the seat for his bag. 'My stop.'

'Here again? You want to walk?'

'Yup.'

'If you insist. I shan't ask.'

'Very wise.' Josh reached for the door handle.

'Have a nice day.'

'I won't.'

A burst of laughter greeted me as I walked in through the gym door. Every machine on the circuit was busy, the room was bright and the music punching. Gwen-the-instructor stood in the middle with her hand over her mouth, feigning shock. 'You wouldn't,' she was saying to Pauline. 'You wouldn't really.'

'I would,' said Pauline. 'And afterwards I wouldn't throw it in a hedge neither. I'd stick it in the mincer. Try sewing *that* back on.'

More laughter. I stuck my car keys and water bottle in the corner and came across to join the girls.

'Margaret's nearly finished,' Gwen told me. 'She'll be off in a sec.'

Change stations now, went the CD player. Margaret stepped off her board and headed for the water cooler, and I took her place.

On the machine opposite, Frances swung her shins backwards and forwards. 'If my husband was trying new things in bed, buying me flowers for no reason and taking more care with his appearance, then, to be honest, I wouldn't care if he was playing away. It'd be worth it.'

Gwen filled me in. 'We're talking about the Tell-Tale Signs your husband's having an affair.'

'I've been reading this article,' said Pauline.

'Yeah. If you tick more than four out of ten, chances are he's up to no good.'

'Problem is,' said Aud, pulling on the bars next to me, 'he can leave no tracks at all. Mine didn't. I hadn't a clue. Not a clue. No funny phone calls, no hiding his credit-card bills. It was because she was at work, it was all so easy for him.'

'How did you find out?'

'He told me. He said he was going, and why. I think he expected me to plead with him to stay. But I just said, "OK then, bugger off." You should've seen his face.'

'Weren't you upset?' said Gwen.

'I was shocked. It was a shock that he'd been lying to me, and to be on my own after so long. But you get used to it, and my sister, same thing had happened to her, so it wasn't too bad. Once, you know, I'd had time to come round.' (*Change stations now*, said the CD.) 'And I lost a stone in weight with the worry, so every cloud has a silver lining.'

'You go, girl,' said Pauline. We were all smiling as we moved round, all nodding our support, and I thought: I could confide if I wanted to. I could tell them how I had no idea Phil was seeing anyone the first time, because you don't expect that kind of behaviour early on in a marriage, especially not when your own parents have been so solidly faithful you never had to think about it. It didn't occur to me he might lie, that he might be going somewhere other than where he said. It had taken Mavis Pearson, Phil's boss's secretary, pulling me to one side at their Christmas dinner. Her emerald blouse, her coral lipstick so bright it was offensive. *I can't stand by and watch it going on, a young girl like you.*

'So it's been good in the long run,' Aud was saying.

'I still miss mine,' said a grey-haired woman whose name I wasn't sure of, though I saw her every week.

'Yeah?'

'I do. Even though it was me who finished it, and it's getting on for twelve years. My daughter, she's in her thirties and she still talks about us getting back together. I say to her, "Why should it matter? You've left home".'

'You can please yourself when you live alone, though, can't you?' said Gwen. (*Change stations now*, went the CD.)

The grey-haired woman climbed off her machine, frowning. 'I know it's fashionable to say you're fine on your own, but I hate it, if I'm being honest. I'm not lonely, I've plenty of friends. But if you go to – oh, say, a party or some do like that – when you get home, there's no one to compare notes with. There's no one to ask, "What did you think of her?" and "Wasn't it funny when such and such happened?". Do you know what I mean?' She stood there, outside the circuit, while we pumped our limbs sympathetically.

Gwen turned to me. 'You don't mind, do you, Carol?'

'What, being on my own?'

'Yeah.'

I let myself think for a moment before I answered, dragging hard on the bars above me and exhaling noisily. Yes, it was better to be alone than with a man like Phil, and his stupid games and continual excuses that ground you down, and it had been like switching a light on when he finally went; I was giddy for days afterwards. And Jaz had gone, 'What took you so long, Mum?' And I'd said, 'I was waiting till you went to college,' and she'd said, 'Well, you needn't have.' Which felt like a slap in the face at the time, but I didn't dwell. Three last-chances he'd had, and he'd blown them all. That's enough for anyone.

'I don't mind it. I'm not often *on* my own. Matty stays over Saturday nights, plus I have him Wednesday afternoons, and I'm at the shop every morning. Evenings I'm here or swimming or Beavers or something else. I don't know how I'd cope with a man on top.'

'Ooh, a man on top!'

I realised what I'd said. 'Honestly, you lot.'

'She means, she doesn't know how she'd fit a man in,' chuckled Pauline.

Now move away from your stations and check your heart rate, said the CD. *Three, two, one – go.*

We stood for ten seconds like mannequins, fingers on throats.

'Everyone OK?' asked Gwen when we'd finished.

'Mine's a little high,' I said.

'You know the best cure for a broken heart,' broke in Sheila from the far end of the room. 'Go out and get laid.'

Shrieks of mirth.

'It's whether you can find someone half-decent, though,' said Aud.

'Oh, I don't let that stand in my way. Use it or lose it, that's my motto.'

'We have noticed,' said Pauline.

'Yeah, well.' Sheila shook her hair back out of her face. 'Get out there, I say, make the most of yourself. Have some fun. You're a long time dead.'

'Thought for the day, ladies,' said Gwen.

Some of us are fine as we are, I wanted to say, but that would have broken the mood. So I just smiled and held my tongue. The music changed to 'Dancing Queen'.

It was my turn for the punchball next.

At least when you're single you can have all your things where you want them.

When Phil lived here it was a house of motoring magazines – stacks of them in the downstairs cloakroom, by the bed, next to the sofa, flooding out of the shoe cupboard every time you opened the doors. His piles of copper were another irritation. I was forever emptying the hollows of ornaments, sweeping coins from the edges of tables, shelves and mantelpieces. The space beneath the sideboard he used for housing not one but three knackered old pairs of slippers; refused to be trained out of the habit. So no matter how scrupulously I tidied the lounge, that area always looked a mess. Then there was his shaving equipment: chargers and spare foils left on the bedroom floor to be trodden on, capsules of gel and bottles of balm and oil spread across sink, bath end, windowsill.

But best of all was when he took his clothes away, and hey presto, I had a whole wardrobe to myself and all the drawers I wanted. Over the years I'd managed to fill them up again: a hanging rail, the shelf above it, the space below, a huge oak press that had been Mum's, and two slide-under-the-bed plastic cases full of clothes.

So it was all the more mystifying that, this afternoon, there was suddenly nothing in the room that suited me. Not one item. It was as though a stranger – conservative, uninspiring – had broken into the house while I was at work, and planted her outfits in place of mine.

I picked up a suede-front cardigan and held it to the light. Decent quality, well looked-after, practical, comfortable, there wasn't anything wrong with it. There was nothing wrong with the four pairs of jeans or the six pairs of cords, the chunky sweaters, the row of white blouses, the black evening tops, my dark jackets. True, there wasn't a lot of colour here – only really my blue going-out skirt, my red wedding suit, and a turquoise patterned dress I'd not worn for over twenty years but was too fond of to throw out. Yet, till today, this collection had functioned perfectly well as a working wardrobe.

Now not even my old favourites felt right. All about me sat heaps of alien clothes with me in the middle, wondering who I'd turned into.

I checked myself in the dressing-table mirror again. No doubt about it, the new haircut was at the root of the problem. Since Wednesday I was flickier, choppier, highlighted and properly coloured, as opposed to home-dyed in twenty minutes while I caught up on the hoovering or sorted my knicker drawer. I'd gone to bed worrying I'd hate my new hair in the morning, dreamed all night about my teeth dropping out, but then, when I got up, the style had fallen into place with a light brush. She'd told me it was low-maintenance, the girl in the salon. 'Takes years off you, too,' she said. And it did, I couldn't argue, only it somehow made me feel all exposed as well. My head no longer matched my body.

A memory of something that had never been popped into my mind: Jaz and me in a café in town, chatting happily, bags of shopping around our chair legs. It shouldn't have been an unreasonable scenario. Other women did these things, mums and daughters together. I thought, We could go round the precinct next week; she could give me advice, I could treat her to something new. Then I remembered how stroppy she'd been on the phone last time we'd spoken. And anyway, who'd look after Matty while we were trailing round the changing rooms? Not Ian, for sure. (A real memory: Jaz at fifteen disappearing into a shop called Scruffy Herbert's, telling me *on no account* to come in after her; me standing in the doorway like a fool while youths in Doc Martens pushed past, knocking my Wallace and Gromit shopping bag.)

I glanced down at my pile of also-wrong shoes. Next to my navy courts was a *Woman's Weekly* back page showing an advert for a locket, one of those collectibles you have to pay for by instalments. *To a precious daughter* was engraved on the gold outside, then, when you opened it, *The day you were born I was truly blessed. Celebrate the special bond that only a mother and daughter can appreciate*, urged the text below. *Imagine her delight when she unwraps this unique gift.* Imagine her falling about laughing, more like.

I kicked the magazine under the bed, sending one of my courts skidding after it. Then I lay back on the duvet and contemplated the ceiling rose for a while. If I turned my head I'd be able to see, above the mirror, the picture Jaz drew for me one Mother's Day when she was about nine. *To Mum*, it said. *I love you.* X X X X X X, the faded felt-tip elephant holding a bunch of flowers in its trunk. Which made me think of some of the presents she'd given me over the years: how she'd scoured the internet to replace the Sylvac bowl I loved but broke; the shoebox she decorated herself with silver-sprayed lace and pressed flowers; the Joanna Trollope novel she'd queued for an hour to get signed.

One of those optical illusions, my daughter was: two black faces in profile or was it one white vase, and you never could see both together at the same time.

CHAPTER 14

Photograph 414, Album Three

Location: Paignton, summer of 1999

Taken by: Eileen

Subject: The sun shines strongly on Carol (oatmeal sundress) and Jaz (thick grey cardigan). They are squashed into the carriage of a miniature train that carts visitors from one side of the zoo to the other. Jaz isn't bothering to smile for the camera and neither, for once, is Carol. Her thoughts are too full of last night's events.

Eileen began it that first evening, mysteriously buying four ice creams, and then passing one to a shabby drunk sitting on the beach steps. 'Well, why not?' she declares gaily. Carol can think of several responses, but daren't voice any of them. It could be the medication that's making her so high, but then Eileen's always had a tendency to make the sweeping gesture.

Of course, every time they go down after that, he's there again and they have to repeat the exercise. Once Eileen adds a cone of chips into the bargain. 'Ketchup,' says the tramp. Not 'Thank you,' Carol notes. She can just imagine what Phil would have to say and wishes, fleetingly, he were on holiday with them. 'It might not be the kindest thing,' she says to

Eileen later. 'Like feeding those stray cats in Portugal. What will he do when we leave?'

The situation resolves itself when, on the penultimate afternoon of the holiday, the drunk man collapses in front of them like a pole-axed heifer. Crack! goes his head against the concrete steps. 'Quick,' says Eileen, reaching for her mobile. 'Make sure he doesn't swallow his tongue.' I'm not putting my fingers in there, Carol thinks, but she does run over to check his airway. He's shivering and his teeth are chattering, despite the day's heat. If only she had something to throw over him, a blanket or a coat, but all she has on is her strappy dress; Eileen's no better, in her shorts and Aertex top. How lucky, then, that Jaz has her thick cardigan (even if she has worn it all week in the face of stifling heat and commonsense). Before her daughter can argue, Carol has whipped it off her shoulders and thrown it down.

'Oh, heavens,' says Eileen, her attention diverted momentarily from the prostrate tramp. 'Carol, whatever are those marks all over Jaz's arms?'

The rockery at the far end of the pond had been there for as long as we'd lived in the house, and I'd never liked it. To me, a garden's for living, flourishing plants, not lumps of stone. It hadn't helped that my thyme had disappeared, and though I'd replaced it twice, the new shoots hadn't taken. Then the heather had become diseased so that meant another bare patch. There was a bindweed infestation coming up one side and now, while the rest of the garden bloomed, the rockery just looked like something mid-moult.

I'd asked Laverne if I could employ Josh to help dismantle it, and she'd immediately volunteered his time for free. I hadn't argued. Instead, Josh and I had come to a private arrangement, involving the minimum wage and my lemon-rind cake. Here he came with the pick, thunking it into the earth and levering away energetically. Under his long-sleeved T-shirt his shoulders were becoming bulky with muscle; only in the western world did we call a fifteen-year-old a child. Yet at the same time it was astonishing he'd so lately been a little boy, whizzing Hot-Wheels cars off the front step and building slug traps. As we worked, I saw again a tiny Jaz toddling along the path; on her first bike riding circuits round the lawn. It felt like all my married life was recorded in this garden.

An hour into the job, the plants had been grubbed up, and the top rocks removed and wheeled down to the scrubby space behind the shed. We still had the sides to deal with and the soil to shift, but it was clear we'd be done before the end of the day.

'Make sure you bend your knees when you lift,' I warned as we hoisted an extra-large slab between us. 'I don't want to have to cart you home in that barrow.'

Josh shook his head. 'All teenagers' spines are made of elastic, didn't you know? We're indestructible, we are.'

Together we inched our way crab-wise towards the bottom fence.

'If we were shifting rocks on the moon,' Josh said, 'we could carry them on our fingertips. We could boot them along like footballs.'

'I remember a man playing golf on the moon.'

'For real?'

'And his friend threw a javelin. It went miles. Are you ready to let go?'

Josh nodded, and the stone thudded onto the turf between our feet. At the same moment I looked up and Jaz was standing by the back door.

'I did ring the bell,' she called, letting go of Matty's hand.

I came forward and held out my arms for my grandson, but

he veered off towards the flowerbed by the fence, after something he'd spied there. Jaz walked up to the blasted rockery and inspected our work.

'Ooh, nice gloves,' she said, tipping her head at Josh. 'Very *floral*.' He coloured immediately.

'They're mine, as you know,' I said. 'He borrowed them to protect his fingers.'

'If you say so.' She poked the soil with her toe. 'Looks like a bomb's gone off here. God, so many worms. Don't let Matty see them.'

Josh pulled off the offending gloves and dropped them in the barrow. He hitched up his trousers nervously.

'Everything all right?' I asked her.

Jaz shrugged. Over her shoulder I watched Matty fish a rubber ball out from the leaves, then start across to us, holding the ball out in front of him. When he got near he held the ball not to me or his mum, but to Josh.

'Oh no, mustn't interrupt the worker,' said Jaz, swiping the ball from Matty's hands.

'Actually,' said Josh, 'I might have to go.'

'So soon? How's school? Getting all gold stars, I hope. Have you got lots of friends? What's your favourite subject? I'm guessing it's not sport. Computers? Maths?'

'He got all As and Bs last year,' I said.

'Oh, jolly good. Mind you, exams are easier than when I was at school.'

'You're only twenty-seven, love.'

'Yeah, but the pass mark gets lowered every year. They were probably twice as hard when I did them.'

Is that why it took you two goes to get your A-levels? I could have said. But that wouldn't have been fair. Or wise.

'I'm trying to think who he reminds me of,' she continued, putting her index finger against her chin.

'Come on,' I said to Josh. 'You can rinse your boots off under the outside tap. I've put the money next to the kettle for you.'

He dithered for a second, then re-hitched his trousers and set off across the lawn.

'Aled Jones,' Jaz shouted after him. 'That's who you look like. Stick a ruff round your neck and you'd be the spit.'

'Leave him alone,' I said, taking the ball from her and passing it back to Matty. 'And hush.'

'What? What have I said? He's a dork, anyway.'

I bent to prise out one of the smaller stones. 'No, he isn't. Why are you being so mean? He's a nice boy.'

'Same thing. A bit of teasing'll do him good. He needs toughening up.'

'He'll get there.'

'I pity him if he doesn't. You can be too soft on people, you know.'

'Like I'm too soft on you?' I said under my breath.

Perhaps she heard me, perhaps she didn't.

'Your hair.'

The stone came loose and I stood up. 'I wasn't sure you'd noticed.'

'God, yeah. I've been considering it. It suits you. It's a shock, because you never change, do you? But, yeah. What prompted the chop?'

'An impulse. *Ten Years Younger*. Who knows?' I set off with the stone towards the shed, and Jaz followed me.

'I used to help you in the garden, didn't I?' she said.

The rock dropped from my hands and I turned round to look at her. 'Oh, Jaz. You aren't jealous, are you? Is that why you chased him away?'

'Course not. I just wanted to talk to you on your own.'

'Oh?'

'Don't get your hopes up. It's nothing new, you've heard it

all before. Only, everything's really bad today, really bad. Like when it first happened. It's like, your anger kind of holds you together for so long, keeps you running, and then all at once you come crashing down?'

I nodded.

'How did you stand it, Mum, being on your own?'

She wasn't after an answer, which was lucky because I didn't have one. 'Here,' I said, reaching over for my spade, and she took the shaft in both fists as though it was a weapon.

'It's not that I want him back,' she said, 'but that doesn't stop me from feeling shit. I've not been sleeping. Everything goes round and round and round in my head till I have to get up even if it's two, three, four in the morning. Sometimes I catch myself talking to Ian out loud, as if he's in the room with me. I can't concentrate on work or anything, keep forgetting stuff. The worst is, I get so I think I'm coming out of it, and then I have a day like this one where I literally can't stand to be in the house on my own. Before I came here, I thought I was going mad. When's it going to get better, Mum? *Will* it get better?'

It was her eyes that worried me. I thought I recognised that look from before.

'Oh, love.' I was pulling off my gloves to hug her when my mobile went. Jaz swore again. 'I'll let it ring,' I said.

'No, go on,' she said. 'You might as well get it.'

So I picked up.

'Hello?' said David's voice. 'Carol? Have I called at a bad time?'

I stood by the sink and watched Jaz through the window. She'd moved to the edge of the pond to throw little pieces of grass and leaves on the water. Matty was still poking around the bottom of the hedge.

'We were just dismantling the rockery.' Guilt had me almost panting.

'And what had the rockery done to offend you?'

'Been a damn mess for years and years. It was when the heather disappeared it began to look really awful. The problem with heather is it tends to spread out and then die in the middle.'

'I know how it feels.'

On Jaz's right was a cherry tree we'd planted over the hamster. I thought of the morning she'd come in from burying him and I'd made her eggy bread and she'd been too sad to eat it. The more parenthood goes on, the more you realise how little you can put right.

'The reason I called,' David was saying, 'is to check whether Wednesday's still OK. You weren't sure, remember? But I could do with getting it in the diary. Ian can take a flexi-day. We could come over after lunch, if that suited.'

'It's fine. I can always give you a ring at the last minute if the situation changes.'

'You can, but please don't. Cancel at the last minute, I mean.' I could hear his breathing down the line. 'You've no idea what these visits mean to Ian.'

'Who was that?' said Jaz, as soon as I stepped through the back door.

I'd meant to lie but I couldn't; not about that, anyway. 'Your father-in-law.'

Her face fell. 'What's he ringing for?'

'For a chat. A chat with me, Jaz. To me.'

I must have overstressed that last bit, because her expression changed to one of puzzlement, then alarm.

'He's a nice man,' I continued, my blood thumping. 'We were talking about gardening.'

Yes, and I was born yesterday, she was clearly thinking. 'Well, I'd rather you didn't see him at the moment.'

'I'm not "seeing" him.'

'Being in contact, whatever. It feels like you're ganging up on me.'

'Don't be ridiculous. I like him, that's all. He's sensible to talk to.' Not a posturing idiot like your father, I could have added.

'I don't like it,' she said. 'Next time you speak to him, tell him from me he can fuck off.'

'Jaz!' I whipped round to see if Matty had heard, but he'd moved to the top of the garden and was digging with a stick near the drain. When I turned back she'd sat down on the grass with her shoulders slumped and her hair hanging. Part of me longed to shake her, to say, *We could all give up, love. Snap out of it, shape yourself.* But the stronger urge was to comfort.

I settled myself next to her.

'Look, Jaz, will you not reconsider?'

Her head came up, sulky and puzzled.

'I'm asking you straight out: please, please think about a reconciliation with Ian. You're so down, you're going to make yourself ill. I know what it's like, the aftermath—'

'How dare you!' she cried, jerking into life. 'What kind of a mother are you to suggest that?'

'One who wants the best for you. For Matty.'

'What, and you think going crawling back to a man who's got zero respect for me is "the best"? That the best thing for Matty is to grow up in a household where the parents loathe each other? I had to do that, and it was hell.'

I struggled to be gentle with her. 'You say that when you look back now, but at the time, you know, you were perfectly OK. You were, Jaz. You're seeing it from an adult's perspective.'

'What fucking planet were you on? How can you say that?

Were you *blind*? Or are you deliberately misremembering because that suits you?'

'I know that when you were older, just before your dad and I split up—'

'What about that time I saw him with Penny in town and I came home practically in tears? How can you not remember that?' She was wild-eyed now, and flushed.

'You did come home upset once – I think you were about twelve? But that was because you'd had a row with Nat.'

'Yes: *over Dad*. We'd argued because she'd told me Penny was *his mistress* and I didn't believe her.'

'You didn't tell me that.'

'I thought you knew! You *did* know. He'd been screwing her for years!'

'I knew about Penny, yes, but not why you were upset. You didn't say.'

'Did you ever ask, Mum? Did you *ever* stop to ask me?'

We were staring at each other then, completely absorbed, so I don't know exactly how it happened. I heard a single terrific splash, no other sound, and when I turned, the water in the pond was slopping the banks and Matty wasn't by the drainpipe any more.

It's not deep, my pond, but Matty's not very tall.

Before I'd struggled to my feet, Jaz had jumped up, thundered onto the plank bridge, scrambled down into the water, and was bending and feeling with her hands. In another second she'd hauled him out, streaming. 'Help me!' she shouted, because he was heavy and slippery and she was weighed down by her own sodden clothes. Her face was distorted, her mouth pulled down in an awful grimace, and her T-shirt was sticking to her skin in shiny folds. The ends of her hair were fused with moisture. At that moment I was completely terrified of her. But I lunged forward and took my grandson, who was writhing and retching, into my arms, and laid him on the grass. I felt the cold stain of him spreading across my blouse.

Jaz hauled herself onto the bank and bent over him. Matty's fair arms were marked with mud and strands of blanketweed; spots of duckweed clung to his cheek. Though I knew it wasn't important right now, I was desperate to wipe them away, to reclaim him from that nasty water.

'We'll get him in the bath,' I said.

She shot me this look, then went back to crouching over him, running her hands over his hair and chafing his fingers. The whole business, from Matty falling in till now, probably took less than a minute, but I knew I'd be re-playing it for the rest of my life.

Matty curled his body round, retched again, and began to howl. Jaz gathered him up and hugged him to her. 'Shhh, shhh,' she said. Their pose was like an old-fashioned painting, *Mother and Sick Child.*

'Let's get him inside,' I said, but they were a closed unit.

With difficulty I stood up – my legs were like rubber – and said, 'I'll start a bath running. He'll be frozen.'

'I *told* you to get it filled in when he was born! Told you!' She tried to shake wet strands of hair off her face but they wouldn't budge. 'Go and call the Health Centre. Tell them he might have inhaled some water. I want him checking over. I'll dry him off, I'll see to him.'

I hovered for a second. 'You're all right,' I said. 'You're all right, sweetheart.'

Matty just yelled harder.

'*Mum*,' Jaz said.

Behind her, the dark water was still churning with cloudy sediment like a collapsing universe. I ran to do as I was told.

CHAPTER 15

Photograph 419, Album Four

Location: Blakemere Moss, Nantwich

Taken by: Carol

Subject: a winter landscape – frozen water, bleached banks, stark trees, featureless sky. The only colour comes from the red light in the corner, which at first looks like a sunset. In fact it is chemical discoloration, caused by Carol leaving the film in the camera too long. It's been a pig of a year (losing Eileen to cancer, Dad's diagnosis, Jaz dropping out, hormones shutting up shop) and she hasn't felt like recording much of it. If ever there was a picture that summed up a moment, it's this.

By the time I told Josh about it on Monday morning, the pond incident was beginning to sound not nearly so bad.

'Of course he was upset, but once we'd got him dry, once Jaz had talked to the doctor and he'd given the OK, we went to the Gingerbread Playbarn afterwards and let Matty loose in the ball pit.'

'I used to love those places.'

'They're great, aren't they? Kids can hurl themselves about for hours and nobody minds.'

'Yeah, but I don't qualify any longer. The curse of somatotropin.'

'The curse of what?'

Josh stretched his legs as far as he could into the cramped space of the Micra's foot well. 'Human growth hormone. The Hungarian was banging on about it last week.'

'And how is our Hungarian? Still picking on that boy?'

He shook his head. 'Had a nasty incident with a sports bag, brought him right down.'

'What happened?'

'He likes to kick our bags out the way, if we leave them between the benches type of thing. He doesn't bend down and shift them, or tell us to, oh no. He just gets his toe in. Biff. Splinter.'

'Is he allowed to do that?'

Josh shrugged. 'We're supposed to stick our bags in the lockers outside, but nobody does because then your stuff goes walkabout. So someone had the idea to fill an old one with bricks, yeah, and plant it in the aisle. The Hungarian, he comes swooping down like a rugby player and gives it an almighty boot – *crunch.* Bones splintering, blood all over his sock, probably. It was excellent. We were killing ourselves.'

'Good God. What did he do?'

'Limped off in agony.'

'Didn't you get into trouble?'

'He didn't want to lose face, did he? Like, if he'd started unzipping the bag and shouting at us, he'd just have looked even more of a wazz than he already did.' Josh must have seen my expression. 'He totally deserved it. Wish it had been his kneecaps.'

'When I was at school,' I said, 'one trick we did was we used to zap each other with compass points.'

'What? Like, stab each other?'

'*No.*' I braked to let a bus pull out in front of me. 'Static electricity. There was this section of nylon carpet outside the Head's office, and if you shuffled your feet and then held out your compass point-first, you could give someone an electric shock. Sparks and all. It nipped, actually.'

'Cool.'

'I don't know who first discovered it, but every Year would pass it onto the kids below. We used to have battles there, although it was risky, what with the Head being just the other side of the door. My friend Eileen was particularly gifted in that department. And my ex-husband.'

'Expelliarmus!'

'Pretty much. Do you still use compasses these days?'

'Yup.'

We were coming to the lay-by where he liked to be let out these days. 'Well,' I said, 'don't let on it was me who told you.'

Josh mimed a compass-point electrocution. 'You may feel a little prick.'

'Have a nice day.'

He dragged his sports kit over the head-rest. 'I won't.'

The door slammed and he loped away.

A stream of lorries and buses kept me stationary, then the traffic came to a halt altogether. I stopped indicating, and put the handbrake back on. Images of Matty floating face down and lifeless in the water immediately covered my vision, and I had to wind down the window and breathe in some cold air to clear my head. 'I'll see about filling in the pond straight away,' I'd promised Jaz. To be fair, she hadn't gone on about it. She hadn't needed to. 'You know, when he's round here, I never take my eyes off him.' That had been the last thing I'd said to her. My eyes welled.

This was no good. Tissues, I needed tissues, and to pull myself together. Ridiculous to churn myself up about what might have been. There was nothing useful in the glove box, or in the door pockets, so I groped behind the passenger seat for the storage compartment there. All I could feel was the packet of wet-wipes I always kept handy for Matty. I unclipped my seat belt and turned to hunt properly, and that's when I saw the plastic bag on the floor, half-hidden under the front seat. I knew without opening it what was inside: Josh's football boots, which he needed today.

Could I still catch him? Forty minutes till I had to open the shop, so I wasn't in a desperate hurry. I wiped my eyes on my cuff, re-buckled my belt, indicated and pulled out into the traffic once more, cruising as slowly as I dared. Luckily it was all stop-start along this stretch anyway, with the crossing by the school and the roundabout up ahead. I crawled past the billboard advertising Thorn Valley Golf Club, past the bus shelter, then the ambulance station, all the while trying to work out how far he could have got during the time I was sitting in the lay-by.

Without warning Josh shot across the road two cars in front of me, straight out into the traffic, like a fugitive in a cop show. He actually jumped over the end of someone's bonnet. Brakes squealed and someone bibbed their horn. I only got a glimpse of his progress because a van was in the way, but after a few awful seconds I saw him reach the far pavement, running.

I'd hardly had time to register that when three other figures appeared in pursuit, dodging crazily between vehicles, swinging sports bags. I had an impression of flying shirts, a white face with the mouth open shouting something I couldn't hear, before they were gone too. Car horns were blaring, and a man in the opposite carriageway had wound down his window to lean out and curse. His lips were making shapes: *Fucking yobs. What the fuck do you think you're doing?*

And I sat there in my Micra, with those football boots on my front seat, not knowing what to do.

'What happened next?' said David, putting his mug down on the table and frowning.

I let my gaze shift to the far end of the room where Ian and Matty were building Duplo towers on the carpet. It had been raining heavily all day, and we had the lights on against the gloom. A stream of water fell from the middle of the gutter where the course was blocked, or damaged: another job I needed to sort out.

'There was a space of about a minute for me to make up my mind,' I told him. 'I thought, I could carry on up to the roundabout, come back on myself, and then either drive on to work, or make a left turn into the school car park. And that's what I did, stop at the school. Because I couldn't just go off and leave things, could I?'

David gave a very slight shrug.

'No, I couldn't. I'd have been thinking about him all day, worrying. With me being the one to drop him off, it felt like my responsibility. And I'm very fond of the lad.'

'I've gathered.'

'So I managed to find the main entrance, and it's not easy because it's such a big building, and all the while I was looking around to see if I could spot him but I couldn't. There were, I don't know, hundreds of children milling about, not always looking where they were going. I got to the secretary's desk but she was on the phone and I had to stand there and wait, all these kids streaming past me, laughing and yelling, and they're so loud I could barely think what I wanted to say. Then she finished the call, but there was another woman in front of me.

'By the time she'd been dealt with, the place was quietening down. I told the secretary I had Josh's boots and I needed to give them to him, and she looked up what room he was in and nabbed a lad going past to take me up there. Just as well she did because I'd never have found my way otherwise. I said to the boy, "It's like a rabbit warren, isn't it?" But he said you got used to it.

'He showed me to a classroom and left me there, and I peeped through the glass and I could see Josh at the back, putting his books out on the table. He seemed all right. So I knocked on the door and the teacher, he was only young himself, said to come in, and I held the bag up and asked if I could have a word with Josh. I thought when Josh saw me he might get up and come over, and I could talk to him outside, in private. But he stayed where he was.'

David had this expression on his face as if to say, 'I know how this story's going to end.'

'I took the bag over and said, "Here's your boots," and he just went, "Thanks." I was trying to catch his eye but he wouldn't look at me. I couldn't stand there for ever, so I said, "OK?" And he said, "*Fine.*" Like that, quite determined. There was nothing I could do without making a fuss, although I did toy with the idea of speaking to the teacher. Then I thought I'd better have a chat with Josh first.'

'What you don't want to do is make the situation worse,' said David.

'No, that's what I was worried about. I haven't mentioned it to his mum yet for the same reason. She's hyper at the best of times.'

'And what's Josh got to say on the matter?'

Over by the window, Matty's tower leaned, toppled, and scattered itself widely across the floor. 'Uh-oh,' he said. 'Cash!' Ian reached across and ruffled his hair.

'I asked him this morning. He says it was nothing. Does it

sound like nothing to you? Do you think he's being bullied? Should I tell Laverne? He is lying, isn't he?'

'Almost certainly he's lying,' said David, swilling his coffee round in its mug. 'But I don't think you should interfere. Not yet, anyway.'

'It's not interfering, it's helping someone who I think's in trouble.'

'Boys have chased other boys since time began, Carol. It's what they do.'

'Across busy roads, in front of cars? Imagine if – And then, I've been thinking: sometimes he tells me about this pupil the teacher picks on, and I think it's him. He tells it as though it's another boy, but it's him, I'm sure of it. So that teacher needs to be dealt with, because he's inflaming the situation, he's giving the bullies licence. It's abuse.'

David drained his cup and set it down decisively.

'Wouldn't you say you've got enough on your plate just at the moment?'

All the fight and the fury went out of me, and I sagged. 'You mean with the pond.'

I had no idea why I kept telling everyone about it. Laverne and Mrs Wynne, Moira and several customers at The Olive, the girls down the gym and the man who called for the Betterware catalogue had all been treated to the story of how I nearly drowned my grandson. I'd even gone so far as to ring Phil and pour out the tale to him.

'To be honest,' said David. 'I was thinking more—'

'The next time you come, it'll be filled in, I promise. I've contacted a landscaping firm, and I'm going to have a word with the Ahernes at the back because they've got a pond and they could take my newts.'

'I don't think you need go that far, Carol.' David stood up and wandered over to the French window. Rain was running down the other side in torrents, creating a weird light, blurring the shapes into each other so that my garden was a fluid landscape of unnatural greens.

'Oh, I do, I do. It'll break my heart to get rid of it, but I can't take the risk.'

'Steel mesh would fix it.' David turned and bent to intercept Matty who was about to collide with his legs. He lifted his grandson off the ground, brought him round to face Ian, then propelled him back the way he'd come, in one neat action.

'You mean a fence?' I asked.

'No. A flat grid over the top. I've installed them in a couple of properties. There are regs about gauge, it's got to be rigid and secure. But I can give you the name of a company who'll fit you one. You don't have to lose your pond unless you want to.'

'Really?' The news lifted my spirits hugely. 'And they're definitely safe that way?'

'RoSPA recommended.'

I thought again of the day Ian dug out my pond, how delighted I'd been then.

'You've a solution for everything, haven't you?'

'No, not quite everything. But a pond's nothing. Ponds can be sorted, like *that*.' He clicked his fingers, then we both looked at each other for a long bleak moment.

Over in the corner, father and son were sorting bricks into piles of different colours, or trying to. Matty was just making piles.

I said: 'Would you believe I'd planned a picnic for this afternoon?'

'Ah.'

'Although Matty would probably like it, splashing about in a downpour. Toddlers do.'

'Well, middle-aged people don't. Anyway, you don't want to spoil your new hairdo.'

I put my hand up to my fringe self-consciously.

'It's very nice,' he said. 'Here's an idea: couldn't you spread a picnic blanket out on the floor in here? Children don't really care what you do as long as you're doing it with them.'

'Doesn't it get wearing, being so brilliant all the time?'

David rewarded me with a thin smile. 'Actually, it's a trick I remember Jeanette pulling once when Ian was little. Do you want a hand putting your sausage rolls out?'

We left Matty and Ian now making a snake or a wall or a lying-down tower, and went into the kitchen to plate up.

Which is how Phil came to find us half an hour later: kneeling round one of my mother's tray cloths, sipping from plastic beakers, while Matty crumbled breadsticks down his front.

I read the look on Ian's face as the bell rang, and rang again. 'She's in Manchester all day,' I said, as I scrambled to my feet. 'She'd an appointment at the university.'

The men exchanged glances. I hurried out into the hall.

'Carol?' said Phil when I opened the door, as though there was some doubt in his mind as to my identity. Water was dripping from the porch down the back of his coat; beyond him the street was a haze of rain.

'What do you want?' I asked, hanging onto the doorframe and blocking the entrance.

'I was passing. You seemed upset.'

'When?'

'On the phone.'

'No.'

'You were. About the pond, and Matty.'

'I'm fine.'

'Oh. Well. Good. I've a present for him, anyway.' Phil jiggled a plastic carrier at me.

Perhaps Matty had heard his name, because a few seconds later he appeared at my side. 'Gappa,' he said.

'Hello, mate,' said Phil, and squatted down so he was at Matty's level. 'Fancy seeing you. Now, what do you think I've got in this bag, eh? Shall I come in and show you?'

I stepped back to allow him a foot of space.

'Yeah?' he said, straightening up again. 'Hey, Matt, what's in the bag?'

Zero response.

'What do you reckon? An elephant? A bus?'

'Oh, for goodness' sake.'

Matty had already lost interest and was wandering over towards the stair gate, so I took the bag off Phil and investigated for myself.

It was a cardboard box with the Lego symbol on the tab. Little pieces shifted inside as I turned it over. The front showed a red robot shooting death rays out of its fingers.

'Bionicle,' said Phil. 'Let him see.'

'No.'

'What?'

'It's not suitable. It's too old.'

Phil gritted his teeth in exasperation. 'You can build it *for him*, Carol. I know he can't manage the construction on his own, but every lad likes a robot.'

'Yes, but it's got small parts. See? *Not suitable for children under 36 months. Choking hazard.*'

'They only say that to cover themselves. Look at what Jaz had to play with when she was little. Your button tin, for one. Beads, plastic figures, pebbles. She never came to any harm, did she?'

'That was when she was older. I'll put it away for him, Phil.'

Now Matty came toddling back over, reaching up to grasp Phil's trouser leg. 'Gappa,' he said again.

'I might have known there'd be something wrong with it,' said Phil. 'My present. I'd have put money on that.'

'You know, you're the one—' I began, but the box slipped out of my hand and fell with a thunk and a rattle onto the carpet. Phil waited till I bent to retrieve it, then took the opportunity to slip past with Matty. 'Oh, hang on, it's not really convenient,' I called after him, but too late because he was standing in the entrance to the living room with his mouth open.

'Carol?'

'It's all right,' I said, even though it wasn't, not by a long chalk.

David stood up as if he was meeting a client, and stretched out his hand. 'Phil.'

'Is Jaz here?'

'No, she's working today,' I said, feeling my face grow hot.

'. . . dropped by,' mumbled Ian in the background.

'We're having a picnic,' went on David.

'Ta,' said Matty, passing up a cherry tomato. Phil took it from him and stared at it.

David gave up on the handshake and sat down again. 'Help yourself,' he said. 'I can recommend the Dairylea.'

I watched Phil dither on the spot, the back of his coat still stained by the rain, and I could tell exactly what was going through his head.

'How's business?' said David. 'This banking thing affecting you at all?'

'Not really,' said Phil. 'Jaz is working, you say, Carol?'

I nodded.

He turned back to David. 'So . . .'

'I came to see my grandson,' said David. 'Incidentally, I think we may have solved the pond problem. Do you want to tell him, Carol?'

Although Phil, as the only man standing, should have had the advantage, he was the one out of place and awkward. He cleared his throat, turned his gaze to Ian. One adulterer to another, I was thinking. David's the only decent one among you. For a few seconds I let myself run a little fantasy: Phil and David locked in physical combat, brawling across the remains of the picnic so that beakers spilled over, fairy cakes were squashed, my mother's ornaments trembled in the display cabinet.

Then Matty, picking his way across the tray cloth, trod on a plate, lost his balance and fell over. He struck his head on the arm of the sofa and began to cry. I started forwards, but Ian was already pulling him onto his lap, shushing and stroking.

Phil's hand was on my arm.

'Come into the kitchen, you,' he said. 'I need a word.'

The light coming in through the window was that golden, pre-sunset type that should make you feel relaxed. Perhaps Dad was relaxed. How was I to know? They'd shifted his chair forward so he could see out of the window, but as the sun dipped lower he'd become dazzled, so I'd turned him side-on. One cheek and ear was gilded, like an angel's.

'Mrs Wynne's granddaughter's not so good,' I said.

In the corridor outside I could hear shouting, and then a nurse's voice, calm and upbeat.

'You remember when her little girl had that fit? Well, Libby's all right, but they don't know if the baby's growing properly. Mrs Wynne says she's got to go in for some tests.' I stretched my fingers out into the shaft of light. 'Which is obviously worrying. When I think about it now, Jaz had an easy pregnancy, didn't she?'

It wasn't my day to be there, but I'd been sitting at home and suddenly I needed to see my dad. Now I was here, I still felt restless and undone.

The glass on the sunburst clock bulged, as if there was too much time inside it, and the earth rolled us towards night. Someone's walking frame tap-tapped along the corridor.

'I just wish I knew,' I said, forgetting the fiction that he could hear, that he could understand, that I'd get any response; forgetting it all and talking to myself. 'Am I doing the right thing? Letting them into my house, going behind her back? She's my daughter.'

You're playing a fucking dangerous game, I heard Phil say again.

'Who should I be supporting here? Who counts the most, Matty, or Jaz?'

Under Dad's eye a nerve flickered, a momentary spasm. That was all. Nothing more.

CHAPTER 16

Photograph: unnumbered, loose inside an old Bunny-Bons toffee tin, the shed, Sunnybank.

Location: outside Jaz's university hall of residence, Leeds

Taken by: Tomasz Ramzinski

Subject: Jaz and her father stand with their backs against the wall, as if they're about to be shot. Phil has his arms folded and Jaz is biting her nails. To Jaz's left, some boy inside the building squashes his face against the window in a grotesque leer.

This has been a disaster of a day.

Phil's intention was to drive his girlfriend, Penny, over to Leeds so she could meet Jaz properly. But on the way there, he apparently said something wrong – he's not sure what – and before he knew it, Pen was accusing him of all sorts. Not taking the relationship seriously, not committing, being ashamed of her, not earning enough money, taking no interest in soft furnishings. After a while he stopped listening. The upshot was, she sat in the car while he went to see his daughter on his own.

Jaz seems OK, as far as he can tell. Has a boyfriend, has a girlfriend, likes her tutor, isn't living in squalor. He'd say she's a bit restless, a bit impatient, but maybe that's just with him. Hasn't she always found him irritating?

Then the boyfriend makes an appearance, and she loses interest in her dad altogether.

Before Phil leaves, he gets the boyfriend – very full of himself, that one – to take a photo. It would be nice to show the picture to Carol; she worries about Jaz being away from home. That he can never do, though. She'd winkle out the details of the trip in no time. For all he's a practised adulterer, he's a lousy liar.

I'd come off the machines and was doing my stretches when Sheila bounced into the gym. (Poor Sheila, whose grandchildren were growing up on the other side of the world.) She clocked in at the computer, looked across, and saw me.

'You drive a blue Micra, don't you?' she said.

My heart sank. 'What's up? Have I been pranged?'

'Not exactly.'

I cut the stretches short, picked up my keys and hurried outside to see.

My car was parked in its usual spot, unharmed, except that tied round the driver's-side wing mirror was a silver helium balloon. It strained and twisted on its string, flashing in the sunlight.

'Looks like someone's got an admirer,' said Sheila behind me.

'Looks like someone's playing silly beggars,' I said.

I walked around and started picking at the knot. It wasn't very secure and soon came loose under my fingernails. I teased out the loop, pulled the tail free and the balloon jerked, jerked again, then floated upwards, off to God knows where. A fraction of a second too late, I realised I could have kept it for Matty.

*

'You know about Monday?' said Laverne over the fence as I was attempting to skim duckweed off my pond.

'Josh not needing a lift? Yes, he reminded me. And it's two weeks, isn't it?'

'That's right.'

'Is he looking forward to his work experience?'

'Yes – well – I don't know. Why he chose the cottage hospital, all those ill people, when he could have gone in a nice clean office.'

'I should imagine he'll be good with the patients, though. Is that what he wants to do when he leaves school? Nursing, something in that line?'

Laverne pursed her lips doubtfully. 'I'm not sure. I don't want to think about it. My little boy, growing up too fast. I've no idea what to do about his birthday, either, that's coming up next month. He's at a funny age. You haven't any suggestions, have you?'

'For his party or his present?'

'Both.' She tilted her head back and looked at the sky, as if inspiration might be writ there. 'It sounds silly to say it about your own son, but – he's strange, in some ways. I don't feel I know him that well.'

'It doesn't sound silly at all,' I said, then wondered whether I'd come across as rude. 'What I mean is, just because someone's part of your family doesn't mean you're privy to their deepest thoughts. It used to be a struggle to buy for Jaz. In the end we just gave her money, and that always went down well.'

'Oh, I'm not giving him *money*,' she said, as though I'd suggested parcelling up some crack cocaine. 'He's got to have a proper present.'

I tried to imagine what might make it onto Laverne's approved list. A book? A non-violent video? 'How about one of those "experience days" where they get to drive a rally car?'

She shuddered. 'Not that.'

'Or zookeeper for a day? Dorothy Wynne's chiropodist did that, said it was amazing. Josh likes animals, doesn't he? And he could invite a few friends to meet him at the zoo afterwards.'

'I'm not . . .' Her face grew vague. 'His friends . . . It's a part of his life that . . . Look, Carol, does he ever talk to you about school? I know you chat in the car.'

The truth was, Josh wasn't talking to me at the moment. Nowadays we mainly sat in silence on the drive to school. The most response I'd had lately was when I told him the story of how Eileen and I had covered our maths books in foil and then flashed them in the eyes of the teacher all lesson long, but even then he was only briefly interested.

'I thought he might have let something slip,' she said. 'To you.'

'What about?'

'I don't know.' She was looking straight at me now, her stringy neck at full stretch, her eyes too wide. I thought of a programme I'd seen about parents who have their kids micro-chipped, and who put up hidden cameras to spy on their childminders. Then I remembered Josh running into the road. What he needed for his birthday were self-defence lessons and a Kevlar vest.

'I think there's something going on. Sometimes he – You would tell me,' she said, 'if you knew there was something wrong?'

The moment teetered on its edge.

'Wouldn't you?'

It was the pause that undid me.

I was actually in bed when the phone went. Not asleep, but settled and wound-down with the lights low. Chilled, as Jaz would say. Then this jaunty blast of music, jerking me into wakefulness. It wasn't the landline, either, it was my mobile, which meant I had to get up, switch on the main light, and hunt the thing down.

'Seriously, though,' went Phil's tinny little voice, as though we'd been in the middle of a conversation, 'I don't think you should be having him round.'

'What?'

'I've been thinking about road signs. You know.'

'No.'

'Those flashing boards that tell you to slow down.'

'Are you drunk, Phil? You sound drunk.'

'A bit.'

I retreated to the bed and climbed back in, pulling the duvet up around myself for decency. 'Where's Penny?'

'Not here.'

Why else would you be calling me so late, I nearly said. 'She's not in hospital, is she?'

'God, why do you say that?' Phil sounded frightened.

'You told me she wasn't well.'

'Oh, no, she's fine. She's, no, she's. Gone to a friend's. Anyway, we're not talking about her.'

'Look, Phil, what do you want?'

There was some scuffly noise and heavy breathing; perhaps he'd dropped the phone. I was on the point of giving up when he spoke again.

'It's bothering me. If you keep having Ian round, Jaz'll find out and then there'll be hell to pay.'

I made myself count to five before I replied.

'So you said, Phil. But if I block him from seeing his son, there'll be trouble from a different direction, trust me. And when I've tried to negotiate between them, that's been disastrous too. Far as I can tell, I'm between a rock and a hard place and another rock.'

'He's not threatened you, has he? Stuck-up bastard. Because if he has—'

'It's not like that. But Ian has rights, and if Jaz ignores them—'

'We can't start telling her what to do or she'll get shirty with us as well.'

'You think I don't know that? For God's sake!'

'I don't have an answer,' said Phil.

'So what's new?'

'Carol, I—'

'Stirring things up, to no purpose! As if you're in any position to adopt the moral high ground. And stop tying balloons to my car, stupid bloody carry-on. And stop calling me when your girlfriend's away. And get my shed cleared out. Why don't you *ever* do anything *useful*?'

I switched the phone off.

Might as well get up and make a drink, do some stretches, maybe sort out some bills. There was no chance of getting a good night's sleep now.

When I'm in a particularly self-destructive mood, I get out the photograph of Penny. No one knows I have it, not even Jaz, and she actually took the damn thing.

It was one afternoon when Phil had dropped by with some message or other (this was after the divorce, when we were supposed to be square and sorted), and Penny was in the car. He told me. 'Pen's outside,' he said. I don't know if he was expecting me to ask her in. I'm ashamed to admit this, but my immediate response was to stalk across and jerk the curtains closed. Then, of course, we'd been plunged into ridiculous gloom. I ought to have taken him through to the kitchen, only that felt like defeat, so whatever it was we needed to talk about we did in semi-darkness, like those ex-cons on TV whose faces have been hidden to protect their identities. I'd been aware of Jaz crashing about upstairs, but my mind had been on other things. Then, when Phil had gone, she came down and showed me what was on my own digital camera: a bored-looking, pudding-faced blonde gazing out of a car window. That was the first time I'd laid eyes on my husband's mistress.

I could have seen her before, if I'd wanted. I'm sure I could have found all kinds of evidence over the years, had I looked for it. I could have hung around near the office, or hired someone to trail her and make a report. Some wives do that, collect files of information; their way of coping. My energy's always gone into blotting Penny out.

Nevertheless some fragments of unwanted information have slipped through. She wears contact lenses; her brother's a nurse; she has to use special shampoo or she gets eczema; she has a mild London accent; her dad once served Dick Emery a tank-full of petrol; she's never wanted children; she's an immoral, unsisterly witch.

I ought to have deleted the picture at once – two presses of a button and it would have gone for ever. But instead I put the camera to one side, waited till Jaz was out one evening, and printed a copy. I wiped the image off the camera, then sat and held the photograph in my hands for an age, just looking at it. This is her? I kept thinking. *This?* Penny's mouth was one of those too-small smug ones, her cheeks plump and going to jowl. Her hair hung to shoulder length, in no particular style. Difficult to tell much about her figure or clothes, but she looked wider than I was, and lumpier. Like me, she was middle-aged. That was all. A completely unremarkable woman.

I remember laughing, at first, in disbelief. Mistresses were supposed to be glamorous and young and willowy. I imagined saying to Phil, *God, is she truly the best you could manage? You junked your marriage for THIS?* After a while I put the photo down, went to my bedroom and, with trembling hands, redid my hair and make-up, as though I was getting ready for the date of my life.

For half an hour after that, I'd been high as a kite. Then, without any warning I was sobbing without restraint, the way I hadn't let go in years. Within minutes my face was a slimy mess, my breath juddering uncontrollably. It felt as though every single tear I'd held back, every spurt of rage I'd stifled over the years was now rushing out of me in a torrent, a huge outpouring that I was physically incapable of stopping.

I have no idea how long this session lasted, but finally I think I just ran out of steam. That was the last occasion I cried over Phil. By the time Jaz came home I'd showered and blow-dried my hair, rubbed on my night cream, and was sitting watching *Blackadder II* in my dressing-gown. 'Everything OK?' she'd asked me. 'Fine,' I'd told her.

I keep meaning to get rid of Penny's photo: burn it, or post it through the floorboards so that, in years to come, strangers will go searching for wires or pipes and find this fragment of an evening's self-harm under a layer of dust and mouse dirt. It's what she deserves. And yet I can't quite bring myself to let the picture go. So it lives in my bureau, face down at the back of the drawer, and whenever I need to stick a knife into myself, out comes Penny again.

I'm well aware I shouldn't, but it's not as if I actually cut myself, the way some women do. The way my daughter did.

CHAPTER 17

Photograph 404, Album Three

Location: a Little Chef car park, half way between Sunnybank and Leeds University

Taken by: Carol

Subject: Jaz leaning against the bonnet of Phil's car. She looks cross, but that's only because she's trying to hide her nerves. Behind her, the boot and half the back seat are crammed with the gear she thinks she will need for her first term.

Phil is not in the picture, even though he is the one doing the driving. As a now officially ex-husband, he shouldn't be on the scene at all, except that Carol's car is suddenly kaput and there seems no other way, at such short notice, of transporting Jaz's goods and chattels across the country. Penny has magnanimously agreed it is OK.

Never have fifty miles seemed so far.

At the previous stop, Carol had to go in search of Phil; found him standing by the side of the road wearing his old fluorescent jacket and holding Jaz's hairdryer to simulate a police speed trap. 'Bloody hilarious watching them slam their brakes on,' was his explanation.

'Why does Dad have to be such a prick?' mutters Jaz, below Phil's hearing, and both women snigger miserably together. It is the one bright spot in a long, long journey.

The kitchen of the Scout hut always smelled of powder paint because it also served as the art storage area. Over the worktop where I was now slicing bread rolls hung a string of papier-maché-covered balloons; both windowsills were jammed with unpainted clay candleholders. Before I'd been able to get at the fridge, I'd had to shift a full-size post box built of corrugated card.

On the other side of the steel serving shutter, the gang show was in full swing. Rows of parents, grandparents and Scout- and Cub-siblings were being entertained by various ropey acts, prior to a sing-along and buffet. One of the mums was supposed to be helping me with the catering, but she hadn't shown. All the leaders were out the front, supervising.

'Two big piles of rolls, one cheese spread and one chocolate, and bugger healthy eating,' Akela had told me. There was also squash to make up and tins of cakes and biscuits to unpack. 'I'm really sorry I can't stay,' she said. 'Another pair of hands would have been useful, wouldn't it?'

Snatches of the show filtered through as I worked. 'Let the audience see your card,' I heard as I punctured the foil on a jar of Nutella. 'Pass me my magic cloth, Wolverine.' The butter had gone hard and I had to beat it with a fork before it was any good. I thought of my mother whisking egg whites by hand and how red and furious her face would turn before she'd finished. 'Was this your card?' the magician cried. 'Oh, hang on.'

Which is when the back door opened and David walked in. I almost dropped my fork in shock.

'Is something wrong?' was my immediate question.

'No.'

'Why are you here?'

'I was passing. I wanted to see you.'

'How did you know where I was?'

'You said yesterday, on the phone.'

His appearance, unannounced and out of context, flustered me and I lost track of where I was up to and knocked over my jar.

'Are you busy?' he said as I scrabbled about.

I raised my eyebrows at the piles of food.

'OK, I'll rephrase that: would you like some help while I'm here?'

'Were you really "just passing"?'

'No.'

'So what is it? Has something happened with Ian or Jaz?'

'Not that I'm aware of, and I only saw Ian half an hour ago. No, I was just at a loose end and I wanted to see you. Should it be so strange?'

You're fooling no one, I thought. Something's rattled you. You've had a row with Ian and you needed a refuge, let everything simmer down. I could just tell.

'All right,' I said. 'Since you're offering, you're more than welcome. Hang your coat up over there and wash your hands. I need those cake tins unpacking, and what's in them arranging on the foil platters in the corner. We've probably got about fifteen minutes till the end of the show and I've not even started on drinks yet.'

David followed my instructions, rolled up his shirt-sleeves and set about plating-up. Skull-jarring music thumped through the wall from next door. 'What in God's name's that?' he asked, peering through the slots between the shutters.

'Charlie Blunt break-dancing. It's all right, he'll be finished in another thirty seconds.'

'You sat through rehearsals?'

'God, no, they do all their rehearsing at home. But I know because he used to do exactly the same act before he became a Cub, while he was still a Beaver.'

I sawed into bread at top speed, careless of the skin between my finger and thumb.

'How did you get into all this in the first place, Carol?'

'The Boy Scout thing? Gosh, well, Sal Vaughan, the original Dove – not this new one who I don't really know yet – was a friend of Laverne's. I started helping Beavers when Josh was in the pack, and stayed on after he left. But I sometimes get drafted in for Cub and Scout dos as well, hence tonight.'

'And you do this for no pay?'

I drew the back of my hand across my brow in a gesture of martyrdom. 'Actually, the ones who deserve medals are the pack leaders who turn up every week and have to organise all the events and be responsible. I just potter in the background.'

The thumping bass stopped at last, to be replaced after a pause by a halting violin solo. David prised the lid off another tin.

'Ah, yet more fairy cakes. How many are we feeding? Five thousand, is it?'

'You have no idea how much these lads can get through at a sitting. It's devastation. They hold competitions to see who can stuff the most in their mouth at once.'

'Does that come under badgework?'

'Scoffers Award.'

A little grin appeared on David's face.

'What?' I said.

'This vast acreage of food. Reminds me of the birthday parties Jeanette used to throw when Ian was small. She always over-catered, always we'd be eating leftovers for a week afterwards.'

'Well, you do. I did, with Jaz.'

'It was like a competition: the table had to be crammed. Hedgehogs out of Matchmakers, jelly goldfish.'

I said, 'How long were you married?'

'Eleven years. Though we met three years before that. She was a secretary in my father's office. I came back from London, and there she was.' His brow furrowed at the memory.

'Was she ill a long time?'

'About two years, from first diagnosis.'

'It must have been hard.'

'Yes.'

'I'm sorry,' I said, as the violin scraped to a conclusion.

David shook his head. 'I'll say what no one else is entitled to: it's twenty years ago, and life moves on. At the time she died I never thought it would, but it does and thank God for it.'

I watched as he carried on laying out cakes to some precise and careful pattern of his own devising. He looked so comfortable with himself, this man in his fifties, with his expensive shirt and sleek haircut, that it was impossible to imagine him young and vulnerable. Twenty years ago, when I was trying to work out whether to dismantle my marriage or not.

The sandwiches finished, I put the butter away and shook the crumbs into the sink. I was about to move the conversation on by asking about work when a Cub on the other side of the screen shouted, 'Hey, mums and dads, want a great family day out, with fun and thrills for all ages?'

'Yeah,' someone yelled back gamely.

There was a brief pause, some whispering, and a giggle.

'Then come to – shurrup, stop it, Tom – come to Knickerworld! The country's only pants-based theme park. Yes, we've got it all at *Knicker*world.'

The audience tittered. David raised his eyebrows at me.

'They write the script themselves,' I said.

'Evidently.'

'*There's millions of knickers all under one roof*,' sang the Cub.

'Kids,' called another one. 'Come and ride in our giant Y-fronts! See our display of famous people's kecks! Marvel at the history of undercrackers in our award-winning museum! And don't forget to pick up some souvenir grundies in the gift shop.'

'Because you're worth it.'

'Try on a selection of smalls from other countries, including porcupine pants, termite trunks, bumblebee boxers and shark-skin Speedos.'

'Knickerworld, the best of both worlds.'

After every line there was shrill laughter, which quickly began to affect the performers themselves. The routine continued, but with gaps of increasing duration where the boys were struck voiceless, convulsed with the hilarity of their own jokes.

'Visit our fabulous café and sample shreddies with a difference—'

'*Maybe she's born with it, maybe it's underpants*.'

'See royal golden pants.'

'*Here come the pants*—'

'And our special room of record-breaking pants.'

'*The pants effect*.'

'– including the smelliest –'

'*The pants of your life*.'

'– your mum's –'

'– big hairy pants –'

The sketch dissolved into helpless sniggering, and Akela took charge. 'Thank you, Robbie and Max, for that very interesting sketch. I'm sure we'll all be saving up to go to, er, Knickerworld in the near future.'

I could hear several boys having what sounded like asthma attacks.

'Easily amused, aren't they?' said David.

'God, yes. Anything at all to do with undercarriages.'

'. . . the part where we ask the families to join in,' Akela was saying, 'as a way of showing their appreciation for the boys' hard work. So if I could ask Martin . . .'

'Quick,' I said, 'we've got about five minutes to sort the drinks.'

While David tore open the polythene wrapper and released the cups, I poured a couple of inches of undiluted juice into an empty gallon container and held the neck under the cold tap. Through the wall came the jolly sound of audience participation.

'There were snakes, snakes, big as garden rakes,

In the store, in the store.'

Once the squash was made up, we started a production line. David held each cup at the base to stop it falling over, and I filled it as far as the plastic crimps.

'In the quartermaster's store.'

After about the first ten we got into a rhythm. 'Anyway, what about you?' said David.

'What about me?'

'Where are you up to?'

'In what way?'

'With your life. The past. Anything.'

'There were gulls, gulls, pecking on your skull.'

My mind at once emptied itself. All I could dredge up at that instant was a random image, a night over thirty years ago, back at Pincroft, trying to write my wedding list during a power cut. When the electricity came on afterwards, my mother found that one of the candles had burned a black spot on the underside of the shelf above and the only person she could blame for it was herself.

'There's nothing to tell,' I said. 'I am who I am: Jaz's mum, Matty's grandma.'

'And?'

'Akela, Akela, Snogging with a sailor.'

'I don't know what you mean, David. I'm fifty-two, I'm divorced. I work in a gift shop. I like photography and gardening, I'm a member of a women's gym – you already know all this.'

'You're telling me your CV. What about *you*?'

'My *eyes are dim, I cannot see*
I have not brought my specs with me
I have not brought my specs with me.'

The song dissolved into screams and whoops and clapping. And then the shutter went up a fraction and Charlie Blunt's face peered underneath. 'Akela says are you ready for us?'

'We are,' I said, with the sense of someone who's had a narrow escape, though I couldn't have told you what from.

The hall was hot and full and a sea of green sweatshirts. Scouts came forward to take the plates and offer them round; the drinks were serve-yourself.

'Are you finished here, or do you have to stick around?' asked David.

'My work here is done. Someone else can wash up.'

The boys were giddy with post-performance relief, high and naughty and fun. I looked out across the rows of chairs and saw parents I recognised, children I'd watched grow up. Martin Clark, a Venture Scout in his last term at school, I'd known since he was a shy ten-year-old with a speech impediment; now he was six feet tall and comfortable playing guitar in front of forty people. I felt my throat tighten at this glow of youth before me. All that energy and promise and clear skin.

'Do you fancy a drink, then?' said David.

I let him lead me back through the kitchen and out of the rear entrance into the car park.

'Where's your Micra?' he asked.

'I walked. It's only twenty minutes.'

He came round to open the passenger door of his Audi. I'd forgotten such courtesies. Inside it was clean and polished, no wet wipes on the floor or muddy marks on the seats. No sweet wrappers in the coin compartment.

'Where shall we go?'

'The Lion's nice.'

'I don't know where that is.'

'Top of the High Street. I'll direct you. Although we're not going anywhere just yet.' In front of us a Saab waited for an ancient Citroën to complete a twelve-point turn. 'Why he doesn't back out . . .'

I wound the window down and breathed in the spring evening.

'How's, you know, your girlfriend who isn't your girlfriend?' I said.

For a few seconds he didn't answer. I thought he was concentrating on the Citroën.

'David?'

'I'm not seeing her any more.'

'Oh. Oh, I'm sorry.'

'I told her this evening.'

So that was why he'd been after my company. As I'd guessed, not for its own pleasure, but because he needed cheering up. Only I'd picked the wrong source of upset. I weighed the thought, decided it was OK; we all require the distraction of the ordinary at times of emotional crisis. 'You should have said.'

'Well.'

'Was it horrible? I'm really sorry.'

'Bloody awful, actually, but it had to be done. And now it's finished.'

I pictured him in some grand hotel foyer speaking urgently with a woman who looked like the model on the Golden Age skin cream ads. Then I thought, Why am I imagining him in a hotel? They'd have been in David's house, or round at hers. I wondered whether she'd cried or shouted, or just been incredibly cool. 'Did she have an idea?'

'She claimed she didn't. I wish I'd never— But I did.'

The Citroën flung itself at the gate-post, stopped with a fraction of an inch to spare.

'Rotten for you,' I said inadequately, 'on top of everything else.'

'No, really, a relief. For me. It's not been – she's not – she wasn't—'

In my imagination I saw the Baroness from *The Sound of Music* flick her cigarette towards Maria.

'I knew something was up, as soon as you came in.'

'There you go, then.'

'As long as you're not too . . . Because whatever the circumstances, these things are always a bit upsetting. You might not realise till later what it's taken out of you.'

'I was sick of the complications, if you want to know,' he said abruptly.

The door of the Scout hut opened and a man walked out onto the steps. I saw the flare of a lighter, then, a beat later, drifting smoke. Midges danced round the security light above. Further off, the orange glow of halogen showed through the horse chestnut trees and there was the sickle moon coming up, like an illustration from one of Matty's bedtime books.

Sick of the complications. *Complications*. The word snagged. A *complicated friend*. Lurch-jerk went the Citroën, backwards and forwards. *Ian hasn't met her*. I remembered the furtive way David had held his shoulders, pacing about my kitchen with his mobile to his ear. *Not really a girlfriend*.

The Citroën shot forward into the open street, and at the same moment, something clicked together in my brain.

'My God,' I said, 'she was married.'

'Well. Yes.'

'You were having an affair with her!'

'I appreciate it's not ideal. That's why I finished it.'

'Not ideal? *Not ideal?*' I stared across at his handsome, serious face, trying to read what I'd missed there. His forehead was creased with dismay.

'All right,' he said. 'I can see why you'd be upset. What you have to say to yourself, though, is, she's an adult, making her own choices, and you don't know the background, and I thought long and hard before I got involved. I'm not about to wreck anyone's marriage. Very much not.'

'Excuse me,' I said. 'If I could speak from the other side. You obviously have no idea.'

'It was insensitive of me to tell you. I should never have said anything.'

'No, no, I'm glad you did.'

'I wouldn't lie to you, Carol. I could have lied, but I chose not to. But you don't know her, it's not as if they're friends of yours. No one's been hurt, because no one knows.'

'That's not the point.'

David gripped the steering wheel. 'Look, I'd *never* have cheated on Jeanette, I've told you that already. Never.'

'And yet you're encouraging this woman to. Bloody funny set of morals.'

'It happened. I didn't plan it, I didn't look for it. It was just – an interaction,' he said.

'God Almighty, I've heard it called some things! "Interaction"? I'll tell you what it is. It's lies and disrespect and deceit and humiliation. It's shoddy and low. No wonder Ian's like he is.' I reached for the door handle.

'Where are you going?'

'Home.' I climbed back out into the car park.

'If I can just—'

'For God's sake! I thought you were one of the decent ones,' I said, and slammed the door against his explanations.

CHAPTER 18

Photograph: clipping inside a wartime edition of Housewife *magazine, marking an article called 'Nerves: The Enemy of Youth and Good Looks'. From Carol's bureau, Sunnybank.*

Location: the foot of Tannerside Brow, Bolton

Taken by: the Wigan Observer, *November 1968*

Subject: New Bypass Open At Last, *says the headline. Despite the promise of sleet, the morning's turned out fine and brisk and every shadow on the tarmac is sharp. Not even British weather can get in the way of progress today. Carol's dad stands shoulder to shoulder with the County Surveyor and Bridgemaster and the mayoral consort, in front of a line of traffic cones. On the other side of the picture, the mayor poses with scissors agape.*

Bob White is here in his capacity as councillor. He is proud of the bypass, proud of his village and of the contribution he and his fellows make to it. Because what a piece of work this is! The area of the new carriageway alone is 37,400 square yards. The total amount of pitching used was 14,000 tons, and before that they laid down 13,500 tons of broken stone and 800 tons of cement. 19,400 cubic yards they had to excavate, in total. Numbers like those make an ordinary man feel nothing's impossible.

He's proud, too, of his recent promotion to foreman at work, and of his new Austin 1100 in coffee and cream. He's proud of his daughter, who'll be reading the second of the Nine Lessons at the school carol service. Even Frieda's managed to be pleased at that bit of news.

When they've packed up here, he'll go back to the council offices for a celebratory sherry, and then it's on to Millie Pharaoh's for a cup of tea, a chat about the old days, and a spell upstairs. Nearly two years have passed since her husband died, eight months since they started with this other arrangement. There's no harm in it, so long as nobody knows.

There are so many things in life just now to be grateful for.

I've never been a fan of Good Fridays. There's always an unsettling and gloomy atmosphere to them, especially when it gets to that dead hour, mid-afternoon. Which I suppose, when you think about it, there ought to be: Jesus had a lot more to contend with than running low on milk and the shops being shut.

In between rain showers I'd been trying to set up an Easter-egg hunt for Matty, because Jaz was going away for the weekend with Nat. I'd offered to keep Matty with me so she could let her hair down for once, have some fun, but she'd got all defensive. 'Of course I'm taking him with me, Mum. Why wouldn't I? It's Easter and I want to be with him. Don't know what kind of a mother you think I am.'

So we were making like it was Sunday, and although Jaz didn't know it, some of the eggs outside were Ian's, delivered to my doorstep while I was at work.

The sun emerged thinly as I was lifting Matty from his high chair, so I parked him by the back door and grabbed the little bucket.

'He's too young,' said Jaz, shaking her head. 'He won't understand what he's supposed to do.'

'I'll help him,' I said. 'You know what an egg is, don't you, Matty?'

'Look,' he said, pointing at the window to where the water was dripping off the top sill. 'Uh-oh.'

'It's only spitting, hardly even that. Here, hold the bucket.'

I knelt to zip his coat. Jaz came round to tie the strings on his hood.

'OK, love?' I said.

'I think I am, yeah.' She smiled, and an indescribable relief washed over me. As we stood up together, I couldn't resist reaching out and drawing her in for a hug. For about five seconds she let me hold her, then she pulled away. 'It's a better day today, Mum,' she said.

'Good.'

'It has to come round eventually, doesn't it?'

'It does.' Though there'll be times you feel as if you've gone back to square one, I thought.

Meanwhile, Matty flapped his arms and pushed against me. I stepped aside and opened the door, and he shot out onto the soggy lawn. 'Your bucket,' I called after him.

'Watch out for that bloody pond,' said Jaz behind me.

I caught up with Matty and tried to hand him the bucket, but he wasn't having any. Two collared doves were stalking about under the feeder like a pair of wind-up toys, and those were what he wanted.

'Can you see any eggs?'

The doves cringed and took off. Matty came to a halt.

'Whatever's under this bush?' I said, for all the world like someone who'd not been crouched next to it ten minutes before. 'Look!'

His eyes swivelled to me for a second, then away again.

'Here's one,' I said, holding it up for him. The sun caught the foil in a brilliant flash, and at last he was interested. He tottered forward. 'Pop it in here, and we'll find some more.'

Matty took the egg, came up to the bucket and peered over the rim. 'Let it go, sweetheart,' I said, and after some hesitation, he did. *Thunk* it went against the bottom of the bucket.

I hooked the handle back over my arm, then steered him in the direction of the fence where my stone squirrel balanced another egg in the V between its tail and its back. This time Matty spotted the prize unaided.

See, Jaz? I thought. I knew she'd be at the window, keeping an eye on us, but that was all right. Matty and I, we were fine, we were blitzing it. So much we had in store over the next few years: treasure hunts, the Science Museum, pantomimes and nature trails, growing seeds, sharing books, constructing a runway for Santa out of tea-lights. My heart contracted with anticipation.

On his way back to me, Matty paused to check out a scrap of orange netting from around an old fat-ball, then lighted on a length of cane, left over from when I'd staked out my sweet peas last year. I rattled the bucket but it failed to register. There's no getting between a boy and his stick.

'Come on,' I said loudly. 'Quick, before the jackdaws get them.'

A few drops of rain speckled my face and within half a minute, the surface of the pond was a mass of radiating circles, the leaves on the bushes quivering again.

'I can see something shiny by the shed. What do you think it might be?'

Matty came forward like a midget king, still clutching his cane and egg, and allowed me to adjust his hood.

'Bucky, Nanna,' he said, and I lowered it for him.

I led him up the other side of the garden where we collected two more eggs.

'How many have we got? Shall we count?' I said, but the shower was getting heavier. Jaz appeared at the door.

'Don't get him soaked,' she called out.

'It's not cold, and he's got spare socks upstairs. Anyway, we're nearly done.'

I'd set the last egg, a larger one, on top of a stone mushroom, and wedged it in place with a couple of brick shards. As soon as Matty saw it, he ran across and began whacking the mushroom with his stick.

'Hoy, stop that,' shouted Jaz.

'He's all right,' I said. Raindrops fizzed on the paving stones around my feet. 'Come on, Matty, grab that big one and let's go back in.'

He turned, but in the wrong direction, and ran off down the garden once more. My grandson may only be small, but he can shift when he wants to. Jaz and I exchanged glances, then she launched herself out of the door after him, while I nipped round the other way with the idea of heading him off. Waves of rain were sweeping across the lawn, and Jaz had no coat on.

Matty got as far as the shed, tripped over his own cane, rolled against the compost heap, righted himself and turned to grin at us. I had one of those moments where your brain goes into camera mode and you know you've captured the scene for ever: his slightly bowed stance as he prepared to take flight again, the highlights on his cheeks, tiny white teeth against the pinkness of his new gums, his miniature thumb against the knobbled cane. There were grass clippings all down the back of one leg. His eyes were slits of mischief.

'You little tinker,' I said. I held my arms open, but he went instead to his mother, and she picked him right up and whirled him round. I could hear him shrieking with excitement, even above the thrumming water.

By now, Jaz was very wet. Shining drops swelled at the ends

of her hair, and her eye make-up was smudged where she'd wiped her face with her sleeve. 'Good heavens, the state of you,' I said as I drew near. 'Give him to me, and run and get yourself inside.'

'I think it's too late for that, Mum.' She was laughing, and Matty was laughing. I took his hand and she held onto the other, and we swung him between us in giant bounds back towards the house.

'What a team, though,' I said, raising my face to the rain and closing my eyes. I imagined how we'd look from above, an aerial view of the three of us, a twisting string of family moving across a green rectangle. I wished I could've had a photograph of that.

When we got inside, I told Jaz she could borrow one of my tops while I changed Matty's footwear. True to form, it was my brand new purple blouse she came down in, a bath towel wrapped round her head. Even like that, she looked lovely.

She pulled at the cuffs, appraising. 'This is nice.'

'No need to sound surprised,' I said.

The television had been playing to itself all the while. Now it showed a man in a white dinner jacket bursting through a giant illuminated mouth onto a stage full of showgirls.

'What on earth's this?'

'How should I know?' said Jaz, dropping the magazine back onto the cushion. She came round and settled herself on the sofa next to Matty, who was lying on his side with his thumb between his lips.

The man in the white jacket raised a silver-topped cane, and H-E-R-O-D appeared above him, spelled out in lights. He wore a white carnation in his lapel, and his bow tie matched his hanky. His hair was slicked back, immaculate.

'Huh.' She nodded at the screen. 'You know who he reminds me of?'

'Don't say it.'

'But he does. Look at him. Look at the way he's kitted out.'

'David does not dress like that.'

'I didn't say he did. I said I was reminded of him.'

The showgirls began a dance routine, their pink dresses shimmering, their diamond collars winking with every gesture.

'You don't still see him, do you, Mum?'

'No,' I said, which was, coincidentally, now the truth.

'Good,' she said. 'Because I was beginning to wonder.'

'Wonder what?'

'You *know.*' Herod jumped onto a grand piano. 'You used to do this funny little smirk whenever you mentioned him. You did. Yes, you did. But there's no way you two would get together, is there?'

'Of course not,' I said.

'It would pretty much be incest. Plus he's such an upper-class twit.'

'He isn't really. Not that.'

'See, you're doing it again. Stop sticking up for him, will you? He's a nob, and his son's a bastard. Just because he's got money, he thinks he's better than us.'

'I don't think that's true, Jaz.' But even as I said it, I was thinking, Why am I bothering to defend him?

'The way he speaks, that thing he does with his eyebrows. So smug. Do you remember how he had to have the last word at the wedding?'

'Only because your dad forgot to toast you at the end of his speech.' (And say how beautiful you looked, or express any kind of confidence in the match.) 'He was too busy telling jokes. Someone had to step in and deliver the line.'

'What about afterwards, when he said Dad ought to have been working the clubs?'

'Yes, all right. That was probably below the belt.'

Our doorbell rang as Herod backed away up the stage, ranting.

'Not that any of it matters now.' I got to my feet. Through the window I could see Josh standing under the porch, and I was glad because it was weeks since I'd had a proper chance to talk to him, what with his work experience and then the school breaking up for the holidays. He was clutching a plastic bag in his hand: Laverne's Easter exchange, that would be. You get into these customs and then it's hard to know when to draw a line under them. I'd always bought a chocolate egg for Josh when he was little, so she started buying one for Matty, and here today was her six-foot son, still the recipient of a Thornton's bunny for which he would be made to write a thank you card. *Oh, for God's sake, knock it on the head*, I imagined Phil saying.

I opened the front door, all smiles. Josh was flushed and breathing hard, as though he'd been running.

'Hello!' I said gaily. 'Enjoying the break? How was work experience? I've got something for you, if you give me a minute.'

'Here,' he said, and thrust out his fist with the bag in it.

'Oh, for me? Well, for Matty. That's lovely, tell your mother thanks. And I've got, hang on a sec, I thought I left yours—'

'Jesus! Take it, will you?' he snapped. And before I could react, he'd hurled the bag past me, into the hall, where it knocked into a bowl of grape hyacinths I'd put on the telephone table ready to take to Dad.

'Oh,' I squeaked in shock.

The bowl had been shunted to the edge but not tipped off. One of the stems looked to be snapped.

When I turned back to the door, Josh was already striding away. Instinct told me not to call after him. Instead I watched him go, my hands on my cheeks, my heart thumping. In my head I heard myself telling Laverne how I thought he wasn't happy at school, remembered that worried crease between her eyebrows, and I knew, I knew exactly what I'd done. 'Oh, Josh,' I said under my breath. 'Oh hell.'

Back in the lounge the TV was still going, but Herod had been replaced by Roly Mo. 'We turned over,' she said. 'Who was it?'

'Josh.' I was almost too shaken to speak the name.

Jaz pulled a face. 'Doughboy? I don't know why he doesn't just move in here. Anyway,' she went on, 'what I was saying was, if you did start seeing David, it would make things impossible for me. With Matty, for one. I wouldn't want to be leaving Matty in a house where David might turn up. Do you understand what I'm saying, Mum?'

I sat down on the sofa next to them, and it felt as though I'd crawled onto an island in the middle of a stormy sea. Every day as a grandmother seemed to bring new anxieties, new traps for me to fall into. Even choosing Matty's egg had been a trial – Jaz might complain it was too big, not ethical, contained E numbers, should have been something else entirely, e.g. an educational toy. Three nights before, and unable to sleep, I'd texted Phil to check again he'd keep his mouth shut about Ian. Even when he'd replied (*No wy dnt wrry*) I couldn't damp down my small-hours terror.

I looked across at Jaz, her hair still spiky from the rain, the yoke of my purple blouse marked with damp smears. She was nodding her head to Roly Mo's song, humming, terrifying in her unconcern.

The rain dried up, and in the end it was such a beautiful evening we took the baby monitor out onto the patio and opened a bottle of wine there.

'What time do you want wakening tomorrow?' I asked her.

'We have to be at Nat's for half-nine, so, eightish.'

'I'll get Matty ready for you.'

We were gearing up to have one of those amazing pink and blue sunsets. I pulled my garden chair closer to hers, and we sat and watched the clouds slowly change colour. For a long time neither of us spoke. A robin was singing from the cypress tree, and the breeze brought us faint snatches of Laverne's piano music. The scent of grass and lilac and flowering currant mingled in a green tang.

I pointed with the toe of my shoe. 'All along the edge of that bed are the tulips Matty helped plant last autumn.'

'Yeah?'

'Well, I held him while he dropped a few bulbs in the right place. They should be coming into flower any day now, I must remember to show him.'

'I'd take that cane off him first.'

'It's locked in the shed.'

'Very wise.'

The lights on the monitor stayed still, and we drank our wine.

'Do you remember that time you put in all those bulbs for me, when I'd broken my arm?' I said. 'You were such a help. I taught you how to load the washer and use the grill, all sorts. You kept us ticking over. I'd never have managed otherwise.'

Jaz leaned back and crossed her ankles. 'You do know, Mum, you're always on about when I was little?'

'Am I?'

'Yup. You bloody live down Memory Lane, you do, it's your permanent address. I wish you wouldn't, sometimes.'

'Why?'

'Because I sometimes feel you only liked me when I was younger.'

'Don't be ridiculous,' I said.

She smoothed the hair from out of her eyes. It was hard to tell how serious she was being. 'You're not telling me you've always felt exactly the same way about me all the way through my life?'

For a moment, I was thrown.

'Of course it changes,' I said, after a few seconds' thought. 'But it's the same, as well. Like a tree going through different seasons; it's always a tree.'

'So I'm a tree, now?'

'No, not you. Us.'

'If you say so.'

A bee dithered through the forget-me-nots at the edge of the pond like a fat woman rooting through jumble.

I said: 'You know that time you were at Leeds?'

'Do you mean during, or after?'

'After, I suppose. When you were poorly.' I paused to let her protest, but she didn't, so I carried on. 'The way you are now, upset – it's not like it was then, is it? You wouldn't let things get so bad again without telling me?'

'No.'

'Because then, you were away from home, on your own. You didn't have the support.'

'I know, that's why I came back. It did help. Eventually.'

I let that last word finish resonating before I spoke again.

'What happened at Leeds, Jaz? You never really told me.'

'I drank too much, I blew my grant on clothes and music. Like students do.'

'Drugs?'

'Never.'

'Honestly?'

'Oh, well, yeah, a bit, at school.'

'I *knew* it.' That drifting-away look she'd worn all the way through Year Twelve, the skulking about and moods.

'Truly, Mum, nothing since the Sixth Form, and only half a dozen roll-ups even then. No big deal. I wouldn't be telling you now if it was. This is, like, ten years ago. What were *you* doing ten years ago?'

Still putting up with my marriage, just. I took her point.

The sky turned pinker, and I poured us more wine.

'I got involved with someone off my course and he let me down, that was all,' she said in a rush. 'And I totally wasn't expecting it, and he told people our private stuff, which was shit, and . . . I just didn't deal with it very well.'

'Oh, love,' I said. 'I wish you'd told me at the time. I thought it must be something—' Something worse, I was thinking, though I didn't dare say it. A broken heart? After all the hoo-ha, that was it? But at the same time I was overwhelmed with relief that it turned out to be such an ordinary kind of tragedy, and that she'd confided at last.

'Funny,' she went on, 'I thought it was such a big deal back then, the end of the world, yeah? And now, against everything that's happened lately, it's a blip. I don't know why I got myself into such a state about it. I should have learned my lesson.'

'How do you mean?'

'That it's obviously me. Obviously I'm destined to fuck up when it comes to men, and that was the warning shot. Or maybe it's not my fault, maybe they're all like that, and it's simply a matter of *when* they cheat on you. They're all bastards, aren't they?'

She sounded so hopeless I couldn't bear it.

'Not all, love. Look at your grandad. Nearly fifty years he was with your grandma.'

'Maybe fidelity's gone out of fashion, then,' she snapped.

I put my glass down and reached across the gap for her hand.

'Listen. Think about this: whatever happens with Ian,

you've got Matty out of it. Same as I had you, when my marriage ended.'

Jaz gave a wan smile. 'A great consolation, was I?'

'Yes,' I said, squeezing her fingers earnestly. 'You were.'

Reeds bent in the breeze, stirring the water's surface. The memory of Josh's outburst came on me like a pain and I swivelled my mind away.

'I just, I get so frightened, Mum.'

'I know.'

'Sometimes I wish I was little again.'

I wish that too, I thought. We all knew where we were in those days.

'Once upon a time,' I said. 'There was a pig called Grunt.'

'God, no, spare us the Grunt stories.'

'Poor Grunt.'

'Poor Grunt nothing. I've got a story for you: once upon a time there was a woman who got bloody everything wrong in her life.'

'Oh, Jaz, you haven't. You've got so much ahead of you.'

'I was talking about you,' she said, laughing. I can't tell you what a good sound it was.

'You, young lady, are sailing very close to the wind,' I said.

'So ground me,' she said.

'You're not too big to put over my knee,' I said.

When the business with Ian was sorted out, whichever way it went, I could start again with her. Without Phil to distract me, I could be the kind of mother I always meant to be. A me of the future waved down from the monorail at Chester Zoo, my face flanked by Matty and Jaz.

My second chance, it was going to be. This time, I'd make good.

CHAPTER 19

Photograph: web print-out, tucked inside a copy of La Symphonie Pastorale *from a box in the loft, Sunnybank*

Location: the Adler-Tate lecture theatre, Modern Languages Department, Leeds University

Taken by: Dr López Covas

Subject: Dr Nick Page posing for his Staff Profile entry. His smile is broad and chipper, though, in truth, this appointment isn't working out quite as he imagined. There are changes he's keen to make, but it's too soon and anyway, he's not senior enough. Still, early days. The second term's bound to be easier.

On the plus side, he's already identified a particularly bright first-year student who looks as though she might prove interesting. Jasmine Morgan, her name is. Dark and troubled, bright and brittle. Those are the kind of students he likes.

Nothing draws him more than a knotty problem, a contradiction.

I had Radio 3 on while I took out the old bedding plants and put in new. Radio 2 was airing an outraged phone-in, and on 4 it was the news, an endless pageant of human suffering, incompetence and doom. I found some piano music that suited the bright day, and I was just about to see off a cockchafer grub with my trowel when the announcer said, '*La Berceuse*, from Fauré's *Dolly Suite*'. Then the opening notes started and it was like an electric shock down my spine: instantly I was by the fire at Pincroft again, shunting around some lead farm animals that had been my dad's. Mum was ironing, there was a wooden maiden draped with pillowcases and underslips, and in the corner, the big radiogram playing the theme tune to *Listen With Mother*. And as I crouched by that planter, trowel-edge poised, I swear I could still smell the hot cloth steaming, and the beeswax polish my mother always used. It was a scene of perfect security and calm.

The loss bloomed inside me, taking my breath for a moment, so that I had to get up and walk about for a while. *Mum may not always have been a ray of sunshine, but there's comfort to be had in normality*, I imagined telling Dad. Except that he wasn't there any more either. I knew that, really.

A noise from next door brought me out of it. Whatever would Laverne say if she came out and found me like this? How would I explain myself? Ridiculous to be upset at fifty-two because you're no longer a child. But there I was.

When I got back to the cockchafer, he'd spied his chance and burrowed away. I dabbed my eyes on the hem of my blouse, and carried on planting.

Lying awake that night, I tried to envisage how Jaz might sum up her childhood. I'd worked so hard to make her days sunny, surely her memories would be positive ones.

If she was here with me now, I'd tell her how vital it is to keep hold of those moments from the past, because they make up who you are. 'That's why Grandad's so lost,' I'd say. 'That's why I take all these photos. You have to hang onto the good times to see you through the bad. Happy memories make a happy person.'

And she'd go, 'Don't be so simple, Mum. You can't *choose* what you remember.'

And I'd say, 'Yes, you can. You just have to make an effort.'

'Dad couldn't come, he says he's sorry,' Ian announced as I took his coat. 'He's got a meeting.'

Ah, I thought. So that's how the land lies. How much had David told him about our last evening together? Ian didn't seem embarrassed by the message.

As soon as he saw his dad, Matty hurled himself across the living room. 'Hey, it's the Mattster!' said Ian, picking him up and swinging him round. I took myself into the kitchen and left them to it. One of the most important skills of being a grandparent is knowing when to melt away.

After a few minutes I returned with a tray of coffee, biscuits and squash.

'Where's Jaz today?' said Ian, as he always did.

'Gone to the university again to have a look at some reference books. Some of those specialist dictionaries cost hundreds, apparently. She can't afford to buy them, so she saves up her vocab queries—'

'She's been getting cash from me every week,' said Ian. 'She's not going short.'

'I never said she was.' I put the tray down carefully.

Ian had knelt down and dragged out the box of plastic rail track. Now he began to hunt through it, separating straight and curved pieces into bundles. At his side, Matty dug around and unearthed random lengths which he thrust in Ian's face. 'Here y'are,' he kept saying. 'Here y'are.'

'I think anyway she's coming round to the idea of sorting out access,' I said.

About time, said Ian's expression.

They made a simple circuit together – Ian constructed, Matty sabotaged, Ian repaired – and set a tunnel over one side.

'What you need now is some trains,' I said.

'Have a look in my jacket pocket, Carol, while I put this bridge together,' said Ian.

I went over to the chair, rummaged, and found a brand new engine, still in its packaging.

'Well, Matty,' I said. 'Look at this! What's this one called?'

'It's Diesel Ten,' said Ian.

'He doesn't look very friendly.'

'That's because he's a baddie. You've got to have baddies.'

'Have you?' I passed it across and Ian set to extracting it from the box.

'There's a battery in the other pocket,' he said.

'I'll say I bought it. If Jaz asks, I mean. Otherwise, obviously, I shan't say anything.' I felt myself blush as I handed him the battery. 'How is your dad?'

'Fine. He's been looking into the legal position. Where I stand.'

The phone started to ring.

'Well. Like I was saying, we might not have to do this much longer,' I said to him over my shoulder.

It was Phil calling. 'I can bring you some steel mesh to go over the pond,' he said. 'I've found someone who does sheets of it. Be a lot less expensive than getting a firm in.'

'Not now,' I told him, too sharply.

'Why? Who's there?'

My delay told him all he needed to know.

'It's not David and Ian, is it? Bloody hell, Carol, you've not got them round again?'

'Ian's here, yes,' I said. 'Not David. Look, I'll call you tonight. It's good about the mesh. Thanks.' And I put the phone down.

'I think there's someone at your back door,' said Ian. 'Someone's knocking.'

So I went through to the kitchen to find Dorothy Wynne's granddaughter Alice rapping on the pane.

'Does Matty want a sunflower?' she said when I opened up. 'Libby's grown a whole bunch of seedlings and we thought Matty might like a couple, you know, to have a race with.'

'That's great. Yes, he'd love that, thanks. Is Libby here?'

'Granny's keeping an eye. Libs is having a nap; she was up in the night, twice, and then she's been so crabby all morning. Let sleeping kids lie, I say. We're all worn out with her.'

'And how are you? How many weeks is it now?'

'Nearly thirty one.' Alice ran her hand over her huge belly.

'You're keeping well?'

Something flickered across her face 'Pretty much. They say I'm on the big side for my dates.'

'Perhaps you're further on than you thought.'

'No, it's not that. There's more fluid than there should be, or something.' She shook her head. 'I don't know. I'm trying not to think about it, 'cause there's nothing I can do. Keeping my feet up, counting the kicks. There's a lot of kicking going on.'

'Well then. I'm sure it'll be fine,' I said, trying a reassuring smile. 'And Libby's OK?'

'She's great, yeah. No time to sit and worry while Libs is around!'

As Alice waddled back down the side of the house, I thought of the last months of my own pregnancy with Jaz, and the nightmares I'd been plagued with. Even now, so many years on, I could remember scenes from them. The fear starts before your children are even born, and it never, ever lets up. That's something nobody tells you till it's too late.

In the living room, Matty was staging more crashes and Ian

was building an extension to the circuit so as to use a set of points he'd discovered.

'My neighbour's granddaughter,' I said.

'Uh-huh.' He carried on slotting sections together.

I found myself glancing at the clock, calculating how long it would be before the visit was up. Still another hour and forty minutes. It definitely wasn't as easy with David missing from the scene. Say what you liked about him, he made things flow.

I turned on the TV for some background noise and it was the news, with a story about a divorced father who'd abducted his children and killed them, before shooting himself. Hastily I flicked through the channels till I found CBeebies, and picked up my coffee, which was now cold.

'Actually, would you mind turning it off, Carol?' said Ian.

The heat rose to my cheeks again. 'Oh, all right. Sorry. Why?'

'Because the time I get with my son is too precious to waste. I want to be able to play with him, properly play with him, and I can't do that if he's gawping at *64 Zoo Lane*.'

My mouth fell open with a mixture of dismay and outrage. I don't have to do this, you know, I could have said. I don't have to have you in my house, behind my daughter's back, with all the hideous stress and guilt that costs me. You should be damn grateful I'm letting you across the threshold at all, my lad, never mind dictating.

Fortunately the doorbell went before I could say any of this, so I simply handed the remote over and went to see who it was.

Laverne. 'Hi,' she said, from the step. Which isn't usual for her; she normally trots straight in.

'Everything OK?' I asked.

'I just wanted to let you know.' She tossed her hair back and clasped her hands in front of her. Even in her casual moments she moves like a dancer. 'Just wanted to say, Carol, term starts on Monday—'

'Yes, I've got it on my calendar. Josh all ready, is he?'

'He, well, he won't be needing a lift in. So you don't have to bother.'

'Is he poorly?'

She gave an awkward little smile. 'He's, no, we've had a chat and he wants to start going on the bus. I mean, it's time, probably. He's at that age.'

Behind me I could hear Matty squealing, and Ian's voice saying over and over, 'No, you don't.'

'That's fine,' I said quickly. 'Yes, of course. No problem.'

'Because it'll be easier for you in the mornings.'

'It will, though it's never been a bother, Laverne.'

'And we're so grateful for all the years you've done it.'

'It's been a pleasure. He's a smashing lad.'

'I wouldn't want you to think we didn't appreciate it.'

'No, really, it's been great.'

As I closed the door I thought, How desperate must Josh be not to come in my car with me any more? The realisation set up a horrible pressure against my breastbone. I wanted to run straight away to their house, apologise, explain that I was only trying to help when I confided in Laverne about the bullying. Because it's what they always say to do: tell someone. She could go down the school now and sort it, and everything would be all right. *Yeah, same as we did with Jaz?* came Phil's sarcastic voice. *I warned you not to get involved*, added David in my head.

Back in the lounge, Ian had the cushions off the sofa and Matty was rolling about on them.

'Sorry,' I said, out of habit. 'It's like Paddy's market here today.'

'No, I'm sorry,' said Ian. 'I shouldn't have, you know, the TV thing. Anyway, I'm going to take him outside. Have a kick-about while it's fine.'

He didn't invite me to join them, and I didn't ask. I sat myself near the window and watched Ian's big hands close round his son's small body, Matty squeaking and wriggling and jerking his short legs as he was lifted in the air. It was a different approach from mine and Jaz's. Rougher, more direct. Lads and dads. And I felt a sudden rush of vindication. If Jaz walked in here now and saw them, I'd simply say, 'This is why they need to be together. Look. Look at Matty's face.'

When they'd gone out, I went and sat in the bay and had five minutes with my eyes closed. Jaz materialised in the chair opposite, as she'd been when she was recovering from her depression, dull-eyed and subdued. *I've always given you trouble, haven't I?* Oh, I told her silently, but you were worth it, in spite of everything. *Honestly?* Then came Eileen's voice: *Raising Jaz has been like swimming upstream all the way; that's what you told me.*

Another, younger Jaz interrupted, swinging through the door: *Hey, Mum, why did the hedgehog cross the road?*

For all the grief with Phil, if I could have snapped my fingers and gone back in time, I would have done. I'd have given anything at that moment to see Jaz when she was little, have that period of my life over again. *Guess what,* said a newly pregnant Jaz. *They gave me a copy of the scan. Do you want to see?*

Before I'd even thought about it, I was out of that chair and kneeling on the carpet, peering at the shelf below the window, looking for my past.

Just before I got married I'd gathered up all the photographs I could find lying around Pincroft. Some were in a biscuit tin in the back bedroom wardrobe, there were a few loose in the bureau, I had my own little cache I kept in my jewellery box. But when I flicked through, there seemed to be a lot of gaps.

'Where are the rest?' I said to my mother. 'Oh, we've never bothered much,' she'd replied. 'We're not a family who takes photographs.' A fact which became self-evident when I began to go through them properly. 'Did you even have a wedding album?' I said. 'Oh yes, we've got one of those,' she said. 'It's in the back room somewhere. Don't ask me to go searching for it.'

In the final count there'd been a couple of dozen of me/us, a few odd ones of my parents from when they were younger, plus a set of very small black and white holiday snaps of castles, mountains, swans, piers, coaching inns, formal gardens, etc. These became my first collection, pasted into a modest ring-bound album with stripy vinyl covers. I don't know why it felt so important to draw the family history together like this, but it did. 'Don't you mind me taking them away?' I'd asked. 'If you want them, love, you have them,' said Dad. 'No,' said Mum.

My next album was bigger, with a hessian front; it began with Early Marriage and ended with Jaz on her first day at secondary school. The camera we owned back then had been Phil's, but after some pestering I'd got him to show me how to use it so that, by the middle of this collection, probably three-quarters of the pictures had been snapped by me. Which was good, because Phil was a careless photographer who regularly missed people's feet off, forgot to prime the flash, let the strap flop over the shutter at the last minute. He never composed a background in his life. Often I had to load the film for him because his fingers weren't patient enough to guide the tiny plastic spokes into the celluloid slots. Finally I got my own Instamatic, and from then on I was official family photographer. I became the person who decided which memories to keep, and which to discard.

My fingers moved along the bookshelf, touching spines for the pleasure of ownership. Here was album five, a posh job in burgundy velvet covers, and pretty much every one of its pages devoted to Matty. Number four – gilt-edged navy leather – was mostly experimental stuff from when I did my evening classes: studies of my father's hands; light through different types of leaves; still-life sequences where I kept changing the shutter speed. I was proud of that collection. It came out of a bad time, but I'd made good.

The album I most needed to look at right now, though, was number three, charting Jaz's older years. I wasn't sure whether Ian had ever seen it. He might be interested. We might all be able to look at it together sometime in the future, when all this was sorted.

The first picture, which I'd stuck onto the inside cover, was a portrait I'd taken of her when she was about twelve. We'd gone to a local folly and climbed a tower there. Then I'd asked her to lean her arm on the stone windowsill and look out across the countryside as though she was lost in thought. Corny, I know, but it made a lovely shot; the skin in particular was amazing. *And this was pre-digital, so there was no enhancement going on*, I imagined telling Ian.

On the next page was a Christmas scene, Jaz and Eileen dancing a waltz across our lounge, both of them wearing false moustaches. 'I've told you about Eileen,' I'd say to Ian. 'My best friend. Jaz's unofficial aunty.' *Among my many other accomplishments*, went Eileen. I flipped the pages.

Dad's birthday: Jaz, Phil and Dad sitting round the table and holding up glasses of wine (Pomagne for Jaz).

Calais: Jaz sitting at a wrought-iron table, sipping a bottle of grenadine through a straw. Phil next to her wearing a child's beach bucket on his head and making a Tommy Cooper gesture with his hands.

Jaz and Phil perched on a flint wall, squinting in the sunshine. Jaz's long limbs are milk-white; Phil is boiled pink.

Jaz dressed as Marceline for a school production of *Le Mariage de Figaro*.

The back page of the school prospectus, showing Jaz in the library with her head bowed over a copy of *Das Beste*.

Jaz and me on the patio, soaking up the sun on the last afternoon before she left for Leeds.

Rare close-up of Jaz without make-up, eyes cast down modestly.

The back inside cover of the album had a pocket for negatives, and in there was a folded newspaper clipping: *Missing Girl Found*. I didn't need to take that one out and look at it because it was burned on my memory.

These albums are my most precious possessions, I imagined telling Ian. *I couldn't put a price on them. They're the first things I'd grab if the house was on fire.*

After Matty, said Ian.

Obviously after Matty. I'd throw myself into an inferno to save Matty. And I saw myself battering down a door – no, running up a burning staircase – no, stumbling through a smoke-filled bedroom, calling his name.

The sound of a diesel engine faded in on the other side of the window; swelled, throbbed, then went ominously dead. As I pushed myself up off the carpet to see who it was had pulled into our drive, a car door slammed.

Jaz's car.

For a split second, all I could do was stare in horror.

Then I was staggering to my feet and throwing myself down the hall towards the back door.

CHAPTER 20

Photograph 256, Album Two

Location: the garden, Sunnybank

Taken by: Carol

Subject: A close-up of seven-year-old Jaz grinning, sans *two of her top teeth. Her hair is in bunches and her lashes are impossibly long. It is about this age people start to recommend child-modelling agencies.*

The teeth have been having adventures all of their own. The first popped out while they were in the car, and promptly fell down the hole at the base of the seat belt. Carol has to ask Phil for his flexible claw and torch (it's lucky he knows his way round that shed, because she certainly doesn't). The second tooth gets mislaid by an idiot dinner lady and is never found, but Carol pretends, by substituting the first in its place, to have discovered it lodged in the front pocket of Jaz's school bag. The third Jaz loses herself, but it turns up in the lining of her coat, a barely detectable lump in the hem. 'Why are they so damn small?' asks Phil, as though there's something personal and deliberate about Jaz's dental dimensions.

The fourth tooth makes it unscathed to the pillow, but Carol, distracted by a bad marital row, forgets and is woken in the morning by howls of outrage as Jaz unwraps the hanky to find the tooth and nothing but the tooth. 'I expect the fairy was called away to a molar emergency,' says Carol, and gives her double-pay the night after.

She's heard recently that some parents leave trails of glitter across the windowsill, make footprints by poking dolls into plant pots, leave gifts of new toothbrushes and certificates and stickers. Well then, Jaz shall have it all. There is nothing Carol won't do to make her daughter's childhood as secure and magical as it can be.

The minute or so Jaz spent hammering on the door was enough for me to get out the back and warn Ian.

All I had to say was her name. His face went rigid and he just stood there, holding the football between his hands while Matty reached up and pawed at it. I thought, Oh God, he's going to argue, he's going to face her out.

'Where's your car?' I hissed at him.

'Round the back of Rydal Avenue. There wasn't room when I—'

'Then she doesn't know for certain you're here,' I said. I was still holding onto the shred of hope that if I got him off the premises, we could bluff our way out. 'Please, Ian, oh, please, go. For me.'

My distress outfaced him, I think. He glanced quickly round the garden as if assessing where he might hide, like some lover in a farce, and I heard him swear under his breath. Then he took off, running at the fence and vaulting it easily. He landed heavily, then righted himself, pelted across Laverne's lawn and disappeared round the side of her house. Immediately I hoisted Matty up into my arms, and hurried back through to let Jaz in.

*

It was Penny who was my undoing. Once again.

She'd heard Phil talking to me on the phone, caught the gist of the conversation, taken herself straight upstairs and called Jaz.

'Why would she *do* that?' I asked Phil later.

'Jealous,' he said.

The irony of that nearly killed me.

'Where is he?' shouted Jaz, bursting in the second I unfastened the door.

'Matty's here,' I said.

She stormed past me and into the lounge. Matty was wriggling to be put down, so I lowered him to the floor and he tottered after Jaz. But she took no notice, almost knocking him over as she doubled back. I watched her grab the newel and swing herself round, her knuckles white. She wrenched open the stair-gate, then her feet were pounding up the steps, and after a moment, I heard doors slamming against walls.

'Come on,' I said to Matty. 'Let's get you some juice.' And I walked him to the kitchen.

I ran the tap to get the water cold and reached for his beaker, at which point Jaz dashed past us, yanked open the back door and threw herself out onto the patio. I carried on making Matty's drink, counting down the last few seconds of calm.

'I know he's been here,' she cried as she came back in. 'I know what you've been up to.'

So here I was, in the scenario I'd never dared rehearse for fear of bringing it on. As Jaz stood and looked at me I thought, I've got to decide, here and now, to lie. Once I'm committed, that's it. 'You don't mean Ian, do you?' I said, as neutrally as I could.

'Of course I bloody mean Ian. Where is he? Where *is* he?'

I snapped the lid on the beaker and passed it down to Matty, who was clinging to my skirt. He refused to take it off me, so I stuck it on the corner of the table, then leaned myself against the sink unit to try and stop my legs shaking.

'He's here,' she said again.

'No, he isn't.'

Jaz seemed uncertain for a moment. She's not used to me lying, and she was probably considering her source, weighing my truth against Penny's. But her eyes were still wild.

'I promise you, Ian isn't here.'

Her hands went to her scalp and she started pulling at her hair. She was breathing very fast. 'If I find he has been.'

'Well, he hasn't. I don't know who's put the idea into your head, but you need to calm down. You're upsetting Matty and you're doing yourself no good. Listen, I'll put some milk on and I'll make us a Horlicks, then you can talk about what's upsetting you.' I managed a weak smile. 'After I've changed someone's nappy, anyway.'

I detached myself from the sink and steered Matty past her, towards the hallway.

'If he's been here—' she said again, menacingly.

Once I was round the corner, my legs nearly gave way. I steadied myself on the back of a chair while my grandson tugged at cushion tassels. 'Come here,' I said to him, and to my surprise he left the tassels at once and edged round till he was up against me. I bent down and held him very tight. 'Nanna loves you, you know,' I said into his hair. *You have no idea how much. There aren't the words to describe it.*

He began to wriggle, but I held on another few seconds.

'I hate Ian,' said Jaz from close behind me. 'It's like a suffocating sensation when I think about him, like I can't breathe. Do you know what I mean?'

I nodded, then let Matty go.

'I couldn't bear the thought of him sneaking round here.'

'Well, I don't know where you got the idea from.'

The changing mat was in the far corner along with the nappies, bags, wipes, cream. I got Matty laid down and commenced removing his trousers.

'Someone rang me,' she said.

'What?'

Jaz looked sheepish. 'Someone. All right. You can guess who.'

For a few seconds, I couldn't. Not for seven years has Penny had any contact with me, made any kind of approach. She took my husband; why would she need to do more?

'Pen said she'd overheard Dad talking to you about it,' Jaz went on.

'So Penny rang you?'

'Yeah.'

'She overheard us talking? She's never been here, how could she?'

'On the phone.'

As understanding dawned, I thought I'd burst into flames with the horror of it. My skin grew hot and my heart banged against my ribs as I pictured Penny hovering on the stairs, ears strained. What had I said? What had Phil said? Oh dear God, dear God.

'I know,' Jaz was saying. 'I should have thought. The woman's a bitch, she'd claim anything to make trouble, wouldn't she?'

Dimly I was aware of Matty rolling and kicking his naked legs against the plastic mat, clean nappies scattering.

'But you get a call like that – You can understand why I came haring round, can't you, Mum? Just the thought.'

I wanted to cry out, run upstairs and shut the bedroom door and howl. Matty, taking advantage of my distracted state, squirmed some more and sent the Sudocrem pot rolling towards the hearth. I bent and placed my hands on his waist to calm him down, and because I needed to hide my face from Jaz till I got myself under control.

'She's a nasty piece of work,' I said, my voice coming out strangled and high.

'It is such a bloody mess, though. All of it. Like, you've made a massive mess of your life and now mine's gone the same way, and they're kind of rebounding off each other.'

I said nothing to that.

'See, I know I'll have to let Ian see Matty at some point, I'm not stupid. But he can bloody well wait on me, till I'm ready, and I'm not ready yet, Mum. I still wake at night thinking of what he did, and replay that bloody text message, and it all sits on my shoulders and weighs me down. I'm never free of it. I can never forget. Some days I'm so depressed I could— But he'll not win, I shan't let him bring me right down. No one's ever going to hurt me like that again.'

I carried on cleaning my grandson, bagging up his nappy, pushing a new one under his hips.

'So he can wait, because he deserves to be kept waiting; he needs to know how it feels to have everything ripped from under you.'

If Jaz would only go, it might be all right. I could close the front door, draw the curtains and have a good furious weep, I could be back in control. From there, we could maybe move the access thing forward so I was never in this position again. I'd sit down and think about a better way. But for now I was wrung out and distressed, and I needed to be on my own.

'I suppose what I mean is, he needs to be hurt before he can understand what he's done.'

'Could you get the Sudocrem for me, love,' I said.

She walked over towards the fireplace. 'See, Matty's the only power I have over him now.'

I reached for Matty's trousers and began feeding his feet through the elasticated bottoms. 'That's not true, Jaz. He loves you.'

'Fuck you.'

'Jaz,' I said urgently. 'Matty's listening.'

'*Fuck you.*'

The trousers had caught under the back fold of the new nappy, but they came free at last and I pulled them up. Then I turned round.

Jaz was holding the jacket Ian had hung on the back of the chair.

We stared at each other for the longest moment.

'Fuck you both,' she said.

If I thought I'd seen Jaz angry before, I was wrong. She seemed to tower above us, raging, a cyclone of furious abuse. You came out of me, I thought as she flailed her arms and yelled. I nursed you on my lap. 'How could you?' she was screaming. 'Behind my back! You lied! I knew something was going on! Whose side are you on? I thought I could trust you!' And I remembered a doctor once asking, the time Jaz was ill, had I noticed how she seemed to direct her emotions inwards rather than outwards. And I hadn't noticed that, no, and I wondered what he'd say if he were here now.

'How many times?' she went on. 'How many lies have you told me? Sneaking behind my back. And to think I was bothered about you seeing David; Jesus! I suppose it was him who fucking talked you into this set-up. It was, wasn't it? I can tell by your face. Jesus fucking wept. What kind of mother are you? Interfering, making me look a bloody fool. This is *worse* than what Ian did. Has he been laughing at me? Have all three of you been? How could you *do* it, Mum? How could you set up something like that after all I've been through. How could you even let him in the house?' I'd have attempted a reply if she'd paused to draw breath, only she didn't. 'I should have expected this,' she shouted, 'this betrayal. After all, it's what my whole life's been about, hasn't it?'

And even though my chief urge was to throw myself at her feet and grovel for forgiveness, at the back of my mind I was thinking, Oh, stop being so melodramatic. I noticed Matty had crawled across to the bay and was twisting himself up in the curtain, and I longed to go over and cuddle him but I didn't dare move. If she'd let me speak I could've explained to her about damage limitation and being frightened of what Ian might do, but she just kept on and on at top volume, like someone blasting a cold water hose directly at me so that my chief instinct was to put my hands up and cover my face.

'I might have expected it,' she said. 'I should have known, because when have you ever, ever stuck up for me? Never, that's when. Not once. When I came home from Leeds you treated me like a bloody nuisance, a hypochondriac—'

'I know, and I apologised for that.'

'You never stuck up for me against the teachers, or when—'

'I did!'

'—those girls were having a go at me.'

'I went in and spoke to the Head.'

'Yeah, and accepted what she said without question, rolled over and took it because you always bloody do.'

'You wouldn't tell me what it was about!'

'I tried to talk to you, but you weren't interested.'

'When? That's not true, I'd always make time for you!'

'You were going to some charity thing. I was following you round the house trying to speak to you and all you were bothered about was the fact that your stupid fucking Stetson wouldn't fit.'

'I don't remember that.'

'Yes, you do. You had to borrow a load of line-dancing gear off Moira. I wanted to talk to you that night and you didn't have time for me.'

'I didn't know! How was I supposed to know?'

'The trouble with you is, you think everyone should just "put up with it and make the best," of whatever's happening, and that's why Dad kept cheating on you, because you never fought back: you just let him walk all over you.'

'That's not fair. I did it for you as much as anyone.'

'Yeah, well, thanks for nothing.' Jaz turned her head, perhaps to check on Matty, and saw my albums out on the floor. 'And as for these!' She aimed a kick at the nearest one, and my stomach flipped over. 'Happy fucking Families.'

'Don't,' I said.

'Your precious bloody photos. Your version of the past. Not mine! Not the truth! Papering over the fucking cracks. Tell you what, I'm going to start an album of my own that tells the real story. 'Cause all these are one great big *lie*, and I'm sick of lies. I've had a lifetime's-worth of them.'

She dropped to her haunches and scowled at the open page. I thought for one awful minute she was going to start ripping the album apart but instead she pointed furiously. 'Look at this one here. Solange bloody Moreau. You let her get away with murder, coming down in the night to watch TV, turning her nose up at everything you put on her plate then raiding the cupboards when she felt like it. Telling me off if I so much as held a fork wrong, like I was about five. You ruined that visit for me. She knew she could do exactly what she liked and you'd say nothing.'

'She was a guest. She was a long way from home.'

'She used to laugh at you, did you know? Behind your back. She thought you were such a pushover. You know she was a thief? That she shoplifted a whole load of stuff? Ooh, but you thought she was Little Girl Lost, away from her mummy. You were pathetic.'

'I didn't know.'

'You'd never have taken any notice if I'd told you.'

'That's not true.'

Over in the corner, Matty was still clinging to the curtain, rolling himself against the wall in a way that made my heart cringe. Jaz whipped the pages over, rewinding, and stabbed at some other crime.

'That fucking red Fiesta. Remember when you first got it and you drove me round to Penny's house and we sat across the street for an hour?'

'I never did that.'

'Oh, yes, you did. You think I'm too young to remember. You bought me a necklace made of sweets. In fact, you had this bag with you, kept bringing stuff out of it, comics and plastic crap. To keep me quiet. You'd come prepared, as ever.'

In all conscience I had forgotten, till she said.

'And this, Seaworld – my birthday treat, supposedly. All smiley smiley in front of the shark tank, but you were in a foul mood with Dad and you wouldn't talk to him. Wouldn't have a proper row with him and get it out in the open, oh no. Sulked and poisoned the day.'

'I wasn't sulking,' I said. 'I was upset and trying to keep myself together. It was very difficult for me sometimes.'

'You think I don't know what it's like to have a husband who screws around? Remember? Except I *deal with it*. I don't *close my eyes and pretend it's not happening*.'

This inventory of all my failings as a parent: I never realised they'd been catalogued so carefully. Somewhere on the edge of my consciousness a voice was saying, 'But you *haven't* been dealing with it, Jaz. That's why I've had to step in.' I didn't dare say that out loud, though. My instinct's always been to appease. I was made that way.

I said: 'You were always the most important thing in my life; always. No question. I put up with your dad because I thought it was best for you.'

'Which is a lie. You were too scared to do anything about it.'

'Because I didn't want to break up the home. I didn't want your childhood disrupted like poor Natalie's. You're only remembering the bad moments. Most of the time we were fine, you had everything you could wish for, and you know, actually for years it worked. Dad and I did care about each other, despite—'

'Oh yeah, it looks like it.' She stood up again and tossed her hair back, and I got a good look at her face. It was white and furious. 'No *wonder* I've never been able to hold down a relationship, the twisted model I grew up with. No wonder I picked a man who let me down. You *taught me* to make bad choices. You fucked up my childhood, and now I'm trying to get myself back on track, you're *interfering and lying and fucking everything up again!*'

Jaz scooped up the nearest album and heaved it at the wall. I heard the spine crack, felt the thud through my feet as the album hit the carpet. Pages fanned messily out like a broken bird's wing.

'That's what I think of your version!' she cried. 'I don't know whose life this is meant to be in here, but it's not mine.'

'Please, love, I'm sorry about Ian. I'm so sorry. I was trying—'

'Too late! Too *fucking* late! Don't you see what you've done? I can never trust you again. At least it's clear what I should do now: I'm not letting you *anywhere near* Matty in future. You're not *fit*. Half-drowning him, standing there while he falls in the pond, letting complete bastards in the house, and all lies lies lies. You'd probably have let Ian take him off abroad, you'd probably be packing his fucking suitcase for him. Who knows what you're capable of? Standing up in court and testifying against me, I wouldn't be surprised. You're not right and you're certainly not fit to be in charge of a grandchild. Oh no. You've shown me where you stand, you've made your choices.'

'Listen, I would never – all it was – I was—'

There was actual spittle on her bottom lip, I noticed.

'No! No excuses! I've had enough of them. I can't believe a word you say any more, so I'm not listening. You take a good look at your grandson, Mum, because I'll tell you now, you're never going to see him again. Ever. That's it. Finished. This farce is over.'

Then she stalked over to the corner where Matty sat rocking, picked him up as though he were a parcel and carried him out of the front door.

Car doors slammed, the engine revved furiously, then they were gone. I don't believe she even paused to strap him into his child seat.

After a moment or two, I staggered into the hall and sank down onto the bottom step. The cold bar of the stair-gate frame dug into my side. I felt as though all my bones had been unjointed.

If I was thinking anything, it was, Let her go, let her have her tantrum, get it out of her system. Give her space before you do anything else.

Which was a mistake, as it turned out, because it gave her time to run.

CHAPTER 21

Photograph 502, Album 5

Location: The Countess hospital, Chester

Taken by: Carol

Subject: Matty aged 6 hours, asleep in his crib under a waffle blanket.

Photograph: 505

Location: the Countess Hospital

Taken by: Carol

Subject: as above, but from close.

Photograph: 512

Location: the Countess Hospital

Taken by: Carol

Subject: the information card above Matty's head showing his name, sex, DOB, birth weight, length, circumference of head.

Photograph 544

Location: Jaz and Ian's lounge

Taken by: Carol

Subject: Matty, four days old, lying on the sofa in a stripy Babygro.

Photograph 585

Location: Jaz and Ian's kitchen

Taken by: Carol

Subject: Matty, one week old, in his car seat, asleep.

Photograph 600

Location: Jaz's bathroom

Taken by: Carol

Subject: Jaz bends over the baby bath, supporting Matty's upper body and head with one hand, and swilling water with the other. Matty is crying.

Photograph 616

Location: Carol's lounge

Taken by: Ian

Subject: Carol stands in the bay window, cradling two-week-old Matty. Her expression is one of ecstasy.

They had a beautiful day for it. Akela was supervising from the canal bank, while Brown Owl, stationed on the bridge above, had charge of the plastic ducks. One of the Beavers had been given the honour of blowing the whistle to start the race. The tow path was packed with spectators.

'Little one not with you today?' asked Dove, pushing past with her clipboard.

I shook my head. 'I did buy him a duck, because he has a set of them in his bath, and I thought he'd like to see them all together.'

But she was gone, headed for the finishing line to adjudicate there. 'Who's got my net?' I heard her shout.

Families milled around. I saw a toddler straining at his reins, a group of older kids poking with a stick at something in the water, two teenage girls strolling hip to hip. There were prams and balloons and ice creams and bunting and a whole lot of flesh on show. Uniformed Scouts and Guides were taking round baskets of raffle tickets. It should have been a perfect afternoon.

The whistle went and there was an extended splashing as Akela tipped the ducks over the parapet. Those nearby yelped and stepped back, laughing and brushing at their clothes. I noticed Alice resting against the wooden arms of the lock gate, and Libby next to her. I hoped they wouldn't see me. I wished I'd never come.

Because I'd been so intent on not pursuing Jaz, on giving her space to come round, it had taken me a couple of days to realise she was gone. I'd thought it was a bad sign Ian hadn't been in touch. When I plucked up the courage to ring him, he told me he'd been waiting on silence, like me.

So she hadn't even paused to blast him out, I thought. Just upped and left. That's how angry she was.

I'd driven over, and the house had been shut up. A neighbour saw me peering through the back window, said Jaz had given him four or five pot plants because she was 'going away and they'd only die if she left them where they were'. Did he know where she was headed? No, he didn't. Of course he didn't. So I'd gone back home and got my emergency key, the key she'd made me swear never to show Ian even though it was his dad's house, and I let myself in.

The first thing I'd done was dash upstairs and check Matty's cot, only to find it stripped. Coming back downstairs, I clocked the pile of post peeping out from behind the door curtain. Even from the hall I could see the kitchen was spookily tidy, no piles of shoes on the mat, no plates to put away. Last, I visited the lounge, stepping over folders of notes and foreign language books. One dictionary was under the table, as though it had been kicked. I'd retrieved it and laid it on the windowsill. The whole place had felt as though it was holding its breath.

Mums and grandmas jostled against me as the crowd moved slowly along the path, following the movement of the ducks. I cast my eye over the bobbing fleet of yellow plastic, wondering which was Matty's, and was crippled suddenly by a fear so intense I could have collapsed there and then on the grass.

'Watch the lady,' someone said behind me, and a split second afterwards I felt a solid warm mass knock into my calves. When I looked down it was a girl about Matty's age, not much older, wearing a sunhat that had fallen over her eyes. 'Sorry,' said the grey-haired woman who was steering her, and she flashed me one of those grandma-to-grandma smiles. It was like a knife in the heart. I had to get away from this tide of cheer.

The tow path being so narrow and the crowd so big, there was almost nowhere for me to go, but I managed to sidestep into the hedge, and from there ease my way back to the wall of the lock-keeper's cottage. Alice and Libby were catching up fast, and I knew I couldn't cope with the encounter. Between the cottage and its breezeblock garage there was a narrow alleyway, what my mother would have called a ginnel, so I slipped quickly into that. This is someone's private property! I was thinking. What in God's name are you doing, Carol? But it didn't stop me. I just kept going.

I emerged round the back of the cottage to face a long, immaculate garden, full of ornaments and add-ons. Stone animals eyed my progress; gravel had never crunched so loud. I dodged a miniature wheelbarrow, hurried past a picture window and started down the path that ran along the side of the lawn, searching for a gate out onto the cinder track.

Almost at once I heard the sound of a top-floor sash being pushed up. I half-turned, lost my balance and stumbled into a bed of lavender.

'Hoy, you!' a man's voice called.

The normal me would have stopped, faced him, and apologised sincerely for trespassing. That wasn't a consideration for now, though. I didn't even bother framing the words.

Instead I charged on through his plants, snapping red hot pokers and lupins and foxgloves like I'd never cared for flowers in my life. Clouds of pollen rose up around me, spider webs wiped themselves across my bare forearms.

'What the hell do you think you're doing?' he shouted.

There was no gate, and the picket fence was too high to stride over unaided. In the corner, though, I could see a stone bench that I thought I might use as a leg-up.

'This is *not* a public right of way. I'm sick of it. I'm calling the police.'

I reached the seat, hoisted up my skirt, climbed on, and jumped forward.

'Bloody sick of it! If there's any damage, you're paying for it, lady!'

He was still yelling as I landed with a thud in the dirt. My ankle went over and I grazed the palm of my hand, but I managed not to go sprawling. When I looked around, the immediate stretch of lane was deserted – no one to identify me or confirm my criminal activity – so I began to hobble between the ruts in the direction of the main road. I didn't look back. Just let him come after me, just let him.

At the end of the track was the A41. I emerged from between the hedges of the lane into a roar of traffic, big lorries thundering past at sixty so you could feel the suck and beat of air from them on your face. My car was parked round the side of the Horse and Jockey; I could see it 300 yards down the hill. I could go home now, if I wanted. Did I want to go home? I didn't know, couldn't think. Another tanker shot past me, whipping my hair about my face. In the gap which followed, I launched myself into the road, limping as fast as I could. A car horn sounded. I was past caring.

Inside the pub it was cool and almost empty, the calm before the duck race finished and everyone piled back. I decided I'd use the loo, splash cold water on my face while I pulled myself together. It was what my mother used to do to calm herself. The number of times I stood in public toilets watching her bend over the sink, wrists offered up to the tap. Sometimes she'd finish by pulling out her Yardley's cologne stick and rubbing it across her temples. 'This is what it's like, being a woman,' she once said to me. 'You'll find out.'

When my face was dry again, I went into a cubicle and locked the door. I put the toilet lid down and sat, listening to the pipes gurgle and the hum of cars through the open window.

'If she's taken Matty without telling me,' Ian had said, 'it's abduction.'

I'd put on this fake no-nonsense tone, even though inside I was panicking.

'Don't be dramatic. She was upset, she needed a break, that's all.'

'Where? Has she been in touch with you?'

'Not yet, but she will.'

Ian had sworn at me, and then David came on. 'Look, do you know where Matty is, or not?'

'I've a good idea,' I lied, outrageously. 'Give her two or three weeks' space, let her calm down, then I'll go up and see her and bring him back.'

'What if she won't let you?'

'I'm his grandmother.'

'And do you know how much that counts for in law?' said David. 'You might as well be the postman or the butcher.'

'I know how her mind works. I'll talk her round.'

'The way you did before, Carol?'

'Give me this chance. You know what she's like when you corner her.'

Seconds ticked by while he considered.

'I understand that,' he said at last, and I thought how strange it was that David seemed to have more of a handle on Jaz than her own father did. 'OK, you win. For now. I'll talk to Ian about it. But come back to me soon. Otherwise—'

He didn't need to complete the threat.

Ever since that call, I'd been living a strung-out life, vibrating between hope and terror, and in no state to tell which was more realistic. I ached, ached for Matty's weight on my lap, the feel of his palm against mine, the scent of his hair. All last night I'd been kept awake by two voices running through my head. My own – *What if she doesn't come back?* – and Eileen's, reciting over and over some line of poetry we'd had to learn at school – *And Lycius' arms were empty of delight*. 'I only ever wanted to help,' I said to Jaz, in my head. 'You know I'd never take sides against you. You and Matty are the world.' But even an imaginary Jaz wouldn't answer me.

I thought of the little rituals Matty and I had going: giving three kisses at bedtime; the Dalmatian-spot towel he used for his bath and how he loved to be rolled up in it; breakfast porridge in his farmyard animals bowl; playing growly tigers through the bars of the stair-gate. And for no reason at all there came to me an image of Dad and Jaz standing in his garden shed, tightening something into a vice – I swear I could smell the oil and rust. (A pictureframe, was he helping her make? A hamster ladder?)

That was all gone now: that was the past and you expected to lose it. It was a sadness you were prepared for. But what I couldn't bear was the thought that I might lose the future, too. Because that's what Matty was, that sense of life continuing, the sense that, however old and decrepit you felt, however many of your peers got ill – or died – there was this new generation carrying it on, and carrying it on for you. A new set of hopes, a job well done, your own small impact on the world secured. And someone, too, who'd look up to you, who always had the time to spend on nothing much and was delighted to spend it with you. Children and grandparents are such a natural fit.

I don't know how long I sat in the gloom like that, trying to articulate, to no one at all, what Matty meant. Then suddenly I heard a swing door thump open. Someone walked into the toilets, clearing their throat, and when I came to myself I was staring at the crinoline lady logo on the hygiene bags, and half-recalling that same motif embroidered on a traycloth of my mother's.

'Carol? Carol?'

My name registered like a shock. I stood up unsteadily, held the wall for a few seconds, then shot the bolt back.

Dove was standing by the sink, waving an envelope at me. 'You've won!' she was saying.

'Won what?'

'The duck race. We've been looking everywhere for you. We thought you'd gone home, but your neighbour said your car was still here. So I thought, I'll just pop and check . . . It's fifty pounds!'

She held out the envelope and I took it. *Number 169: Matty Reid (via Carol Morgan)*, it said on the front. Someone had drawn a smiling duck in the top right-hand corner.

'Fifty pounds,' said Dove again. I suppose she was waiting for a more dramatic response.

'Thanks.'

'I bet you can't believe it. We had nearly three hundred ducks, you know. Fantastic support. A really good turn-out. And this weather, can you believe it? What a shame Matty isn't here. He'd have loved it. He'd have been cheering.'

'Yes.'

Her eyes scanned my face. Just go, I was thinking. Leave me alone.

'First prize, eh?' she said. 'Fantastic. All those toys you can buy him.'

'Yes.'

She gave up on me and half-turned away. *Should've seen her reaction*, she'd tell the others later. *Never even cracked a smile, can you believe it? Fifty quid!*

'Anyway,' she said, 'you've obviously got the lucky touch this week, haven't you? Lucky Granny.'

I waited till the door hissed shut behind her.

'Looks like it,' I said.

Natalie was currently living back at her mum's, a Seventies semi on the Bowbrook Estate where every street was named after a bird. 'Skylark Rise! Like there were ever skylarks anywhere near there,' I remembered saying to Phil once. 'Oh, there were, apparently,' he'd said. 'All up that side of the town was fields. Some woman at work was telling me.'

Some Woman at Work: it was months before I cottoned on. Now I never walked along this road without thinking of Penny. It had become another area her existence had polluted.

I'd called ahead to say I was coming, so I knew Nat would be in, she couldn't pretend she wasn't. Her small face showed briefly at the window, and I thought what a hard look she'd always had about her, even as a child. Now she was twenty-seven, and her features had settled into a scowl. All the highlighting and tanning beds and nail polish in the world couldn't offset her vinegar soul.

'I don't know where she is,' were her first words as she opened the door. 'I told you that on the phone.'

'Yes, I'd love a coffee,' I said brightly, stepping forward so she had no choice but to let me across the threshold.

Nat frowned, grudging. 'OK. It'll have to be a quick one. I've to be back at work at two.'

I took myself through to their lounge and waited for her to make the drinks. I wanted a minute to get my head straight.

Last time I ruined everything by losing my temper. It had been Phil who'd got the information out of her, in the end.

Phil who'd grabbed my arm as I went to slap her. Twelve years ago I'd sat in this same room, on this same cream leather sofa, under that David Shepherd print of lion cubs, desperate to know where on God's earth my daughter was.

Nat came in with one cup only and put it on the coffee-table next to me. 'You tried ringing her?'

Of course I've bloody tried ringing her. What kind of an idiot do you take me for?

'Yes,' I said. 'There's no answer. I've left messages. Has she been in touch with you?'

'No.'

'And she didn't speak to you before she took off?'

'No.' Nat perched herself on the arm of the chair opposite. 'I know you won't believe me.'

Can you blame me?

The ghosts of before shifted through the room. Skinny Nat in her school uniform, her shrew of a mother standing by the telephone with her arms folded. Me, shouting in their faces.

'She's a grown woman,' said Nat. 'It's not the same.'

'No, I know that.'

Last time Jaz had been intercepted at Lancaster services on the M6, having cadged a lift with a lorry driver. She'd told him she was eighteen. Thank God he'd been a decent sort, who'd called as soon as he realised something wasn't right. Daughters of his own, he had. But before that, Nat had let slip Jaz was headed north. Why north? Nat didn't know, or said she didn't. Jaz would never tell.

'Do you think,' I said, 'she might have gone in the same direction?'

Nat shrugged.

I tried again. 'When you last spoke, was there anything she said, any clue she might have given about her plans? Did she tell you about Ian?'

'What about him?'

'Me letting him see Matty at my house.'

'Oh, that, yeah.' She let her gaze drift over to the window.

So, I thought, she did speak to you before she went. You bloody little liar, Natalie Gardiner. I took a deep breath.

'What did she say?'

'She was really pissed off. Like, really really. I've never seen her as . . . Jesus, she was mad. With you, mostly.'

'I was trying to help, Nat.'

'Yeah,' she said. 'I know you were.'

That unexpected sympathy made my eyes prick with tears. 'I was worried about Ian. That he might retaliate. You hear stories in the news.'

She nodded.

'At the very least, David was talking about involving the courts. And if Jaz doesn't come back soon—'

'He could get shitty.'

'Which is the last thing Jaz needs right now. So can you see what I was trying to do, Nat?'

I thought I had her on my side for a moment. She squinted at me, as if considering. 'You shouldn't have done it behind her back, though.'

'I know.'

The room blurred.

'I'm sorry,' I said, wiping at my eyes with my knuckle. 'Only I miss her. I miss Matty. I just want to know where they are. I know I've messed up, I know I should have stuck up for her more, and she's been saying about how she hated me staying married to her dad. I had no idea. Did you know, did she ever tell you? She didn't tell me. At least, I don't think she did. What I thought was, if I let Ian come round a couple of times, it would keep him sweet, stop him getting too resentful while he waited for her to get herself together. It would take the pressure off. She wouldn't move an inch, you know, wouldn't even talk to him. I couldn't sit by and do nothing, could I? All my life, I've been trying to do the right thing and it's never good enough. Whatever I do, turns out I should have done the opposite. I must have been a really bad mother. Sometimes I think I might as well not have tried.' My voice was thick with self-pity. 'I just want them back, how it was, together. That's all I want.'

'Tell you something,' said Nat, as I attempted to fish out a hanky from my sleeve, 'I'm never having any fucking children. Seems like one big fucking load of grief to me.'

When I'd dabbed my face dry and looked up, she was watching me with what might have been pity, or boredom.

'Please,' I said. 'I'm begging you. If you know anything.'

There followed a long moment where Nat stared up at the ceiling, down at the carpet, and finally settled her gaze on the lion picture above my head.

'She could be in Leeds.'

'Leeds?'

'There's a guy.'

'Who?' I never knew any of the boys she dated then. 'What's he called?'

'Not sure.'

'Did she say she was going to see him?'

'No. She mentioned him a few times.'

'And he's still in Leeds?'

'He might be.' Nat was twisting a strand of hair round and round her finger. 'I don't know for definite. It's just, like I said, she was talking about him before she went.'

'What did she say?'

'I can't remember.'

The urge to rise up, grab her by the shoulders and shake her till her teeth rattled was tremendous. At the same time, my mind was racing ahead. Where did Jaz keep her address book? Might she have left it behind?

'Nat, is there anything else I need to know? Anything at all, *please*. Do you think he's all right, this man? Is Jaz safe?'

She gave a nervous sort of giggle. 'I don't know him. She might not be there, anyway. I've told you all I can.'

I thought I'd better go before I slapped her again.

On the doorstep, she said to me: 'Sorry. It must be shit.'

'Yes,' I said. 'It is.'

I walked to the end of the road, counted thirty, then retraced my steps. This time, instead of marching up the front path, I slipped down the side of the house and round the back. I ducked under the kitchen window, then crouched down behind the door. Gingerly I rose and peered through the glass. The kitchen was empty.

I pressed the handle down by degrees, pushed, and the door gave. I opened it as stealthily as I could, holding my breath, hearing nothing over the pounding of my heart. Then I stepped inside.

'—your fucking mother,' I heard Nat say, from the lounge. 'Oh, going on at me, you know.'

I went faint.

'No,' she said. '*No*. No, I *didn't*.'

A pause.

'Well, where *are* you?'

Slam slam slam slam went the blood in my ears.

'No, I won't. I *won't*. I promise.'

I moved forwards.

'Suit yourself,' said Nat hotly. 'But I'm not having—' That was when she turned round and saw me in the doorway.

'Oh, fuck,' she said, taking the mobile away from her cheek.

'Give it to me!' I shouted. 'Give it to me!'

I don't know whether it was fear or spite made her drop the

phone, but the next second I was scrabbling across the carpet for it. My hands were shaking so badly, and the thing was so bloody tiny, I could barely pick it up.

At last I managed to jam the speaker against my ear. 'Jaz? Jaz? Are you there? Jaz?' All the concentration I had was focused on that moment, as if I could conjure my daughter's voice by sheer force of will. My eyes were screwed tight shut, and my shoulders hunched away from Nat, blocking her out. 'Jaz, please,' I said into the silence.

I stood that way for what seemed like a long time.

When I opened my eyes, Nat was picking up her car keys from the table, and the phone was dead in my hands.

CHAPTER 22

Photograph: unnumbered, wedged between pages 40 and 41 of La Symphonie Pastorale, *in a box in the loft, Sunnybank*

Location: Hunger Hills, Horsforth, Leeds

Taken by: Stephanie Page

Subject: a group of students in hiking gear pose at the base of a huge oak tree. Jaz is on the extreme right, in borrowed boots, borrowed socks, borrowed cagoule. Next to her stands Dr Nick Page, the youngest tutor in the department and a man who has not yet quite sorted out his staff-pupil boundaries. A hearty man, a muscular Christian, mens sana in corpore sano *is his motto and he likes to encourage these academic young people out of the library (or the bar, or bed) and up a hillside once in a while. Luckily, his wife enjoys this sort of caper too.*

'Having fun?' Mrs Page *asks Jaz as the group begins to move apart. 'Yes,' says Jaz, and finds, to her surprise, it's true. Up here, on this high ground, the situation with Tomasz doesn't seem quite so serious, though she knows that every step of the descent will bring it back into focus.*

But maybe it will work itself out. There must be something she can do to get Tomasz all to herself. The fresh air is help-

ing to clear her head, and she thinks she might be on the verge of a plan.

She hitches up her rucksack and sets off down the track. Dr Page soon falls in next to her.

'Let me tell you,' he says eagerly, 'how this place got its name.'

You know the sensation when you bite down with an amalgam filling against tinfoil? That's how I felt all the time now, only from inside my chest: a poisonous, sick fizzing of nerves below my ribcage. Food lodged in my throat; trying to get to sleep was like sprawling on jagged stone. When I watched TV or read, nothing went in. I'd have liked to go to the gym, see the girls, but I couldn't face them. My own fault. I'd made Matty the centre of so many stories, it was the first question people asked. *How's your grandson?* And what could I say? 'My daughter's so disgusted with me that she's taken him away and I don't know where he is. Yes, I'm that bad a parent.' Shame layered on grief layered on fear layered on anger. I didn't know what to do with myself.

If Jaz had been taking photographs for her unhappy album, she'd have had a field day. Daft Carol getting to the supermarket checkout and finding six pots of Splat in her basket, when there's no one now to eat them; rooting like a madwoman through her bag at two in the morning to check again for non-existent phone messages; eating toast over the sink because she can't bear to get a plate from the cupboard where Matty's cup and dish are kept; driving straight into the back of a 4 × 4 and crumpling her bonnet to buggery.

And now I was on this train to Leeds. When Jaz was at the university, I used to drive up, but my head being the way it was, I didn't trust myself not to have an accident. Aside from the prang, I'd had two near-misses in the previous three days. So the train was safer, but on the other hand it meant there was nothing to do but stare out of the window and think. The magazine I'd bought at the station was no go: first headline in it turned out to be *My Ex Stole Our Daughters*. I rolled it up and stuck it in the bin between the seats.

We flicked past rows of terraces that reminded me of Bolton, and housing estates that made me think of Nat. Sometimes in the gardens there were ride-on toys, or climbing frames, or swings. A group of children waved from a cycle track. Look, Matty! I wanted to say. A stadium! A weir! Rabbits! Narrowboats! The loss of him was a solid space sitting in the carriage with me, and outside it, and all around, in everything.

When I'd gone back to Jaz's, the first thing I'd done was run upstairs and check the cot again. I knew it would still be stripped, but I had to see anyway. The times I'd stood listening to Matty's wind-up night light, watching for his eyes to close. I fought the temptation to put it on – to drop the cot side, kneel with my cheek against the bare mattress – and instead turned and walked across the landing, into Jaz's bedroom.

The train jolted, bringing me out of myself. In front of me a red-headed woman about my age was struggling through the inter-connecting door with a hot drink in each hand and a large bag over the crook of one arm. She paused to hitch up the bag and, as she did so, the doors started to slide shut. I thought that, like lift doors, they'd spring apart when they encountered the least resistance, but these swept on, thumping hard into her shoulder. She stumbled against the wall and winced. But then she quickly righted herself to carry on down the aisle, her spine straight, flicking her eyes away from my gaze in a way I knew meant, *This is not how life treats me. That was not a representative scene. I'm really not the kind of person who spends her time being humiliated and pushed about. Stop looking.*

We plunged into a tunnel, and all I could see through the window was my own anxious reflection. Let me say, I would never normally have gone into Jaz's bedroom without being asked, or searched through her dressing-table drawers or the bottom of the wardrobe or under her bed. I'm not that kind of a mother. All through her teens she'd kept a candy-striped hat box full of private bits and pieces – love letters, diaries, that sort of caper – and I'd never so much as run a duster across the lid. But the shelf by the phone had been empty, her address book gone, so where else could I look? I remembered a Filofax with a pair of lips on the cover that she'd still been using in her first year at Leeds. I thought, if I could locate that, I might be in with a chance.

The train came out into daylight again, and the memory of Phil's voice: *Oh, come on, you know Jaz. She likes to make a statement. She'll be back. Try not to get so worked up.* As he'd been speaking, I'd glanced out of the kitchen door and seen Matty's tulips, straight and bright like a row of scarlet soldiers. How long would it be before the petals dropped? Would he get to see them? Would he be back playing in my garden next week, next month, never? I said to Phil, 'It *feels* bad. She was livid with me, you've no idea. You don't understand Jaz the way I do.' 'So you're always telling me,' he'd said.

In the Filofax I'd found just two Leeds addresses: a crossed-out one for her personal tutor, a man I dimly remembered meeting once while she was showing me round the union, and one for a Sam Barnett. Not a name that rang any bells, but then Jaz had kept her university life strictly private and she was rarely at home, even in the holidays. Every week I'd written to her or rung, but all I ever had in return was a handful of texts and the occasional request to send up something she'd forgotten. She'd pass on odd incidents – there was this boy who played his guitar on the roof, there was this girl who got drunk and fell down the faculty stairs – and sometimes let slip names or nicknames, but never the same one twice. Bright enquiries only made her clam up. 'She was that way at school,' Phil had said. 'Just be grateful she's settled. Don't keep digging.' It's hard when they're not around to keep an eye on, though.

The Sam address had been updated twice, which seemed hopeful. I'd written it down, and placed the book back in the hat box, wiping my fingermarks off the lid guiltily. As though that would make any difference.

The carriage door opened again and a young woman walked through with a boy of about seven or eight. She was holding him by the shoulders, a light, protective contact to steady him as we rocked from side to side. I wanted to put out my hand to touch him as well, but that would have looked mad. My limbs twitched uselessly. Huge smooth fields flashed by, one after another, and a line of pylons, and a scrapyard and a lake, and Phil's voice came again: *Try not to get so worked up.* Then my own voice, snapping down the phone line: *Oh, it must be marvellous not to care.* His hurt silence. My parting shot: *And while you're at it, you can tell Penny to piss off.*

'She already has,' he'd said. 'She walked out six days ago.'

The red-headed woman blundered past me again, a coffee stain down her blouse. She saw me looking, smiled slightly and raised her eyebrows in a gesture of complicity. *This tricky world, eh?*

I turned my face away. I wasn't like her, I wasn't a victim. I was going to find my daughter and put things right.

'You're a girl,' I said, staring at the person who called herself Sam Barnett. The boy-toddler she was holding shifted on her hip. Her free hand was on the door, ready to close it in my face.

'Uh huh.'

I looked round to see if my taxi was still there, but it had gone. The terraced street stretched empty.

'Do you mind telling me who you are?' she said.

This woman could almost have been Jaz's sister. Her face was rounder, and her eyes had an oriental look about them, but her hair and colouring were the same. The likeness made me shiver. Jaz would never have worn slippers with tracksuit bottoms and a shirt with sauce stains at the cuff, though.

'Carol Morgan. I'm looking for my daughter,' I said.

The child whimpered and squirmed. 'Jesus,' she said under her breath.

'I think you used to know her?'

'Now's not very—'

'I won't keep you. I only want to know she's OK.'

Sam let the boy slide down her body onto the tiled floor, where he sat leaning against her, whining. 'Sorry, who are we talking about, here?'

'Jaz Morgan. Jasmine. You were at university together.'

'Jaz? Yeah. God. Sheesh.'

'Do you know where she is?'

She shook her head. 'No, no idea. Haven't spoken to her for ages; you're asking the wrong person. You should've rung, saved yourself a journey.'

Except, I could have said, when your daughter won't even answer the phone to you, your best bet is to turn up without warning and try and catch her out. I needed to come and walk these streets between Hyde Park and Headingly anyway, just in case she was magically there, simply because, once upon a time, she had been.

'I'm looking for a man she used to know.'

'Can't help you. That was all years ago. Another life. And like I said, now isn't a good time.' She nodded down at the boy.

'We've only just got back from the doctor's; I've had no sleep for two nights.'

'What's the matter with him?' I said quickly, as her hand tightened on the door.

Both of us peered at the child, who was now lolling his head from side to side and breathing noisily through his mouth. His cheeks were bright red.

'The doctor says it's a virus. He said we have to let it run its course. There's all sorts of bugs going round. Do you reckon he's teething?'

'I don't know. Could be.'

'He won't eat, won't play, can't seem to drop off. It's completely fucking knackering.'

'When exactly did you last speak to Jaz?' I said, dropping to my haunches so I could take a better look.

'I told you; I haven't talked to her for about, ooh, three years. We kept in touch a bit after she left, but it petered out.'

'You were her friend?'

'Sort of. But then—'

Without warning, the child leaned forward and vomited onto the doorstep. Milky drool spattered across the grey stone next to me.

'Oh, shit,' she said. She took a step forward and I knew she was preparing to draw him inside and close the door on me.

'Hang on a minute,' I said. I lifted the hair up on his forehead because I thought I'd glimpsed something there. 'What did the doctor say again?'

'A virus. Why?'

'Can we take him inside and get his T-shirt off?'

I must have frightened her, because she didn't hesitate.

The house was tidier than I'd imagined, and the décor modern, plain and light. Even so, the back room was poky and I had to bring him up to the window to see properly. Sam sat him on the table and peeled off his top while I hunted my reading glasses out of my handbag. You could tell he was poorly because he barely protested.

'How old is he?' I asked.

'Two next month. He's had a lot of ear infections, we're always up at the surgery with him. You get so you think, I don't want to bother them again. But then, when it's night time and he's burning up . . .'

I put my palms to the butter-soft skin of his chest. Then I checked under his fringe again. 'See that?' I said, pointing above his eyebrow.

There was a tiny clear blister marking the fair skin.

'My God,' she said. 'What is it?'

'Chickenpox, I think.'

'I thought that was red spots?'

The child twisted away from us, and we caught sight of his back. 'Like those?'

There weren't many, just three or four, like flea bites.

Sam frowned. 'When I had it, I was absolutely covered. I remember.'

'It can vary. Jaz had hardly any at all.'

'Should I try that glass test thing?'

'You can if you want to.'

She poked one of the spots with her finger experimentally. The redness vanished for a second, then flushed back.

'So what do you do for chickenpox?'

'There isn't really anything, other than ride it out. Oh, cut his nails as short as you can so he doesn't scratch himself into a nasty mess. And keep him cool, don't cover him up with thick blankets. Have you any calamine lotion?'

'No.'

'Don't worry, you can get it in any chemist. Sudocrem'll do in the meantime.'

'And the being sick?'

I shrugged. 'Toddlers do tend to, for no special reason. But if you're at all concerned, get him back to the doctor's. They won't mind. It's better than worrying all night.'

She sat down heavily, then she slid the boy towards her and onto her lap. Both of them looked exhausted. 'Are you a health visitor or something?'

'Just a grandma who's seen lots of cases of chickenpox over the years.'

'Well, if that's all it is . . . Sometimes he seems to go from one infection to another with no pause in between. And there's no one to ask.'

'Your mum?'

'Lives in Spain. Too busy having a good time to bother with grandchildren.' Her eyelids closed. 'I'd make a cup of tea if I had the energy.'

'Stay there,' I said.

When I came back, she'd laid him out on the sofa, and he looked to be almost asleep. His long lashes quivered against his cheeks, and he kept making long, juddery sighs. Up and down his little chest went, his fingers curled and relaxed. What would she say if I reached down and stroked his hair?

'You seem like a nice woman,' she said suddenly. 'I don't know why Jaz always had such a downer on you.'

'Me neither. Look, Sam, are you absolutely sure you can't help me? I really could do with a lead.'

The boy's breathing seemed to fill the room.

She said, 'You'd better let me have your story. Then maybe we'll take it from there.'

'OK, well, I should tell you now,' she said when I'd finished. 'Jaz and I had a – a fall-out. I was pretty pissed off at the time.

I'm sorry about her marriage. If it's any consolation, though, I think she can look after herself.'

'Do you?' I wondered what version of Jaz she'd known.

'God, yeah. She's got a core of steel.'

'Why did she drop out of the course?'

'Didn't she tell you?'

'No.' I felt foolish saying it. 'We didn't even realise she had dropped out, at first. It's not like school, where the teachers ring the parents and send out letters if anything's wrong.' The whole thing was conducted in private, between the university and Jaz. Data protection, I was told when I phoned the department. She was an adult, it was her business, and nothing to do with me. Unless she wanted to involve me, which she didn't.

'Didn't she mention my name at all?'

I struggled to remember. 'I don't think so. I mean, not especially. She used to come at me with a whole list, all funny-sounding nick-names. Slothy was one, and there was another called Meat. She shared a house in the second year with two Zoology students, I do know that, but she was only with them a term.'

Flashback to Jaz that Christmas before she left Leeds, slouching over her plate. I was furious that I'd gone to the trouble of cooking a proper dinner for the two of us, and then she wouldn't eat it. *Nothing I do is ever good enough*, I'd said to her.

'She was supposed to share with me,' said Sam. 'Me and Tomasz. We were – friends. It's complicated.'

'I might have heard her mention Tom.'

'You would have.'

'He was her boyfriend?'

Sam's eyes were dark and clouded. 'He was my boyfriend. Then he was hers, then he was mine again. Although it wasn't as clear as that. It wasn't like anyone drew a line, you know?

Sometimes it was this, sometimes that. Mainly we were friends. That was when it was best. Brilliant, actually.'

'Sounds complicated.'

'It wasn't, though, that was the thing. We just hung around together. Went up Majestyks or Heaven and Hell or the Union; best time of my life, really.'

'Until?'

She looked away. 'It was tricky to keep the balance going long-term. We dated other people, me and Jaz, but never anyone serious. I think we both really loved Tomasz. I think secretly we were each hoping he'd choose us and that the other one would be OK with it. Like that was ever going to come off. I'm sure he found the whole situation . . . you know. Two women, mad for him.

'Jaz had a lot of little flings, and there was this one guy, Andy, I went out with a few times. She set us up, then kept pushing us together, even though I wasn't totally sold on the idea. I knew what she was up to. But Andy was too . . . he wasn't Tomasz, basically. I finished with him to get back with Tomasz—'

'Was Jaz going out with Tomasz then?'

'Like I said, it was a sort of fluid situation. I suppose they were closer at that point. Well, obviously . . .' She gave a funny sort of laugh.

'And Jaz was upset?'

'She was OK with it. It had happened before. What you have to realise is, it was like we were playing some stupid game of tennis, with Tomasz as the ball. I think she assumed she'd get him back, but she wasn't that serious, you know? We were all still going round together. Having a laugh.'

Sam shifted in her chair. A worry line had formed between her brows.

'This,' she went on, 'is where it gets tricky. The other guy I'd been seeing, Andy, he came round to the house and gave me this big speech about love, how we were meant to be together and stuff. He got himself in a total state. Now I look back, I can see he wasn't balanced – he was ill, really, but I didn't pick up on the clues. And then it was coming up to the end of term, and we were supposed to be doing exams, and that's when he killed himself.'

'Good God,' I said.

Against the ordinariness of this pale, neat living room came scenes I'd caught on television: a figure climbing over a railway bridge; a washbasin spattered with blood; a young man's body sprawled across a bed.

'An overdose,' she said, cutting into my thoughts. 'He'd tried it before, when he was in the sixth form. There wasn't a note. Some people are wired that way, it's no one's fault. It wasn't my fault I didn't want to go out with him, was it? Was it?'

'No.' My mouth was very dry. 'And Jaz? Was she involved at all?'

Sam ignored me. 'There was an inquest, obviously. Have you ever been to one of those? Fucking awful. Like a court. Fucking big room. But they said no one was to blame.'

'Did Jaz go?'

'No. I had to. I had to stand up in public and tell them what he'd been like. His parents were there – I had to do all that on my own.'

So much of my daughter's life that I knew nothing about. It was as though a huge gong had been struck inside my head and was reverberating, on and on.

'It must have been awful for you,' I said.

'Yeah, it fucking was. Talking like this – you think something's in the past and then it all comes back.'

'I can imagine,' I said carefully, 'you must feel, even if it's nothing to do with you, a sense of guilt.'

'It wasn't my fault. They said.'

'No, it wasn't. But nevertheless, very distressing for everyone involved.'

'I didn't last much longer than Jaz, you know. One more term and I was back at my mum's. At the time I just wanted to get away. Then I meet someone, get married and find myself here again. There's irony for you.'

'So do you think that's why Jaz became ill? Do you think she was affected by what happened to this boy?'

Sam raised her head and looked at me directly. A bitter triumph gleamed in her eyes.

'I reckon that was probably more to do with the abortion,' she said.

CHAPTER 23

Photograph: unnumbered, stuffed down the back of the immersion heater, Sunnybank

Location: Bar Coda, the Student Union, Leeds

Taken by: Tomasz

Subject: Jaz and Sam lean in together, grinning. Sam has her arm round Jaz's neck, and there is a good deal of bare shoulder and décolleté on view. 'Go on,' urges Tomasz, 'kiss her.' Which one is he addressing? In practical terms, it doesn't matter. Jaz lays her head against Sam's neck because she doesn't want to snog a girl, even for Tomasz. He says he's drunk, but she's been watching him and she thinks otherwise.

'Mmm, my mate,' says Sam, swaying slightly. All at once Jaz is desperate to remove Sam's clammy arm from against her skin. She wants to escape this hot loud room, break out into the panoramic night, and run and run. But that would mean leaving the other two on their own.

It's not the evening any of them have been hoping for.

I sat holding Dad's limp hand and told him all about it.

'How could she not have confided in me? How could I not have known? If she'd come to me, I could have helped, we could have talked it through. She didn't need to have got rid of the baby; I could have supported her. Surely she didn't think I'd be angry with her. *Would* I have been angry with her?'

Dad blinked.

'I wouldn't, would I? I might have said she'd been a bit silly, but I wouldn't have gone on about it. If she'd come home and announced, "Mum, I'm pregnant",' I paused for a moment to construct the scene, trying to imagine myself saying, 'There there, not to worry, we'll see you through.' How likely would that response have been? To have held my tongue about how hard she'd worked to get to university, or how we'd all struggled to get her through those re-takes, or the cash Phil and I had scraped together to start her off? Would I really have been able to pretend unalloyed delight?

Then I thought of Matty, newborn, and what a rush of love I'd felt when I'd held him. That faint prickle of remembered lactation as I held him against my breasts, the endless marvelling at his miniature perfection. Feeling almost drowned in the weight of pride, responsibility and privilege. All that lost to me, to us both: it was an intolerable thought.

Eh, our little Jaz, I heard Dad saying, from across time.

'But I'm speaking from the other side of experience,' I said to him. 'I know now what it's like to be a grandma. That wouldn't have been the case if she'd come to me when she was only twenty-one. I was just a mother then, and that would have made all the difference. Having a grandchild around puts, I don't know, a layer of tolerance between you somehow. Perhaps it's because you're speaking more on a level with each other. You're both mums, so you've a better understanding. Or she's grown up, or you've understood that she's grown up. I can't pin down exactly why, but it alters things right down to the core. So, obviously, I wouldn't have felt the same about a pregnancy as I do now.'

We were all different people back then, love, said Dad.

'See, what counselling did she have, that's what I want to know. Where did she go to have it done? Was he around for her, this Tomasz? God, if he was here now—'

Sam had been infuriatingly short on detail. Yes, the baby was Tomasz's; yes, she thought he might have taken Jaz to the clinic but she didn't know if he'd stayed or not. 'We'd all kind of fallen out by then,' she said. As though they'd been kids having some stupid spat, instead of adults dealing with a matter of life or death. 'Have you got his address?' I'd asked her. 'No,' she said, 'I've no idea where he is.' 'Do you think there's any chance Jaz might be with him now?' I said. 'I wouldn't have thought so,' she'd said. Then she'd turned away from me deliberately and bent over her sleeping boy. She'd done the damage. The discussion was closed.

I squeezed Dad's fingers in mine. 'I need to see this man who hurt Jaz,' I said.

Why?

'Because she might be with him. And because I need to understand her more. No wonder she was angry when she came home. I thought it was with me. But if I'd known. If only I'd known, Dad.'

I couldn't have told you what was bothering me the most: the loss of a baby who I could only conjure in the form of Matty; the idea of Jaz, hurt and lonely and going through such an ordeal on her own; guilt at the way I'd treated her when she dropped out; resentment that by keeping silent, she'd put me in that position. Fear that I knew my daughter so little.

The door opened suddenly and one of the care assistants came in holding a pair of hair clippers. 'Oh!' she said. 'It's so quiet in here I thought he was on his own. Sorry.'

I struggled to come out of my thoughts. Had I not been speaking aloud?

'We're—' I started, but she'd already gone, closing the door softly.

Dad shivered. I kept hold of his hand.

I don't know how much longer we sat like that, talking to each other in silence.

Phil was, as usual, more pragmatic.

'Plenty of girls have abortions. Thousands every year. It's a standard medical procedure, perfectly safe, perfectly legal. Don't get yourself in a state about it, Carol.'

He knelt by the pond, retractable tape measure in one hand, squared paper in the other, a pencil stuck behind his ear. Out of nowhere had come this baking hot day; even the pale grey paving slabs were dazzling.

'But why didn't she tell me?'

Phil paused in his calculations and looked at me, his eyebrows raised.

'Oh, don't start,' I said.

'All I was going to say is, she doesn't like a fuss. She knew she'd messed up and didn't need you to ram it home.'

'I would *never* have told her she'd "messed up". How could you think I'd say such a thing?'

He sighed, took out his pencil and began to mark points on the sheet.

'I know Jaz,' I went on, 'and I know she couldn't have gone through an abortion without being emotionally scarred by it, never mind the physical side. And for her to have faced it on her own – that's what gets me, Phil. I was sitting at home in ignorance while she was going through hell.'

'You were sorting your dad out, as I remember,' he said grimly. 'And there was – Well, you had a few things on your mind that year.'

'Eileen,' I said, to stop him mentioning the divorce.

'Yes, Eileen.'

Insects skated across the surface of the pond inside sliding rings of light.

Phil said: 'Do you not think Jaz might have been keeping schtum to protect you?'

'I wouldn't have thought so. She doesn't operate like that. Oh, God, where did I go wrong, Phil? When she was little we got on really well. Even when she became a teenager it wasn't so bad—'

'Only because you let her have her own way and a bag to put it in.'

'I did not.'

He shrugged, pulled out a length of tape. 'OK.'

'But when she hit nineteen, twenty, I was the devil incarnate. You weren't there to see, but I tell you, I couldn't do a thing right. If I said "good morning" to her, she'd bristle like I'd sworn in her face.'

'I wouldn't take it personally,' said Phil. 'She always dismissed *me* as a fool.' And for a second he looked so forlorn I could almost have gone across and put my arms round him.

He sighed, scrambled stiffly to his feet and then stood looking at me.

'Are you all right?' I said.

'Trying to remember if I've any four-inch staples in the shed.'

I was still imagining what would have happened if I had walked up and touched him.

'Six-inch would do it, but I don't want to go any bigger than that.'

'Don't ask me,' I said. 'No one but you knows their way round that place. One day I'll drag everything out and make a bonfire.'

'I do hope you're joking, Carol.'

'Or alternatively, you could get on and clear it like you've promised so many times.'

'And then every time you needed a job doing, I'd have to bring all my tools round with me. Do you want me to fit this grid over your pond, or not?'

We weren't comfortable enough with each other for this kind of banter. *You moved out of this house, you should have taken all your stuff with you*, my head was going. *Sticking your foot in the door, that's what it amounts to. God knows why I've put up with it all these years*.

Ungrateful cow, he was thinking; I could see it in his face.

I waved a hand in a vague sort of 'have it your own way' gesture, and he disappeared into the shed.

It was much cooler in the kitchen, but I still stood with the cold tap running over my wrists. Tomasz Ramzinski had been easy to track down via Friends Reunited, and then the phone book. But again, I wasn't going to risk calling first.

'Are you sure you want to pursue this?' Phil had said when I first told him. 'If she's not there, you'll have wasted your time, got all wound up for nothing. If she is, she'll be that pissed off with you.'

I hated him for being right, but I didn't seem able to help myself. 'I'll talk her round,' I'd said. 'She's not going to climb out of the back window and run off, is she? Maybe I could just see Matty for a little while. Get my fix.' Give Phil his due, he'd let that comment lie.

When he emerged from the shed, shielding his eyes against the sun, I went out with a glass of water.

'Here,' I said. 'You don't want to get a headache.'

'Ta.' He took it from me, and nodded towards a clump of glyceria. 'I'm going to need to drill some holes around the edge. That all right? It shouldn't affect your liner or anything.'

When I didn't reply, he knelt back down at the pond's edge

and started counting squares on his diagram. His lips moved in silent calculation.

I said: 'I can't believe you're taking it all so calmly.'

'Taking what?'

'Jaz going off with Matty. What she said to me. Anyone would think you didn't care.'

Phil stopped dead and put down his drawing. 'Never say that, Carol. Never say that again.'

He went back to marking his diagram.

'I'm sorry,' I said lamely. 'You just don't seem to get worked up the way I do.'

'Look,' he said, tucking his pencil behind his ear again, 'how about I go down to Bristol with you? You don't want to be messing about on trains; let me drive you. It'll be moral support. Someone to chat to.'

I thought of Sam's face, that tight half-smile as she realised the impact of what she was delivering. Watching me as I struggled to take everything in. It would have been good to have had someone with me that day. Even Phil.

'Well,' I said.

'I could tell you about Pen on the way,' he added carelessly.

You can take a running jump, I thought. I snatched up his almost empty glass and flung the dregs onto the dusty flagstones where they left a dark-blotched trail, like a nursery painting of a caterpillar. 'You come,' I said, 'on condition you don't say a word about her. I don't want to hear her name. I don't want to know.'

'I thought you'd want—'

'Your problem, nothing to do with me any more, Phil. That was me in another life.'

All those times I'd prayed she'd bugger off and leave us. At first so he'd stay, then that he'd come back to me, and finally that he'd show up just so I could tell him to get lost. Now, like so many events you desperately wish for, the nothingness when it arrived was staggering.

'You come with me because you're Jaz's dad, yes?'

He dropped his gaze. 'She might still ring or text. You never know.'

'She won't.'

'I'll see you Saturday, then,' he said, and turned away again to study his figures, his bent back towards me.

I'd no intention of telling David, but it came out anyway.

'I came to ask whether there was any news,' he said, walking into my hallway with a clipboard in one hand and calculator in the other. As if the last time I'd seen him I hadn't slammed a car door in his face.

'What are those for?' I asked.

'I thought I'd measure your pond so we could price up a grid. Might as well get something useful done.'

'Oh,' I said, 'Phil's seeing to it.'

'He's getting professionals in?'

'No, he's fitting something himself.'

David pressed his lips together disapprovingly.

I said, 'He's checked the gauge, it's the proper stuff. If it doesn't look a hundred per cent safe in the finish, I'll take it up and start again.'

'OK.' He pocketed the calculator, laid the clipboard on the windowsill, and sat down. 'So, have you heard from Jasmine yet?'

The stand-by lines I'd rehearsed dissolved from my memory and I found myself mouthing like a fish.

'That'll be a no, then.'

'I did go – she wasn't where I thought she was. But probably—' I began. He interrupted me.

'Look, Carol, I'm here to fight Ian's corner. My son needs to see his child. There's no argument about that. But I'm also on your side, the side that wants Jasmine and Ian talking again, even if it's only to engineer an amicable and fair break-up plan with minimum damage to all parties. So you have to be straight with me. It's really important that you are.'

The open concern on his face made me feel shabby. 'I didn't set out to deceive you.'

He waved his hand. 'Let's just re-cap. You don't know where Matty is right at this moment. That's the state of play, isn't it?'

'Yes, but there's a man . . .'

David raised his eyebrows.

'. . . an old friend, lives in Bristol. It's possible she might be staying with him. I'm going down tomorrow.'

'And you think Jasmine will be there?'

'I don't know. I can't get her to answer my calls. There's a good chance.'

He gave me a searching look. 'You're going tomorrow?'

'First thing.'

'Ring me when you get down there.'

'Soon as I know anything. I promise.'

He stood up. 'Well. I'll report back to Ian. What can I say, except I hope for everyone's sake she's there.'

Before he stepped through the front door, I slid my keys off the hall table, snapped Jaz's spare key off the fob and, without explanation, fumbled it into his hand. He pocketed it without comment or fuss; I can't tell you how grateful I was for that.

The evening was another warm one, so I went round opening upstairs windows to let some air through. In the back bedroom that had once been Jaz's, I unhooked the latch and leaned out over the garden. The light was fading and fine textures were more or less gone, but I could still make out distinct colours and shapes. House martins gabbled under the eaves somewhere near, and traffic passed distantly. Then, overlaying these sounds, came a strange, light, repetitive thumping from the direction of Laverne's. It was one of those noises you don't notice at first, like a tap dripping – and then when you do, you can't hear anything else. *Thunk, du-dum. Thunk, du-dum.*

I craned to see what it was. Funny she wasn't out herself, because it must be driving her mad, what with her artistic nature. *Thunk, du-dum.* After thirty seconds there was a lull, and a football rolled into view across their lawn. Josh appeared, slouching after it, bending and scooping. As he turned he raised his face in my direction, but he didn't acknowledge me. He walked back out of sight with the ball under his arm, and then the noise started again. Kick, hit-bounce. Kick, hit-bounce. A troubled boy booting a football against brick in the gathering dark, his mother inside, registering each sulky resonance. *Fuck you all, fuck you all.*

I closed the window against the sound, and went downstairs to turn on the TV.

CHAPTER 24

Photograph 122, Album Two

Location: woodland, Alnwick, 1976

Taken by: Carol

Subject: Phil, wearing a maroon velvet jacket, sitting astride a tree trunk and pretending he's on a horse.

Earlier that afternoon, he made the mistake of asking why she looked so down when they're supposed to be on holiday and enjoying themselves.

Out it all pours, how she's thought over and over she was pregnant then found she wasn't, how she might never have children, how she's failed as a wife. 'If I don't have children, I think I'll die,' she says melodramatically.

'Rubbish,' he says, ruffling her hair. 'We've not been married five minutes.'

Over a year, thinks Carol. Long enough.

But Phil doesn't seem the slightest bit concerned that he might be hitched to a barren woman. Instead he starts talking about his so-called super-sperm, demonic white tadpoles that wear little cloaks and have magical powers. 'They're waiting,' he says, 'for that special egg. An everyday egg won't do. It's got to be a top-grade one. Nothing but the best.' He mimes the sperm's wiggly journey, acts their expressions as they search and reject, and search again. He gives them the voice of David Niven in A Matter of Life and Death.

Then he takes her in his arms and puts his lips to hers. The clouds scud over their heads and the grass quivers around them.

This is what he's good at: when she leans on him, when she lets him be the man.

I put on old clothes for travelling, then swapped them for something smarter, then changed back into old again. Bristol was a long way. I was standing in front of the mirror, wondering how I wanted to look when I met the man who'd wrecked my daughter's head, when the doorbell rang.

To my surprise, it was David.

'I'm going out,' I said.

'I know. That's why I'm here.'

It took me a moment before I understood. 'You want to come with me?'

'If you'll let me, I'd like to drive you down. It's a good three hours and I know your car's still crimped. I'd wait outside when we got there. I wouldn't interfere – that's very much not my agenda – or I'd come in with you, if that's what you wanted. Whatever suited you. I'd just like to be involved.'

I said, 'Phil's taking me.'

'I see.'

'Sorry,' I said. 'I should have mentioned it. But thanks ever so much for coming round.'

'All right. But you will give me a ring when you get there? To let me know what's . . .' He trailed off, frowning. 'Can you hear music? Or am I hallucinating?'

He was right, it was my mobile. By the time I'd hunted it down, the screen was displaying Missed Call, but I knew it was

Phil. I left David where he stood, took myself into the kitchen and rang straight back.

'Ah, Carol,' said Phil. 'I am still coming round, but I might be a bit late. Something's happened.'

'Something?'

There was shouting in the background, a woman's voice.

'Pen's here. She wants— *No, it isn't. Wait. Wait! There's no need!*' I heard him mutter an aside, then his voice became loud again. 'I didn't know she was coming. She wants to pick up some stuff.'

'Phil, I need to get down there.'

'Yeah, I'll be with you, soon as I've got rid of her.'

'Fine,' I said crisply.

'Don't be like that.'

'I'm not being like anything. Obviously there are still things you need to sort out. Don't bother coming over, I'm setting off now.'

And I clicked the phone closed.

I came back out into the hall where David was writing something on my telephone pad. 'I was going to see myself out,' he said.

'If it's three hours to Bristol,' I said to him, 'we'd better get going, hadn't we?'

The first part of the drive was completed in silence. My head was all Phil, all anger and humiliation and disappointment and images of bloody Penny, bloody bloody Pen, jowly cow blundering into my life, buggering everything up again and again and again! God, I hated her.

Two feet away from David I sat and stewed in my own thick fog of loathing; when that began to disperse, I remembered where we were going, and then it was fear enveloped me instead. I sat clutching the seat belt, trying to work out how I'd cope if we got there and there was no Matty, no Jaz, and why should she be there? This was a longer-than-long shot, I was only setting myself up for a fall. I tried not to imagine her opening the door to me, Matty behind her, peeping round her legs. I tried not to imagine my grandson tottering forward for a hug, me lifting him up and squeezing him to my chest, his hair against my cheek, his hot smooth skin brushing my lips as I kissed him and kissed him. And the more I strained to banish the pictures, the clearer they became till they were as sharp as real memories.

David was saying something. It was like someone speaking to you from the poolside when your head's underwater: '—if you get car sick. Wind the window down if you need it.'

'I'm fine,' I snapped. I felt as though his interruption had foiled an actual reunion. When I glanced across, his expression was completely neutral. Was it just a front? Was he, secretly, as churned up as me? Why did he have to call me out of myself like that? Now I was wrong-footed, on top of everything else. The miles were rolling away under us and I wasn't prepared. 'Sorry, I'm a bit tense.'

'Or we can have the radio on if you want background noise.' He pushed a button on his dashboard, and something busy and classical came out of the speakers.

'No, thanks.'

He switched the music off. We covered another silent mile.

'Who are we going to see, exactly?'

'Oh. Her ex, sort of. Although she's not been in touch with him since she was married, her friend told me.'

'And what do we know about him?'

'Only that Jaz dated him at university, and that it was quite serious. The break-up was what started her illness, I think.'

I wasn't going to tell David about the abortion. No one was hearing that.

I said, 'I suppose Ian's in a state.'

'He's pretty wound up, yes. Though still very aware that whatever Jaz is up to, he started the whole business. That's holding him down at the moment. I don't know how long for.'

'Does he know about today?'

'He's had to go into work.'

'On a Saturday?'

'Some kind of project crisis that won't wait. No point dragging him away from that, stressing him out over what might be a wild-goose chase. I'll tell him when I get home,' said David, as if there were nothing to debate about such a strategy. Imagine having offspring who respected your opinion like that, who assumed you knew what you were doing, who were prepared to put their life into your hands.

By the outskirts of Birmingham, the traffic had grown much heavier. We passed huge, thundering lorries with wheel arches as high as my head. The landscape on either side was hoardings and warehouses and factories and banks of transformers. Wires criss-crossed the skyline.

I said, 'One thing I've realised, I don't know my son-in-law at all. Not even slightly.'

'If it's any consolation, I think he took us all by surprise.'

Here came a truck with a yellow digger on the back, but I had no one to point it out to.

'When you look back, though, can you see where the affair came from?'

David was silent for a long while. I thought he'd decided not to answer, or perhaps he'd shaken his head and I'd not seen. The traffic became mesmerising if you gazed at it for too long.

Suddenly he said, 'What you have to understand about Ian is, he has absolutely no self-confidence.'

'I can't believe that,' I said. 'His background. His education.'

'You're confusing confidence with being well turned-out, polite, nicely spoken. It's not the same thing, Carol. I've trained Ian over the years to come across as relatively easy with himself, but it's a veneer. I don't know how far even Jasmine appreciates that, for all the time they've spent together. She may not. He's become adept at disguise.'

I found myself staring at a row of grey and beige tower blocks, imagining myself transported there, my own face to the window, watching the distant cars.

'Do you think it comes down to having a difficult childhood? Losing his mum?'

'Oh, it started before that. Long before. When Ian was born, there were babies in cribs either side who lay like dolls and never made a murmur. Ian was fretful from the minute he came out; I could almost have told you then we'd have trouble at nursery, and starting school, and changing classes, and that every little setback would be a crisis. In a sense he didn't cope too badly with Jeanette dying, in that his life then was one drama after another, so that just became one more to deal with. I did my best, under the circumstances.

'He calmed down as he got older, grew a thicker skin, learned the social graces. I'd say he enjoyed certainly the sixth form and university. Barring a couple of hiccups.

'Then he married your daughter, a woman – let's be frank – in a completely different league from anyone else he's ever dated. Not that he'd had many girlfriends to begin with.'

'Surely if he felt like that, he'd have hung onto Jaz all the more tightly?'

'Why do some women who've had a violent upbringing go on to choose a violent partner? Or girls whose mothers had them too young fall pregnant themselves before they're able to cope with a baby? Why do people drink too much, or take harmful drugs, or get themselves repeatedly into debt? We all come with a self-destruct button, Carol, it's just that some of us are better at resisting than others. My guess is that when this woman threw herself at him, flattery scrambled his brains. The boost to his confidence eclipsed everything else. Even, momentarily, his love for Jasmine and Matty.'

Excuse-lines from Phil echoed in the back of my mind: *You and Jaz make me feel the odd one out. Sometimes I think I'm invisible to you. It's like I come last in this house.*

'I hope you're not suggesting Jaz is to blame?' I said. 'It's not her fault she's beautiful. You know, he's had *nothing* but kindness off our family.'

'It's not an excuse,' said David. 'Just an attempt at explanation. Anyway, I could be wrong. He doesn't speak to me about it. By the way,' he nodded at the plaster across my knuckles, 'what happened to your hand?'

'Oh. Silly accident.'

'Argument with a cheese-grater?'

'Not exactly.'

To tell him, or not. He waited while I decided, and it was knowing I didn't have to say any more that made me want to.

'God, it's so stupid. I punched a wall.'

'And why did you do that?'

'I don't know. I had this mad moment last night where suddenly I didn't know what to do with myself, I just needed to thump something. I hope that doesn't sound too disturbed.'

'Can I suggest a cushion next time?'

In spite of everything, he made me smile. 'It's not me. I don't do things like that. Unless I'm someone different from who I thought I was.'

'That's always possible.'

We were out of the city now and into countryside. The pressure in the car was less somehow, even though every revolution of the wheels brought me closer to Jaz, or to her absence.

'A month after Jeanette died,' said David, 'I tried to dig up a tree root in the garden. That was idiotic of me, because really it needed experts in with proper equipment. But I wasn't bothered about that, I just wanted to attack something. I used a pick and a spade and I went at it non-stop for two hours, and by the end I'd taken all the skin off the palms of both hands. They were so bad I had to go up to the surgery to have them dressed. I couldn't drive for a week.'

'Oh, God.'

'Time moves on. This too shall pass. It will, Carol.'

Much later, as we were getting ready to come off the motorway, I realised there was something else I needed to get off my chest.

'I feel as though I should say sorry.'

'What for?'

'Shouting at you. What I said about, you know.' *No wonder Ian's like he is*.

'You feel you should, but you don't especially want to?'

I blushed. 'That's about it, yes. It seemed important at the time. Now, compared with everything else that's happened – And it wasn't really my business anyway. And I should have let you have your say. Those are the bits I'm sorry for.'

'A selective apology.' He rubbed his wrist strap, stretched his shoulders back in his seat. 'Well, you were selectively right, if it's any consolation. Not about all of it; you don't know the details and I'm not prepared to share those because it would mean breaking a promise. Although, if anyone would have understood, it would have been you.'

'I don't want to hear.'

But I was thinking about those stories you read in magazines: people with partners who were very badly disabled or ill, open marriages, marriages where one person simply didn't want sex and the other had been left stranded. Perhaps it was one of these he was talking about. Perhaps not. Perhaps you could never ever justify that kind of deceit.

He said, 'I hope you know me well enough by now to appreciate I'm not wholly devoid of morals. There were special circumstances. It wasn't a bad thing I was doing, at least I didn't think it was when it started, but I ended it because it didn't sit right with me. I got drawn in against my better judgement. The way it began, I thought I couldn't say no without hurting someone I thought a lot of . . . No, I've already said too much.'

'Let's leave it there, then,' I said.

'Let's,' he said.

At last I sat back and let my mind drift. Ian showing me the picture of the pram he'd marked in the catalogue. Ian opening their fridge and counting up the jars of cling peach pieces Jaz had stockpiled to satisfy her pregnancy cravings. Jaz lifting up her skirt and showing me the veins in her legs. Jaz unfolding the kick chart that the midwife had given her, the little blocks shaded with ink that meant the baby was alive. Meeting Ian at the entrance to the maternity ward, neither of us able to shape a coherent sentence. Laughing at Phil because he brought in a packet of make-up remover tissues instead of baby wipes. The way Ian leaned protectively over Jaz to shield her when she was breastfeeding. Her expression as the wedding car drove off. Ian sitting next to Dad's bed, reading him articles from the local paper. Ian reading to Matty at bedtime and putting on a high-pitched voice for a mouse. Matty standing up in his cot, pointing at a teddy he'd thrown onto the floor. Six-week-old Matty strapped into his baby carrier, asleep on Ian's back. Matty asleep on my sofa, while I sat by him and watched over him.

'It's saying junction nineteen.' David nodded at the satnav screen. 'So the next one.'

I pulled down the mirror to check my lipstick. Behind me on the back seat Jacky materialised, wedding hat and all. She became the Baroness, who became Penny. *You're nothing, any of you*, I told them, pushing the mirror back up and vanishing them with a flip.

When I looked out of the window, we were crossing the estuary, into Bristol.

CHAPTER 25

Photograph 468, Album Four

Location: the back garden, Sunnybank

Taken by: Carol

Subject: Jaz and Ian, the week before their wedding. Jaz is throwing her head back at something Ian's said, and he's smiling because he's pleased he's made her laugh, and oh, the look of love in his eyes.

Clifton turned out to be a place of Georgian terraces set on hills. As we cruised along, counting off street names, I turned my head this way and that, hoping against sanity to catch a glimpse of Jaz and Matty. Was that Spar one she'd been in, buying milk, bread, bananas for Matty? Every young woman we passed had me leaning forward, eyes screwed up for maximum focus. If I could have conjured her through mere wanting, she'd have been there in an instant.

'We're here,' said David as we turned down a lane of tall pastel houses. 'Are you all right?'

I'd had my eyes closed for a moment, praying. 'Not really.'

'Shall I walk you across?'

'No, I'll be fine. Watch for me, though.'

'Of course.' He reached across and opened the door for me.

Tomasz won't be in, I thought. He'll still be at work or with friends or in town or whatever it is young men do these days. The desperation to see Jaz and Matty again was like the heel of a hand pressing against my throat. Let them be there, I thought. I'll do anything. Then: He won't be in, he won't be in. These games we play with fate, as if we have any control over anything.

The building that had looked smart from a distance was shabbier when you got close up, the lawn scraggy and full of weeds. Multiple buzzers and name tags revealed flats, not a single house. I pressed *Ramzinski*, and waited.

He was in. The door opened and a broad, good-looking blond man in an open-necked shirt hung onto the doorframe. 'Yeah?' he said. An excited sports commentary boomed somewhere behind him.

The words were sticky in my mouth. 'Is Jasmine in?'

His look told me she wasn't.

'You are Tomasz Ramzinski?'

'Yeah.'

'I'm looking for Jaz Morgan.'

'*Jaz*? She isn't here. Why would she be?'

'I'm her mother.' Knowing David was across the road, looking out for me, made me braver. 'Has she been in touch? Do you know where she is?'

'No, no idea. Don't know. Sorry, I can't help you.' He started to close the door.

'Could I come in for just a minute?'

Tomasz looked doubtful.

'Just for a minute, please. I won't keep you. I'm really desperate.'

He backed off enough for me to step up and inside, and we stood in the open hallway, eyeing each other.

'I'll be blunt,' I said. 'My daughter's missing and I'm concerned over her whereabouts.'

'Shit,' he said, with a nod at sympathy. Behind him, the high ceiling was cracked between the coving and picture rail, and there was dust on the skirting, old flyers littering the floor tiles.

'I know you were . . . involved at one point. When did you last speak to her?'

He shrugged. 'Not for ages. Since she was going to get married. We used to email, but then she met this guy and it stopped. Nothing since then. We're talking, I dunno, maybe three years. When you say missing, is it, like, you should go to the police or something?'

I shook my head quickly. 'We had a row. I only want to find her and say sorry. Know she's OK. She has a little boy. My grandson.'

'Shit,' he said again.

'Have you any idea at all where she might be?'

'Nope.'

'You can't think of anyone she might have gone to? Anyone from Leeds? Anyone you used to email about?'

He folded his muscular arms and leaned against the grubby wall. 'God, I don't know. She used to hang about with a girl called Sam, ages back; no idea where she is, though.'

'I know where Sam is.'

All at once I had his attention. He detached himself from the wall and let his arms drop to his sides. 'Yeah? Holy fuck, where?'

'She didn't go far. Headingly.'

'No way! She left – did she come back, then?'

'Evidently.'

'Aw, for real?' He grinned and shook his head at the marvellous irony. 'She doing all right?'

'Yes, she's fine. She has a baby. But what I need to know is—'

'A kid? No way.'

'A little boy, yes. She seemed to be doing fine. But what I—'

'How did you know where to find her?'

'In my daughter's address book.'

'What? Jaz had her address? All that time?' Tomasz's expression changed to one of disbelief. 'Fucking hell. So when I was emailing her and Sam got mentioned and she said she didn't know – Fuck. Do you know it? Can you remember the house number and the street?'

I took a step forward. 'What can you tell me about my daughter? What don't I know that might help me find her?'

His lips puckered round half-formed words as he weighed up the deal.

'Come up,' he said.

What I saw first as I walked into his flat was a huge black and white photograph. It hung above the marble mantel, dominating the room: Tomasz, during a game of rugby, mid-pass. His fair hair flicked out as he turned to grasp the ball, and his jaw was set, the cords in his neck standing out. The thighs were rounded, straining against his shorts, and his boots dug into mud, a sliding pivot before his blurred team mates. It was a moment beautifully captured; when your own muscles react in sympathy, that's a good action shot. He saw me looking, and smiled briefly. He just likes the photo because it's of himself, I thought.

The rest of the room was decently furnished, but messy. He'd spread all the sections of a weekend newspaper across the floor, and there was a plate of crumbs beside it. Golf clubs leaned against the chimney-breast and a series of trophies lined the mantelpiece. The rest of the clutter was mainly magazines and mugs and items of clothing. The sweater draped over the back of the chair was surely a woman's.

Tomasz muted the widescreen TV while I sat on the edge of his man-size sofa.

'So how was she?' he said. 'Is she married?'

For a mad second I thought he meant Jaz. 'I'll give you Sam's address and you can see for yourself,' I said coldly, struggling to contain my temper.

He was scrabbling for a pen almost before I'd finished the sentence.

'I can't believe Jaz never let on they were still in touch. I can't believe she kept it from me.' Then he paused, Biro in hand. 'Actually, yeah, I can.'

I said: 'You must know you hurt my daughter very much.'

'We split up. People do. It's shit, but there you go.'

I was imagining myself unsheathing one of his golf clubs and swinging it full pelt against his TV screen, his portrait, his pretty face. 'Sam told me about the abortion.'

He looked sick then.

'What can I say?'

'You can tell me why you didn't give her the support she needed. Why didn't you go with her?'

'Where to?'

'The clinic. It was your baby.'

'She didn't want me to.'

'I find that hard to believe,' I said. I watched his neck grow pinker, his eyes flick away from me.

'She went with her personal tutor. That's who she wanted.'

'Jaz wasn't on her own, then?'

'No. She stayed with him and his wife afterwards.'

'What: in his house?'

'Yeah.'

'How long for?'

'A couple of days.'

'What was his name? Where did he live?'

'Dunno. Can't remember.'

I hate you, I thought. I hate you so much it's all I can do not to leap up and attack you. 'How was she?'

'OK.'

'OK? You're telling me that my daughter went through an operation as traumatic as that and she was *perfectly fine* with it?'

He shook his head in irritation. 'I'm not saying it was nothing! I mean, it wasn't something she'd have chosen to go through, obviously, but she really wasn't that cut up about it. I think she saw it as something she had to get done. Like, like going to the dentist.' He saw my face, forestalled me. 'Just, don't, yeah? Don't even say it. You might not want to hear all this, Mrs Morgan, but it's how it was, that's how it was for her. I was there, I saw. I fucking saw, right? She was strung out and pissed off, but she wasn't running round in tears.'

'Some people show grief in different ways!'

'Sure, but – honestly, Jaz wasn't that affected.'

'So not affected she had a breakdown when she came home.'

'Did she?' He looked properly taken aback then. 'Shit. She never said. I didn't know that.'

'Well, you wouldn't, would you? I presume you didn't bother contacting her in those months after she left Leeds, or you'd have known.'

Tomasz shifted, and hooked his thumbs defensively in his jeans pockets.

'Look, don't try and pin that on me. None of us were in touch at that time. I don't know what Sam told you, but the three of us got blown apart. It all just went – it was a fucking mess. Jaz didn't want to see me. Boy, did she not want to see me. Then Sam disappeared off the map. Then I start getting emails from Jaz again, then a couple of years down the line she meets this bloke she wants to marry and I'm dropped again. Seems to me like she was the one calling the shots. Took me all my time just to keep up with her.'

'Then why was she so desperately upset? Why did she lie in bed for weeks and need me to help get her up and dressed every day as though she was some kind of invalid? Tell me that!'

As I sat looking up at him, trembling with rage, he only shook his head pityingly. 'You really don't get your daughter at all, do you?' Then he walked away from me so he was standing in front of the hearth, underneath his own vast image.

'It was Andy Spicer dying,' he said. 'Did Sam fill you in on that stuff?'

'But that wasn't Jaz's fault!'

'Not that Sam knew, really, not the whole story. I'll tell you why Jaz was wrecked over it: because she thought she was responsible.'

I tried again to protest, but he spoke right over me, his tone low and dangerous.

'And she was responsible, in a way. Those two, her and Sam, teasing him and drawing him in. Big old joke that was. Then – and this is the bit Sam doesn't know, God help her – Jaz went round to his flat and spun him this lie about how Sam really did love him, and if he went back and crawled to her, she'd be his for the taking. Totally set the poor bastard up. 'Cause he was like, he was really into her – into Sam, I mean. Then afterwards, the two of them were laughing about him to his face. *To his face*, Mrs Morgan. Within his hearing, anyway.'

'They didn't know he was going to—'

'No, none of us did. None of us did.' His face creased up in disgust. I could only guess what scenes he was playing out in his head.

'And you didn't tell anyone about what Jaz had said to this boy?'

'For fuck's sake, it was enough of a mess!'

I was floundering, trying to imagine why she'd have done something so cruel. Whatever I didn't understand about her, I knew she was never like that. It must have been Sam's fault, or Tomasz's, or maybe she thought this Andy really did stand a chance. His parents standing in a courtroom to hear how he died. Maybe the whole tale was all lies, from start to finish.

'Did Jaz love you very much?' I heard myself say.

Tomasz exhaled raggedly, the breath of someone struggling to contain themselves in the face of unbelievable provocation, and for a moment I experienced a flicker of fear. But then he shrugged and half-turned away towards his row of shiny trophies. He said, 'We were really young, everything was weird – you could never tell who was being serious.'

Did you love her? I wanted to ask, but I didn't dare. I think I knew the answer.

'Anyway, that's all there is,' he said, facing me again, straightening his back aggressively. 'I've told you everything I can think of, whether you like it or not. Can I have Sam's address now?'

Your version, I thought, that's what you've told me. I took the pad of paper he'd placed on the sofa arm and scribbled something down off the top of my head. There was no way I was letting him near Sam's little boy. I'd have liked to tear the page out, screw it into a tight ball and throw it at him, but I was afraid that once I gave full vent, I'd not be able to stop. The moment I'd put my pen down, Tomasz lunged and snatched the pad off me, scanning it greedily.

'Are you sure this is right?' he snapped.

'Quite sure.'

I wondered whether he could tell I was lying, and what he might do to me if he guessed.

'Good. Get out, then.'

I stood up, and tottered towards the door.

'Oh, and Mrs Morgan,' I heard him say behind me. 'One last thing. When you leave here, yeah, go to the end of the street, turn left, and then *fuck off out of my life*.'

'Drive,' I said to David as I closed the car door. He revved the engine the way they do in cop shows, and the car shot forward.

'Where?' he said.

I didn't answer.

We travelled through wide and gracious streets that took us gradually upwards. On another day it would have been pleasant to look out at the cream-coloured houses with their balconies and hanging baskets, the shops with their striped awnings, but my vision was all poisoned with Tomasz.

After a few minutes, David pulled in under a line of trees, braked, and switched off the engine. 'Come here,' he said, turning in his seat. I leaned across and he gathered me in against his chest.

'She wasn't there,' he said.

'No.'

'Have you found out where they are?'

'No.'

'Do you want to tell me what happened?'

'I can't, not all of it. He's a horrible man. Let me just—'

His grip tightened. 'I'm sorry, Carol.'

'For Ian, you mean.'

'For all of us. For you.'

He went on holding me, and I imagined a pair of satellite

beams coming down, one on our car and one fixing Jaz wherever she was, like a mathematical compass. All it came down to was two points on a map; a simple straight line could connect us, if only I had that knowledge. Sometimes it's the straightforwardness of a situation that drives you mad.

CHAPTER 26

Photograph 632, Album Five

Location: Carol's sofa

Taken by: Laverne

Subject: baby Matty, swaddled like a papoose, lying across Carol's lap with his eyes closed in blissful sleep. Everyone is sagging with relief because the marathon crying session's finally over. 'You've certainly got the magic touch, Carol,' Laverne says as she squints through the viewfinder. 'Oh yes, Grandma knows best,' says Dorothy Wynne.

At the edge of the shot you can see Jaz's hand reaching across to reclaim him.

When the call came next day it was David, not Ian.

'What was his reaction?' I asked fearfully.

'I need to see you, to explain,' he said. 'Are you in this afternoon?'

'Helping at the County Show. Akela's dad's been rushed into hospital, and they're an adult short to oversee the hot drinks.'

'And you can't get out of it?'

'I promised, they're expecting me.'

'I'll see you there, then.'

Which is why he found me with my ear against a tea urn, trying to listen for sounds of bubbling. 'I don't know whether this is working,' I explained. 'How long do you think it takes to boil something this size?'

David touched the side lightly with his fingertips. 'When did you switch it on?'

'Half an hour ago.'

'Should be on the way by now.'

'That's what I thought.'

Boys in green sweatshirts buzzed around the tables shaking out paper cloths, setting down sugar bowls, unstacking chairs in a scene of cheery industry.

'And the generator's working?' David was saying.

'Definitely. Can't you hear it?'

He left the urn and followed the lead to the back of the tent while I made up two big containers of orange squash. A minute later he was back.

'I've pressed the re-set button. It should be fine now,' he said. 'Is there anything else I can do to speed things up here? When can you get away?'

'Soon as Dove gets here, but she was having a replacement windscreen fitted this morning so she can't come till that's finished.'

'It really is all go, isn't it?'

'Chaos in every area.' And I thought of the clearing I'd been doing at two that morning, unable to sleep and so turning out more of the accumulated junk of the last eight years.

Charlie Blunt appeared at my elbow with a column of shrink-wrapped plastic cups he couldn't open. While I was wrestling with that, two Cubs larking about burst a full bag of sugar over the grass.

'I'll go and have a wander,' said David, 'come back when

you're less rushed. You need to give your full attention to what I've got to tell you.'

As he walked away, I felt the panic begin to unstring me again.

He was waiting by the birds of prey tent opposite. I came up by his side, and we watched a falconer trying to coax a buzzard off his glove and onto a perch. The bird kept baulking and flapping its wings, but the man persisted until at last the buzzard settled where he wanted it. Then it sat, swivelling its head in a way that made me feel ashamed for looking.

'Ian's making an appointment with a solicitor first thing,' said David. 'I think it's time. I feel that if she'd had any intention of getting back with him, she'd have been in contact.'

'We don't know that for sure.'

'Some men would have been to the police by now.'

'Ian wouldn't do that.'

'He's talked about it. I've told him to wait.'

I couldn't help marvelling once again at the level of influence David held over his son.

'But if the situation carries on much longer, Carol—'

'I know.'

'So he'll get an application for contact in place, and the moment Jasmine reappears, we can start it moving through the courts.'

What if she still blocks him? I was thinking. But David was ahead of me.

'If the application's approved,' he went on, 'and I can't see any reason why it wouldn't be, then she'll have to comply. Breaking the terms of a contact order can be serious. Ultimately, you can go to prison for it.'

'Oh my God.'

'I don't mean to frighten you, I'm just saying, that's the law.

Fathers' rights. Ian's rights.' He patted my shoulder in what I assumed was an attempt to reassure.

'I wish she'd just come home!' I burst out.

Some of the birds shifted on their perches, talons flexing nervously.

'She'll have to, sooner or later. There's too much needs attention. Her books, her work, Ian says half her clothes are still in the wardrobe. There are people she'd need to notify, health visitors and such. Even if you don't know exactly where she is right now, Carol, she hasn't vanished into the ether.'

'She'd leave clothes, she wouldn't be bothered about coming back for them. Not if she's decided to keep away.'

'I agree if she was on her own she might be able to melt into the crowds, but she's got Matty with her. He has no passport, he'll need registering with a doctor if she settles for any length of time. We know Jasmine's car registration. When her savings run out she'll have to start using cash machines, and then we can check the joint bank statements.' David counted off each point on his fingers. 'It might take a little while, but we'd find her.'

He took my arm and began to lead me back from the pen, away from the tents and people, towards the boundary of the field. As we drew near the hawthorn hedge he said, 'And look at it this way, Carol: once a proper framework's in place, it'll be easier for them to talk to each other.'

'Jaz hates being told what to do, though.'

'It wouldn't be a case of that. I'm talking about a formal dialogue, Jasmine working with a solicitor to draw up terms and responses she approves.'

'So the marriage is over.'

His pause told me all I needed to know.

'But even if they divorce, they can still work as a team for Matty. I believe Jasmine will do that, when it comes to the crunch. Don't you?'

'I want to say yes.'

Soon the showground would be open. Marshalls in fluorescent jackets stalked between the stands, reeled out cables, consulted clipboards, spoke into two-way radios. The public would stream in: hundreds of families enjoying a sunny day, with no idea how lucky they were.

'There's one thing I need to ask you,' I went on. 'You know what you said once, about me being like the postman or the butcher?'

David looked puzzled.

'You said,' I went on, 'that if I tried to get access to Matty, I'd have no chance because I had no legal rights. Was that it, or did I misunderstand? Because I was thinking, maybe *I* could apply for a contact order as well, if necessary.'

He was looking puzzled. 'You? A contact order?'

'She was pretty cross with me before she went.'

'Not so cross she'd block you from seeing Matty.'

I'm never letting you near him again, I heard her say. *You just can't be trusted, can you?* 'I only want to make sure where I stand.'

'What exactly did she say to you, Carol? Did she say she wouldn't let you see him?'

Over the rustling of the trees I could hear the megaphone squawking a way off, and someone playing 'Heaven is a Place on Earth'. I said, 'She came out with a lot of things, the way you do when you've had a shock. When she comes home, we can talk it through. But I thought it was as well to know the legal position. That's all.'

We began to walk along the edge of the field. It felt pleasant to match his pace, to be physically close to someone bigger and stronger than myself, who smelled of good aftershave and who knew where he was going.

'A couple of years back,' he said, 'I was on a train to

London. There was a lad, a youth, swearing into his phone, legs sprawling out in the aisle so everyone who went past had to step over them. The carriage was packed and the language wasn't nice. No one said anything for a while; you know what people are like. But then he started playing thumping music with offensive lyrics, very aggressive. An elderly man in the seat behind him stood up, looked over and asked him politely to turn it down or put his headphones on. The boy ignored him, so the man's friend, also in his sixties or seventies, I'd guess, stood up and repeated the request. This time, the response was a volley of abuse and the volume cranked up.'

'What did you do?' I was waiting for some tale of heroism on his part: how David, the voice of confident reason, saved the day.

'Nothing, to my shame. The boy was a few rows down from me, and I was busy working on my laptop. I suppose I decided it wasn't my problem.'

'Well,' I said, 'people get knifed for interfering these days. So what happened?'

'The two old men started singing.'

'Singing?'

'That's right. I hadn't realised before, but they were part of a group, some choir or other. When I looked properly, the carriage was full of white-haired men in blue blazers – on their way to a performance, I assume, or back from one. These two struck up with "Bye Bye Blackbird", and within a few bars there were twenty, thirty doing all the descants. It was loud, too. A *capella* can be deafening at close quarters. They completely drowned out the boy. By the time they'd got to the third verse, he'd gathered his stuff together and stomped off to another section of the train. We never saw him for the rest of the journey.'

As David had been speaking, I was seeing it unfold, watching the delighted expressions spread from seat to seat, hearing the swelling chords, feeling the buzz that comes from being united. 'Oh, I love that song. My dad used to sing it when he was working in the garden.'

'After they'd finished, everyone broke into a round of applause, so they launched into "The Black Hills of Dakota", and then "If I Had a Hammer". Other passengers were joining in. The whole atmosphere was like a carnival. I've never forgotten it.' David was staring into the middle distance thoughtfully. 'The shift in who controlled that carriage was amazing.'

'And?'

'It taught me a lesson. I suppose what I'm coming round to is that you mustn't ever think you're powerless. You should never sit back and assume there's no hope. If it comes to it that you do need to fight for Matty, I'll be right behind you; we'll work together, and whatever's ahead, we'll give it our best shot. Yes?'

The gates ahead of us had opened and people were streaming onto the field.

'Do you want to know something terrible?' I said. 'There are moments I think I hate my own daughter. She was such a lovely baby, I had control of her then. I suppose you think I'm awful for saying that.'

'Not awful, just honest.'

'Does it all boil down to power, in the end? All the relationships we ever have, is that what they're about?'

'You need a drink,' he said. 'So do I. Let's go find one.'

'Life is a Roller Coaster' sang the Tannoy as we picked our way forward.

I shouldn't have worn a skirt and mules, or I should have chosen a different place to go walking. Last time I'd been down the public footpath by the old railway bridge had been with

Matty, early spring, when the grass and weeds were still short. We'd watched a jackdaw pulling a tuft of wool off barbed wire, and Matty had found a pile of ash from a bonfire and paddled around in it till his shoes went grey.

Now, coming towards the end of summer, the track was waist-high nettles and sticky burr and thistles, and my calves and shins were striped with welts. It was madness to keep going, but I did, stamping down the taller stalks so they snapped and lay prone. Every one of them felt my wrath. Ten times I'd tried phoning Jaz this evening, all the while knowing I'd get the same recorded message, but unable to stop myself.

'The difference is,' David had explained, 'Ian's name is on the birth certificate. Yours isn't. It's a crucial difference, in law.'

'But all the hundreds of hours I've spent with Matty, all the love I've given him. That counts for nothing?'

I didn't believe him, but afterwards he'd helped me Google the facts. Thirteen and a half million grandparents there were in the UK, providing a massive 60 per cent of all the country's childcare. Without our input, the job market would collapse and families go under, lose their houses, fall apart. If grandparents ever chose to go on strike, there'd be economic crisis.

And that was only looking at cold finance. What about the emotional stability we gave our grandchildren? The continuous sense of who they were, where they'd come from? We were the ones with time to spend, and experience. We held the family stories. We were the ones who passed on the great secrets of their parents' youth: that their mum was once a naughty girl, or their dad a frightened little boy. It was from us the very young often had their first exposure to disability, learning how to work round a physical restriction with practical good humour.

The love we gave was different, too: less judgemental, unclouded. Some of us had got it wrong with our own kids, but we knew the way forward now and were determined to make good. All this we did willingly and for free.

Yet if Jaz did ban me from seeing Matty, I wouldn't have a leg to stand on.

Theoretically, as David said, I could try for a contact order, but to do that I'd first have to approach the court and request permission to apply for one. Like having to ask for a key to a cupboard in which was locked the key to your door. Throughout the legal proceedings, the onus would be on me to prove I had a meaningful relationship with my grandson (even though I worked five days a week and only had him in my spare time and had once nearly drowned him). Matty, my very best advocate, would be able to contribute nothing.

I'd read that, in the end, the vast majority of applications by grandparents were unsuccessful, and even where they won, the order for access was often ignored. The whole process would involve officials and reports and standing up in court, and would last for months, and cost a small fortune. And there were a million others like me, denied contact with the people they most loved in the world. The unfairness of it beggared belief.

A shadow fell across the field in front of me, and I looked up. Against the summer evening sky a red balloon drifted, clean and bright, like an illustration from a children's book. 'Look', I longed to say to Matty. 'Give them a wave!'

The balloon was rising steadily as I watched, the basket suspended like a matchbox underneath. Then the flame shot up, orange against the blue, and I thought, How amazing that a tiny jet of fire can raise that huge structure hundreds of feet. Incredible. For a few moments I was up there with them, out of myself and carried along.

I head Eileen's voice: *If you had the chance to see into your own future, would you take it? God, I would!* We'd had a weekend at Blackpool, just after I was married – her, me, Phil – and she'd been eyeing up the clairvoyants' caravans along the sea-front. 'No,' I'd said, in answer to her question. She'd laughed at me and called me a coward. Later that night, and drunk, she'd laid half a chicken pie on the top step of a caravan. 'Let's see if Gypsy Romana predicts *that* when she comes skipping out tomorrow morning.' 'Like they sleep in their vans,' Phil had scoffed, and they'd had a bit of a fight. She never did have a reading, though, for all her talk.

The balloon passed over the allotments, and on towards town. Ahead of me the track ended in a stile, but so lost in nettles I knew I'd never stand a chance of getting near. I'd gone as far as I could. The light was changing, and it was time to go home.

On the way back towards the bridge, I began toying with the idea of ringing Jaz again. Part of me knew this was not the way, that she hated any kind of pursuit. Then again, if I didn't try, would she realise how desperately I was missing her? Maybe, in the end, I'd wear her down. Maybe I'd catch her at a mellow moment, if she had any mellow moments these days. All of a sudden, a hot flare engulfed me at the injustice, the sheer cruelty of her behaviour. *She used to cut her arms, you know*, I imagined telling a courtroom. *There's a history of instability. He'd be much better off with me*.

The next second I was shaking the picture away, appalled.

'If you want an exchange of confessions,' David had said, 'then listen to this: when Jeanette died, I was relieved. I loved her, I would have gone to the ends of the earth for her, but the truth was I was weary of the months of pain and suffering and the broken nights and the visitors trooping through the house and the sense of death hanging over all of us, stringing us out. Now, does that make you think any less of me?'

I was shaken out of memory by a sudden, violent shout coming from somewhere near the bridge. 'You FUCK-ing wanker!' a girl yelled, her voice ripping across the evening. 'You *fucking* dickhead.'

The atmosphere of the evening changed at once. Suddenly I saw myself as I was: a lone middle-aged woman more than a mile from the nearest house and without a mobile phone. A figure shot out from under the arch, then ran back under, laughing. There was more calling, more swearing, the clatter of pebbles against stone.

'I'll *fuck*ing kill you for that! Tosser.'

I hesitated, considering whether to go forward or stay where I was. You heard about these gangs, and what they got up to. There were always stories in the paper. A man near us had literally been frightened to death by a bunch of youths; they hadn't even needed to lay a finger on him.

'You stupid fucking *prick*!'

No, better keep going. I needed to pass them to get back to the main road. If they came out and saw me, if they started shouting at me, what I'd do would be feign deafness. They wanted you to talk back, so I wouldn't give them the satisfaction. Dumbness was my best defence.

'Oi, stop! STOP!'

Was that to me? I made myself look straight ahead, my pace fast but steady. Turning back wasn't an option; the path was too overgrown. I could walk out into the middle of the field, but that would only make me more conspicuous, and if they did spot me it would be obvious what I was doing, which would attract comment in itself. Mad sandal-shod woman, flattening crops.

Best to stick with it, and hope. The path went up and over the top of the bridge, so provided these kids stayed where they were, I had no need to cross their line of vision. I risked a quick glance to the side. No sign of anyone.

'You utter fucking twat,' said the girl again.

'I can make a match burn twice,' I heard a boy say.

'Fuck off.'

More laughter, and a whoop. It was impossible to tell how many of them there were, or how old. I moved my steps away from the centre of the path, where the grit crunched, onto the muffled grass.

'That was my hair,' whined the girl.

'Aw, kiss it better.' There was a burst of tinny music, and someone threw what might have been a coloured plastic lighter out onto the grass.

I visualised David's train carriage, the blue-suited white-haired men standing to defeat the forces of yobbism. Where was a passing *a capella* group when you needed one? A memory flashed on me of Dad humming while he shaved in the kitchen, his mirror propped on the eye-level grill pan and a dish of water on the cold gas ring. Black and white tiles, the kitchenette with the fold-down front and built-in shopping reminder. When I was safe and small and knew what lay in front of me each day.

'Give it us back, you little shit!'

And David's voice went, *Get a grip, Carol. This is a public footpath and you have every right to be here, just as much as whoever it is howling and cursing under the arch. Look, they probably won't come out, and even if they do, why should they be interested in you? You're not hassling them. You're quite clearly walking away, minding your own business. Forget what you've read in the newspapers; they have to scare to sell. Kids being noisy in a deserted spot isn't the crime of the century. They're not harming anyone. Just keep going. Put your shoulders back. Steady your breathing.*

In my mind, Dad still hummed 'Bye Bye Blackbird', hauntingly. I slowed my pace to match the rhythm of the song, and lifted my chin. It did help, a bit.

At the start of the bridge rise, a track strewn with litter

branched off down the bank and, as I passed it, a boy wandered out from under the arch, scanning the ground. I watched him nervously out of the corner of my eye. There was something familiar about the back of his head.

'Give it up,' called the girl. 'It was knackered anyway.'

The boy lifted his head to shout back, and caught sight of me standing above him. I saw his lips form the word *fuck*. Josh.

'Oh my God,' continued the girl. 'See this, will you?'

Josh and I carried on staring at each other.

'I've got a text from Vic. Oh my God. Oh my God.'

Do not speak, his eyes said. *Do not go home and mention this to my mum. I don't know you and you don't know me. You owe me. Shut it.* At the same time I was taking all this in, I was thinking, He's done something to his fringe since I last saw him, it's made his face look squarer. Is that a cigarette between his fingers? Where does Laverne think he is tonight? Drama group?

'Hoy, Joshy. Come see this.'

He gave me a tiny shake of the head, just as the girl wandered out. I turned and began to walk quickly away.

'I don't fucking believe her. If she fucking thinks I'm taking any notice . . .' The girl's sentence trailed off. 'What you looking at? Who was that?'

The balloon was a red football vanishing behind far-off trees.

'No one,' I heard him say. 'It wasn't anybody.'

CHAPTER 27

Photograph 217, Album Two

Location: James House Hospice, Worsley, Manchester

Taken by: Carol

Subject: Jaz, six, is sitting on a slatted white bench, holding on to her grandma's elbow crutch. Behind her, an impressive wisteria drapes its loaded arms over the stonework of the rear wall. The hospice manager is a keen horticulturalist himself, and knows the value of a well-kept garden for those in need of earthly balm. No one crosses these soft and level lawns without feeling a degree better. A blackbird sings each evening in the conifer, as if by arrangement, and worms send up their inoffensive casts between the patients' feet. Peonies bud, bloom, drop and seed by the path; tiny nymphs squirm across the surface of the bird bath. If Carol and her mother could make any kind of peace, it would be here.

And they do find something like it, in that Carol's so far managed not to ask anything provocative – why did you have children if you didn't want them, for instance – and Frieda's refrained from making any final sour quips. It's the best that could be hoped for.

During this particular visit, her mother consents to sit outside for quarter of an hour. Once she's made it to the bench, Jaz climbs up alongside her and asks her what it's like to be dying. You'd think Frieda would be offended, but she takes the question in her stride. It may be that she's too tired to object.

'Don't they favour each other?' observes Bob.

'No,' says Carol, appalled.

'I meant the eyes, round the eyes,' he says. 'I've never really noticed before.'

Carol looks, but won't see. Four to six weeks, the doctor's said, so it makes no odds anyway.

So there we were, working alongside each other like the married couple we used to be. Phil was unwrapping Rawlbolts on the patio, and I was turning out kitchen drawers and cupboards and attempting to rationalise the contents. Like that married couple, we were holding an icy, singing silence between us that had us both clattering about and clearing our throats just for the relief of sound. Fit the grid and bugger off, I was thinking. I could hear his thoughts, too, clamouring back: Bloody hell, I come round here to help her out and she acts like she's the one doing *me* a favour. The quarrels where no one speaks are always the noisiest.

After a while I put the radio on, and tried to follow a discussion about the European Union.

Meanwhile I pulled out tea towels still in their wrapping, icing-bag nozzles, yet more of my mother's embroidered cloths. Three hand-whisks, it turned out I owned – not including the K beater for a defunct Kenwood Chef – plus four incomplete canteens of cutlery, and a set of unused American measuring cups. As I peeled away old lining paper, David's voice floated in over the rest: *Why did you stay so long with Phil?*

The question, spoken in the dim back room of a country pub, had caught me off-guard. 'For Jaz,' I'd said, as I always did. 'I thought the disruption would be too damaging for her.'

'That must have taken a lot of strength.'

'Except now Jaz claims I stayed out of cowardice, and that I ruined her childhood because I was scared to strike out on my own.'

'Wouldn't she have been disturbed if you'd split up?'

'Probably. She didn't want me to change my name after the divorce; how's that for inconsistency?'

'Had you intended to?'

'I wasn't sure. I didn't want Jaz and me not to match. And I didn't want to go backwards, to be Carol White again. Hobson's choice, really. They should let you have a special divorce name that you choose. A naming party, you could have, a special dinner or something.'

David had said that was a good idea, and then we'd just sat for ages, listening to the blare and clatter of the fruit machine round the corner, sipping our drinks. A different kind of not-talking.

The kitchen door banging against the wall made me jump.

'For God's sake!' I said.

Phil looked guilty, then irritated. 'You want a new stopper,' he said, glancing at the floor. 'You'll end up with a hole in your plaster otherwise.'

'No, because no one else flings the door open like you.'

'Two minutes of a job to screw one in.'

'I don't need one!'

We glared at each other.

This is not your house! Screw a bloody stopper in your own floor!

Jesus wept, woman, I was only making a suggestion.

'What do you want, anyway?' I said ungraciously.

'A slash,' he said, and pushed past me.

I carried on with the clearing, piling up crockery into sets.

As he came back down the stairs I could hear him whistling 'Tie a Yellow Ribbon'. Its jauntiness, and the sheer tactlessness of his choice, infuriated me beyond sanity.

'I don't think you're remotely bothered about Matty,' I snapped.

Phil's step faltered in the doorway. 'Eh?'

'You don't love Matty as much as I do, and that's the reason you're not concerned.'

He closed his eyes. 'Don't start, Carol.'

'Well, you can't do,' I said, my fingers tightening on one of my mother's Coalport plates. 'Otherwise you'd be as upset as me. Wouldn't you? *Wouldn't you?*'

'Look,' he said, 'how many times do I have to repeat myself? I love my grandson and I'll be glad when he comes home.'

'You think she'll bring him back?'

'Of course she will.'

'And let us see him?'

'I expect so.'

'"Expect so"? Dear God, have you no feelings at all?'

He put his palm to his forehead. 'I meant she will do. Jesus. You take her too seriously. You give her too much power over you.'

'That's because she *has* power!' I cried, flinging the plate downwards so it smashed onto the floor. The impact was startling. Shards of white china shot across the tiles in all directions.

'Jesus wept, Carol,' he said. 'Listen to me. I'll say it for the last time: I love Matty. Right?' I gripped the edge of the table, trembling. 'I'm just maybe not as obsessed with him as you are.'

'I'm NOT obsessed!'

'You've seen a lot of him, had him round two, three times a week—'

'Which makes it harder.'

'So, like, you've had a good run—'

I threw a second plate and it exploded into the jamb near his feet, making him jerk with shock. 'Shit. There was no need for that.'

'Had a good run? Had a *good run*?' I yelled.

'I didn't mean – oh, I don't know what I meant. Only, you're always on about him. Always. But the bottom line is, he's not your child.'

'He's my *grandson*! If it wasn't for me, he wouldn't *exist*!'

'That still doesn't make him yours.'

Images whirled around my head of Matty, me, Jaz. I thought of the early days when I'd watched her trying to breastfeed, and how I'd tried so hard not to show disappointment when she gave up at three months. I remembered him taking his first steps and not telling her because I wanted her to think they happened when she was there, and how I had to pretend surprise when she showed me his first tooth breaking through the gum. Stocking up with the very particular brand of baby food she wanted him to have, taking off the cot bumper because she said it might make him over-heat. Doing as I was told, to the letter, on every occasion. 'You talk as though I'm one of these interfering types who flout their daughter's rules and constantly tell them where they're going wrong. I've never done that. I never would.'

'It's more subtle than that, Carol. You, you act as if he's yours.'

'But—' I floundered for a moment. 'Don't all grandparents feel that way? It's a special bond, it's like *double* the family tie. That's why Matty's so special: he's mine, and mine again.'

When I looked up, Phil's eyes were roving over the mess of splinters that fanned out across the floor.

'Oh,' I said, 'this is pointless. I can see you don't get it at all. But then, why should you? You were a bloody awful dad, so why should you be any better at being a grandad?'

Accusation crackled between us. Snatches of past rows needled back through the airwaves, as though the house had absorbed and kept them inside its walls, waiting for a fresh bout of fighting. Suddenly the desire to hurt Phil overwhelmed any sense of the damage I might do to myself. Even when you think everything's been said about a break-up, it's amazing how much more can be dredged to the surface by a burst of real temper. Here came the rest of it, unstoppable:

'If you'd been a better father to Jaz, I bet you this situation would never have happened. She wouldn't have grown up so resentful, she'd have chosen a better husband, we'd have been a normal, stable family.'

'Jaz is just Jaz; she is who she is. Same as your mother was just your mother. You're not being fair.'

'What's fairness got to do with anything? When was fairness ever a factor in our marriage?' I saw again Mavis Pearson, that bright green blouse, her coral lipstick mouth making sympathetic shapes at me, and felt the hot prickle that comes from realising you're an object of someone's pity. 'Twenty-four years of shambles and lies; what a bloody waste of everyone's time!'

'So why did you stay, Carol?'

'I don't bloody know. Because when you want to believe someone, you do. I kept thinking it would peter out, you'd come to your senses. But you didn't.'

He was shaking his head as if he couldn't fathom things either.

'I mean, why *her*?' I'd rehearsed the question a thousand times, but never spoken it out loud because it sounded too humiliating. Now, though, I felt I had nothing to lose. '*Why her*? What in God's name makes you prefer *her* to me?'

'I don't. Not now. Not for a long time.'

'You did; of course you did. You made a choice.'

'It wasn't as simple as that. I got, I don't know, tangled up.'

'See, I can understand a slip, a one-off, like Ian made. But to go back to her, and keep going back when you said you wouldn't, and the lies are worse than the infidelity, they hurt a hell of a lot more. And everything you could have wanted was here. God, when you think of how some wives are.'

'I couldn't seem to get myself out of it.'

'You didn't want to.'

'I did. It was difficult. She wasn't—'

'Wasn't what?' I hissed.

'She wasn't strong like you are. You always got on with things. She fell apart every time I tried to finish. She couldn't cope. She needed me.'

I couldn't believe my ears. '*We* needed you! Jaz and I. Your *family*.'

'She used to threaten suicide, all sorts.'

'And you fell for it.'

'She's not—'

'Not what?'

'Stable,' he said, avoiding my gaze. 'Well, you know, don't you? Ringing Jaz up. She's very jealous, very unpredictable. She does stuff, and then she's sorry afterwards.'

'And this is the woman you chose over me?' I caught sight of my face in the glass of the oven door and I hardly recognised myself. 'So what you're saying here is, my mistake was to behave too well? I was too dignified and contained? That if I'd thrown myself down on the floor, wailing and carrying on like a lunatic, you'd have stayed? Bloody hell, Phil. Have you any idea what you've just said?' I took a step towards him, and he flinched. 'You know what? Don't *ever* let her come round here because I will kill her.'

'I've not seen you like this before,' he said in a small voice.

Before I could say any more, a tower of Worcester tea cups I'd stacked earlier toppled over, and two fell off the edge of the table and broke.

'Fuck you,' I heard myself say. Then I sat down and covered my face with my hands. I wasn't crying, I just needed to block him out for a moment.

'What if I told you,' he said cautiously, 'that she really had gone this time. For good.'

I kept my hands where they were and spoke between my fingers.

'You say what you *want* to be true.'

Now I sensed him come forward, heard him pull the chair out from under the other side of the table and sit down.

'This time it's different, Carol: I told her to go. She's taken all her gear.'

'Yeah yeah.'

'Come round and see.'

'The day hell freezes over.'

'I haven't even a washing machine.'

'You're confusing me with someone who gives a damn.'

Faint thudding rap music was coming from Laverne's. Through the open back door I could hear a lawnmower doing the last cut of the season. Opposite me, Phil sighed noisily.

'I don't know what I can say.'

'Best keep it shut, then. You've done enough damage.'

'Carol, I always loved you. I still do. It just got complicated. I painted myself into a corner.'

'Stop, please.'

'I'm sorry.'

'I'm damn sure you are.'

'If you ever took me back—'

'I said, stop it.'

He shifted on his chair and cleared his throat.

'Well. Whatever – whatever *we* are, I'm still Jaz's dad and I'm still Matty's grandad, and I'll do what I can to help you get them back. I'm fitting this grid so if you have to go to court, you can say you've taken safety measures, yeah? . . . I'm doing my best.'

When I took my fingers away from my eyes, he was bowed over the table. 'God,' he said, 'I wouldn't mind, but I've been that fucking miserable.'

It was the line I'd waited nearly all my married life to hear. I pictured him sitting alone in his empty flat, the walls marked with the shape of departed furniture, the carpets dented and unhoovered. Excellent. Served him right.

'Anyway,' he said lamely. 'It's a fucking mess, in't it?'

The rap music from Laverne's rose in volume.

'I'd best get on and finish the grid.' He pushed the chair back, got to his feet and lumbered out.

There I sat between my trembling towers of china. Outside, the drill began to whine again.

In the end I went and fetched a dustpan and brush, and began to sweep up the shards of my marriage.

'Do you mind if I ask you something?' said David as we strolled back down the High Street together one quiet Sunday afternoon. Once again he had charge of my clipboard; this time we were taking photographs of town landmarks for the Beavers' Local History Hunt.

I snapped my lens cap over the shutter.

'Go on.'

'Do you think I'm too controlling, Carol?'

The question took me by surprise. 'Controlling?'

'A controlling person.'

'In what way?'

'With Ian.'

'Whatever's made you say that?'

'It's something he came out with yesterday evening.'

I waited for more, but he obviously felt he'd given me enough, that any more detail was superfluous.

We walked on a few paces while I thought about what he'd said. In one sense it was deeply flattering he trusted me to answer a question like that, a question which admitted a vulnerability I hadn't seen before. But at the same time I was alarmed because I wasn't at all sure what to say. *Was* David too controlling a father? I had no idea. Not from where I stood, certainly. No, no, he wasn't. In fact, the more I considered, the crosser I felt on his behalf.

'You're not, no,' I said. 'And I hope you stuck up for yourself.'

'I told him it was nonsense.'

'Good. What was his reaction?'

David shrugged. 'Hard to tell; he didn't say a great deal after that. He's fine today. I was just interested in your take.'

We walked on past the card shop with its oriel window and 1720 date stone, past Healey's café and the Civic Centre, till we were within sight of the Victorian arcade.

'I'm sure it's the stress talking, that's all. Ian's lashing out at you because you're around, you're available to be lashed out at.'

'Yes, it might be that.'

'Hey, don't you lose confidence, or we're all done for.' I smiled to show this was a joke, even though I kind of meant it. I'd come to rely on his mild brand of arrogance over the past weeks. Another ditherer like me on the case would have spelled disaster.

David gazed past me, down towards the precinct with its hanging baskets and new heritage-style litter bins. After a moment, I slid my arm through his, and the furrows on his brow eased a fraction. He looked down at my arm, and laughed ruefully.

'What?' I asked.

'Well, God help us, Carol, someone needs to pretend they know what they're doing,' he said.

CHAPTER 28

Photograph: unnumbered, from a page inside a pile of old newspapers at the bottom of Carol's cleaning cupboard

Location: the Long Room, Chester Race Course

Taken by: the Chester Chronicle

Subject: a crowd of people in evening dress, including Pippa Williams, her husband Lionel, and David, stand grouped around a signed football shirt donated by Wayne Rooney. The shirt is the star prize in the after-dinner charity auction, which they hope will raise in the region of £2,000 towards the Wirral and North Cheshire Prostate Cancer Group's Doppler Scanner appeal.

'It's the most common male cancer,' Pippa tells the reporter. 'Very treatable if caught early, so it's vital we raise public awareness.'

Lionel says nothing. Even before he became ill he wasn't the sort to stand up and give speeches. He simply watches from the sidelines, full of admiration. His wife's been a marvel, as tireless in the role of campaigner as she's been in nursing him. She could not have been more supportive, more loving. As yet they have not talked about how she'll manage when he's gone, but she seems so strong he can't imagine her not coping and that gives him some relief.

Pippa is not feeling strong at all. Two evenings before, she was sobbing in David's kitchen. 'It's so bloody awful, trying to put on a brave face. So exhausting. Never letting up. You must know what that's like.'

David does. He loves them both. He hates seeing his friends suffer like this. He puts his arms around her and lets her cry it all out against his shoulder.

'I need somewhere to come sometimes,' she says. 'Lionel mustn't see me like this.'

'Whatever I can do to help,' says David.

He feels her grip tighten around him, her hot breathing in his ear; then, hesitantly at first, her lips moving across the fresh-shaved skin of his neck.

He does not know how to push her away.

My parents' most important documents – the birth and wedding certificates, their old insurance policies and household receipts – were in an old briefcase under the spare bed. When someone dies, it's not always easy to know what to throw away and what to keep, and a lot of my mother's everyday bits and pieces had been bundled up and stowed away in odd corners. Over the years I'd disposed of a few items, a few pockets, as I came across them, but the bureau was where most of her things lived, and I'd forgotten what I'd stowed away in there.

In starting to clear it now I'd already unearthed a bag of hairnets, several dozen parish magazines, a sealed packet of triple-absorbent-super-mega-maxi Dr Whites, assorted cigarette cards, nine sachets of Atrixo, six cologne sticks used and unused, corn plasters, a felt corsage, her second-best purse, a giant bottle of Quink and a bundle of memorial service sheets. Rubbish, it was. Tat, junk. Why ever had we both given it house room?

Then there were her ancient magazines: *Housewife*, *Mother and Home*, the *Homecraft Book*, all pushing a routine where every day your letterbox must be wiped free of fingerprints, the doorstep scrubbed, the porch swept; where every week all metal items and light bulbs had to be polished, lace mats rinsed and ironed, walls and ceilings brushed down. Where washing your clothes involved steeping, blueing and starching, and cleaning your fireplace required blacklead, methylated spirits and wax. *Use two dusters, one in each hand for speed*, one article advised. *Wallpaper can be rubbed clean with a simple flour-and-water dough. And why not hem old shirts and use them as kitchen towels? Or quilt worn towels into bath mats?* suggested another.

Thank God I was born when I was, I thought smugly. What a bloody dull existence it must have been.

A picture came to me of a future Jaz clearing out this house, and what she might find, and how she might assess me by the remnants of my life.

And then the bell rang.

'You're not moving, are you?' Laverne stared round the living room at the assorted boxes and bin bags, the emptied bureau and the dislocated drawers. Behind her, in the doorway, lurked Josh.

'No,' I said. 'Just having a clear-out.'

On the rug by my feet was strewn more evidence of my mother: piles of *Picture Post* and *Everybody's Magazine*, *Bairnswear* paper bags of half-used embroidery silks, bundles of cotton cloth cut into strips with pinking shears, packets of Coverax jam seals, a St Bruno's Flake tobacco tin of little horn buttons, a Keating's Powder pot containing twenty or thirty suspender clips. Old Sylko cotton reels, bright as the day Mum must have bought them, spilled out of a Coredoxa cigar box, along with several packets of Co-operative needles and a box of birthday cake candles. One large, scratched Coronation tin contained about two hundred recipe clippings, some of which obviously dated from the days of rationing. Cauliflower Fool, Spaghetti Mould, Semolina Soup.

Laverne frowned sympathetically. 'You haven't heard anything from Jaz, still?'

'No.'

'Well,' said Laverne, and stopped, because what comment can you make in such a situation that doesn't sound either trite or alarmist?

'Would Josh like a slice of lemon cake?' I said, more brightly than I felt.

He shook his head emphatically. 'I have to go in a minute.'

'He has to be at Healey's for eleven,' she said. 'I'm giving him a lift in. He's got an interview.'

'Not an interview, Mum.'

'Healey's coffee shop?' I asked.

'That's right,' said Laverne. 'They want more Saturday kitchen staff – waiters, washers up. I wasn't sure, because, you know, if he wants something, I can buy it for him – well, we can talk about it – but he thinks he should be earning.'

'Mum,' said Josh.

'So I said he could pop along and see, although I wasn't sure it would suit him. It's not a particularly pleasant job, is it? But I suppose they need to try these things for themselves.'

She turned a searching gaze on him, trying no doubt to imagine him in a steaming kitchen with a swearing chef. Self-conscious, Josh put his hand up to check his fringe. As he did so, the cuff of his shirt flopped open.

'Do your button up, at least,' said Laverne.

'Haven't got one.'

'Haven't you? You'll need to go and change, then.'

'I'll roll my sleeves up, it'll be fine.'

'No, it won't. Oh, see, Carol, he hasn't got a button on that one, either.'

'It doesn't matter,' he said. 'They won't care.'

'I'm not taking you like that. Go home and put your green shirt on.'

I could see the temper gathering on Josh's face. 'Hey,' I said. 'I've cotton and a threaded needle here, ready. There's buttons in that tobacco tin; I can have one sewn on before you've reached the top of your stairs.'

'It's both cuffs,' said Laverne.

'Then you do one and I'll do the other. Come on, Josh. Sit at the table and we'll have you sorted in two minutes. I promise.'

Jesus, he mouthed, but he went over and slumped down, wrists out in front of him like someone awaiting the application of thumbscrews. 'Eleven o' clock, I have to be there,' he muttered.

'Heaps of time yet,' I said, handing a needle to Laverne. She pulled a chair round and we positioned ourselves either side of him so there was no escape.

For half a minute there was just the movement of cloth being punctured and thread drawn tight. Then Laverne said: 'The reason I actually came round was, I heard some awful news this morning.'

I kept up my careful rhythm with the needle. Logic told me, if she had any information about my daughter and grandson, she'd have come straight out with it. In fact, she'd asked *me*, hadn't she? Even so, I felt the panic surge.

'What, Laverne? What is it?'

'Alice.'

'Alice?' Not Jaz.

'Dorothy Wynne's Alice.'

'Oh, yes. Sorry. Is she all right? Has she had the baby? I knew it must be any time soon.'

'She's had a little boy, but he's very poorly. There's something wrong. A disability of some sort, I'm not sure what exactly. It's serious, though, I do know that. Mrs Wynne caught me as I was wheeling the bin round. She's ever so upset. I said I'd tell you, save her having to.'

'God, that's awful. I am sorry. Is Alice all right?'

'Physically I think she's OK. It's the baby. And obviously she's very distressed, as you would be.'

Between us, Josh studied the table-top.

'The thing is,' Laverne was saying, 'you expect babies these days to be healthy, don't you? It never crosses your mind that anything might go wrong.'

It used to cross mine, I thought. Every day I was pregnant with Jaz, I scared myself stupid, imagining the worst. When she was born perfect, I couldn't believe it. And when, afterwards, we tried for another baby and it never happened, I didn't dare rail against fate in case what I already had was taken away from me. Did I ever worry for unborn Matty? No: somehow I always trusted he'd be all right. Jaz worried, though. She told me some nights she was wakened several times with bad dreams. Perhaps it's something to do with feeling another heartbeat beneath your ribs; that's enough to send anyone's mind off-balance.

'Joshy came out blue, with oxygen deprivation. They brought him round, but it was – I can't imagine what Alice must be going through, can you?'

'No,' I said.

'And she's so young, isn't she? It's such a lot for anyone, let alone – should we send a card? What do you say? Not congratulations. Or should we? I don't know.' She looked about for scissors, found none, wound the cotton round her finger and tugged. Then she sat back, her eyes searching my face.

'Let me have a word with Mrs Wynne,' I said. 'I suppose a

lot depends on how the baby's doing. You know, the long term.'

'However is she going to cope, though?'

'I don't know,' I said, and broke off the last piece of thread.

Released at last, Josh jerked his chair back and stood up. 'Great. Can we get going now, Mum?'

'In a minute,' she said. 'I'm sorry, Carol. He's been really stroppy lately – Oh, it's just so sad. Should we send some flowers?'

'Flowers would be good. Maybe some for Mrs Wynne, too.'

'You ask yourself why on earth these things have to happen to good people.' Laverne gazed round the room as though the answer might be lying somewhere among my piles of paper and junk. Then she sighed and stood up.

'Will you order the flowers?' she began, moving towards the door. But in squeezing past the edge of the table, she knocked off an ancient Kestos Nursing Brassière box. There was a sound like marbles clicking together, and a whole heap of miniature light bulbs spilled out onto the carpet.

Josh made a growling noise. 'Nice one, Mum.'

'Watch where you're treading,' I said hastily, imagining how tiny the glass splinters might be if any of the bulbs got crushed.

'Oh, heavens, Carol,' she said. 'What are they? I can barely see them. Josh, stick that light on, would you?'

'Leave them, I'll do it,' I said, conscious of her son loitering.

'No, it's all right, we're still early. We are, Josh.' Laverne bent down and began swishing her palms over the carpet. With extreme care I lowered myself onto my knees next to her and we hunted about blindly. 'Don't move your left foot,' she'd go. 'There's something glinting.' And I'd freeze, and she'd say, 'Oh no, it was a speck of glitter.' Or I'd say, 'Under the sofa end, near your hand. A bit further. A bit further.' They were like dolls' bulbs, and I wondered where they'd fitted and why the filaments were different colours and how many of them still worked. This was exactly why all the rubbish needed to go.

From somewhere above me Josh went, 'Is this Jaz?'

'Where?'

I scrambled to my feet at once, but he was only holding up a photograph.

He passed it to me and I peered into the picture, my heart contracting painfully. It was Jaz, aged about thirteen, almost unrecognisable with her round, unmade-up face and her hair in little plaits like dreadlocks. She was sitting with Nat on the steps of a shabby caravan, holding a bottle of Coke aloft as if she was offering up a toast. On her feet, which were stretched out in front of her, she sported a pair of men's boots, much too big for her.

'Where did you find it?'

'Here.' He pointed at a yellow Kodak envelope which I'd balanced on the back of the sofa. 'That one was stuck against another.'

I took the wedge of prints and flicked through them. They were ones I'd found when I was going through Dad's boxes in the shed, but I'd mislaid them in the panic over Libby. How had they ended up in the bureau? I lost all sorts these days. Here again were the frog, the toadstool, the horse, Nat astride a gate, but the shot Josh had asked about was new to me.

'She looks like a gypsy,' said Josh.

'You shouldn't go through people's personal things,' said Laverne, pulling herself upright and brushing at her jeans.

'It was out on top, I was only looking. Can we go now?'

'He means "thank you, Carol, for sewing my shirt",' said Laverne.

'Yeah, cheers.'

'Any time,' I said, and winked at him. I did get the tiniest of smiles back, so that was something.

After I'd seen them out I went back into the lounge, piled all my mother's belongings back into the bureau, and shut the door on them. Today was not the day for getting rid of the past.

CHAPTER 29

Photograph: loose inside a Cook Electric! *brochure at the bottom of the bureau, Sunnybank*

Location: Canterbury

Taken by: Reverend Pendlebury

Subject: the exterior of the cathedral, south-west aspect.

It's been a long journey, but worth it. Frieda had thought, on the coach, with the rest of the Mothers' Union, that she had another headache starting, but the pain vanishes once she's in the nave. The cathedral is blissfully cool, and dim. If everyone will just leave her alone, she'll be fine.

'How long are we going to be?' asks Carol, pulling down on Frieda's bag so the strap cuts into her shoulder.

'I don't know,' says Frieda.

'I need the toilet,' whines Carol.

So they have to go and look for the ladies', and as they hurry along the aisles, Frieda feels a flush starting, and when they get to the washrooms she realises she's left her cologne stick at home. 'Why didn't you go when we got off the bus?' she says to the cubicle door, but gets no answer.

By the time they make it back to the nave, she's incandescent with heat. Sliding into a pew, she lowers her burning brow to the back of her hand, and prays.

'The vicar says Jesus was born in a cellar,' Carol whispers suddenly in her ear, making her jump.

Frieda raises her head and Carol skips off.

After a while, the glow subsides. Other women, her friends, come and go without fuss. Kneelers sag under the weight of pious knees, sending up little spurts of dust into the light. Someone starts to play the organ quietly and the notes are like a thread of silver beads unravelling in her soul.

Partially restored, she stands and steps out into the aisle, which is when she sees her daughter spinning like a Dervish among the tombs in the Warrior Chapel. What does she think she's doing? People are looking.

'This is NOT a playground!' she snaps, and drags Carol outside to retch over the grass and her own shoes.

'Did you see the pelican?' asks Carol, when everything's come up.

Behind them, a woman exclaims with delight over some small feat of ordinariness her baby has just performed.

'There's a pelican in the window,' Carol continues. 'It's a symbol of the Redeemer, because it tears its own breast that the young may feed. A man told me. Wouldn't it die, though? And the babies starve? Joyce Whittle's rabbit ate its babies, did I tell you?'

Five minutes – five minutes' peace was all Frieda wanted.

'And Joyce says spiders eat each other. If you were a pelican, would you tear your own flesh? Say we had no food and we were starving to death, except we had one slice of bread between us, would you give it all to me?'

'Of course I would,' says Frieda. But Carol is picking at a scab on her knee and doesn't bother listening to the answer.

*

The last time I'd been round to David's house for dinner, it was Jacky who'd let us in. Jacky had shown us through, made us drinks, talked about wedding venues and hire cars and menus, while David stood by the grand fireplace, overseeing the discussion, master of this hall. 'Bloody lording it around,' Phil had said afterwards. And I'd replied, 'Get a taxi back to Penny's; you're drunk.'

Even though I knew Jacky was long gone, it's hard to shift the idea that places stay as they were when you last saw them, so I was still relieved when David answered the door.

'I did mean to tidy up,' he said.

A glance round his hallway showed only a pair of shoes on the parquet by the door and a folded sweater on the stairs. 'Get away. You should see my place at the moment. House Clearances R Us.'

He took my coat. 'There's a lot to be said for keeping busy. Ian's been stripping wallpaper.'

The large sitting room I remembered as a palette of calm, of pale lemon and white and oatmeal slub, where Jacky had placed a huge arrangement of lilies and gerbera on the table in front of the window, and set two or three of those church candles burning on the marble hearth. This evening there were none of these feminine traces, only papers spread across the table-top, a calculator and a receipt spike, and books and cups and whisky tumblers dotted about. 'Tax return,' he said. 'Demands a lot of surface area.'

'And I had you down as one of those types who lines up their pencils in order.'

'Think again,' he said.

While he was getting me a drink I walked around, taking in the detail. When Jacky was semi-resident, she'd streamlined this place so it was like a show home. Since then, the house had returned to what I guessed was its more normal

David-state, so instead of matching beige vases on the mantelpiece we had scissors and an iPod dock, a tube of Superglue, a glasses case. Towers of DVDs jostled his Art Deco clock; the Georgian slops bowl I'd admired now contained cufflinks and a bottle of tea tree oil.

And on the chimney breast, a selection of photographs I'd never seen before.

In the centre of the arrangement hung the largest picture, Ian the infant, lighter-haired and minus some teeth and with a face you'd almost have called chubby. Then, above that, primary school Ian, sporting a too-short trim and a wide, nervous grimace. Higher still was a sharper-featured Ian with imperfect teenage skin. They were glossy, well-framed images, yet there was something in the pitch of his eyebrows, or the apologetic hunch of his shoulders, that seemed to cancel out the smile every time. Even as late as his degree portrait, you could see the pinch of anxiety on his face. By the wedding, he'd managed to straighten his posture and relax his frown into the Ian I knew, or thought I knew. The wide eyes, the tightness of his lips, you'd just have put down to usual wedding-day jitters. Which, obviously, I did. I wanted him to be right so I made him right.

'My gallery,' said David, setting down two wine glasses. 'A work in progress.'

'They weren't up last time.'

'You've shamed me into sorting out my collection. Most of my photographs have been living loose in wallets or on my hard drive; it's about time I imposed some order.'

'I treasure my albums,' I said.

'I know you do.' He opened a drawer in the side of the table. 'Here. I have to finish up next door, but in the meantime, you might be interested in these.'

He pressed a wad of pictures into my hand, and left me.

It was an intimacy I'd not been expecting.

The top few were the older, smaller type of prints with a white border. David I was able to pick out immediately, even though he was in short trousers and had his hair in a side parting. A family posed against a holly hedge, then on a beach, by a bridge, outside a church: mother, father, two boys and an older girl. And as I looked at each scene, I had the curious sensation of standing between two doorways, with David's life playing out in front of me and my own somewhere behind my back. So when I studied his parents' large Victorian house, I was also seeing Tannerside's old vicarage and the garden parties where my mother served the teas, and the ancient grey pony they used to have giving rides round the lower lawn; and then I thought of Pincroft itself, one Deco semi in a street full of the same, and how we wore our ordinariness proudly, like a union badge. David's father, with his broad shoulders and confident, lifted chin, seemed to emphasise my dad's slight frame, while the mother, elegant in pencil skirt and plain blouse, showed me that even back then, women in their thirties didn't have to look two decades older, the way my mother had done.

There was a class photograph much like my own, except all the pupils were boys and the teacher's face a whole lot sterner. It took me a moment to locate David because now (at fifteen – sixteen?) he wore his hair combed forward in a mop top. His hands in his lap, his shoulders back, he stared moodily at the camera, looking exactly like the kind of student who'd have been made a prefect and then demoted shortly afterwards.

My laughter at the next batch brought David into the room again. 'OK,' he said, 'what's so hilarious?'

I pointed at the shot of him standing in front of a farm gate, his hair lapping his collar, sideburns adorning his cheeks. 'Tan jacket and a black polo neck? You look as though you're posing for an album cover.'

'Meanwhile you were dressing like Sandy Denny. Go on, admit it, you used to wear shawls and Indian shirts.'

'It was against the law not to in those days.'

The next picture was of a young woman standing on a canal tow-path. She was kitted out in jeans and a long coat and a crocheted hat, and carried a patchwork shoulder bag. 'She's pretty. Is this Jeanette?'

'No, pre-Jeanette. I was still in London then. The next one should be her.'

And there she was, his late wife, a fresh-faced brunette with bobbed hair, apple-cheeked and wide-hipped. Where her pinafore dress ended she had on maroon patent knee boots that reminded me of a pair I used to own myself. I don't know what I'd been expecting, but she still took me by surprise. 'Gosh, she's young,' I said.

'Twenty-one when I met her, twenty-four when we married.' He took the bundle of photos off me and began to move more swiftly through them. 'Some of these I used to have on display, and then I took them down. It became . . . It's not as if I need them to remember. You don't forget the things that have mattered, do you? But perhaps I should put one or two up again.'

I wondered whether Jacky had asked for them to be packed away. Or maybe David felt that when Ian left home, it was time to move on. Duty to the present balanced against duty to the past.

'This is our wedding . . . wedding . . . wedding again . . . reception, honeymoon – all these honeymoon. This is in Dumfries with my sister, at our mother's seventieth, my brother on his boat, Jeanette passing her driving test, Jeanette pregnant, Ian, Ian, Ian, Ian in his new uniform – he fell down the stairs the day that was taken and gave himself a bloody nose. This one's shortly after we discovered Jeanette was ill.'

We paused at a Christmas dinner scene. Ian was waving his

hands in the air, after some comic effect, while his mother clutched the stem of her wine glass and smiled at the camera. 'Did she know it was serious?'

'Oh yes.'

'Did Ian?'

'I thought he should be told, but Jeanette didn't agree. In the end I went against her. That was hard.'

'You're better being honest in these situations, even with children.'

David nodded. 'Thank you for saying that. I still believe it was the right course of action. Although my motivations were partly selfish, I confess.'

'In what way?'

'I appreciate this sounds terrible, but at the time I felt it wasn't fair of her to "escape" and leave me to deal with Ian. I know, it's a dreadful thing to admit. But I really truly believed she needed to shoulder some of his grief, not leave it all for me to mop up afterwards. He had questions I wouldn't have known how to answer. Do you understand? But that was cruel of me when she was so sick. I should have let her have her way.'

'No,' I said. 'I'm absolutely sure your instinct was correct. They needed to say a proper goodbye, didn't they? Ian would have been devastated if you'd denied him that.'

David only cleared his throat and flicked onto the next photo, but I knew for once I'd said just the right thing.

The next two dozen shots featured a succession of women. First it was a long-faced blonde who favoured ponytails and jeans, and who liked pub lunches and picnics and vintage car rallies. ('Susannah,' said David.) She gave way to a plump, dark woman, older than him, with a motherly face and a hairstyle not unlike Jeanette's. In the first few pictures she was playing with Ian – beach cricket, hoisting him onto a tree branch, bike riding together – and I began to think perhaps she'd been a nanny, or even that this was the sister, put on weight. But no, because here they were dressed up to the nines and he had his arm around her, and her beaming smile told me this was not a sibling embrace. ('Fiona,' said David. 'A Scot.') Then there was a Sloaney type, frilled collars and navy V-necks, slightly pronounced chin, who'd shared a Christmas with them and at least one family holiday. ('Rachel,' said David.) Lastly we had Jacky, the lovely Jacky, immaculate even when she was crouched in between the geese and ducks by the Old Dee Bridge, holding a Value bread bag. Sometimes Sloaney Rachel appeared with them, and once or twice a fortysomething grey-blonde I recognised as Susannah, aged.

I wanted to say something like, 'Great, good for you,' or 'At least you weren't lonely,' or 'Well, life's for living,' but however I tried to frame my words I sounded trite or, worse, sarcastic. Luckily, David summed up for me.

'Yes, they were nice girls, and much-needed company at the time. Some of them are friends to this day.'

'But not Jacky.'

'Not Jacky.'

Or the other one, I thought.

He glanced at his watch. 'I need to go and stick some broccoli on. Give me another five minutes.'

He took himself off again, leaving me to finish the photos alone.

From now on they were all of Ian: at a friend's wedding; pushing an elderly lady in a wheelchair; in sunglasses leaning against a white stone column; feeding a lamb; pointing at a tor; climbing into the basket of a hot air balloon; patting the roof of a blue Fiat Panda; waving from Chester city walls; in running gear; in university cap and gown; holding the hand of a girl with an oversized forehead.

And lastly, with Jaz. They sat outside the Rocket at a wrought-iron table, eyes screwed up against the dazzle of the whitewashed walls. Jaz must have been working that day because she was wearing an apron, but they were never very busy there and staff often used to come and sit with customers for a chat. Ian was lifting up a chunky mug, and Jaz had her head on his shoulder. Behind them bloomed bright baskets of geraniums.

Even though I'd anticipated coming across such a picture, the sight of her still safe in the past brought on a pang of pure agony.

'Carol?' I heard David calling.

'Coming.'

Just before I set them down, I turned the prints over and riffled through them to check the backs. I don't know what I was hoping, or fearing, to find. Every one turned out to be unmarked; he'd added not a word of commentary or identification anywhere. But then, I thought, why should he? I never needed such prompts either. I always remembered exactly what had been happening in all of mine.

We sat in his kitchen to eat.

'This is nice,' I said, looking round me.

'Stew or kitchen?'

'Both.'

'Jacky used to say the kitchen was dated. I suppose it is, but I don't honestly care as long as everything's clean and works.'

'Quite right too.'

I wanted to say it was good he'd learned to cook, but I was worried that might come across as patronising. My head was still buzzing with his photographs, random scenes that I was struggling to place in their proper sequence. Which girlfriend had he liked the most? Who was it had ended each relationship, and under what circumstances? Had any of them broken his heart?

'OK, Carol?'

Worried he might somehow see inside my head, I caught at the first topic that floated past. 'Why did you get stripped of your school prefect badge?'

David let out a short, yelping laugh. 'How on earth did you know about that?'

'You told me. When we were walking with Matty on the Moss.'

'Did I? Good Lord. Now why would I have brought up that event, of all things?' He looked at me quizzically.

'Hey, if you don't want to tell me, say so. But of course, now I'm imagining all sorts—'

'I should make something up, then, something spectacular. It's going to be such a let-down.'

'Oh, get on with it.'

'If you really want to know, I was given the boot for helping produce a satirical magazine mocking the staff and governors.'

'Blimey. Like *Oz*?'

'Not like *Oz* at all. Nothing terribly bad, actually, but containing opinions which deviated somewhat from the official school line. Rude rather than libellous. The print quality was so poor I'm amazed anyone could decipher it. You know what it's like when you photocopy a photocopy of a photograph, especially when you've added a pair of horns.'

'Sounds fun.'

'It was a total rubbish. We thought we were being edgy, when in fact we were just being boorish. But I was already in trouble for smuggling out percussion instruments for our band to borrow.'

'Tambourine up the jumper?'

'Castanets down the trousers, something like that.'

'I didn't know you were in a band.'

'Yes, and we were pretty bloody awful at that, too. Six English grammar-school boys pretending to be Aphrodite's Child. We'd never have stood an actual gig. Anyway, the upshot was, I was suspended for three days and permanently demoted. I had to behave after that or I'd have been expelled. Even my father wouldn't have been able to save me.'

'I was always too scared to be naughty at school,' I said. 'Too scared and too unimaginative. Mrs Blind Obedience, I was.'

David clicked his tongue. 'There you go again, doing yourself down.'

'And what have you just been doing? The band was "awful", the magazine was "indecipherable".'

'Yes, but I was stating the truth.'

'So was I.'

We frowned at each other across the table.

'I still say you've a tendency to rubbish yourself unnecessarily. It's like a reflex response. You can't help yourself.'

'Do you charge by the hour?'

'I only meant, you're better than you think you are. There. Will that do? One day, perhaps, I'll learn to master the art of giving a straight compliment, and you'll master the art of accepting one.'

'Quits.'

'You're looking very nice this evening, Carol.'

'Thank you.'

I smiled into my stew, and fought down the urge to tell him my blouse had come from the Scope shop. Let him admire uninterrupted.

Evening wore on, the sky darkened. When we were both straining to see our plates in front of us, he got up and drew the blinds and switched on the lights. The gloom had been friendly, the brightness felt like an intrusion. 'Shall I leave the hall light on, and these ones off?' he asked.

I nodded. 'Though I should warn you, there's a risk I'll go to sleep.'

'I'll try and be more stimulating company for you.'

'It's the wine,' I said, 'not you. Anyway, you should take it as a compliment. You put me at my ease.'

'Likewise.'

The house was stiller than mine, I noticed; no noise from next door, no grumbling joists or musical pipework. Perhaps it had absorbed less drama into its walls over the years. I said, 'I wish we'd got to know each other better, sooner.'

David leaned forward and topped up my glass. 'It wasn't the right time.'

'No. I wish it wasn't the right time now, if you know what I mean.'

'Because of Jasmine and Ian.'

'But since we don't have a choice, I'm glad, for us. I'm drunk.'

'You're not.'

I am, I thought.

He made coffee, and I told him about Josh's find.

'I think Nat must have taken the photograph. They look like they're in a gypsy camp.'

'A gypsy camp?'

'When Jaz was about ten, some travellers set up on the field behind the surgery – not that it's a field now – but anyway, Jaz was fascinated. I think for two pins she'd have moved in with them. Phil had to ban her from going there, in the end. She was getting very intense.'

'In what way?'

'She seemed to feel we'd let her down. There was opposition, petitions and letters in the paper, but we weren't involved. I suppose she wanted us to pile in on the gypsies' side. Then the camp moved on, and we thought she'd forgotten about it. Five years later, she ran away; we never found out where she'd been headed. I've been turning it over in my mind all afternoon.'

'Do you think she might have joined up with some travellers?'

'God, I don't know. I'm grasping at straws.'

Jaz reading out snippets from *Local News and Views* in a loud, scandalised voice. Jaz in the courtyard of the Rocket, convinced she'd found the love of her life. All at once my mood plummeted, and I felt overwhelmed with despair.

'Oh, David, I miss them so much it's like being ill. There are some days I don't know what to do with myself. I'm angry with her, I'm angry with Ian, I'm sick of feeling anxious and churned up and frightened of a future I thought was going to bring us so much joy.

'And it's everywhere I turn, you know? Wall-to-wall grimness and suffering. My dad, stuck in that home with no idea who he is. Eileen gone; your wife. Good people! I heard this afternoon that my neighbour's grand-daughter's had a disabled baby. She's such a lovely girl and we were all thrilled for her when she told us she was expecting, and now she's sitting in intensive care not knowing what the next hour'll bring. I just thought, Is there anything that's safe to believe in? Why do we risk being optimistic, and getting close to people, and trying to do a bit of good in the world? What's the point of any of it? Because even if Jaz comes back, she and I are broken, her marriage is gone. It all comes to nothing. It all seems to turn bad eventually.'

He listened without interrupting. Then I heard the scrape of his chair, saw his shadow as he passed between me and the light, felt his touch on my arm.

Please don't claim everything's going to be fine, I prayed. *Don't make glib promises about things which aren't in your power. I don't think I could stand it if you did.*

'All I know, Carol, is, whatever's ahead, you're not on your own. I'll do whatever I practically can to support you. You do understand that?'

I gave a faint nod.

'It's the only certainty I can give you, truthfully.'

His hand fumbled for mine, and I clasped it hard.

'Listen, I have a proposition for you,' he went on.

'What?' I struggled to concentrate over the roar of my own emotion.

'Well, one contribution I could make is to supply funds – no, hear me out – to cover legal procedures, private investigators, whatever you need. I've hesitated to offer till now because of – dealings – at the wedding.'

'Oh, God. That.' Phil grumbling and muttering about passing on receipts, me making comments about Jacky's clothing budget. It made me wince to remember. 'I didn't mean to come across as ungrateful.'

'You didn't. Well, it's water under the bridge. But the point is, whatever you decide you need to do here, I don't want you to feel constrained by finances.'

'That's very generous. I can't take money from you, though.'

'It wouldn't be like that. Matty's my grandson too. It's in my interests to see him reunited with his family. All of his family, on both sides.'

If it would help get Jaz back, I'd have agreed to anything. 'I'll think about it,' I said. 'It's incredibly kind of you.'

'No strings.'

'No.'

'I mean, absolutely none.'

'OK.'

'Good. I wanted to be clear on that. It's a practical arrangement first and foremost, there's no payback, no one's in anyone's debt. A job needs doing, simply that. Because the other thing you need to be aware of . . .' David's face was strained, and for the first time ever, I thought I glimpsed his son in him '. . . I should probably say at this stage. It's possible I may have fallen a little bit in love with you. Do you think that's going to be a problem?'

Strange what rises to the surface of your mind at moments of crisis.

Once, when I was a little girl, my mother and I went on a day trip to somewhere with a cathedral. There are no photographs of this expedition, which I think might have been organised by the Mothers' Union, but I remember it vividly all the same. Not the name of the place, only details: the carved screens, the smell of the wood polish, the ice-smooth veiny columns, the clank of the grating underfoot. While my mother was fishing for loose change to donate, I tiptoed into a side chapel to stroke the carvings of dead knights. Ahead was a vast arched window, through which beams of coloured light slanted down, and the walls on either side of me glowed with embroidered flags. You could see why God chose to hang out here.

Looking above me, I was awed by the vast height of the ceiling, and the way the vaulting at the tops of the pillars seemed to draw together like crystal fans. The scale was humbling and exhilarating at the same time. A surge of excitement rose up in me, and I wanted to shout at the top of my voice (at least till I spotted my mother standing under the central tower, studying the information leaflets). So instead, overwhelmed by spiritual energy, I began to turn on the spot. I tipped my head back, focused on one of the painted bosses, spread my arms out wide, and revolved. I remember spinning faster and faster, till my surroundings were lost in a holy smudge. At the same moment, someone started to play the treble line to 'Jesu, Joy of Man's Desiring'. I was on the verge of being Taken Up.

My mother's voice jerked me out of it. I staggered and fell against a tomb, the scenery still whizzing past in nauseating feints. Closing my eyes made no difference. Nothing was stationary any more.

'I think I've had a religious experience,' I told her.

'You're confusing God with dizziness,' she said, and took me outside so she could tell me off properly.

I don't know why that memory came back so keenly now, unless it was to warn me how easy it is to confuse different sensations, especially when they're very strong. You can think you've received Divine Communion when, in fact, you're just giddy. You can think you've fallen in love when the truth is you're grateful, tired and lonely. *Not him, Mum, anyone but him*, said Jaz, in my head.

3.30 a.m. and I was still prowling round the house, unable to sleep. Couldn't find anything on the internet about imminent gypsy gatherings, except for the Stow Horse Fair – and that was still a month off. And what would I do if I went there? Walk round with a loud-hailer? I kept seeing David's face, the sad lines round his eyes. Thought of kissing Phil, that first time on the bridge as a teenager, and years later in the B&B where we stayed on honeymoon, those funny damp patches on the ceiling paper, and me trembling with nerves under the sheets in case the owners could hear us doing it.

'Not now,' I'd told David. Under the intensity of his gaze I'd felt almost hysterical. 'Everything's complicated. It's a weird, bad time.'

'I know. That's why you have to seize the day, though. Life's short.' He squeezed my fingers in time to the last two syllables.

'No. But it's—' *Everything*, I wanted to say. 'Too much. You're my friend.'

'And I can't be anything else?'

His face was so close I could have kissed him. I wanted to, dear God, I really did. My whole body was charged with longing and fear.

Instead I got up in a rush, stumbled into the hall, and without even picking up my coat, ran out of the house like some idiot schoolgirl.

I don't know who he thinks he is, went Phil.

Next time you speak to him, tell him from me he can fuck off – Jaz.

I've no time for all this love stuff – Eileen, in a deckchair, her eyes hidden behind sunglasses. *It's like dancing on a cliff edge*.

Dad's face as it used to be, animated and keen – *As long as you're happy, that's all that matters*. Are *you happy?*

These pre-dawn hours were like another dimension altogether. Every second could last an hour, you could live a lifetime in one night.

I wandered back over to the computer and shut it down. Then I started a bath running, and did some stretches while I waited. Would David be in bed still, or pacing round the house, like me? What was he doing at this exact moment? My mind whirred insanely. It's past four! I kept thinking. You've got till seven to get through. I'd have given the world to be able to flick an off-switch, blot everything out for even a couple of hours.

But then, if I'd been asleep, I'd never have heard the text come in.

CHAPTER 30

Photograph 180, Album Two

Location: the back garden, Sunnybank

Taken by: Carol

Subject: Jaz, strapped into her toddler reins, and swiping at a dandelion clock. Technically speaking, it's an excellent piece of composition, even though it's one of Carol's earliest attempts at portrait. She's captured Jaz's chubby profile, the anticipatory parting of her young lips as her open grasp bears down on the seed head. It's a perfect scene of summer.

Would you believe that, only the previous night, Jaz is at death's door? That she brews up a mysterious fever with such rapidity even Phil, dismisser of panic, is alarmed? The screaming doesn't help: high-pitched, unnatural, distressing beyond sanity. When she's still screaming at midnight, Phil tells Carol he's driving them up to the cottage hospital.

So they bundle her and her car seat into the night air, and almost immediately she settles. By the time they get to hospital, she's cooing and chattering like a normal three-year-old. The doctor lifts her onto the examination table and she giggles in his face.

On their way home, the radio starts to play Neil Young's

'Heart of Gold'. Phil pulls the car into a lay-by opposite the park and, with the engine still running, climbs out, unclips Jaz from her seat, and carries her onto the municipal lawns. Then he holds her against his chest, and begins to twirl round in a lop-sided waltz. The moon and stars behind them are picture-book-bright.

'Don't let her catch cold,' Carol shouts.

What is this strange, unpleasant sensation in the pit of her stomach? Surely it should be her *job to dance with her daughter in the moonlight?*

My instinct would have been to phone David, but after what he'd said, I couldn't bring myself to dial. I was too frightened.

I paced around for a couple of minutes, then I tried Phil. He was, after all, Jaz's dad, and I needed someone with me. When I got no response, I tried again. Eventually he answered, groggily.

'It's me,' I gushed. 'I know where Jaz is. She's sent me her address. Can you drive me there?'

There was a long silence. 'Carol?'

I said, 'Can you drive me to Harrogate?'

'When?'

'Now.'

'Jesus.'

I waited, listening for sounds to show he might be with someone, but there was nothing. No female voice asking what was going on.

'It's half past four in the morning,' he said. 'Can you give me time to have a coffee and some breakfast? If she's sent you her address, she's not going to be skipping off, is she? We can wait till it gets light, at least.' Probably he was twitching the curtain aside to look out, because there was a pause and I heard him swear under his breath. 'I need to look at an atlas, anyway.'

He turned up later than he said he would, by which time I was climbing the walls.

'You said six-thirty at the latest.'

'And it's six forty-three, Carol. Now tell me what's up.'

'In the car,' I said, pushing him out of the front door and slamming it behind us. How lucky, in the end, that I wasn't tied any more to taking Josh into school. Moira I could call on the way, ask her to open the shop. All that mattered was getting to my daughter.

Once we were on the road I read out the text. Just Jaz's name, and an address. No message.

'You tried to ring back?'

'Of course I bloody did.'

'No luck?'

'What do you think?'

'And it was her number?'

'Yes.'

The streetlamps flicked past as we sped down the dual carriageway.

I said, 'You don't think she's being held prisoner, do you?'

Phil snorted with laughter, which was annoying as hell and reassuring at the same time. 'Don't be daft.'

'We could ring the police, ask them to be on stand-by.'

'No, Carol.'

I glanced across, took in his grey-streaked hair, his sagging jawline, the creases round his eyes and mouth. Then I pulled down the sunshade mirror and studied my own tired face. I felt old and stupid and not up to the job. I wanted it to be David in the driving seat.

'You're shivering,' he said. 'There's a coat in the back if you want.'

'One of Pen's?'

His knuckles tightened on the steering wheel. 'For the last

time, she isn't around any more. How many times do I have to keep saying it?'

I scowled, and reached round for the overcoat.

'And there's a flask in the glove compartment. Help yourself,' he muttered.

'Tea? Coffee?'

'Brandy.'

We drove on under a grey, uncertain sky. All I could feel, as the miles clocked up, was terror: of Jaz not being there, or her being there but still not letting me see Matty, of her changing her mind and fleeing again, of her being in some terrible trouble. It seemed as though I'd spent all my life as a mother in a state of churning fear. Labour pain's nothing to what comes after. From the first moment you're pregnant, everyone seems to have a horror story to tell you. *They did a scan and found there was no head*, I remember overhearing someone in the shop say, and I had to go home early that day and had weeks of terrible nightmares. And the potential for pain starts even before you're pregnant, from the second you admit that you want a child. Moira tried for years, had miscarriage after miscarriage and all sorts of tests and humiliating procedures, and in the end had to learn to live without. I can't imagine what that must have been like. All I ever wanted was a baby.

And yet, when I got home from hospital with newborn Jaz, I remember looking at her and thinking, Dear God, I don't know what to do with her. That awful lurch when the idea that you truly have got an actual baby sinks in, and that what you've done, in having a child, is open yourself up forever to the worst hurt imaginable (and I saw again Jaz hauling Matty out of the water, his drenched clothes streaming and his face streaked with weed). There's no magic age where you can stop worrying, either, because after falling in ponds and meningitis and choking there's paedophiles and bullying and drugs and car crashes. Teenage boys getting knifed and shot, girls getting raped. I thought of Alice's little baby, pictured him lying in an incubator with a name tag round his tender ankle, and wondered how on earth she would bear it.

Having a child was like building a house on an unexploded bomb. At any moment, the possibility for devastation was part of your life. In some ways, Eileen had been clever to steer clear of it all.

'I'm not sure I can cope with this,' I said. We were coming onto the motorway, and Phil was looking away from me, over his shoulder.

'Course you can,' he said, flicking the indicator.

'I daren't let myself think Matty might be there, because if he's not, if it's like last time when I went down to Bristol—'

Lorries roared into line beside us, and behind us, and ahead. Danger was everywhere.

'Tell you who I was dreaming about when I got your call. You remember that chemistry teacher, the one with the lisp? God knows why she made an appearance after all these years.'

'I know what you're trying to do,' I said.

'In the dream she was really friendly, not like she was when we were at school. Mary bloody Whitehouse in a lab coat. God, she went ballistic over that chlorine gas business, didn't she? Absolutely livid. I got the cane for that.'

'You deserved it.'

'It wasn't me who didn't close the fume cupboard properly. That was her.'

'Yes, but you didn't have to fall off your stool and pretend you were choking to death, did you? Dribbling everywhere, jerking around. Even I thought you were a gonner.'

Phil grinned. 'Hey, do you remember that assembly when we

had that ex-pupil come to talk to us about how he'd won the war?'

'You got the cane for that as well,' I said. I could see him now, tie askew, making a dash across the playground to where the tall man with the military bearing stood conversing with the Headmaster. Phil had tagged the man on the arm, for all the world as though they were playing a game of chase, then run off shouting at the top of his voice, 'I'm cured! It's a miracle! I was blind and now I can see!'

'Grand days, eh?'

'If you say so.'

'They never did find out who added Hitler moustaches to all the photos in the entrance hall.'

'It's nothing to be proud of.'

'I seem to recall you finding it pretty funny at the time. In fact, didn't you and Eileen get a bit creative yourselves with the speech-day programmes at one point?' Phil raised an eyebrow at me, and my lips twitched, in spite of myself. It was nerves, though, that was all.

There were hold-ups on the M62. As the car slowed down, then halted, I gripped the handle of my bag so tight I left fingernail marks in the leather.

'I saw Edith Hilton last week,' said Phil. 'Coming out of Aldi.'

'Is she still alive?'

'Unless what I saw was a zombie.'

'Very amusing. I meant she must be getting on.'

He reached into the pocket between the seats, hooked out an elderly Polo and stuck it in his mouth. 'How long's Laverne been living next door? It's only about twelve years, and Edith would have been, what, sixty when she moved out? So she'll be in her seventies, that's all. Still a way to go before she's a contender for Britain's Oldest Woman.'

'Britain's Oldest Bag, more like.'

'You weren't fond of her, were you?' Clicky-click went the mint against his teeth.

'No. She was horrible to Jaz. Horrible full stop.'

'Do you remember that time you swapped all her flower bulbs for pickling onions?'

'You told me to.'

'Yeah. Good, wasn't it?'

The traffic started to move again. I thought of Edith Hilton peering suspiciously over the new green shoots in her border, bending to pinch the leaves and then sniffing her fingers, while Phil and I hooted with laughter from behind the front-room curtain. She'd had a son, a nasty piece of work, who complained about Jaz more or less constantly. Didn't like her climbing the tree in our garden because he thought she was spying on his mother; objected to the noise they made when Nat came round; claimed they were poking fun, when they were just giggling like young girls do. I always tried to be polite, but it wasn't easy. One time he banged on the door to moan they were playing their music with the window open and his mother didn't like it. I'd stood there on the step for five minutes, explaining it was a new birthday CD-player, and reassuring him it wouldn't happen again, and apologising for any disturbance. Then Phil had come up behind me and said to him, 'Tell you what, Norman: why don't you just fuck off?' and shut the door in his face. And that, astonishingly, was the last we'd heard of him. For all his failings as a husband, Phil sometimes hit the nail on the head.

'Poor woman, such trouble she had with her lawn,' he said now as we came onto the M60.

I looked sideways at him. 'Was that you?'

'Yup.'

'How?'

'Coca Cola. Kills the grass. Takes it ages to grow back properly. She went bonkers trying to work out what caused those lines. I saw her putting down fertilizer, extra turf, all sorts. Always those lines came back, though. What a mystery, eh?'

'Why didn't you tell me at the time?'

'I thought it would be more convincing if you were mystified too.'

At last he'd made me smile properly. 'Do you think there's any chance you'll ever grow up?'

'God, no.'

When we came off the motorway, there was another hold-up: some roadworks with a complicated three-way lights system and traffic backing up for miles.

'Keep calm,' he said. 'Have a Polo.'

'You know I hate them.'

'We used to play that car game with Murray mints, do you remember? Who could make their sweet last the longest. And we always let Jaz win because that way you got the maximum amount of peace. It chipped away another twenty minutes or so off a long journey.'

'What if that text's a wind-up, Phil?'

'It won't be. Try not to think about it. There's no mileage in getting yourself upset before we've even got there. Is there?'

'No,' I said reluctantly.

He switched the radio on, and twiddled the dial till he found 'Stuck in the Middle With You'. 'Hey, what about that time Natalie sat on the dolls'-house roof and the whole thing collapsed? All those bloody miniature spindles for the banisters; I was months putting them right. And I got Superglue on your mother's tablecloth, do you remember?'

I let him prattle on because it was easier than trying to shut him up. How he used to wind Jaz up by singing *Take my paw, I'm a hamster in paradise* whenever she cleaned Mojo out; how once, when we were courting, my mother had invited him to Sunday lunch and he'd choked spectacularly on a string of beef fat; that time he'd been changing on the beach in Fowey, larking about, and had overbalanced and given everyone a flash.

But as we came into the outskirts of Harrogate finally, even he went quiet. Only when Neil Young's 'Heart of Gold' came on the radio did he break the silence. 'Hey, do you remember when Jaz cooked up that massive temperature out of nowhere, and we had to do a midnight dash to hospital?'

'I do,' I said. I could recall the scene so clearly. 'The minute we walked through the door she was right as rain. Then, on the way home, you stopped the car and I took her out into the park and whirled her round. I was that relieved.'

Phil opened his mouth as if to speak, but then shook his head and stayed silent.

We were driving between rows of tall stone houses. In one of these, or something like it, Jaz and Matty were waiting for us.

'It wasn't all bad, was it?' said Phil, after a while.

'No.'

'I mean, we've history, haven't we?'

'Too much,' I said.

After that, neither of us spoke till we saw Soulton Street.

I'd printed out the directions from the computer, but now I came to look at the detail, one side had been cut off and some of it we were having to guess. The stone houses gave way to a modern estate, then to rows of semis like Sunnybank, then a council estate. Then we seemed to be passing through the edge of Harrogate and out into the countryside again. I was about to say I thought we must have gone wrong when I recognised a road number, and understood where we were. A couple more turnings, one, two, and the next one was us.

We found ourselves in a cul-de-sac flanked by terraced grey cottages, all with little porches and square front gardens, fields and moorland behind. Phil slowed the car to a crawl so I could peer at house numbers.

'It's on your side,' I said, swinging round in my seat to face him.

He was leaning forward, frowning, his lips drawn into a kind of snarl. It was the first evidence I'd seen that he might be under stress. 'Over there. That's Jaz's car,' he said.

I started to shake.

Within the next second my focus shifted to something moving just beyond the car in one of the gardens: a small white figure behind black railings. 'Matty', I tried to say, but only a whisper came out. Blindly I felt for the handle and pushed the door open even though the car was still moving, but my seat belt locked and held me back. I scrabbled for the release clip.

'Wait,' said Phil.

'There! Look!' I said.

He pulled up, and turned the engine off. 'What are you planning to do, Carol?'

It was as if he could read my mind. He looked into my eyes and saw the film play out: me running across the road, grabbing Matty, lifting him over the fence, dashing back to our getaway car with my grandson in my arms.

'No,' he said sternly.

'What's he doing out on his own? He's not safe.'

'There are railings all round, and a gate.'

'Who's keeping an eye on him, though?'

'The front door's open. Someone'll be watching out, trust me.'

It was impossible to see anything in the windows from this angle, bar reflections of the sky. The porch was empty.

'Take a moment or two,' said Phil, placing his hand on my arm. 'How are you going to do this? You want me to come over with you? You're not going to get hysterical, are you?'

'I'm not going to get hysterical, no. I just need to—' Again I felt for the handle. The physical urge to hold Matty was becoming overpowering, eclipsing even, for that moment, the risk of upsetting Jaz.

'I'll walk across with you. We'll put our heads round the door and see what happens.'

'Let me have a minute with him first.'

He sighed, then shook his head. 'You know, Jaz is my daughter too. I'd quite like to see she's OK.'

'You told me she was fine!'

'Carol. Calm down.' He took my wrists in his hands and held them, and I let my eyes close while I counted to ten. My breathing was too fast, my heart pounding. When I opened my eyes, Matty was still there. I shivered violently.

'Now,' I said. 'Please.'

'Come on, then.'

I climbed out, and Phil escorted me across the road as if I were an invalid. My legs were weak with nerves, and when I got to the railings I had to hold onto them for support. Matty was crouched on the lawn, two-handedly bashing some gourd-shaped object against the ground. His hair had grown, and he was wearing a cream-coloured outfit I hadn't seen before, with grass stains on the knees. So absorbed was he that he didn't look up till the gate creaked open.

'Hello,' I said, trying to keep my voice steady.

'Macca, Nanna, look,' he said, straightening up and holding out his gourd. In one swooping movement I reached down, lifted and pulled him tightly to me, nestling my face into his curls, and his weight and shape were such a blissful sensation against me I could have cried out. There's no feeling on earth like holding a child you love. It's a comfort beyond anything else, a crucial jigsaw piece slotted home. Matty smelled of shampoo and butter and soil and himself. I breathed him in, and thanked God.

Somewhere in the background I was aware of Phil shifting about; then I heard the sound of footsteps in the porch. I knew we only had seconds left, and I kept my eyes screwed shut.

And then Jaz's voice went, 'Jesus wept, *you*!' and the game was up.

CHAPTER 31

Photograph 155, Album Two

Location: the back garden, Sunnybank

Taken by: Carol

Subject: Eileen under the lilac tree, holding newborn Jaz. She looks so utterly absurd with a baby in her arms that, at first, Carol laughs out loud. Eileen wants to know what's so funny. Carol realises, in the nick of time, that the truth might not be diplomatic. 'I'm just a bit giddy,' she says instead. And because Carol has been high as a kite since the birth, manically so, Eileen accepts this explanation.

She does look bloody odd, though; there's no getting away from it.

I kept my face buried against my grandson, counting down the last few moments.

'Hey up,' said Phil.

When I mustered the courage to peep, Jaz was, astonishingly, in the process of embracing him. He looked caught out and embarrassed, and relieved. 'Dad!' she said. 'What are *you* doing here?'

'You sent a text.'

'No, I didn't.'

She moved over to me and I thought maybe I was going to get a hug too. But the outstretched arms were for Matty. Of course. It was all I could do not to cling onto him and fight her. A part of myself tore away with him, and I was left standing there, exposed and frightened.

'Jaz didn't send a text. I did.' A short man with a frank, pleasant face was advancing across the lawn towards Phil.

I waited for Jaz to explode with fury, but she just went, 'Oh! I should have known.'

'Well, someone had to.' He smiled at me as he shook Phil's hand. 'Nick Page, pleased to meet you. Shall we go in?'

I glanced at Phil. *I don't know, should we? Are you getting any of this?*

He gave a tiny shrug. At the same time, Nick Page took my elbow and began to draw me towards the door. As we walked, I was gaining the impression of someone who liked to act older than his years. In spite of the slightly receded hairline, he didn't look much past thirty-five. *Who is this guy? Do we know him? How should I be playing this?* said Phil's expression. *No idea*, I signalled back.

We funnelled through the porch straight into a wide, light room with cream walls and a bare wooden floor. Books filled almost every available horizontal space except for the mantelpiece, which had been used to display a collection of African masks and statuettes. Above the fireplace was a mirror with a blue and green mosaic frame, while near the opposite skirting board, a stone painted with a rainbow served as a doorstop. Hippy, I was thinking. Intellectual, middle-class. Everything here's ethically sourced and unprocessed; I'd seen rooms like this in the Sunday magazines. What a contrast from Sunnybank's chintz cushions and Beswick budgies. No china cabinets here, I'd be prepared to bet.

Indignation rose up in me. I was who I was, I'd done my best and if all Jaz valued in the end turned out to be a certain set of lifestyle trappings, then that was her failing, not mine. To come across the country to this man and seek shelter here, when the ones she'd left at home were beside themselves—

'What can I get you?' asked Nick, clasping his hands like a hearty waiter.

'Tea, please,' I said feebly.

'Tea,' echoed Phil.

Nick took himself off, leaving us to our awkwardness, and that's when I registered the little shrivelled palm cross tacked to the chimney breast.

'For God's sake, sit down,' said Jaz, and plonked herself on the large squashy sofa with Matty on her knee. At once he slid himself onto the cushion next to her, and reached up for me. He was still holding his gourd.

'What is it, love?' I asked, bending to see. My heart was thudding as though I'd swum ten lengths.

'African maracas,' replied Jaz. 'Nick spent some time in Kenya.'

Who is he? I wanted to ask, but didn't dare voice the question yet.

'Who is he?' said Phil.

Jaz laughed, as if we were being particularly dense. 'Nick Page. You do know him. Dr Page. When I was at Leeds? You met him, Mum.'

I thought about it, and tried to recall the detail: standing with Jaz in the Union building, being hailed by a man in a moss-green jacket. I couldn't have told you another thing about the encounter, though. *Yes, Jaz, I did meet him, for about ten seconds, more than six years ago. If I'd known you were going to run off with him, I'd have paid a sight more attention.* How much older than her was he, for a start? Wasn't it against the rules, or something? Could she possibly have stepped straight from Ian to an old fogey like this?

Then, in a rush of understanding, I heard Tomasz's voice once more: *She went to the clinic with her personal tutor*.

Back he came into the lounge, Dr Page, with a tray of cups and a bright smile for everyone. 'That's the kettle on,' he said, placing the cups on the coffee-table and settling himself on a carved stool by the fender. 'Now. I'm guessing there are probably lots of questions you'd like to ask.'

'I'll say,' growled Phil.

For God's sake, don't ruin it, I thought. I held onto Matty, who'd decided to study the bobbles on my jumper, and stroked his hair in an effort to calm myself.

'You're Jaz's teacher?' I said.

'I was.' They exchanged a smile that made my heart contract with jealousy. 'I had that privilege.'

Phil addressed Jaz. 'Have you been here all the time, then?'

'About a fortnight. I went to Whitby, first off.'

'*Whitby?* Why?'

'I felt like going to the seaside. We stayed in a hotel.'

'Who did?'

'Me and Matty. Who do you think?'

'What hotel was it?'

'Just a hotel, I dunno.'

I said, 'I wish you'd let me know where you were. It was – really difficult.' That was as much protest as I dared.

'Yeah.' Again she cast her eyes towards Dr Page. 'Sorry.'

'Nanna bag. Here y'are, Nanna,' said Matty, struggling to pull up the strap he was sitting on.

'Are you coming home, Jaz?'

At that moment, the door in the far corner was pushed open and a young woman walked in carrying a teapot. Her blonde hair fell forward as she put the pot down, a process that involved her bending at the knee rather than the waist, since she was heavily pregnant.

'This is my wife, Steph,' said Dr Page.

Oh thank God, I nearly said out loud. I don't know how Phil was feeling at that moment, but I could have whooped with relief. Now I knew for certain we weren't looking at a predatory tutor taking advantage of an ex-student; I wouldn't have to go back to David and Ian and break the news that Jaz had moved in with a new lover a hundred miles away, and field their outrage and dismay. Simply, Jaz had been with friends, people who knew her history and accepted her, who were in a position to offer practical help.

'Nice to meet you,' I said, meaning it.

'I must tell you,' she said. 'Jaz has been such a help to me these last two weeks.'

'She contacted me to ask if she could drop by for a chat, catch up on old times,' continued Dr Page. 'Then, when she got here . . . well, she ended up staying. Turns out there was quite a lot to talk about! Not that it's put us out in any way. As Steph says, she's actually been a tremendous help. Although we didn't know till yesterday that she hadn't told you where she was.'

'I was *going* to phone,' said Jaz, rolling her eyes as if she was fourteen again.

'Well, you don't need to now, do you? Mrs Morgan, your daughter and I had a very long discussion late last night.'

'You're telling me.'

'And I'd say she resolved quite a few issues that were troubling her. Is that a fair summary, Jaz?'

Another of those looks passed between them.

'Yeah, I'm feeling loads better,' she said. 'I've got a lot of stuff into perspective. Sometimes you have to, you know, get right away.'

'You certainly did that,' said Phil. 'Your mum—'

'Shh,' I said.

Dr Page nodded understandingly. 'So we've done a lot of talking, and a little bit of praying, and I think Jaz feels it might be time to come home.'

Jaz nodded. 'I'm much more straightened out. I'm in a better place now.'

I heard Phil snort under his breath. *A little bit of praying?* I was thinking. Is this the same person who told me not eighteen months ago that having a child christened was a form of bullying? Who as a teenager, for spite, once picked the cross off a hot cross bun before eating it? Then again, hadn't she begged me last Advent for my Nativity set, and put it on display in the front-room window? I closed my eyes and thought of us all gathered round the table for Christmas dinner. Dear God, that it might happen.

'When do you think you might be ready?' I asked.

'Oh, I reckon she's pretty much ready now,' said Dr Page. 'Is that right, Jaz? You could pop upstairs and pack your stuff while your mum and dad finish their tea. Then you can all set off home together. A merry convoy. Steph'll help you gather your bits and pieces. Leave Matty down here, eh?'

'Oh, I don't know. It feels a bit sudden. Maybe tomorrow, so I can sort a few more things.'

'Didn't we say last night that delay becomes, in the end, an additional burden?'

'Yeah, I know. I can see that. But it's still—'

'The truth is, you'll never be as ready as you are right now. You admitted that yourself, not twelve hours ago. Take control of the moment, eh?' He leaned forward encouragingly. 'I know you can do this, or I shouldn't ask you.'

She went like a lamb.

Once she was gone, he said, 'I'm sorry I couldn't let you

know earlier. We weren't aware of the full situation. But I want you to be clear, I didn't go behind her back in contacting you; she had said she would ring you within the next couple of days. I just felt it might be difficult for her to make the call, and I didn't want you worrying even a minute longer than necessary.'

'If we could have talked to you before we came up,' Phil began.

'Yes, I did consider that. But I decided, on balance, it would be better if she could explain to you herself, here. I didn't want to overstep my remit.' His manner was so candid, so disarming. All those years ago my daughter must have sat in his study, pouring out crisis after crisis: Tomasz, the boy who killed himself, a positive pregnancy test. This man and his wife drove her to the clinic and stayed with her till the abortion was done. Took her back home with them, tucked her up in bed, brought her painkillers and sanitary towels, mopped her tears. Things I should have done myself, but wasn't allowed. Gratitude struggled with jealousy, and shame.

'You were her *personal* tutor?' I asked carefully.

'I was.' He looked at me for a long moment. *Don't ask me what I've promised to keep confidential*, his eyes said.

'It was a damn shame she packed in her degree,' said Phil. 'That you couldn't have talked her round. Whatever the circumstances.'

Dr Page stepped across to the window and addressed himself to the far hills.

'She did what she felt she had to, at the time. I agree, it was a great shame she didn't complete her course. She was one of the best students in her year. But she's using her languages, and enjoying them – not every graduate can claim that. And you know, Steph and I are very fond of her.' After a pause, his focus came back to us and he smiled. 'I really do believe Jaz has turned an important corner these last few weeks. I know she'll want to talk a lot more when she gets home.'

'I suppose we should say thank you,' said Phil.

Dr Page spread his hands, like a vicar giving a blessing. 'You must have my number before you go.'

Damn right, said Phil's expression.

Matty lolled against me and drummed his heels against the sofa arm. 'Shh,' I said. He burrowed his face against my stomach, and it was as though we'd never been apart.

'Tell you what, let him take those maracas,' said Dr Page. 'He seems to have developed a fancy for them.'

Ten minutes later we were all back in the porch.

'Is it OK if I ring Ian? Or do you want to do it?' I asked Jaz. I'd been rehearsing the question all the while she was upstairs.

'Yeah, you do it.'

'You know, I had to give him the key.'

'Well, obviously.'

'Right.' I took in her pretty, heart-shaped face and my heart clenched with hope. 'Oh, you've had a proper fringe cut.'

'Have you only just noticed?' She shook her hair out of her eyes, and took hold of Matty by his coat sleeve.

We shuffled at Matty-speed towards the gate. Phil took the opportunity to slip his hand in mine and I didn't pull away. 'Come on,' he said, drawing me ahead. 'It's a long drive home.'

'What if she doesn't follow us?' I whispered. When I turned back, Dr Page had lifted open her car boot and was swinging cases and bags inside.

'She will.'

Together we walked across the street.

I'm glad you were with me today, I thought. But I didn't say the words out loud.

CHAPTER 32

Photograph: unnumbered, from Carol's wedding album

Location: round the back of St Stephen's C of E, Tannerside, Bolton

Taken by: Ribble Photographic Studios

Subject: Carol stands in full-length white, white-capped, with a bouquet of irises, freesia and roses. Although she is smiling, there's a slight clenching of the jaw that betrays the fact she's frozen, as cold as the granite memorial tablets beneath the soles of her inadequate slippers. Her feet are in pain. 'It's almost June,' she mutters to bridesmaid Eileen, 'but it's like crossing the Arctic. It's not what you expect.'

'Nothing ever is,' says Eileen. The wind whips through the weave of their thin silk gowns and the ribbons round Carol's veil tangle madly. 'I'll be as blue as my dress by the time this photographer's sorted,' adds Eileen.

Earlier, when they are trying to warm themselves in the ladies', Carol says: 'Don't let people boss you about when it's your turn. Have the wedding you want.'

'If I ever get married,' Eileen replies, 'which I doubt. I'm running away to Jamaica and doing it on the beach. In a white

bikini, to a Sean Connery lookalike, and we'll leave for our honeymoon on a jet ski.'

She's really weird today, thinks Carol. Jittery, distracted, near the edge. Snapped Phil's head off earlier over nothing. You wouldn't think she'd get so keyed up about being a bridesmaid, at her age.

'Best avoid the bouquet, then,' says Carol archly. She's too full of her own happiness to care much anyway.

The first thing I noticed, on returning to Jaz and Ian's house, was that the gate had been replaced. An unpainted wooden one now hung from the hinges, while the old wrought-iron one lay flat on the lawn, grass poking up through the scrolls.

I paused on the step to listen. Some toy of Matty's sounded a klaxon repeatedly, and I could hear Ian's irritated tones over the top of it.

The door was on the latch so I knocked loudly, then let myself in.

It was the light that struck me. Where the hall used to be papered with a dark, embossed design, the walls were now a plain milk-coffee colour, and the woodwork gleaming white. The changes made the place seem much bigger, despite the stairs being once more cluttered with toys and washing and books. It was wonderful to see again Matty's plastic bits and pieces strewn about, though I noticed with a jolt that the wedding photo had been taken down from the wall.

'Then get someone in to *fix it*!' shouted Jaz from the top of the stairs. Which is when she saw me. 'Oh, Mum, hi. I was just sorting out Matty's stuff. I'll be with you in a minute.' She raised her voice unpleasantly. 'Ian, can you stick the kettle on?'

Ian emerged from the lounge. He rearranged his features into a smile, nodded a greeting and headed for the kitchen. I could guess what his face was doing once he'd turned his back on me.

I went to find Matty.

He was in the living room playing with one of those big multicoloured learning centres. The top section had a row of chunky talking buttons in various shapes, and the lower half was all farmyard animals that made the appropriate noises when you pressed them. Along the bottom was a flashing keyboard.

I lowered myself onto the carpet next to him and began to pick out the tune of 'Baa Baa Black Sheep', while my grandson provided a descant of moos and quacks. It was a bit of a racket, to be honest, but no one else was in the room.

Even though he'd only been away a season, Matty had changed. His development had leaped forward. He knew all sorts of new words, plus a fragment of a song I'd not taught him, with accompanying actions. He could negotiate my back step without needing his hand held. He could turn the pages of a book by himself and build a four-block tower out of bricks. Every time he stayed over we had a marathon bedtime reading session, and after I'd tucked him in I'd go up four or five times just to lean over his cot and look at him. For a week and a half I'd had the bitter pleasure of discovering what I'd missed. And all the while, in the background, I was aware of Jaz still poised to deliver our fates.

Here she came now, stropping into the room, her colour high. I snatched my hand away from the keyboard.

'Heating's playing up,' she said.

'Oh, love. You look tired.'

'Yeah, well.' She dropped onto the sofa. 'I'm not sleeping. No one is. Matty won't settle when I'm in the room and I seem to be waking at every little squeak or sniffle he makes. So the nights are pretty long, aren't they, old chap?'

'Why are you sleeping in there? Has he not been well?'

'Ian's got our bed,' she said.

I didn't know what to say to that.

Instead I told her about Moira's sister's mini-trampoline she was getting rid of, and did Matty want it. 'It's nearly new, it folds away, and it's got safety bars on the side. It's a decent one, ELC.'

'Great,' said Jaz flatly. 'Tell her thanks.'

I heard the back door judder open and shut, and assumed Ian had gone outside for something. But a few moments later, it was David who walked in on us. He must have left his shoes on the mat but he still wore his coat. From his gloved hand dangled a pair of secateurs.

'Carol!' He laid the secateurs on the chair arm by Jaz, and opened his arms for me. I started forward, then panicked. Jaz was watching me with eyes like flint. I faltered, took a few more steps till I was within his range, and submitted to a brief embrace.

'Nice to see you.' I pushed him away and stepped back.

'And you,' he said, frowning.

'How are you getting on?' Jaz asked him, pointedly moving the secateurs to the top of the bookcase where they'd be out of Matty's reach.

'I need a hacksaw, I've come in to ask for one.'

Jaz turned to me. 'We're taking out the elder tree by the kitchen window, Mum. It's making the room dark and rotting the sill outside. Cut out the *dead wood*.'

'I thought you said you were getting another loaf,' said Ian, coming in with a tray of mugs and setting it down. 'We've only crusts left. I can't do Matty toast with that.'

'Well, you know, I've had a few other jobs to do.'

I said, 'He's coming home with me in a minute. I can give him dinner.'

David was still standing in the corner, watching me. 'It's been a while since I've seen you, Carol.'

'Only a week,' I said, for Jaz's benefit.

'A fortnight,' he said. 'I thought we might have had a chance to catch up.'

'I've been really busy, I've not caught my breath yet.'

'It does seem to be all go.'

'Ian,' said Jaz, 'if you're going back into the kitchen, can you get Matty's coat off the hall radiator and stick it by the door, ready?'

He went out of the room, there was a pause, then he shouted back, 'It's not there.'

'What do you mean?'

'I mean it's not there.' His face reappeared round the jamb.

'I told you to take it out of the machine.'

'No, you didn't.'

'Yes, I did. Oh, for God's sake. I knew you weren't listening. Now it'll be wringing wet!'

She hauled herself up off the sofa, and as she bent her head I saw the blueish-grey skin under her lower lids.

Don't leave me alone with David! I wanted to shout, but she was already gone.

'Well,' he said.

Matty was prodding at the flashing lights on his board. I scrambled up stiffly, saying, 'It must be difficult for both of them—'

'Carol.'

'I'd better go help out, if you can keep an eye on this one.' Quickly I slid past him and into the hall.

'Carol?' he said behind me. 'Carol!' But I pretended not to hear.

Afterwards, he phoned. 'Let me come round and see you,' he said.

'Wait till we hear what's happening. Wait till Jaz makes her decision.'

'She's back home. She's made it.'

'I don't think she has.'

'Why won't you meet me, Carol?'

'Let's just wait,' I said.

Sometimes I'd get out the wedding album and look at his picture, one hand covering Jacky. If the photos had been loose, I'd have got the scissors and cut her off.

I don't know why I assumed she'd invited me to go shopping and have lunch, like a regular mum and grown-up daughter.

'I want you to come and see a flat with me,' Jaz said when I met her by the Civic Centre.

My hopes plummeted, there and then.

'Don't panic,' she continued. 'I'm not going far. But it'll be easier all round. Ian and I'll be able to talk to each other better if we have some space. At the moment it's just grim. The atmosphere's like you wouldn't believe. I've got to go or it'll do my head in.'

She took my bag for me, a small, unlooked-for kindness, and we began to walk up the High Street together.

'It's bound to be difficult at first,' I said, 'when you think what's gone on. I'm sure things'll get easier. Can you not give it a bit longer?'

'Nope. This isn't a snap decision, Mum, I've thought it through. It's the best way.'

'OK, well, how about you move in with me for a few weeks? And then that's saving you money, and you're not tied up in a contract or anything.'

'Thanks, but I want to go with the flat.' She smiled tightly at me. 'It's all right, you know, I'm not about to take off again.'

'I don't think I could bear it if you did, Jaz.'

I glimpsed our reflection in the butcher's window, caught the way she lowered her head guiltily.

'How will you afford it?' I said.

'Ian. Benefits. I'll work something out.'

'Does he know what you're planning?'

'Yes.'

'What does he think?'

'He agrees. It's been too much of a shock coming together again. And he's angry with me, so fucking angry, and I'm angry with him and we've so much to sort out but all we're doing is fighting. So I've told him it's our best chance.'

'Did you mean it?'

'Yeah, I do.'

We passed the shop where I bought my grandson's Moses basket and his first car seat. Behind the window a couple stooped to examine the mechanism on a collapsible pram.

'How's Matty with it all?'

Jaz shrugged. 'He was having a tantrum when I left. Didn't want to wear his shoes, wanted to keep his slippers on all day. I've left Ian dealing with it.'

'That's normal, coming up to two. You were a nightmare at that age. What are you doing for his birthday?'

'I'm not sure.'

'You could have some of his little friends round from nursery.'

'Maybe.'

Please be together for him, I wanted to say. *There's no better gift for a child.* 'I could bake some muffins.'

'Can't think that far ahead right now, Mum.'

We passed Boots, and Healey's café, and the side street that led down to Bark End and The Olive.

I said, 'See the pet shop across the road? That used to be Falkirk's, where we bought your first school uniform.

Do you remember? Gosh, you were a little scrap in those days.'

'Nick said you phoned him last week,' she said. 'Don't worry, he wouldn't tell me what you talked about. He never breaks a confidence.'

Bully for him, I thought. Saint Page. 'What do you reckon to him?' Phil had asked me on the drive back. 'Is he on the level or what?' 'I think he is on the level,' I'd replied. That didn't mean I had to like him, though.

'It was only to thank him again.'

'I don't mind you discussing me, Mum.'

What's he got that I haven't? I wanted to say. *How come you'll listen to him and not to me?* 'I expect he confirmed you'd had a terrible upbringing and everything that had happened to you was my fault.'

Jaz shook her head. 'He gave me a right bollocking, actually. In a nice way. He told me to grow up.'

'Oh,' I said.

'But he was fantastic with me. Not just letting me stay; more than that. The way he listens and just sort of suggests things subtly, so you can work out what you think without being hassled. Not telling you what to do, but, you know, guiding you. He's laid-back, *and* super-moral. It's difficult to explain. When I was at uni . . .'

'What?'

'He was very kind. He's been like a dad.'

'You've got a dad.'

'Yeah, right.' She pulled a sneery face.

'You never give him a chance,' I heard myself say. 'He cares a lot about you.'

Jaz raised her eyebrows, but she didn't say anything.

We reached the top of the High Street. 'Where do we go from here?' I asked.

'Down Overdale Road. It's near the Catholic church.'

A side of town I hadn't visited since the days of the divorce. This was the back of the library and the health centre, a row of Georgian buildings housing law firms and accountants. Makinson & Todd had been my solicitors. The brass plate was still up, and I wondered whether at this moment, a woman like me was sitting in Mr Todd's office, unpicking her marriage.

'David cares about you too,' I added recklessly, as we crossed to the opposite pavement.

'He can fuck off.'

'Jaz, if it wasn't for his intervention, Ian would have had the police after you.'

She sighed and swapped the bag to her other hand.

You don't seem to realise what a bloody dangerous game you were playing, or how I had to fight to keep you out of trouble, I wanted to shout at her. But before I could marshal the right words, she changed the subject.

'You've been moving stuff round.'

'Where?'

'Your house.'

'I've been having a clear-out.'

'It's good, it looks bigger.'

'It should do. I've been right through, taken eleven bags to the tip and five to the charity shop. There were still a load of your dad's car mags in the hall cupboard, plus all my mother's sewing patterns, balls and balls of dish-cloth yarn, parish magazines going back to the Seventies. Suddenly I have all this extra storage space. Just the shed to tackle. Although, I might leave that now.'

Now you're home, I meant.

We turned onto Overdale Road.

'Tell you what, Mum: I wish I could go through my head like that and drag out all the bad memories. Sort through and dump the rubbish. Why should I have to cart it round with me all my life?'

I guessed she was imagining Ian with the other woman, or recalling the night she found out, or the rows afterwards. Or maybe it was Tomasz she couldn't shake out of her mind, or Sam, or the boy who killed himself. Into my own consciousness came, unbidden, a memory of Dad standing in his living room, unable to tell me where he was and near to tears. I had no clever answers to offer my daughter.

Instead I said, 'Ian must be glad to have Matty back.'

Something softened in her face. 'Uh-huh.'

'And Matty pleased to see his daddy.'

'Yeah.'

'He must have missed him so much.'

'Don't push it, Mum,' she said, but without real heat. Then, 'Here we are. This is it.'

We were standing outside a large cream and orange Edwardian villa. 'Can we go in?'

'The estate agent's due any time now. What do you reckon so far?'

'Fine,' I said, trying not to look at the unloved square of lawn. 'It's a quiet road. I can't imagine the Catholics get very rowdy.'

She put down my bag and leaned against the coping stones. 'I meant to ask, are you free tomorrow afternoon?'

'Yes. Why? Do you want me to go look at another flat with you?'

'I need to see Grandad.'

To my shame, I almost said, *Why*? 'He's no better, there's no change in him.'

'I want to go anyway.'

'Come round when you're ready, then.'

'Should I bring Matty?'

I gave her a look, mock-despairing. 'What on earth do you think I'm going to say to that, hey?'

At least I got a proper smile out of her.

The day was fine, sharp and bright, and, as if in response, Dad seemed on better form than I'd seen him for a while. He was up in his chair, shaved and dressed, apparently watching the birds on the feeder outside his window. He didn't look up when we came in, but he hasn't done for nearly two years now. I know the way things are with him, though it doesn't stop me hoping.

'You're looking well,' I said, kissing his cheek. Jaz came in behind me with her changing bag in one hand and Matty's reins in the other, plus a carrier of toys and snacks to keep him entertained. I watched as she unpacked, laying out his Duplo first.

'He likes the stones in the yucca pot,' I said, but this time Matty only glanced at the corner, and settled down in the middle of the floor.

Meanwhile Jaz drew out what I thought at first was a large black book, and propped it on the table: speakers for her iPod.

'Are we having music?' I asked, with some slight anxiety. Jaz's tastes could be off-beat.

'Uh-huh,' was all she said.

While she scrolled and fiddled with the cursor, I set to unfastening Matty's reins. He hardly registered my interference, so focused was he on separating two blocks. I thought, That's changed too. He wouldn't have been able to concentrate at that level three months ago. Then, out of the speakers, a ribbon of violin started, so pure it was like a pang of grief.

'Bing Crosby,' said Jaz, 'Pennies from Heaven.'

'Oh, Jaz,' I said. Even Matty paused to listen for a few moments as Bing's low voice cut in over the orchestra.

'Thought it might cheer Grandad up.'

Both of us shifted our chairs round so we were half-facing him, and I took his hand. His eyes stayed fixed on the feeder. 'Matty's here,' I said. 'And Jaz. Come to see you.'

'Plus, I don't like it when it's too quiet,' she said.

'Your generation, you need a soundtrack wherever you go.'

'Silence does my head in after a bit. Doesn't it yours?'

'When you live on your own, you have to make friends with silence. I rather like it.' Bash bash, went Matty. 'Although, when he was away . . .'

The music played on, sweetly.

'I've been thinking,' said Jaz, 'about when I was little. Did you know, Nick was brought up by his grandparents? His mum and dad were missionaries. Like Victorians or something. And where they were working wasn't always safe, so they left him with his mother's parents, which was fine with him because he loved it there. He says that family is the most important thing there is, after God. Family's a gift. People don't appreciate what they have.'

Matty was gathering his blocks together, corralling them into a pile in the centre of the carpet.

Jaz said, 'I think I can understand now what you were trying to do, Mum. When you let Ian see Matty behind my back.'

A fearful hope surged inside my chest. 'Can you?'

'I told Nick about it, and he said I hadn't thought it through. What might have happened if I'd shut Ian out completely, how he might have retaliated. The damage. To all of us. I couldn't see that.'

'That's what I was worried about; I tried to tell you.'

'I know. You still shouldn't have done it, but—'

'And David. David was only ever trying to help.'

'He's just a git.'

'Why do you hate him so much, Jaz?'

'Why do you *like* him so much, Mum?'

She held my gaze till I looked away.

Suddenly Dad cleared his throat and we both jumped. Bing was 'Ac-Cent-Tchu-Ating the Positive', a track I knew was one of his all-time favourites.

'Gosh, can you remember Grandad singing this in his shed?' I asked. Jaz still eyed me suspiciously, but I carried on. 'It was a summer afternoon, probably a couple of years after Grandma died; you'd have been about eight. He was making some sort of rack for his beans, working with the door open because the day was hot, and you and I were on the lawn making daisy chains, except you couldn't because your nails were bitten to nothing and you couldn't split the stems. There'd be a burst of hammering, then a couple of lines, then more hammering. It made you laugh. And later on you were asking about the picture on the syrup tin he used to keep his nails in, and he told you the story of Samson killing the lion, and the bees making a nest in the carcase.'

'*And out of the strong came forth sweetness*. God, yes, I do remember that. I used to love going to Grandad's. He always did fun things. I was never in trouble at his house.' She was leaning over the arm of the chair, in a posture that reminded me of how she used to ask for a bedtime story. 'I wish I could remember more from that time. You think you'll never forget something, or that it'll never end, and the next minute it's gone. Why do we let the good stuff slip away?'

'That's why I take my photographs,' I said. 'Pin down the past.'

Jaz closed her eyes. 'Tell me about when I was little, Mum.'

'What about it?'

'Anything, really. I want to see if I can get it back again.'

So I told her, off the top of my head, some random memories: taking her when she was a toddler to Eileen's, and finding her in the kitchen eating cat biscuits from the bowl; about Mojo hanging by his teeth off Phil's thumb; her first words, how she learned to swim in the sea at Weymouth, the llama in Paignton Zoo that spat down Eileen's coat, the time she made a Hallowe'en mask and accidentally cut a hole in the bedspread beneath. While my dad gazed out of the window, and Matty sorted and re-sorted his bricks, the past pulled up the past the way roots pull up soil.

In turn she told me about wetting her knickers once when we were on a picnic, and throwing them in a hedge. How she'd watched Phil pour Coke on next door's lawn, and how he'd sworn her to secrecy and given her five pounds to keep schtum. How she'd killed my lobivia cactus out of revenge because it had spiked her. She talked about seeing us in the audience at the school play, and how it had distracted her but she'd also been pleased we were there. She recounted a sledging session with Eileen, and how Nat had once tried to get her to bleach the ends of her hair with Toilet Duck.

Matty moved between us, sometimes offering Duplo to me, sometimes to his mum. At one point he dropped a piece and, in pursuing it, he bumped into Dad's knee. He might as well have walked into a table leg, and I ached for the acknowledgement that would never come: the freckled hand coming down to caress the curls, the friendly word.

'Let's not leave Grandad out,' I said.

'No.'

Jaz moved her chair again till it was very close, and spoke into his face. 'Do you remember when you let me practise bandaging on you, Grandad? And I did your arm in a sling and I made you keep it on all through teatime?'

'I didn't know about that,' I said.

'Oh yeah. I wanted to do him up like a mummy, head to toe, but there wasn't enough bandage.'

'Otherwise he'd probably have let you do it.'

'And those pigeons,' she went on, speaking loudly as though he was deaf. 'Do you remember taking me to see your friend's racing pigeons? We had to go down this long path between people's gardens and then there was a massive shed, and all this noise coming out. You said it sounded like a bunch of Grandma's friends, tutting and moaning.'

'Car,' said Matty. 'Car, Mummy.'

Jaz indicated over her shoulder at the bag on the floor. 'Oh, could you get it out for him?'

'Of course.'

I knelt down and opened the bag, and Matty shuffled in next to me. Together we made a performance of peering inside. 'Uh-oh, I think there's a mouse in here,' I said, making my hand scuttle under the canvas. 'Watch out!'

When he giggled, I whipped my hand out and tickled him so that within seconds I had him shrieking with laughter, bucking and flailing against me, butting me in the chest with his head. I put my arms round his solid little body and squeezed him to try and restore some calm, but he still wriggled like a demon. 'Watch out,' he said, making his own mouse and aiming it at my stomach. 'Watch out, Nanna!'

'Honestly, you two,' went Jaz, behind me. Part of me was screwing myself up against a telling-off, but she only said, 'Get that car of yours, Matty, then you can run Nanna's mouse over if it starts being naughty again.'

I laughed, partly from relief.

You let her rule you, I heard Phil say again. Yes, I thought, perhaps I do. Perhaps other grandmothers don't tread on eggshells the way I have to. But I'm so damn grateful to have Matty back, and so petrified she'll take him away again, that I'll do anything it takes not to rock the boat. She can impose any condition she likes. I'll drain the pond dry, cut my hours at work, have him any nights she decides, at the drop of a hat. She only has to name her terms. If that makes me feeble, then that's too bad.

I knew now there was no way I could carry on seeing David. His gentle kindness and support belonged to a very particular time that was gone. Already some of the memories were patchy and imperfect, though I could still conjure the modulations of his voice, his confident stride, the detail of his mouth and eyes. I should have taken some pictures of him, but there were too many events and revelations in those months that I didn't want to acknowledge; photographs would have fixed them more firmly into reality. Jaz was right, the bad images would hang around longer, but it would all pass away eventually. Everything would go. New hurts and new happinesses would overlay each other, till the weeks without Matty, with David, were almost nothing. That was the way it had to be.

'And you used to have this joke about the coasters I made for you,' Jaz was telling Dad, 'the little felt ones with the cross stitch round the edge. You'd pick one up and you'd go— Oh, Mum, look! *Look!*'

Panic shot through me as Jaz bent forward. What could she see on my father's face? A heart-attack? A stroke?

She drew back from him and turned to me, her face triumphant. 'He's rocking himself to the song, Mum. He can hear it. He knows it.'

'*Don't fence me in*,' crooned Bing.

'Dad?' I said, touching his fingers lightly. His eyes were still vacant, but there was no doubt about it, he was marking time to the music.

'Isn't it fantastic?' Jaz said. 'Has he ever done this before?'

'No,' I said.

We sat entranced by the tiny movement of his shoulders, as though we were witnessing some incredible feat of gymnastics.

Meanwhile Bing spoke of wide skies and blissful solitude, of a life at ease and without boundaries or grief.

The song played out its jaunty amble, and I let myself imagine, for those two minutes, my dad's spirit roaming free across any landscape he cared to call up. Inside his silence, he must still be moored by a thread of memory; not floating, lost and nowhere. Even if he wasn't with us, he was himself, somewhere.

A weight lifted in me for the first time in ages.

'I have my uses, don't I? I'm not just a thorn in your side,' said Jaz over the closing chords. She passed me a tissue from Dad's locker, and I dabbed at my eyes.

'Rewind it, oh please, rewind it.'

'See,' she said, bending once more to the iPod, 'how something good can happen even after you've given up hoping?'

It wasn't till hours afterwards that I saw the irony of what she'd said. And I don't think Jaz got it at all.

CHAPTER 33

Photograph 352, Album Three

Location: Carol's dining room

Taken by: Carol

Subject: Eileen's birthday. A triple celebration because the biopsy seems clear, she's been promoted at work, and today she's twenty-one for the nineteenth time. Jaz brings in plates and cutlery, sets them down, and Eileen catches her hand playfully. 'Why do you bite your nails?' she asks.

Jaz raises her eyebrows. 'Why don't you get your roots re-touched?'

'Touché,' laughs Eileen.

At the far end of the table, Carol's stomach turns over with jealousy.

'You're so good with her. I bet she wishes you were her mother,' she says that evening, when Jaz is in bed and both women have had a fair bit to drink.

'Don't be daft,' says Eileen. 'I'm more like a substitute granny. I just hover on the edges. I'd be a useless mother. I'd be a useless wife.'

'You would not,' protests Carol. She'd like to know why Eileen thinks this, and also why there have been so very few

boyfriends over the years. After all, she dated at school. This is a bright, sparky, good-humoured woman with a decent figure and all her own teeth. 'Not the marrying kind, your Eileen,' Carol's mother once remarked. Meaning what? Now, under this friendly gauze of drunkenness, might be the time to probe. But in leaning forward to pursue her point, Carol knocks her glass off the chair arm. By the time they've mopped up and re-poured, the moment's gone. Some instinct tells her not to return to it.

It was only when I came to trawl through my hard drive to make up a special album, a thank you to Jaz, that I realised how many photographs I'd actually taken of Matty. Already there were hundreds.

Of my own first twenty-three months of life there existed just two snaps. One was a studio portrait of me as a baby, which my mother only had done because a friend was getting one of her little girl and wanted the company. The other shows me as a toddler in a knitted pixie cap with ear flaps, and an A-line coat. I'm holding onto my father's hand and we're outside church watching a neighbour's wedding. Heaven knows who took the photograph, or how we came by a copy.

It's difficult not to feel hard done by when I flip between that early album and the most recent. My childhood versus Matty's. There *are* snaps from the Fifties and Sixties, but they're pretty much all holiday vistas, rarely troubled by human figures. Very occasionally the minute form of my mother appears at the bottom of a sweeping landscape or a historical monument. Later on I pop up in a couple of beach shots, once underneath an archway in Ludlow Castle, and in the entrance to the Blue John Cavern. But the ordinary, everyday activities – the sort of thing I snap Matty doing, and treasure – never merited recording.

I just don't think there was the same level of interest in children then. Eileen and I used to play in the quarry, and round the lonely deep pond in the middle of Copper's Field, and clamber over farm equipment and throw branches at pylons. What freedom, you might say, how lucky we were. I know for a fact, though, that a lot of my personal liberty stemmed from my mother's indifference. Stop ironing and play a game? Switch off the vac and go for a walk? Don't be soft. She'd no more have got down on her knees to be a growly lion than she would have performed a striptease down the nave of St Stephen's. The nearest she and I ever came to spending quality time was when I became old enough to learn baking, sewing and cleaning (and there's not much entertainment to be had out of a wad of Duraglit, I can tell you).

What was it about those decades that made mums and dads so blasé? My mother thought I was mad to rush to Jaz as soon as she cried. Couldn't understand why I was cutting trailing ribbons off her baby clothes, shifting bottles of bleach out the way, screwing the bookcase to the wall. 'You wonder how any of us managed to make it through infancy,' she used to scoff. *Your bloody good luck*, I'd think.

I let myself be frightened; stoked it, revelled in it. My reasoning was, if I remembered to be consciously grateful for Jaz from the moment she was born, then some Higher Power might recognise my appreciation and keep her safe.

I realise now you can't make bargains like that. Fate laughs in the face of such tactics.

I asked David to meet me by Pettymere Lake. I couldn't face seeing him in private, where heaven knows what might get said – or in a public place like a restaurant, with other people listening in. The wide bowl of the Moss was the only space I felt I could cope with.

We were both early, but I'd got there first and was able to watch him walk from the car park, round through the bare trees and across the bridge to the bench where I was sitting. I'd rehearsed a hundred lines and still I didn't know what to say. As he came towards me, his hands in the pockets of his big overcoat and a scarf at his neck, my mind went as blank as the sky. I was all October cloud and chill.

When he reached the bench, he didn't kiss me or say any kind of greeting. He sat down next me, his eyes on the lake.

'Shall I begin?' he said after a few moments.

Pointless to pretend I didn't know what he meant. I nodded.

In cool, straightforward terms, David spelled out what I'd been about to say: that I couldn't contemplate a relationship with him because I was scared of my daughter.

'It sounds so cowardly when you put it like that,' I said.

He made no comment.

'Let me try and explain,' I said. 'It's not just that I *love* Matty – obviously I do. It goes right beyond that. When I'm with him, it's almost as though I'm – I'm taken out of myself. I don't mean he makes me young. He makes me *no* age, and I can act how I want, I don't have to watch the implications of every damn thing I say. I see the world through his eyes and it's new and magical, and we're discovering it together. I go into the garden and Matty's pointing out, oh, spider webs, as though they're the most brilliant creation ever, and it lifts me right up. It's a kind of energy he gives off. Or happiness. I'm recharged. When he was away it was . . . well, you know what it was like. I was lost. A really important part of me was missing. So I daren't contemplate being without him again, I really daren't. I don't know what I'd do.'

'I can't possibly compete with that,' he said.

'You're Matty's grandad. Don't you feel the same way?'

'I don't think I do, no. Not to the same degree. I love my grandson, too, of course, but not so – ferociously.'

What had Phil said? *He's not your child. You're obsessed.* Why could neither of them understand?

I tried a different tack.

'OK, look at it this way, David. Are you prepared to risk all the ground we've won?'

'It wouldn't come to that.' He spread his palms in a dismissive gesture. 'I know what you're trying to do here: bargain with the future. Sacrifice one happiness against another. But it doesn't work like that. You can have both.'

'I wish I could be so confident.'

'Try it, Carol.'

Dead leaves lay clumped round our feet, rotting into blackness; bare branches scraped against each other.

'You know,' he went on, 'some people would say you've hung me out to dry.'

'That's not fair!'

'Tell me, what is fair about this business?'

On the other side of the lake an elderly couple walked a dog, a retriever or a golden labrador, which ran back and forth excitedly along the water's margin. As I watched, the woman stopped and spoke to her companion, and in response he held out his arm to her while she leaned against him and shook a stone from her shoe. It was one of those small, tender, everyday gestures that you take for granted when you're in a relationship, but which viewed from the outside can strike you through your breastbone with longing.

'I feel terrible enough as it is,' I said. 'I *do* understand what you did for me over the summer, of course I do. Do you honestly think I've forgotten the phone calls and chats and meals? The fact you drove me all the way down to see Tomasz and back again, found out all that information on legal rights, offered me money? I will *never* forget those things. How you talked Ian round. Jaz and I couldn't have managed without you. I count my blessings every day that you were there to help us through. Whatever else, please don't think I'm not intensely grateful.'

'It's not gratitude I'm after.'

'This is hurting me, too.'

'And I'm supposed to be pleased by that?'

At every turn he blocked me. The lines I'd prepared, I didn't dare deliver. I sat there with the cold slats of the bench digging into my back, feeling like the meanest woman born. My only consolation was my own, deserved, pain.

I said: 'You know, I spent two dozen years married to a man who never listened. Unless you've lived in a relationship like that, you have no idea how lonely it is. Every serious conversation I ever started, he'd derail with his jokes and daft asides, till eventually I stopped bothering; I used to get more sense out of Jaz. And that was in the days when we were getting on, never mind what came later. Then I started talking, really talking, to you, and I found I could tell you things I'd not told anyone since Eileen died.'

'But isn't that exactly—'

'Wait,' I said. 'Let me finish. It's worked the other way, too. I've got so much out of listening to you. Some of the things you've said have gone right through me, and changed me. You've made me feel more confident in myself, I've been better at making decisions. Essentially, you've become the best friend I've had in years. Although I know it's more than friendship.' I blushed. 'And I never thought, after Phil—'

Say it, went Eileen. *You owe him*. But I couldn't get the words out.

'You're making me sound awfully altruistic. Do you think I've got nothing back from this relationship, Carol?'

'I don't know.'

'Oh, for God's sake. Why do you imagine Jacky left me? Can you really not guess?' I shifted my gaze away from him, embarrassed. 'It was because I "wouldn't commit". Her words. She was right. I admired her, we got on well, but for me it went no further. She wanted more and she got fed up of waiting. So she went. Like the others. Do you see?'

'Not really.'

'I thought, when Jeanette died, that was it. That I'd been incredibly lucky to have met her and to have had that time with her, and the flipside of that was that I'd never experience anything like it again. Every woman I've dated since then has confirmed that belief. Until you.'

'I don't see why I'm so special. Compared with someone like Susannah.' I meant her long, poetic face, that sleek hair, the expensive coat.

'There you go again. I'll tell you what the difference was: she didn't have your warmth, Carol. I look at you and I see a woman who's natural and instinctive and straightforward and true, and, when you're not tying yourself up in knots over Jaz, damn good company. You don't hold back, or scheme or calculate. There's nothing *artful* about you. You have this tremendous warmth, it just pours out of you—'

'Holds me hostage,' I said.

'Yes, but it *needn't*.'

I laughed bitterly. 'You're the one who believes people are born as they are. Well, I wish I wasn't. I wish I could turn my emotions off. I wish I was cool and calculating and all the rest of it, because it would be a damn sight less distressing, that's for sure.'

At last he lifted his arm and put it round my shoulders, and the simple pressure was so comforting I wanted to cry.

Laverne's voice came through the muddle of noise in my head: *Imagine the hassle of dating again. I'd hate to start over, wouldn't you? The stress of someone moving into your house. Or you moving into theirs. Interfering with your systems, always around you. Seeing you in all states. The s-e-x.* It was true, it would have been hard to begin all that business after so long on my own. I would have been prepared to face those fears for David, though.

I made myself shift away from him, out of reach of his arm. Probably he knew then.

'David, it's taken me a long time to get where I am. Settled, I mean, and calm. I had a difficult marriage, years of trouble with Jaz, this latest upset. Finally I can see a bit of clear water ahead. What I have is enough. And although I do want to be with you – believe me, you have no idea how much – I can't risk losing what I have. I daren't. I really daren't. You don't know my daughter, even now.'

'I see.' He clasped his hands in his lap, a man defeated.

'I'm sorry.'

'Yes, I know you are. Is there anything, anything at all I can say to persuade you?'

'I don't think so.'

'Then I shan't drag this out any longer. It's unpleasant for us both.' He rose and stood, looking down on me. 'Thank you for being honest, at least. I shan't bother you with it again. Next week I'm off to the States for a few months to see my sister, so that should give us all some space to recover. I'm sorry if I've distressed you; that was never my intention. But will you do one thing for me, Carol?'

'What?'

'Will you try and make Jasmine confront what she's done? What she did to you when she took Matty away, and what it's cost you this afternoon? And what she means to you, how much it matters that she's fair and decent in her dealings with you. I don't think she sees any of it, and she needs to.'

'She's not a bad person.'

'Will you speak to her?'

'I can't promise.'

'Then you won't have any peace till you do.'

And he turned and walked away into the trees.

Waste of time crying for the moon, said my mother's voice.

CHAPTER 34

Photograph 67, Album One

Location: outside Phil's mother's terraced house, Tannerside, Bolton

Taken by: Phil

Subject: The other Mrs Morgan, Betty, stands with her arms folded and a cigarette between the index and third finger of her right hand. She reminds Carol slightly of Eileen's mother – a slattern – but where Eileen's mother is built on a large scale, Phil's is little and shrunken. She's older than Frieda, but dresses younger, to ghastly effect.

No one's really expecting this visit to be a success.

Husbandless Betty's on a lower rank to start with, and she knows it. There was never any point in trying to impress. So she doesn't. 'You've to take me as you find me,' she says, elbowing Frieda jocularly in the ribs.

Engagement celebration it may be, but they eat across two folding, clothless tables, while ITV plays in the background. The first course is potted meat barmcakes, during which Betty tells a joke about a man refusing to eat tongue because he doesn't like the idea of anything that's been in an animal's mouth and so asks instead for a nice boiled egg. Frieda absolutely does not laugh; the room is filled with the loudness of her not-laughing. Bob pretends absorption in the exploits of Black Beauty. Phil laughs uproariously, even though he's heard the gag before, because he means to show whose side he's on. He's fed up of Frieda's narrowed eyes scrutinising, finding fault; she must think she's the Queen or something.

When Carol finally gets the joke, she laughs too, and Phil loves her for it.

Dessert is tinned pears plonked in cereal bowls and eaten with soup spoons. By now Phil and Carol have got the giggles and cannot stop. Pear juice comes out of Phil's nose, and despite the pain and disgrace, he remains helpless.

By Sale of the Century*, everyone's had enough and the coats are brought back in. Carol stands looking round the room, tries to imagine through Frieda's eyes the matted shagpile rug, the collection of trolls, the porcelain cat climbing the green brandy glass, the unravelling raffia plant-holder. The Whites are not well-off, by any stretch of the imagination, but they make a better fist of things than this. She feels simultaneously proud of her mother, and ashamed of her.*

'Come again, it's open house,' says Mrs Morgan, flicking ash into a chrome-plated pedestal ashtray. Carol suspects sarcasm, but passes Phil the camera anyway. It's unlikely there will be any more visits between the in-laws, so they'd better commemorate this one.

I pulled the car up outside Phil's place, and sat, considering.

In all the years he'd lived there, I'd never once been inside. There was no need. It wasn't as if Jaz was a kid and needing to be shuttled between households. Phil's new life was all his own, I didn't want any part of it. *I haven't even a washing machine*, went Phil, making me think of a derelict flat I'd seen on TV the night before. What would it be like inside, the place where my husband had chosen to set up home with his spiteful, lumpen mistress? For everything she'd taken with her, would there still be evidence of her decoration, her tastes?

Did I dare go up and ring the bell?

And what if he'd been lying, and she was still there? What in God's name would I do then? For a few moments I let a fantasy run of Penny opening the door and me punching my car keys into her face. *Ha! Weren't expecting that, were you?* Perhaps if I'd carried on like that from the start, kicked and screamed and fought, brawled in the street like a fishwife, I'd have saved my marriage. If I'd wanted a husband brought to heel that way, if I thought he'd wanted such a wife.

I'd have given anything to turn the keys in the ignition now and drive straight up to Chester, and David.

But that was a chapter closed.

I needed to see my ex.

He wasn't expecting me; I didn't want to give him chance to hide anything. As soon as he let me through the door, though, I could see he hadn't been lying.

'It's a mess,' he said.

There were gaps everywhere, and dirty marks along the walls. Sometimes you could guess at what had been there before: some sort of arched dresser in that corner, a bureau or bookshelf along that side. There were dents in the door where it must have opened repeatedly against a table edge. 'How much a month do you spend on car magazines?' I asked because random stacks of them rose up everywhere, some on the floor, others on chairs or balanced on the windowsill. Despite the clutter, the middle of the room felt empty; there was no sofa, though you could see from the hollows in the carpet where one had been. No curtains, either. He followed my gaze. 'I keep meaning to get a blind,' he said. 'This weekend. Maybe. I don't spend that much time in here.'

The kitchen wasn't as bad as I expected in that, although the drainer was full, the sink was empty and clean, the lino swept.

'I'll get sorted in the end,' he said.

'I thought you said she'd taken the washing machine.'

'It's new. I wasn't going to start mauling with launderettes. Funny, in some ways, it's quite nice to have everything stripped away. Makes you re-evaluate what you need. It's almost like you could start again.' He looked hopefully in my direction.

'Or not.'

'Yeah, well.'

There were only tall stools to sit on. I tried perching on one but it felt unnatural and exposed so I got up again and stood, shuffling my feet.

'Where's she gone?'

'She's at her mum's. That's where she was headed, first off. Although she might have gone on somewhere else, I'm not sure. It's nowt to do with me any more. She can go camp on the moon as far as I'm concerned.'

'So that really is it?'

'It really is.' He licked his lips nervously. 'Listen, do you want to come through?' I wasn't sure what he meant. Then it clicked he was talking about the bedroom. 'Only I'm all set up there. This is no good, in here. I promise, no funny business.'

He was inviting me to see the room where he'd lain with Penny.

For a second I was too appalled to answer, but I didn't want him to see that. 'I came to give you the latest on Jaz,' I said.

'About Ian mending her hot-water tank? Yeah, she told me. Hopeful, eh? She was round earlier.'

'What, here?'

'She dropped in for half an hour with Matty. I played bowls with him, Matty-style. You know, crash, fling, wallop, thump.' He nodded at a small cardboard box that I hadn't noticed before because it was tucked between the bin and the wall. The flaps of the box were pushed half-open by a selection of cheap toys, bright and out of place in this shabby kitchen. 'She'd never come round when Pen was living here, but now she's popping in every week or so. I keep that lot for the entertainment of his lordship.'

'Oh,' I said. 'Great, that's great.' It shouldn't have been a surprise that Jaz was visiting her dad, that Matty was getting to know his grandad better. It was a good thing. It just felt odd.

'Come on,' he said. 'Let me take you through.'

And suddenly the compulsion to see the life he'd led without me was overwhelming.

'OK,' I said, shrugging in case he thought it was a big deal.

When I saw the bedroom I understood at once why the lounge was so neglected. This room was almost twice as big, with a (curtained) bay window, a two-seater sofa, TV, computer workstation. It was moderately tidy, too, though the television screen was dusty and the window panes could have done with a wipe.

'You have made yourself at home, haven't you?'

'It's all right.' Phil seemed pleased, shyly proud.

I made myself turn and look at the bed.

'That's new too,' he said. 'Brand new.' He walked over to the swivel chair by the monitor and sat down. 'You won't find anything of hers anywhere.'

'Makes no odds to me.'

'I'm only saying. It's all how I want it now. Everything around me, to hand. I can put something down and it stays there. Hey, I've even a mini-fridge next to the bed. In fact, do you fancy a can?'

He urged the chair forward on its rollers and leaned down to open the fridge door. 'Ice cold, yeah? It's really good.'

His naked delight amused me. 'No, thanks.'

'Oh, go on. You used to love a cider. When we were first married, it was your tipple of choice . . . Do you remember the White Swan in Alnwick? That swanky dining room that had come off an old ship? I can see you now, in your leather coat, all those grand fittings round you, sipping half a pint of Woodpecker. Yeah? You remember that, Carol?'

I did. As soon as he'd mentioned it, I could see the wood panelling and the gracious columns, the thick red carpet and the snowy tablecloths. Afterwards we'd gone for a walk up to the castle where he'd run about the grounds, re-enacting scenes from Robin Hood, till an elderly couple told him off. So then he stalked them, pulling faces, till they stropped off to the car park and we collapsed, hysterical with laughter.

'Sure you won't have a little sip?' said Phil, waggling the can at me.

'Oh, go on, if it'll shut you up. But I can't have much, I'm driving.'

He grinned, and tossed the can over to me. I settled into the sofa and tried to ease back the ring-pull without the contents exploding. Phil selected a bottle of Stella for himself.

He said, 'It is weird, though, isn't it?'

'How do you mean?'

'Well – life. How are you, in yourself, Carol? What are your plans?'

'Keep my head down, now Matty's back. If I can just untangle things between Jaz and Ian.'

'Yeah. I meant, how are *you*, though?'

'I'm all right. Don't try and be clever.'

'I'm not. I'm only asking.' He sighed. 'Looking back to when you were starting out, you know, in your twenties and such, did you have any idea your fifties were going to be like this?'

'Like what?'

'A bit of a fucking shower.'

'Speak for yourself.'

'Aw, come on. You know what I mean. Is this what you envisaged when you imagined yourself at fifty-odd?'

'What do you think?'

Again he sighed. 'It's a bugger, isn't it?'

The can flexed cold under my palm. 'I always thought your middle age was a time of calm and wisdom,' I said slowly, 'when you'd have everything important in its proper place. I never dreamed there'd be any of this – this upheaval. There are days I feel I don't know who I am, which is ridiculous at my age. Like some confused teenager. I said to someone this week I was a coward, and I waited for them to disagree and they didn't. Served me right.'

'That's bollocks,' said Phil. 'Who was it? Laverne?'

'No one you know,' I said hastily.

'Well, it is bollocks. God, when I think of some women.'

'Don't bring *her* into it.'

'The way you dealt with Jaz growing up . . .'

'You were always criticising me for that!'

'How you coped with your dad's illness, how you supported Eileen at the end. You were a rock. And putting up with me. Even I can see I must have been a tricky sod to live with.'

His expression was so rueful it was almost funny.

'Don't think for one minute that admitting it wipes it all away,' I said sternly.

'As if. Seriously, though, the last thing you are is a coward.'

'I am with Jaz.'

He seemed to consider this; at least he took another long swig of lager, and then stared up at the ceiling rose. 'You're not a coward. But I've told you before, you don't stand up to her like you should. You've got balls, but sometimes you need to strap them on a bit tighter.'

'Charming turn of phrase.'

'It's true. You forget, I've known you since forever. The daft thing is, she'd respect you more if you did take a bit of a harder line.'

He was so wrong. I thought of Jaz's face twisted with fury, her fist gripping Ian's jacket and shaking it like a dog. The memory still made me feel sick.

'I asked Dr Page if she'd got religion – trying to find my bearings. He said not as far as he was aware, but he thought she might have developed a better sense of perspective. Maybe if I understood her more . . .'

'What's to understand?' He waved his bottle. 'Understand yourself, Carol. Put yourself first, for once in your life.'

'Thank you, Marjorie Proops.'

This time it was he who laughed. 'I reckon we could both do with seeing a trick-cyclist. Family therapy. What do you say?'

'Bog off. I do owe you a sort of thank you, though.'

'How's that?'

'Well, you never once said to me, "I told you so", did you?'

'Over what?'

'Letting Ian come round and see Matty. And you had every right.'

He scratched his neck. 'You were trying your best – do you think I'd have done any better? You're the one who knows how people work. I look at our Jaz and I haven't a bloody clue.'

Phil had been edging his chair back across the room till he was by the computer. He wiggled the mouse and, after a few seconds, I heard music.

'Hey, what do you reckon to that?'

'What is it?'

'Shh. Listen.'

A jaunty guitar riff, punctuated by claps, then Marc Bolan's reedy voice: 'Ride a White Swan'.

'Good God, this takes me back,' I said. 'What year was it? Were we still at school?'

'I think so.'

'Yes, we must have been, because I remember Eileen and me going into town after last lesson to buy the single, and being embarrassed because we were in our uniforms. She'd pulled her shirt open and had her tie wrapped round her wrist, I don't know what we must have looked like. And we went to that little record shop in St Andrew's Square, do you remember it? I bet it's long gone now.'

Phil took another swig, wiped his mouth, and said, 'This mess we're in, do you think there's any good to come out?'

'With Jaz and Ian?'

'You and me.'

I put my can down on the carpet. 'Oh, Phil. I'm too tired to argue.'

''Cause it wasn't all bad, was it?'

'No, but the bad bits spoiled the rest.'

'What I'm saying is, though, you don't have to make that the last word. You don't *have* to let the past rule your entire future. We're not the same people we were, even this time last year, are we? Are we?'

I found myself feeling with my left thumb for the tiny dent that still marked my ring finger.

'You think,' he went on, 'what a team we made when we went to fetch Matty back. I'd never have managed without you. I don't think you'd have managed without me. We did it together.'

He stood up, and my heart began to beat faster. Keep away, I thought. But I stayed where I was.

'All I'm asking, Carol, is that you give it some consideration.'

'I have considered it. The answer's no.'

With extreme care he lowered himself down next to me, a man keen not to make any sudden moves. Nevertheless, his hip was against mine, and I felt the contact acutely. 'I'm just trying to be honest with you. I thought it would help if you knew where you stand. No messing, I'm telling you: I'll do anything at all—'

He took my hand. Still I didn't pull away.

'See, the man I was then isn't who I am now, any more than you're that girl in her teens or twenties. You're not, though, are you? And it's madness to let that hang over us when we could make a fresh start. The time's right. Jaz is home, she's back with Ian – kind of – you've got Matty. Everything's how you want it. But you're more than a "grandma" and a "mum" anyway. You have a life of your own.'

I do have a life, I wanted to say. *Don't unbalance it again*. And another part of my brain was saying, *Why did you come round here, Carol? What were you expecting?*

'Are you really saying you want to shut the door on this?' He leaned in and kissed my hair. 'And this?' He put his lips to my forehead. 'And this?' He kissed the side of my mouth. By now I'd closed my eyes to shut him out, but that only made the sensations more intense. His fingertips crept round to caress the back of my neck, circling the top vertebrae, smoothing along the collarbone. A groan stifled in my throat. When someone's that familiar with your body, they know exactly what works.

Stop, oh, stop, I said, but no words came out.

'I tell you, we're different people now,' he said again, breathing into my hair.

You're wrong, I thought. I am that girl in her teens, her twenties, her thirties. I'm fooling with a scarf on the motorway bridge, waiting outside the Odeon, being snogged against a tree, walking up the aisle, crying in your arms, passing you your baby daughter, cracking your photo over the newel post. I'm a blank-faced future me, watching.

He pulled away, and the unexpected action made me open my eyes. His brow was creased with hope.

'Oh, please, Carol,' he said.

At last, the power was all mine.

CHAPTER 35

Photograph: unnumbered – loose inside an old Bunny-Bons toffee tin, Sunnybank

Location: Blackpool

Taken by: Phil

Subject: Eileen leans against an iron railing with the sea at her back. Her hair is blowing about, her fun-fur coat flattened down one side by the strong breeze, and her grin is as wide as the Golden Mile. This weekend she has the Key of the Door; all her life stretches in front of her, starting with this coming Saturday night.

Newly-married Carol should be standing next to her, in her long leather coat, only she's been cut off the photo. You can just make out the crook of her elbow, and the fluttering end of a belt.

It was my last chaotic area. This afternoon I was determined to have one big push, clear the shed, and then at last that small aspect of my life would be under control. As usual I was equipped with my three sets of bin bags – Keep, Throw and Charity Shop – and this time my mood was ruthless. Space had to be forged, my house reclaimed from the past. A new era beckoned.

I dragged the first box towards me and flipped it open.

There's a displacement activity, if ever there was one, went Eileen.

You'll be telling me to take a cold shower next, I said to her.

When you live alone and don't date, your body learns to accept the situation, and deals with it accordingly. The dying days of my marriage had run my libido down for me; nothing damps your sex drive like living in simmering resentment month in, month out. Then, after the divorce came Jaz's illness, plus the stress of losing both Eileen and, after a fashion, my dad. By the time I felt anything approaching normal, my hormones had shut down. Sex seemed an activity I'd grown out of, the idea of me stripping naked in front of a man ludicrous, remote and petrifying.

Now, though—

Are you really saying you want to shut the door on this? I heard Phil say again. And my own response, *I'm not taking Penny's leftovers*.

'Not worthy of you, Carol,' he'd said. 'Pen left because she couldn't compete. We both know it's always been you. That's why I couldn't leave you, why you had to kick me out. I didn't want to go – I've missed you like hell. It's been crap.'

This kiss should have been David's had come into my head and I thought, If I spoke that out loud, it would really hurt you. 'Tell me again why Penny left,' I'd said.

Something clattering onto the floor made me jump. In moving the box I'd disturbed a pile of refuse sacks, and they'd been gradually sagging against one of the shelves, shoving the contents towards the edge in the manner of one of those coin waterfall arcade games. A tin of Back to Black lay rocking on the concrete with its cap off.

I looked down at the box I was supposed to be sorting. It was full of crumpled newspaper, which I knew meant crockery:

Dad's. There was no need to go through it because I remembered the kind of thing he kept in his kitchen cupboards towards the end – mis-matched pieces from the Sixties and Seventies, ugly and utilitarian. He'd made me take the best when Mum died, said he was frightened of breaking them. Of course I should have slung this lot as soon as he moved out, but I couldn't bear to. Getting rid meant he was never coming back.

But he wasn't coming back. He was where he was, ambling across some great twilit plain towards a dark horizon. With one hand I opened the door, and with the other I pulled the box right out of the shed onto the flags. Perhaps a charity shop could use old plates and mugs, or a homeless shelter. Jaz might know of somewhere.

The next bag was his clothes. When I cleared out Dad's wardrobe, it seemed to me he must have kept every garment he'd ever worn in his life. The care home's always sweltering, so we only took a handful of outfits, light summer wear, and bought him new where necessary. But here were his old overalls, stained with creosote, and his gardening boots, and his rough tweed jacket. He used to sit in that jacket rolling cigarettes, I could see him now. Once he caught me on the lawn with a square of blotting paper, trying to construct a tube out of bits of grass and clover. Not long after that, he quit smoking.

The box behind, when I tore it open, was solid with books: Alistair MacLean, George MacDonald Fraser, Dennis Wheatley, the old familiar covers. I wasn't getting rid of these, for all the spines had softened and the pages swelled. Dad loved his paperbacks. I felt guilty for leaving them out here in the damp for so long. *The Ka of Gifford Hillary* I lifted out, and it flopped open unresistingly. 'They make paper out of rags,' I remembered him saying. The edges of the pages were furry, like felt.

Underneath the top layers I found, not action novels, but a more eclectic mix of sizes, conditions, bindings and genres. Strange books I didn't recognise. Perhaps Phil had packed these away. *The Grapes of Wrath*, I uncovered; *Brave New World*, *Sons and Lovers*, *Middlemarch*. They had me frowning because, to tell the truth, I couldn't recall anyone reading the classics at Pincroft. But these had been read, you could tell by their state. *A Room of One's Own* was positively tatty, dog-eared, the picture of the woman on the front creased right down the middle. Delving deeper, I found Doris Lessing's *The Golden Notebook*, A. S. Byatt's *The Virgin in the Garden*, Fay Weldon's *Down Among the Women*. There was something severe and grand about these titles, despite their dated fonts and colour-ways, as if they knew I hadn't read them and held me to account for it. One had been covered with brown paper in place of a jacket; when I opened it to find out what it was – Margaret Drabble's *The Millstone* – I saw, not my father's, but my mother's name inked possessively on the flyleaf. I put it down and picked up an ex-library copy of *The Selfish Gene*, only to find she'd gone further, marking sections with pencil underlinings and crabbed, illegible notes. Frieda White versus Richard Dawkins.

I hadn't known her as a reader. When had I last seen her absorbed in a book? All I could conjure at that precise moment was my mother up a stepladder shouting for curtain clips; holding her forearm under the cold tap where she'd caught herself with the iron; hacking viciously at the lilac which hung over our front path. Or sunk against the hospice pillow, her drip swaying on its tall stand. They might almost have been memories of someone else's mother, or a character from a drama on TV. At the very bottom of the pile was a battered paperback edition of *The Second Sex*, which I put gingerly to one side, as if it were a grenade.

To my relief, the next box turned out to be not Dad's, but Jaz's: schoolbooks and ringbinders and coursework folders. I flicked one open and my heart gave a twinge at the rounded, childish handwriting, at the doodles in the margin of cartoon bombs and eyes and wasp-waisted women. 'What would Jaz say if she could see us now?' I'd asked Phil as he tried to kiss my neck.

'Stop thinking about her,' he'd said. 'You always think about her first. Think about yourself.'

I managed to dispatch two more boxes (old books and ornaments, tea towels and bedding) and three bags of clothes before Phil intruded again. This time it was a memory of very early sex, a clumsy attempt to use a condom that wouldn't roll down because it was on inside out. I honestly thought I'd die of embarrassment, but he made me laugh, and it was OK. It was always OK in those first years (and, God, we were young when we started out). He was still the only man I'd ever slept with. That counted for something, whether I liked it or not.

What would David say about that? If we were in a room, kissing, and I broke away and said, 'You should know, I've only ever been with my husband.'

I needed to keep telling myself, though. He wasn't mine: Phil was.

Take all the time you need, Phil had said. *I'm going nowhere*.

I hadn't slept with Phil, but I knew I was going to, sooner or later.

By the time I'd stopped for lunch and washed up and put away, I knew I only had another four hours before dark. The shed floor was now clear and I was about three-quarters of the way through the mezzanine section; this despite the voices in my head keeping up a hysterical and disjointed commentary throughout. I replayed Eileen's advice about how I should treat Phil's affair like a battle, and on no account let this other woman take him off me. 'You've come too far, you belong together,' she used to say. So un-Eileen-like, in many ways. Then it was Moira, talking about her ex and how she blamed herself for the break-up because she got obsessed with wanting a baby. And Faith from the gym, confiding to a general audience that her husband complained she put the children first, which is what Phil always said I did. I still couldn't see how that was wrong, so perhaps I had been a bad wife. Perhaps I did bring it on myself.

Towards the end wall of the boarded-off section I discovered a small disaster. A drum of varnish Phil had used to renovate the bedroom floor had fallen over and emptied itself. Everything in the immediate vicinity, I could see at a glance, was ruined – the fan heater, the fish tank, Mojo's cage, the spare shower head. Worse than that, the varnish had soaked into the hardboard and dripped through the join.

I came down to investigate the damage below. This was an area of the shed I hadn't bothered looking at before because it was all Phil's odds and sods, tins and jars of loose screws, nails, nuts, staples, bolts, drill bits, unidentifiable twists and fragments of metal. 'Don't *ever* move my gear around,' he'd warned me repeatedly. But it was clear that a lot of it was now covered in a film of varnish, and that the contents of the top two shelves at least would need throwing. There was no point leaving it when I had a rubbish pile going. I picked up an open Walkers Shortbread tin and tipped it experimentally. Nothing inside moved. The mess of panel pins was stuck solid, like flies in amber.

So I set to, working my way down the wall where the varnish had flowed in a sticky river, tossing into the centre of the floor anything that was beyond redemption. If Phil had wanted any of it, I reasoned, he should have come and taken it years ago. Sealant tube was welded to bracket, brush to bottle, sanding disc to match pot. In one corner a batch of oily rags had soaked up some of the varnish, and now they were stuck fast against the wall, and crispy. I had to pull hard to get them to lift, and even then they only came because the varnish cracking tore some of the threads. I was thinking, Phil'll need to get a chisel to this, when they ripped completely away, and I half-lost my balance and knocked a tin nearby right off.

It seemed to fly in slow motion, while my hand swiped ineffectually, striking against glass jars, skinning my knuckle on the sharp metal edge of the shelf. The tin crashed to the floor and the lid popped open, spilling out the contents. *Riley's Bunny-Bons* said the ancient label, over a badly scratched picture of a rabbit in a top hat and spats. Pre-war toffees, it must once have held. Now it seemed to be full of postcards and clippings.

I squatted down, turned over the first piece of paper.

It was an old photo, from the early Seventies, of Eileen and Phil together. He was dressed in a Homburg and a mackintosh, while she had on a man's pinstriped suit and a bowler hat. I recognised the occasion at once: Stackholme Grammar End of Year Review, and the Social Classes sketch from *Frost Over England*. They'd cast me as Common Man, in my dad's flat cap and muffler, and I remember it wasn't a role I was very comfortable with because it seemed to me they were mocking people like Dad, decent ordinary folk who kept their heads down and worked hard and were the backbone of the country. Every time I had to say the line 'I know my place', it made me wince. Phil and Eileen hadn't been able to see the problem. In fact, they found rehearsals so wildly hilarious I used to wonder how we'd get through the actual performance.

I should have been on the end of this photograph, but someone had cut me off.

I drew the print aside, only to find that under it was another photo of Eileen, this time on her own, in our garden.

Then Eileen in her Vauxhall Viva, waving through the windscreen.

And underneath that, there were dozens more pictures of Eileen, not one of them put there by me.

Nowhere is as lonely as the middle of the night. While Matty slumbered upstairs, I sat on my living-room carpet reviewing the hundred thousand lies inside my photo albums. All those Eileens, smug with secrets. All those Phils with their scheming sideways glances and their hearts entirely full of self.

At ten I'd called my ex-husband and told him what I'd found.

'Was it Eileen, or you?' I asked.

'I haven't looked at them for years,' he said.

'Was it Eileen, or you?'

'Nothing happened, I swear.'

'Why should I believe you?'

'It just didn't. As God's my witness. On my life. On Jaz's life.'

'Don't you *dare*!'

'I'm trying to get you to see. I never so much as kissed her, nothing. She wouldn't let me. I made a pass, she said no. That's it.'

'And the photos?'

'I had a little crush for a couple of years.'

'If she'd said yes?'

No answer.

And there I'd sat, feeling I should have been relieved, when in fact hearing the truth was more painful than I could have imagined.

'Don't blame her,' Phil had said.

I'd slammed the receiver down on him.

Twenty-six pictures he'd stored in his bloody tin. In some he'd physically sheared me off with scissors, so I was no more than an arm, or a scrap of material, or a shadow. Once, unforgivably, he'd cut away Jaz. I never knew betrayal could go so deep.

Eileen stared back at me, sometimes darkly, sometimes sunny and mischievous. There she was holding my arm, my wedding bouquet, my baby girl. You knew about this, I said to her, and you kept quiet. Why? Eileen tipped her head to one side and smirked at something lost to the camera. At least when you were dying, you could have told me then, I said.

What purpose would that have served? she said.

I'd have known where I stood!

You weren't ready.

It would have been honest of you, then.

Is honesty always the best policy, Carol?

I flung the album from me by its spine but I couldn't stop the photographs chattering. They had their own agenda.

CHAPTER 36

Photograph: unnumbered, loose in a Bunny-Bons toffee tin

Location: Grimeford Lane, Tannerside

Taken by: Phil

Subject: nothing except the empty road, stretching up towards the moors.

Phil wants this photo for a souvenir. It's the best he's going to get. Eileen refuses to be in it, doesn't want to be here, is livid with him. She can't imagine why he'd want a reminder of this day.

She thought she was coming up to help him take pictures of childhood haunts, as a surprise for his wife. 'You invited me here on false pretences,' she rages. 'If I'd had any idea you were going to start spouting this rubbish, I'd never have come near.'

Because he's claiming he's in love with her suddenly, à propos of nothing at all. He's sorry about the lie, but he's desperate.

'Don't be so stupid,' she tells him.

'You know what I'm talking about,' he says. 'You've felt it too. We're two of a kind. When we were at school—'

'When we were at school,' says Eileen dryly, 'you had

every opportunity. But you chose Carol. She thinks the sun shines out of you.'

'What if I made the wrong choice?' he says.

'Too late,' she says.

'It might not be,' he says.

'It is,' she says. 'Sod off.'

Eventually she convinces him to go, and he drives away, watching her grow smaller in the rear-view mirror. He has no idea what he's doing. Is he simply scratching an itch? Is it just a crush, a product of post-wedding-panic? If she'd said yes, would the affair have burned itself out? The years are his to wonder.

Eileen walks alone across the fields to the station and catches the train home.

No one must ever know what it's cost her to turn this man away. You can't help who you fall for; he may be a fool, but he's a bloody handsome one. From the Second Form up, she thinks she's been in love with him. Not that he's ever looked at her in that way. Till now.

She prays she was convincing enough, so that he feels too embarrassed to try again, because she doesn't know if she'll be able to resist him a second time.

It was half-past midnight when I heard my doorbell go. Luckily I was still up, pottering about doing a final tidy because I hate coming down in the morning to a messy room. I can't sleep if I know there's washing not put away.

My heart jumped at the sudden noise. I dropped the pile of tea towels I was holding and ran out into the hall. It crossed my mind that the shape behind the glass might be a criminal, a madman come to rape me in my bed, except from what I understood, such types didn't tend to announce their arrival and formally request entrance. The letterbox opened, a pair of fingers poked through and Josh's voice went, 'Carol? Are you there?'

I let him in at once.

'What in God's name are you up to?' I asked.

He grinned sheepishly. 'I got locked out.'

'Your mother locked you out?'

'Sort of.'

'Is she not in?'

'Oh, she's in.'

I was having some trouble with the idea that if Josh was out after dark, Laverne would be tucked up peacefully in bed. Impossible.

I brought him through and switched the main light back on. Josh was wearing a jacket I hadn't seen before, and his T-shirt was tucked in on one side only. 'You've not been in a fight, have you?'

He shook his head. 'I was round my girlfriend's.'

'I didn't know you had a girlfriend.'

'Yeah, well.'

'Not that one I saw you with at the bridge?' I remembered that sneering female shout, and shuddered inwardly.

'God, no, not her. Sheesh. Not her. Kirsty's *nice*.'

'OK. And where does Kirsty live?'

'Near the park. Bargates.'

'So what happened?'

'That's it.'

'And your mother knows you're out?'

Josh treated that question with the contempt it deserved. 'Can I borrow your front door key, Carol?'

'You went out without a key?'

'No, I have a key, but it's to the back door and Mum's put the bolt on. I left via the front. I failed to think my strategy through.' His face was very open and friendly, the way it used to be when I gave him lifts to school. He might have been asking me to help with a tricky piece of homework.

'But you'll wake her up, she'll hear you.'

'No, she won't, because she's taking sleeping tablets and they knock her out. She had one tonight, I watched her take it.'

'And then you sneaked out?'

'Yup.'

I noticed that all the while he was talking, he was struggling not to smile. I didn't know what to make of it.

'But if she wakes up and I'm not there,' he went on, 'she'll freak. The shock'll send her mental. Then she'll be on tranx as well as sleeping pills.'

That was true enough.

'Oh, honestly, Josh. Right, listen, I will let you in, *this once*, but for Laverne's sake. And I'm not thrilled about being put in this position. You're not in any sort of trouble, are you?'

'Do I look like I've been in trouble?'

'You look a bit drunk, if I'm being honest.'

'I'm not. I've not been near any booze. Smell my breath.' He opened his mouth wide and huffed over me.

'No thanks,' I said, stepping back. All I could pick up were mints and body-spray.

I left him in the lounge while I went to fetch from the kitchen the biscuit tin with Laverne's key inside it. When I came back he was grinning to himself again.

'Hey, do you like shortbread, Carol?'

'Why?'

''Cause I can get you a load from Healey's. A carrier bag full, if you want. They throw them when they get to their sell-by date, and there's nothing wrong with them.'

'I don't want paying,' I said sternly. 'Especially in dodgy biscuits. You know, you're damn lucky I was awake.'

'Mum goes to bed at ten.'

'Well, I had a few things on my mind this evening.' I extracted the key and put the tin down. 'Do you absolutely promise me you've not been doing anything illegal? Because you're putting me in a very difficult situation here.'

Josh hung his head. 'I know. You're a mate, Carol, you really are. I just lost track of time, that's all it was, I swear.'

'And this girl's parents?'

'On holiday.' Again, that smirk.

'You know, you could try asking your mum straight out whether you can go round to your girlfriend's house.'

'I could, couldn't I?'

I held out the key to him. 'Wherever did that good little boy who used to live next door go?'

'He got wazzed off at being pushed around all the time.'

'I see.'

'So he pushed back and found he liked it.'

'And while we're on the subject, that teacher who used to make bother?'

'Oh, the Hungarian? Currently the subject of a formal complaint. With any luck, he'll be suspended, his career in ruins. Couldn't happen to a nicer bloke. I'll post your key back tomorrow.'

'You'll open up and then you'll bring it straight back now,' I said.

I waited on my front step, listened for his trainers crunching along their path, silence, the clicking of metal against metal, his footsteps coming back.

'And if your mum finds out,' I said, 'I shall claim you stole my key. I'm not being held responsible. She'll have my guts for garters.'

He flicked his fringe to one side, roguish in my porch light. 'In that case, you'll just have to stand up to her, won't you? Don't let yourself be bullied, Carol. That would never do.'

Then he turned and disappeared into the dark.

The evening after Matty's second birthday, Ian and Jaz brought him round for his usual Saturday night sleepover. I had everything ready for him, the curtains were drawn and the fire lit.

Ian carried him in, swooping him round the room like a human battering ram before dropping him onto the sofa. This kind of treatment always made me wince to watch, but Matty loved it. For a split second I remembered Phil holding a squealing infant Jaz upside down, the ribbons on her bunches streaming down his trouser legs. Then the image was gone. Matty was standing against the back of the settee, holding up his arms for more.

'How's he getting on with his electronic book?' I asked. They'd bought him a device to help accelerate his reading, a ring-bound contraption with a wand that spoke the words as you pointed at them. Terrifically complicated, it looked to me.

Jaz pulled off her coat and laid it on the chair arm. 'Not shown much interest in it yet. It does say "age three or over", but he's bright, I thought he'd be able to cope with it.'

'Don't wish his time away,' I said. 'He'll be there soon enough.'

'He likes the bead frame you bought him, though. He's never been off that.'

'Wanted it in the bath last night,' said Ian, sitting down opposite her.

'Did he?' Jaz smiled.

'Oh yes. I had to distract him with Squirty Fish.'

'Well, I hope Squirty Fish confined his exploits to the tiles, and not the carpet or the wallpaper like last time. You should have seen the state, Mum.'

'It was him,' said Ian, pointing at Matty. 'He led me on.'

They were laughing together, just like a real family.

'Are you staying for a drink?' I asked hopefully.

A signal passed between them.

'No,' said Ian. 'I have to get off. I'm working tomorrow, this project where they've brought the deadline forward and we're all scrambling to get it finished. So I need to make tracks. Sooner it's started, better chance we have of nailing it.' He ruffled his son's hair, and stood up. 'Bye, Mattster. Be good.'

Jaz stayed where she was. 'See you Tuesday,' she said. Then she saw my expression. 'We came in separate cars, Mum. I'll have a coffee, if you're making one.'

Looking back, I suppose that's the point I should have twigged.

After I'd got Matty in bed, I came down to find Jaz standing by the back window with the light off. She'd opened the curtains and was staring across the garden.

'I was checking out the stars,' she said. 'It's a really clear night.'

'Frosty.'

'I'll say. It was bitter coming over.'

'Has Matty got a hat?'

'Yes, Mum, he's got a hat. And mittens, and a quilted coat and boots and a scarf. So no need to worry.'

'My mother once accidentally locked me out on a night like this, then blamed me. I was too small to reach the door knocker. A neighbour let me in, in the end.'

Jaz snorted. 'She always sounds a bit of a cow, does Grandma.'

'I think she was just one of those people who's born discontented. And maybe I was a disappointment to her.'

'In what way?'

'I don't know. We never talked about things like that. She just gave that impression.'

'Am I a disappointment to you?'

'Oh, love,' I said, 'how could you think so?'

She spoke without turning her head. 'Ian and I are getting a divorce. I'm sorry.'

The stars beyond my daughter's silhouette stayed where they were, unblinking.

'He's OK with that?' I managed to make myself say.

'We've spent a long time talking it over and he can see it's best. I'm not being awkward, Mum. I need to start again. With someone I can trust, if there is anyone out there. I'd never be able to trust Ian again, not totally, and I can't stay in a marriage like that. It would destroy me. I'd rather be on my own.'

Tears threatened, but I fought them back. This was not the time to load her with my distress.

'Matty can see his dad when he wants?'

'Oh, yeah, that's key. I figure it'll be less damaging to him if he grows up knowing we're separated, than if we try again and Ian and I split later. Two houses'll be normal for him because it'll be all he's ever known.'

'You know you'll need to cite this woman in the divorce papers, like I had to do with Penny. You'll have to see her address and everything. It'll rake a lot back up again.'

'Yeah, I know. It's got to be done, though.'

I sat myself down in the armchair.

'You always said I should have divorced when you were little, Jaz. I want you to know that I would have done if I'd seen – the whole—'

'Oh, that's the past, don't beat yourself up about it,' she said carelessly, as if she couldn't hear how those words echoed round the room, rebounding off walls and colliding against themselves till it hurt my head.

Or perhaps she did realise, because she came away from the window and stood by me. Her hand came out of the dimness and touched my shoulder.

'You're being really good about all this. I thought you'd have hysterics or something. Did you already guess?'

History was splitting off into decisions made and not made. Other versions of my life spooled out against the gloom.

She bent and peered into my face. 'Are you OK?'

'Yes.'

'Look, I'm going to pop upstairs and check on Matty,' she said. 'Then we'll talk some more.'

I don't know how long she was gone, it could have been a minute or an hour. When she came down she said, 'Someone's letting off fireworks on the cricket field.'

I glanced over at the window as a spectacular rocket burst, on cue, into a golden chrysanthemum. 'Early for Bonfire Night. Mind you, that seems to last about a fortnight these days.'

Three glittering green stars bloomed, and faded.

'It might be a wedding reception, or a party,' I said. 'Draw the curtain right back so we can see properly.'

'Why don't we go out? I could put the monitor on the patio.'

'We'll freeze.'

'Stick your coat on. I could do with breathing some cold air,' she said.

We leaned over the back fence. The larch lap panels were already glistening with ice.

'You can smell the cordite,' she said, 'or whatever it is.'

'They must have a bonfire, too. You can see the glow.'

Fireworks screeched upward, little bright nuggets tracking across the wide sky, to explode into fleeting brilliance. The night cracked and whistled around us.

'There was something else,' said Jaz, below the whine of

rockets. Her face lit red, then green, then was dark again. 'Sam's been in touch with me.'

'It was when I was looking for you,' I said quickly. 'I was trying any avenue I could think of.'

'What did she tell you?'

'About some of the things that made you leave university.'

'The abortion?'

'Yes.' My breath came out in a puff of white.

Jaz shifted against the fence, and I wondered if I should put my arm round her.

'I know what you want me to say, Mum. You want me to say it was terrible and I was really upset, and it's haunted me forever after.'

'Oh, Jaz, you know I'd *never* wish for that.'

'Didn't you think I'd "let you down"?'

'No! Good grief, no. Just sorry I wasn't there to help you. Have you any idea how it made me feel, as your mother, hearing that you were upset and frightened, and I wasn't with you? There's nothing worse, believe me. You wait till something happens to hurt Matty and you can't make it better. See how that cuts you up.'

'You need to hear how it was,' she said, and it was a kind of challenge.

Smoke hung in a pall over the far gardens, like the remnants of a battle.

'It was dire, Mum, having to go to the clinic. It's quick, the actual . . . but there's a lot of stuff beforehand, talking to people, which churns you up, and then you feel pretty shit for a few days after. I wouldn't have managed without Nick and Steph.'

'They've been good friends to you.'

'You think I don't know that? But the abortion wasn't anything compared with the rest. It was Tom who broke my heart. That's what did the damage.'

'And the boy who died?'

'Sam told you about him too. Oh, God.' She buried her face in her hands. Then she raised her head and said, 'It's like it never goes away. Will it ever go away?'

This time I did touch her arm. She stiffened immediately.

'I don't want your sympathy, I'm just telling you how it was because you need to hear. It was really, really shit. I couldn't think about anything else for weeks, Sam just kept going on and on about Andy dying, and I was sick in case Tom told her what I'd done. But I only lied to Andy because I was desperate to get her out of the way. I thought she quite liked him. I thought if Sam was hooked up, she'd leave Tom alone, and then— None of us knew Andy was ill. And a lot of it was Sam's fault; she didn't have to be so fucking vile with him. Trying to impress Tom, mocking Andy because she thought Tom would find it funny. I actually said to her, "Don't be such a bitch." He didn't deserve it. He didn't deserve any of it. It was so fucking awful, what happened.'

'Oh, Jaz,' I said. 'I can see why you got poorly, keeping all this to yourself.'

'Then, when I came home, you didn't understand.'

'How could I, love? I didn't know! Why didn't you tell me?'

'Because.'

I closed my eyes for a moment, thought again about Andy Spicer's parents standing in that courtroom. But the picture hardly touched me. The instinct to protect my own child obliterated any connection with their pain, to a degree I never could have credited. 'Have you talked about this with Nick?'

'He says it wasn't my fault, people get knock-backs every day but they don't all take their own lives, and how could I have known? That if I'd had any idea of the result, I'd never have taken that course of action.'

'Well, then.'

'But if I hadn't made up the story. I keep coming back to that.'

'Jaz,' I said, feeling for the right words, letting my breath rise and fall in time with hers, 'you have to believe me when I say it was pure horrible awful luck.'

'No, Mum.'

'*Yes*. You might just as well have spoken to Andy and had him laugh in your face or tell Sam to get lost or drink himself into oblivion for two days and then be fine. The leap to – to that particular outcome was one you could never have anticipated. Not everything links up to this person's fault or that person's action. Most events just happen. The idea you can trace them back and make yourself responsible's a fallacy. David taught me that.'

She turned on me. 'Oh, *David*. Well then, it must be true. I suppose you told him what I did at Leeds?'

'Not the private stuff, not the things you hadn't confided to me yourself. Honestly, Jaz! I didn't even tell your dad about the boy who died.'

'Because it was that shameful.'

'No, because there was no need. Who would it have benefited? It's in the past, it's terribly sad but it's done with. As Nick said.'

Rockets were blasting the sky apart in front of us; there was no pause now between explosions. At my side, Jaz was shivering.

'Let's go in,' I said.

'Wait,' she said. 'You know, it's been hard in the past to talk to you about anything upsetting. You're so bloody cheerful, Mum, so bloody brave. Even when your life's falling apart, you're smile, smile, smile. It's outfacing.'

'Seems like I can't do right for doing wrong,' I said.

'I'm only trying to explain.'

An aeroplane passed over the far rooftops, navigation lights winking red and white. 'When you were little, you used to think planes at night were Santa's sleigh,' I said.

'That's a long time ago,' she said. 'Look, the fireworks are over.'

I took her hand and led her across the lawn, back to the house.

CHAPTER 37

Photograph 35, Album One

Location: 22 Manchester Road, Tannerside, Bolton

Taken by: Mr Ainscough from the Black Horse

Subject: the village snow plough, at the junction of Halfacre Lane and Church Street. This is the winter of 1947, and the snow lies in drifts that reach some second-storey windows. When Frieda's mother went shopping this morning, she tripped over the rung on a gas lamp post, that's how deep this snow is. The children have been forced to pick coal off the slag heap on the Brow, while the men cut down hedges and trees to burn. The roads are impassable.

But here comes the plough, so perhaps the worst is over. Two cart-horses pull not only the wooden wedge but half a dozen children, who've been invited to sit inside for ballast. Frieda watches, half-jealous. She's too old for such activities now, although a snowball fight isn't out of the question, especially if it's with a certain young man living six doors down. She fizzes with energy and excitement at the thought.

One thing's for sure: never, never will she moan about

snow, the way old people do. Why they can't see the magic of it is beyond her.

It was with gladness I made up the spare bed for Jaz, unwrapped a spare toothbrush, laid out fresh towels, located Kitten. 'I'm too tired to drive back now,' she said. 'My head's all over the place.'

I said, 'I meant it when I said you could always stay here for a while, till you get yourself sorted. This is your home.'

She closed her eyes. 'I need to be moving forwards, not backwards. So do you, Mum.'

The next morning, while I was feeding Matty his breakfast, she had all my photograph albums out. I picked up straight away a sort of giddiness about her, a relief that last night's confession was out of the way.

'Oh my God, look at this,' she said, as I brought Matty in and plonked him on the sofa.

Reluctantly I craned my neck to see. I'd been avoiding photos recently.

It was a picture of the four of us: me, Phil, Jaz and Eileen, standing on Chester city walls. It must have been a hot day because all of us were in short sleeves and Phil was wearing sunglasses. 'How old were you there?' I asked her.

'Fourteen, fifteen. That was the afternoon you dropped your earring and we had to go all the way back round. We found it, though. It was on the steps by the river.'

I switched on CBeebies for Matty and he settled back, sucking his thumb. 'Who took the picture, then?'

'Some old granny in a sheepskin coat. Do you not remember? Dad said she must have been walking round with an ice pack strapped to her vest.'

The day was a void as far as I was concerned. 'Eileen looks pleased with herself.'

Jaz went to turn the page, but I stopped her. 'What?' she said.

'It's just—' Phil's real expression was hidden by the glasses. Eileen stood, honest-faced, her arm draped round Jaz's shoulder.

'What, Mum?'

'Sometimes I think she'd have made a better mother for you.'

Jaz glanced my way. 'You're not serious?'

'You got on better with her, a lot of the time.'

'Oh yeah. You know what she used to say to me? That if I'd been hers, she'd have kicked me out on the streets. Handed me a washbag and a tenner and told me to sod off.'

'She didn't say that.'

'She bloody well did. She was a laugh, Eileen, but pretty useless in the maternal department. Once I asked her advice about some girls at school—'

'When?'

'You know. When I was getting bother, when you went in and saw the Head. Not long after this photo, as it happens. Half of that mess was Eileen's fault, because she told me to fight back so I did and I got into more trouble than the bullies. It was the crappest tip ever.'

'You confided in her, rather than me?'

'Only because she overheard me and Nat talking.'

'And she didn't think to let me in on it.'

'No,' said Jaz patiently. 'It wasn't like that. What she made me do was promise to speak to you myself if I couldn't sort things on my own. Which I did. Jeez, Mum, what's eating you?'

'I've been wondering about her and your dad,' I muttered, pushing the album away.

'What do you mean? Oh!' This time Jaz laughed out loud. '*Eileen?*'

'It's possible.'

Jaz was shaking her head. 'No way. No *way*! I always assumed Eileen was gay. Wasn't she?'

'No. She had boyfriends sometimes.'

'Did you ever ask?'

'Don't be ridiculous.'

'Well, gay or straight, she certainly didn't have the hots for Dad, absolutely not. She couldn't stick him. Used to call him all sorts behind his back. If she did fancy him, Mum, she was a bloody good actress.'

'What about if he fancied her?'

'Makes no odds, if she wouldn't play ball, does it?'

The sick ache in my stomach eased fractionally, for the first time in weeks. I leaned over and hugged her.

'What was that for?'

'Being my daughter.'

She sighed, like someone who endures unimaginable provocation. 'Big fan of yours, Eileen. Always going on about what a great mother you were and how I should be thankful, not that it made much difference . . . Hey, look at Dad, here,' she said, lifting the book up for me to get a better view. She was pointing to a group shot of herself, Solange Moreau, Nat and Phil, all crowded into the hall. Solange's suitcases were by the door; it must have been her last day. Behind Nat's head, Phil held up two black dinner plates to give her Mickey Mouse ears. 'He was funny, Dad. Do you remember the Exploding Taco?'

'I do.'

'He made us laugh.'

'Sometimes.'

'It wasn't enough, though, was it?'

'No, it wasn't.'

Flick, flick went the pages. I glimpsed a photo of Mum holding my new baby like a sack of potatoes; Dad pushing Jaz's

Christmas bike through tiny islands of melting snow; Prom Night, and Jaz kitted out like a trollop.

I said, 'You know that first time you ran away, when you were still at school? Where was it you were headed?'

She didn't look up. 'I have no idea.'

'Please. Since we're clearing the air.'

'Honestly. I didn't have a clue.'

'You weren't meeting up with someone?'

'Nope. I was bored, I was getting hassle from some girls in my class, I took off. That's all it was. Teenage dramatics. I told you at the time.'

'You told me a lot of stuff,' I said.

She closed the book and set it down.

'I'm sorry. I'm sorry for all the crappy things I've done to you, Mum. All right?'

Now would have been my chance. I could speak out, tell her my side of events, tip the balance back. If she could be made to see—

I glanced at Matty, rolling his head against the sofa arm, and my courage evaporated into nothing. 'Someone's still a bit sleepy this morning,' I said. I got up and sat close to him, so that his small feet were in my lap. 'You used to like having your feet tickled, do you remember? You'd poke me with your toes every time I stopped. You were a devil for it.'

Jaz began to pile the albums back onto the shelf. 'Do you think he'll turn out optimistic, like you, or gloomy, like me and Grandma? Dark and light. It's like a pattern. Each generation reacts against the other.'

'I think my optimism's been fear, a lot of the time. Not being able to face the worst possibility.'

She pushed the last album home, then came over to the sofa and squeezed in on Matty's other side.

'Matty'll grow up to be what he'll be,' I said. 'And he'll be a little treasure.' I gave him a cuddle, and got no reaction at all. On television, a man in a pink sweater waved over the battlements of a pink castle. As I watched, he became Eileen, speaking Eileen's words: *You and Phil belong together*. Then Phil: *Not even a kiss. Don't blame her.* What had Jaz said? *If she did fancy him, Mum, she was a bloody good actress.*

'So what was it David was on about?' asked Jaz suddenly, jerking me back to reality.

'David?'

'What you said last night, about events not being causal. What was he referring to? Was it me?'

'Oh,' I said. 'No.'

'What, then?'

'It doesn't matter now.'

The TV showed two small girls spreading glue on purple sugar paper. One had her neck in a kind of metal brace, but she seemed to be coping all right. The children took dried leaves from a pile at the side and stuck them down randomly. Then we had a short film showing frost on hedges, trees, grass and cobwebs, while Prokofiev's Troika played in the background. When the cameras came back to the girls, they were dribbling glue on the leaves while a lady bent between them with a saucer of glitter. The next shot was a close-up of their fists against the saucer. 'We're like Jack Frost,' said the one wearing the brace. I put my hand against Matty's leg to stop him kicking.

'When's he back from the States?' said Jaz, her eyes on the screen.

'I don't know.'

The lady helped the girls hold their pictures up and shake them onto paper. Swathes of glitter fell away, leaving random lines and blobs of sparkle across the brown leaves. "It's a winter picture," said the second girl, as the camera closed in.

A sharp rap on the window made us both jump. When I looked up, Laverne was peering through the glass.

'I've come to ask if you're around over Christmas,' she said, as I was leading her through to the lounge. Josh shuffled in behind her.

'We're thinking of booking a mini-cruise,' she went on, perching herself on the chair arm. 'One of these last-minute deals. Only I don't like to leave the house without someone to keep an eye on it. So, would it be possible for you to pick up my post from behind the door, check my pipes haven't frozen, that kind of thing? It would stop me worrying.'

'Of course,' I said.

Jaz had turned in her seat and was staring at Josh. I knew what she was thinking. His outline had changed. These days he filled the doorway, and no longer with puppy fat.

Laverne was still talking. 'I know we usually go to my sister's at Abersoch in the summer, but I think it's time for a change. Josh has never been abroad, have you, love? And all his friends go on about France, and America and – You have to keep up, these days.'

'How's the job going?' I asked him.

He shifted his weight from one foot to the other. 'All right.'

'You're loving it, aren't you?' said Laverne. 'And he's loving his drama group in the evenings. And he's got himself a little girlfriend. Little Kirsty. She's very nice. I know, I know, I shan't go on – he gets embarrassed – but you're enjoying this school year a lot better, aren't you? One boy he didn't like so much has left, and another one who was – You've palled up with him, haven't you? Mind you, he's not getting quite such good reports as he was, so I don't know whether that's altogether a good thing. Detention last week, his first ever. I was mortified. He wasn't, though. Took someone's rugby kit out of their bag and filled it with lost property, so when they got off the coach, all they had—'

'Mum,' said Josh, warningly.

I looked from one to the other. Against him, she was tiny and frail. Lines were forming round her eyes. He looked as if he could swallow her up in a single bite.

'Not my little boy any longer, is he?'

'That's the way it goes,' I said.

Matty sneezed, and for the first time Laverne seemed to notice him properly.

'Ooh, look at this young man here. Hello, Matty. Are you watching television? Who's that? Is it La La?'

'Wrong programme,' said Jaz.

'And did he enjoy his birthday party?'

'He did, yeah. He loved the Talking Thomas: thanks.'

'It's nice to have someone small to buy for. They're not babies long. You need to make the most of every minute.'

Laverne and I exchanged the glances of women who've been through it, and know.

She stood up. 'Well.'

'Have you heard any more about how Alice is getting on?' I asked as we got to the front door. Josh made good his escape, slipping through ahead of us.

'Oh, yes. The baby's home.'

'He's better?'

'Better than he was, but he's still needing all sorts of specialist care. Tanks of oxygen, tubes. They're seeing how he goes.'

'And long term?'

'I don't think they can tell yet. Connor, his name is. Bonny little boy, really blond hair. Has Dorothy shown you the photos?'

'No.' I pictured again her young, scared face. 'Oh, poor Alice.'

'I keep thinking, you know, if it was me, I'd never manage.'

'If you had to, though. If it was your child. Maybe when the absolute worst happens, you do just get on with it.'

We stood in silence, two mums trying to imagine how we'd cope if fate had charged to us a desperately poorly baby.

'I suppose—' Laverne hovered on the step, frowning as she tried to frame some idea of a way forward, some positive comment where almost nothing positive can be said, 'I suppose all she can do is love, and hope.'

Which is really all any of us can do, I thought, when it comes to it.

I shut the door against the world, and went to sit with my family.

CHAPTER 38

Photograph: unnumbered, part of a postcard-sized wedding album, wrapped in a tea towel inside a Fox's biscuit tin

Location: St Stephen's C of E Church

Taken by: Imperial Photographic Studios, Chapel St, Adlington, Lancashire

Subject: Frieda and Bob's wedding day. The couple stand in the centre of the picture, flanked by family from both sides. What an abundance of middle-aged women there are, too, all in their hats and gloves and long flared coats. 'Smile,' Frieda's mother hisses from time to time, when she thinks no one's listening, but once again she could do with taking a leaf out of her own book.

If I'd been able to talk to you, thinks Frieda furiously, I wouldn't be in this situation. I wouldn't have accepted an offer of marriage I didn't want.

Has it been poor nutrition, or stress, or simply being underweight that's caused Frieda's periods temporarily to stop? In these post-war days there are girls so slender they move in and out of fertility, the way the sun passes through clouds. Since no doctor's been involved, they'll never know. At any rate, when her monthly visitor does show up again, it's much too late to cancel the church.

'You'd better not mention this to anyone,' says her mother when Frieda hands her the laundry basket with its bloody news. 'Just be glad. You've been lucky.'

'But I don't want to get married,' says Frieda hopelessly.

'What's wrong with Bob all of a sudden?' says her mother. 'You liked him before.'

'Nothing. I just don't want to get married. Ever. To anyone.'

'Don't talk soft,' her mother snaps, shaking the dirty clothes into the tub. And with that, the subject's closed and Frieda finds herself prematurely vaulted into womanhood. She must put away her girlish dreams of – what? It doesn't matter now. A life circumscribed by Windolene and Brasso awaits.

For now, she's a vision in white, clutching hard at the arm of a young man who has no idea the world is anything but grand. On her other side stand Aunties Edie and Flo, her mother and her grandmother, like a set of disapproving Russian dolls.

'Where's Matty?' I asked as Jaz climbed into the Micra.

'With Nat. Brewing up a cold and pretty grouchy about it; I didn't think any of us would enjoy ourselves if he came along. Plus it's forecast snow. He's better staying in.'

'Is he OK to leave?'

'It's a cold, Mum. I've got my phone.' She unbuttoned her thick coat and pulled the seat belt across her body, slotted it home. 'Have you got your camera?'

I'd had an idea to make an illustrated family history, with Jaz, for Matty. He'd appreciate it when he was older, I'd said to Jaz. And if she helped, it'd be her chance to get the story down right.

So a trip to Tannerside was needed, for background. We hadn't been up there for nearly five years.

'Will there be pages about Ian, too?' she'd asked.

'That's up to you. Only, it's for Matty, remember. What do you think he'd want?'

She'd looked away, out of the window. Yes, I thought, one day he'll be grown up and standing there like a recording angel, listing all your deficiencies. Missing photos won't be the half of it.

The place I grew up in had gone from being an unpicturesque village, built off the back of cotton and coal, to one of the remoter suburbs of New Enterprise Bolton. Building developments had sprung up everywhere; the fields I'd played in had vanished under housing estates and bypasses and supermarkets. Streams we fished and poked about in had been culverted, trees we used to swing from chopped down, their roots blasted out. You couldn't blame Dad for becoming disorientated. When they erase key landmarks from your childhood, it becomes harder to trust your own memory.

Tannerside's original vicarage was now an old people's home, with a bungalow where the main lawn used to be. Jaz and I stood at the bottom of the drive, underneath leafless horse chestnut trees, reading the sign.

'Is this where you want putting when you reach your dotage?'

'You're to stick me on a cruise ship, you know that.'

'Why do you want a photo of this place, then?'

'It reminds me of your grandma,' I said. 'They used to hold Mothers' Union meetings here, and let us kids loose in the garden. It was terrifically grand. For Tannerside.'

Between the upper and lower lawns there'd been wide stone steps, but we always chose to run down the grass bank instead. Every visit began with a game of hide and seek. Round the back of the house, near the kitchen, I remembered a compost heap where Joseph Critchley found a nest of grass snakes and threw gravel at them till the vicar's wife made him stop. There were fruit canes at the back, too; one time Margaret Wardle ate so many raspberries she vomited red on the doorstep, and panicked because she thought it was part of her insides. We always got a high tea before we went home, with miniature sandwiches and fairy cakes, so it was almost like going to someone's birthday party. Uneaten food was parcelled up for us to take home. Eileen was never part of these afternoons because her family didn't go to church. For some reason my mother, normally a keen recruiter, would never approach hers. So to make up, I'd share any stale sponge left over and give Eileen a blow-by-blow account of what we'd all been up to in the vicarage grounds. I did try to include her that way. Perhaps, in retrospect, it might have been better if I'd kept the details of our revelry to myself.

St Stephen's Primary was now a private residence called 'The Old Schoolhouse', had a black and gold name plaque on the gatepost. 'Boys still got the slipper in those days,' I said to Jaz, bringing the gable end into focus through my viewfinder. 'Girls just lost their playtime for being naughty. Though your dad once famously got both.'

'What for?'

'He carried one of the reception class up to the top of the oil tank and left him there.'

'Why would he do that?'

'Oh, he never needed a reason. It was me who went to get a teacher, but I've never told him that. Don't you say, either.'

'Like it matters now.'

Greenhalgh's was still there, still with a queue coming out the door. Hot pasties glistened in the window.

'You're not taking a picture of a bakery, Mum?' said Jaz.

'We used to go there every Friday dinnertime to get the bread for the weekend. Never cake, though; your grandma made all our cakes herself. Drop scones, she was always very good at. I've still got her griddle. One day it'll be yours.'

'Gee, thanks.'

We strolled on down to the wool shop, but it was a chiropodist's.

'How much do you remember of your grandma?' I asked.

Jaz shrugged. 'Nothing, really. She walked with a stick.'

'When she got poorly, yes. Nothing else?'

'Don't think so. She wasn't very nice to you, was she?'

'She did what she was capable of.'

'You've got a bit of an issue there, haven't you?'

'I wouldn't say so.'

At the start of the next terrace was Eileen's old house, unchanged except for a satellite dish above the upstairs window. I'd meant to stop, take a snap, but as we drew near I changed my mind and kept my camera by my side. Bevelled glass doors, the smell of hairspray, plastic flowers and charity shop shoes with dirty insoles bring her mother back to me. 'By the time I turn twenty-one, I want to be out of this village,' Eileen had told me. But it was me who'd left first, for Phil's job.

As we passed the low front wall I had a sudden memory of Jaz returning from a sleepover at Nat's and saying, 'I'm glad I live here and not there.' I think she may even have hugged me, although I might be imagining that.

St Stephen's Church looked the same as ever from the outside, but when we went in I discovered the interior had been dramatically refurbished. There were now indoor toilets, and a proper enclosed meeting area, and what looked like a crèche. The austere feeling I remembered from childhood had gone, banished by deep orange carpet in the entrance hall and proper heating. My mother would have hated it.

'I knew you'd come here,' said Jaz, putting her bag down by the baize display board.

'I wanted a shot of the village quilt,' I said. 'If it's still on display. Come and help me find it.'

Two years it had taken the Mothers' Union to complete the quilt and they'd hung it in the Lady Chapel, with a spotlight of its own. It depicted historical landmarks of Tannerside, bordered by scenes from the Christian Year. In the top left-hand corner, the Nativity hovered above a set of pit winding gear; bottom left were harvest sheaves, veg, fish, and the original council offices with their bowed walls and cobbled front. St Stephen's itself had been given centre spot, along with Cappelthorne Hall where they started holding the church fete after the old vicarage was sold off.

'The middle right side is Grandma's,' I said, pointing. My mother had used a mixture of embroidery and appliqué to render the Passiontide: a basin and towel, a bag of coins, a whip, a sword, a crown of thorns, some nails, a sponge, a blindfold and a sign saying *King of the Jews*.

'How neat is that?' said Jaz.

'Oh, she was a whizz with a needle, before her hands got bad. She taught me to sew when I was still in the Infants.'

'You never taught me.'

'I tried. Anyway, you can manage the basics, can't you? You can mend a seam, sew on a button.'

Jaz smirked. 'Nat's got this thing with buttons.'

'How do you mean?'

'I'm not sure I should say in a church.'

So we went outside into the freezing graveyard, and while

I hunted for ancient family headstones, she told me how Nat liked to secretly cull a button from every man she slept with. 'She keeps them in a box,' said Jaz.

'Good grief. How many are we talking about?' I was picturing something the size of a shoebox, filled to the brim.

Jaz sketched cigarette packet dimensions with her fingers. She was grinning.

'Well,' I said, 'I don't think that's very nice.'

'I know, it's cheap. I wouldn't do it. Not that I'd have a lot of buttons in the first place.'

'If it was me, it'd be the one button only. I'd need a single compartment of a pill box, that's all.'

She goggled at me. 'God, honestly?'

'Yes.'

'Only my dad?'

'Yes. Stop looking at me like that.'

'No one else, before or after? Jeez. That's amazing.'

'Not really.'

She followed me as I picked my way through stone memorials.

'I suppose there's a lot of stuff like that I don't know about you,' she said.

'I'm your mum. There's nothing else for you to know.'

I stood for a moment in front of my Great-aunty Florence's grave and thought about the drive to the crematorium after my mother's funeral, then all those po-faced elderly ladies standing round the chapel foyer. *You'll not remember me, Carol, but I lived next door to Flo Viner . . .* Phil stiff and awkward in his suit; Dad with his head bowed over the pew, one hand laid across the other. Moira had looked after Jaz that day. I'd been so glad to get back to her.

'Do you think I should start going to church?' said Jaz.

I tried not to look taken aback. 'If you want to.'

'Why did you stop going?'

'I was too busy.'

'That's rubbish.'

'All right: I lost heart, then. Things got in the way.'

'But Nick says—' She saw my expression. 'Obviously it's your choice.'

'It is.'

'Can we talk about it sometime?'

'Yes, but not today,' I said, clicking the lens cap back into place. 'Today we have other fish to fry.'

The rendering on Pincroft's top half had been re-painted pale yellow and the front lawn paved in that compressed concrete they have nowadays. I thought of my mother's continual war with grass and dandelions and lilac and privet, how she'd don a pair of pink rubber gloves and re-do the bedding from scratch every season, and wondered whether she'd have been pleased at the innovation. It's possible she might have approved.

'Haven't you got photos of the house already?' asked Jaz.

'Not of the front, looking from the road.'

'Is it the same people Grandad sold it to? They were going to move the bathroom upstairs.'

In my head I was clearing piles of old newspaper from under the stairs while Dad, his shirt hanging loose from his trousers, paced anxiously up and down the hallway. The next instant I was sitting on the back step in my Ladybird nightie cutting the robin motifs off a box of starch.

'It's a strange process, getting old,' I said.

'Do you want to have a look inside? Shall I go knock on the door?'

'No!'

'Go on. I'll do it, you can wait here. What's there to lose?'

'I don't want to see what they've changed, Jaz.'

The grey carpet with black, white and red drizzles would have gone for sure, and the kitchen cupboards with their rickety sliding doors, and the old Fifties bathroom suite. Probably everything I knew would have been stripped and junked.

'It's not my house any more.'

'Fair enough,' she said. 'Can we get something to eat soon? I'm frozen and I'm starving.'

She let me take her arm and we retraced our steps towards the High Street. There was a café-cum-gift shop I'd noted, where, as well as having a snack, I could check out product lines and displays to report back to Moira. After lunch I intended taking Jaz along the canal, see if the woods were still there, and the stone dovecote, and we could loop back via the main road to where the car was parked, taking in Cappelthorne Brow where Dad once took me blackberrying when the works were on strike.

'You look nice today,' she said, as we drew near the church again. 'Your hair's so much better than it was when you used to try and do it yourself.'

'Job's complimenter.'

'The jacket's neat, too. I've not seen you in that colour before.'

'It's funny,' I said, pausing before we crossed the road, 'you might think you'd get to an age where you'd have sorted your style for good. You'd just know what suited you, and that would be it. But actually, the older you are, the more need there seems to be for reinvention and makeover. I can't decide whether that's a positive thing or not.'

'I'm getting old,' said Jaz. 'I'll be thirty in a couple of years.'

I made a mock-swipe at her, and she laughed.

Together we stood outside the gift-shop window, eyeing the pearlescent vases and floral pigs. Behind the front shelf our reflections hovered.

'You know,' she said, 'Nick's a friend, not a rival. He really rates you.'

'That's lucky, then.'

'It's been fun today, hasn't it? We could do it again, with Matty when he's a bit older.'

And I thought, This is my reward, this is my life as it is now. It's enough. I'm happy. I am.

CHAPTER 39

Photo 185, Album Two

Location: the lounge, Sunnybank

Taken by: Carol

Subject: It's Christmas 1983 and Frieda's stationed in an armchair, clasping a cerise paper hat to her bosom. How did she get here? she's thinking. Who are these people gathered around her? Perhaps this is how dementia begins. Not with a lack of recognition, exactly – that woman there's her daughter, that man there's her no-good son-in-law – but with a lack of explanation for your life. What has this scene got to do with who she is, and the things she wanted? She could surely have done more with these past four decades than shift dust from surface to surface, wring out the days over a Belfast sink.

If she closes her eyes, she feels it: only the thinnest of filaments tethers her to this room and this family.

Now Carol's talking, she's offering round a box of Eat Me dates, but it's as if she's stretching her hand out from a mile away. Bob's taken refuge in a nap. Even the jolly piano music to All Creatures Great and Small *fails to provide its usual faint comfort. The only object that stirs Frieda here is the little girl playing on the hearthrug. She can't say why.*

It was dark by the time we got back to Jaz's.

'I hate these winter evenings,' she said as the car pulled up. 'After I've put Matty to bed.'

'I'm only ever a phone call away, you know.'

'Yeah. I've got to learn to cope, though, haven't I?'

I couldn't answer her. Bloody rotten shame, I was thinking, when she'd had it all, their lovely first home just how she wanted it, and no mortgage or rent to pay so they weren't struggling like so many young couples; happy and loved and safe and optimistic. Sometimes these sudden and massive waves of anger against Ian still knocked me off-balance: the injustice, the waste. What must my daughter feel every time she unlocked the front door of this flat to be presented with grubby walls, worn carpet, other people's post?

When we got inside, Nat was feeding Matty chocolate buttons in front of the TV. The arms of the sofa were covered in scrunched-up tissues. 'How's he been?' asked Jaz, bending to kiss his filthy face.

'Snotty,' said Nat.

'Apart from that?'

'Yeah, fine. We went into town, looked at the Christmas lights. But it was brass monkeys so we didn't hang around long.'

'Shall I go run his bath?' I said.

Jaz nodded. 'That would be a help. I'll be there in a minute.'

I made my way to their poky bathroom and started the water running, then I went next door to Matty's room to collect his slippers and pyjamas. Those I laid out on the bathroom floor ready, and then I thought I'd have a quick tidy round while I was there. I was on my knees cleaning the base of the sink pedestal with a sheet of baby wipes when Jaz appeared, carrying a pile of towels.

'I keep thinking about Grandma,' she said.

'What about her?'

'That she can't have been happily married if she was always such a misery-guts.'

I struggled to my feet and dropped the wet wipe in the toilet bowl.

'So I reckon,' she continued, 'it *is* a pattern. I'm unlucky in love; you were; Grandma was. It's genetic. Either that or I'm cursed.'

'Don't be silly,' I said. 'Grandma and Grandad got along fine. It may not have been a movie-style romance, but they stuck it out for thirty-six years. Anyway, Grandad's lovely, he'd never have done anything to hurt Grandma, never. And Ian – Ian's situation isn't the same as your dad's. For all sorts of reasons.'

Jaz sighed, opened the airing-cupboard door and began to stack the towels on the top shelf.

I said, 'I understand the urge to look for a broader explanation, but sometimes there is none.'

'I'll go get Matty,' she said.

She kept his bath toys in a colander near the taps, so I picked out a few I knew he liked – a polythene kitchen jug and funnel, a wind-up turtle, a flannel frog – and dropped them in the water. Matty burst in, trouserless, and peered over the edge while I swirled the water round. 'Froggy all wet,' he said. He bobbed against the bath rim in anticipation.

'Let's get your top off,' I told him.

He stood, jiggling impatiently, while I knelt again to undo the press-studs at his neck. His mouth was smeared with chocolate and his nose was running. When I reached for a wipe, he saw it coming and jerked his head away.

'No, come on, be a good boy, let Nanna clean you up.'

'Determined, isn't he?' said Jaz, poking her head round the door and watching us wrestle.

'Oh yes. I can't think who he reminds me of.'

While Jaz moved back and forth between rooms putting away dried washing, I whipped off his nappy, hooked my hands under his armpits and lowered him gently into the bath. 'Not too hot?' I asked him. For answer Matty grabbed the jug and splashed it base-first into the water.

'Watch out,' he said. 'Watch out!'

I pretended to duck, and shake my hair, which pleased him. He splashed some more, rubbed his eyes, then his attention lighted on the soggy frog. He pulled it out so it lay across his leg.

'Is Froggy having a rest from swimming?' I asked.

Matty said something I didn't understand, and raised his knee so the frog slid off with a plop. 'Oh dear,' he said. Then he scooped the frog back out and repeated the exercise. I got hold of the turtle and began to wind its key.

Suddenly he raised his head and said, 'Where Swir-Fish, Nanna?'

I looked about me. 'I'm not sure, love.'

'Swir-Fish.'

'Let's see if he's in the colander.' I reached over and rummaged about.

'Swir-*Fish*, Nanna.'

'I know, sweetheart, I'm doing my best.'

'Swir-Fish!'

I stood up and cast my eyes around the room; there wasn't much room for even a small toy to hide itself. Without much hope I peeped inside the airing cupboard, but there was nothing in there except towels and toiletries.

'Nanna!'

'OK, OK, I'll just nip and have a look in your room,' I told him.

Matty's bedroom was probably no smaller than his old one had been, but it felt cramped because Jaz had put a lot of her belongings in there. Some of it was boxed and some wasn't: some of it spilled out over the floor. A pile of clothes lay across a pair of speakers, and behind those she'd stacked half a dozen framed prints and a weekly planner blackboard. There was a suitcase labelled *imp docs*, another labelled *cupboard 2*, and a beaten copper umbrella stand she'd filched from Sunnybank and seemed to be using to store DVDs. She'd pushed piles of foreign language books between the end of Matty's bed and the wall. His dismantled cot she'd shoved down the side of the wardrobe. And overlaying all this was what looked like an upended bin-full of toys and toddler equipment. I didn't know where to start.

Speedily I began to work my way across to the bed, shifting this bag of Duplo, that basket of trains, this dislocated drawer of socks, that bundle of parenting magazines. The item I was trying to locate was only three inches long, but on the plus side, it was bright orange.

Something I trod on mooed, and a tower of boxed games fell over. I gained the low bed where Dawg lay flat on his back, legs splayed as though pinned for dissection. Then I pulled down the sheets and scuffled a few teddies aside. Nothing. I lifted the pillow, and there was the blessed fish. 'Got him!' I called.

Jaz met me at the bathroom door. 'You shouldn't leave Matty on his own in the bath,' she said.

'I went to get this,' I said, waving the toy at her. 'He was asking for it.'

'Then you should have called for me.'

'I was only gone thirty seconds.'

'More than that. It's OK, I've been here, I saw you go so I

left the washing and came to watch him. But don't do it again, Mum.'

'I was twenty steps away.'

'Makes no odds. You shouldn't leave him in water even for a moment.' She must have seen the upset on my face because her tone softened. 'Like I said, I was here, he's all right. Just, in future—'

Limply I held out the plastic fish. 'I'm really sorry.'

'OK, well. I'll see to him now. There's no harm done. But you really mustn't leave him unattended like that, ever – yeah?'

I nodded.

'After all,' she said playfully, 'I don't want to have to cut you off again, do I?' She pulled a mock-tragic face, and disappeared into the bathroom.

For a moment I couldn't take in what she meant. Then the impact of her words hit me, and I had to steady myself against the wall. I could hear Matty twittering, and Jaz responding, the slosh of water, the gurgle and clunk of the plug coming out. I pictured her lifting him up, setting him on the bathmat, wrapping the towel around his pink body. Her tone was bright and cheery, untroubled. And all the time the heat of rage was spreading over me like a fever, leaving my throat tight, my breath shallow. After a minute, she came out carrying him, his pyjama bottoms draped over her arm. 'These have got porridge stains down them,' she said as she passed me. I stayed where I was.

His bedroom light went on again, then dimmed as the curtains rattled against the rail. His musical bear-lamp started up, and when the tune finished, I could make out the story she was reading, *Runaway Bunny*. Found myself mouthing the words, while inside my head raged and whirled. Silence after, as she closed the book, took him over to the bed, then Matty asking some sort of question, too low for me to hear, Jaz murmuring something soothing. She'd be kissing him now, patting Dawg, pulling the cover up tight. I waited.

I caught her as she was closing the door.

'Oh!' she said. 'You made me jump.'

'How dare you,' I said.

'What?'

'How *dare* you joke about it.'

'How dare I joke about what, Mum? What's up? You look—'

'Joke about cutting me off from Matty. Stopping me from seeing him. *It's nothing to joke about.*'

Jaz's eyes had gone wide with surprise. I let her steer me away from Matty's bedroom door and round the corner, into the lounge.

'Sit down,' she said.

'No.'

She hovered uncertainly by the sofa. 'Look, I'm sorry. It was a stupid thing to say. Obviously I didn't mean it, I wouldn't take Matty away again.'

'How do I know that, Jaz?' I shouted. 'How am I supposed to know? I never guessed you were going to do it before! Why should now be different from then?'

She began to say something, but I swept on.

'You have no idea, *no idea* what it did to me when you and Matty went on the run. I didn't know where you were, whether you were safe, whether I'd see either of you again. You could have been lying dead somewhere – anything. You'd told me I'd never see my grandson again – yes, you did, it was your parting shot, don't deny it. And you meant it.'

'I didn't.'

'You did when you said it.'

I'd backed her up against the edge of the sofa; she had nowhere to go.

'I didn't, Mum. I was just really angry. I get angry, it's the way I am.'

'We *all* get bloody angry, Jaz! *I* get angry! What am I supposed to do? Swallow it down, smile? Carry on pretending it doesn't matter; forgiving-and-forgetting? Oh, I forgot, that's another of my failings, isn't it, stoicism? Well, I've *had* it. I'm sick of you taking advantage of my honest concern. You turned your own son into a weapon, your own son, it's unforgivable. What you did to me was horrible. You took my love and used it to hurt me, when you know I'd do *anything* for you and Matty, lay down my life if need be, and that's not being dramatic, it's a simple statement of fact.

'You had no *right* to threaten me that way! Not answering my calls, no word, nothing. If you'd planned for weeks, you couldn't have hurt me more profoundly. You need to be told. It was beyond cruel.'

Behind Jaz, on the cushion, I could see one of Matty's socks, sky blue with a penguin motif on the ankle. For a second I imagined him next door, his lashes fluttering against his cheek, his thumb in his mouth, and my momentum faltered. What in God's name was I doing, risking everything after I'd been so careful all these months to keep control?

But this wasn't just a matter of indulging my temper. I thought of a letter in a problem page I'd read a few days ago, where a woman had written in to ask about tackling agoraphobia. 'It's like a bully,' the agony aunt had told her. 'Step back to give it room, and it'll only advance further.' The comparison had stuck in my mind. If I spent the rest of my life avoiding confrontation with my daughter out of fear, I'd always be in this same place: a click of her fingers away from losing Matty. David was right. I had to make a stand.

'Since you were born,' I said, 'you've been my first priority. Everything I've done has had you as the central consideration.

You must know that. If I've made mistakes, it's not because I haven't cared, it's because I'm human, and we all make mistakes.'

I saw again Jaz raging about my living room, kicking my albums, barking accusations at me while Matty cowered behind the long curtain. Gathering now were all the lines I'd rehearsed over and over, the defences I never got to deliver, till they'd become a litany which sent me nearly mad. 'Good God, love, how could you possibly accuse me of not sticking up for you or protecting you? You've been my *life*. I've done my damnedest to give you the best of everything – maybe I tried too hard and spoiled you, that's what your dad always said. But to claim I taught you to make bad choices, just because I was trying to protect you! Would you really have been happy if your dad and I had split up, like Nat's parents did? No, you wouldn't, and you'd have blamed that on me as well. Oh yes, you would. I'm sorry, desperately sorry about what happened with Ian, but to argue it's somehow my fault is as ridiculous as it's insulting. And the idea that I'd *ever* deliberately want to hurt you – it would be like hurting myself, Jaz, only worse.

'I would *never* betray you, I would never stand aside and watch someone cause you pain. How could you even contemplate those things? All I've ever wanted, from the moment I first held you when you were a tiny baby, was your happiness. That's been my focus and my direction. I can't imagine how you could ever think otherwise. To say the things you've said to me, to treat me the way you have – it's got to stop. Enough. I don't want a medal, I just want you to be fair and decent, *the way you were brought up*.'

Jaz hadn't moved at all while I was speaking. Her face was rigid now, her pupils shrunk to tiny unreadable points. I needed my words to have gone below the surface, snagged somewhere in her conscience. Out of nowhere I remembered

Dad reaching through brambles to get me blackberries, pulling his hand back and there being a line of welling red beads across his knuckles.

A swoop of dizziness passed over me and I knew I had to get out. Without waiting for her to respond, I grabbed my coat and turned towards the hall.

The last detail I saw, out of the corner of my eye, was the kitchen door opening a fraction, and Nat's shocked face peering out. I'd completely forgotten she was there.

CHAPTER 40

Photograph 315, Album Three

Location: Jaz's bedroom

Taken by: Nat

Subject: a head and shoulders shot of Jaz, draped in a red velvet dressing gown, her hair crimped and swagged up on each side with enamel combs. Today she is the Lady of Shalott, because they have been doing it at school and Jaz thinks it is the most tragically beautiful story she has ever heard. The death scene's obviously interesting, and the hazy circumstances of the curse, but it's the twist in the end that's bothering her most, the fact that Lancelot kills her and he doesn't even realise it. How could you inflict that amount of damage on someone and not be aware of what you'd done? How might he be made to find out, and pay? She's been turning the question over in her mind ever since.

Nat's plain bored with the whole Camelotty business. She thinks Jaz is only going on about castles and webs and greaves and mighty bugles because of Mr Bryant. All the girls (except for Nat) are in love with Mr Bryant.

'How old do you think he is?' asks Jaz dreamily.

'Dunno. Twenty-three?' Nat has no idea how long teacher

training lasts, but Mr B looks like a student to her. He wears tour T-shirts under his jackets, and a leather strap round his wrist. 'You just want to shag him,' says Nat, seizing her chance with the crimpers.

'Already have done,' says Jaz.

It's an idiotic boast. She's still only fourteen, hasn't even French-kissed yet.

'You can get into trouble for making up stories like that,' warns Nat. Tirra Lirra by the river. It's all bollocks, all of it.

For years I've had a recurring dream where I come across a whole set of extra rooms to Sunnybank I hadn't realised were there. Sometimes it's a bedroom suite, sometimes a dining room featuring a great banqueting table; once I discovered, against all logic, a sea view. Even though I love my house, it's always a mild disappointment to wake up within its real confines. Disorientating, too. For a day or two after, I'll flick through home improvement magazines till the sensation passes.

You get to my age, you think you know yourself pretty well. But in that half-hour at Jaz's, I'd found a side to my personality I'd never suspected. I strode out of her flat and climbed into my car without hesitation. As I drove back through the sleety darkness I began making plans: how, if the worst came to the very worst, I could contact Grandparents Apart, engage a mediator, get myself a lawyer, take my access case to court. Remortgage Sunnybank if I had to. *You mustn't ever think you're powerless. You should never assume there's no hope*, I heard David say again. Then: *I'll be right behind you*. 'I can do it on my own, you taught me that,' I said out loud into the night, and the windscreen wipers marked the seconds between what I'd done, and the consequences.

When I got home I had a glass of brandy, spent three hours on the internet researching useful organisations, then took myself to bed. Against all the odds, I fell into a deep sleep that took me through till morning.

I woke with a crushing sense that I'd done something awful. But when I recalled the details, I didn't panic. I made myself breakfast, using some of my mother's Royal Worcester that normally lived in the back of the cupboard and never saw the light of day. I took the time to set the table properly. I opened a jar of posh jam I'd been saving, and I read the opening chapter of a Mavis Cheek novel while I ate my toast. Then I set off for work. What I didn't do was go rushing to the phone to plead my daughter's forgiveness, or trawl round the house stroking Matty's things, or pore over his albums, weeping.

How long I'd be able to keep it up I had no idea. Was I confusing courage with numbness? Had I been brave, or unbelievably, irredeemably stupid? Would I be spending Christmas alone? I had no way of knowing till Jaz made her move, whatever that might be.

Days passed, five of them, and I heard nothing. She could have been in her flat, or she could be at the other end of the country. She could be carrying on as normal, unconcerned beyond a lingering sense of annoyance, or beside herself, downing pills with the curtains closed and daytime TV on for company. She could even now be applying for Matty's passport, with a view to emigrating thousands of miles away. That would teach me.

She won't cut you off, you're too useful, said David's voice, reasonably. And another voice, possibly my own: *Come on, you're her mother, she loves you.* 'Then why hasn't she been in touch?' I asked the woman frowning back at me from the mirror. None of the voices in my head had a convincing answer to that.

In my bleakest moments, I found myself wondering how long it would take for Matty to forget me entirely. Time operates differently for two-year-olds. Within the space of a few months, I guessed, those hundreds of hours we'd spent together would evaporate to nothing. By the time he started school, he'd have virtually no recollection of his grandma. Fifty-four, I'd be, then. Sixty-one when he went up to secondary school, sixty-six by the time he sat his GCSEs. How old when he married? I tried to picture it but the image was too remote. Matty was just a misty shape and the only Jaz I could conjure was younger than she was now, a sulking, flash-eyed teen. I couldn't get near either of them.

Repeatedly I forced my thoughts away from the worst possibilities, but even so, the temptation to at least phone Nat or Ian and check up on her was continuous and almost overpowering.

I started re-organising the loft, took more clothes to the charity shop, and binned all my mother's old recipe books and magazines. For all her hours spent carefully copying out ingredients, what use were they now? *Everyday Eggless Cooking*, for God's sake. Her other books – the novels, the de Beauvoir, the annotated Dawkins – I stowed in my bedside cabinet because one day I did intend to read those, if only for themselves.

On the Wednesday evening, when I should have been having Matty to stay, I retrieved the photograph of Penny and, without looking at her, folded it in two and dropped her on the fire. A brief yellow flare and she was gone. She really didn't matter any more. So little did, when it came down to it.

I was in freefall, I could have been any woman except the one I had been.

On the sixth day I was in Healey's picking at my ham sandwich when Josh came over and plonked a plate of sponge cake in front of me.

'I didn't order that,' I said.

'No,' he said, 'but you looked like you needed something. And we're not allowed to serve alcohol.'

He winked at me, and I was just thinking what a lovely boy he was after all when suddenly his head jerked up and I saw him mouth 'Fuck off' in the direction of the window. I turned to see three youths flicking Vs and grinning. When I looked again at Josh, he was grinning too. He snatched my laminated menu and held it with his middle finger up the back, towards them. The boys jostled each other, slapped the glass, jeered, and carried on past the window.

'You won't last long if you start making obscene gestures at the public,' I observed.

'I won't do it to real customers.'

'You'd better not.'

'Madam.' He draped a serviette over his forearm and bowed deeply. 'Sometimes a waiter's got to do what a waiter's got to do. Enjoy your cake.'

I did my best to eat it, but the buttercream was an inch thick and tasted oily. Only last week, when Jaz was still at primary school, she'd stood in my kitchen sifting cocoa powder and icing sugar into a mixing bowl to decorate her first ever batch of fairy cakes. You know these years are going to come to an end, but you don't believe it. One day Matty would be a stroppy, gangling youth, and Jaz would be stranded out of time, bewildered and unsure.

I was trying again to visualise an adult Matty, when the café door tinkled open and Nat walked in.

Nat didn't come in Healey's, it wasn't her sort of place. Was she here for me? Did she bring bad news? I didn't know if I dared meet her gaze or not, but I had no chance to pretend indifference because she came straight over to my table and sat down.

'That woman in the shop told me you were here,' she announced.

I swallowed nervously. 'Everything all right?'

'With Jaz?'

Of course with Jaz. Good God, what else would I mean? 'And Matty.'

'Oh, they're fine. Matty's still got a cold so he's off nursery. But he's all right.'

'They're – around?'

'She hasn't gone off anywhere. She's in the flat. I thought you'd want to know.'

'Yes, yes I do. Thank you.'

''S all right.' A brief twitch of the lips that was Nat smiling.

'What state's she in? Is she angry?'

'She was, yeah. Now she's just, sort of crushed.'

That single syllable was like a stab to the ribs. 'Depressed?'

'I dunno. She wants to say sorry,' Nat continued, 'but she can't, you know, make the move.'

'So she's sent you?'

'God, no. She doesn't know I'm talking to you. You mustn't tell her. She'd be – shit. No, don't say anything.'

I watched her fidgeting, nudging the salt and pepper pots around with her French-polished nails. Two narrow strips of bleached-white hair hung down around her cheekbones. She said, 'I'm a little bit frightened of Jaz, to tell you the truth, Mrs Morgan.'

I don't want your confidences, I thought, I haven't the energy for them. In and out of Sunnybank for years, this girl had been; she was part of Jaz's childhood. There should have been a connection between us, but I looked at her and felt nothing.

'What should I do?' I asked.

Nat shrugged. *How should I know?* her expression said.

'Is she very upset?'

'She was crying last night. She needs you.'

I felt like the worst mother in the world. 'You're a good friend to her,' was all I could think to say, and that nearly choked me.

'Yeah, well.'

Nat was studying me with narrowed eyes. Clearly there was something else she needed to add.

'Do you remember,' she said at last, 'when I used to come round your house?'

'Well, yes.'

'I bet you don't, really.'

'Of course I do,' I said.

'Not all of it. Like, in the summer, going to school, yeah, if it was hot, you'd put suncream on Jaz and then you'd put some on me too.'

'That was no—'

'My mum never bothered. And sometimes you cleaned my shoes when you cleaned hers. And once I didn't have the stuff I needed for Food Technology, and you sorted me out, pots of butter and that.'

Dimly I recalled standing in the kitchen amongst the breakfast remains, hunting out Tupperware boxes while the girls hovered behind me.

'And if it was a non-uniform day and I'd forgotten, you'd let me wear Jaz's clothes. And you lent me a hat for the Year Seven play, and you made me a packed lunch for a trip when my mum hadn't done me one. I think you paid for a trip, too, didn't you? Because I had to have the cash that morning or I wouldn't have been allowed on the coach and Jaz didn't have anything in her money box. Did you ever get that back? I don't think I ever paid you back.'

'It was no trouble,' I said. They were light, unthinking kindnesses I'd barely registered.

'You don't even remember, do you?'

'Some of it. I'm glad if I helped.'

Her face was irritated, disappointed. 'I used to love your house. I tried to say about it to Jaz, sometimes, but she just laughed at me. She didn't get it.'

Nat paused there. If it had been anyone else, I might have put a supportive arm around them.

I struggled for a moment, decency against instinct, and then I withdrew my hand from under the table and laid my fingers across hers. Her brow pinched into its usual tight lines. Then she pulled away, scraped back her chair and got to her feet.

'Basically, my mum's never been able to give a shit. Far as I can see, Jaz is bloody lucky.'

I stared down at the uneaten cake, embarrassed.

'It's very nice of you,' I began, but when I raised my head she was already halfway to the door.

So on the seventh day I went to my daughter because she was unable to come to me.

I stood in the porch, surrounded by thick cobwebs and dead leaves, stamping my feet with nerves. When Jaz came to the door I took a deep breath and said, 'Does Matty want a walk to the back field, see the horses?'

There was old gritty make-up round her eyes and a tiny smudge of ink under her chin, but I was relieved to see she was properly dressed, that her clothes and hair were clean. She was OK.

She said, 'Shouldn't you be working?'

'Moira's in this afternoon. I'm back again this evening for late-night opening.'

'Oh,' she said.

'I thought I could take him off your hands for an hour.'

'I've got this translation to finish,' she said, her voice gruff and tired-sounding. 'So that would be good, yeah.'

I waited on the doorstep while she got him ready. At last he trotted out, his face small between thick folds of scarf and woolly hat. His mittened hand reached straight up for mine and I took it and clasped it.

'I've got my phone,' I said, patting my pocket.

Jaz nodded and stepped back into the hall, but she didn't close the door. She leaned on the jamb, watching us as we picked our way down the stone steps, and I knew without turning round that she stayed like that till we reached the end of the road.

The traffic was busy and I kept Matty well away from the kerb. We used the pelican crossing, Matty pushing the button, and shouting when the green man lit up. We looked both ways till we got to the other side.

An alleyway between two houses took us onto the broken tarmac of the public footpath, and there were iced-over puddles to step on, and a holly hedge covered in berries, and someone had dumped a wheel trim in the grass that needed investigating. We saw a flock of small birds land on a telegraph wire and take off again, and we heard a police siren far away, and just before we got to the field we discovered a wall with an air vent that was belting out a column of steam. I lifted Matty while he swiped and blew at it, but the effort made him cough so we left it and moved on.

Soon we came to the end of the estate and the path became cindery gravel, then opened into fields. 'This is where the horses live,' I told him. 'If they're around today.' There'd been horses here as long as I could remember; I used to take Jaz to see them when she was six or seven. She'd clamber up on the gate to reach, and stroke them confidently down their noses and flanks. The grey one she liked better than the black because he was smaller and friendlier. She'd given them names, and made up stories about them.

Here came two horses now, both tall and glossy-brown, sleeker than their predecessors but making those same chomping, clodding, huffing noises, their breath coming in cloudy snorts. 'Look,' I said to Matty. 'They want to say hello.'

From my bag I extracted an apple and showed Matty how to offer it, palm flat. 'So they don't accidentally bite your fingers,' I told him. I held the apple over the gate and the lead horse dipped his head, nostrils flaring. The next moment, the apple was snatched off my hand and crunched to slobbery pulp behind black rubber lips. The horse behind shuffled its hooves and tried to push nearer.

'Shall we give his friend one?' I asked. Matty jigged up and down excitedly.

I loved the rippling sheen of their coats as they shifted on the hard, rutted ground, and the expressive way they swivelled their ears. I presented the second apple.

'Horsey's hungry,' said Matty.

'He is, isn't he? Goodness. What a big wet mouth. I think Nanna might need to wipe her hand with a tissue, don't you?'

'Bleauh,' said Matty.

When Jaz was little, I used to pretend the horses were answering back. I'd a high voice for the grey one and a low voice for the black. It always made her laugh.

Matty pulled dead beech leaves off a twig, and I extemporised about the stable the horses slept in at night, and the people who came to feed them, and the wild animals who sometimes visited the field. I don't know whether he was listening or not. Snack time over, the horses drifted away to the side of the field and I was able to hoist him onto the top bar of the gate for a better view. I put my arm round his shoulders to steady him. 'I won't let you fall,' I said.

Footsteps crunching behind us made me look round: it was Jaz, walking towards us in her long black winter coat with her hands in her pockets. Her head was lowered, but I could see she'd scrubbed the make-up off her face and her eyes were pink and bare. She looked clean and young and penitent. I knew then it was going to be all right.

She came up against the gate, on Matty's other side. For a while all three of us stood there, watching the sky change from bright to dull to bright again. There was, when I looked across at her, something in her profile, in the earnest set of her jaw, that put me in mind of an old wartime propaganda poster. *Women of Britain Fight On!*

Matty began to tell her in his garbled way about the horses and I stayed where I was, my hand against his back. I'm sorry, Mum, she would say, I will never take your grandson away from you again. I understand how you must have felt. I know you were only trying to help.

And I might explain how horrible it was to have to say goodbye to David, to have such a decent man think of me as a coward and an ingrate, and how I didn't blame her for it but that she needed to know what it had cost me to turn him away.

Not quite yet, though.

With infinite gentleness, she slid her arms round her son, drew him off the gate, set him back down on the ground, steadied him, and took his hand. I came up and took his other one.

Then, still without speaking, we began to make our way home, swinging Matty between us every few paces. Anyone watching would have thought we were the most normal family in the world.

CHAPTER 41

Photograph 839, Album Six

Location: Carol's spare bedroom

Taken by: Carol

Subject: Matty asleep in his cot with Dawg and the gourd-rattle

I'm not naïve, whatever Jaz thinks. I know my albums are more than just memory prompts. I'm well aware I've been manipulating history to make it more upbeat. In that estimation, she was right, and I make no apologies for it.

But even edited narratives don't remain stable for long. Event overlays event, it's impossible to view any incident in isolation. Some hurt or failure here, a triumph there, the cutting of ties, a resolution or a reunion, every experience creates another version of the past. Sometimes I remembered Jaz's boast, how one day she would make an album which told the Real Truth. Good luck with that, I thought.

I took albums two and three and went through them, systematically removing all the photos that included my ex-husband. I scanned each one, cropped him out, and replaced it on the page with a Phil-free version. Although the idea of a bonfire or tearing-up session was tempting, I found myself keeping the originals for the same reason I'd never excised him before: my marriage was too big a part of my history. But neither was I prepared any longer to give him an official place in my book of memories. You can't undo the past, but you can choose how you move on from it.

On the last page of album five I added, defiantly, a portrait of David, taken from one of the wedding shots. Twice I'd written to him since he'd left, once to say thank you again for all his support, and then to tell him some of the things I'd said to Jaz. He hadn't replied to either letter. Which was an answer in itself, of course. *You've made your bed*, went my mother.

Meanwhile.

Matty learned how to run, kick a ball, climb the stairs one at a time if I was behind him. He could speak in almost-sentences, and if you gave him a felt-tip and paper, he'd do you a circular scribble, holding the pen in his fist like a dagger. I bought a cardboard wallet to keep his pictures in, and Jaz laughed because I'd spent so many hours clearing the house and here I was, filling it up again.

Jaz and Ian met at a solicitor's office and agreed terms of contact and maintenance. Jaz filled in the first set of forms and submitted them. Ian returned the form that acknowledged receipt. Jaz completed an affidavit confirming his signature, and sent it back to court.

Dad caught another chest infection and needed antibiotics.

Moira changed the opening hours of the shop so we started at ten. Our rent went up. The main window had to be replaced after it got smashed by drunks.

Gwen at the gym handed in her notice to train as a fire-fighter.

Josh was in the local paper for saving a woman customer from choking. *Service with a Thump* said the headline, which

Laverne felt trivialised the incident. The woman wanted him entering for a Local Heroes competition, but Josh refused.

Connor went back into hospital, and came out again.

Dr Page and his wife had a baby girl called Amelia Catherine.

Dove at Beavers announced she was getting engaged.

I had an awful, awful dream about Andy Spicer.

Jaz had her hair cut short, like a boy's.

I went to strim the ugly dead reeds from round the pond, and there were already new green shoots coming up underneath. I cried for a little bit, but then I was fine.

Spring had been a long time coming. The crocus bulbs Matty and I planted in December had come up, flowered, and died away to a purple slime. I'd cleared out the winter bedding and installed lobelia plugs and primulas, snapdragons and petunias. All the shrubs I'd hacked back hard a few months before were flushing into leaf again. We watched a blackbird build a nest in Laverne's hedge, and we took in half a handful of frog spawn so we could see it developing. 'I wish we'd had a pond when I was little,' said Jaz, watching a tadpole suck on a fragment of beef. She's never been good at identifying irony, for all she's clever.

Mostly she was up – more buoyant than she'd been for a year – but there were days she was as snappy and downbeat as ever. I had those too. When I knew she was going round to Phil's, for instance. I bore it, but I no longer bothered pretending it didn't get to me. This was the new understanding I'd reached with my daughter.

One warm May morning we were walking across the centre of Nantwich to deliver Matty to his dad.

'You know Penny's back on the scene, do you?' said Jaz over her shoulder, as we cut through the lawn of St Mary's Church, me pushing the empty buggy behind them.

I think I might have stumbled; in any case, Jaz turned round and halted. Matty tugged at her hand but she ignored him.

'Oh, Mum.'

'It's all right.'

'I shouldn't have said anything.'

'No, really, it's all right. I should have guessed he'd go that way.'

She squatted to adjust Matty's coat. 'I've told him he's a fool. Pen's moving her stuff back in, the place is a tip. You know, the daft thing is, they don't even like each other.'

'So, why?'

'Scared of being on his own, isn't he? It's pathetic. I'm not scared of living alone. You're not. The trouble with Dad is, he's never grown up.'

Pigeons stalked near us, curious and hopeful. I said, 'Do you mind if we don't talk about him?'

'Nope,' said Jaz, and stood up.

The market was on, so we took a stroll through that.

'Need any more sheets?' I asked, pointing to the linen stall. 'Or tea towels, dish cloths? Have you a pair of oven gloves? I'll treat you.'

She laughed. 'I'm fine. In fact, I'd say I've got the flat pretty much as I want it. Well, aside from the décor, but I'm not shelling out for new wallpaper when I'm only renting. That would be mad.'

'When you've your own place again, we can make it like a palace.'

'I'm not rushing, Mum.'

As we walked past a stall selling carpets and runners, Matty spotted a sheepskin oval and broke free from his mother's grasp to bury his face extravagantly against the wool. We had to haul him away, with apologies. 'Thank God he doesn't have a cold,' I said. 'Then we'd have had to buy a snotty rug.'

Next door was a stand of baby clothes and equipment.

'Did I tell you, I sent a parcel of Matty's old sleepsuits to Nick and Steph,' said Jaz, pausing to finger the little vests. 'They'd hardly been worn, it seemed a shame to have them sitting in the drawer.'

'You don't think you might be needing them again sometime?'

Immediately she dropped the giraffe bib she'd been examining. 'Let's not even go there, Mum. Hey, I know what I meant to ask. How's Alice doing?'

'She brought the baby round, little Connor. He's gorgeous. Except he's got this tracheostomy, this tube taped to his throat.'

'Oh, God.'

'He smiles, though. He's got a beautiful smile. Libby tickles him and he just beams.'

'What does she think of her brother?'

'Libby? She's very good. I was nervous about holding him, but Libby went, "He won't break, you know". It's something she must have heard her mum say.'

'And Alice?'

'Tired to death, strung out. But getting on with it. Mind, I don't know if she has any other choice. He's scheduled for an operation when he's a bit bigger, and that should improve his breathing.'

'Must be awful,' said Jaz, drawing Matty nearer and stroking his hair.

'It's a tough road ahead, that's for sure.'

I thought of Alice sitting in my armchair, her face grown older than her years, older than mine somehow, yet how the dark shadows under her eyes melted away when she smiled down at her baby and he smiled back. A very different sort of family, with very different problems and tensions and struggles and fears, but as full of love and the possibility of ordinary joy as the next. 'Well, he's gorgeous,' I'd said to her, not because I felt I ought to say it, but because he was. 'He is, isn't he?' she said, shining with pride. 'And so is Libs.' And with her free arm she'd reached out and hugged her daughter, and I'd felt the brittle tension of all their gathered hopes, like a bright glass ball surrounding them.

'What time is it?' asked Jaz. 'Only I said I'd be in the park by eleven.'

'We've still got twenty minutes,' I said. 'Do you want to stick Matty in his pushchair?'

'No. He naps better in the afternoons if he's had an active morning. See, I'm that considerate of my ex.'

The precinct was busy, but we weren't in a hurry.

She said, 'You know, Ian's thinking of having counselling. He reckons his personality was subsumed by his dad, and that's why he has no confidence. He's decided the input of a professional might help.'

'Oh, we're all failed parents now, aren't we?' I flashed. 'For God's sake! Everyone's a victim. Alternatively, Ian could try taking full responsibility for his actions as an adult.'

Jaz eyed me, then let Matty pull her away to the centre of the square where a man was selling balloons. I was left on my own to stew. It took some deep breathing, and a run-through of my eight-to-twelve times tables before I was calm enough to catch them up.

'All right, are we?' asked Jaz.

I ignored the tone. 'What are Ian's plans for the weekend? Has he said?'

She nodded. 'He always gives me a run-down of where he's going. I do the same for him, as much as I can. Making the point. So it's back to the house this afternoon, and then tomorrow he's taking Matty to one of these farm shops where they let you stroke the lambs and feed the chickens.'

'He'll be in his element. I hope Ian takes some photos.'

'Yeah.' Her hand went up to fiddle with her hair, but her new style was so short there was nothing to play with. Perhaps she was hoping to break a lifetime's habit. 'What'll you be up to this weekend?'

'The usual. Visiting Grandad, getting the food shop in. I want to price up fence panels because that section behind the shed's on its last legs, and I said I'd pop round and see Moira's new house, have lunch there.'

'A packed programme?'

'I shan't sit around and pine for Matty, if that's what you're worried about. I appreciate he needs time with his dad.'

She flashed me a grateful look. 'It's hard, sharing him out.'

You're telling me, I thought.

We were making our way down Mill Street when she said, 'Tell me to mind my own business, but did you ever hear again from David?'

'Mind your own business,' I said pleasantly.

I'd been ahead of her because she was trailing Matty, but she caught up and came in close to my side. 'I deserved that, didn't I?'

'Well. Yes. It doesn't matter any more. Truly.'

Jaz looked down at her feet.

'It'll be awkward for you, seeing him again.'

'If I ever bump into him, yes, it'll be awkward. But I know he'd go out of his way to make things as easy as possible, because he's like that.'

I half-expected a response to that, a rebuttal, but again she said nothing. Good, I thought. We've got somewhere.

The main road was busy and we had to wait a long time for a gap in the traffic. Neither of us spoke till we'd got Matty safely across, then Jaz halted on the verge and cleared her throat. Again her hand moved to her head, seeking tresses that were no longer there.

'Mum?'

'Yes?'

'I need to warn you about something.'

'What?' That instant shot of dread.

'David's back. I didn't tell you before. He's here.'

'You mean, in the UK?'

'Over there, with Ian.'

A few yards in front of us lay the shelf of the riverbank, then a stretch of green, a bench, a path, a line of trees bright with new leaf. It was under these trees that two figures stood. One was tall and lean, his hands in his pockets and his shoulders hunched forward. The other stood straighter, was shorter and more solidly built.

My legs started to tremble. 'Oh,' I said.

I'm not prepared, I wanted to say. *You ought to have let me know in advance. Ian should have rung and tipped me off. I look a mess!* If I could have had half an hour, even, to get myself together.

'He knows you're coming.'

'Does he.'

'Are you OK?'

'I don't know.'

When I'd rehearsed the moment of reunion, I thought the only real emotion I'd feel would be embarrassment. I assumed I'd have to force myself to approach him and then I'd be standing like an idiot, struck dumb under the weight of shaming memories. I'd not counted on this rush of painful pleasure, so intense it made me light-headed. There he was, in plain and shocking sight, and all I wanted to do was go to him.

'Ian was saying he's only been back a couple of days—'

I swallowed hard, touched my daughter's arm. 'Can you take the pram?'

'Mum?'

'It's all right,' I said.

'What are you going to do?'

One, two, three, four swans I counted on the grass ahead. *All mouth and trousers, your swan*, Dad used to say.

I'll tell you what I'm going to do, I thought. I'm going to take a stupid long-shot chance. I'm going to walk over there and tell him properly, to his face, that I was wrong to make him go, that I regret my decision and I wish like mad I had the power to undo it. I don't care who's listening in, Ian or you – let everyone hear. And if David sneers or shouts at me, or worse, if he's kind and shakes his head and says gently that it's too late, then I'll have done my best. I'm no worse off.

I thought of my mother, a life spent skewered on her own martyrdom, it occurring to no one around her to ask what was wrong, not that she'd have spoken up anyway. I thought of Dad, shackled for decades to a woman to whom he was patently unsuited, and without any form of romantic consolation. I thought of the years I'd wasted with Phil. What Jaz said was true: I wasn't afraid to be alone. It was the risks associated with commitment that scared me witless. But at this moment I wasn't motivated by fear. It was purely and simply a need to set something right.

'Jaz,' I said. 'Listen, I have to speak to him. I have to try and take this opportunity to make good. I don't know whether I can – I'm fairly sure it's too late, actually – but I want him to know I appreciate the chance he gave me, and how much I regret its loss. If you don't agree with that, then I'm sorry, but I still have to do it, and you really should be supporting me because I've always tried so hard to support you, and I'd never deliberately stand in the way of your happiness, especially if you wanted to start again with a new man, which is damned hard to do when your confidence has been knocked into the ground the way mine has, and yours, both of us, really—'

I ran out of breath.

'Jesus,' she said, frowning. Matty pulled on her wrist impatiently. 'I was going to tell you to go. If you must.'

And with those brief syllables, I was suddenly left to fend for myself.

When I looked over, David's face was turned in my direction, waiting. I tried to read his stance: was it disappointed, defensive, calculatedly indifferent? The space between us was wide and unobstructed, the clear sky gave no cover.

I began to pick my way across the lumpy grass, all too aware of how clumsy I must look, lurching on weak ankles, clinging onto the shoulder strap of my bag as though it were a parachute ripcord. The skirt I'd chosen, a dull corduroy thing, was riding up over my knees, my coat flapping open. My lipstick needed re-applying. Ill-equipped fiftysomething, floundering.

The field seemed to elongate as I struggled on; two swans whipped their heads up and hissed me spitefully on my way. What would happen when I reached him? He might use any one of a dozen put-downs, all deserved. He might say, 'You'll have heard about—' and then some woman's name, some American piece whose hair was not in desperate need of recolouring, and who was smart enough to hold onto a good man when she saw one. Perhaps he'd pull out a photograph of them together for me to admire, while my insides dissolved in acid remorse. If I was going to get my speech out, I'd need to say it quickly. Or would that be worse, blurting out my feelings with no idea of their appropriateness? I lowered my gaze and concentrated on where I was putting my feet, so at least I didn't go sprawling in front of him.

When I dared look up next I was near enough to see David's face. What struck me first was his tanned skin, and the fact that his hairline seemed further back than I remembered. His expression was stern and my confidence faltered. There was no hope. He had not replied to my letters because there was nothing more to say. This whole exercise was a pointless humiliation.

It might be better never to speak again.

Suddenly he broke into a grin and said something to Ian, who smiled too. Was it a real smile, or a mocking one? Were they just amused by the state I'd got myself into? Somehow I made myself keep going towards them, until at last I could make out the expression in his eyes. Then I knew.

'You know it's a myth about a swan being able to break your arm,' I panted. My chest was heaving and sweat prickled between my breasts.

David took one step forward, and opened his arms for me.

'God, I'm such an *idiot*,' I said.

'Shh, shh,' he went, holding me tight against him.

'It's taken me till now,' I said. 'All this time. Did you get my letters?'

'I did,' he said.

And?

In the background I could hear Ian beginning to exclaim in that exaggerated voice grown-ups use with small children, Jaz calling instructions about nap times and clothing and pick-up. Underneath ran a piping descant from Matty, thrilled once more to be with his dad, too young to understand that for every reunion there must also be a parting. There was this child, surrounded by adults, all trying their best to build a world around him that made sense, even when their own didn't.

I touched the side of David's face, still terrified he hadn't understood.

'Can we go somewhere and talk? I've all sorts I need to tell you.'

'I'd say you and I could go anywhere you like, when you're ready,' he said.

EPILOGUE

Photograph 899, Album Seven

Location: the park, Nantwich

Taken by: Carol

Subject: It is a glorious spring Saturday, the culmination of a week of unseasonably warm weather. People are calling it a reward for last year's wash-out summer. But meteorology doesn't go in for checks and balances, thinks Carol, as she attempts to trap her family inside the camera's viewfinder. For the previous half-hour she's been sitting on a bench holding hands with David, a pose she's found simultaneously foolish and thrilling, given it's in the presence of her daughter. Hovering at the edge of her consciousness comes an ancient memory: the mortifying moment her dad opened the front door and discovered her mid-snog with Phil. But she waves the image away because those days are long gone, irrelevant.

'Why didn't you reply to my letters?' she asked, as soon as they were out of earshot.

'I wanted to be sure you meant it. I thought you might be just surfing a wave of guilt, and you'd change your mind back again as soon as you were challenged. I don't think I could have stood that.'

'But the silence. That was cruel.'

No consoling reply. All he'd done was take her hand possessively.

There's something steely and triumphant about him; she's noticed the sideways glances passing between him and her daughter. God knows how they are going to work this. Another picture comes: Dad showing Jaz the lion on the syrup tin, tracing the minuscule lettering with his soily finger. And out of the strong came forth sweetness.

Jaz and Ian are talking, or not talking, over by the river's edge; Matty is mooching about halfway between bank and bench.

'Every time you let yourself love, it's like being held hostage,' Carol observed earlier. 'Laying yourself open. We must be mad to do it, and keep on and on.'

'And yet we do,' he said.

David observes her now. Matty is plodding over to his grandma, holding some suspicious brown nugget between his finger and thumb. He has the air of a naturalist, discoverer of rare and significant species, who's anxious to log his findings with a colleague.

'Look, Nanna,' he says, holding it out to her. 'Snail's gone.'

'No,' says Carol. 'He's hiding in his shell because he's frightened. That's what they do. He'll come out soon, though, you wait.'

Matty drops the snail on the grass and crouches, frowning, waiting for the future to unfurl.

Carol raises the camera again. She has forgotten everything outside the viewfinder. Just before she presses the shutter, her face is illuminated.